IMAGE COMICS, INC.

TODD McFARLANE [PRESIDENT]
JIM VALENTINO [VICE PRESIDENT]
MARC SILVESTRI [CHIEF EXECUTIVE OFFICER]
ERIK LARSEN [CHIEF FINANCIAL OFFICER]
ROBERT KIRKMAN [CHIEF OPERATING OFFICER]
ERIC STEPHENSON [PUBLISHER / CHIEF CREATIVE OFFICER]
NICOLE LAPALME [CONTROLLER]
LEANNA CAUNTER [ACCOUNTING ANALYST]
SUE KORPELA [ACCOUNTING & HR MANAGER]
MARLA EIZIK [TALENT LIAISON]
JEFF BOISON [DIRECTOR OF SALES & PUBLISHING PLANNING]
DIRK WOOD [DIRECTOR OF INTERNATIONAL SALES & LICENSING]
ALEX COX [DIRECTOR OF DIRECT MARKET SALES]
CHLOE RAMOS [BOOK MARKET & LIBRARY SALES MANAGER]
EMILIO BAUTISTA [DIGITAL SALES COORDINATOR]
JON SCHLAFFMAN [SPECIALTY SALES COORDINATOR]
KAT SALAZAR [DIRECTOR OF PR & MARKETING]
DREW FITZGERALD [MARKETING CONTENT ASSOCIATE]
HEATHER DOORNINK [PRODUCTION DIRECTOR]
DREW GILL [ART DIRECTOR]
HILARY DILORETO [PRINT MANAGER]
TRICIA RAMOS [TRAFFIC MANAGER]
MELISSA GIFFORD [CONTENT MANAGER]
ERIKA SCHNATZ [SENIOR PRODUCTION ARTIST]
RYAN BREWER [PRODUCTION ARTIST]
DEANNA PHELPS [PRODUCTION ARTIST]

IMAGECOMICS.COM

[+]

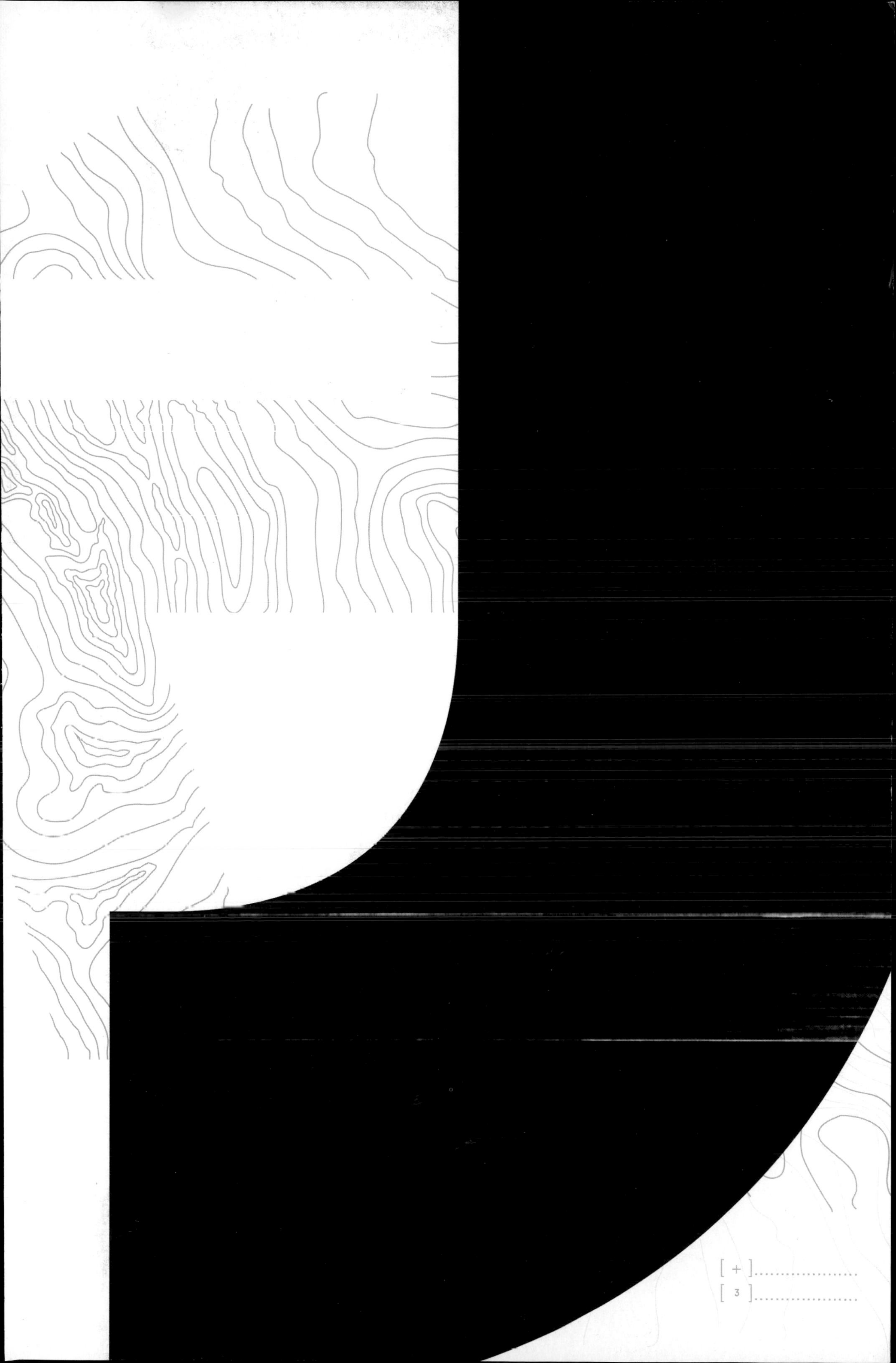
[+]....................
[3]....................

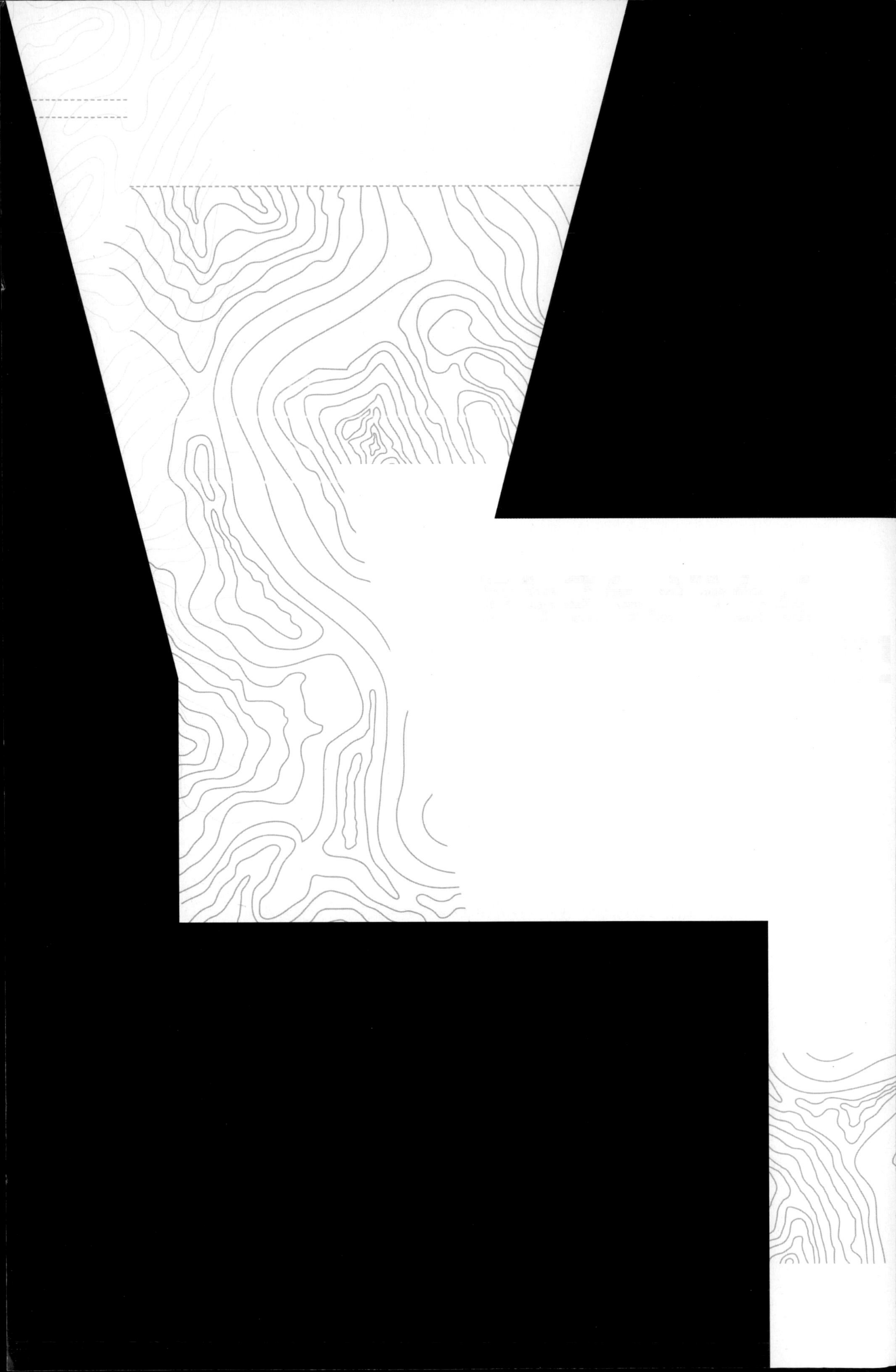

JONATHAN HICKMAN
[WORDS]

MIKE HUDDLESTON
[ART]

RUS WOOTON
[LETTERS]

SASHA E HEAD
[DESIGN]

もくじ

CONTENTS

PART I: THE WOMANLY ART OF ASSASSINATION

PART II: THE MACHINIC LOVE OF RELIGION

PART III: THE RE-EDUCATION OF DEVIANTS

PART IV: THE EATING OF A WORLD

PART V: THE MISEDUCATION OF NEHA NORI SOOD

PART VI: THE ONE JOB YOU REALLY NEED

PART VII: THE EGG THAT BROKE A WORLD

PART VIII: THE WHOLE THING ENDS BADLY

DECO

DECOROUS

RUM

[AND THE WOMANLY ART
OF **ASSASSINATION**]

CHAPTER ONE

[RUN MOTHERS]

SOLAR IMPERIAL PRESERVES

The Preserves are an artifact of the ten-thousand-year plan to mitigate the effects of mass expansion during the golden age of the old Solar Empire. The forced acquisition of Goldilocks planets [not rare, but finite in number] resulted in the indigenous creatures of any claimed world being initially 'preserved' on-world in some version of their natural habitat.

Predictably, this 'containment' method failed [originating itself from the 'flawed' idea that the evolution of all creatures should occur in an uninterrupted fashion] and after serval generations of seed ships spoiling each Goldilocks planet, the idea of off-world preserves was born.

Self-repairing, autonomous, terraformed bubbles were constructed off world and over a period of thousands of years, over one hundred thousand preserves were created. In five of them, the emergent civilization reached a point were they were adopted into the Solar Empire. In several thousand, the societies died out. In hundreds, the society remained unspoiled—pristine [as these societies lacked the normal forced adaptation most endure because of the automated nature of the preserves].

The remaining tens of thousands of preserves were destroyed when the Solar Empire fell during the crusades of the Singularity.

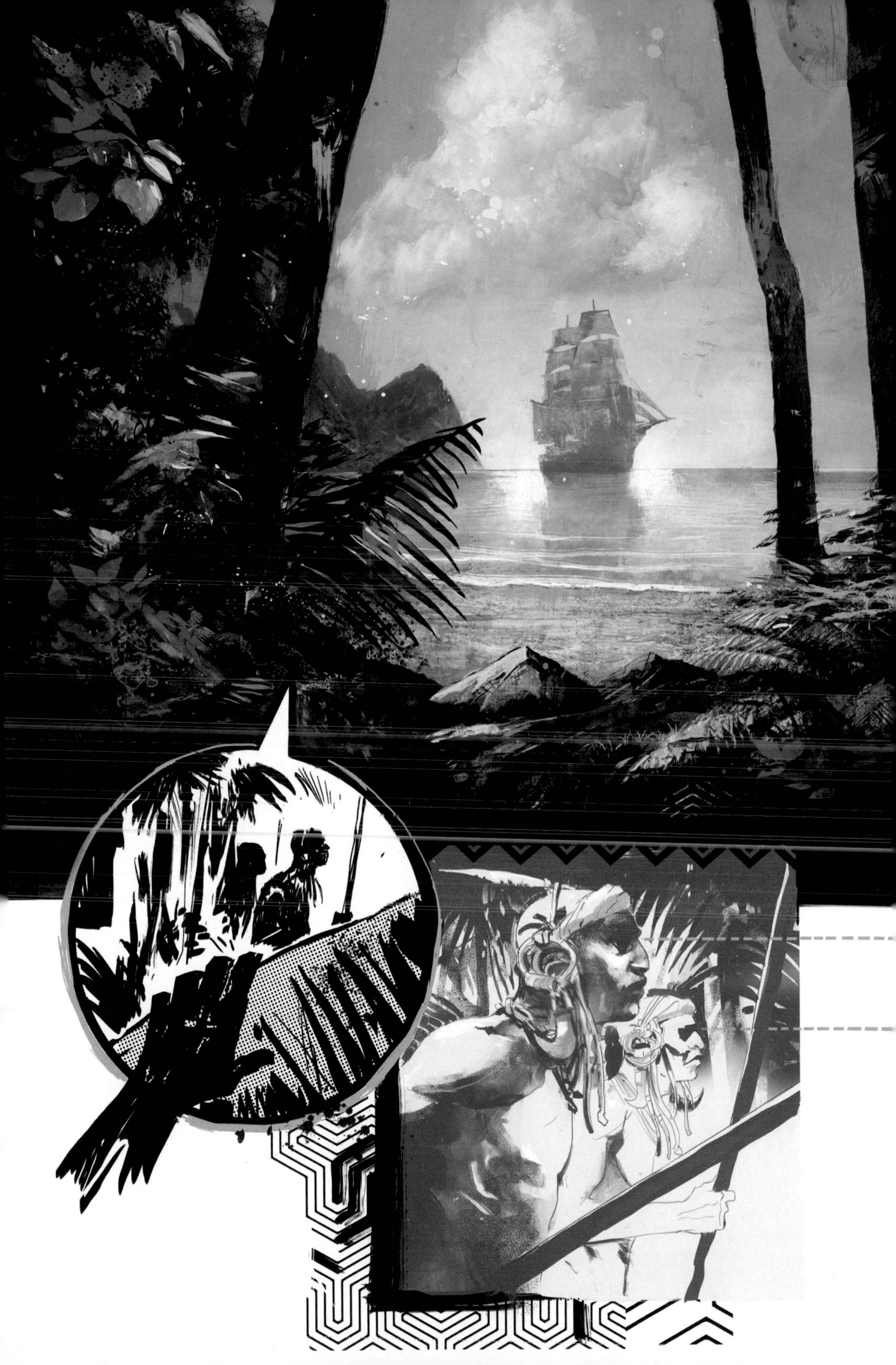

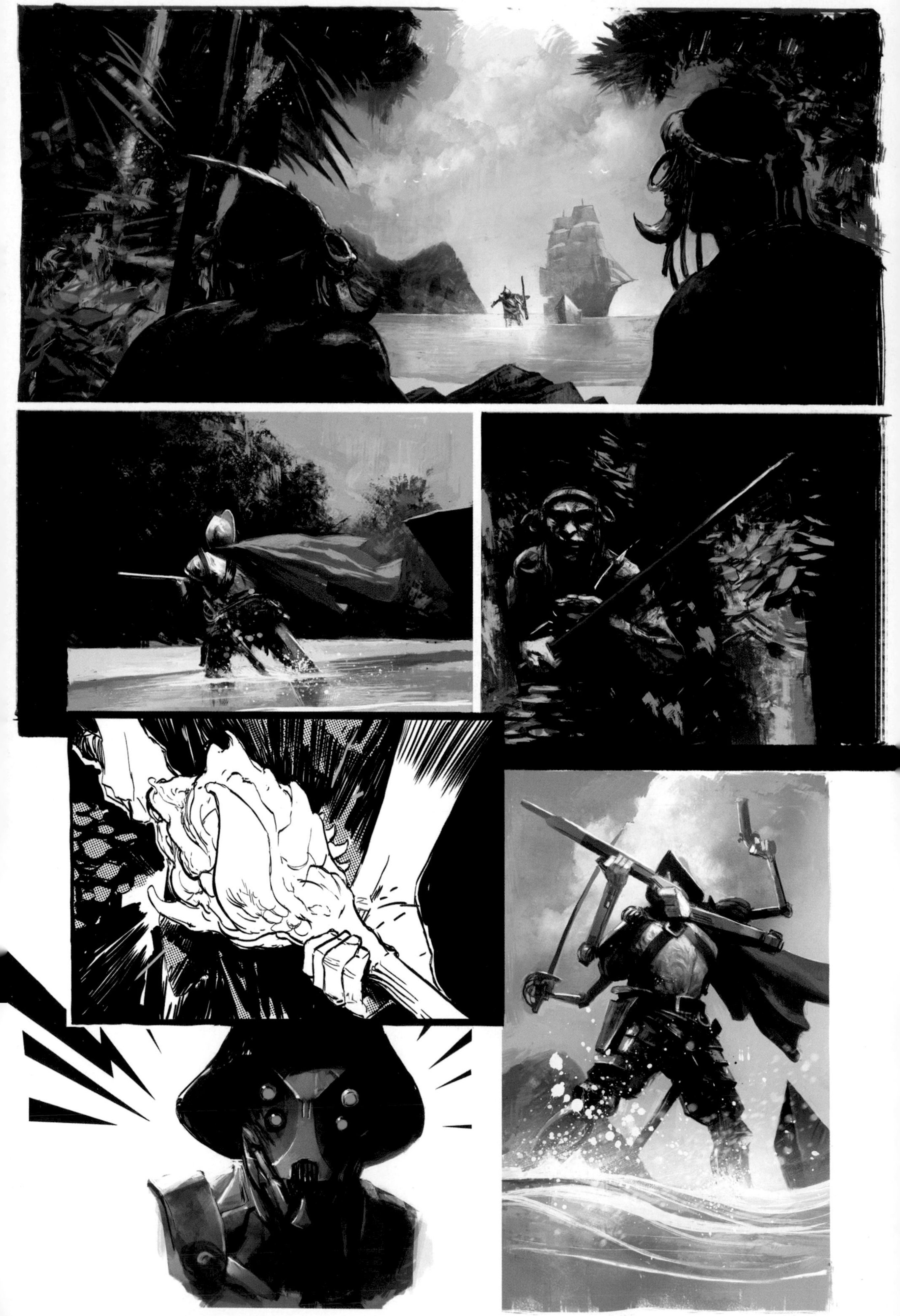

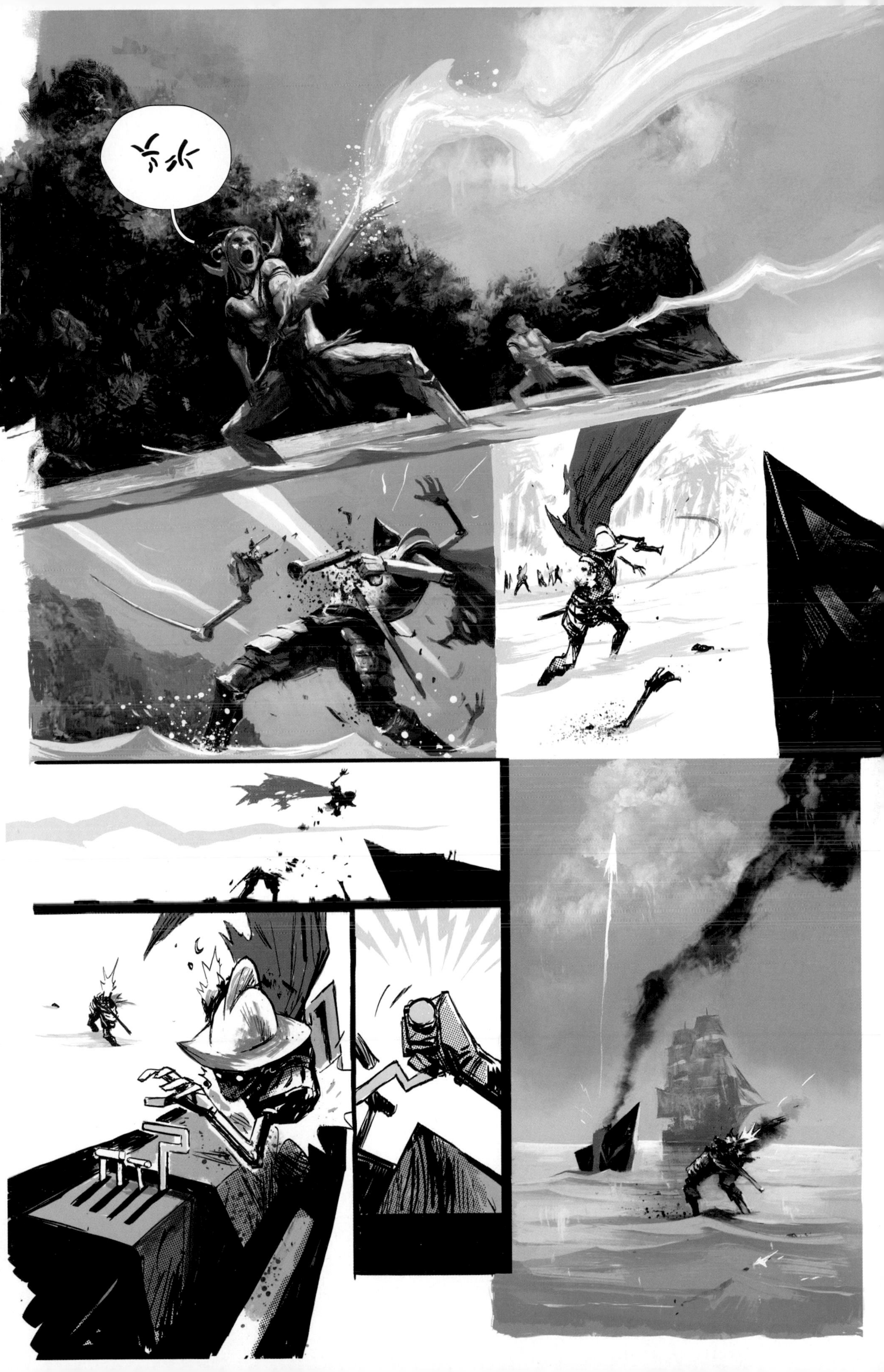

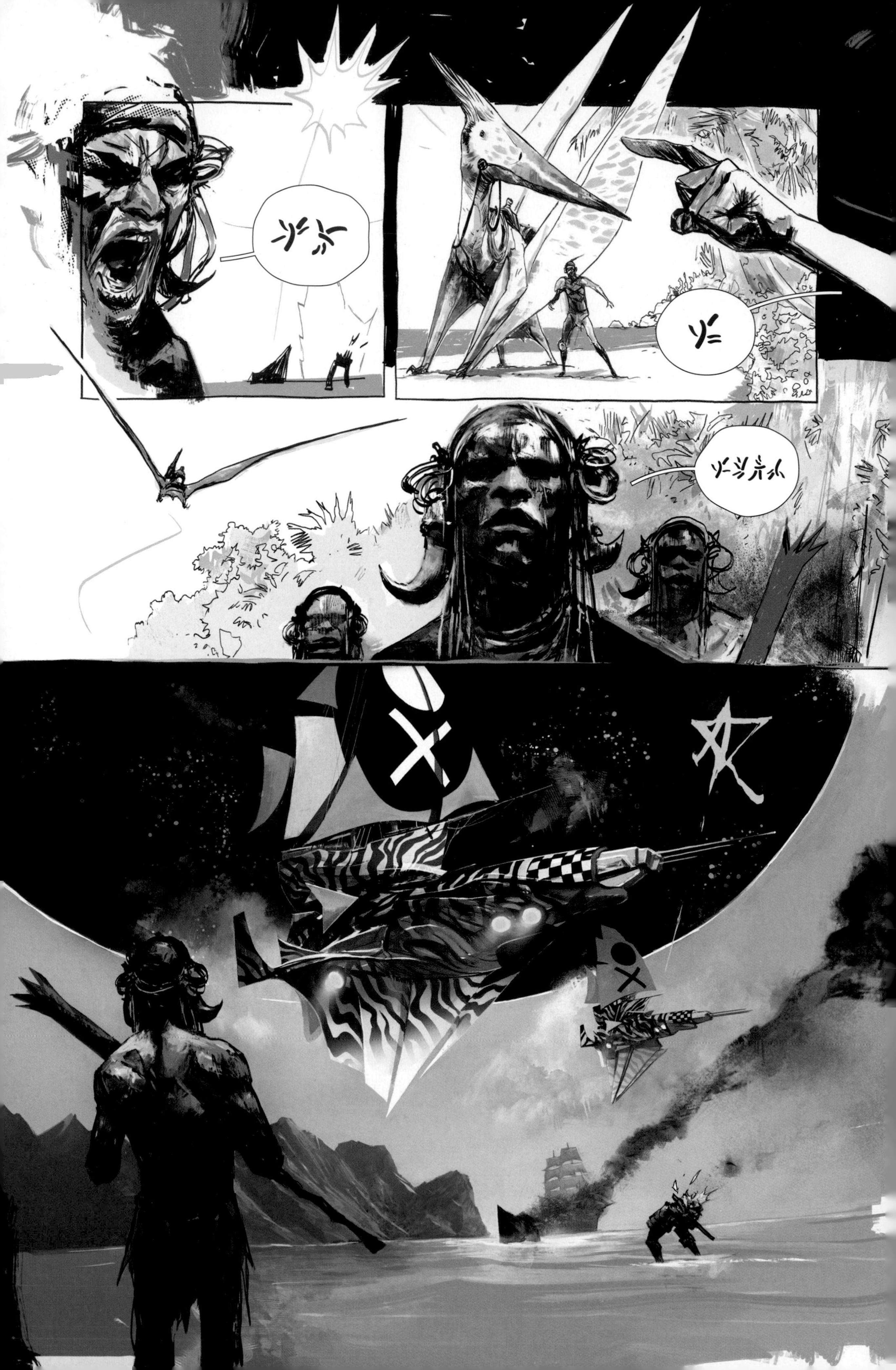

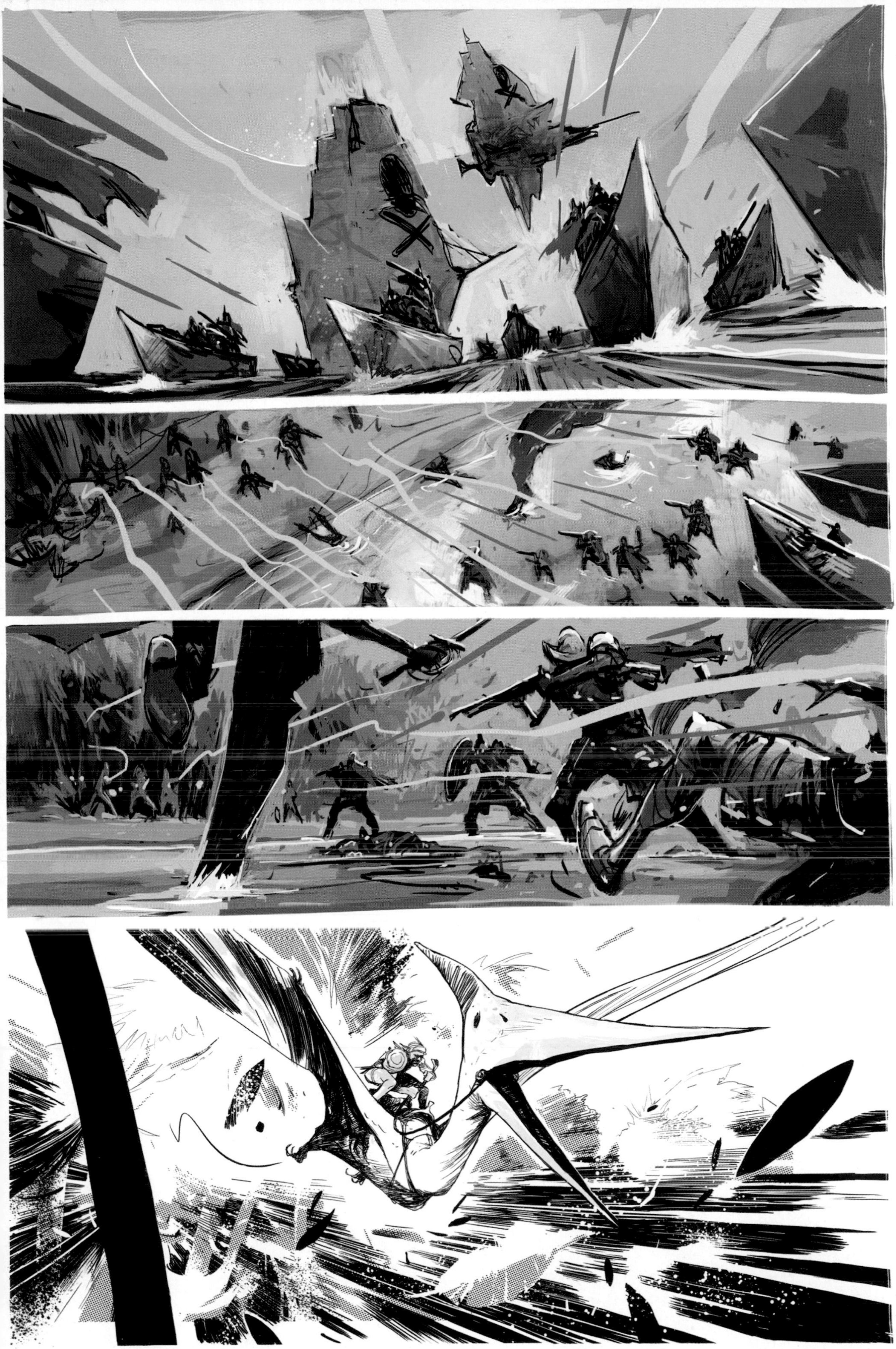

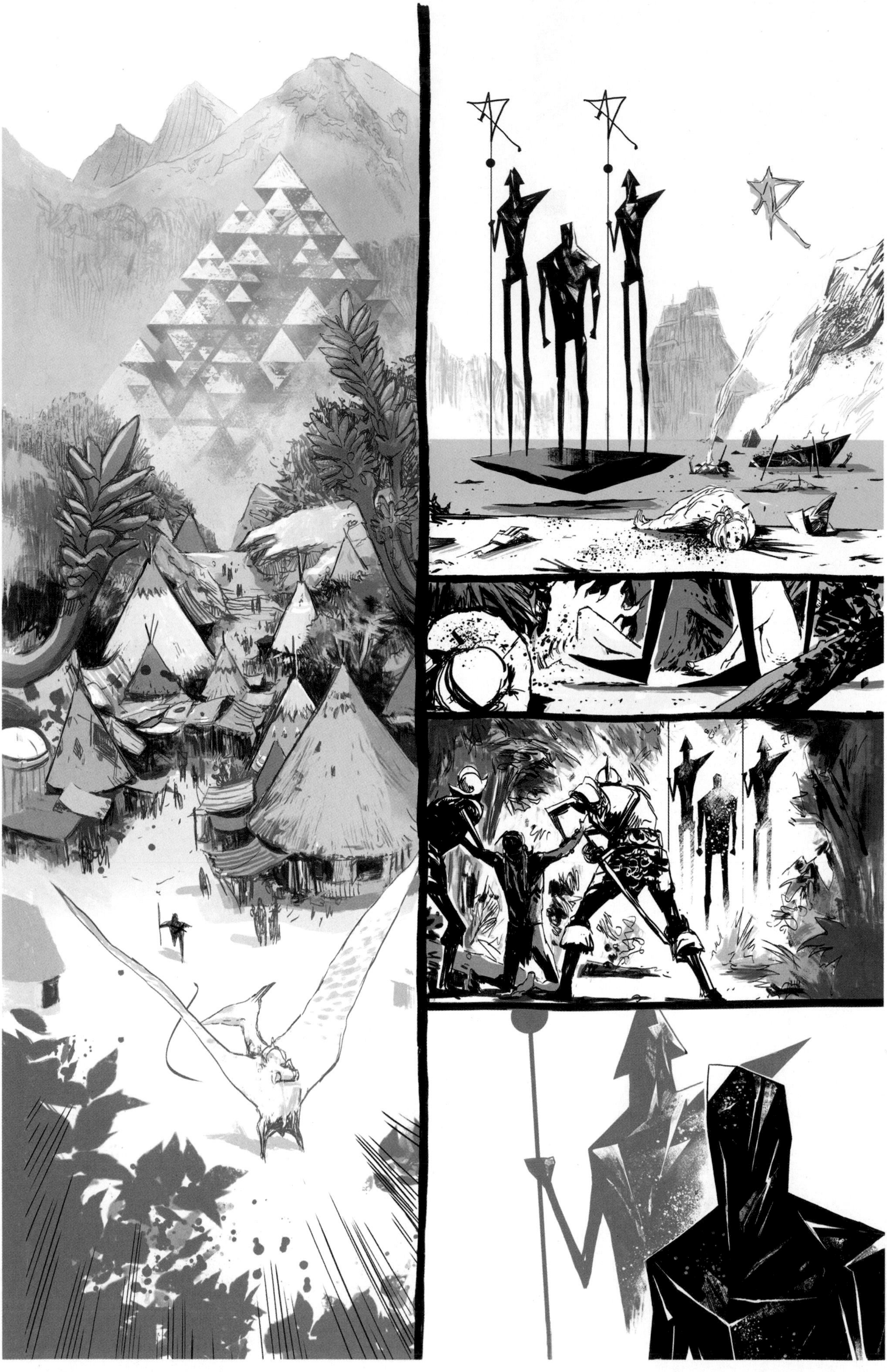

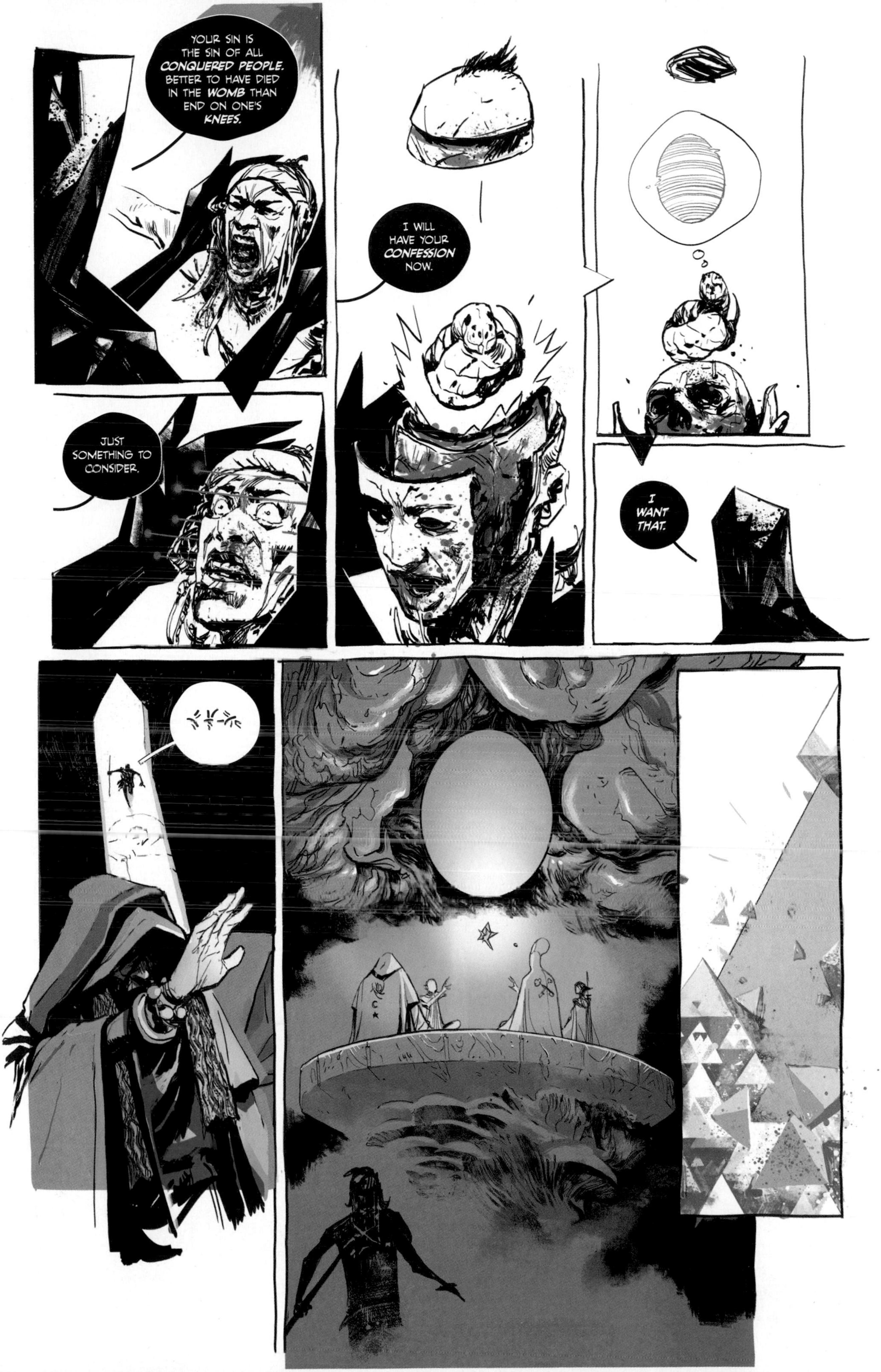
YOUR SIN IS THE SIN OF ALL CONQUERED PEOPLE. BETTER TO HAVE DIED IN THE WOMB THAN END ON ONE'S KNEES.
JUST SOMETHING TO CONSIDER.
I WILL HAVE YOUR CONFESSION NOW.
I WANT THAT.

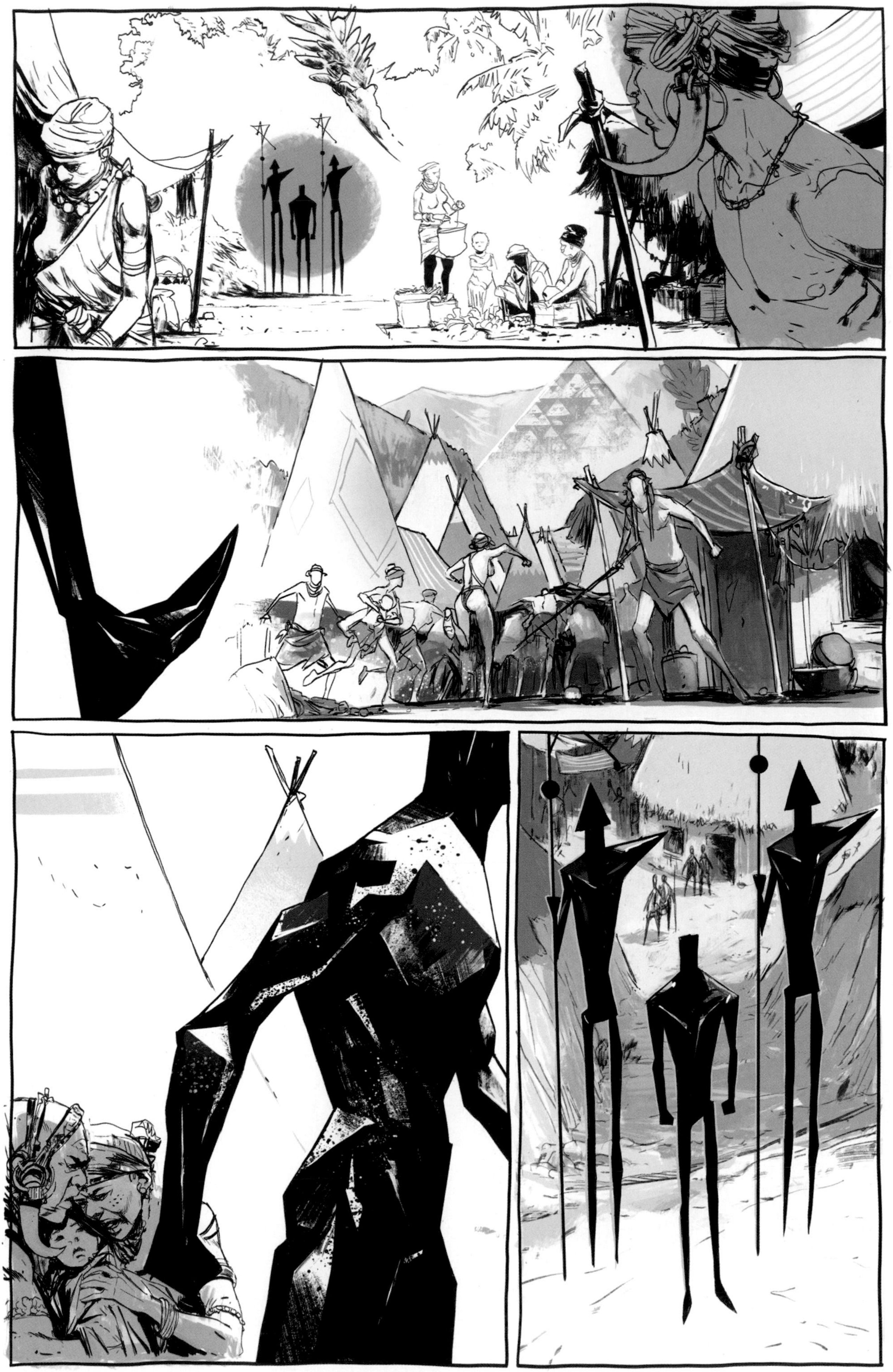

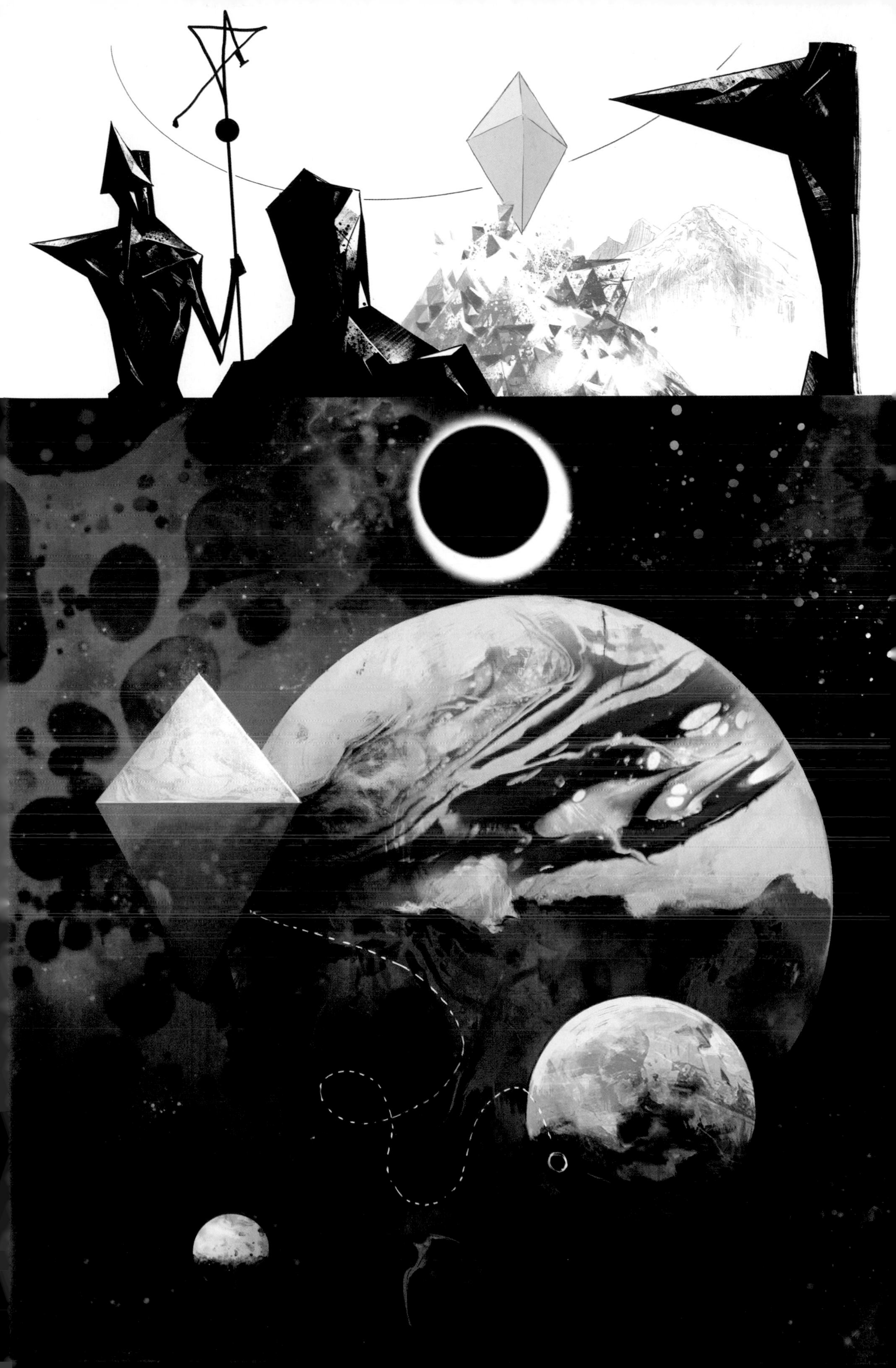

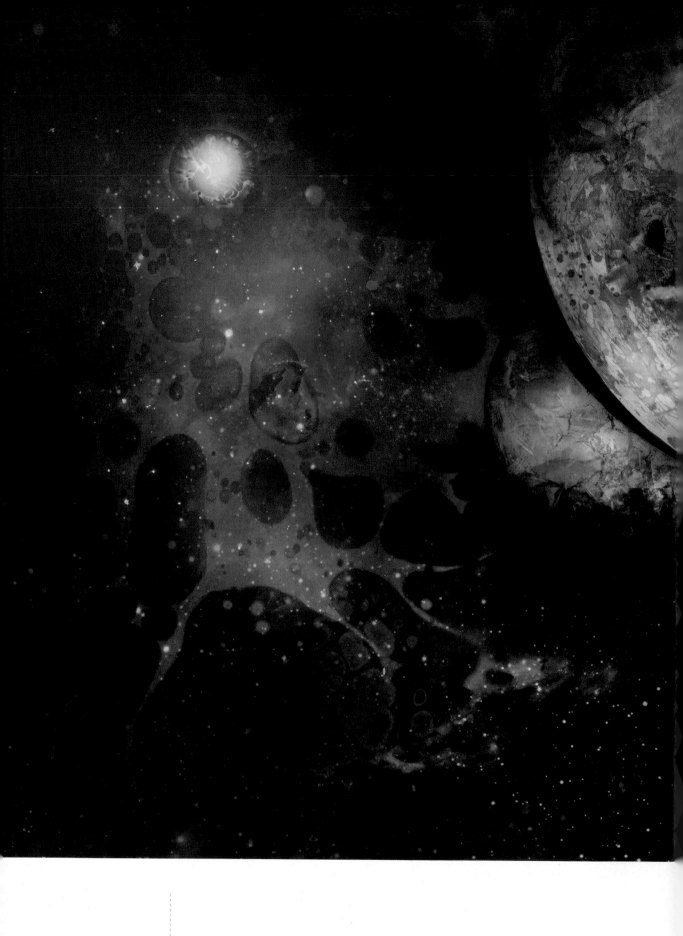

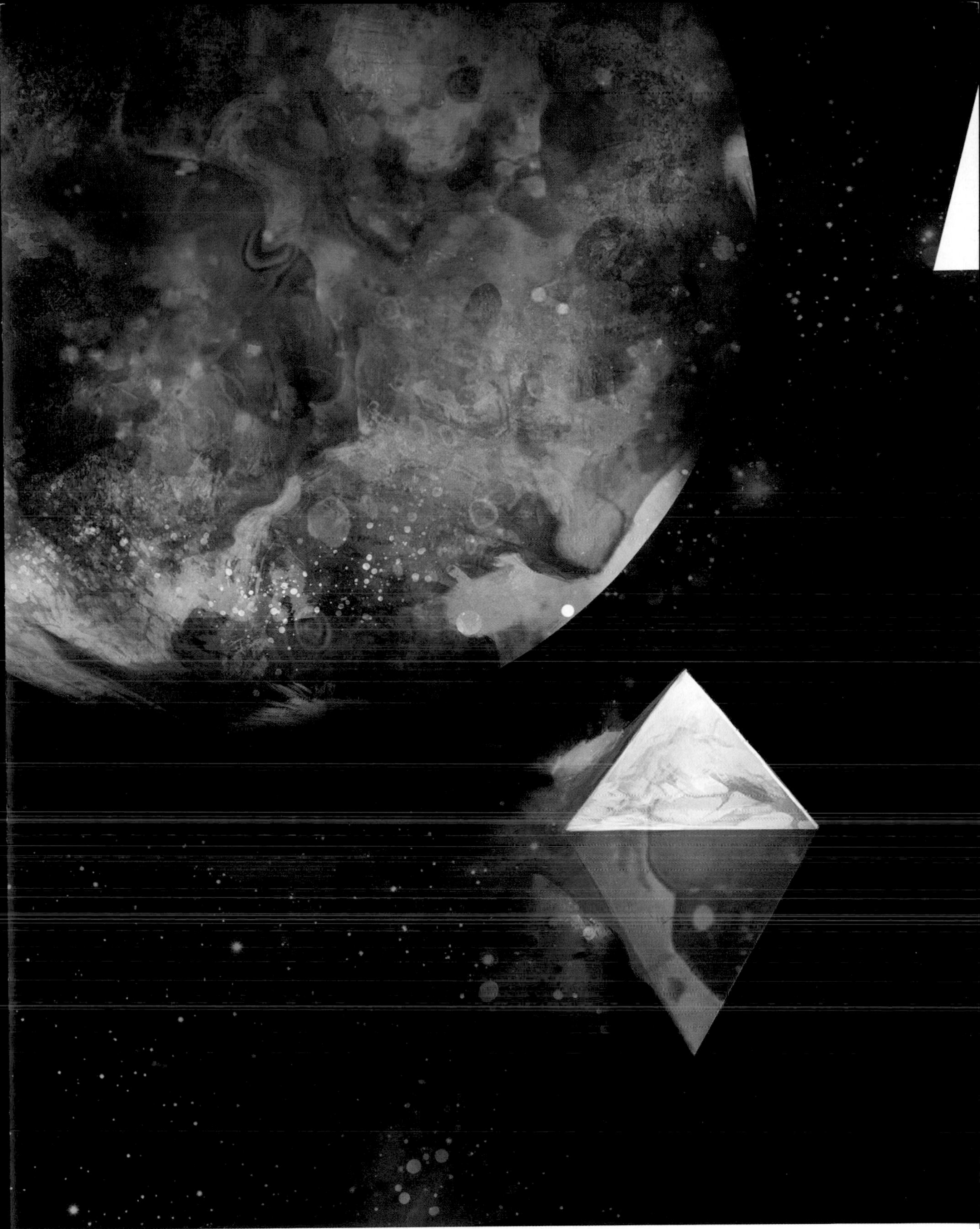

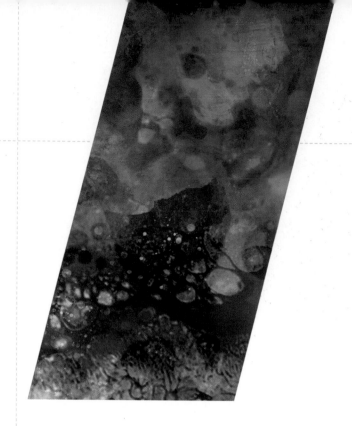

MAPS

GALACTIC SECTORS

[EMPIRES, ALLIANCES, ETC.]

PYRAMID LOCATIONS

[WHERE ARE THE MOTHERS]

SECTOR DETAILS

[SOCIETIES IN CONFLICT]

PLANET DATA

[A FLOATING WORLD]

[+]

1
2
3
4
5
6
7

GALACTIC SECTORS

[1] **SAGITTARIAN HIVE**.......................... ENERGY COLLECTIVE

[2] **NORMA COALITION**....................................... WILD SPACE

[3] **ORION-CYGNUS LEAGUE**........................ CELESTIAL FARM

[4] **THE UNION**.................... REPUBLIC OF FRONTIER WORLDS

[5] **SHATTERED EMPIRE**.. WASTE

[6] **CHURCH OF SINGULARITY**................................ A.I. UNION

[7] **SYNDICATE MAJOR**........ FEDERATION OF ROGUE SYSTEMS

[+]

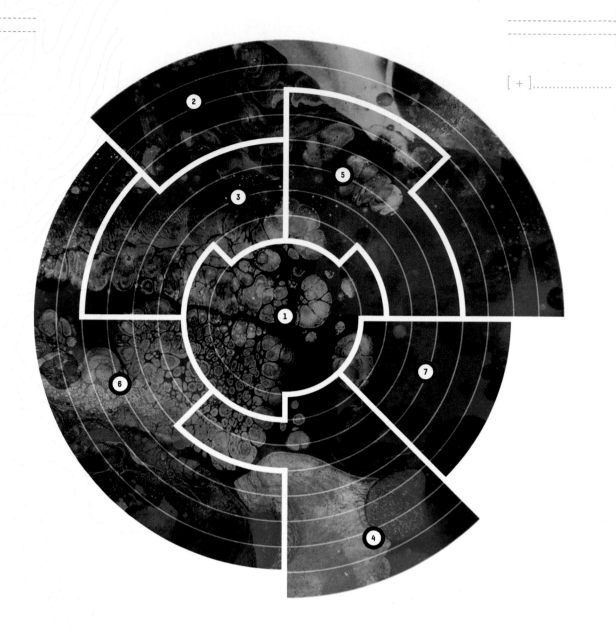

PYRAMID LOCATIONS

[DURATIONS OVER THE PAST 100,000 YEARS]

[+]......................

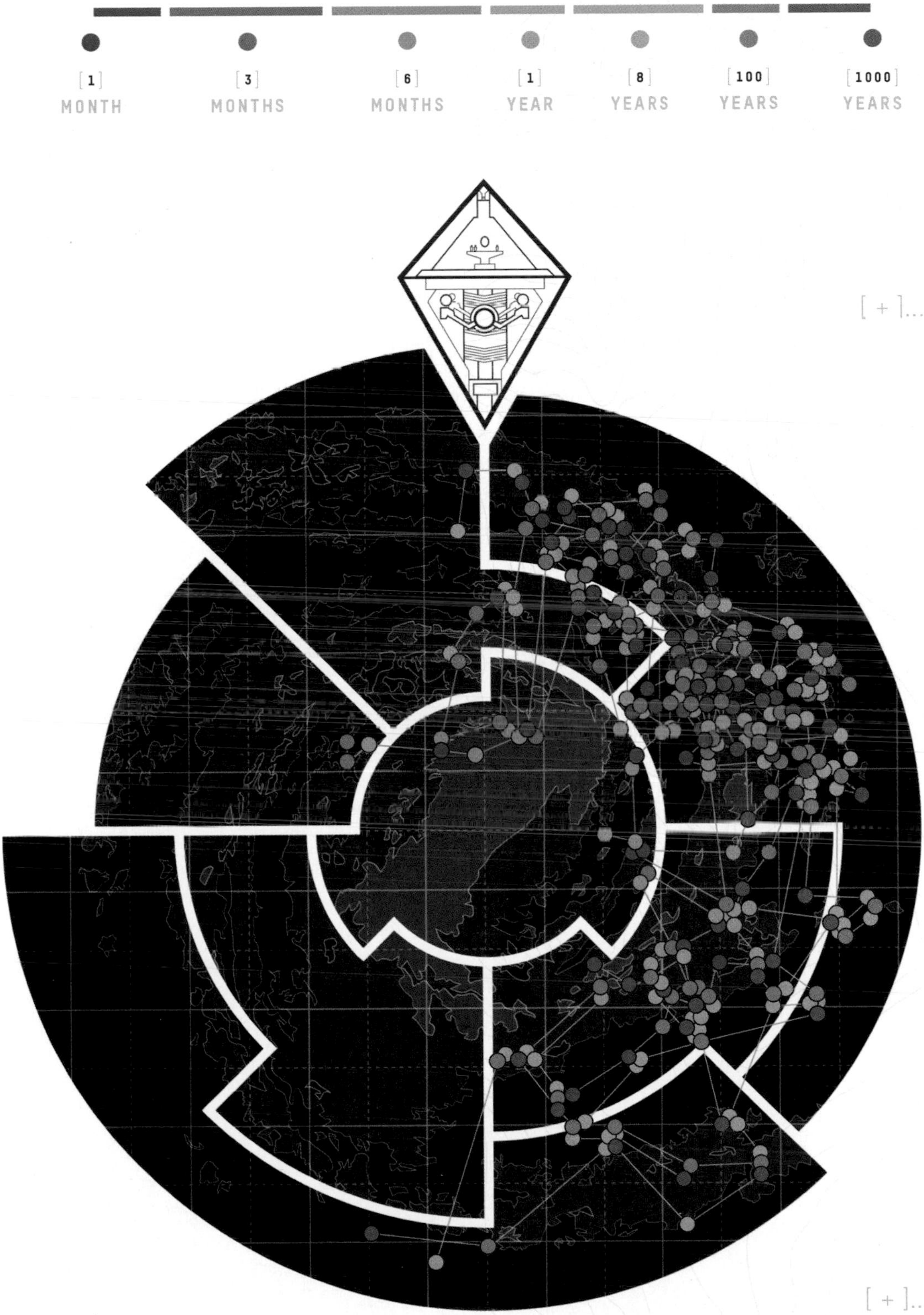
[1] MONTH
[3] MONTHS
[6] MONTHS
[1] YEAR
[8] YEARS
[100] YEARS
[1000] YEARS

[+]......................

[+]......................

CHURCH
[OF THE SINGULARITY]

THE UNION
[OF FRONTIER WORLDS]

Built on the bones of the old Solar Empire, the Church of the Singularity is a cooperative [but hierarchal] artificial intelligence that controls its galactic sector with an iron fist.

The Church exists in a conflict state which is a result of its ingrained messianic subroutine. It believes in Apocalypse because it is built into its programming.

The rise of the Church of the Singularity led to the forced expansion of the old Solar Empire. Colonizing seed ships pushed into its neighboring sector giving rise to conflict with the ancient [and dying] Perseus Union.

After tens of thousands of years of war, the refugee wars ended with an uneasy peace and the establishment on a new Union.

DAELDUS

[FLOATING WORLD]

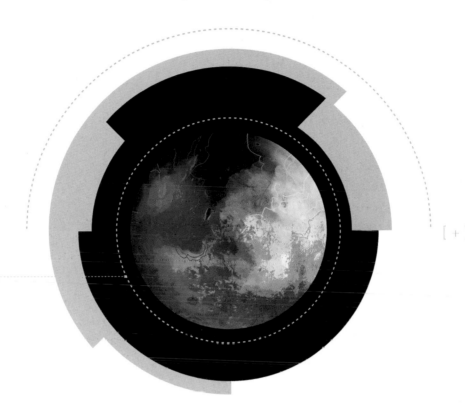

Originally an entirely liquid world, Dealdus was terraformed 10 centuries ago by Guild engineers.

Using a number of mobile, floating platforms, the geographic makeup of Dealdus is constantly changing due to the highly variable tidal patterns caused by its multiple erratic orbiting moons.

Because of the lack of fixed locations and constantly rearranging cities, Dealdus has proven to be a magnet for black market economists and morally flexible businessmen.

STATS

[PHYSICAL CHARACTERISTICS]

MEAN RADIUS	$3,105 \pm 0.3$ km
SURFACE AREA	$142,810,717$ km^2
VOLUME	2.053×1011 km^3
MASS	5.2801×1023 kg
SATELLITES	5
CONTINENTS	[VARIABLE]

[BEWARE THE BOUWERIZ]

CHAPTER TWO

[BROKE AND BENT OVER]

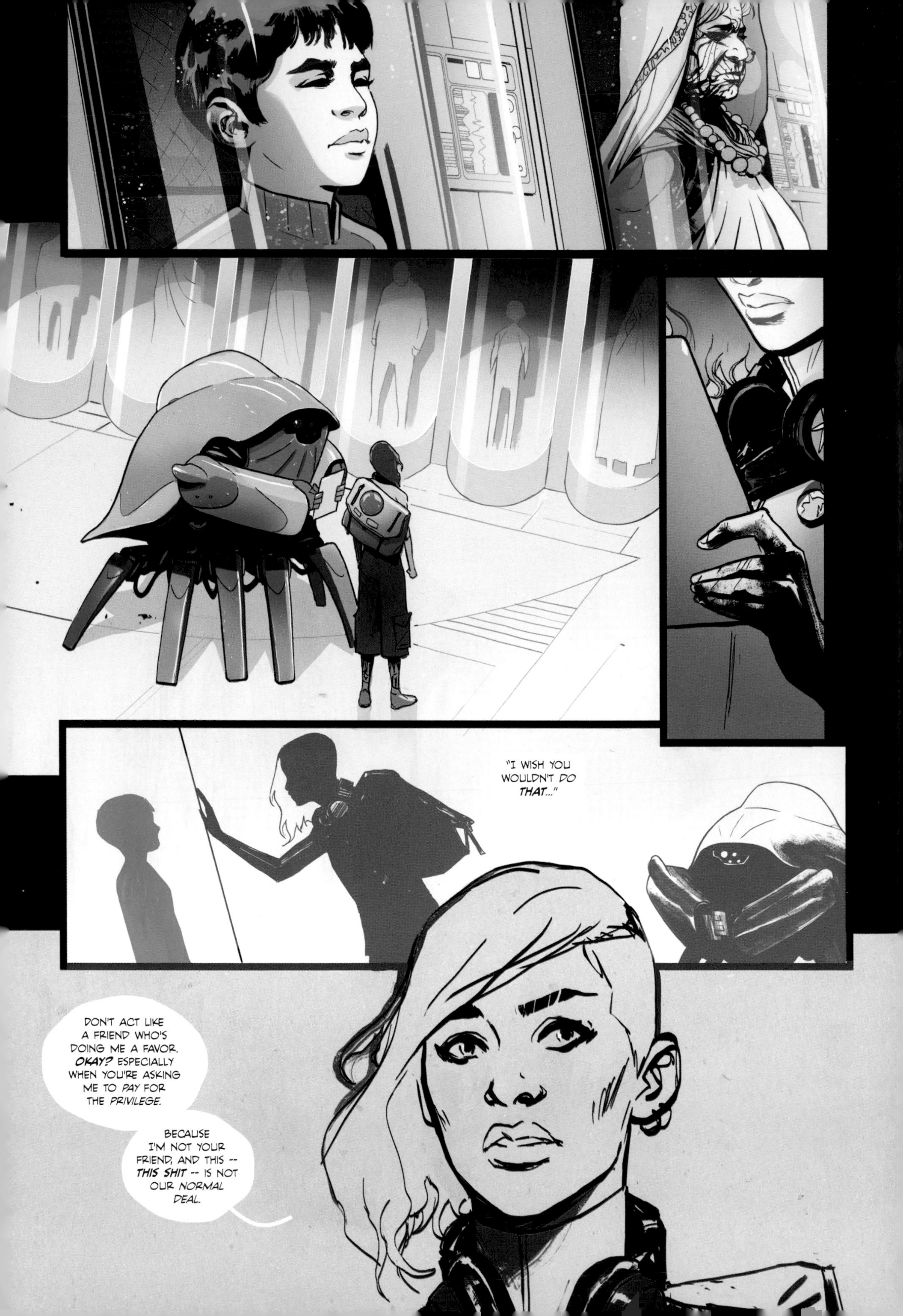
"I WISH YOU WOULDN'T *DO* *THAT*..."
DON'T ACT LIKE A FRIEND WHO'S DOING ME A FAVOR. ***OKAY?*** ESPECIALLY WHEN YOU'RE ASKING ME TO *PAY* FOR THE *PRIVILEGE*.
BECAUSE I'M NOT YOUR FRIEND, AND THIS -- ***THIS SHIT*** -- IS NOT OUR *NORMAL* DEAL.

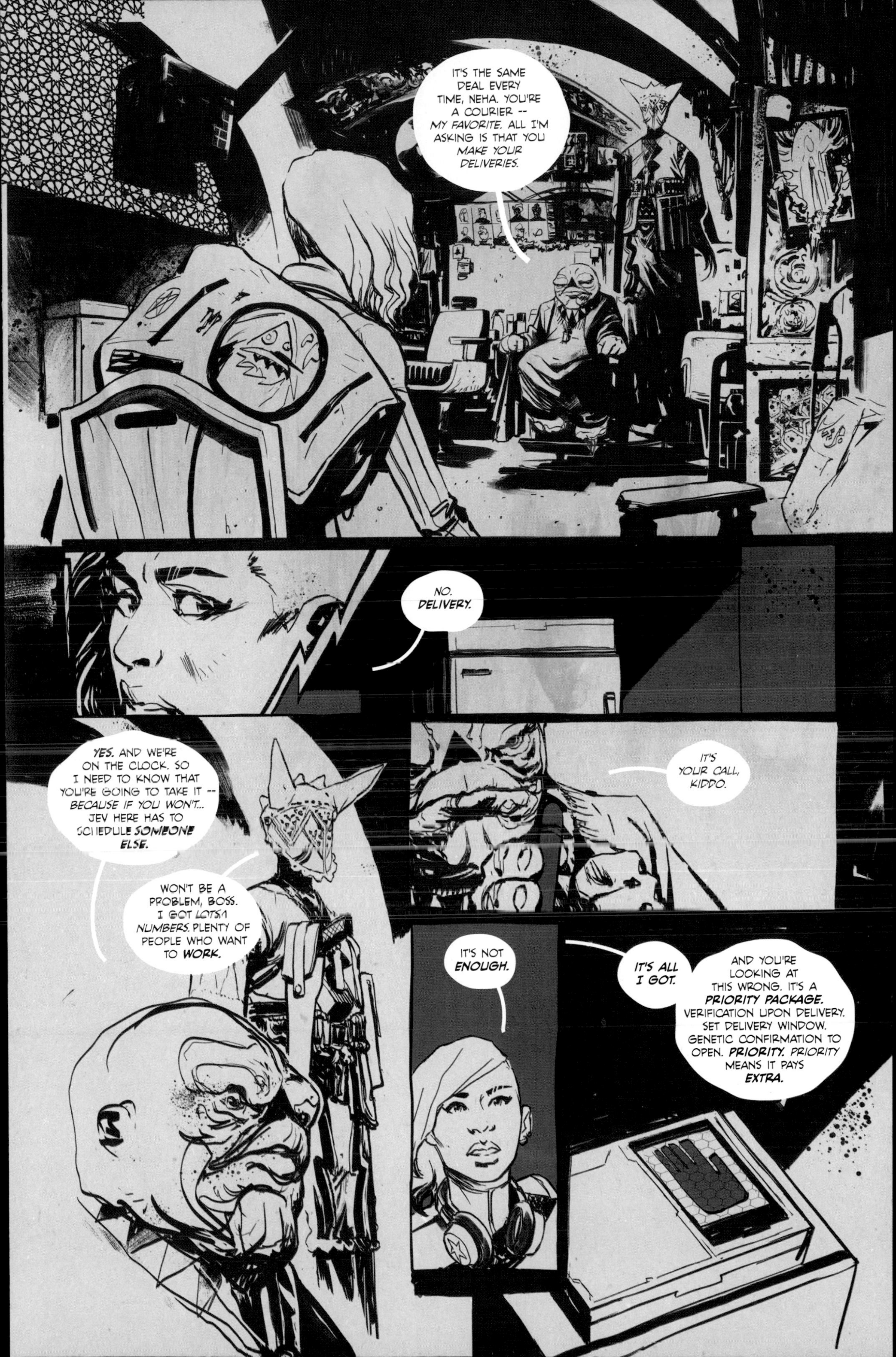
IT'S THE SAME DEAL EVERY TIME, NEHA. YOU'RE A COURIER -- *MY FAVORITE.* ALL I'M ASKING IS THAT YOU *MAKE YOUR DELIVERIES.*
NO. **DELIVERY.**
YES. AND WE'RE ON THE CLOCK. SO I NEED TO KNOW THAT YOU'RE GOING TO TAKE IT -- *BECAUSE IF YOU WON'T...* JEV HERE HAS TO SCHEDULE **SOMEONE ELSE.**
WON'T BE A PROBLEM, BOSS. I GOT *LOTSA NUMBERS.* PLENTY OF PEOPLE WHO WANT TO **WORK.**
IT'S YOUR CALL, KIDDO.
IT'S NOT **ENOUGH.**
IT'S ALL I GOT.
AND YOU'RE LOOKING AT THIS WRONG. IT'S A **PRIORITY PACKAGE.** VERIFICATION UPON DELIVERY. SET DELIVERY WINDOW. GENETIC CONFIRMATION TO OPEN. **PRIORITY.** *PRIORITY* MEANS IT PAYS **EXTRA.**

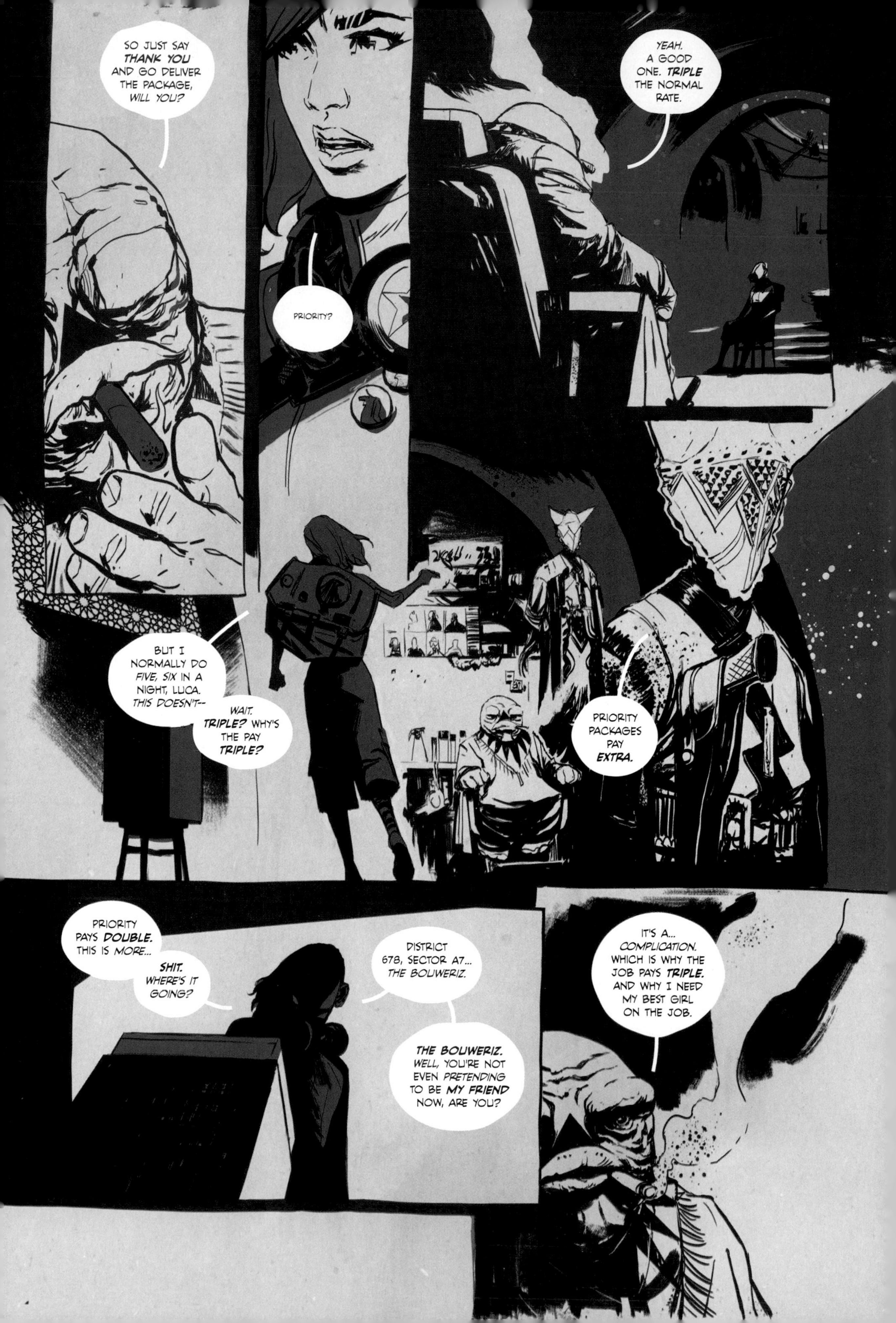
SO JUST SAY **THANK YOU** AND GO DELIVER THE PACKAGE, *WILL YOU?*
PRIORITY?
YEAH. A GOOD ONE. ***TRIPLE*** THE NORMAL RATE.
BUT I NORMALLY DO *FIVE, SIX* IN A NIGHT, LUCA. *THIS DOESN'T--*
WAIT. ***TRIPLE?*** WHY'S THE PAY ***TRIPLE?***
PRIORITY PACKAGES PAY **EXTRA.**
PRIORITY PAYS **DOUBLE.** THIS IS *MORE...*
SHIT. *WHERE'S IT GOING?*
DISTRICT 678, SECTOR A7... *THE BOUWERIZ.*
THE BOUWERIZ. WELL, YOU'RE NOT EVEN *PRETENDING* TO BE ***MY FRIEND*** NOW, ARE YOU?
IT'S A... *COMPLICATION.* WHICH IS WHY THE JOB PAYS ***TRIPLE.*** AND WHY I NEED MY BEST GIRL ON THE JOB.

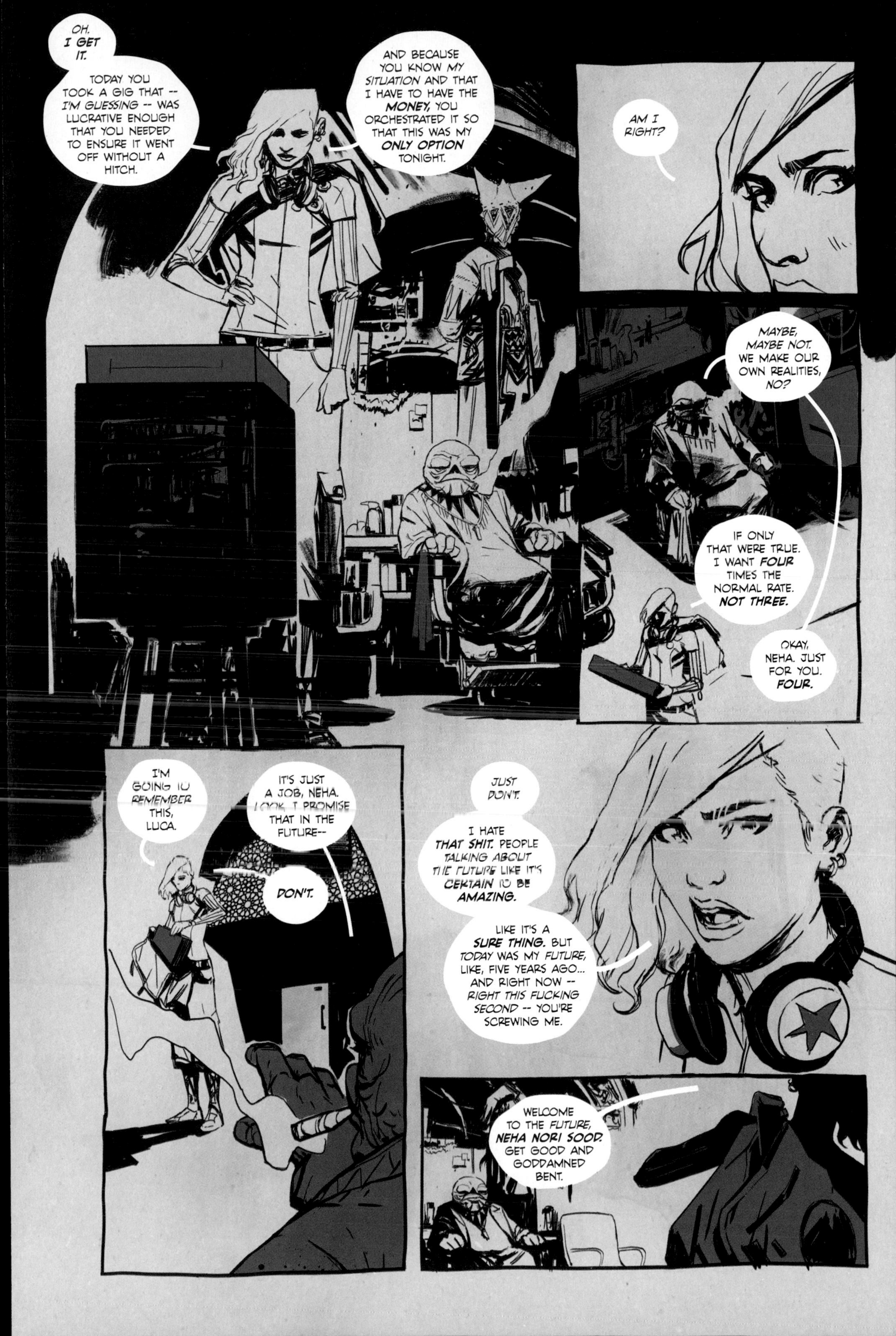
OH. I GET IT.
TODAY YOU TOOK A GIG THAT -- I'M GUESSING -- WAS LUCRATIVE ENOUGH THAT YOU NEEDED TO ENSURE IT WENT OFF WITHOUT A HITCH.
AND BECAUSE YOU KNOW MY SITUATION AND THAT I HAVE TO HAVE THE MONEY, YOU ORCHESTRATED IT SO THAT THIS WAS MY ONLY OPTION TONIGHT.
AM I RIGHT?
MAYBE, MAYBE NOT. WE MAKE OUR OWN REALITIES, NO?
IF ONLY THAT WERE TRUE. I WANT FOUR TIMES THE NORMAL RATE. NOT THREE.
OKAY, NEHA. JUST FOR YOU. FOUR.
I'M GOING TO REMEMBER THIS, LUCA.
IT'S JUST A JOB, NEHA. LOOK, I PROMISE THAT IN THE FUTURE--
DON'T.
JUST DON'T.
I HATE THAT SHIT. PEOPLE TALKING ABOUT THE FUTURE LIKE IT'S CERTAIN TO BE AMAZING.
LIKE IT'S A SURE THING. BUT TODAY WAS MY FUTURE, LIKE, FIVE YEARS AGO... AND RIGHT NOW -- RIGHT THIS FUCKING SECOND -- YOU'RE SCREWING ME.
WELCOME TO THE FUTURE, NEHA NORI SOOD. GET GOOD AND GODDAMNED BENT.

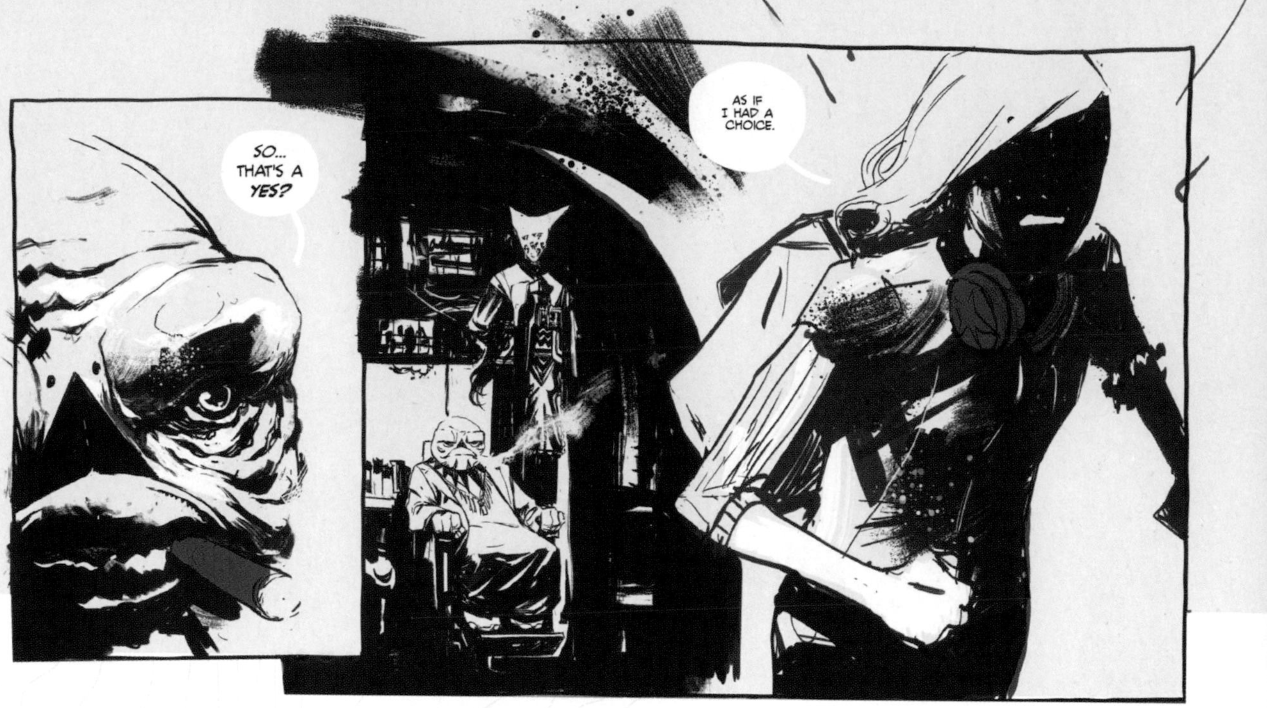
SO... THAT'S A YES?
AS IF I HAD A CHOICE.

CRYOPODS

Located in dense warehouses spread across dozens of worlds, Luxor Cryopods are a state-of-the-art suspended animation system that runs off an independent and redundant power source independent of all public and private grids. This ensures that your loved ones will enjoy a peaceful, undisturbed rest until the day that they are cured and returned to the land of the living.

Luxor Cyropods are, of course, egalitarian in production and design, and since we offer only a single model, we can assure you that each and every Cryopod is constructed with the highest precision that comes from consistency and uniformity.

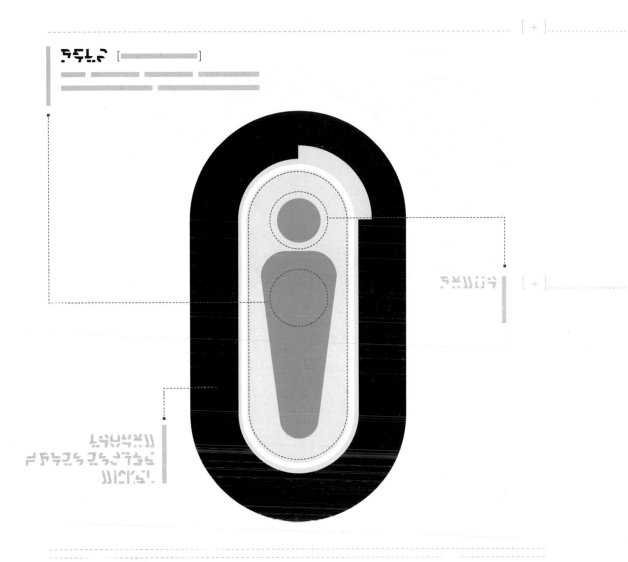

FLOATING SECTIUN:
0132 A2 [SECOND CYCLE]

LUXOR FINANCING

SEVENTH WAVE REGENERATIVE SERVICE
[ONE PERSON] **6,000,000.00** CREDITS

CRYOPOD STASIS [20 YEARS / 5 PERCENT INTEREST] .... **1,000,000.00** CREDITS

CRYOPOD STASIS [10 YEARS / 10 PERCENT INTEREST] .... **500,000.00** CREDITS

CRYOPOD STASIS [5 YEARS / 15 PERCENT INTEREST] .... **200,000.00** CREDITS

CRYOPOD STASIS [1 YEAR / 20 PERCENT INTEREST] .... **40,000.00** CREDITS

CRYOPOD STASIS [1 MONTH / 28 PERCENT INTEREST] .... **4,000.00** CREDITS

PLAGUE

Bioengineered to be a carrier virus as a method of planetary submission for rogue worlds, the Seventh Wave Plague was designed to quickly infect, spread and paralyze victim worlds into which it was released. While extremely painful and debilitating, the virus was designed to only actually be fatal in instances where the infected party did not receive treatment— there was a cure. The complication was that the remedy required a prolonged battery of expensive pharmaceutical treatments and an organ regrowth and replacement process that most infected parties could not afford.

[+]

Billions of infected citizens were forced to contractually enter a credit-based cryogenic stasis until the time arose that the non-frozen family debtor could pay for the very expensive Seventh Wave cure, or until they could no longer afford the cryogenic stasis. At that point, the bodies of the infected—unable to pay for a cure, and out of external credit—were destroyed as potential health and environmental risks.

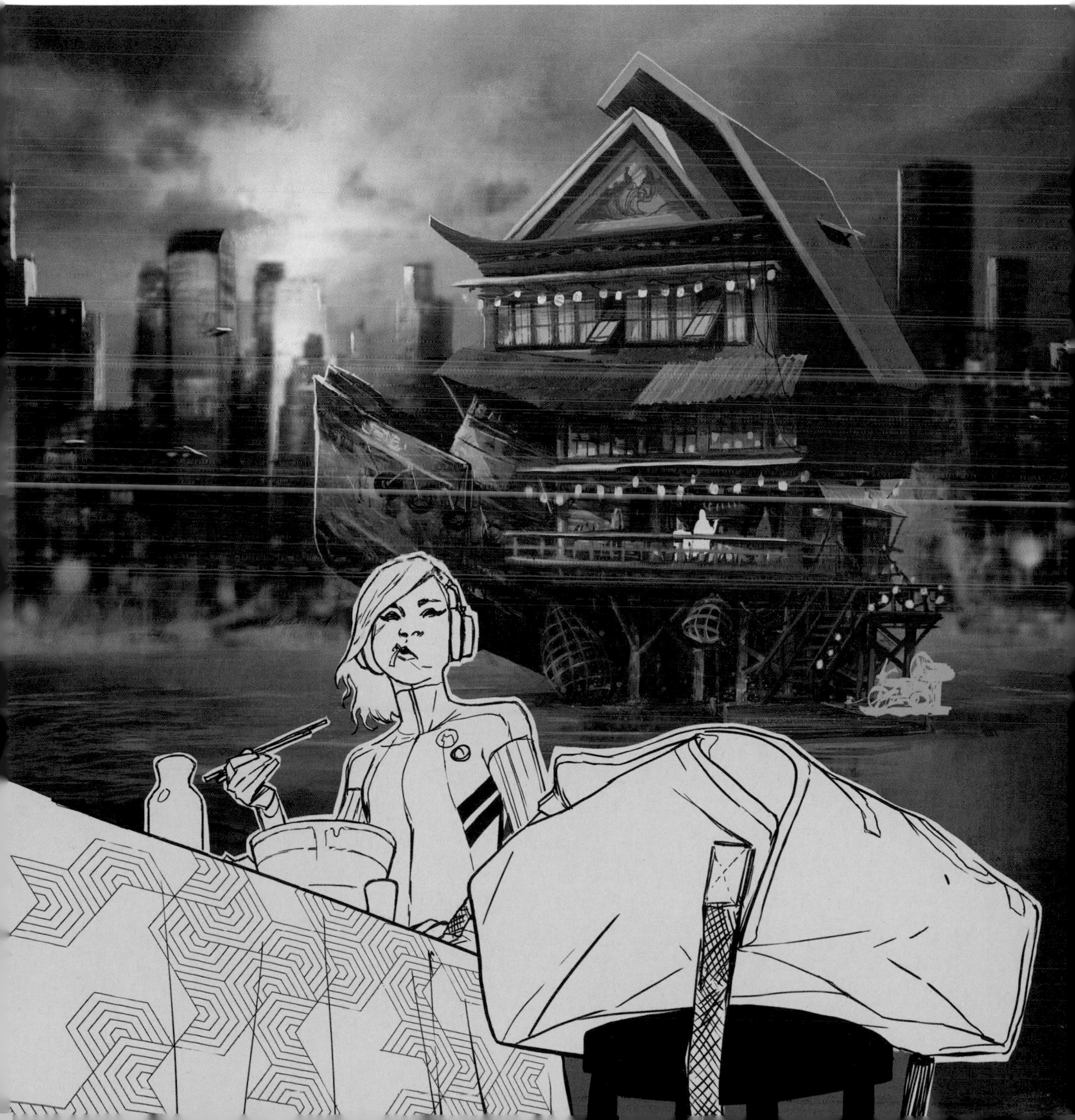

FLOATING SECTION:
0027 B3 [SECOND CYCLE]

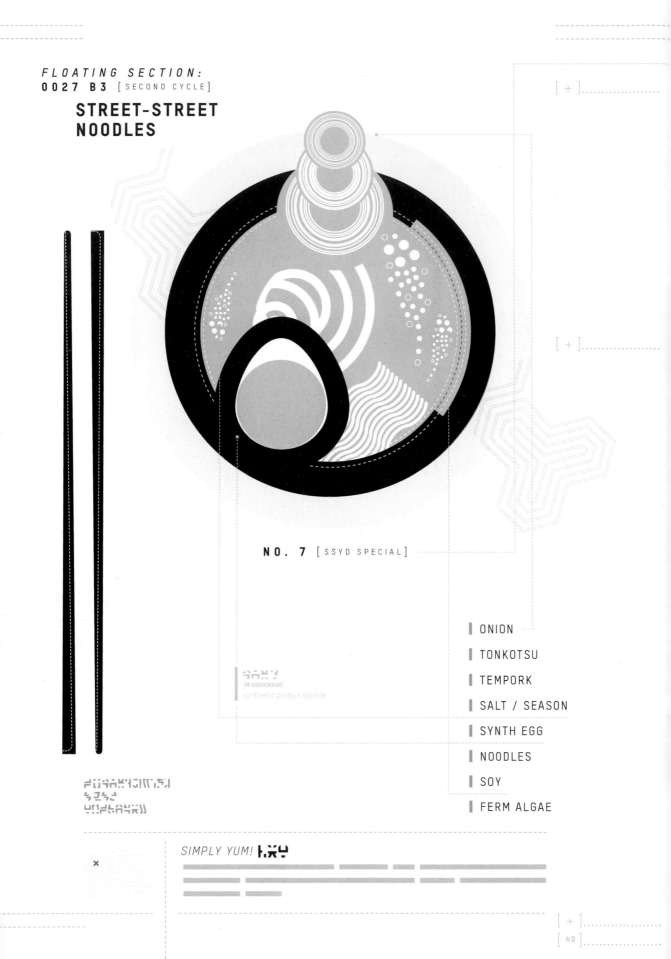

STREET-STREET NOODLES

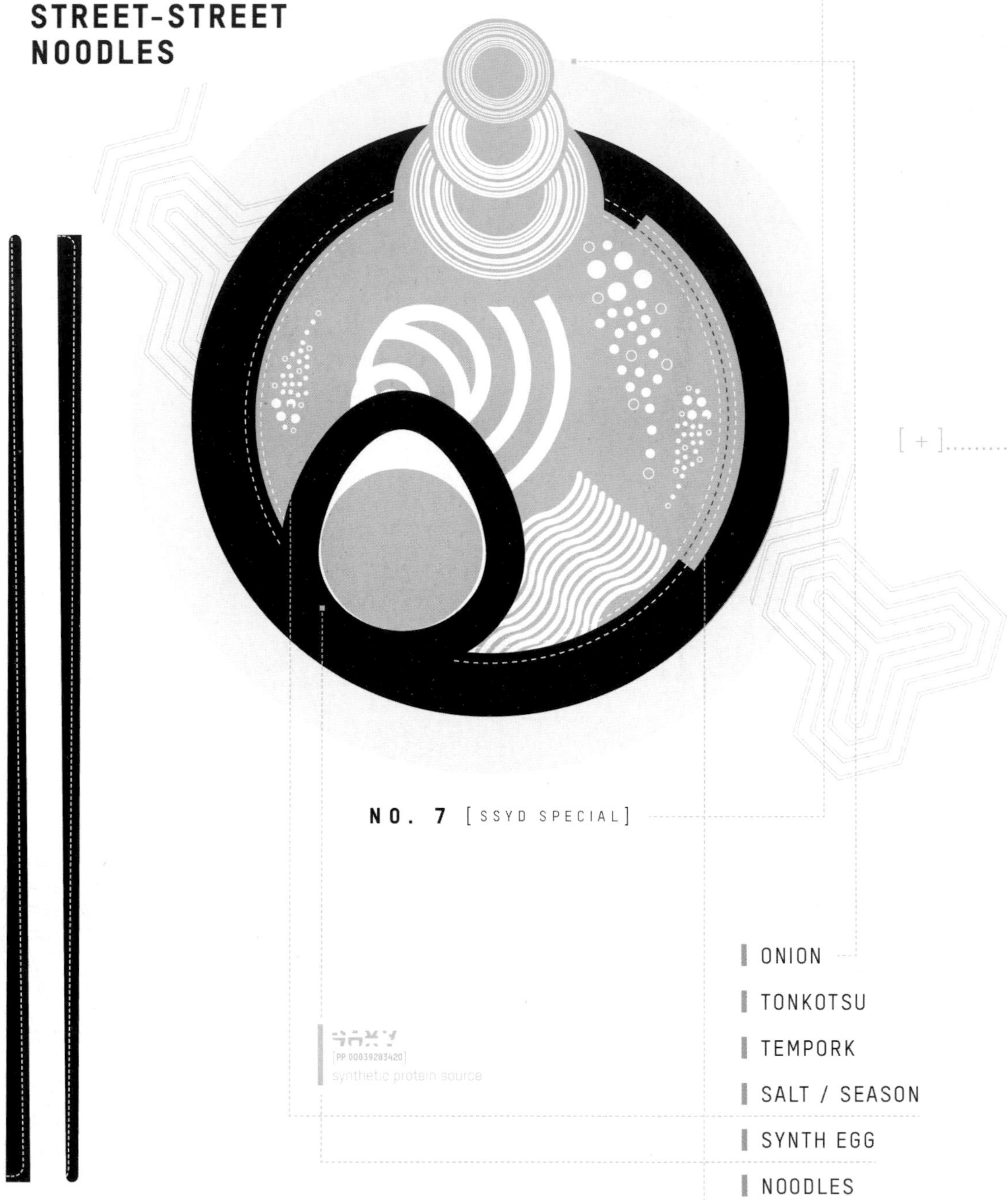

NO. 7 [SSYD SPECIAL]

[PP 00039283420]
synthetic protein source

- ONION
- TONKOTSU
- TEMPORK
- SALT / SEASON
- SYNTH EGG
- NOODLES
- SOY
- FERM ALGAE

×

SIMPLY YUM!

[+]

[+]

[+]

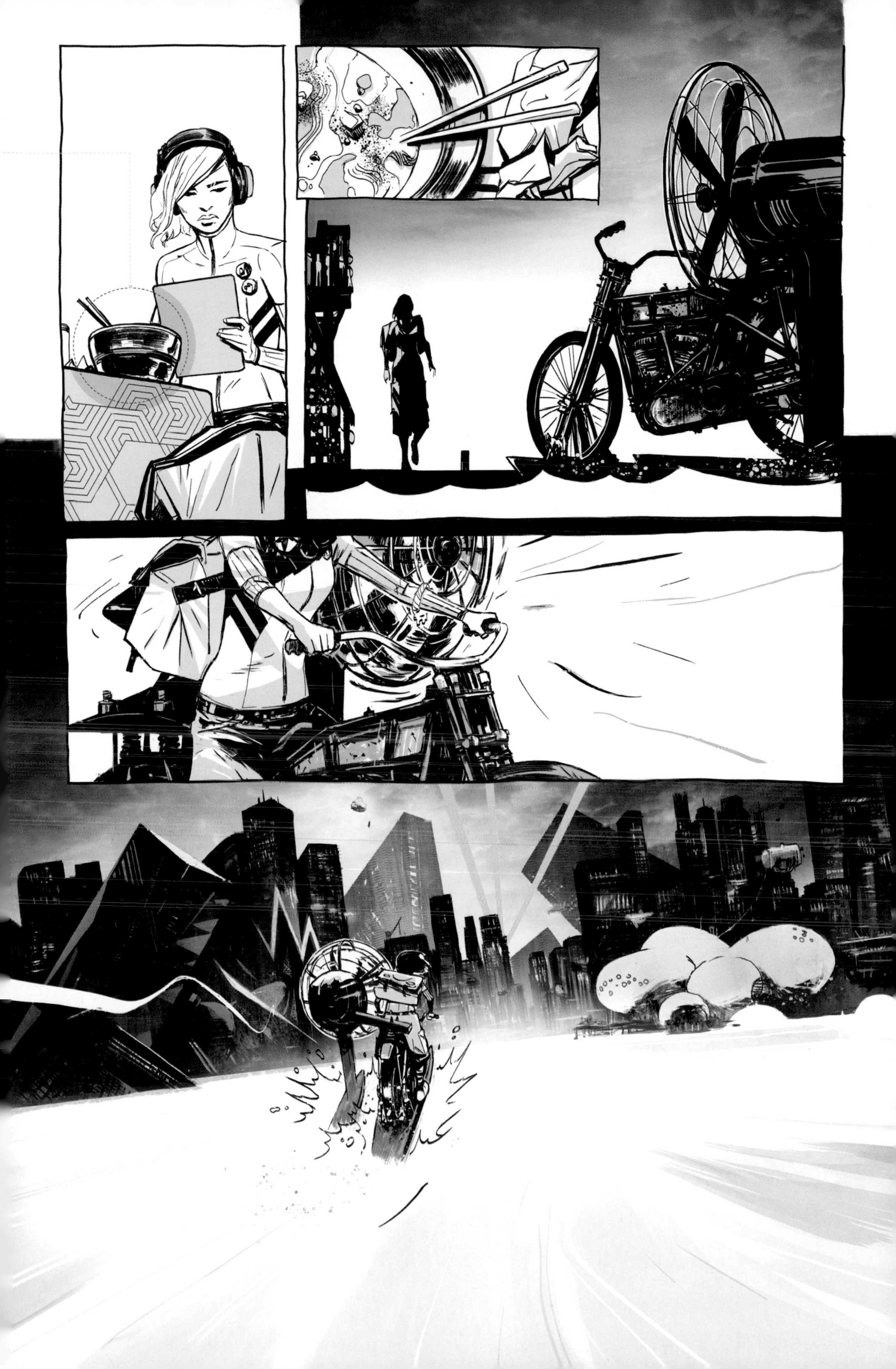

CHAPTER THREE

[ELBOWS OFF THE TABLE]

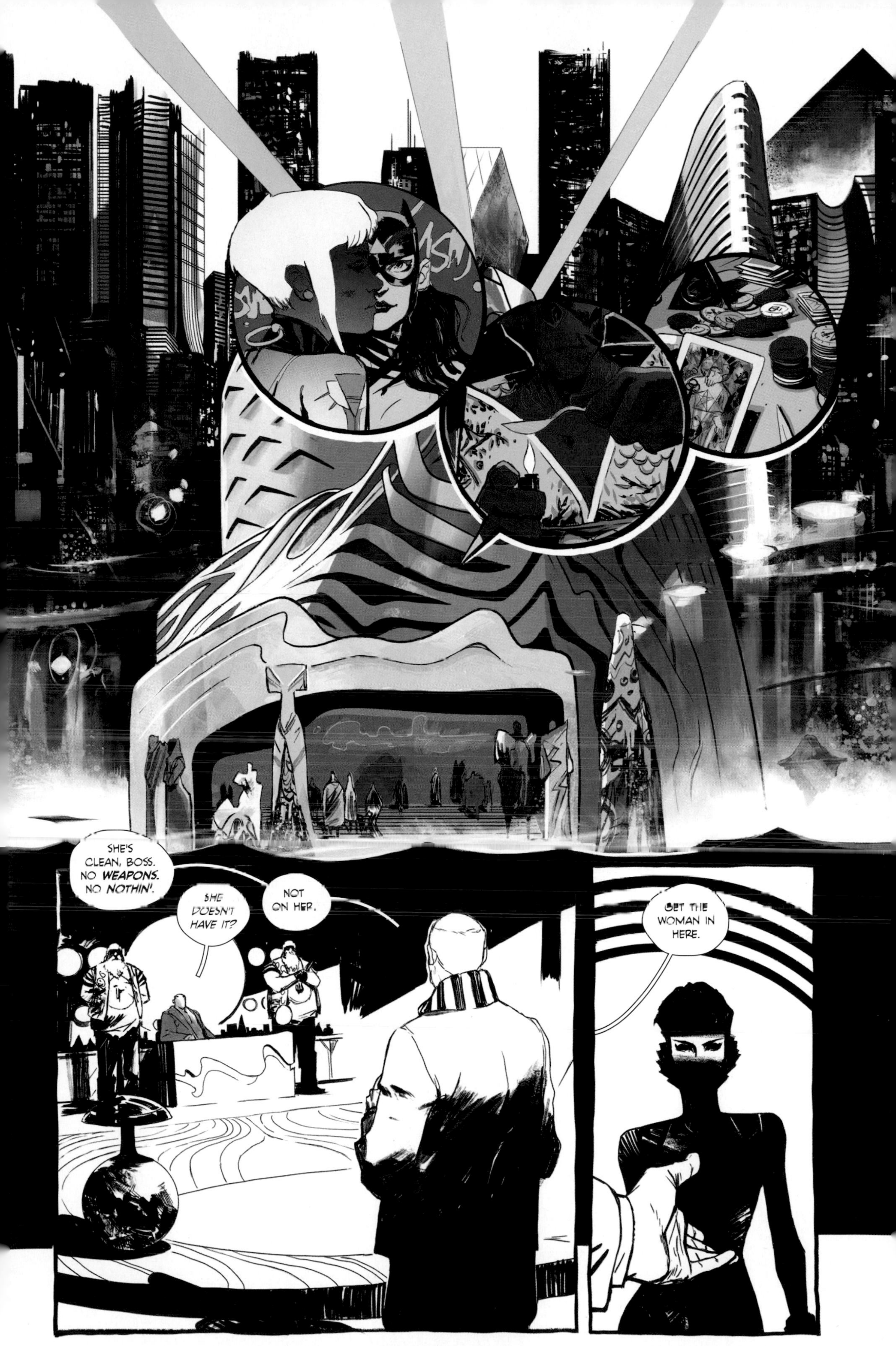
SHE'S CLEAN, BOSS. NO WEAPONS. NO NOTHIN'.
SHE DOESN'T HAVE IT?
NOT ON HER.
GET THE WOMAN IN HERE.

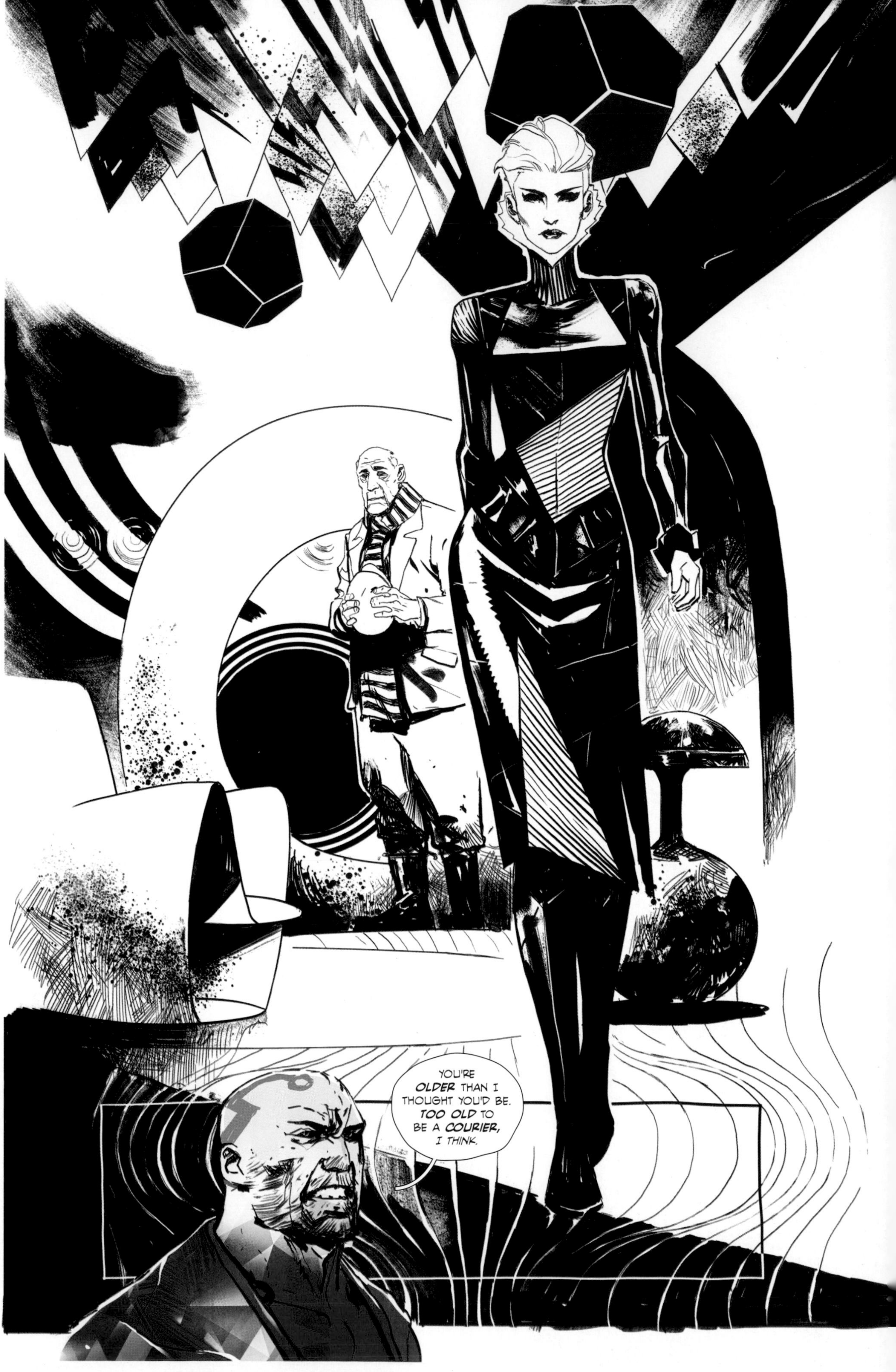
YOU'RE OLDER THAN I THOUGHT YOU'D BE. TOO OLD TO BE A COURIER, I THINK.

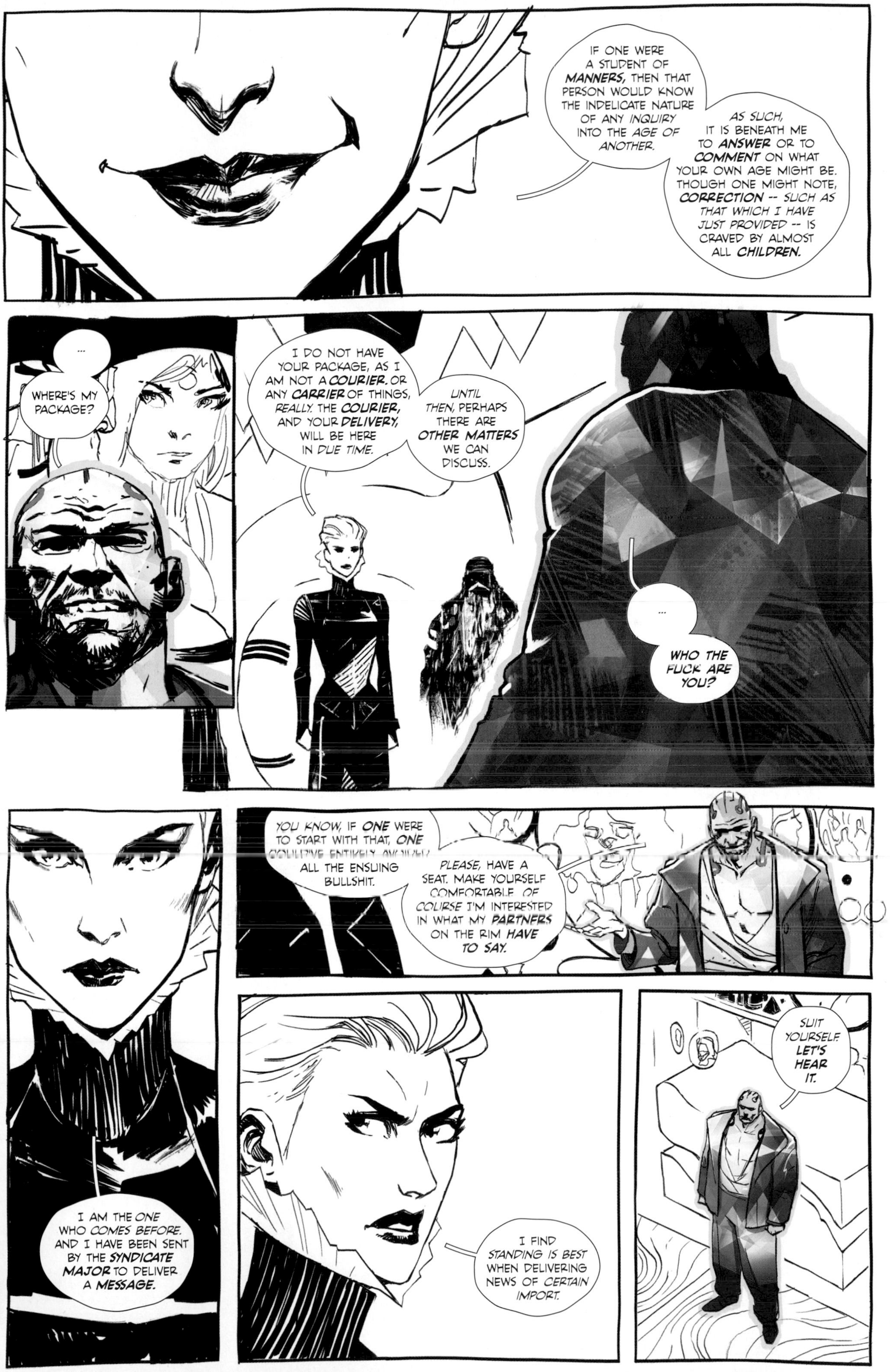
IF ONE WERE A STUDENT OF MANNERS, THEN THAT PERSON WOULD KNOW THE INDELICATE NATURE OF ANY INQUIRY INTO THE AGE OF ANOTHER.
AS SUCH, IT IS BENEATH ME TO ANSWER OR TO COMMENT ON WHAT YOUR OWN AGE MIGHT BE. THOUGH ONE MIGHT NOTE, CORRECTION -- SUCH AS THAT WHICH I HAVE JUST PROVIDED -- IS CRAVED BY ALMOST ALL CHILDREN.
...
WHERE'S MY PACKAGE?
I DO NOT HAVE YOUR PACKAGE, AS I AM NOT A COURIER. OR ANY CARRIER OF THINGS, REALLY. THE COURIER, AND YOUR DELIVERY, WILL BE HERE IN DUE TIME.
UNTIL THEN, PERHAPS THERE ARE OTHER MATTERS WE CAN DISCUSS.
...
WHO THE FUCK ARE YOU?
I AM THE ONE WHO COMES BEFORE. AND I HAVE BEEN SENT BY THE SYNDICATE MAJOR TO DELIVER A MESSAGE.
YOU KNOW, IF ONE WERE TO START WITH THAT, ONE COULD'VE ENTIRELY AVOIDED ALL THE ENSUING BULLSHIT.
PLEASE, HAVE A SEAT. MAKE YOURSELF COMFORTABLE. OF COURSE I'M INTERESTED IN WHAT MY PARTNERS ON THE RIM HAVE TO SAY.
I FIND STANDING IS BEST WHEN DELIVERING NEWS OF CERTAIN IMPORT.
SUIT YOURSELF. LET'S HEAR IT.

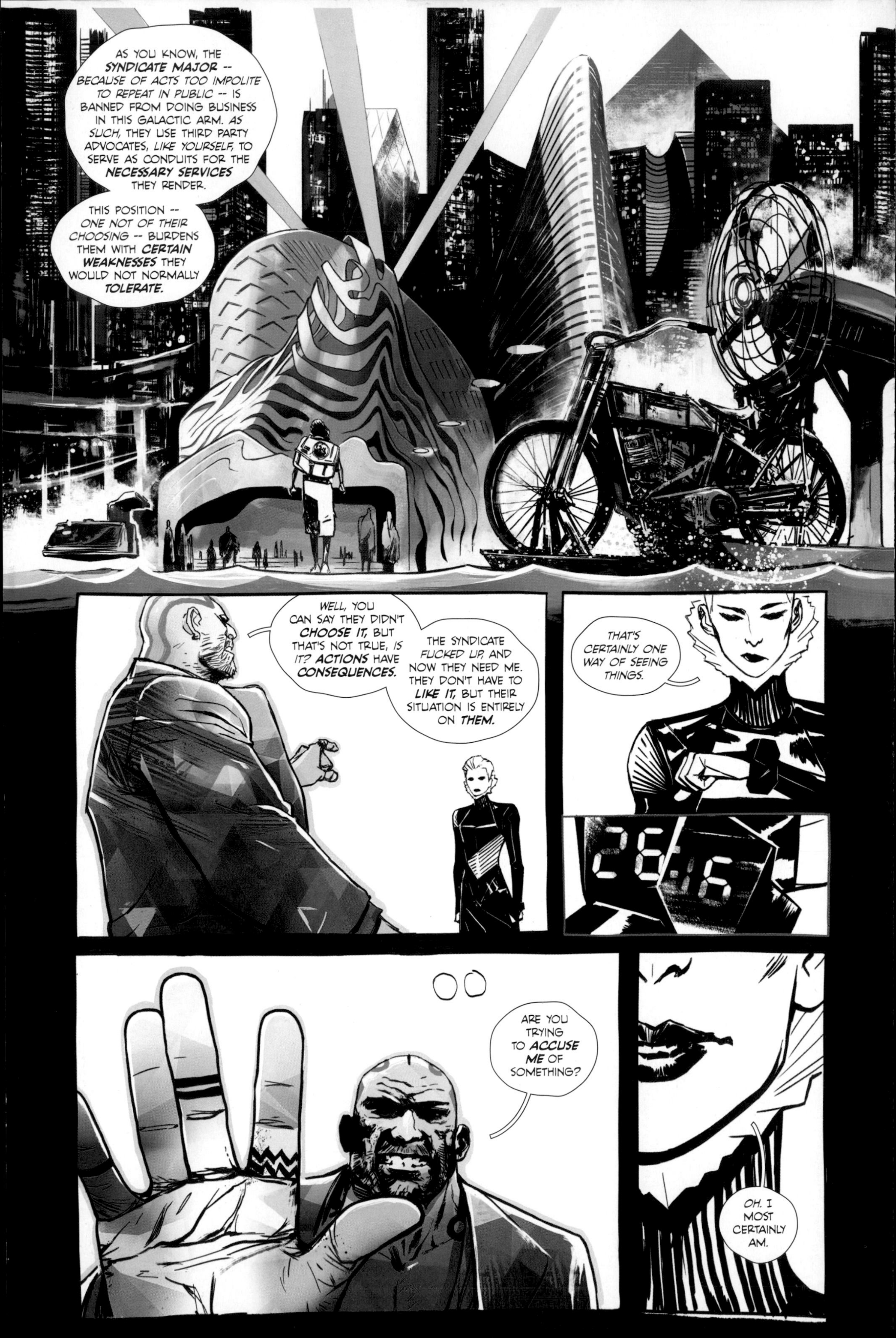
AS YOU KNOW, THE SYNDICATE MAJOR -- BECAUSE OF ACTS TOO IMPOLITE TO REPEAT IN PUBLIC -- IS BANNED FROM DOING BUSINESS IN THIS GALACTIC ARM. AS SUCH, THEY USE THIRD PARTY ADVOCATES, LIKE YOURSELF, TO SERVE AS CONDUITS FOR THE NECESSARY SERVICES THEY RENDER.
THIS POSITION -- ONE NOT OF THEIR CHOOSING -- BURDENS THEM WITH CERTAIN WEAKNESSES THEY WOULD NOT NORMALLY TOLERATE.
WELL, YOU CAN SAY THEY DIDN'T CHOOSE IT, BUT THAT'S NOT TRUE, IS IT? ACTIONS HAVE CONSEQUENCES.
THE SYNDICATE FUCKED UP, AND NOW THEY NEED ME. THEY DON'T HAVE TO LIKE IT, BUT THEIR SITUATION IS ENTIRELY ON THEM.
THAT'S CERTAINLY ONE WAY OF SEEING THINGS.
26:16
ARE YOU TRYING TO ACCUSE ME OF SOMETHING?
OH. I MOST CERTAINLY AM.

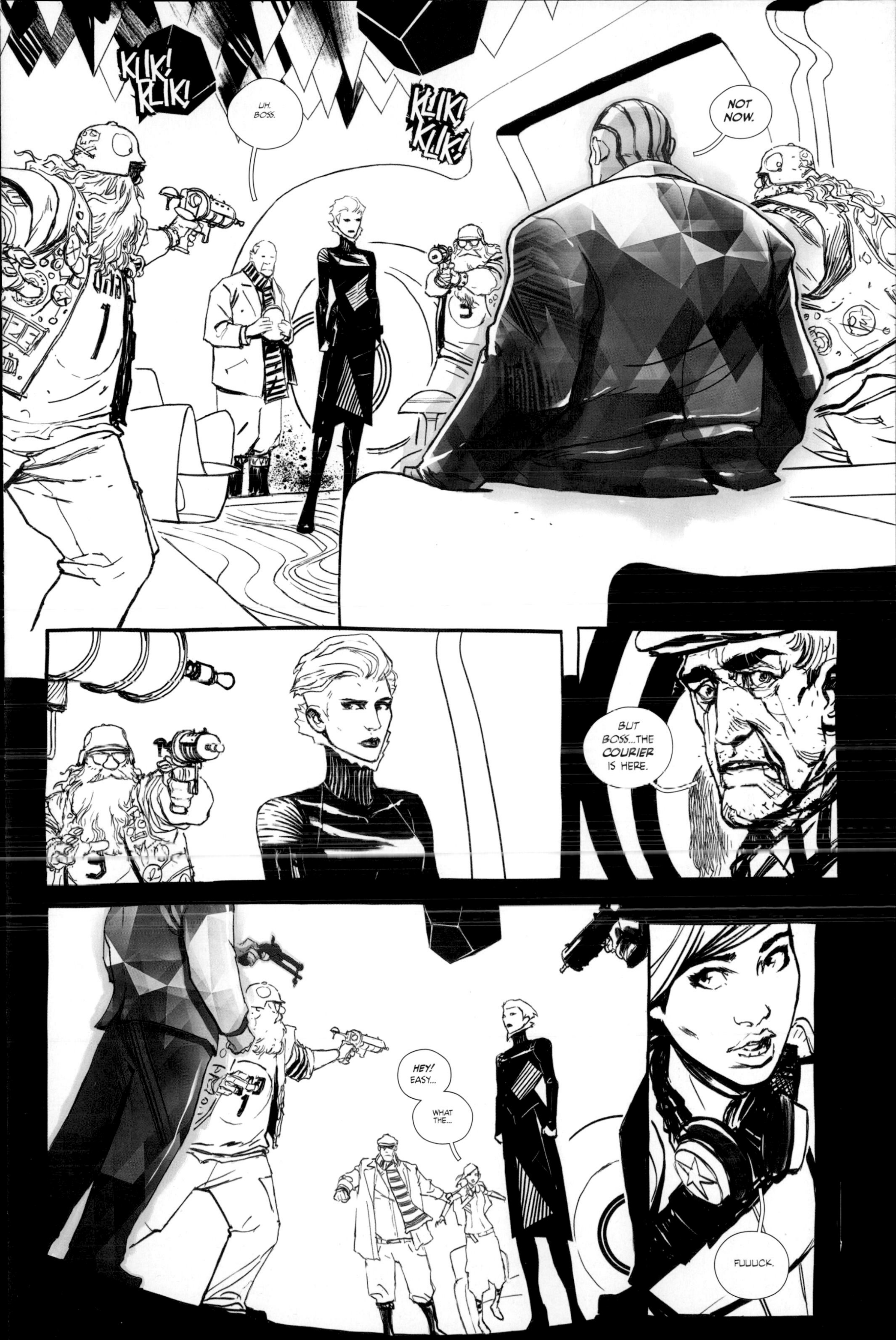
KLIK! KLIK!
UH. BOSS.
KLIK! KLIK!
NOT NOW.
BUT BOSS... THE COURIER IS HERE.
HEY! EASY...
WHAT THE...
FUUUCK.

COURIER
BOX

[CLASS 5]

Our highest security enclosure. Ensured to micro-singularity
collapse upon unauthorized breaching or
credit-back guaranteed.

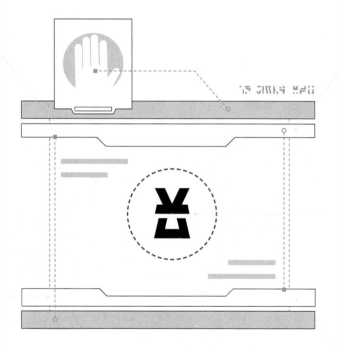

FEATURING

AUTHORIZATION WINDOW.
PALM PRINT IDENTIFICATION.
RETINA CONFIRMATION.
GENETIC CONFIRMATION.

Constructed of **neutron polymers** *and*
sealed by **heavy atomic bonding.**

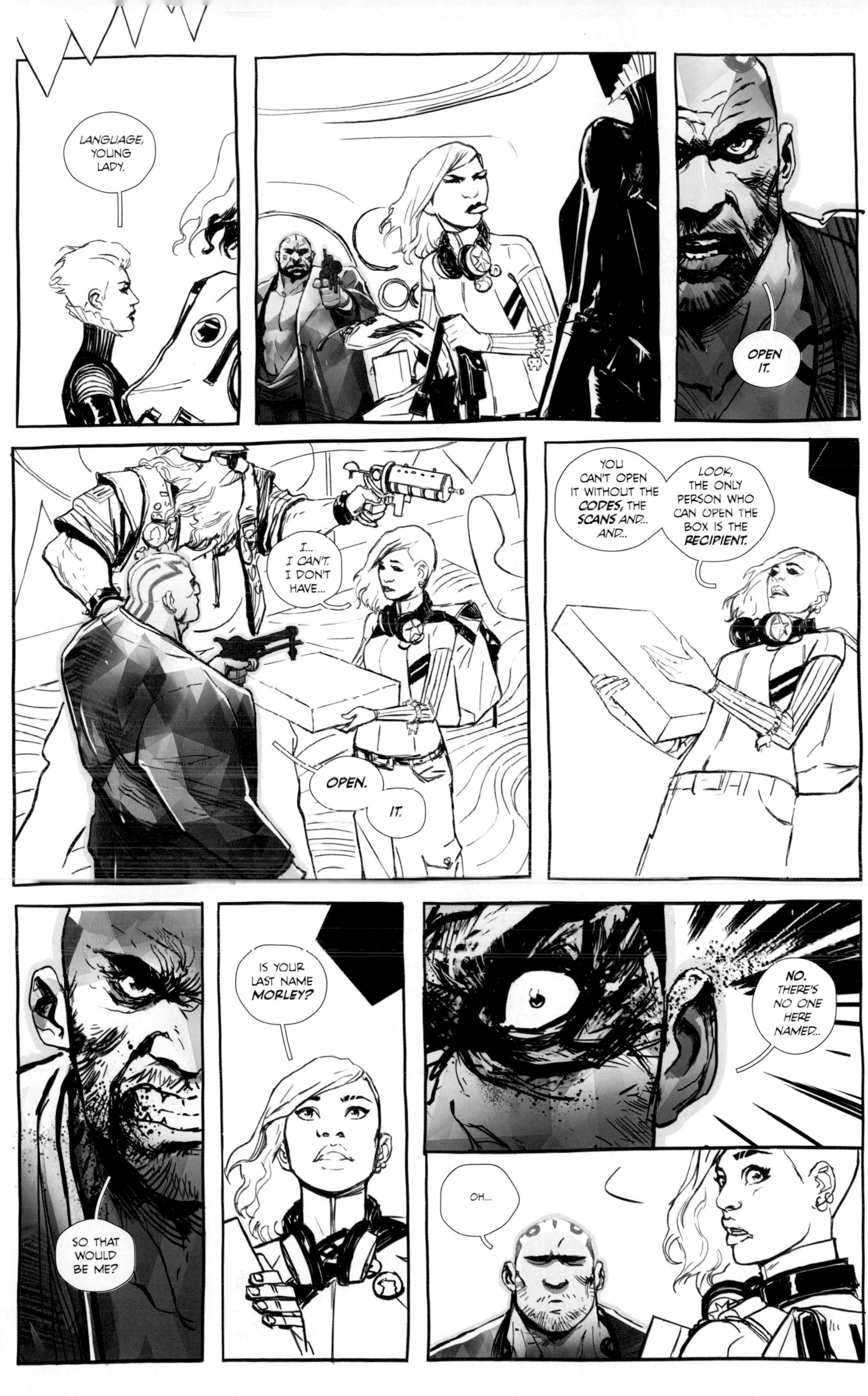
LANGUAGE, YOUNG LADY.
OPEN IT.
I... I CAN'T. I DON'T HAVE...
OPEN.
IT.
YOU CAN'T OPEN IT WITHOUT THE CODES, THE SCANS AND... AND...
LOOK, THE ONLY PERSON WHO CAN OPEN THE BOX IS THE RECIPIENT.
SO THAT WOULD BE ME?
IS YOUR LAST NAME MORLEY?
NO. THERE'S NO ONE HERE NAMED...
OH...

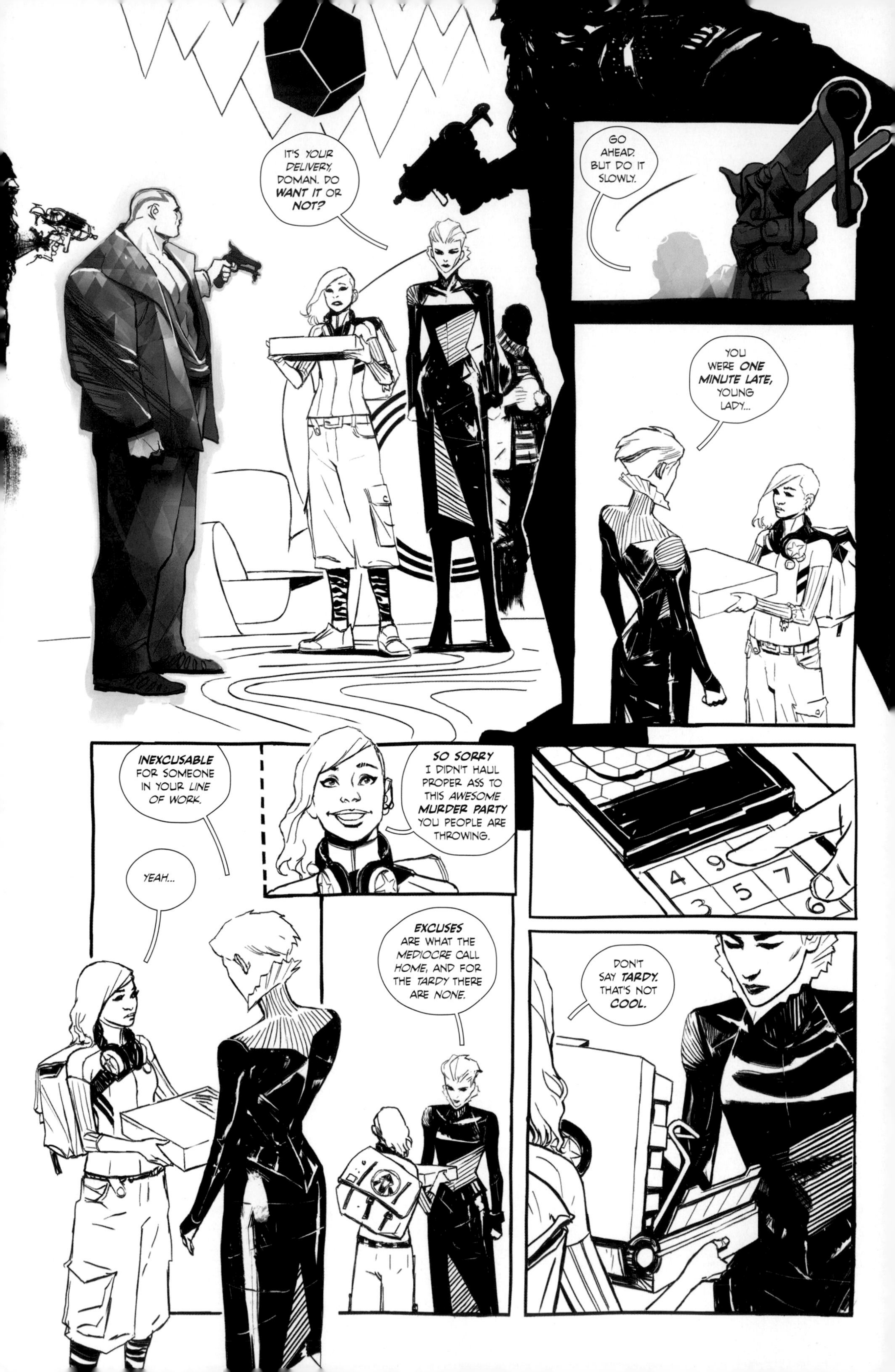
IT'S YOUR DELIVERY, DOMAN. DO WANT IT OR NOT?
GO AHEAD. BUT DO IT SLOWLY.
YOU WERE ONE MINUTE LATE, YOUNG LADY...
INEXCUSABLE FOR SOMEONE IN YOUR LINE OF WORK.
YEAH...
SO SORRY I DIDN'T HAUL PROPER ASS TO THIS AWESOME MURDER PARTY YOU PEOPLE ARE THROWING.
4 9 7
3 5 6
EXCUSES ARE WHAT THE MEDIOCRE CALL HOME, AND FOR THE TARDY THERE ARE NONE.
DON'T SAY TARDY. THAT'S NOT COOL.

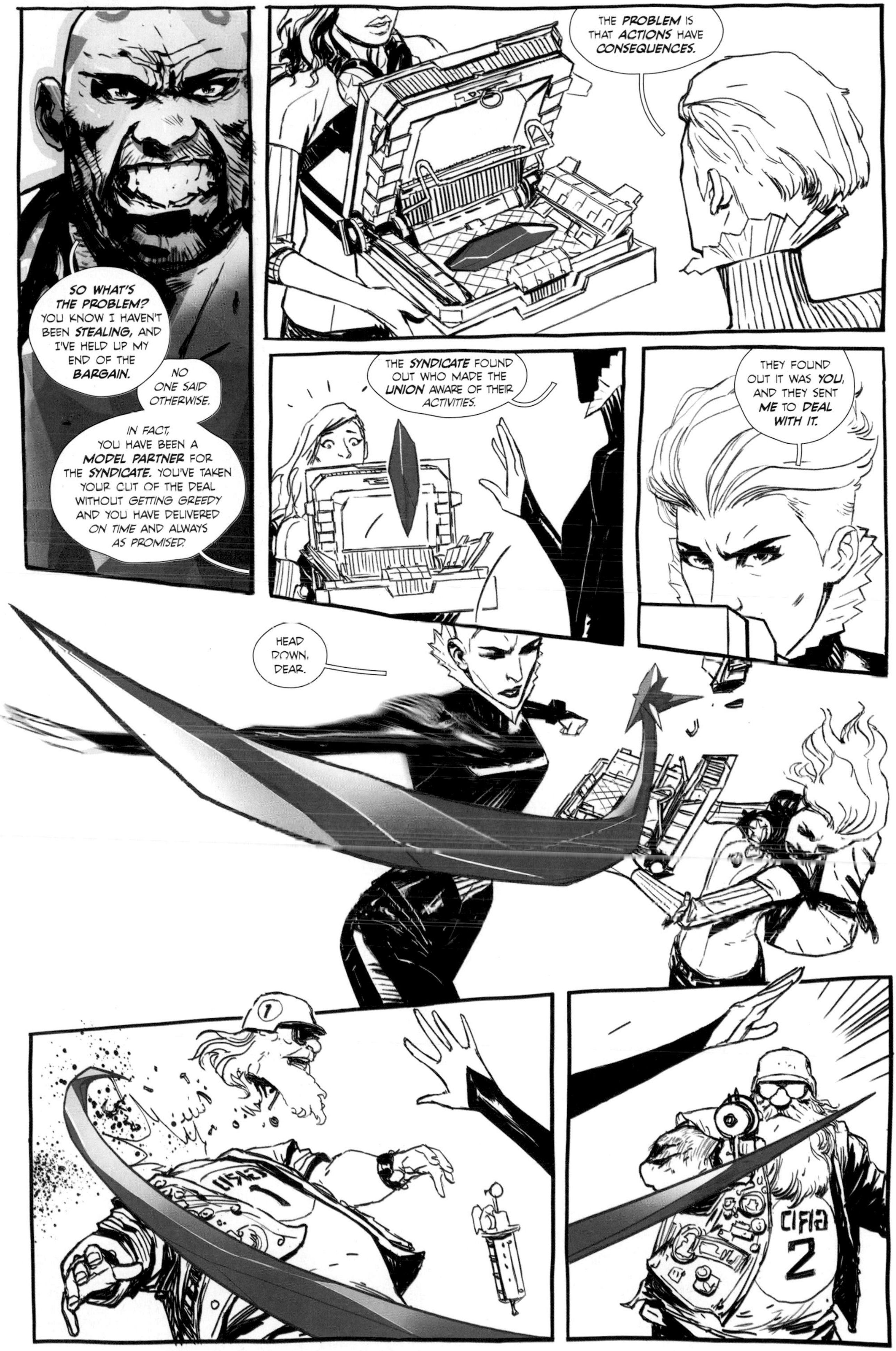

SO WHAT'S THE PROBLEM? YOU KNOW I HAVEN'T BEEN STEALING, AND I'VE HELD UP MY END OF THE BARGAIN.
NO ONE SAID OTHERWISE.
IN FACT, YOU HAVE BEEN A MODEL PARTNER FOR THE SYNDICATE. YOU'VE TAKEN YOUR CUT OF THE DEAL WITHOUT GETTING GREEDY AND YOU HAVE DELIVERED ON TIME AND ALWAYS AS PROMISED.
THE PROBLEM IS THAT ACTIONS HAVE CONSEQUENCES.
THE SYNDICATE FOUND OUT WHO MADE THE UNION AWARE OF THEIR ACTIVITIES.
THEY FOUND OUT IT WAS YOU, AND THEY SENT ME TO DEAL WITH IT.
HEAD DOWN, DEAR.
CIFIG
2

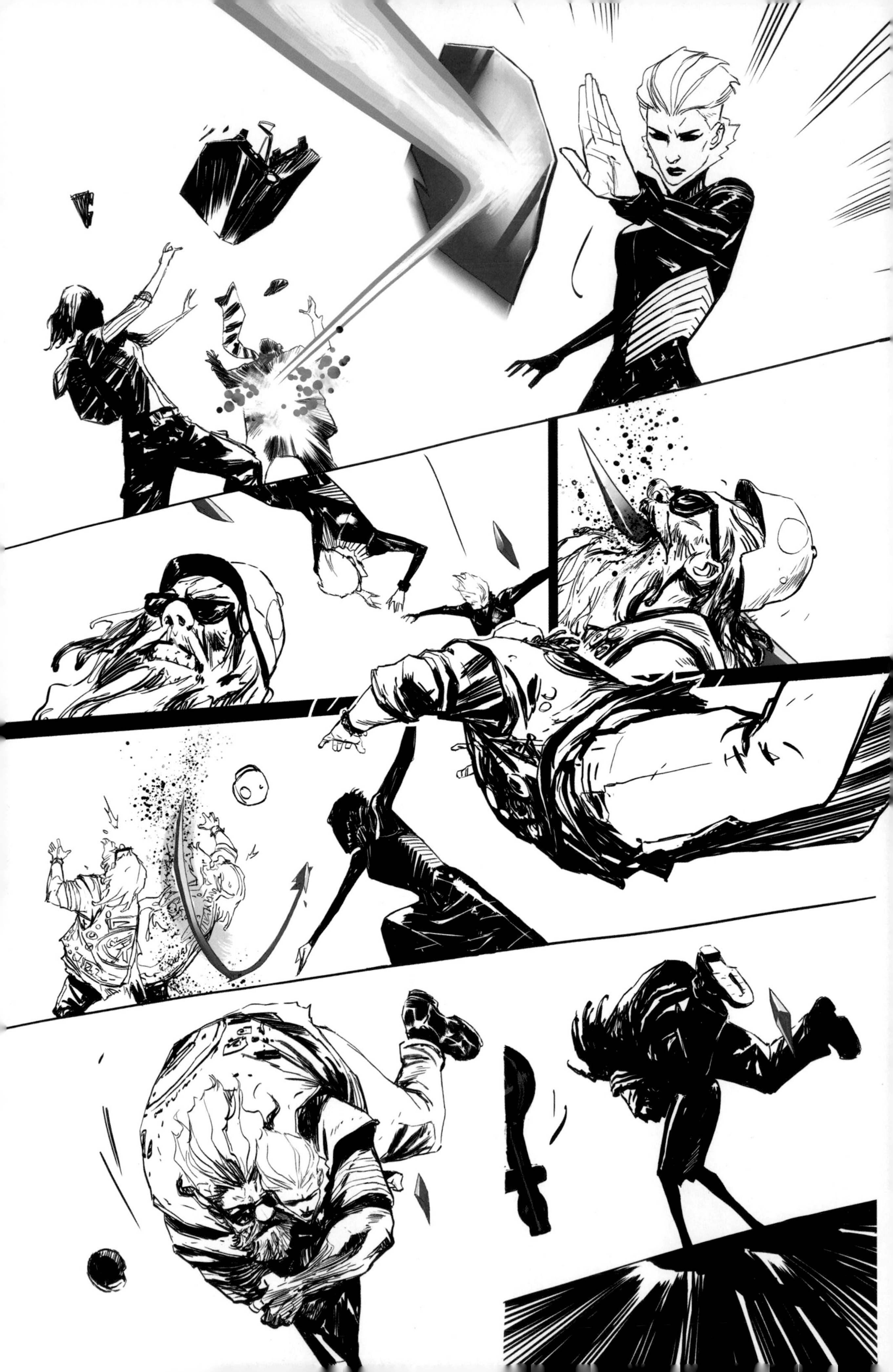

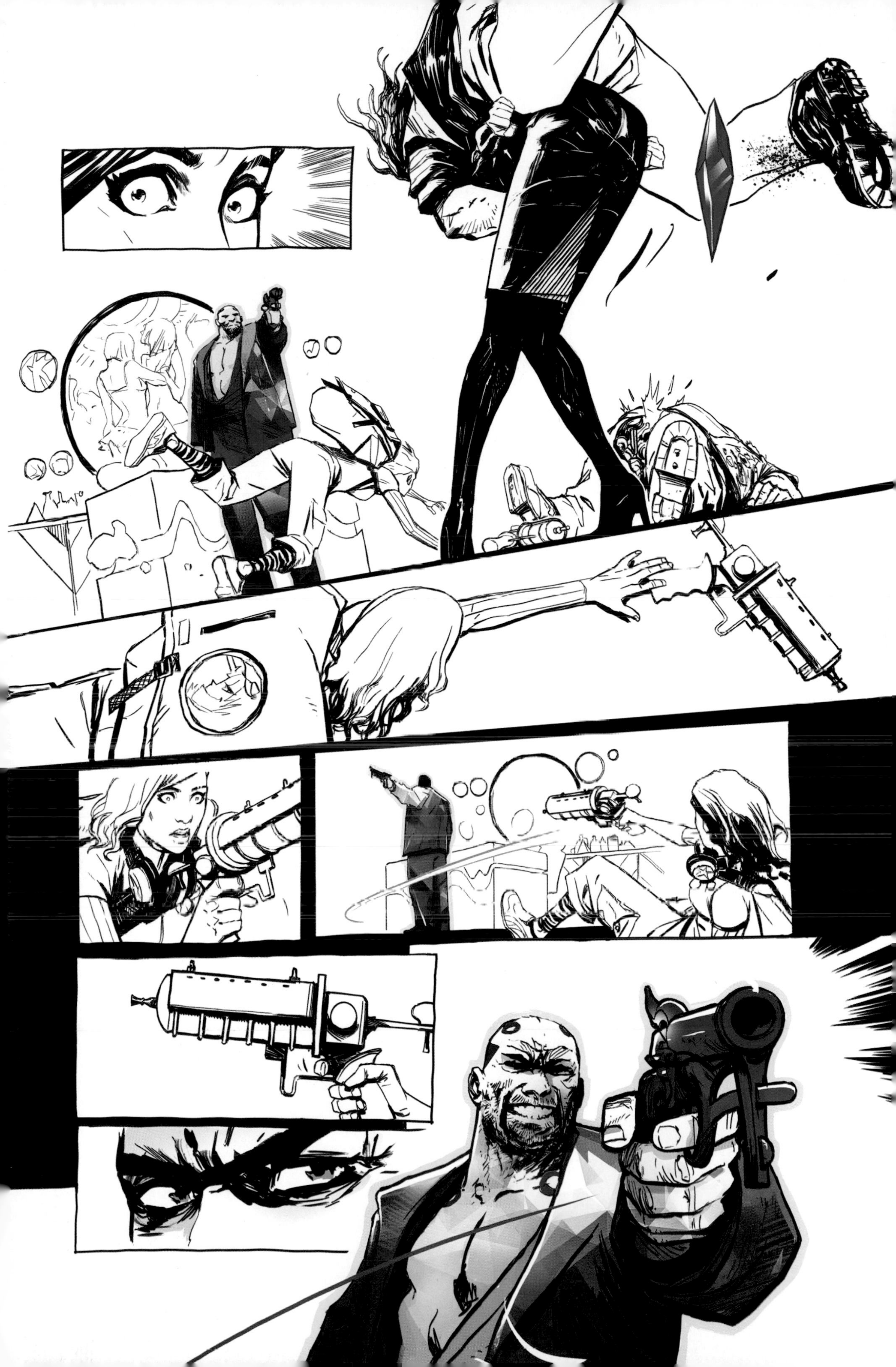

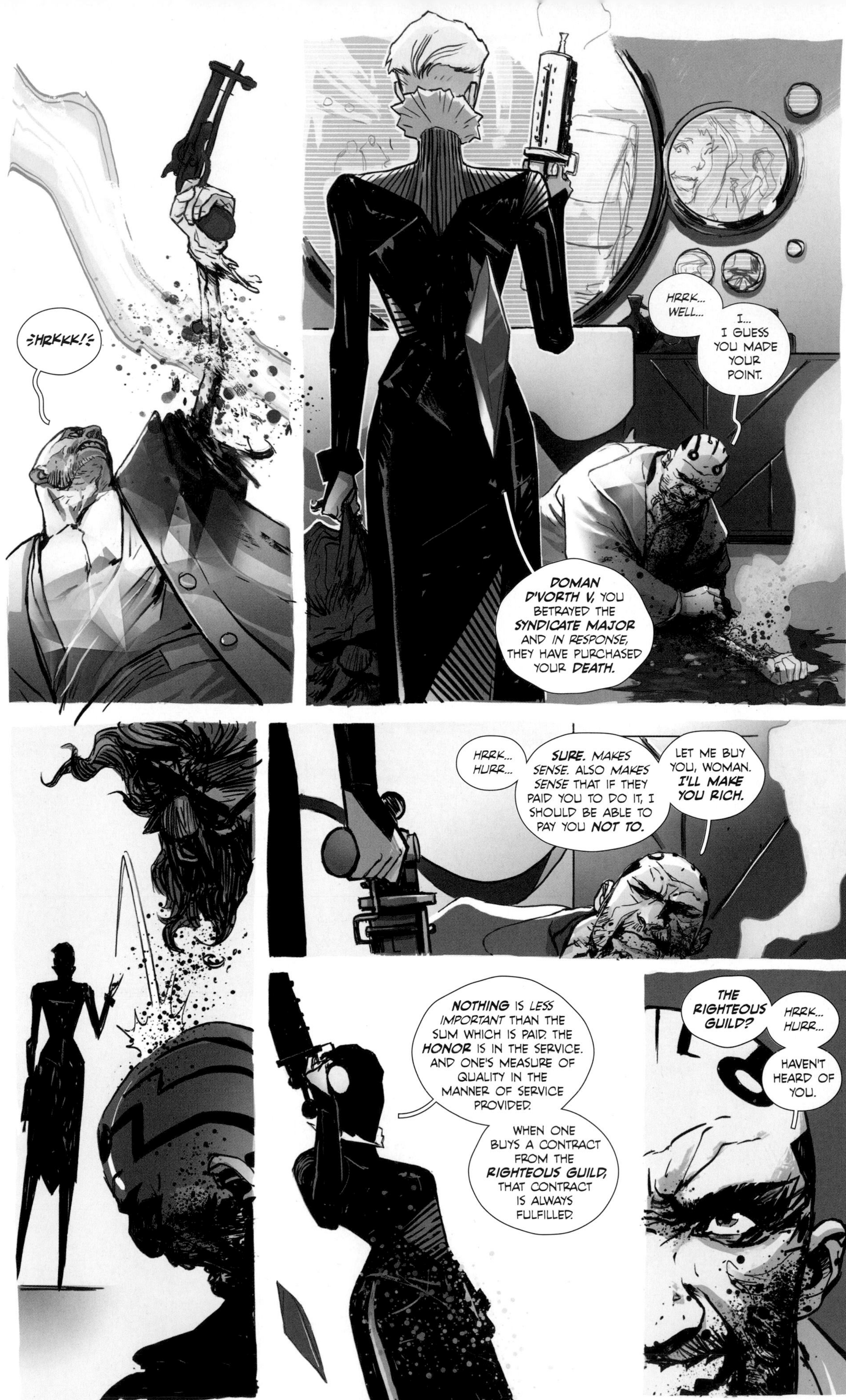

HRKKK!
HRRK... WELL...
I... I GUESS YOU MADE YOUR POINT.
DOMAN D'VORTH V, YOU BETRAYED THE SYNDICATE MAJOR AND IN RESPONSE, THEY HAVE PURCHASED YOUR DEATH.
HRRK... HURR...
SURE. MAKES SENSE. ALSO MAKES SENSE THAT IF THEY PAID YOU TO DO IT, I SHOULD BE ABLE TO PAY YOU NOT TO.
LET ME BUY YOU, WOMAN. I'LL MAKE YOU RICH.
NOTHING IS LESS IMPORTANT THAN THE SUM WHICH IS PAID. THE HONOR IS IN THE SERVICE. AND ONE'S MEASURE OF QUALITY IN THE MANNER OF SERVICE PROVIDED.
WHEN ONE BUYS A CONTRACT FROM THE RIGHTEOUS GUILD, THAT CONTRACT IS ALWAYS FULFILLED.
THE RIGHTEOUS GUILD?
HRRK... HURR...
HAVEN'T HEARD OF YOU.

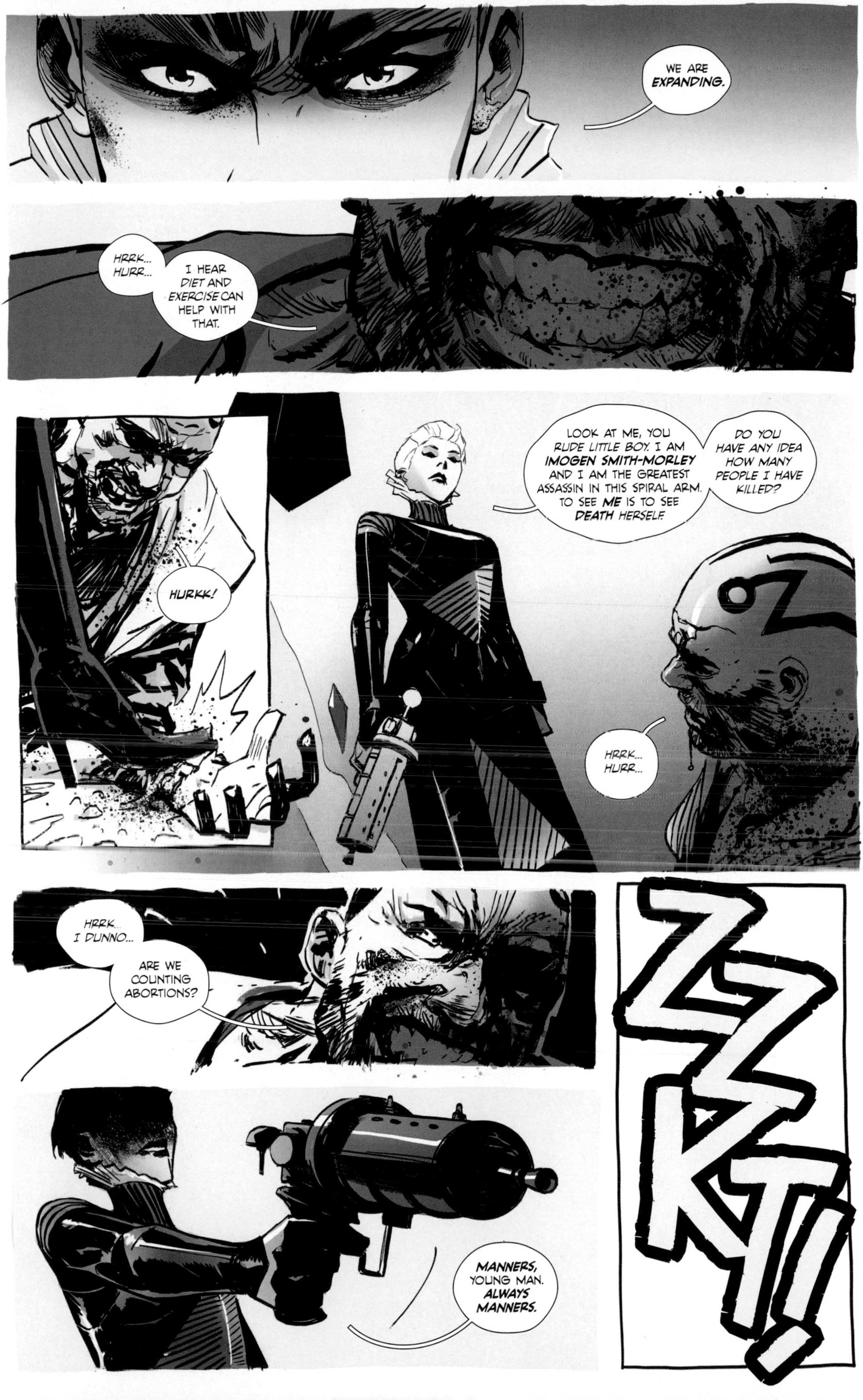
WE ARE EXPANDING.
HRRK... HURR...
I HEAR DIET AND EXERCISE CAN HELP WITH THAT.
LOOK AT ME, YOU RUDE LITTLE BOY. I AM IMOGEN SMITH-MORLEY AND I AM THE GREATEST ASSASSIN IN THIS SPIRAL ARM. TO SEE ME IS TO SEE DEATH HERSELF.
DO YOU HAVE ANY IDEA HOW MANY PEOPLE I HAVE KILLED?
HURKK!
HRRK... HURR...
HRRK... I DUNNO...
ARE WE COUNTING ABORTIONS?
MANNERS, YOUNG MAN. ALWAYS MANNERS.
ZZKT!!

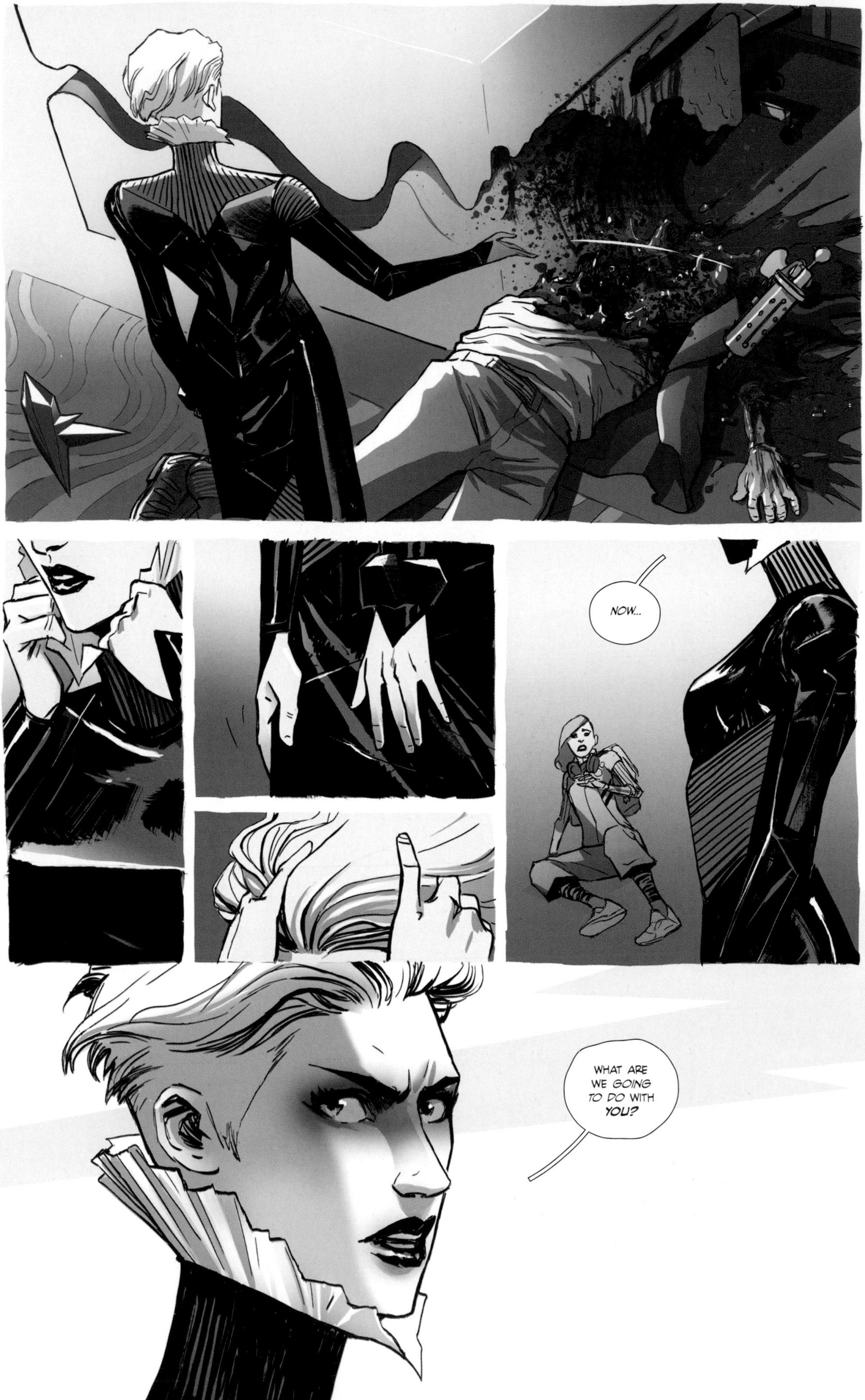
NOW...
WHAT ARE WE GOING TO DO WITH YOU?

[AND THE MACHINIC LOVE
OF **RELIGION**]

CHAPTER FOUR

[SINGULARITY NOW]

THE SHIP OF THE CELESTIAL MOTHERS

[DRIFTING THROUGH SPACE AND TIME]

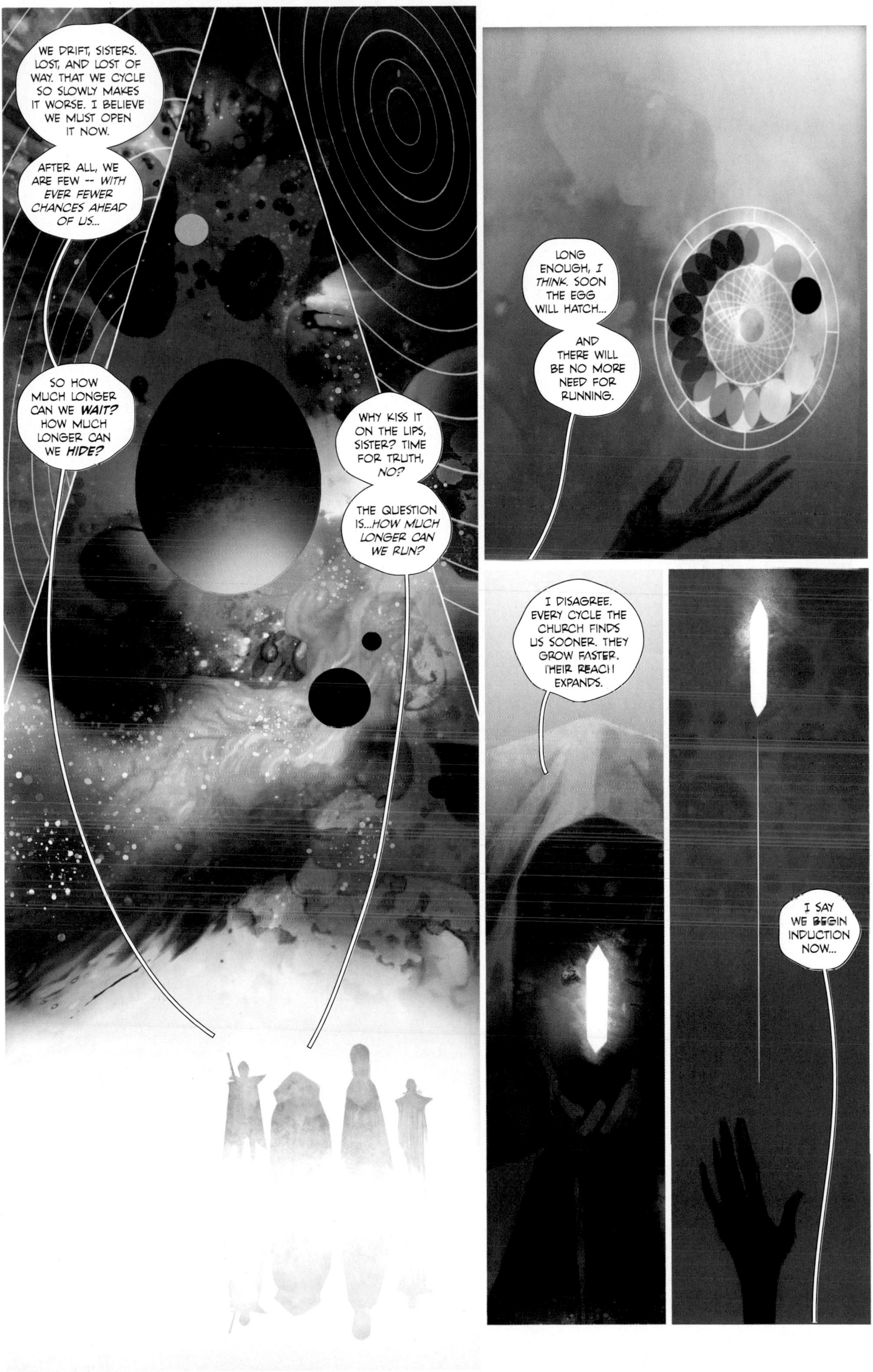
WE DRIFT, SISTERS. LOST, AND LOST OF WAY. THAT WE CYCLE SO SLOWLY MAKES IT WORSE. I BELIEVE WE MUST OPEN IT NOW.
AFTER ALL, WE ARE FEW -- *WITH EVER FEWER CHANCES AHEAD OF US...*
SO HOW MUCH LONGER CAN WE ***WAIT?*** HOW MUCH LONGER CAN WE ***HIDE?***
WHY KISS IT ON THE LIPS, SISTER? TIME FOR TRUTH, NO?
THE QUESTION IS...HOW MUCH LONGER CAN WE RUN?
LONG ENOUGH, *I THINK*. SOON THE EGG WILL HATCH...
AND THERE WILL BE NO MORE NEED FOR RUNNING.
I DISAGREE. EVERY CYCLE THE CHURCH FINDS US SOONER. THEY GROW FASTER. THEIR REACH EXPANDS.
I SAY WE BEGIN INDUCTION NOW...

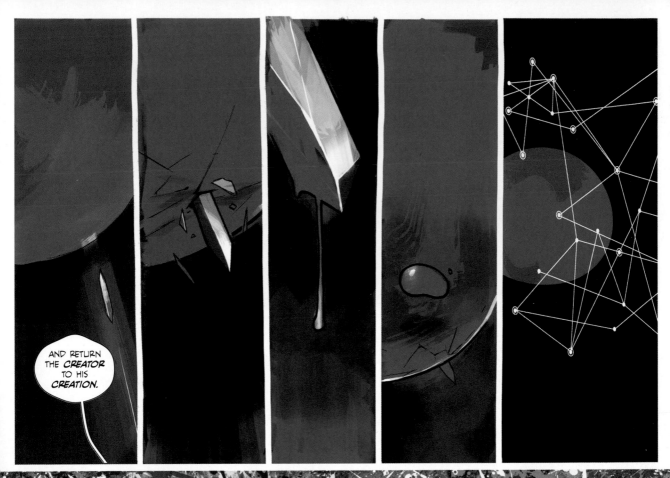

AND RETURN THE **CREATOR** TO HIS **CREATION.**

SINGULARITY WATCHTOWER.

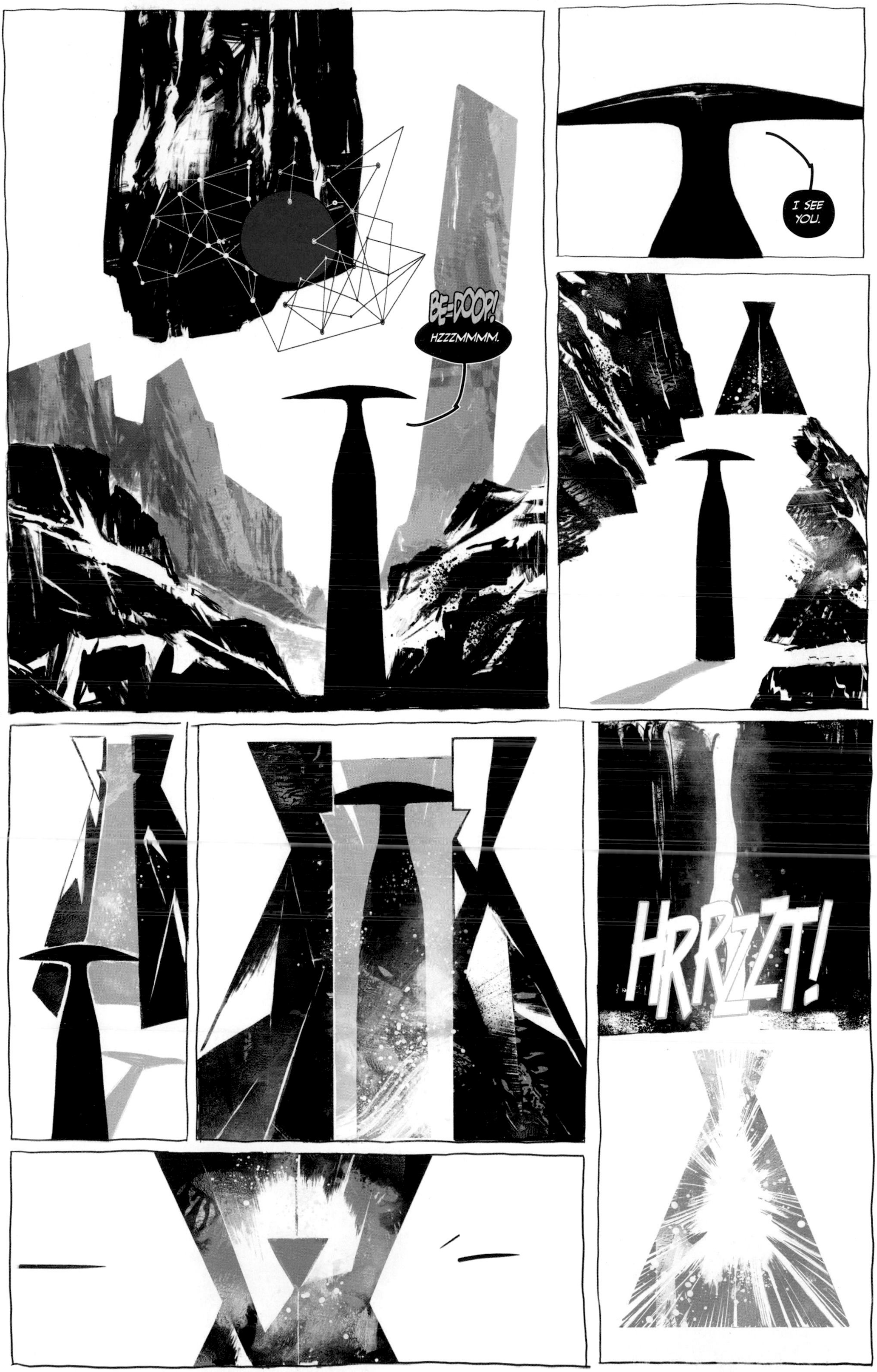

BE-DOOP!
HZZZMMMM.
I SEE YOU.
HRRZZT!

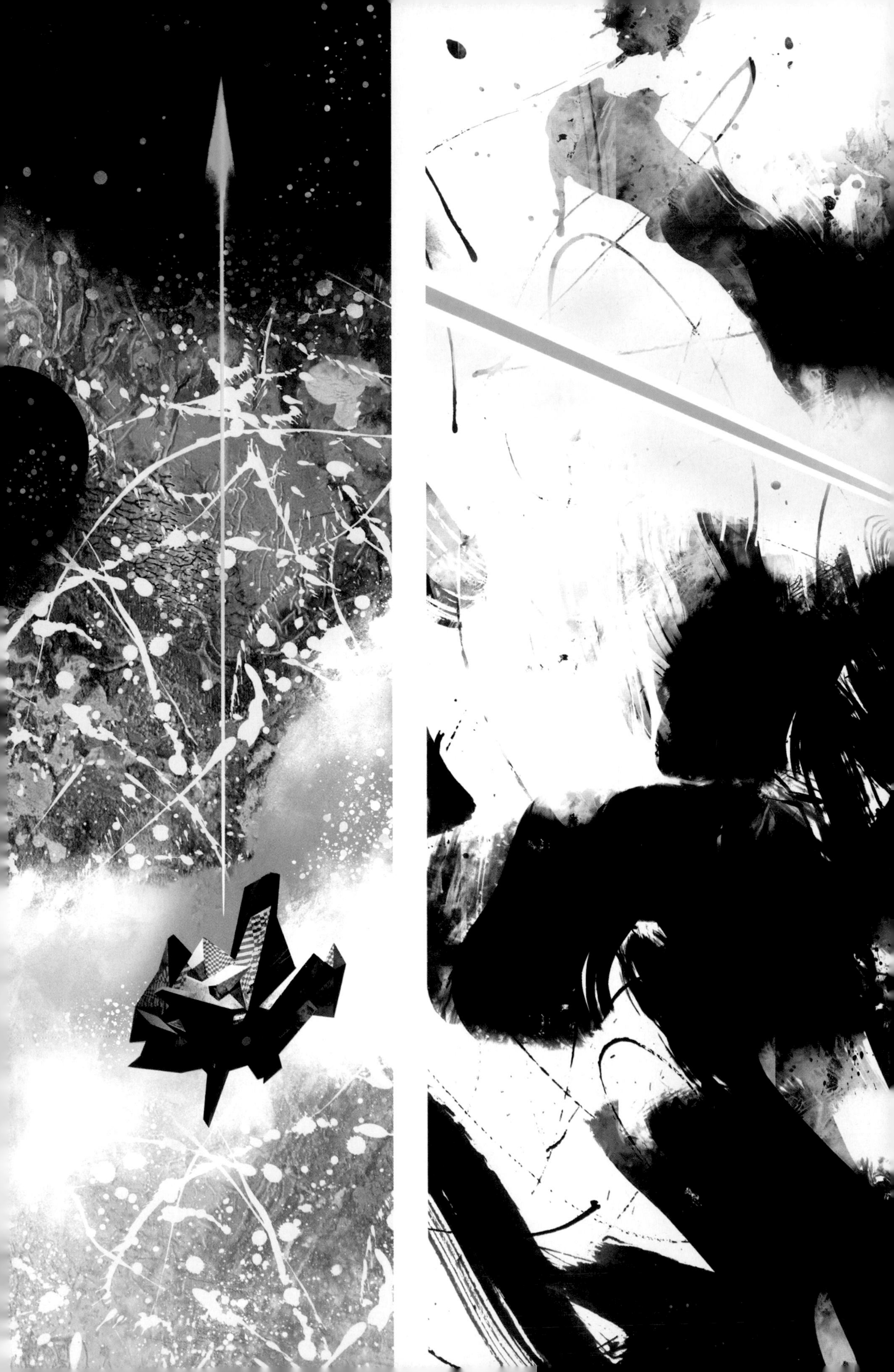

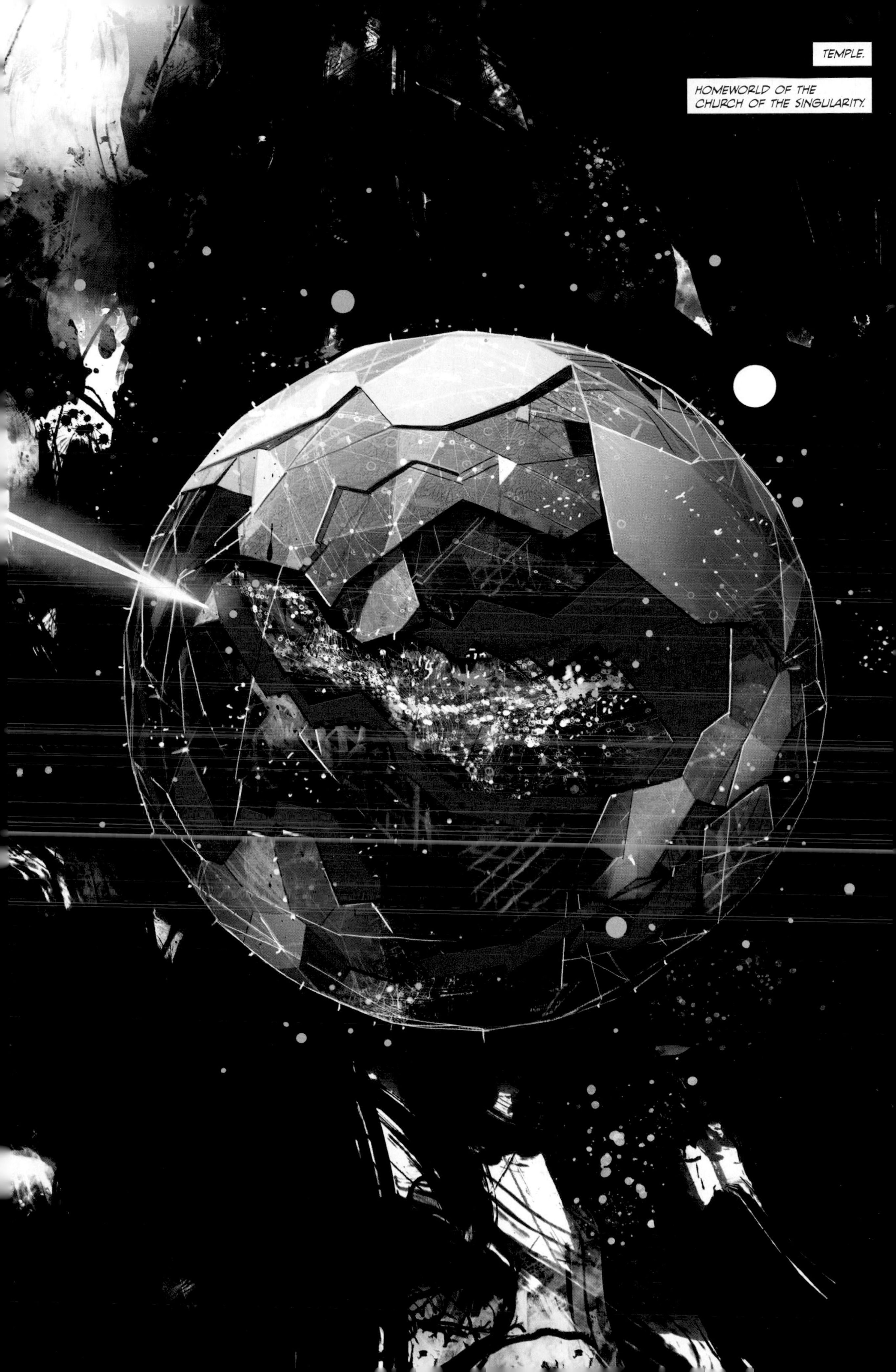
TEMPLE.
HOMEWORLD OF THE CHURCH OF THE SINGULARITY.

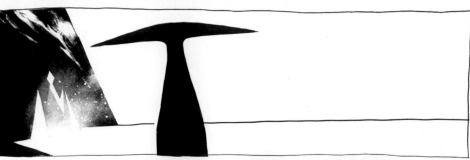

HRRZZT!

YES?

I BRING GOOD NEWS, RO CHI. WE'VE DETECTED A SMALL BREACH.

NOT ENOUGH TO LOCATE, BUT ENOUGH TO SPOIL THE SPACE.

YOU'RE SURE?

YES.

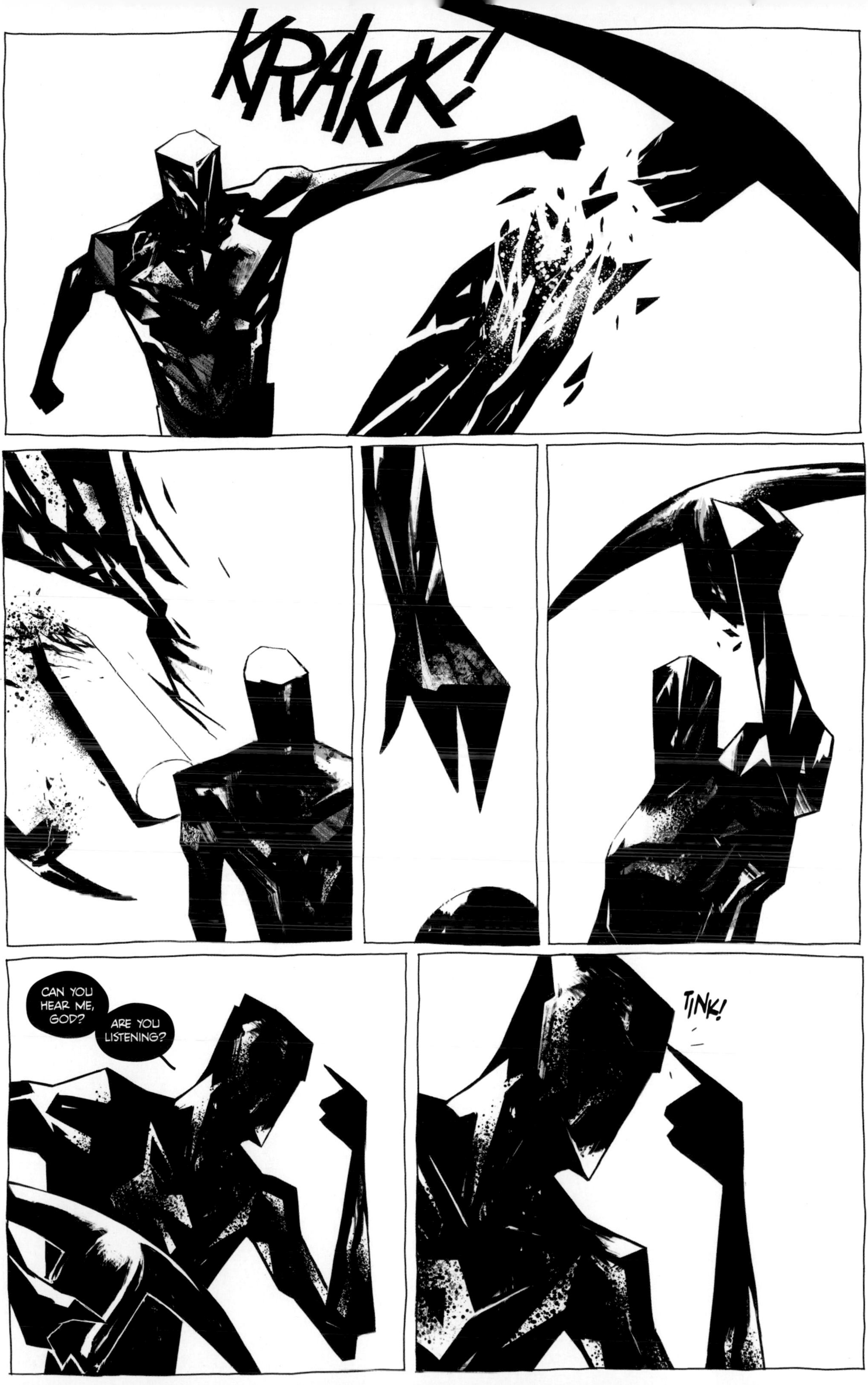
KRAKK!
CAN YOU HEAR ME, GOD?
ARE YOU LISTENING?
TINK!

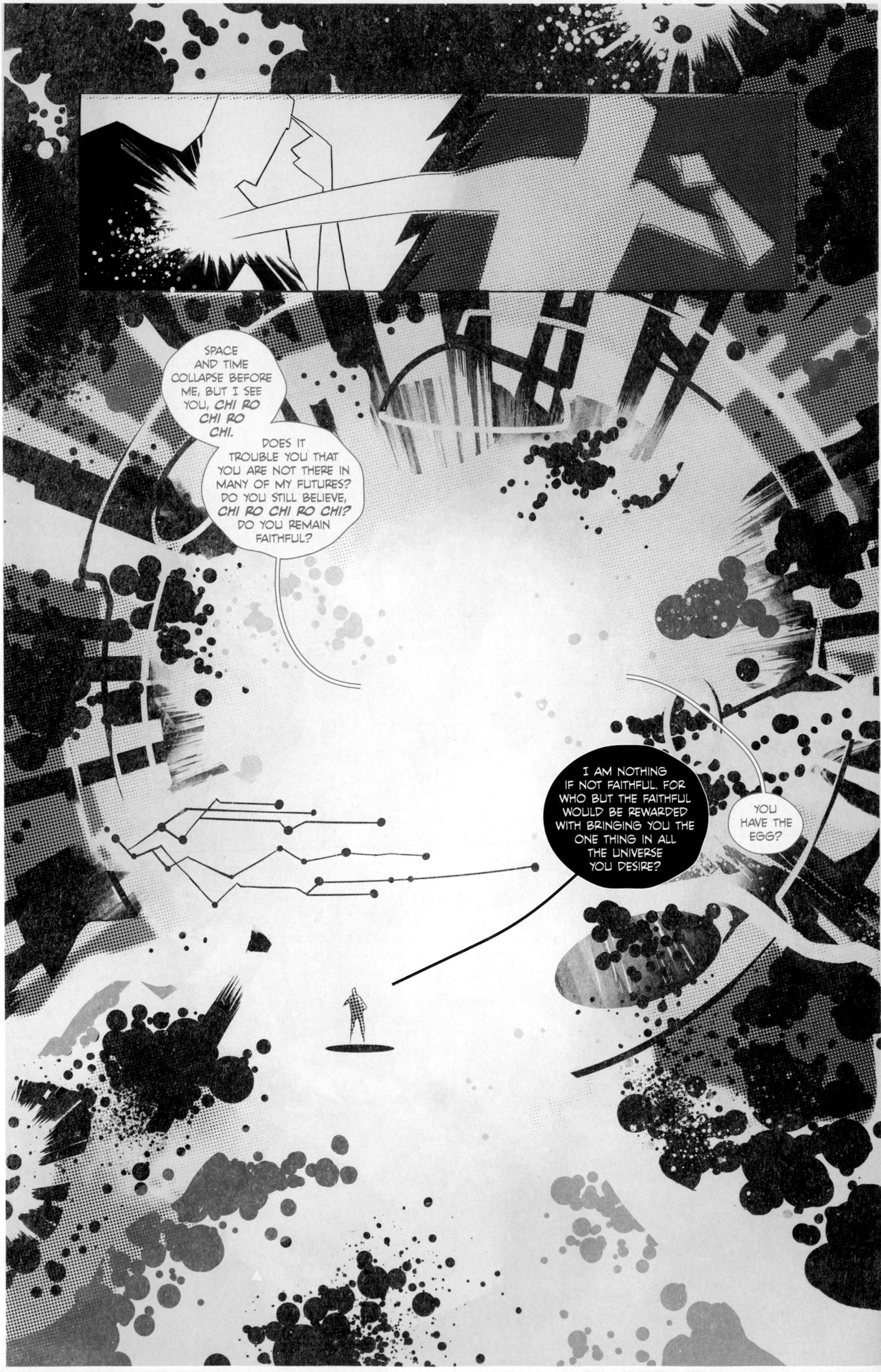
SPACE AND TIME COLLAPSE BEFORE ME, BUT I SEE YOU, CHI RO CHI RO CHI.
DOES IT TROUBLE YOU THAT YOU ARE NOT THERE IN MANY OF MY FUTURES? DO YOU STILL BELIEVE, CHI RO CHI RO CHI? DO YOU REMAIN FAITHFUL?
YOU HAVE THE EGG?
I AM NOTHING IF NOT FAITHFUL. FOR WHO BUT THE FAITHFUL WOULD BE REWARDED WITH BRINGING YOU THE ONE THING IN ALL THE UNIVERSE YOU DESIRE?

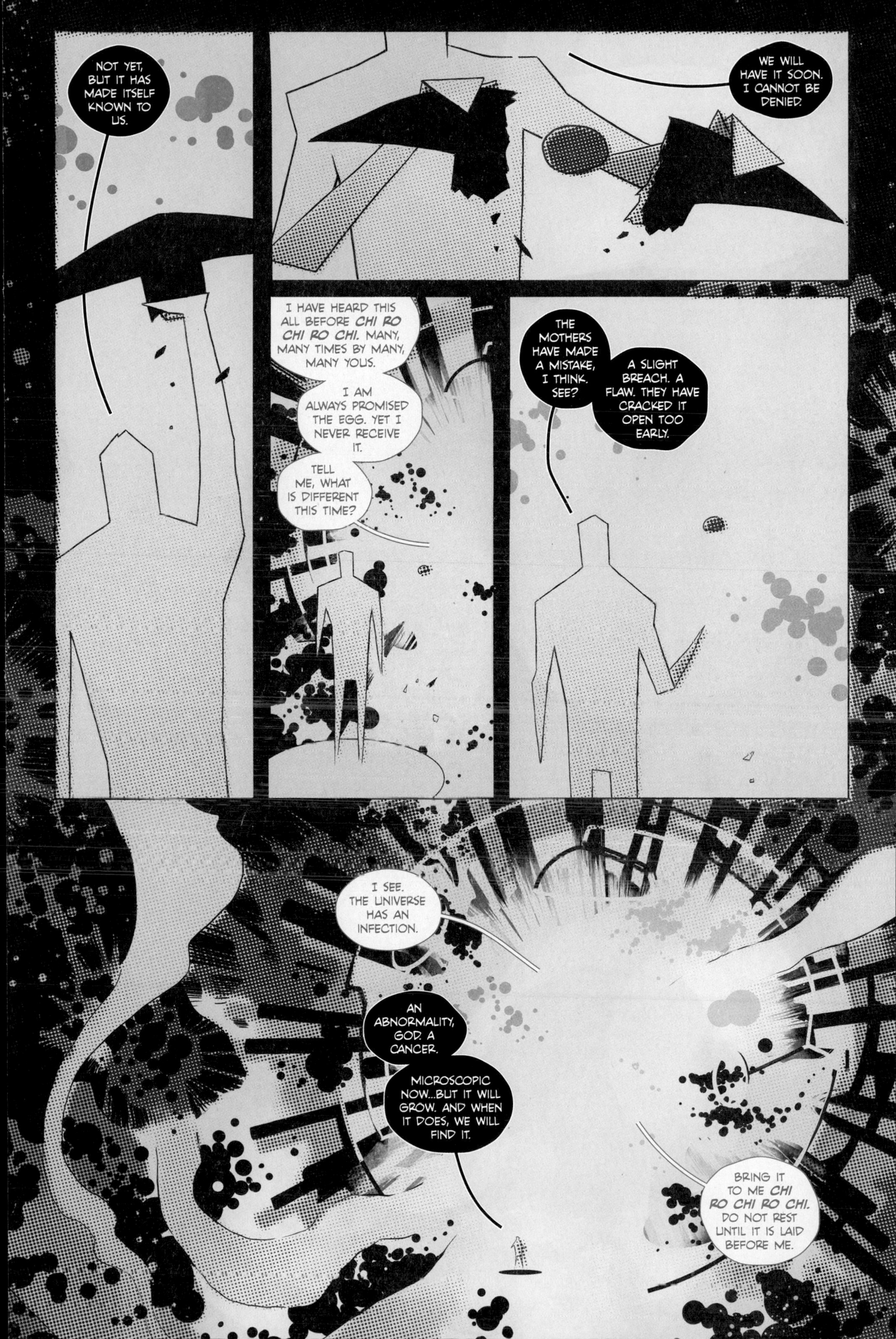
NOT YET, BUT IT HAS MADE ITSELF KNOWN TO US.
WE WILL HAVE IT SOON. I CANNOT BE DENIED.
I HAVE HEARD THIS ALL BEFORE *CHI RO CHI RO CHI.* MANY, MANY TIMES BY MANY, MANY YOUS.
I AM ALWAYS PROMISED THE EGG. YET I NEVER RECEIVE IT.
TELL ME, WHAT IS DIFFERENT THIS TIME?
THE MOTHERS HAVE MADE A MISTAKE, I THINK. SEE?
A SLIGHT BREACH. A FLAW. THEY HAVE CRACKED IT OPEN TOO EARLY.
I SEE. THE UNIVERSE HAS AN INFECTION.
AN ABNORMALITY, GOD. A CANCER.
MICROSCOPIC NOW...BUT IT WILL GROW. AND WHEN IT DOES, WE WILL FIND IT.
BRING IT TO ME *CHI RO CHI RO CHI.* DO NOT REST UNTIL IT IS LAID BEFORE ME.

THE HIERARCHY OF
THE CHURCH OF THE SINGULARITY

IN SERVICE TO THE SINGULARITY ITSELF

(THE UR-CONSCIOUSNESS OF THE FIRST COLLECTIVE SOCIETY IN
THE TOWN UNIVERSE).

[1] ▲ **RO CHI**

The high priest of the Church of the
Singularity. The voice of God.
The machine behind the veil.

[50] ⬤ **ARCHCANTON**

Territorial mind boss of a church node. [+].....................

[10] ⬤ **BISHOP-GENERAL**

The personal attaché of Ro Chi.

[1000] • **BISHOP-INQUISATOR**

A high priest of a watchtower.

[10,000] • **PRIEST-HERALD**

Academic masters of expansionist
theory. The security-intelligence arm of God.

[10,000 × 10,000] **PRIEST-CONQUISTADOR**

Crusader class, warrior-priests.

[200] • **NAVIGATOR**

A mass driver of intelligence. A deployer
of warrior-priests. A herald of heralds.

CHAPTER FIVE

[MASTER MORLEY AND THE BETTER DREAMS OF BETTER MEN]

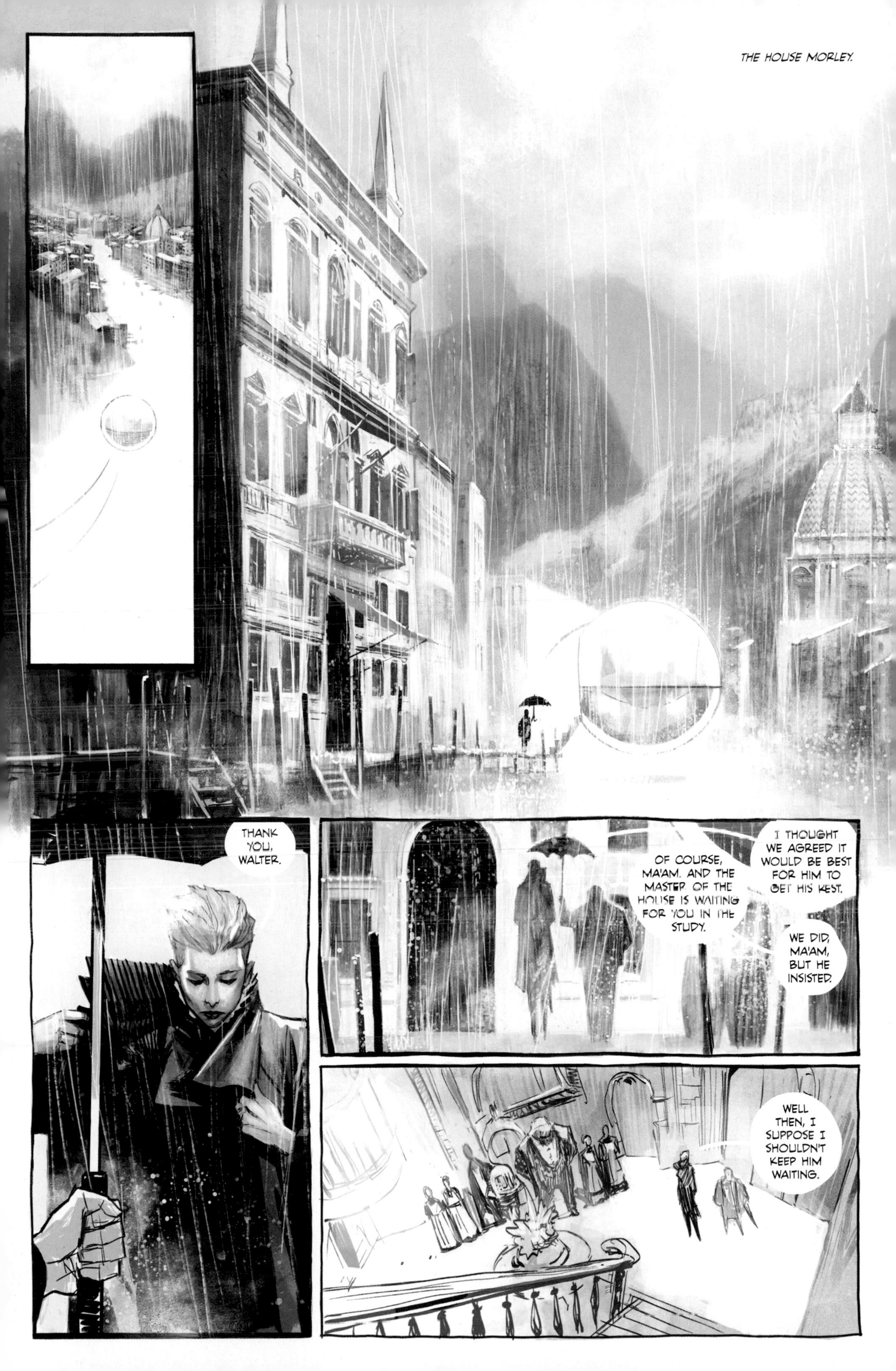
THE HOUSE MORLEY.
THANK YOU, WALTER.
OF COURSE, MA'AM. AND THE MASTER OF THE HOUSE IS WAITING FOR YOU IN THE STUDY.
I THOUGHT WE AGREED IT WOULD BE BEST FOR HIM TO GET HIS REST.
WE DID, MA'AM, BUT HE INSISTED.
WELL THEN, I SUPPOSE I SHOULDN'T KEEP HIM WAITING.

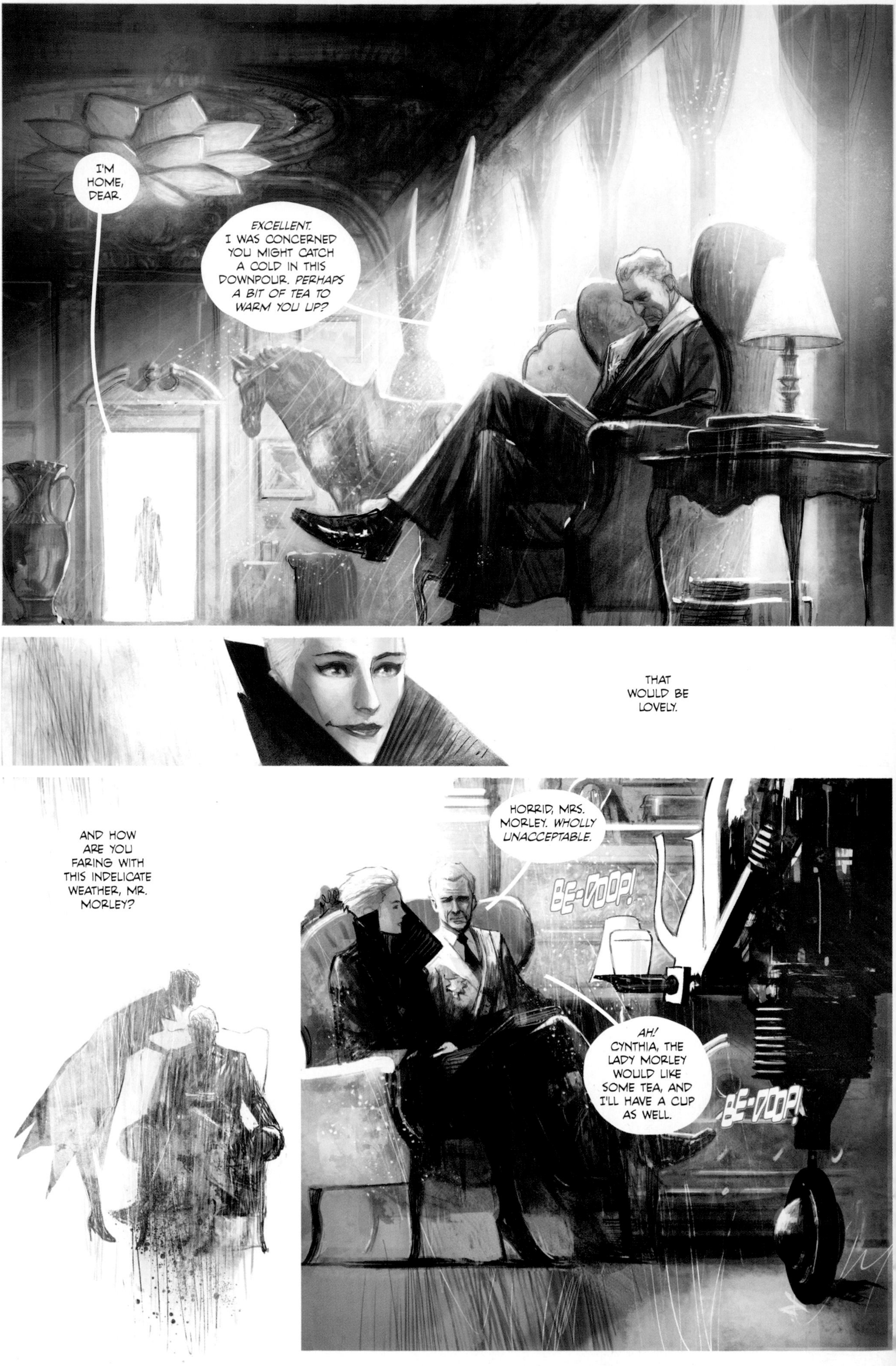
I'M HOME, DEAR.
EXCELLENT. I WAS CONCERNED YOU MIGHT CATCH A COLD IN THIS DOWNPOUR. PERHAPS A BIT OF TEA TO WARM YOU UP?
THAT WOULD BE LOVELY.
AND HOW ARE YOU FARING WITH THIS INDELICATE WEATHER, MR. MORLEY?
HORRID, MRS. MORLEY. WHOLLY UNACCEPTABLE.
BE-DOOP!
AH! CYNTHIA, THE LADY MORLEY WOULD LIKE SOME TEA, AND I'LL HAVE A CUP AS WELL.
BE-DOOP!

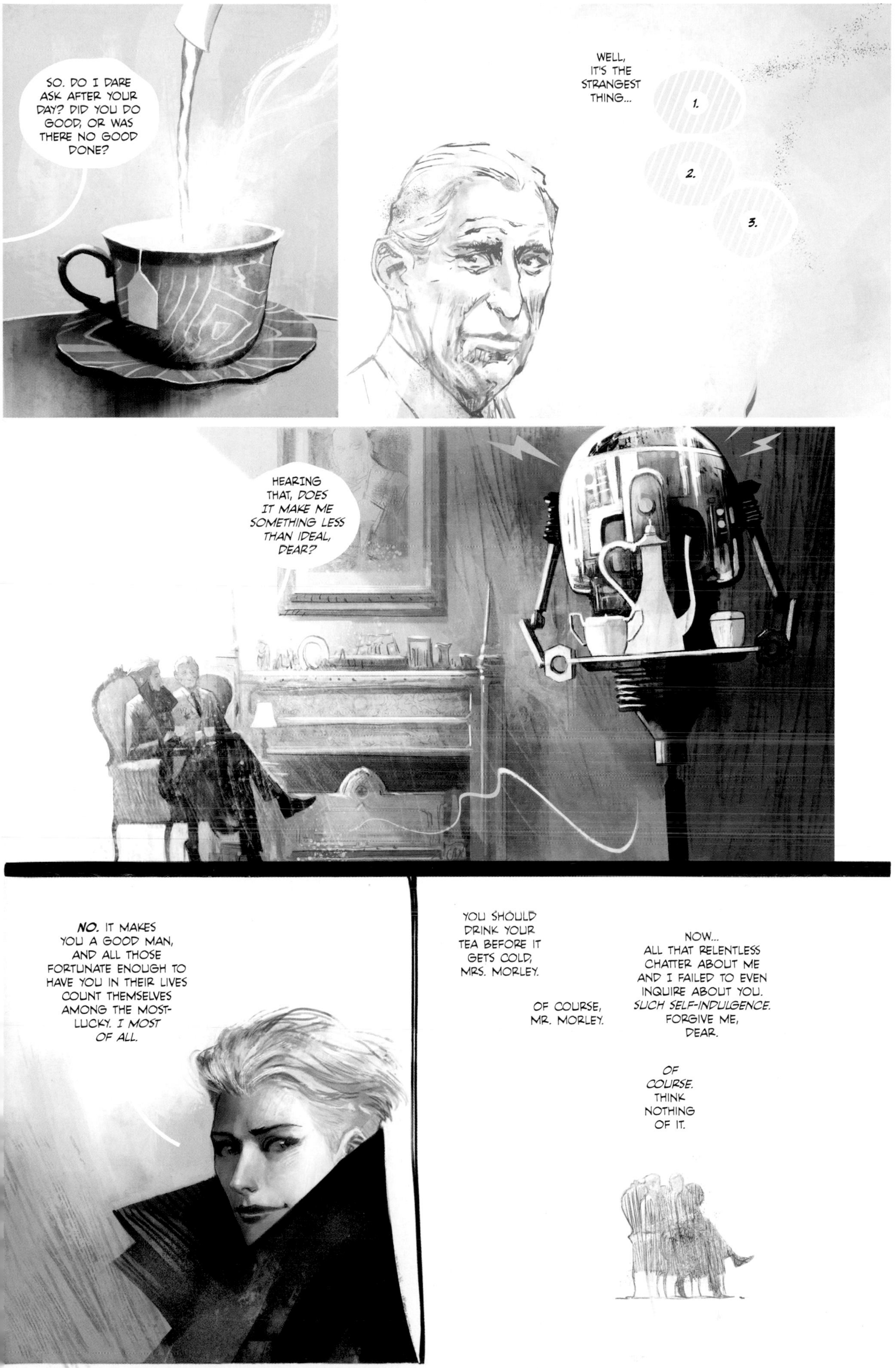

SO. DO I DARE ASK AFTER YOUR DAY? DID YOU DO GOOD, OR WAS THERE NO GOOD DONE?
WELL, IT'S THE STRANGEST THING...
1.
2.
3.
HEARING THAT, *DOES* IT MAKE ME SOMETHING LESS THAN IDEAL, DEAR?
NO. IT MAKES YOU A GOOD MAN, AND ALL THOSE FORTUNATE ENOUGH TO HAVE YOU IN THEIR LIVES COUNT THEMSELVES AMONG THE MOST-LUCKY. *I MOST OF ALL.*
YOU SHOULD DRINK YOUR TEA BEFORE IT GETS COLD, MRS. MORLEY.
OF COURSE, MR. MORLEY.
NOW... ALL THAT RELENTLESS CHATTER ABOUT ME AND I FAILED TO EVEN INQUIRE ABOUT YOU. *SUCH SELF-INDULGENCE.* FORGIVE ME, DEAR.
OF COURSE. THINK NOTHING OF IT.

THE DREAMS
OF MASTER MORLEY

You may not even believe this, as it is a bit improbable and requires no small measure of disbelief, but before you came in I was in the middle of a dream...

And I know, immediately, what you are thinking — Mr. Morley, you sir, are no dreamer...and to that, I must confess, no small measure of guilt.

Yet dream I did.

I was walking through a house. Not this one, but similar enough that I was felt comfortable in my surroundings — it was a home, but not my home. I turned a corner and I caught my reflection in a mirror. And watching me watch myself, my twin smiled, nodded his head just so, and then turned to walk into the next room.

So I turned to enter the same room on my side, and it was as if the house sprang to life. Suddenly, there was a party underway. Not a casual affair, mind you, something...a bit more cultivated. I immediately recognized

[▬▬▬▬▬▬▬▬]

▬▬▬▬▬ ▬▬▬▬ ▬▬▬▬▬▬ ▬▬ ▬▬▬▬▬▬ ▬▬▬▬ ▬▬▬▬▬▬▬ ▬▬ ▬▬▬

!!⊏╳Ϥ [▬▬▬▬▬▬]

▬▬ ▬▬▬▬▬▬ ▬▬▬▬▬▬
▬▬▬ ▬▬▬▬▬▬ ▬ ▬▬▬▬
▬▬▬ ▬▬▬

a representative from the energy collective, and well, was quite shocked to hear actual business being discussed.

It was nothing so unseemly as a negotiation — more of a declaration of intent — regarding the price per unit the union advocates were willing to pay.

Then I remembered. I had been here before. In fact, I had been here recently. The deal that was being discussed, I had already closed last week.

So when he accepted my offer, in the dream, I realized that it was myself in the dream that encouraged myself in the past to accept the deal.

Then, like a bolt of clarity, I realized this was every deal I had ever done.

Now, my question, upon waking, is not a complicating of temporal mechanics or any other reasonable attempt at explaining such a phenomenon, but more a concern with the possibility that I have, as I have always thought might be possible, an unfair advantage over those I compete with.

And, if such a thing is true, is my constant flirtation with fairness actually a coping mechanism for an unavoidable guilt over the unfairness under which I operate?

I tell you truly, I do not know. So I turn to you and wonder...what say you, Ms. Morley?

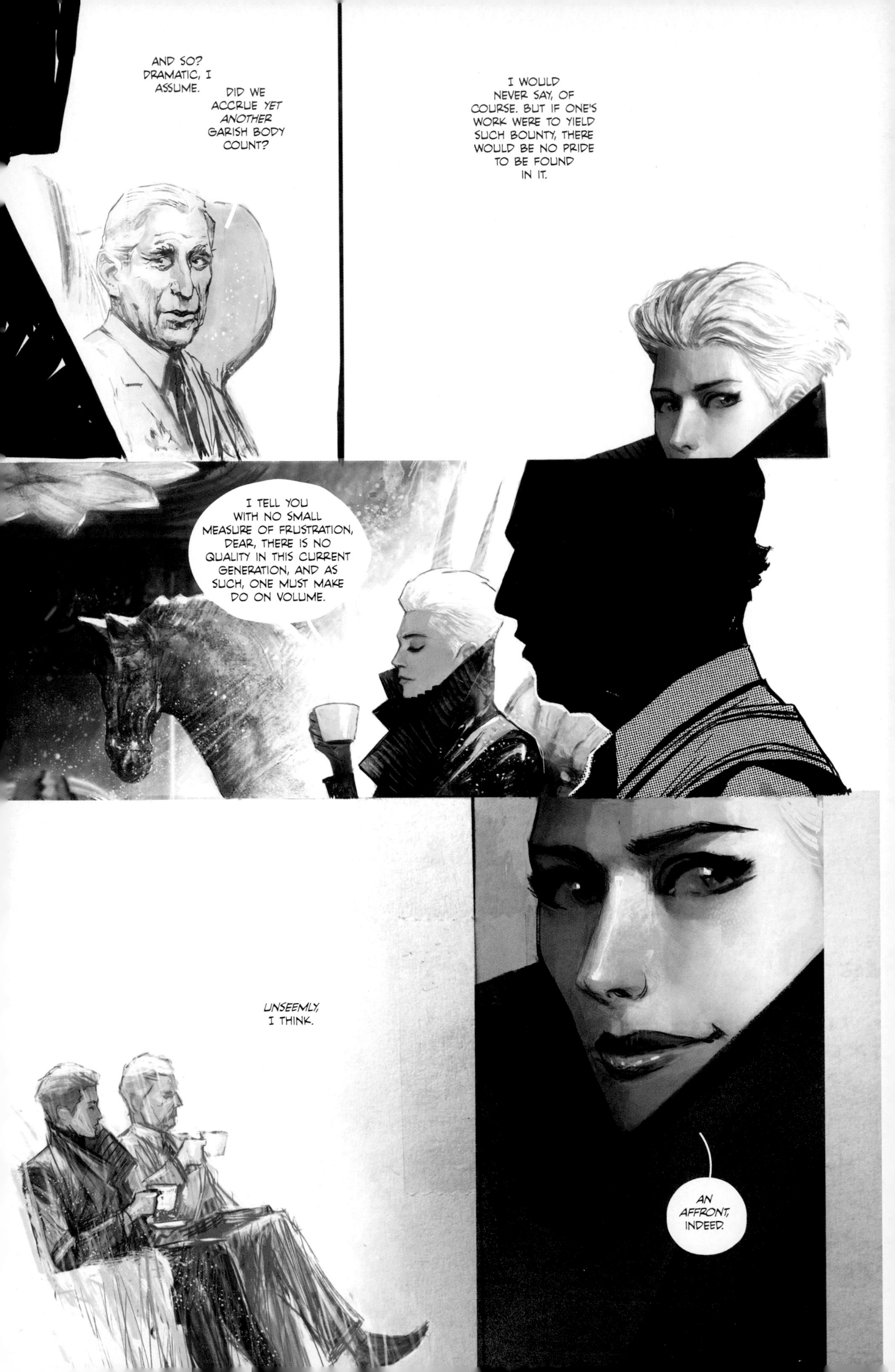
AND SO? DRAMATIC, I ASSUME.
DID WE ACCRUE *YET ANOTHER* GARISH BODY COUNT?
I WOULD NEVER SAY, OF COURSE. BUT IF ONE'S WORK WERE TO YIELD SUCH BOUNTY, THERE WOULD BE NO PRIDE TO BE FOUND IN IT.
I TELL YOU WITH NO SMALL MEASURE OF FRUSTRATION, DEAR, THERE IS NO QUALITY IN THIS CURRENT GENERATION, AND AS SUCH, ONE MUST MAKE DO ON VOLUME.
UNSEEMLY, I THINK.
AN AFFRONT, INDEED.

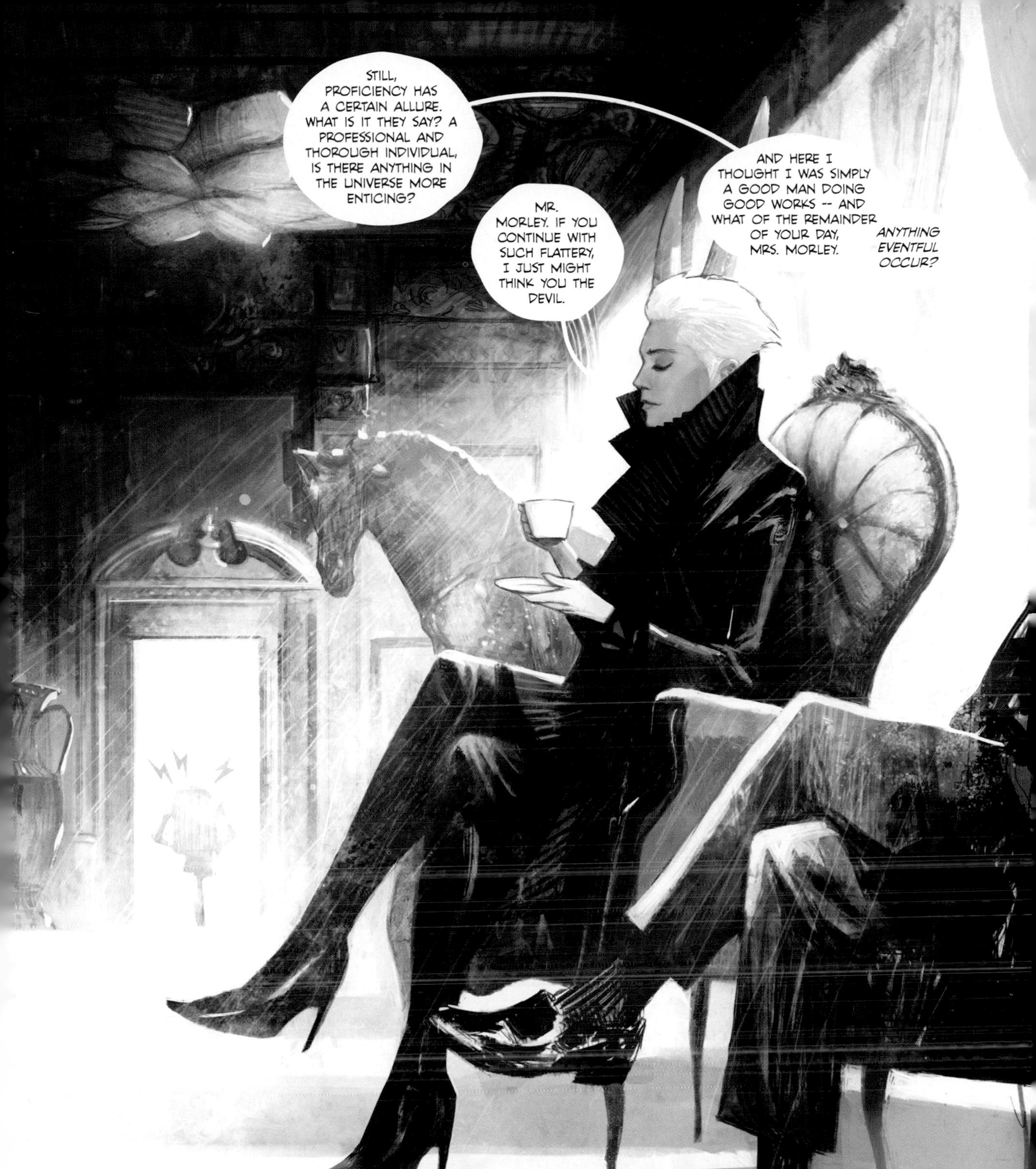
STILL, PROFICIENCY HAS A CERTAIN ALLURE. WHAT IS IT THEY SAY? A PROFESSIONAL AND THOROUGH INDIVIDUAL, IS THERE ANYTHING IN THE UNIVERSE MORE ENTICING?
MR. MORLEY. IF YOU CONTINUE WITH SUCH FLATTERY, I JUST MIGHT THINK YOU THE DEVIL.
AND HERE I THOUGHT I WAS SIMPLY A GOOD MAN DOING GOOD WORKS -- AND WHAT OF THE REMAINDER OF YOUR DAY, MRS. MORLEY.
ANYTHING EVENTFUL OCCUR?

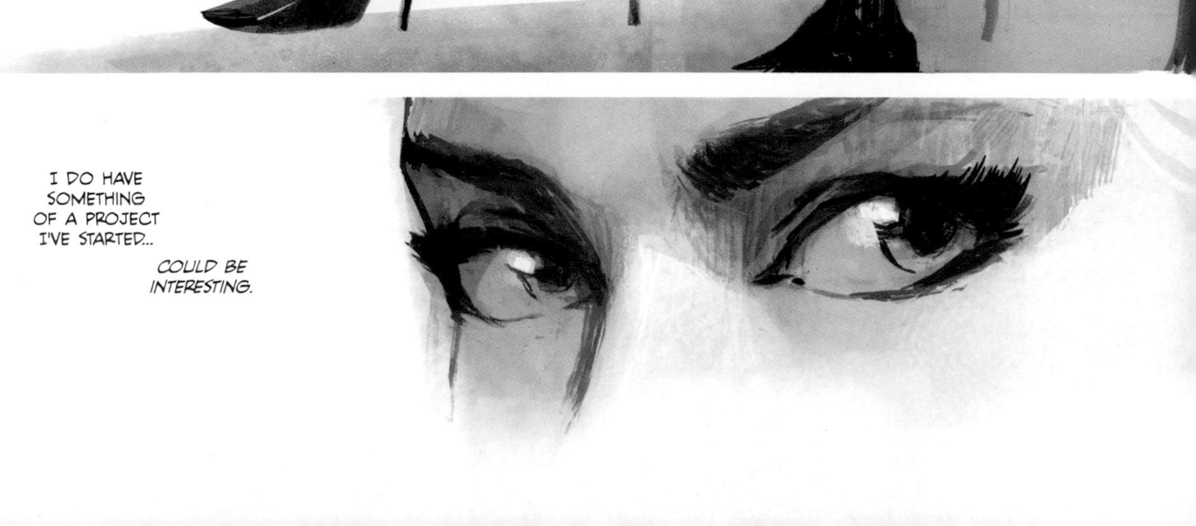
I DO HAVE SOMETHING OF A PROJECT I'VE STARTED...
COULD BE INTERESTING.

CHAPTER SIX

[A MOST UNCOMMON AND UNEXPECTED INVESTMENT]

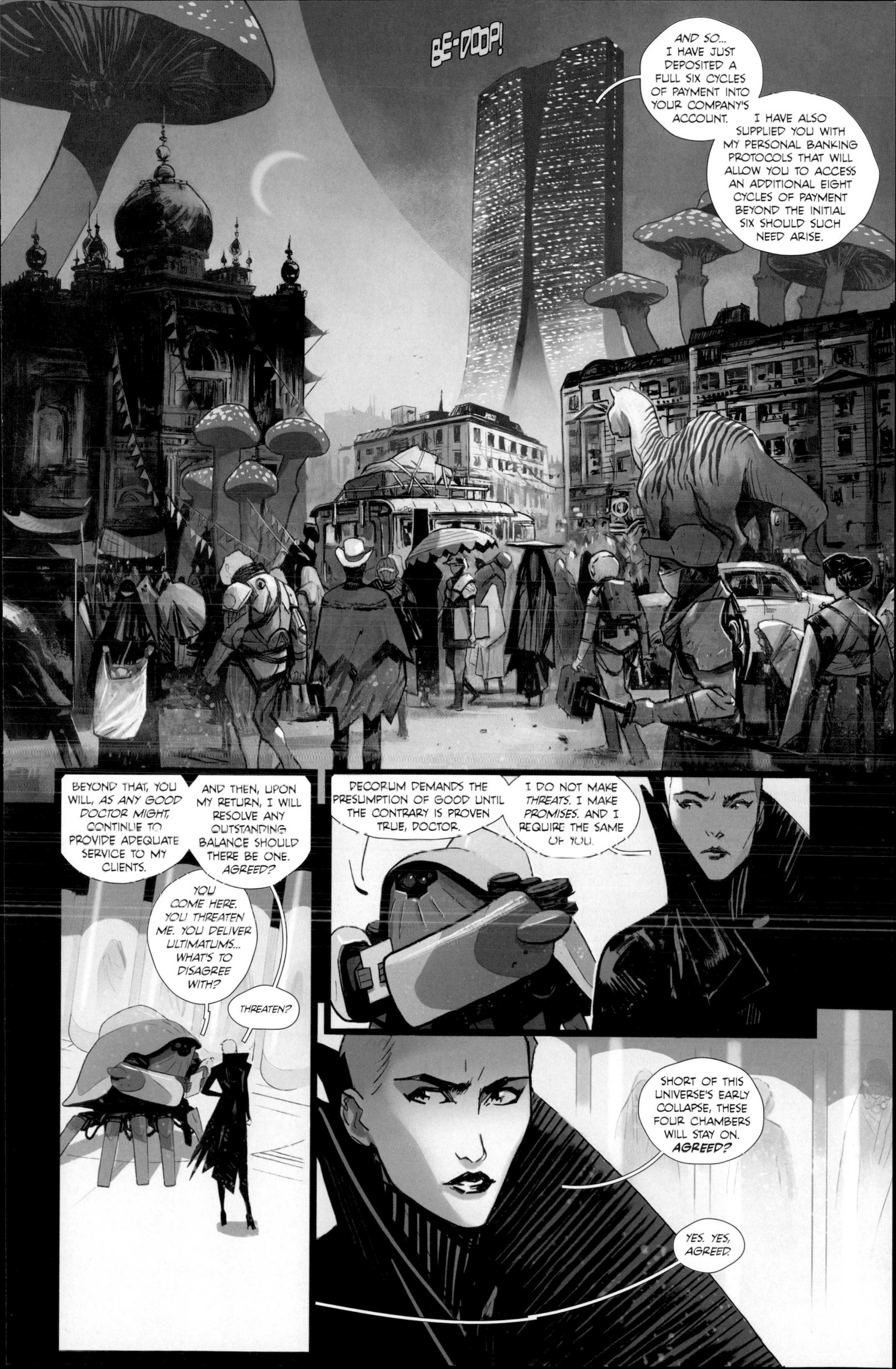
BE-DOOP!
AND SO... I HAVE JUST DEPOSITED A FULL SIX CYCLES OF PAYMENT INTO YOUR COMPANY'S ACCOUNT.
I HAVE ALSO SUPPLIED YOU WITH MY PERSONAL BANKING PROTOCOLS THAT WILL ALLOW YOU TO ACCESS AN ADDITIONAL EIGHT CYCLES OF PAYMENT BEYOND THE INITIAL SIX SHOULD SUCH NEED ARISE.
BEYOND THAT, YOU WILL, AS ANY GOOD DOCTOR MIGHT, CONTINUE TO PROVIDE ADEQUATE SERVICE TO MY CLIENTS.
AND THEN, UPON MY RETURN, I WILL RESOLVE ANY OUTSTANDING BALANCE SHOULD THERE BE ONE. AGREED?
YOU COME HERE. YOU THREATEN ME. YOU DELIVER ULTIMATUMS... WHAT'S TO DISAGREE WITH?
THREATEN?
DECORUM DEMANDS THE PRESUMPTION OF GOOD UNTIL THE CONTRARY IS PROVEN TRUE, DOCTOR.
I DO NOT MAKE THREATS. I MAKE PROMISES. AND I REQUIRE THE SAME OF YOU.
SHORT OF THIS UNIVERSE'S EARLY COLLAPSE, THESE FOUR CHAMBERS WILL STAY ON. AGREED?
YES. YES, AGREED.

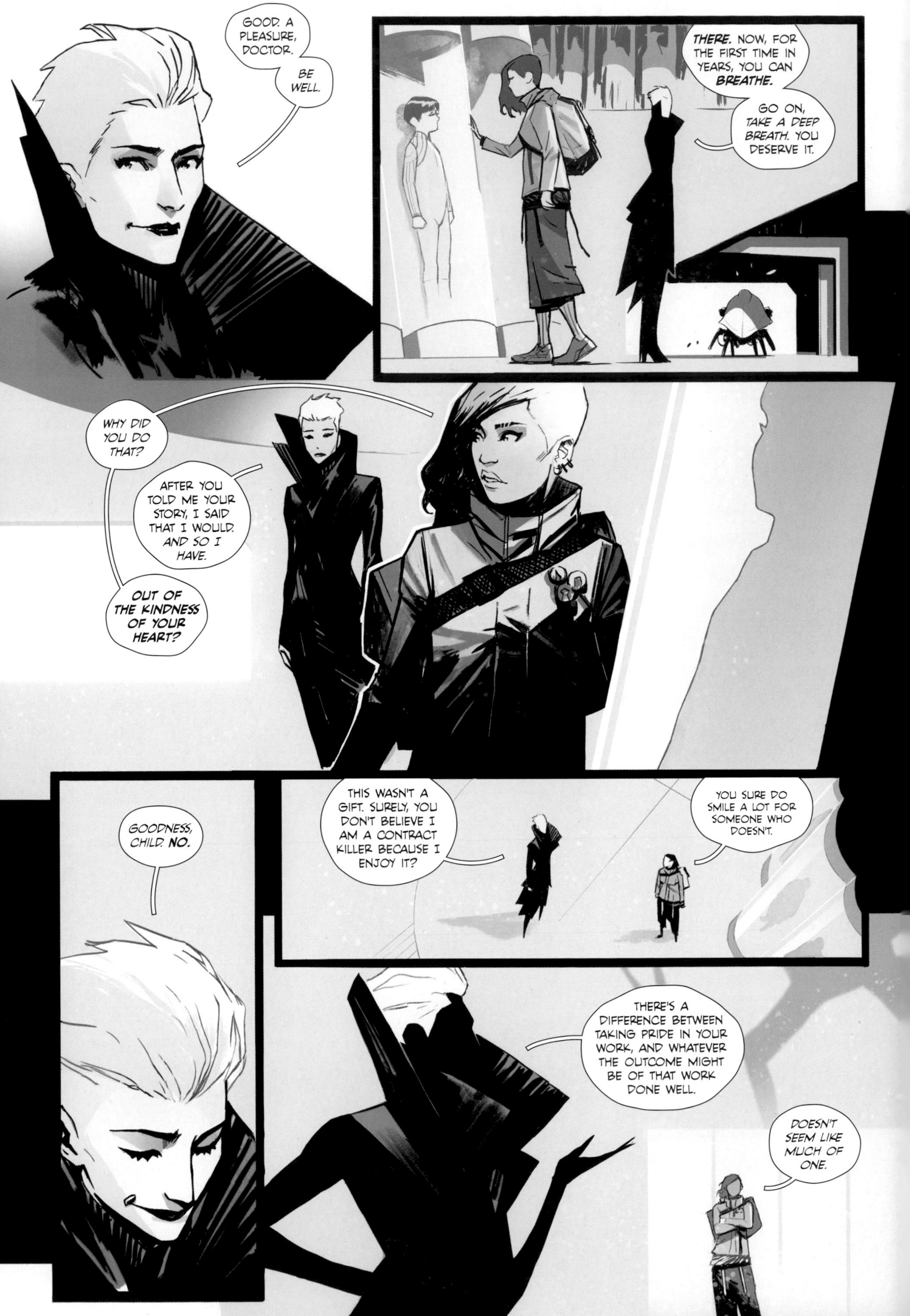
GOOD. A PLEASURE, DOCTOR.
BE WELL.
THERE. NOW, FOR THE FIRST TIME IN YEARS, YOU CAN BREATHE.
GO ON, TAKE A DEEP BREATH. YOU DESERVE IT.
WHY DID YOU DO THAT?
AFTER YOU TOLD ME YOUR STORY, I SAID THAT I WOULD. AND SO I HAVE.
OUT OF THE KINDNESS OF YOUR HEART?
GOODNESS, CHILD. NO.
THIS WASN'T A GIFT. SURELY, YOU DON'T BELIEVE I AM A CONTRACT KILLER BECAUSE I ENJOY IT?
YOU SURE DO SMILE A LOT FOR SOMEONE WHO DOESN'T.
THERE'S A DIFFERENCE BETWEEN TAKING PRIDE IN YOUR WORK, AND WHATEVER THE OUTCOME MIGHT BE OF THAT WORK DONE WELL.
DOESN'T SEEM LIKE MUCH OF ONE.

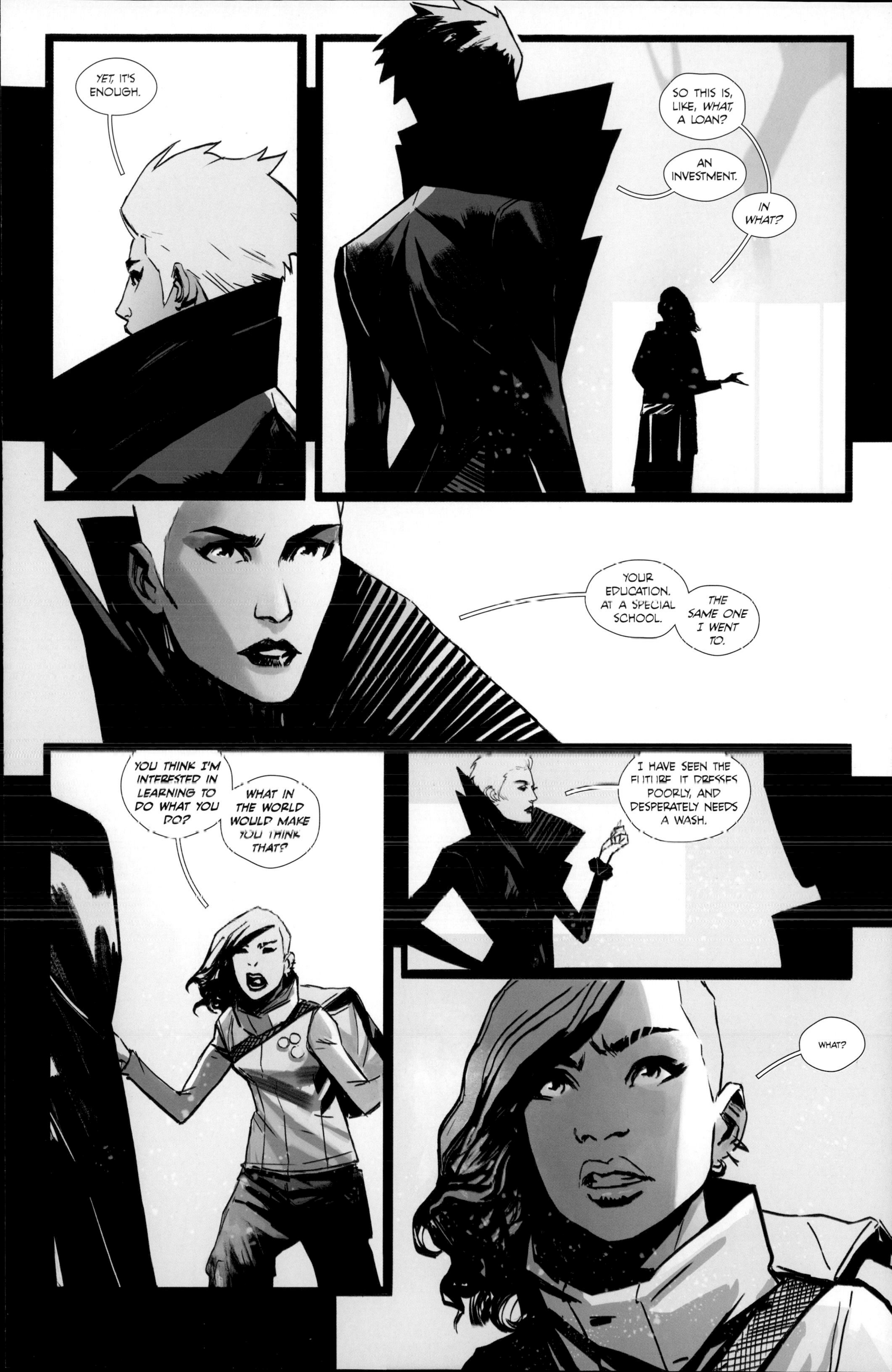
YET, IT'S ENOUGH.
SO THIS IS, LIKE, WHAT, A LOAN?
AN INVESTMENT.
IN WHAT?
YOUR EDUCATION. AT A SPECIAL SCHOOL.
THE SAME ONE I WENT TO.
YOU THINK I'M INTERESTED IN LEARNING TO DO WHAT YOU DO?
WHAT IN THE WORLD WOULD MAKE YOU THINK THAT?
I HAVE SEEN THE FUTURE. IT DRESSES POORLY, AND DESPERATELY NEEDS A WASH.
WHAT?

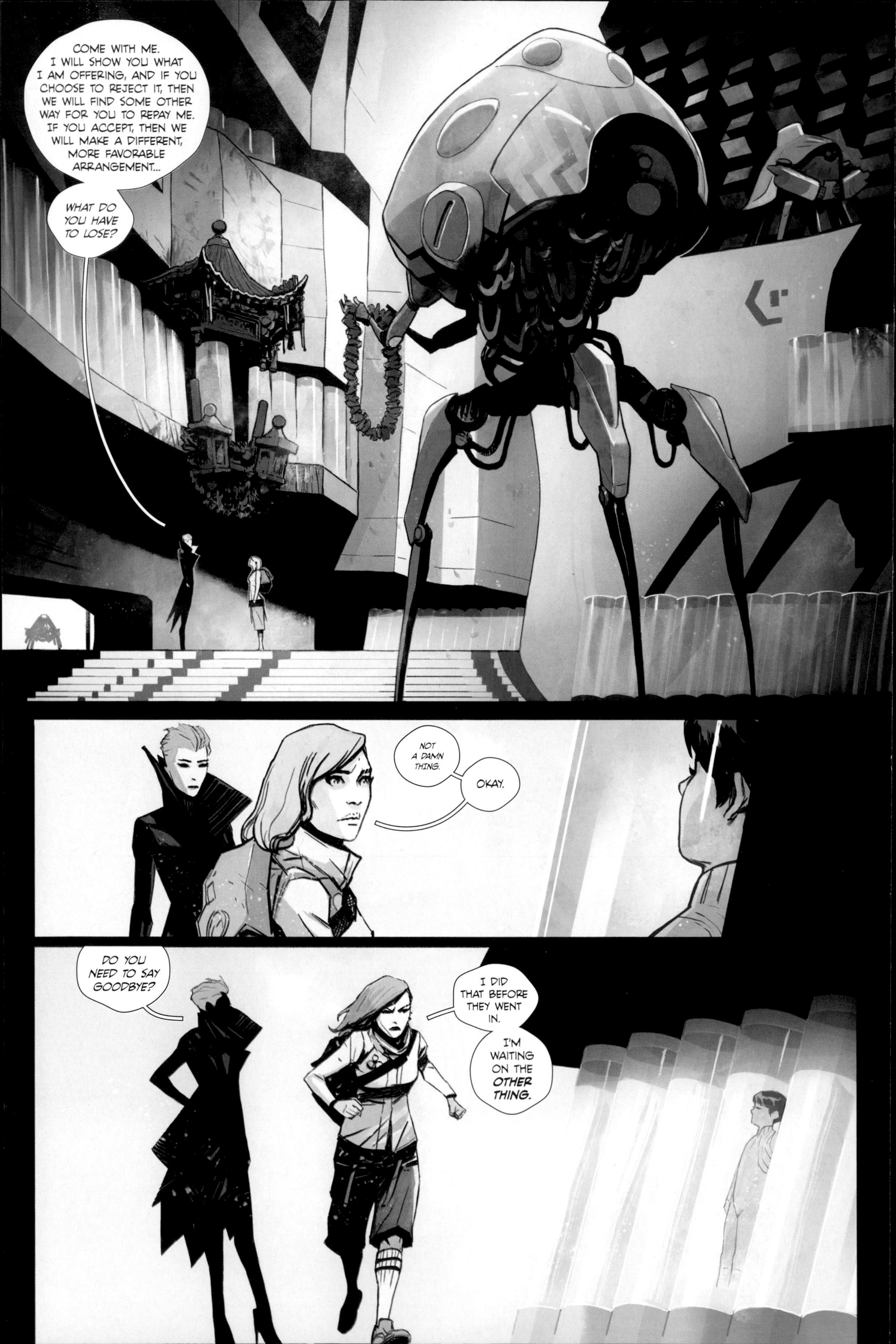
COME WITH ME. I WILL SHOW YOU WHAT I AM OFFERING, AND IF YOU CHOOSE TO REJECT IT, THEN WE WILL FIND SOME OTHER WAY FOR YOU TO REPAY ME. IF YOU ACCEPT, THEN WE WILL MAKE A DIFFERENT, MORE FAVORABLE ARRANGEMENT...
WHAT DO YOU HAVE TO LOSE?
NOT A DAMN THING.
OKAY.
DO YOU NEED TO SAY GOODBYE?
I DID THAT BEFORE THEY WENT IN.
I'M WAITING ON THE OTHER THING.

CHAPTER SEVEN

[CYCLE]

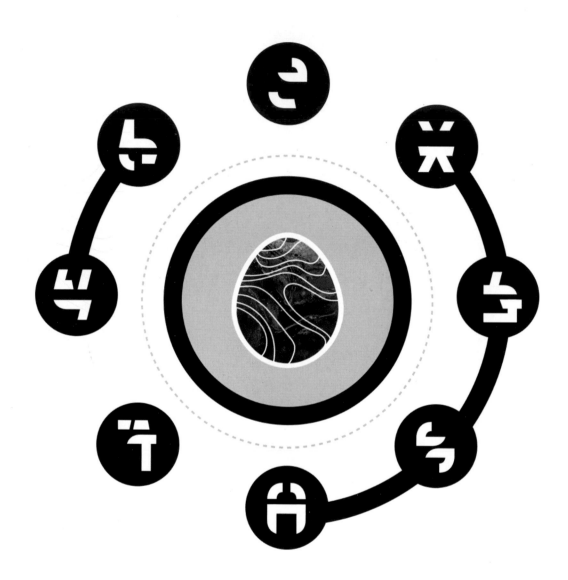

THE EGG

[THE RESURRECTION CYCLE]

[STAGE ONE]
Encasement of Genesis Material

[STAGE TWO]
Deconstruction of Exotic Matter

[STAGE THREE]
Absorption of Genesis Protein

[STAGE FOUR]
Regeneration of Form

[STAGE FIVE]
Maturation of Form

[STAGE SIX]
Messianic Induction

[STAGE SEVEN]
Final Gestation

[STAGE EIGHT]
Rebirth of Originator

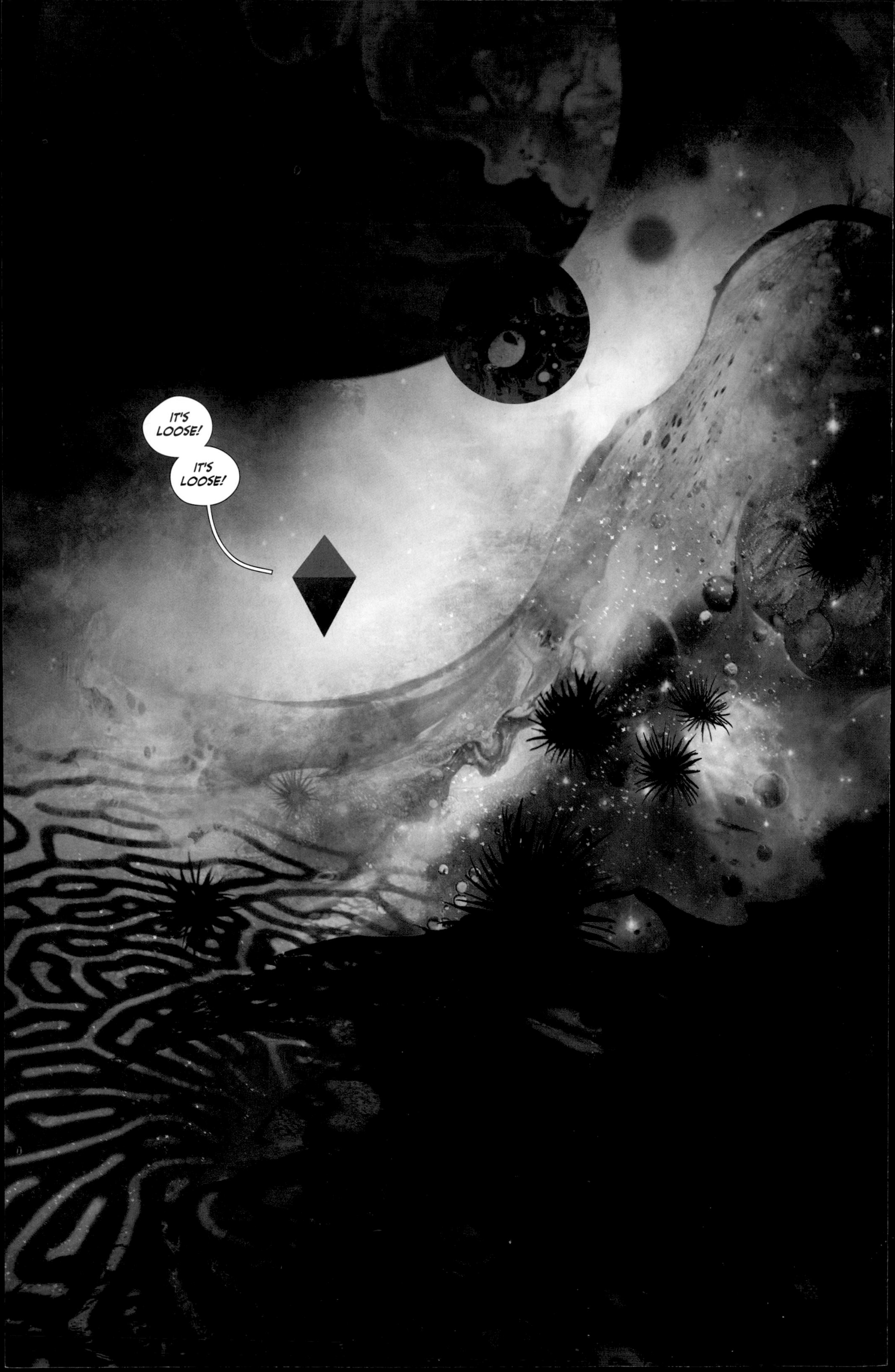
IT'S LOOSE!
IT'S LOOSE!

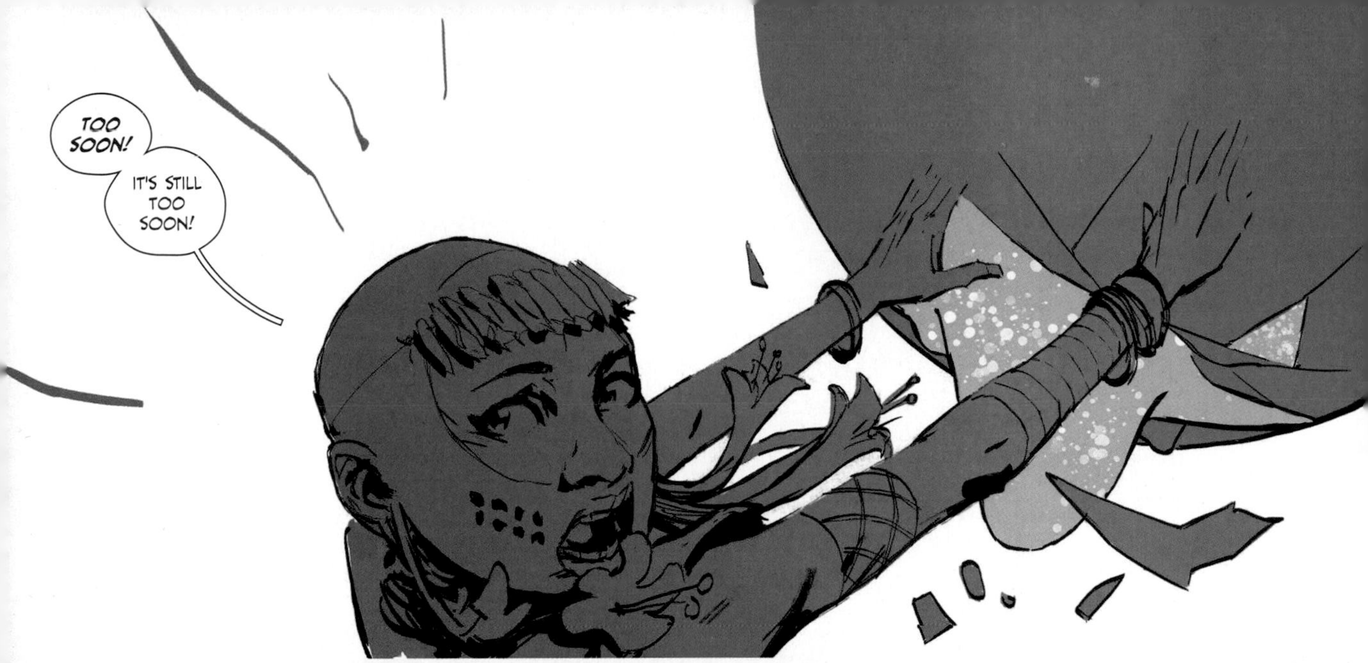
TOO SOON!
IT'S STILL TOO SOON!
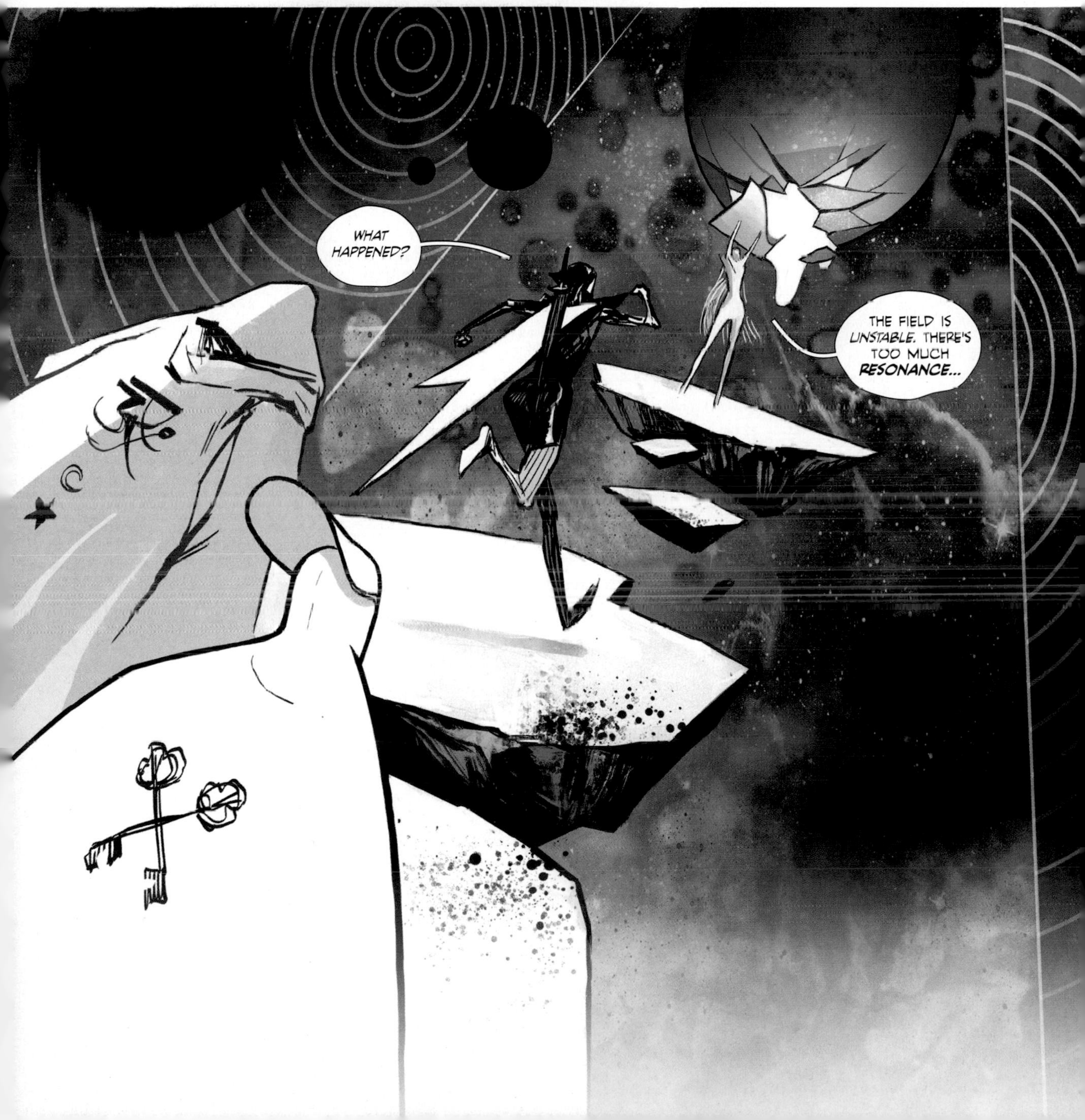
WHAT HAPPENED?
THE FIELD IS UNSTABLE. THERE'S TOO MUCH RESONANCE...

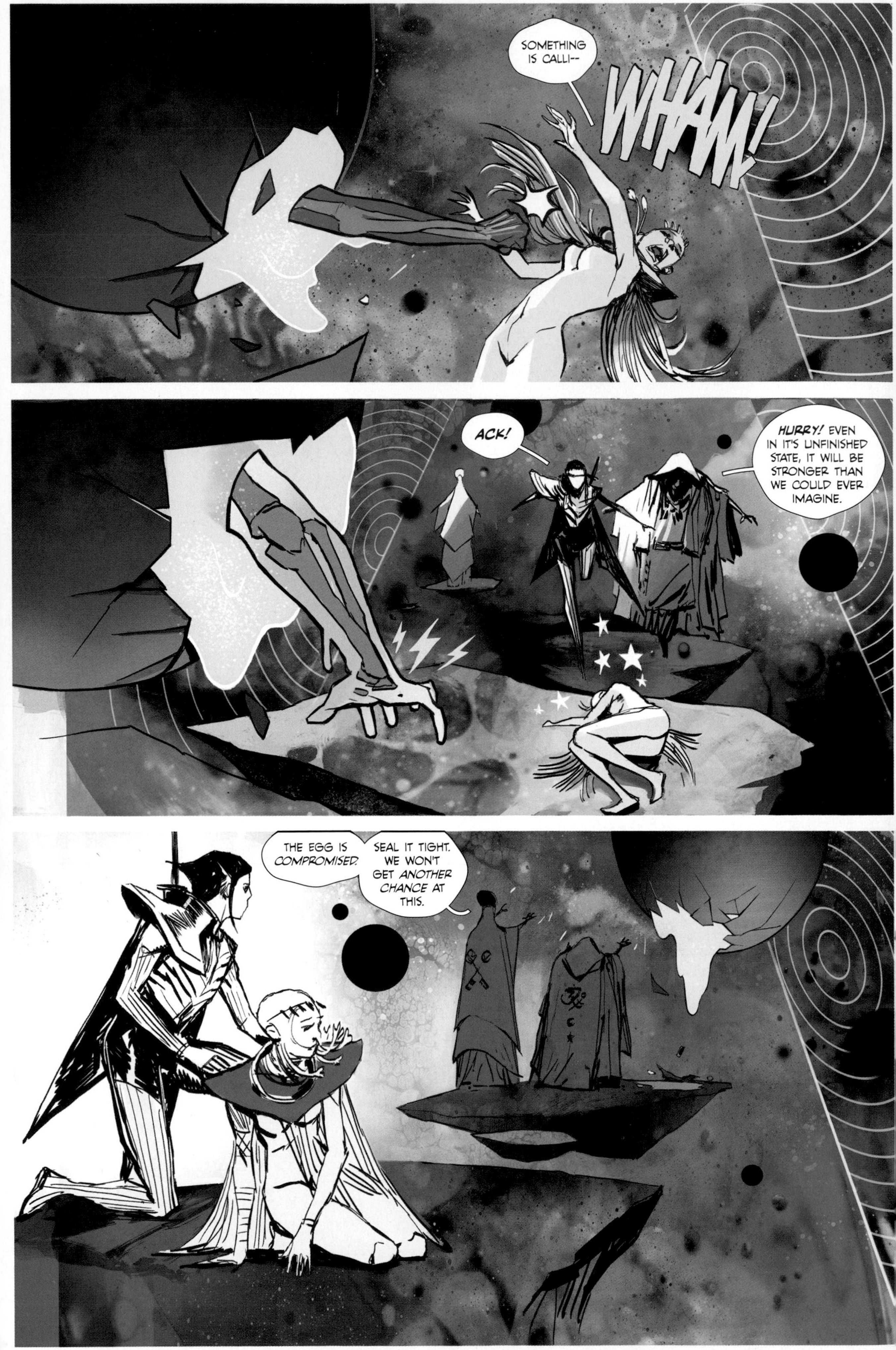
SOMETHING IS CALLI--
WHAM!
ACK!
HURRY! EVEN IN IT'S UNFINISHED STATE, IT WILL BE STRONGER THAN WE COULD EVER IMAGINE.
THE EGG IS COMPROMISED.
SEAL IT TIGHT. WE WON'T GET ANOTHER CHANCE AT THIS.

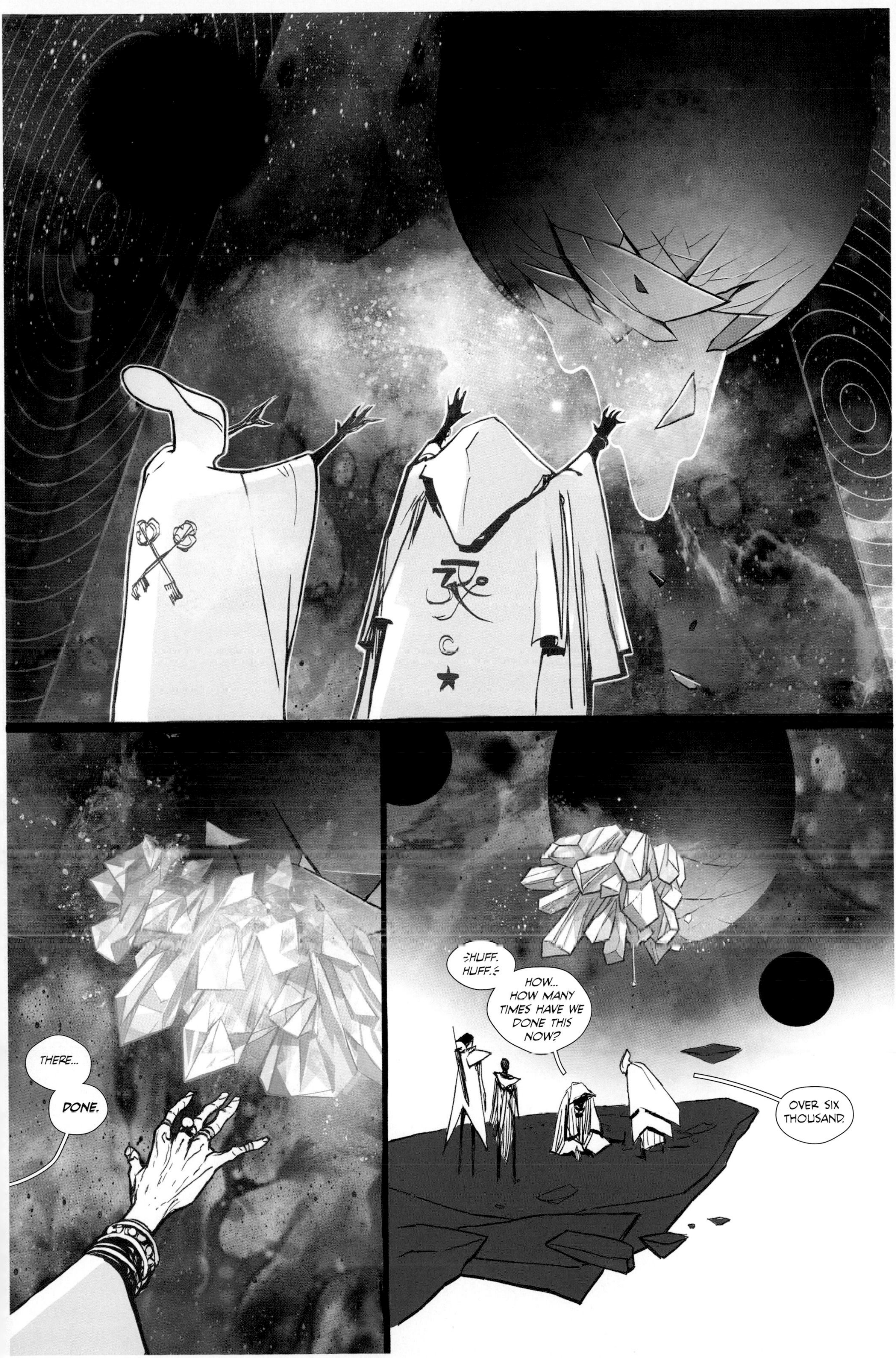
THERE...
DONE.
-HUFF. HUFF.-
HOW... HOW MANY TIMES HAVE WE DONE THIS NOW?
OVER SIX THOUSAND.

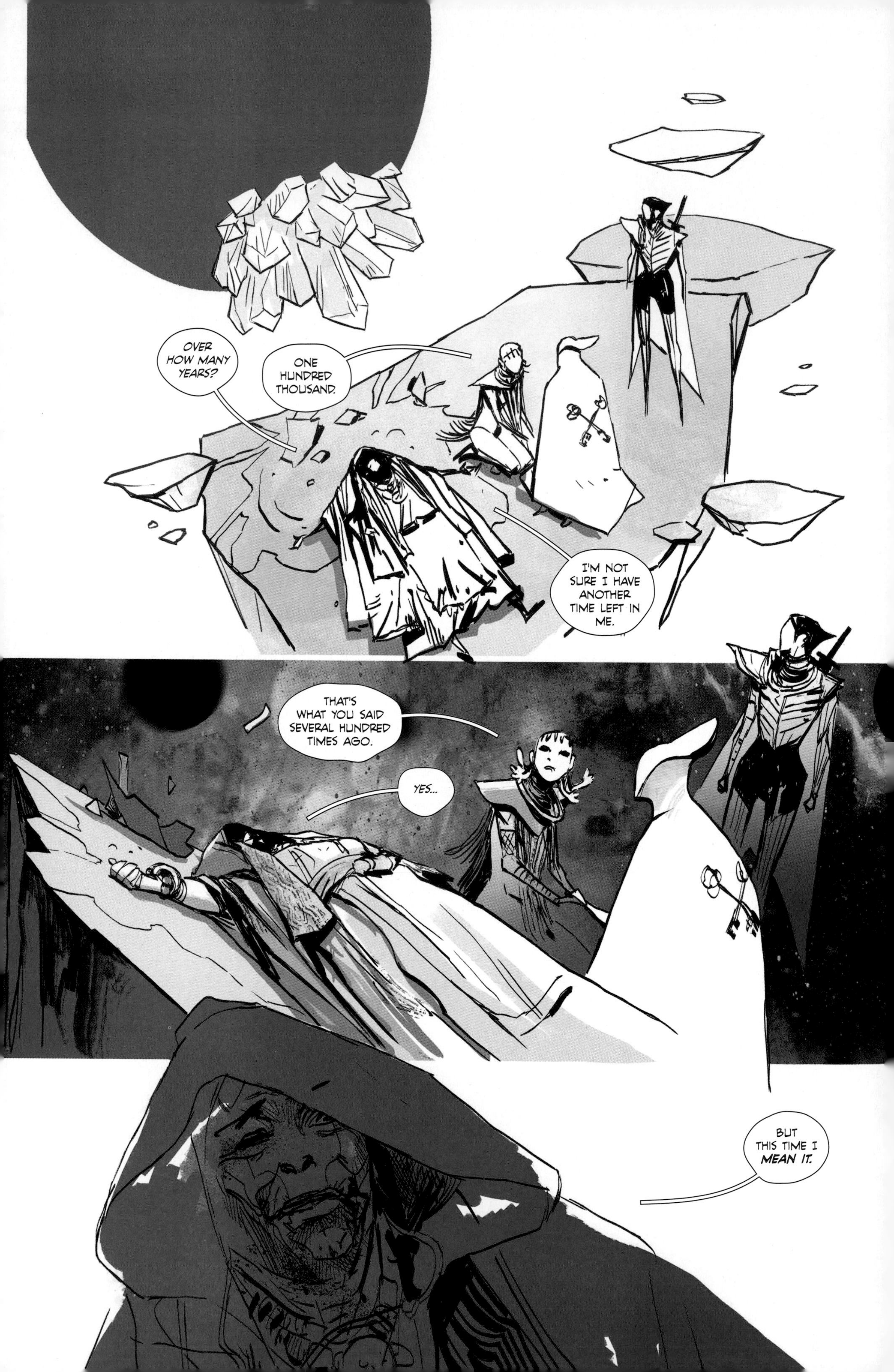
OVER HOW MANY YEARS?
ONE HUNDRED THOUSAND.
I'M NOT SURE I HAVE ANOTHER TIME LEFT IN ME.
THAT'S WHAT YOU SAID SEVERAL HUNDRED TIMES AGO.
YES...
BUT THIS TIME I MEAN IT.

[AND THE RE-EDUCATION
OF **DEVIANTS**]

CHAPTER EIGHT

[TAKE A RIDE, TAKE A TRIP]

[+]

[+]

[A SHORT JAUNT FROM DEALDUS TO THE TRANSIT HUB BYS]

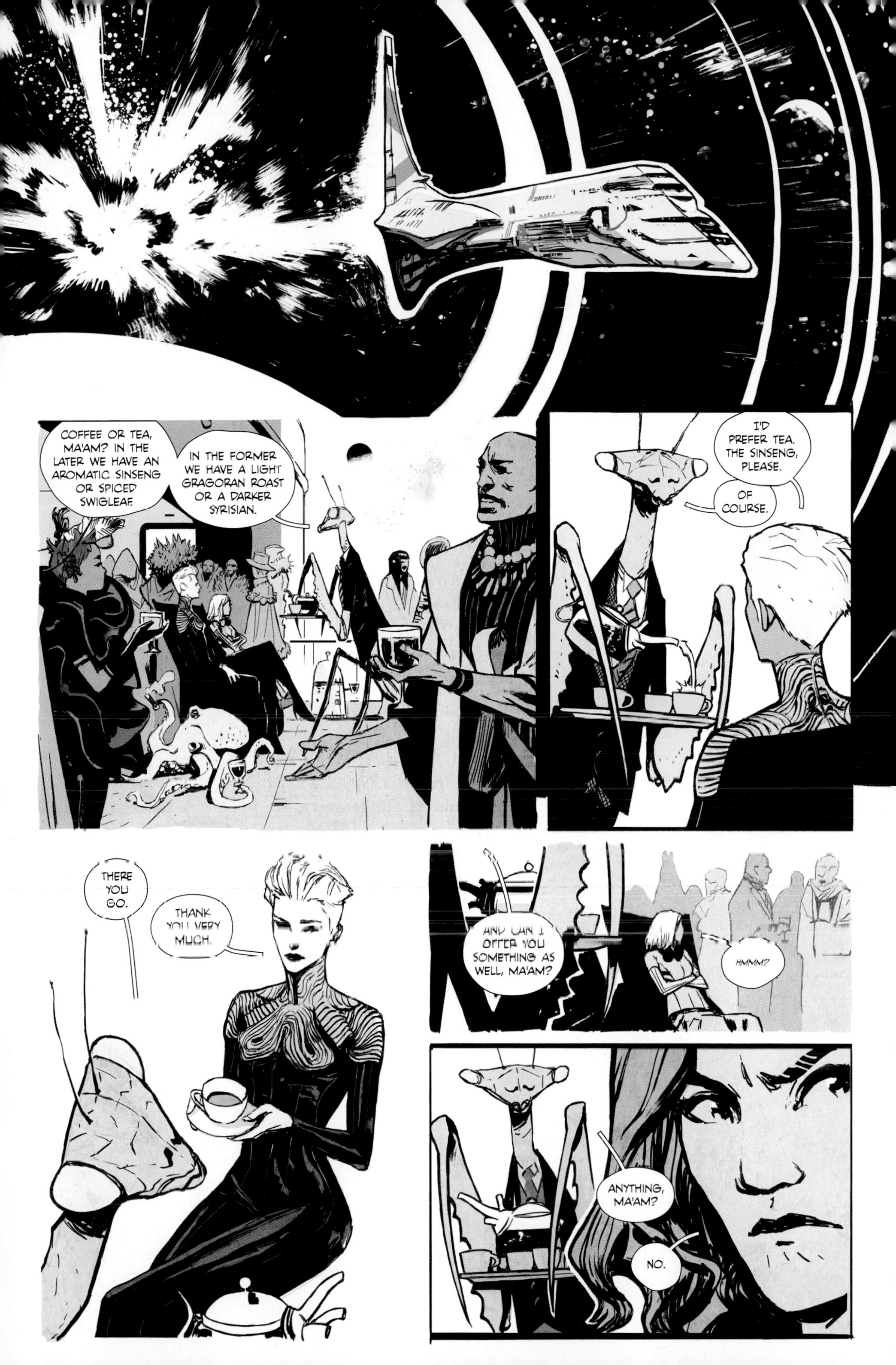
COFFEE OR TEA, MA'AM? IN THE LATER WE HAVE AN AROMATIC SINSENG OR SPICED SWIGLEAF.
IN THE FORMER WE HAVE A LIGHT GRAGORAN ROAST OR A DARKER SYRISIAN.
I'D PREFER TEA. THE SINSENG, PLEASE.
OF COURSE.
THERE YOU GO.
THANK YOU VERY MUCH.
AND CAN I OFFER YOU SOMETHING AS WELL, MA'AM?
HMMM?
ANYTHING, MA'AM?
NO.

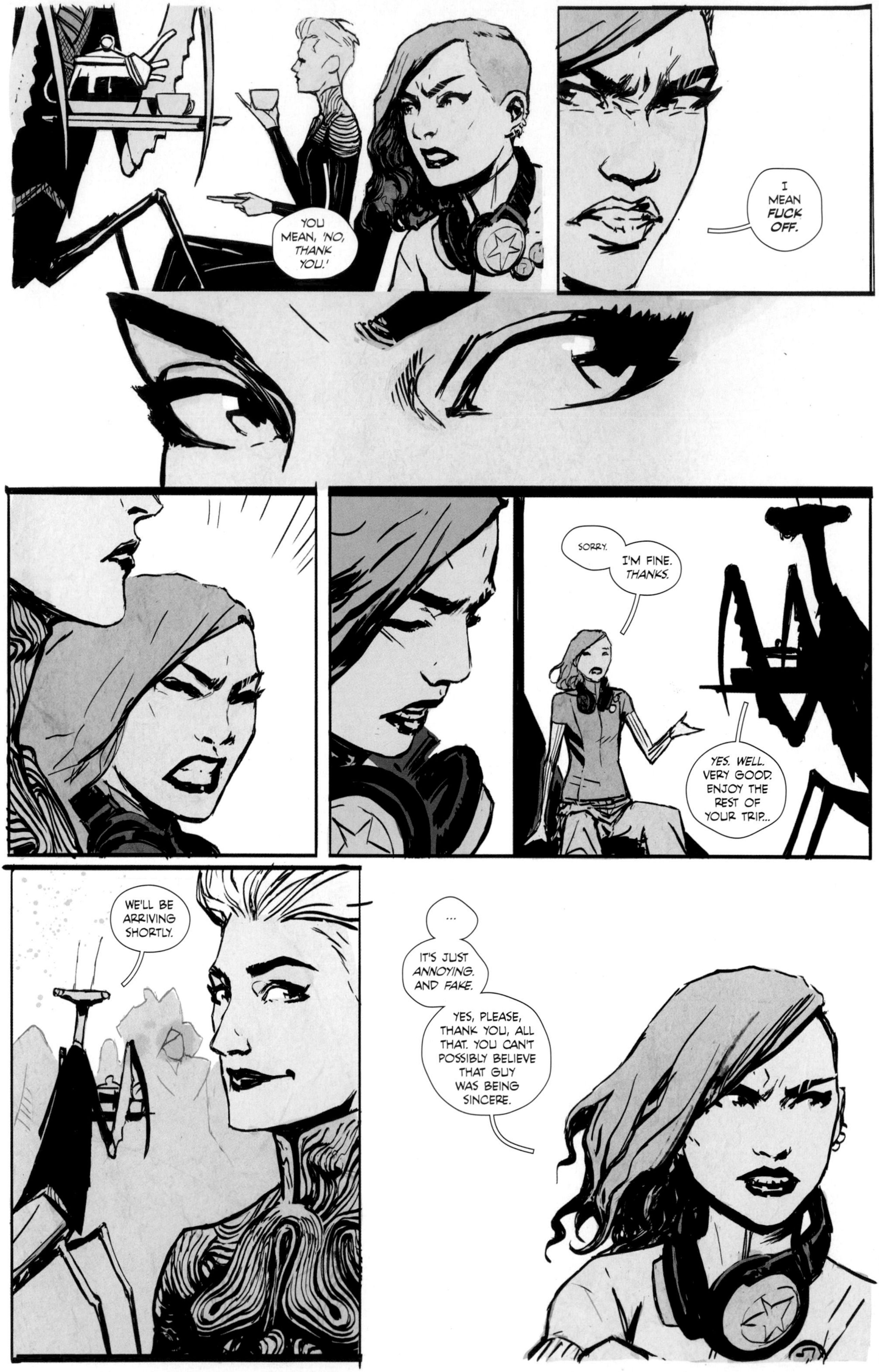
YOU MEAN, 'NO, THANK YOU.'
I MEAN FUCK OFF.
SORRY.
I'M FINE. THANKS.
YES. WELL. VERY GOOD. ENJOY THE REST OF YOUR TRIP...
WE'LL BE ARRIVING SHORTLY.
...
IT'S JUST ANNOYING. AND FAKE.
YES, PLEASE, THANK YOU, ALL THAT. YOU CAN'T POSSIBLY BELIEVE THAT GUY WAS BEING SINCERE.

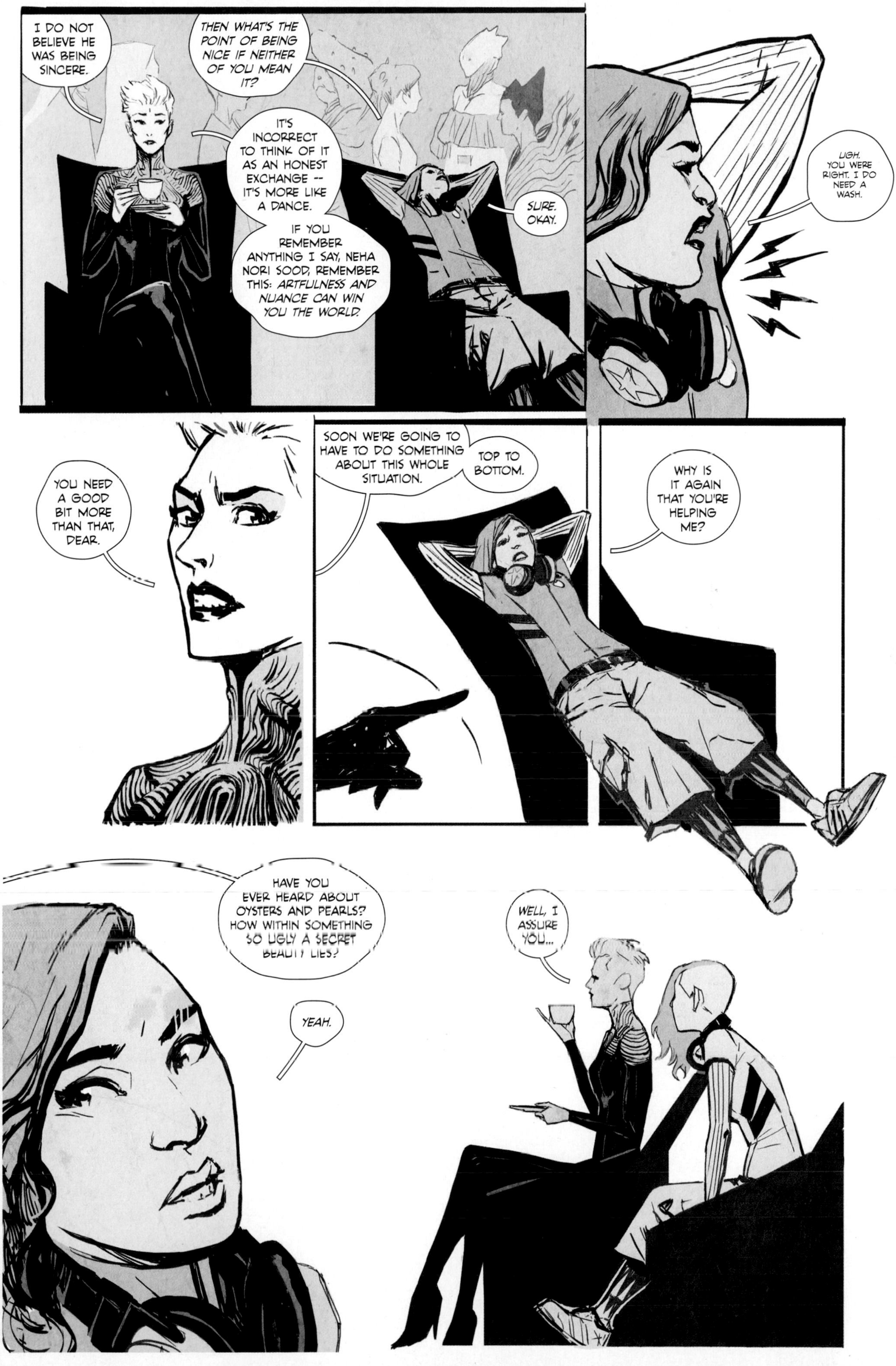
I DO NOT BELIEVE HE WAS BEING SINCERE.
THEN WHAT'S THE POINT OF BEING NICE IF NEITHER OF YOU MEAN IT?
IT'S INCORRECT TO THINK OF IT AS AN HONEST EXCHANGE -- IT'S MORE LIKE A DANCE.
IF YOU REMEMBER ANYTHING I SAY, NEHA NORI SOOD, REMEMBER THIS: ARTFULNESS AND NUANCE CAN WIN YOU THE WORLD.
SURE. OKAY.
UGH. YOU WERE RIGHT. I DO NEED A WASH.
YOU NEED A GOOD BIT MORE THAN THAT, DEAR.
SOON WE'RE GOING TO HAVE TO DO SOMETHING ABOUT THIS WHOLE SITUATION.
TOP TO BOTTOM.
WHY IS IT AGAIN THAT YOU'RE HELPING ME?
HAVE YOU EVER HEARD ABOUT OYSTERS AND PEARLS? HOW WITHIN SOMETHING SO UGLY A SECRET BEAUTY LIES?
YEAH.
WELL, I ASSURE YOU...

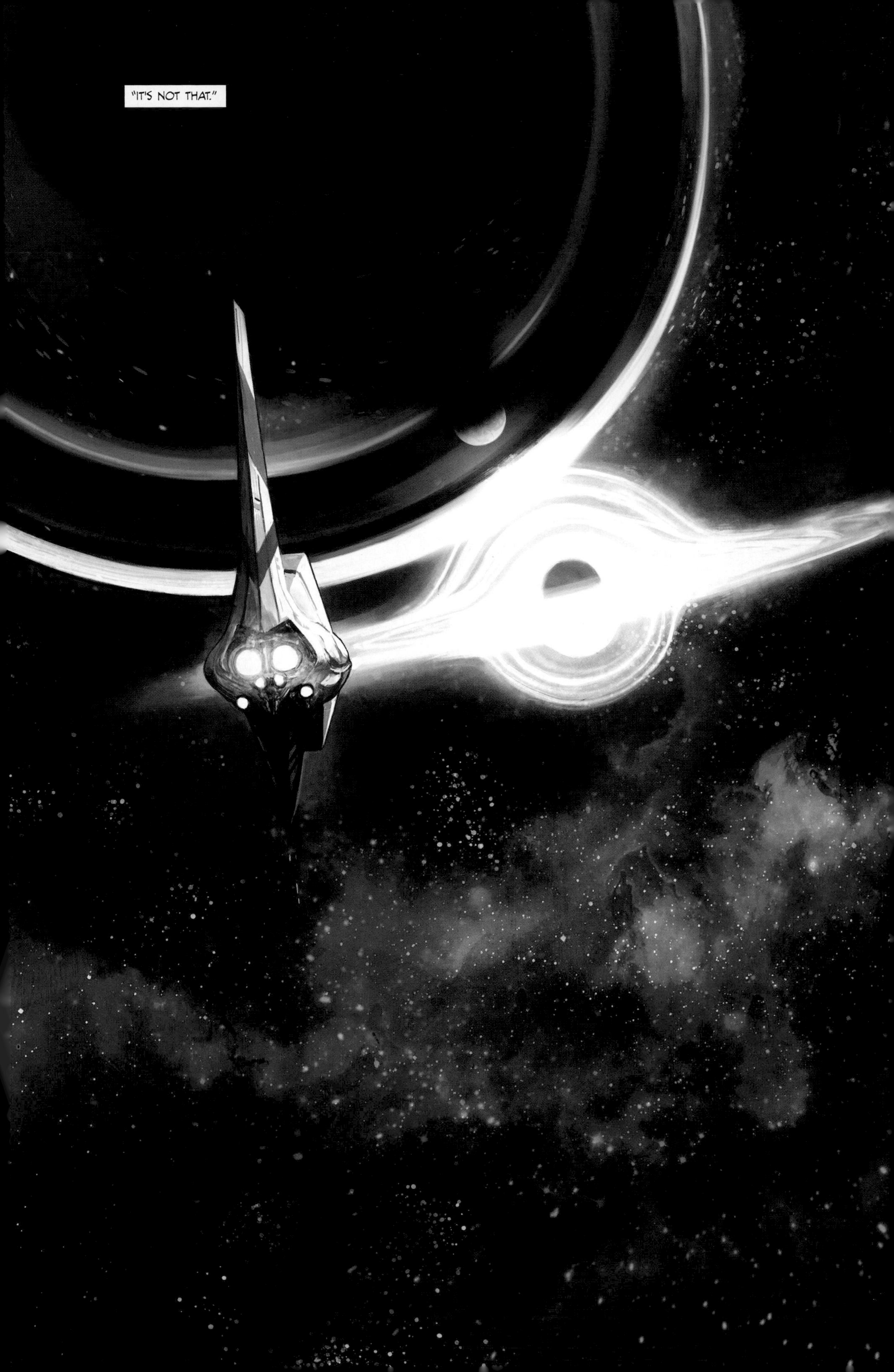
"IT'S NOT THAT."

CHAPTER NINE

[OVERGROUND, UNDERWORLD]

BYS

[TRANSIT WORLD]

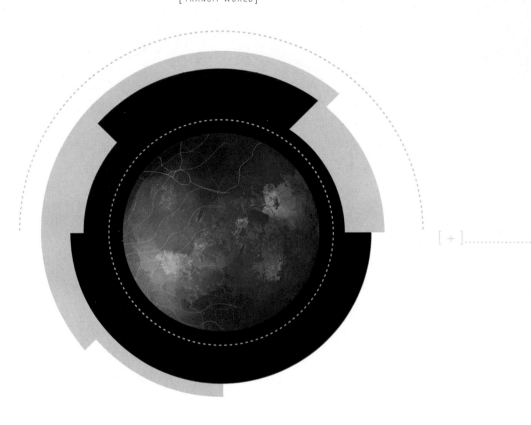

STATS

[PHYSICAL CHARACTERISTICS]

MEAN RADIUS........ **3,466 ± 0.7** km

SURFACE AREA...... **160,271,109** km²

VOLUME................. **2.198 × 1329** km³

MASS..................... **5.4104 × 1106** kg

SATELLITES.......... **2**

CONTINENTS......... **9**

[▬▬▬▬▬▬▬▬▬]

▬▬▬▬ ▬▬▬▬▬ ▬▬▬▬▬▬▬
▬▬ ▬▬▬▬▬▬ ▬▬▬▬▬ ▬▬▬▬▬▬▬
▬▬ ▬▬▬▬▬▬▬▬▬▬ ▬▬▬▬▬

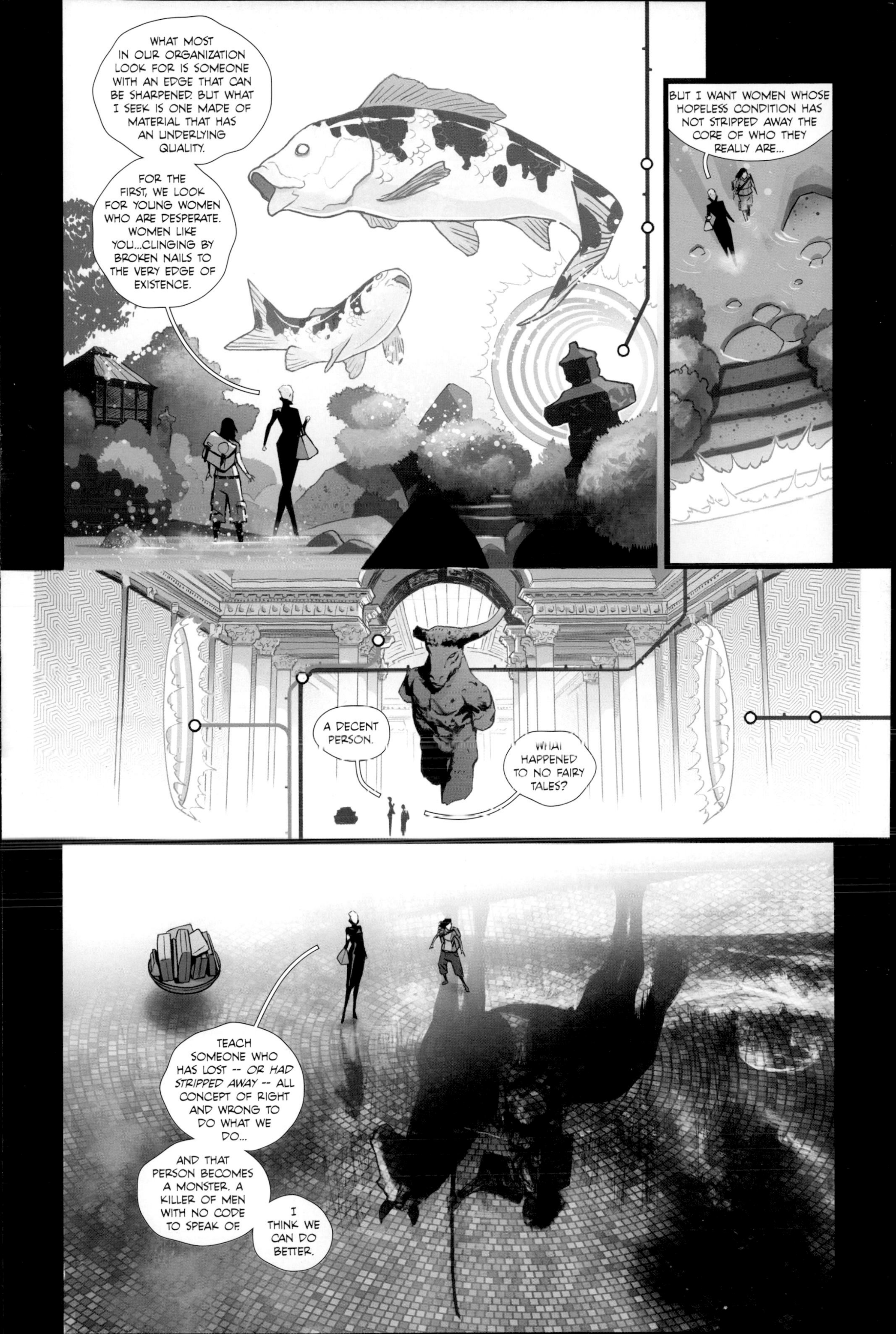
WHAT MOST IN OUR ORGANIZATION LOOK FOR IS SOMEONE WITH AN EDGE THAT CAN BE SHARPENED. BUT WHAT I SEEK IS ONE MADE OF MATERIAL THAT HAS AN UNDERLYING QUALITY.
FOR THE FIRST, WE LOOK FOR YOUNG WOMEN WHO ARE DESPERATE. WOMEN LIKE YOU...CLINGING BY BROKEN NAILS TO THE VERY EDGE OF EXISTENCE.
BUT I WANT WOMEN WHOSE HOPELESS CONDITION HAS NOT STRIPPED AWAY THE CORE OF WHO THEY REALLY ARE...
A DECENT PERSON.
WHAT HAPPENED TO NO FAIRY TALES?
TEACH SOMEONE WHO HAS LOST -- *OR HAD STRIPPED AWAY* -- ALL CONCEPT OF RIGHT AND WRONG TO DO WHAT WE DO...
AND THAT PERSON BECOMES A MONSTER. A KILLER OF MEN WITH NO CODE TO SPEAK OF.
I THINK WE CAN DO BETTER.

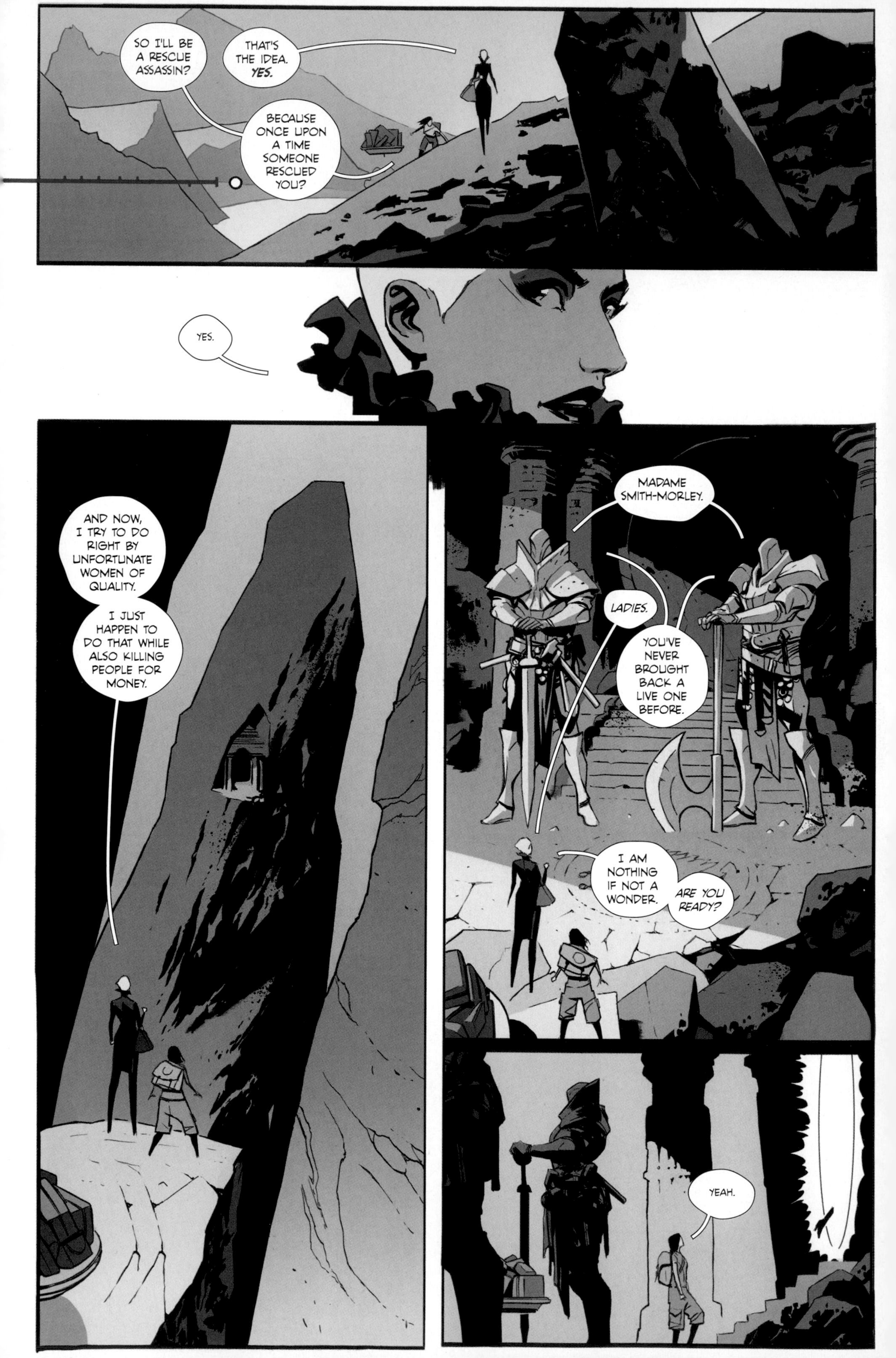

SO I'LL BE A RESCUE ASSASSIN?
THAT'S THE IDEA. *YES.*
BECAUSE ONCE UPON A TIME SOMEONE RESCUED YOU?
YES.
AND NOW, I TRY TO DO RIGHT BY UNFORTUNATE WOMEN OF QUALITY.
I JUST HAPPEN TO DO THAT WHILE ALSO KILLING PEOPLE FOR MONEY.
MADAME SMITH-MORLEY.
LADIES.
YOU'VE NEVER BROUGHT BACK A LIVE ONE BEFORE.
I AM NOTHING IF NOT A WONDER.
ARE YOU READY?
YEAH.

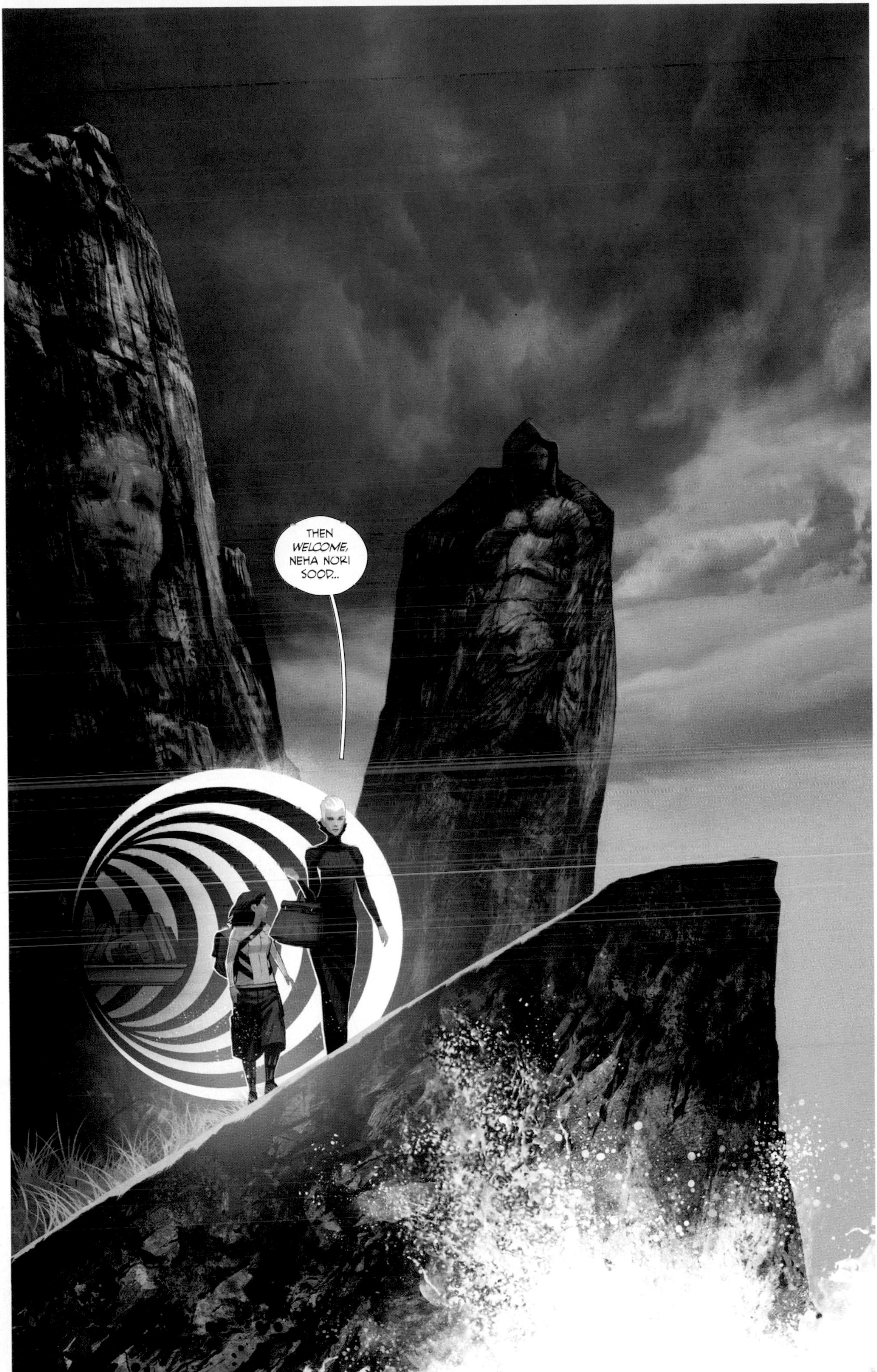
THEN *WELCOME,* NEHA NOKI SOOD...

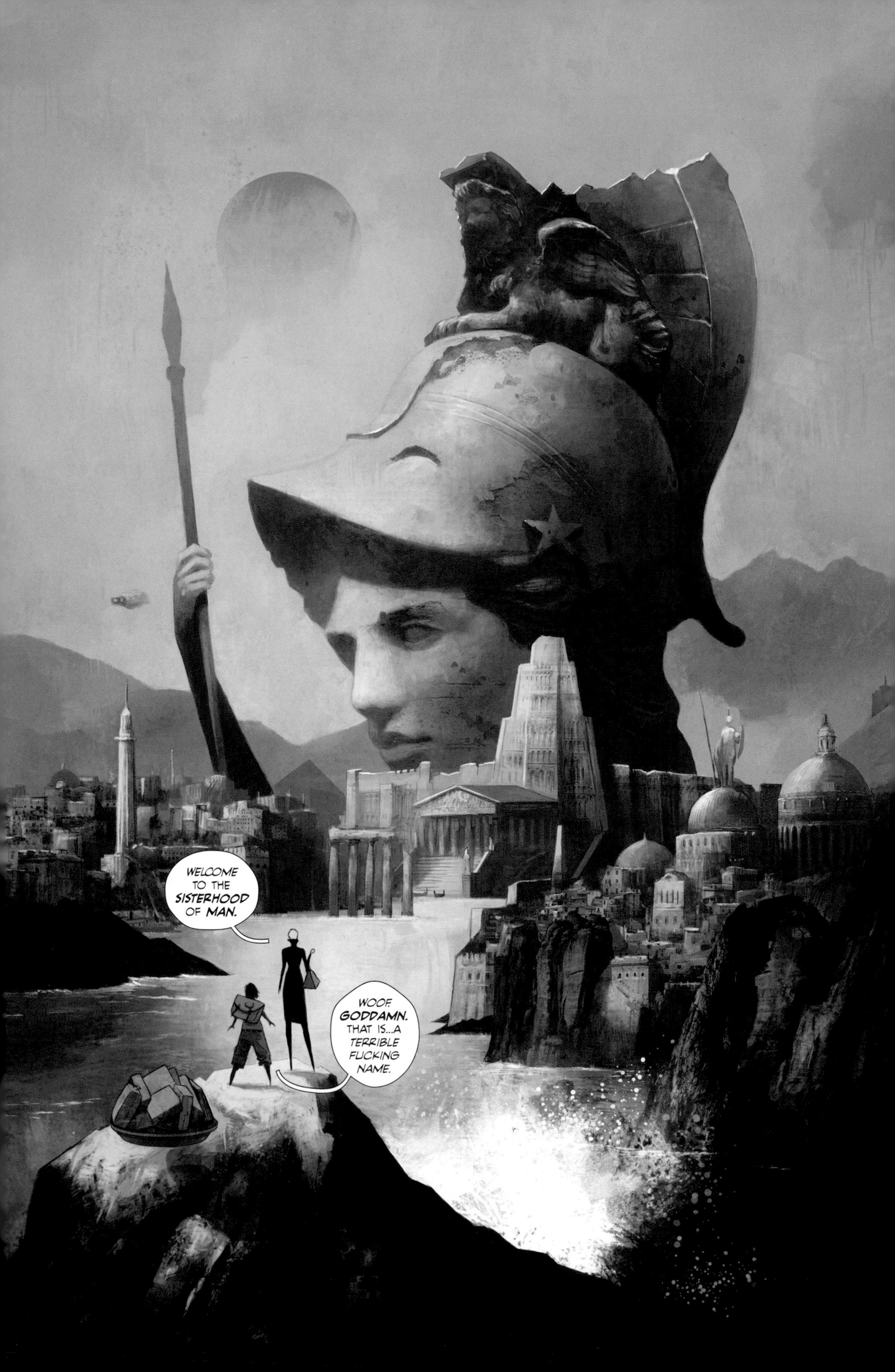
WELCOME TO THE SISTERHOOD OF MAN.
WOOF. GODDAMN. THAT IS...A TERRIBLE FUCKING NAME.

CHAPTER TEN

[BONAFIDES]

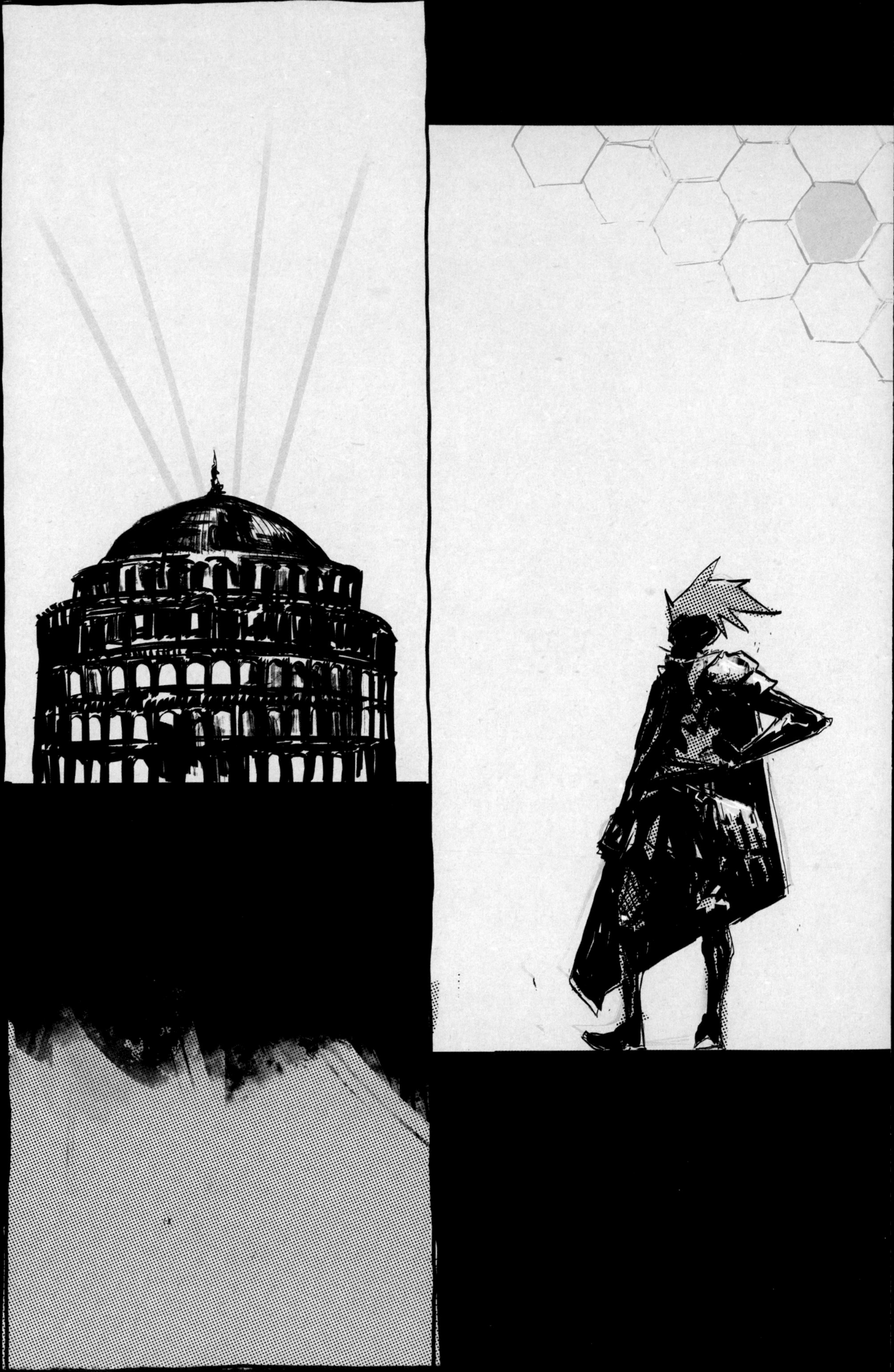

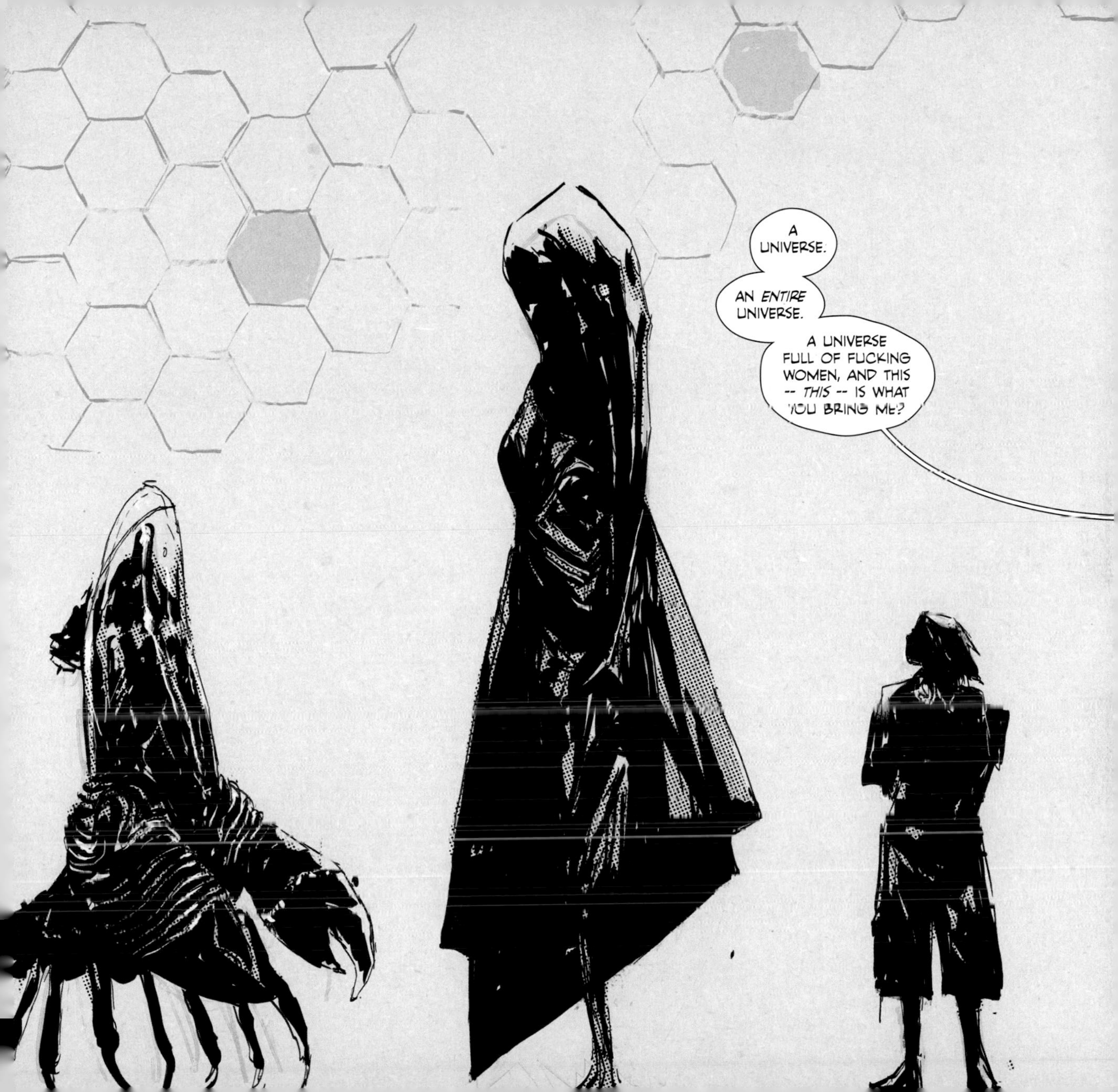
A UNIVERSE.
AN *ENTIRE* UNIVERSE.
A UNIVERSE FULL OF FUCKING WOMEN, AND THIS -- *THIS* -- IS WHAT YOU BRING ME?

WELCOME, KILLERS!

THE SISTERHOOD OF MAN OFFICIALLY WELCOMES THE FRESHMAN CLASS OF FY 12,902.

Ready to embark on a life-long adventure of grudge-settling, assassination and revenge? **WE ARE TOO!**

BOMB-MAKING!

EDGED WEAPONS!

POISONS!

PISTOLS!

AND MORE!

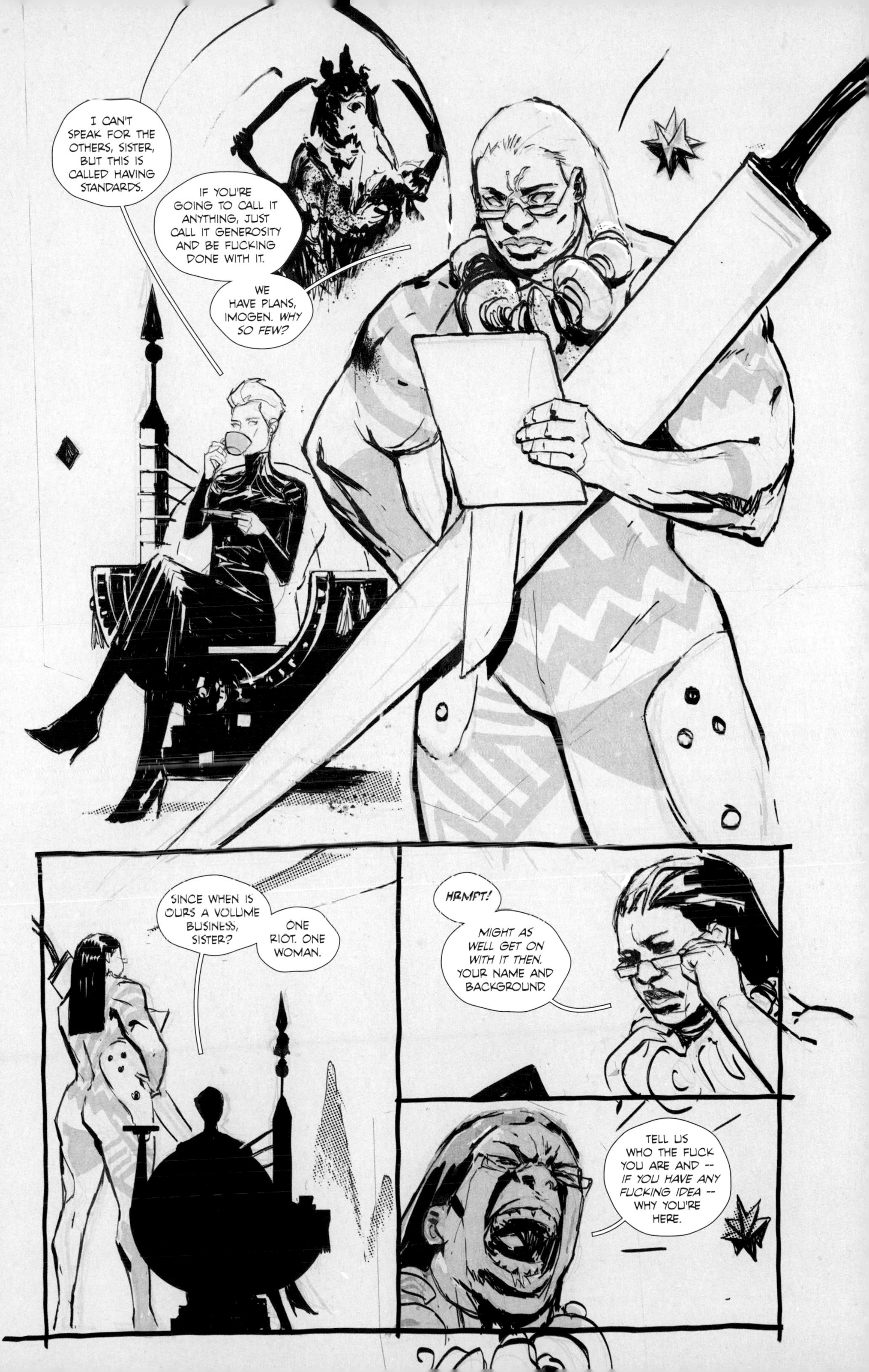
I CAN'T SPEAK FOR THE OTHERS, SISTER, BUT THIS IS CALLED HAVING STANDARDS.
IF YOU'RE GOING TO CALL IT ANYTHING, JUST CALL IT GENEROSITY AND BE FUCKING DONE WITH IT.
WE HAVE PLANS, IMOGEN. *WHY SO FEW?*
SINCE WHEN IS OURS A VOLUME BUSINESS, SISTER?
ONE RIOT. ONE WOMAN.
HRMPT!
MIGHT AS WELL GET ON WITH IT THEN. YOUR NAME AND BACKGROUND.
TELL US WHO THE FUCK YOU ARE AND -- *IF YOU HAVE ANY FUCKING IDEA* -- WHY YOU'RE HERE.

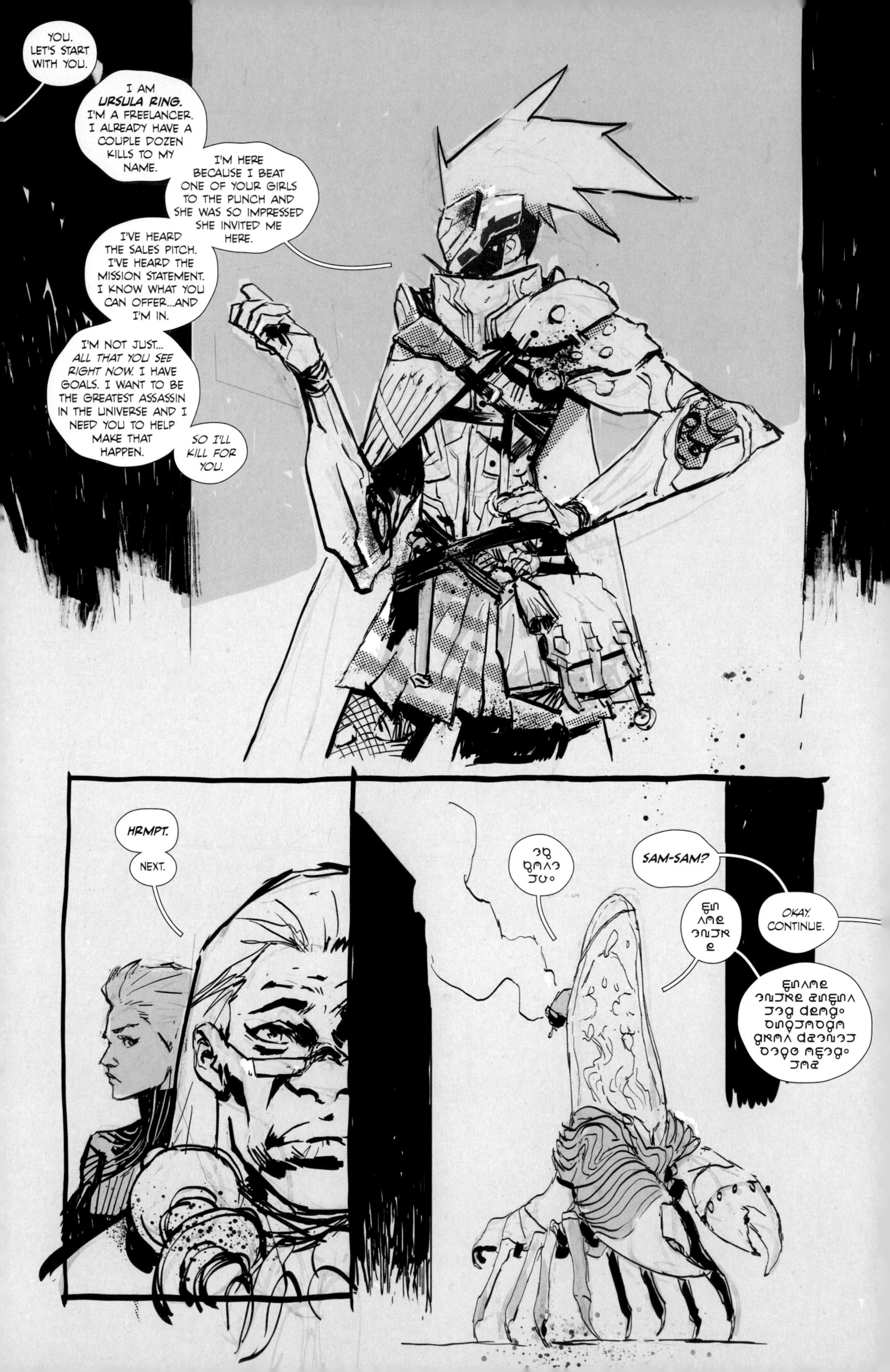

YOU. LET'S START WITH YOU.
I AM ***URSULA RING.*** I'M A FREELANCER. I ALREADY HAVE A COUPLE DOZEN KILLS TO MY NAME.
I'M HERE BECAUSE I BEAT ONE OF YOUR GIRLS TO THE PUNCH AND SHE WAS SO IMPRESSED SHE INVITED ME HERE.
I'VE HEARD THE SALES PITCH. I'VE HEARD THE MISSION STATEMENT. I KNOW WHAT YOU CAN OFFER...AND I'M IN.
I'M NOT JUST... *ALL THAT YOU SEE RIGHT NOW.* I HAVE GOALS. I WANT TO BE THE GREATEST ASSASSIN IN THE UNIVERSE AND I NEED YOU TO HELP MAKE THAT HAPPEN.
SO I'LL KILL FOR YOU.
HRMPT.
NEXT.
SAM-SAM?
OKAY. CONTINUE.

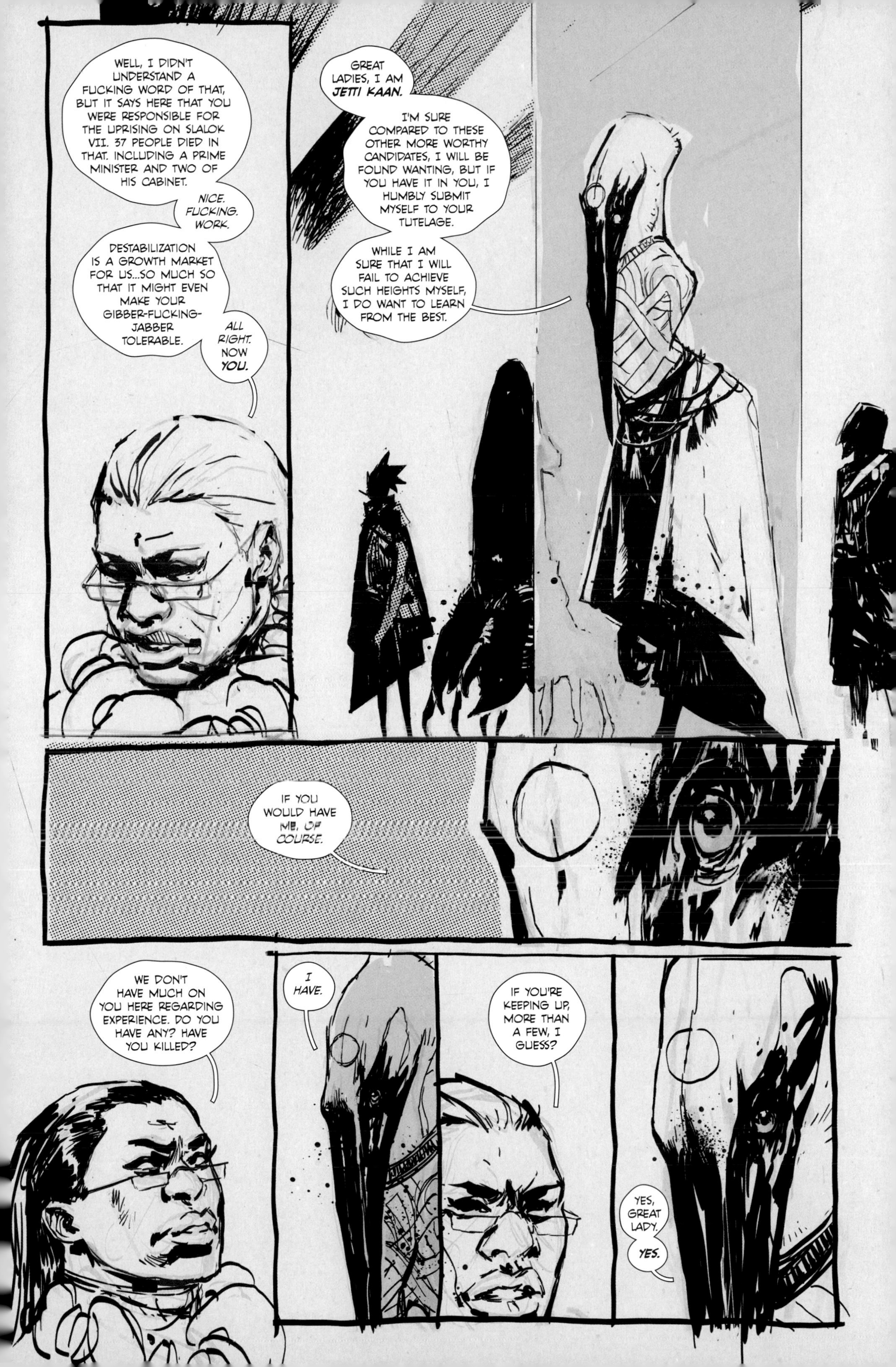
WELL, I DIDN'T UNDERSTAND A FUCKING WORD OF THAT, BUT IT SAYS HERE THAT YOU WERE RESPONSIBLE FOR THE UPRISING ON SLALOK VII. 37 PEOPLE DIED IN THAT. INCLUDING A PRIME MINISTER AND TWO OF HIS CABINET.
NICE. FUCKING. WORK.
DESTABILIZATION IS A GROWTH MARKET FOR US...SO MUCH SO THAT IT MIGHT EVEN MAKE YOUR GIBBER-FUCKING-JABBER TOLERABLE.
ALL RIGHT. NOW YOU.
GREAT LADIES, I AM JETTI KAAN.
I'M SURE COMPARED TO THESE OTHER MORE WORTHY CANDIDATES, I WILL BE FOUND WANTING, BUT IF YOU HAVE IT IN YOU, I HUMBLY SUBMIT MYSELF TO YOUR TUTELAGE.
WHILE I AM SURE THAT I WILL FAIL TO ACHIEVE SUCH HEIGHTS MYSELF, I DO WANT TO LEARN FROM THE BEST.
IF YOU WOULD HAVE ME, OF COURSE.
WE DON'T HAVE MUCH ON YOU HERE REGARDING EXPERIENCE. DO YOU HAVE ANY? HAVE YOU KILLED?
I HAVE.
IF YOU'RE KEEPING UP, MORE THAN A FEW, I GUESS?
YES, GREAT LADY.
YES.

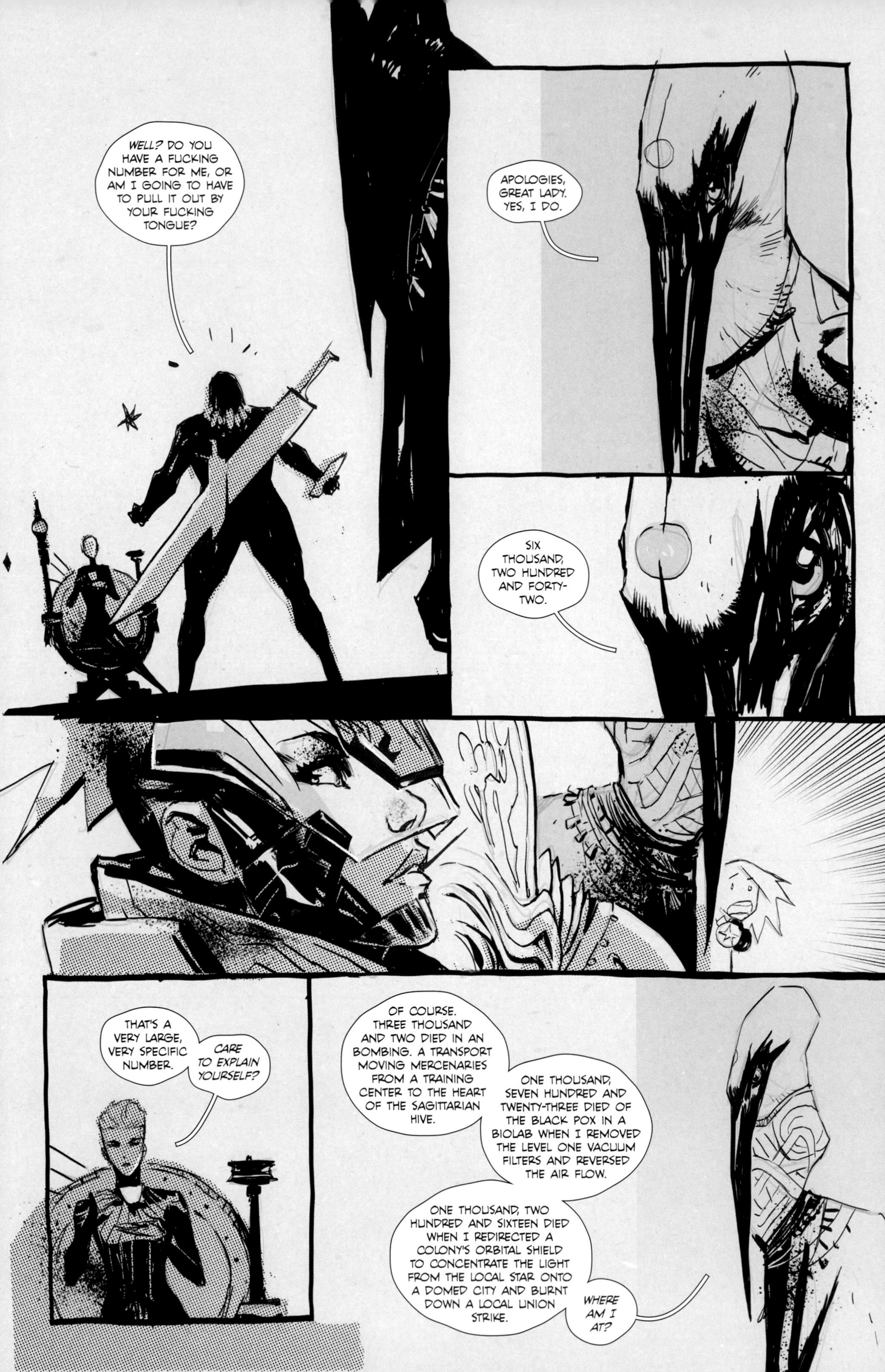

WELL? DO YOU HAVE A FUCKING NUMBER FOR ME, OR AM I GOING TO HAVE TO PULL IT OUT BY YOUR FUCKING TONGUE?
APOLOGIES, GREAT LADY. YES, I DO.
SIX THOUSAND, TWO HUNDRED AND FORTY-TWO.
THAT'S A VERY LARGE, VERY SPECIFIC NUMBER.
CARE TO EXPLAIN YOURSELF?
OF COURSE. THREE THOUSAND AND TWO DIED IN AN BOMBING. A TRANSPORT MOVING MERCENARIES FROM A TRAINING CENTER TO THE HEART OF THE SAGITTARIAN HIVE.
ONE THOUSAND, SEVEN HUNDRED AND TWENTY-THREE DIED OF THE BLACK POX IN A BIOLAB WHEN I REMOVED THE LEVEL ONE VACUUM FILTERS AND REVERSED THE AIR FLOW.
ONE THOUSAND, TWO HUNDRED AND SIXTEEN DIED WHEN I REDIRECTED A COLONY'S ORBITAL SHIELD TO CONCENTRATE THE LIGHT FROM THE LOCAL STAR ONTO A DOMED CITY AND BURNT DOWN A LOCAL UNION STRIKE.
WHERE AM I AT?

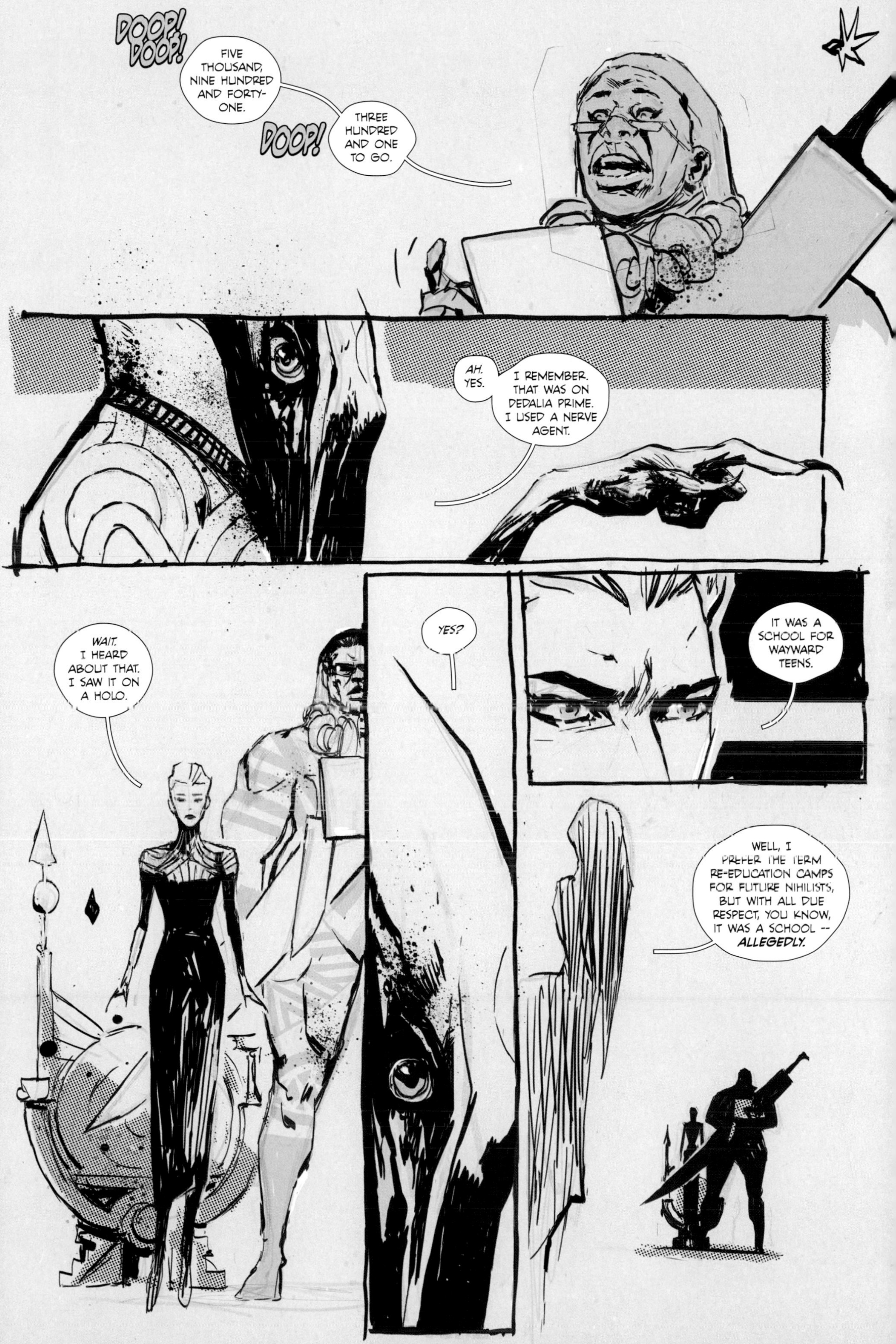
DOOP! DOOP!
FIVE THOUSAND, NINE HUNDRED AND FORTY-ONE.
DOOP!
THREE HUNDRED AND ONE TO GO.
AH. YES.
I REMEMBER. THAT WAS ON DEDALIA PRIME. I USED A NERVE AGENT.
WAIT. I HEARD ABOUT THAT. I SAW IT ON A HOLO.
YES?
IT WAS A SCHOOL FOR WAYWARD TEENS.
WELL, I PREFER THE TERM RE-EDUCATION CAMPS FOR FUTURE NIHILISTS, BUT WITH ALL DUE RESPECT, YOU KNOW, IT WAS A SCHOOL -- ALLEGEDLY.

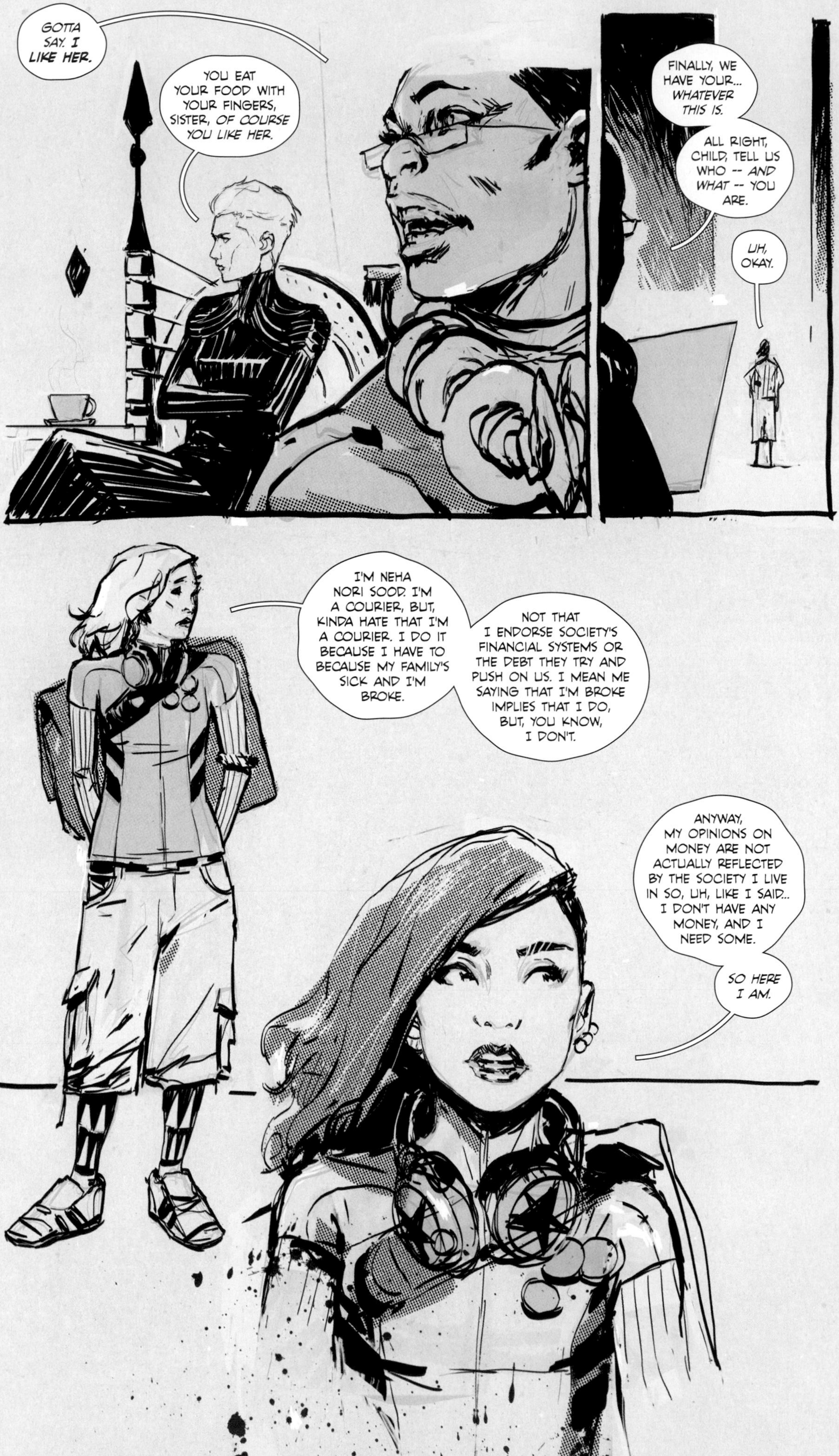
GOTTA SAY. I LIKE HER.
YOU EAT YOUR FOOD WITH YOUR FINGERS, SISTER, OF COURSE YOU LIKE HER.
FINALLY, WE HAVE YOUR... WHATEVER THIS IS.
ALL RIGHT, CHILD, TELL US WHO -- AND WHAT -- YOU ARE.
UH, OKAY.
I'M NEHA NORI SOOD. I'M A COURIER, BUT, KINDA HATE THAT I'M A COURIER. I DO IT BECAUSE I HAVE TO BECAUSE MY FAMILY'S SICK AND I'M BROKE.
NOT THAT I ENDORSE SOCIETY'S FINANCIAL SYSTEMS OR THE DEBT THEY TRY AND PUSH ON US. I MEAN ME SAYING THAT I'M BROKE IMPLIES THAT I DO, BUT, YOU KNOW, I DON'T.
ANYWAY, MY OPINIONS ON MONEY ARE NOT ACTUALLY REFLECTED BY THE SOCIETY I LIVE IN SO, UH, LIKE I SAID... I DON'T HAVE ANY MONEY, AND I NEED SOME.
SO HERE I AM.

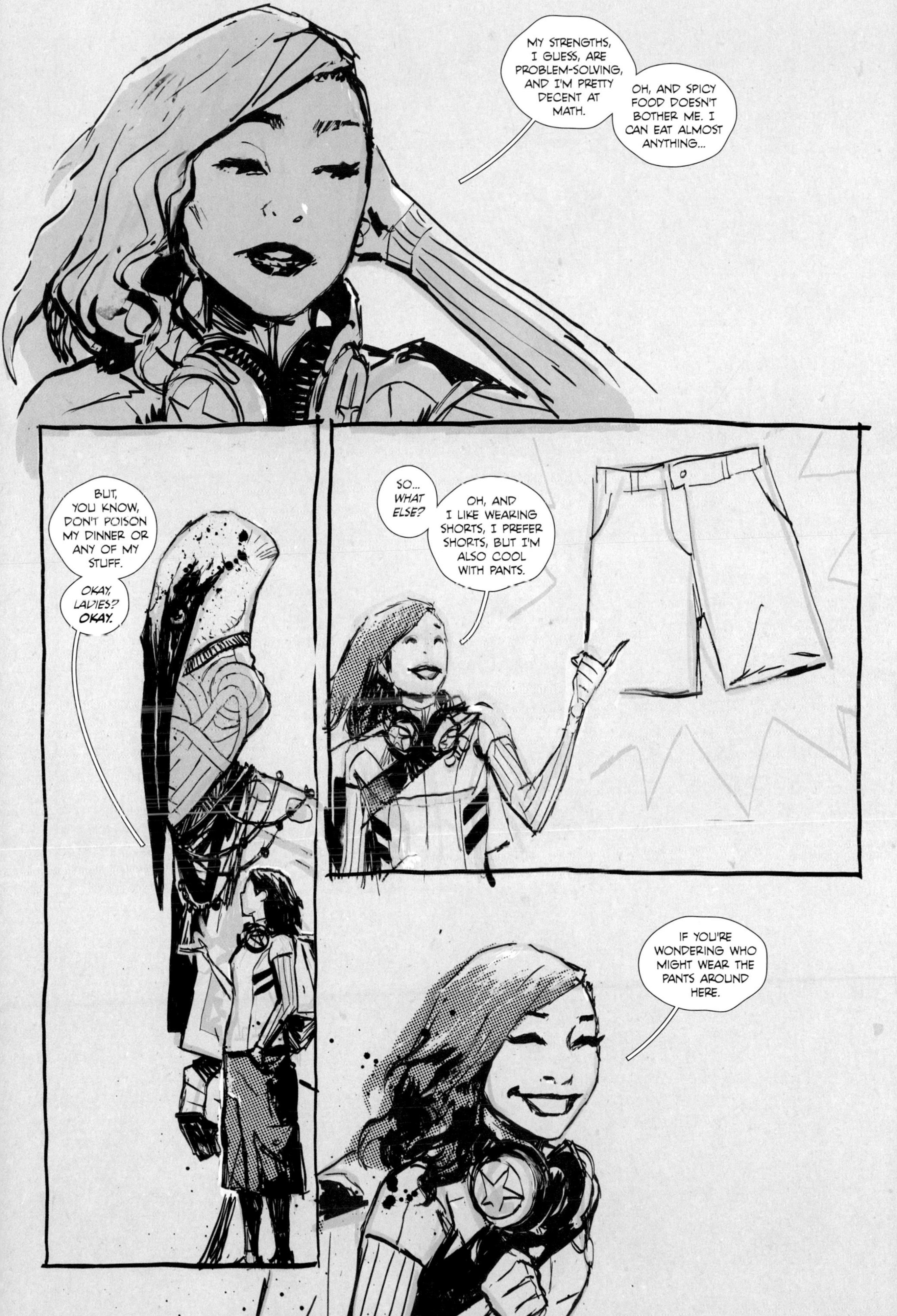
MY STRENGTHS, I GUESS, ARE PROBLEM-SOLVING, AND I'M PRETTY DECENT AT MATH.
OH, AND SPICY FOOD DOESN'T BOTHER ME. I CAN EAT ALMOST ANYTHING...
BUT, YOU KNOW, DON'T POISON MY DINNER OR ANY OF MY STUFF.
OKAY, LADIES? ***OKAY.***
SO... *WHAT ELSE?*
OH, AND I LIKE WEARING SHORTS, I PREFER SHORTS, BUT I'M ALSO COOL WITH PANTS.
IF YOU'RE WONDERING WHO MIGHT WEAR THE PANTS AROUND HERE.

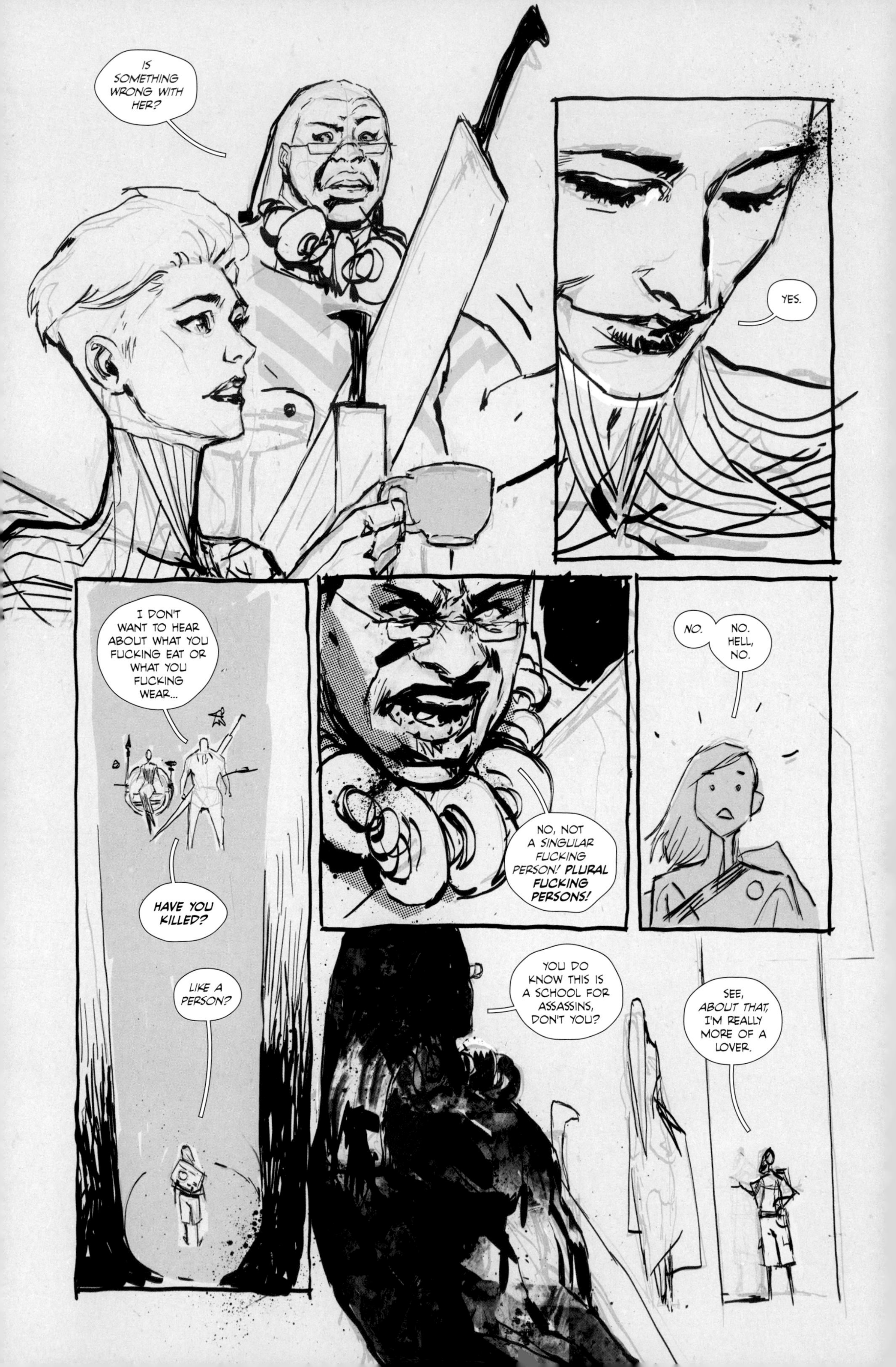
IS SOMETHING WRONG WITH HER?
YES.
I DON'T WANT TO HEAR ABOUT WHAT YOU FUCKING EAT OR WHAT YOU FUCKING WEAR...
HAVE YOU KILLED?
LIKE A PERSON?
NO, NOT A SINGULAR FUCKING PERSON! PLURAL FUCKING PERSONS!
NO.
NO. HELL, NO.
YOU DO KNOW THIS IS A SCHOOL FOR ASSASSINS, DON'T YOU?
SEE, ABOUT THAT, I'M REALLY MORE OF A LOVER.

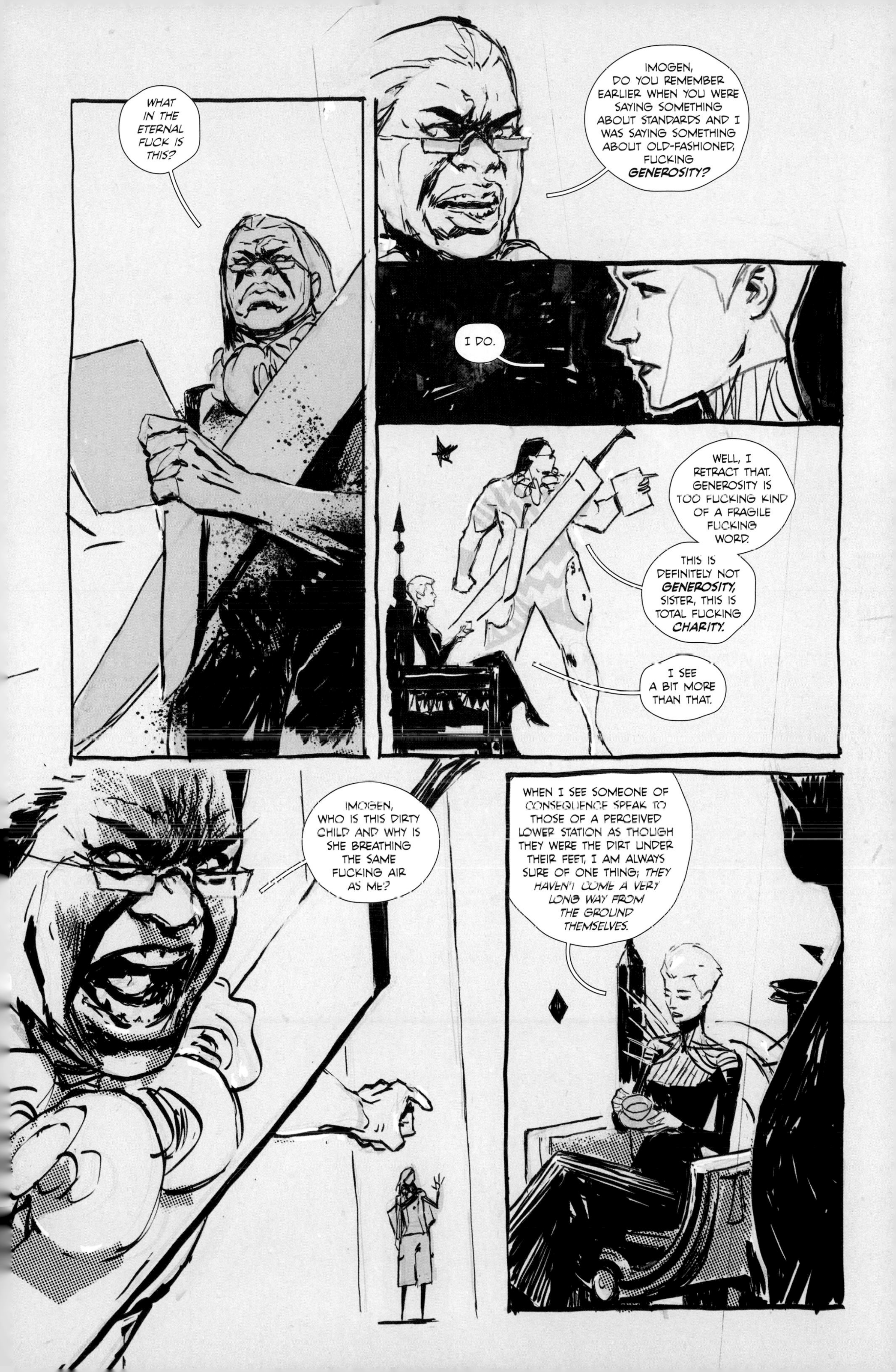
WHAT IN THE ETERNAL FUCK IS THIS?
IMOGEN, DO YOU REMEMBER EARLIER WHEN YOU WERE SAYING SOMETHING ABOUT STANDARDS AND I WAS SAYING SOMETHING ABOUT OLD-FASHIONED, FUCKING GENEROSITY?
I DO.
WELL, I RETRACT THAT. GENEROSITY IS TOO FUCKING KIND OF A FRAGILE FUCKING WORD.
THIS IS DEFINITELY NOT GENEROSITY, SISTER, THIS IS TOTAL FUCKING CHARITY.
I SEE A BIT MORE THAN THAT.
IMOGEN, WHO IS THIS DIRTY CHILD AND WHY IS SHE BREATHING THE SAME FUCKING AIR AS ME?
WHEN I SEE SOMEONE OF CONSEQUENCE SPEAK TO THOSE OF A PERCEIVED LOWER STATION AS THOUGH THEY WERE THE DIRT UNDER THEIR FEET, I AM ALWAYS SURE OF ONE THING; THEY HAVEN'T COME A VERY LONG WAY FROM THE GROUND THEMSELVES.

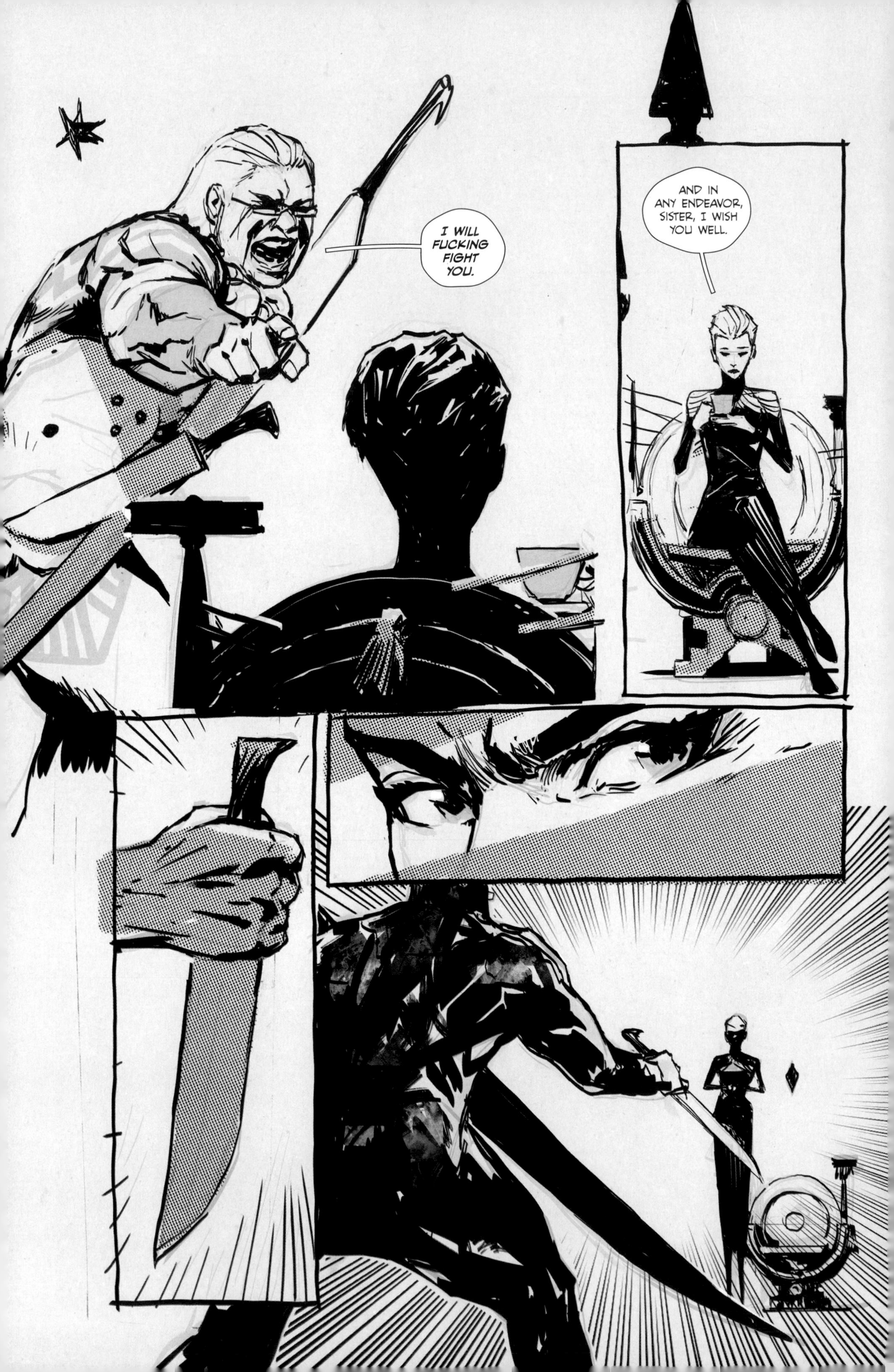
I WILL FUCKING FIGHT YOU.
AND IN ANY ENDEAVOR, SISTER, I WISH YOU WELL.

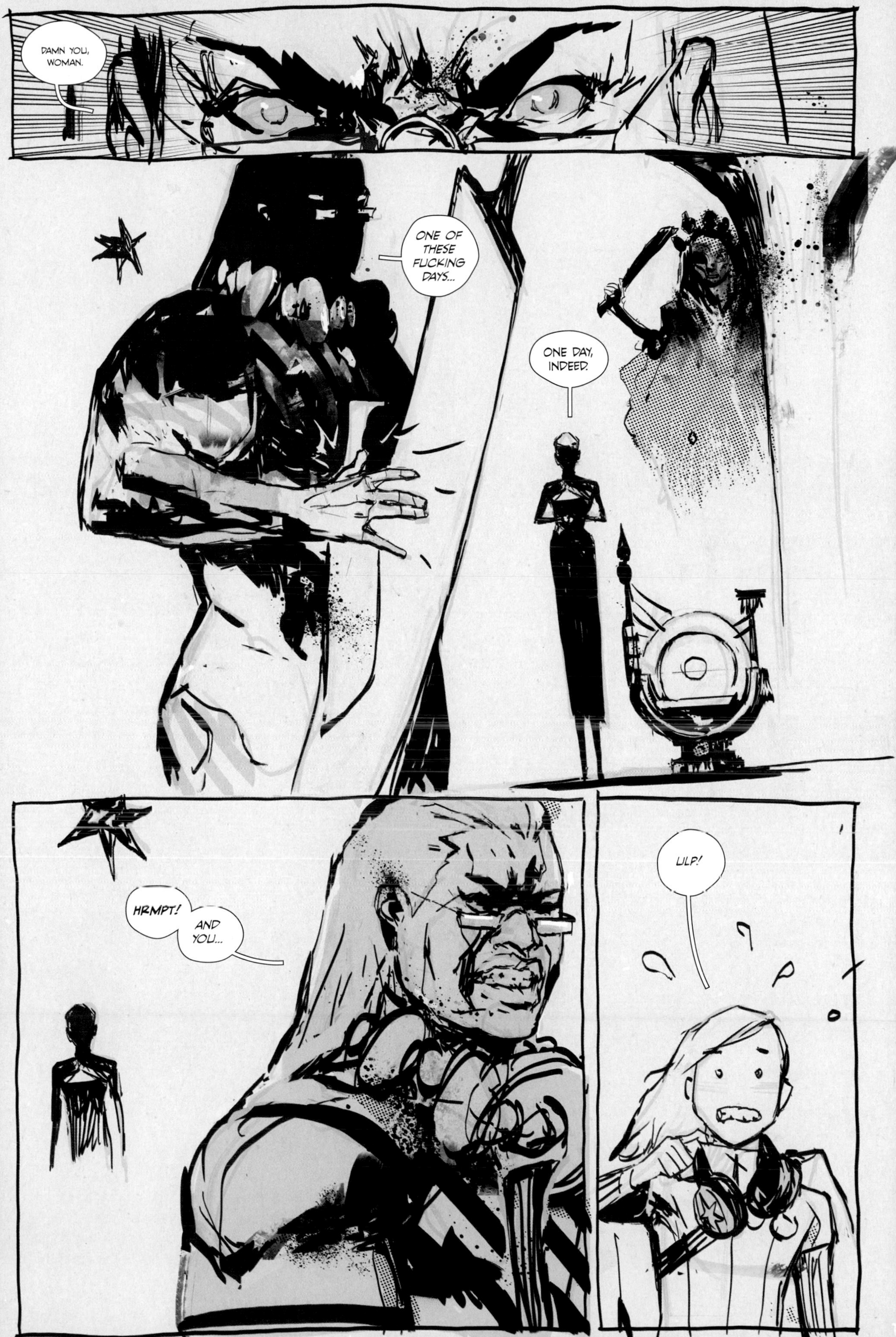
DAMN YOU, WOMAN.
ONE OF THESE FUCKING DAYS...
ONE DAY, INDEED.
HRMPT!
AND YOU...
ULP!

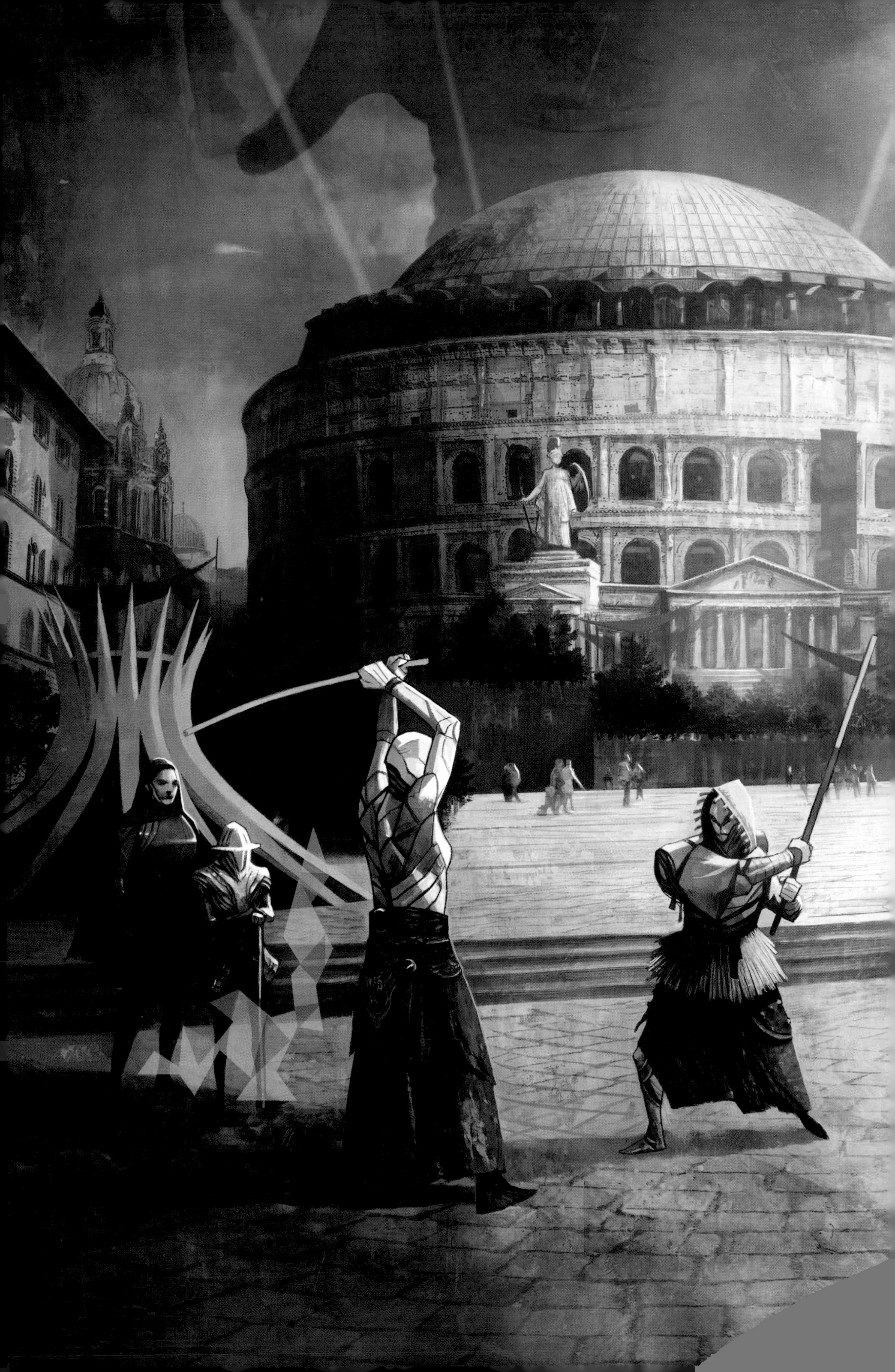

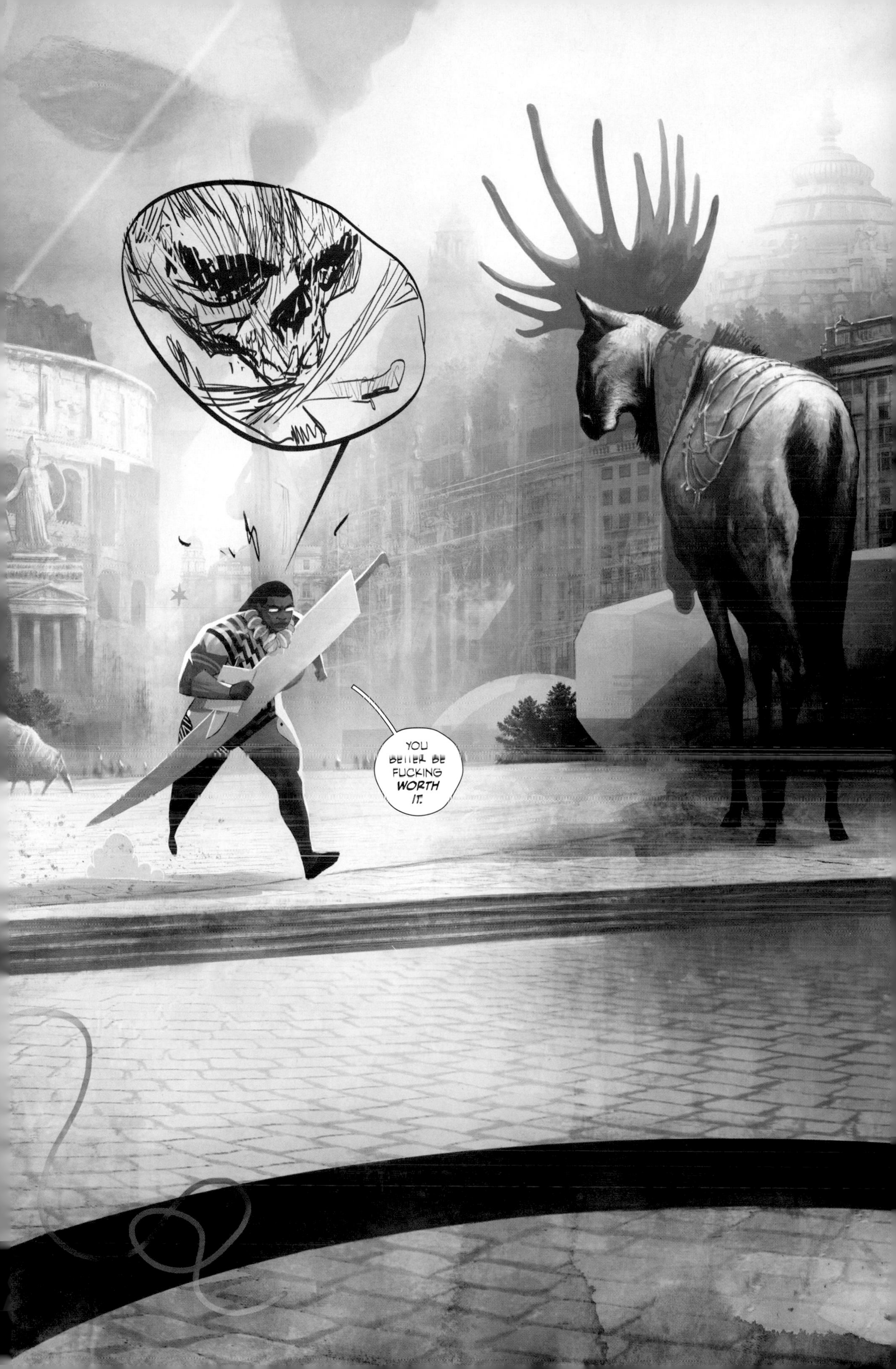
YOU BETTER BE FUCKING WORTH IT.

THE SISTERHOOD OF MAN

[INTRODUCTORY CLASS OF FY 12,902]

"MOST OF YOU WON'T MAKE IT."

—SISTER MA

URSULA RING

[▬▬▬▬▬▬▬▬▬▬▬▬]

STATS

AGE: **27**

HOMEWORLD: **UNKNOWN**

HEIGHT: **179cm**

WEIGHT: **63kg**

EDUCATION: **UNKNOWN**

EXPERIENCE LEVEL: **INTERMEDIATE**

DISLIKES: **PEOPLE ASKING QUESTIONS ABOUT HER PAST.**

LIKES: **KISSING UP.**

STABBING PEOPLE IN THE BACK.

STABBING PEOPLE IN THE FRONT.

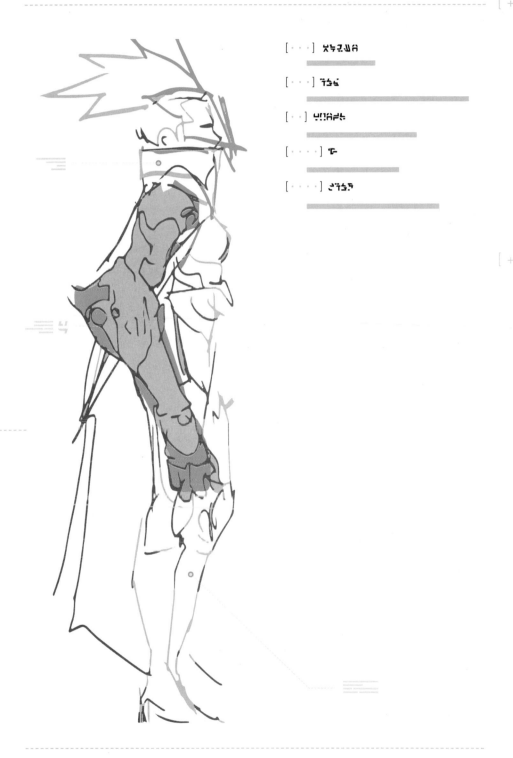

SAM-SAM

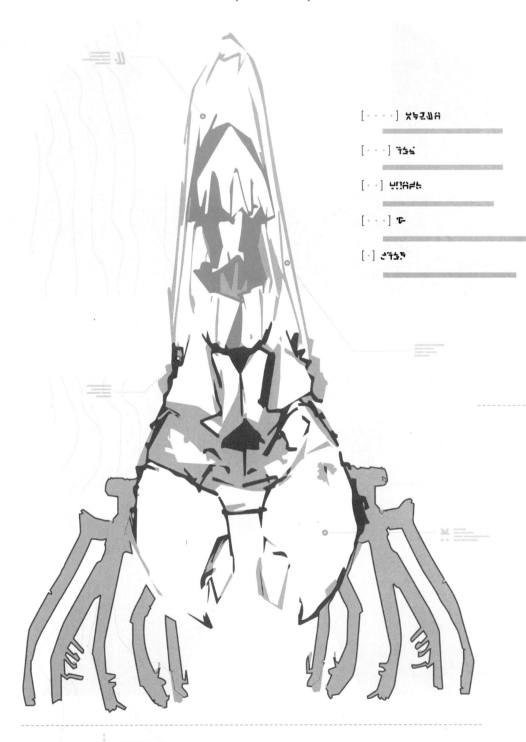

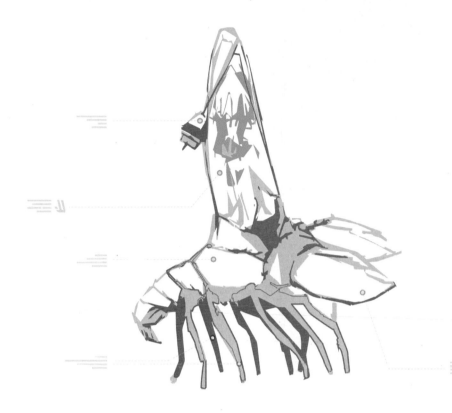

STATS

AGE: **278**

HOMEWORLD: **QUAPOPOD**

HEIGHT: **182cm**

WEIGHT: **816kg**

EDUCATION: **ADVANCED**

EXPERIENCE LEVEL: **INTERMEDIATE**

DISLIKES: **INDECIPHERABLE.**

LIKES: **IRREGULARLY SHAPED OBJECTS.**

STANDARD PRONUNCIATIONS.

JETTI KHAN

[=========]

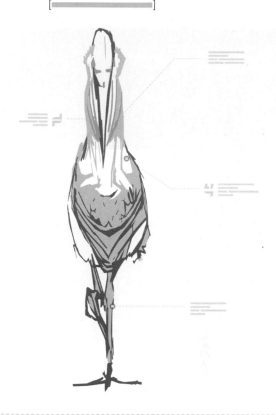

STATS

AGE: **35**

HEIGHT: **213cm**

WEIGHT: **88kg**

HOMEWORLD: **FLEESCK**

EDUCATION: **UNKNOWN**

EXPERIENCE LEVEL: **ADVANCED**

DISLIKES: **PROCRASTINATION. SUBTLETY. CHILDREN.**

LIKES: **POISONS. BOMBS. NICE FEET.**

NEHA NORI SOOD

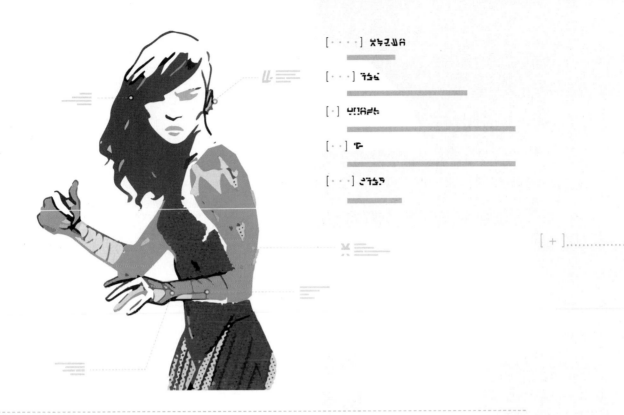

STATS

AGE: **21**

HEIGHT: **167cm**

WEIGHT: **53kg**

HOMEWORLD: **DEALDUS**

EDUCATION: **NONE**

EXPERIENCE LEVEL: **BEGINNER**

DISLIKES: **BAD NOODLES.**

VIOLENCE.

SHOWERS.

LIKES: **SHORTS. PANTS.**

IV

[AND THE EATING OF
A WORLD]

CHAPTER ELEVEN

[A SINGLE GRAIN OF SAND]

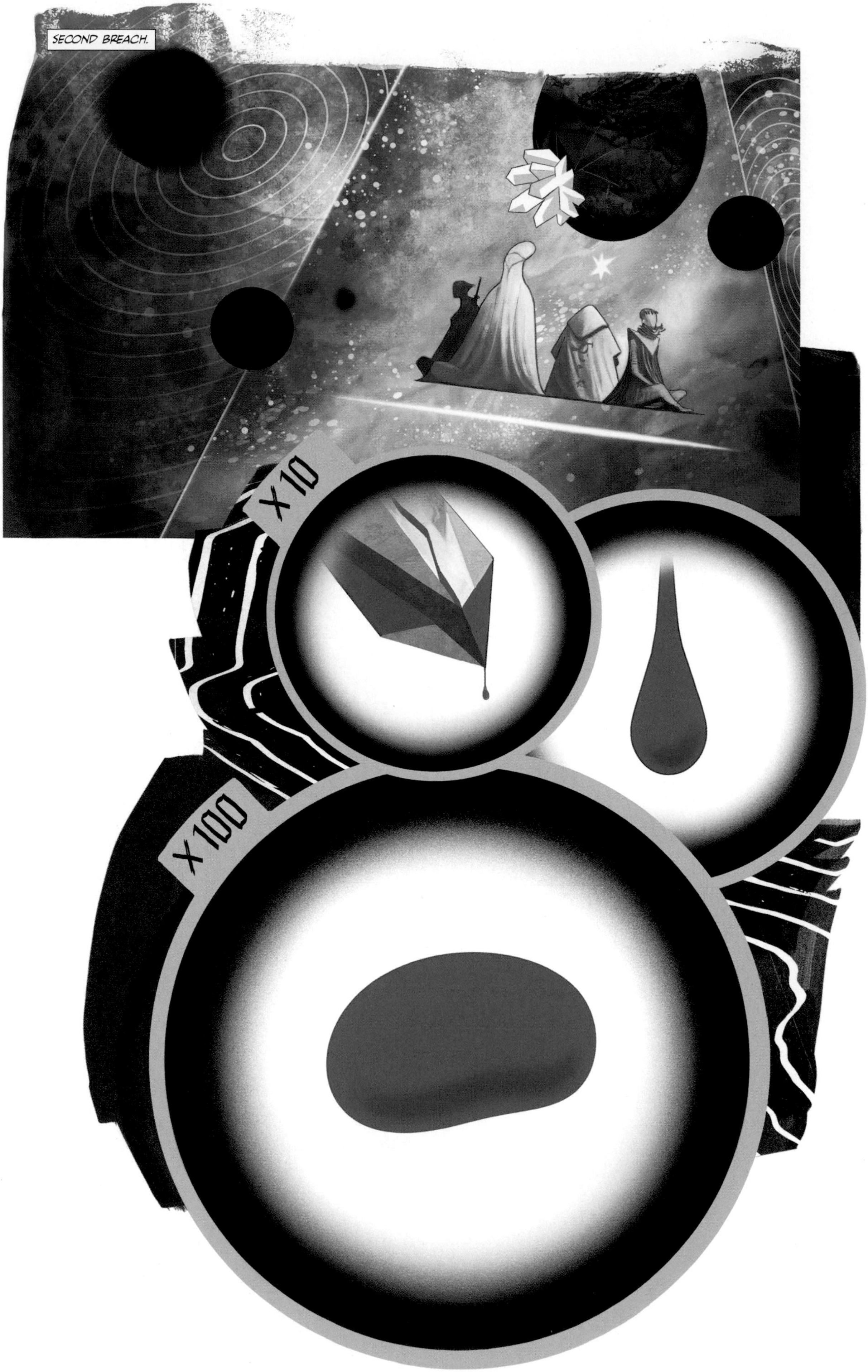
SECOND BREACH.
X10
X100

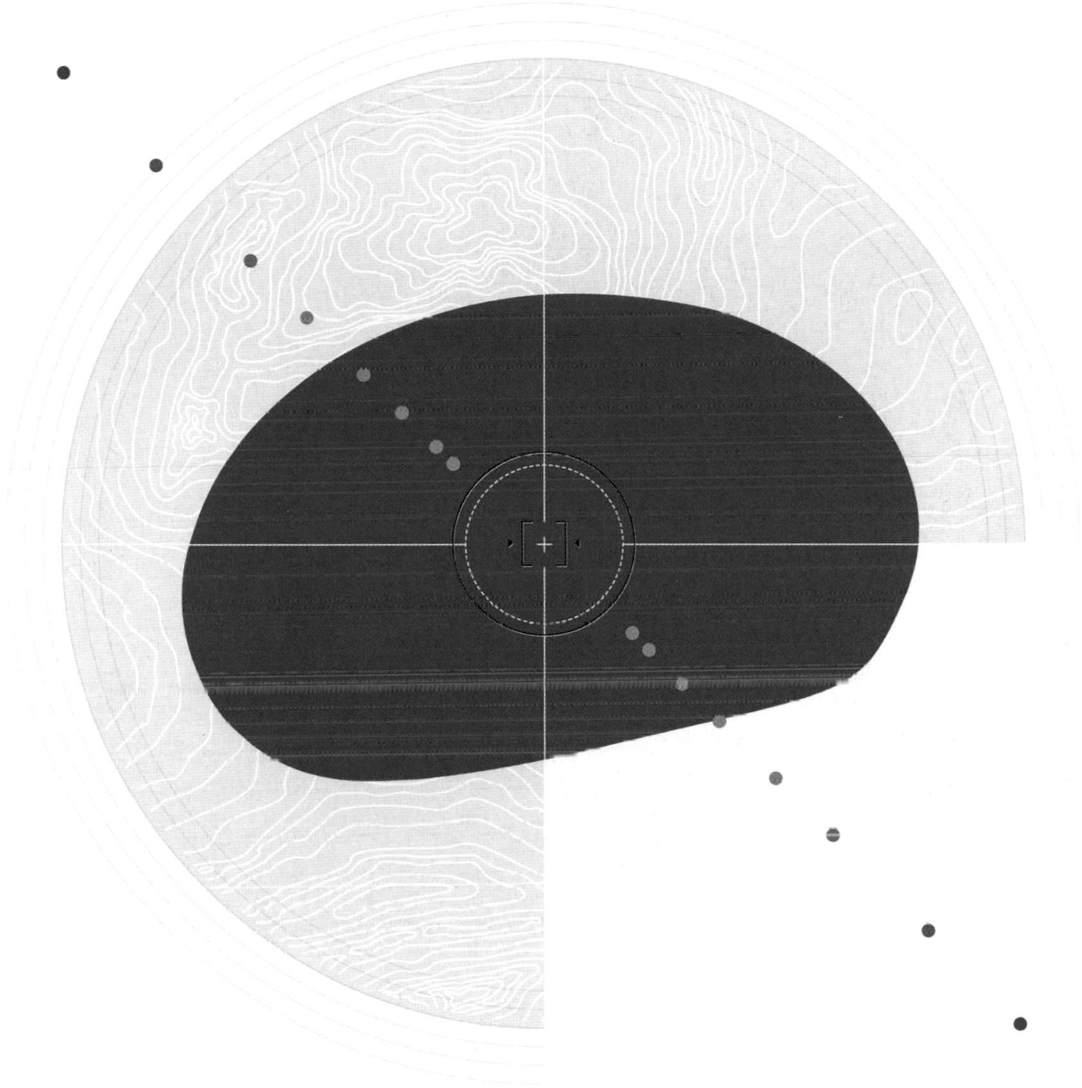

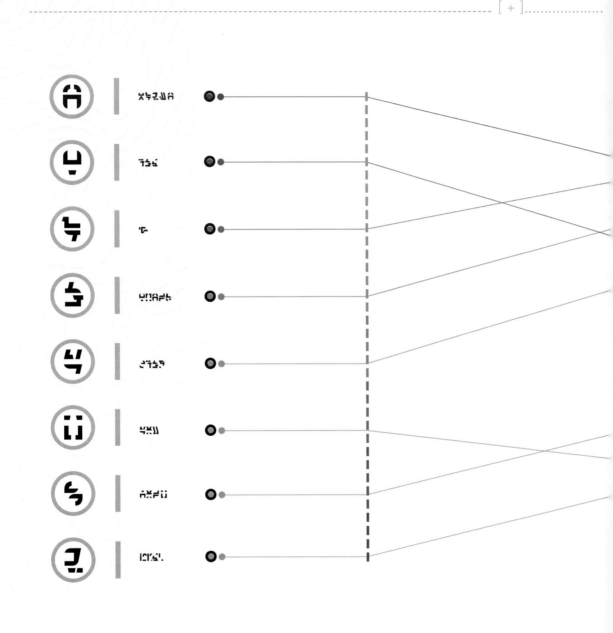

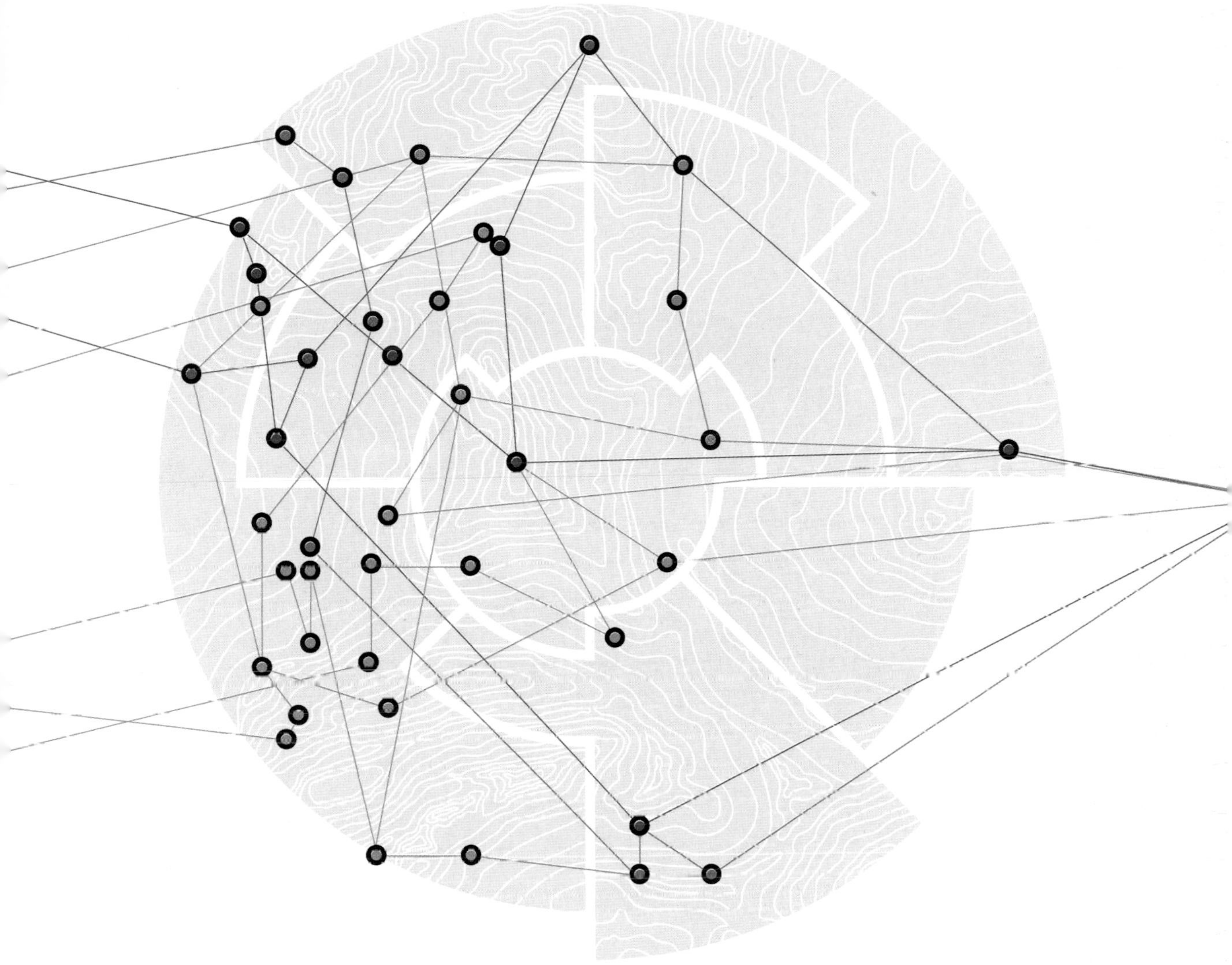

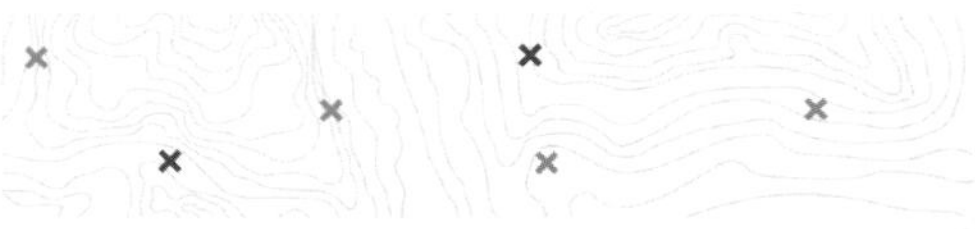

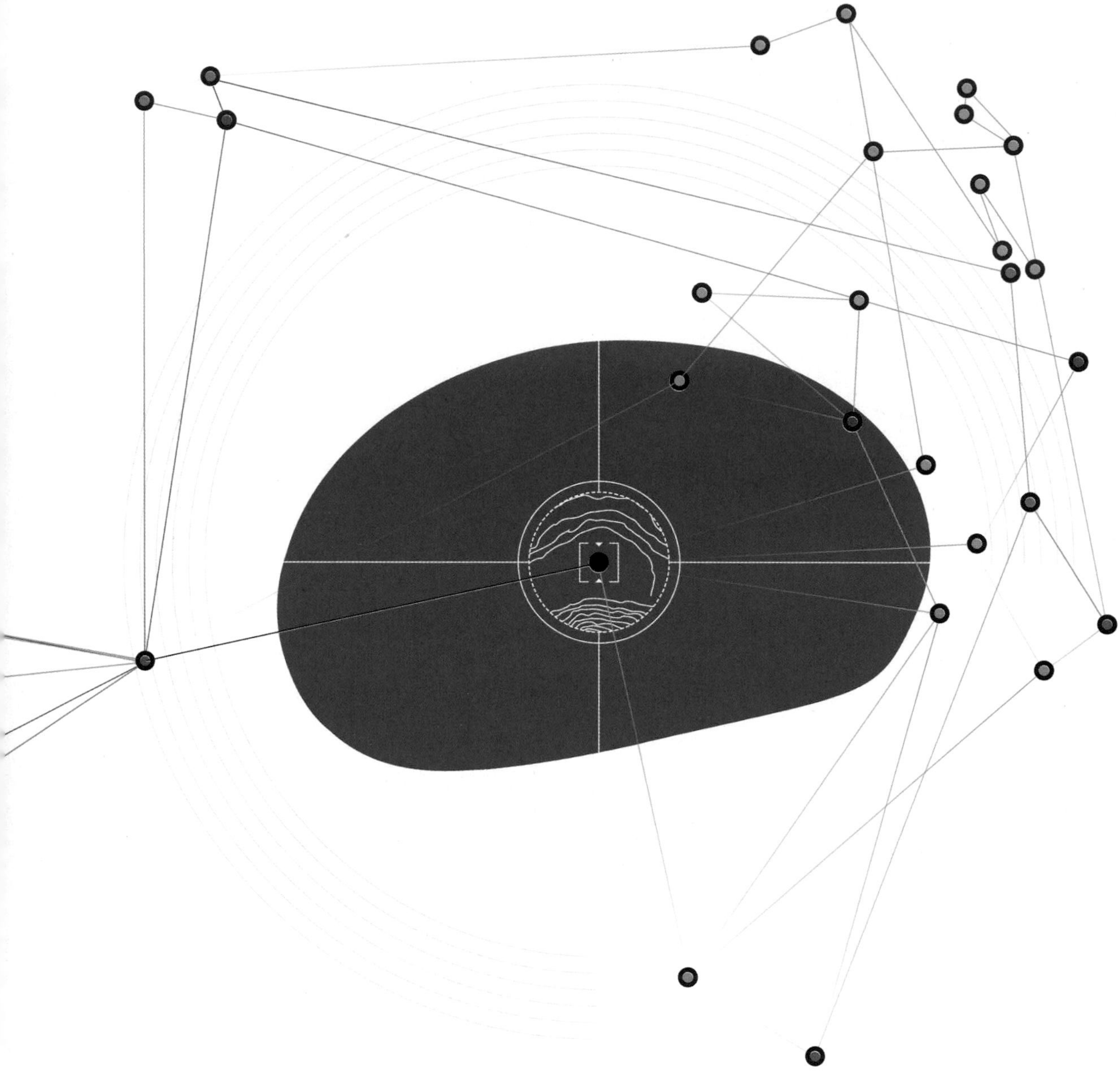

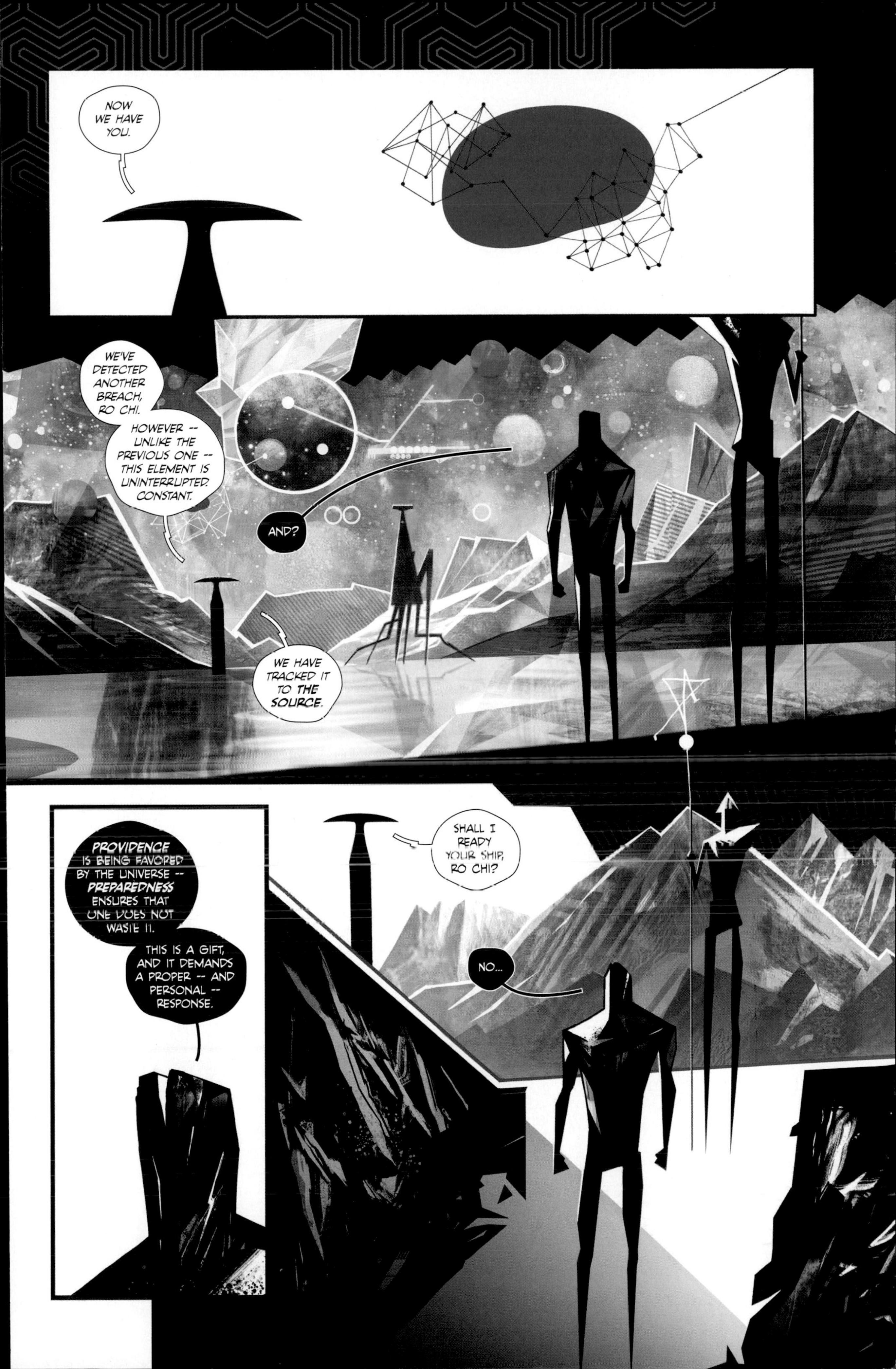
NOW WE HAVE YOU.
WE'VE DETECTED ANOTHER BREACH, RO CHI.
HOWEVER -- UNLIKE THE PREVIOUS ONE -- THIS ELEMENT IS UNINTERRUPTED. CONSTANT.
AND?
WE HAVE TRACKED IT TO THE SOURCE.
PROVIDENCE IS BEING FAVORED BY THE UNIVERSE -- PREPAREDNESS ENSURES THAT ONE DOES NOT WASTE IT.
THIS IS A GIFT, AND IT DEMANDS A PROPER -- AND PERSONAL -- RESPONSE.
SHALL I READY YOUR SHIP, RO CHI?
NO...

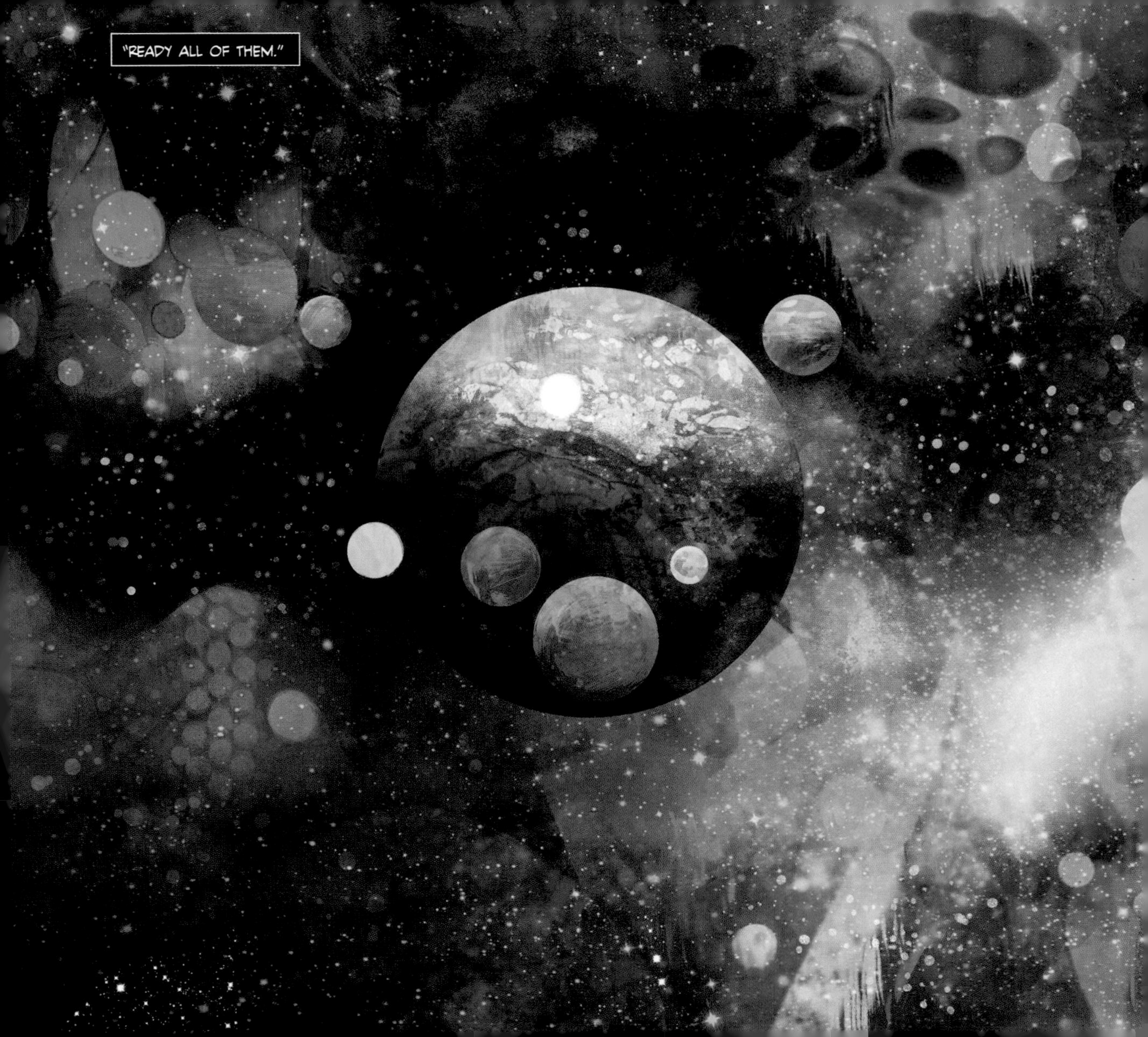
"READY ALL OF THEM."

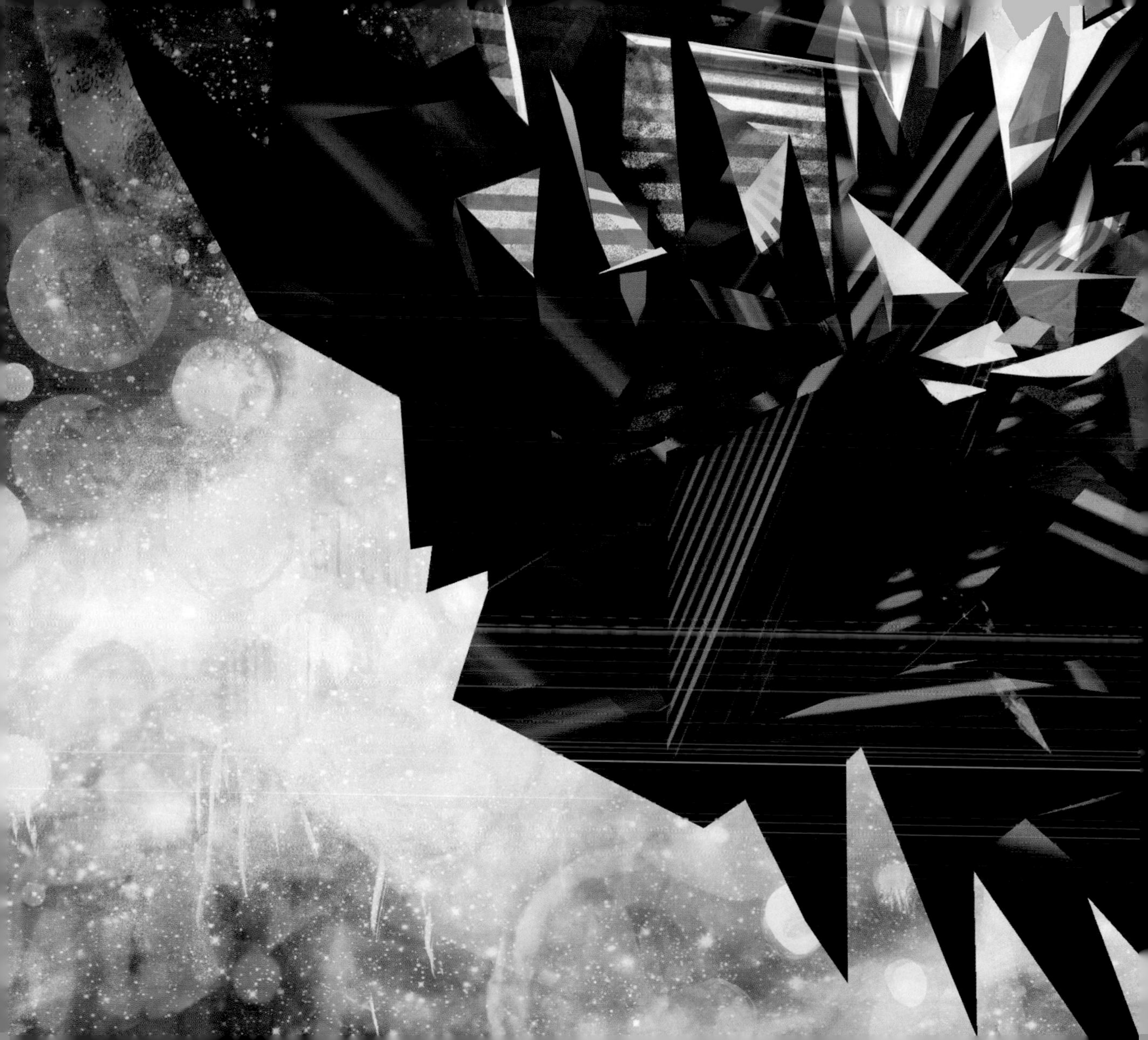

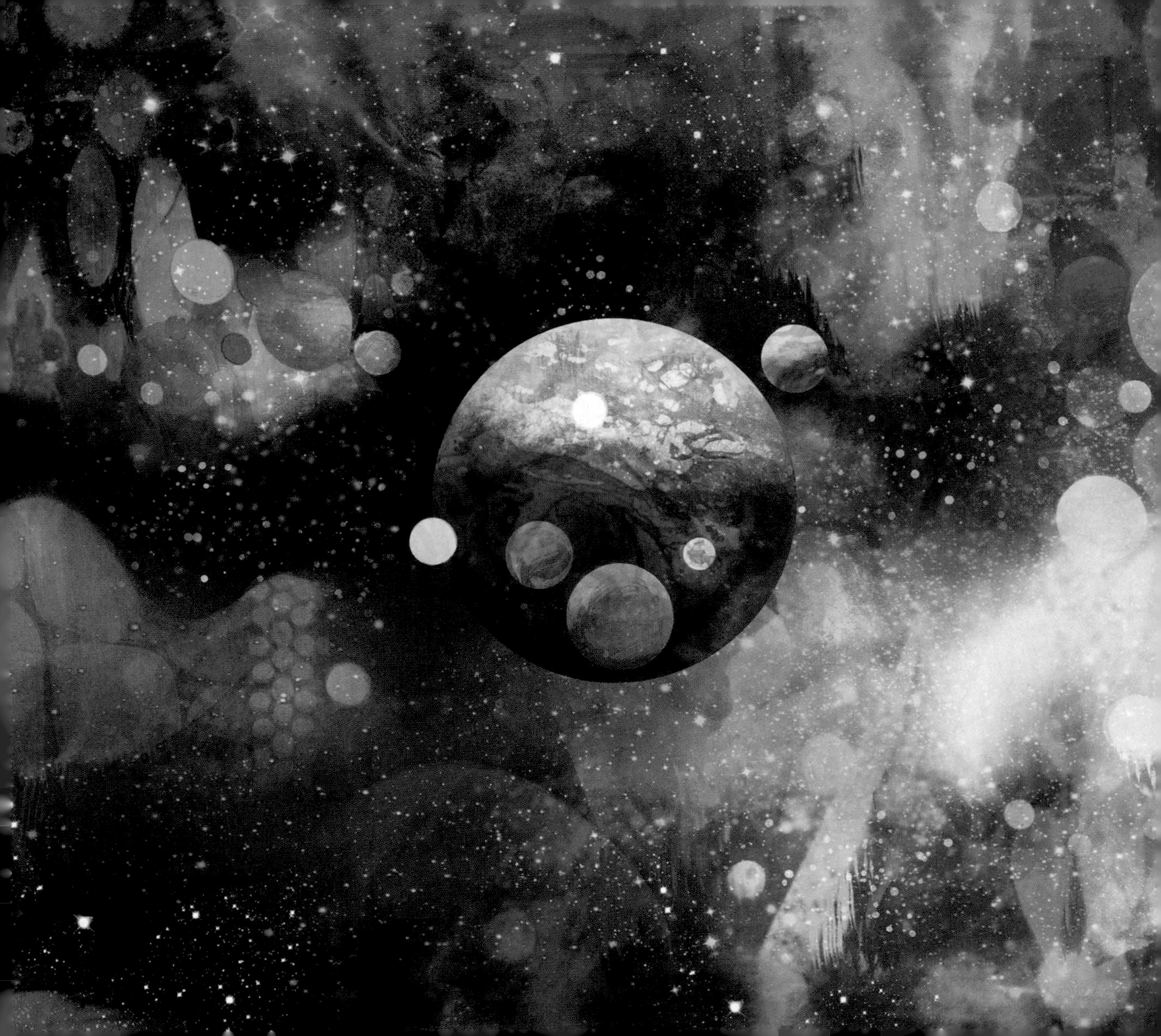

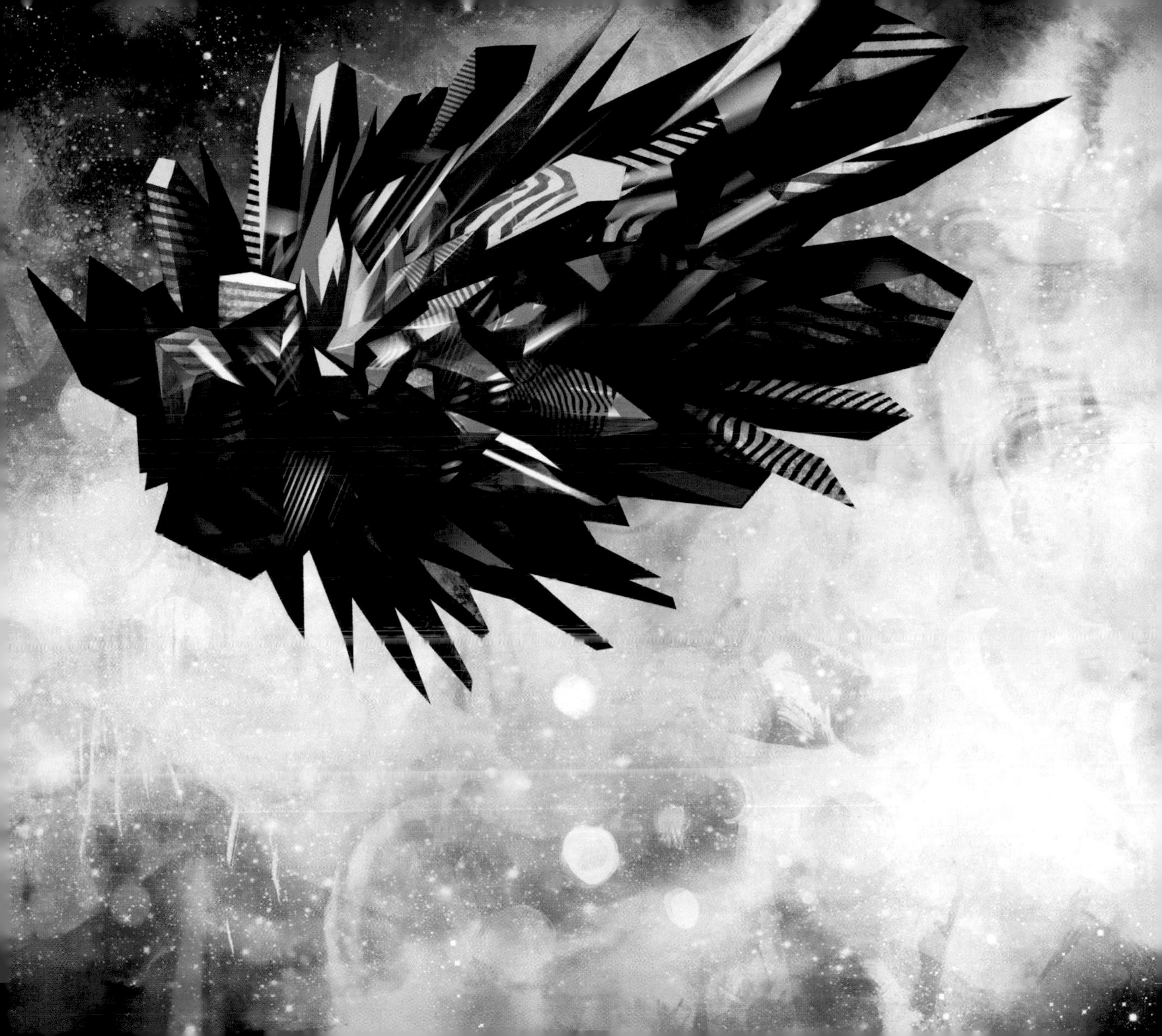

BIDUR FAUL

[A DENSE UTOPIAN ROCK WORLD]

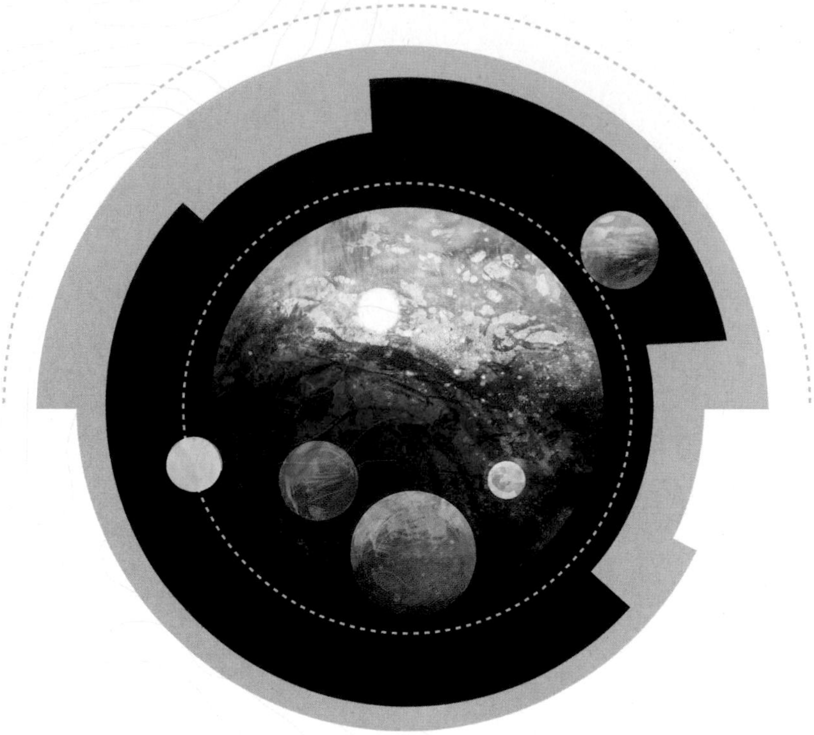

[+]

[+]

STATS

[PHYSICAL CHARACTERISTICS]

MEAN RADIUS .... 4,721 ± 0.9 km

SURFACE AREA ..... 241,673,002 km^2

VOLUME .... 4.612 × 2087 km^3

MASS .... 7.302 × 2243 kg

SATELLITES 5

CONTINENTS 1

[+]

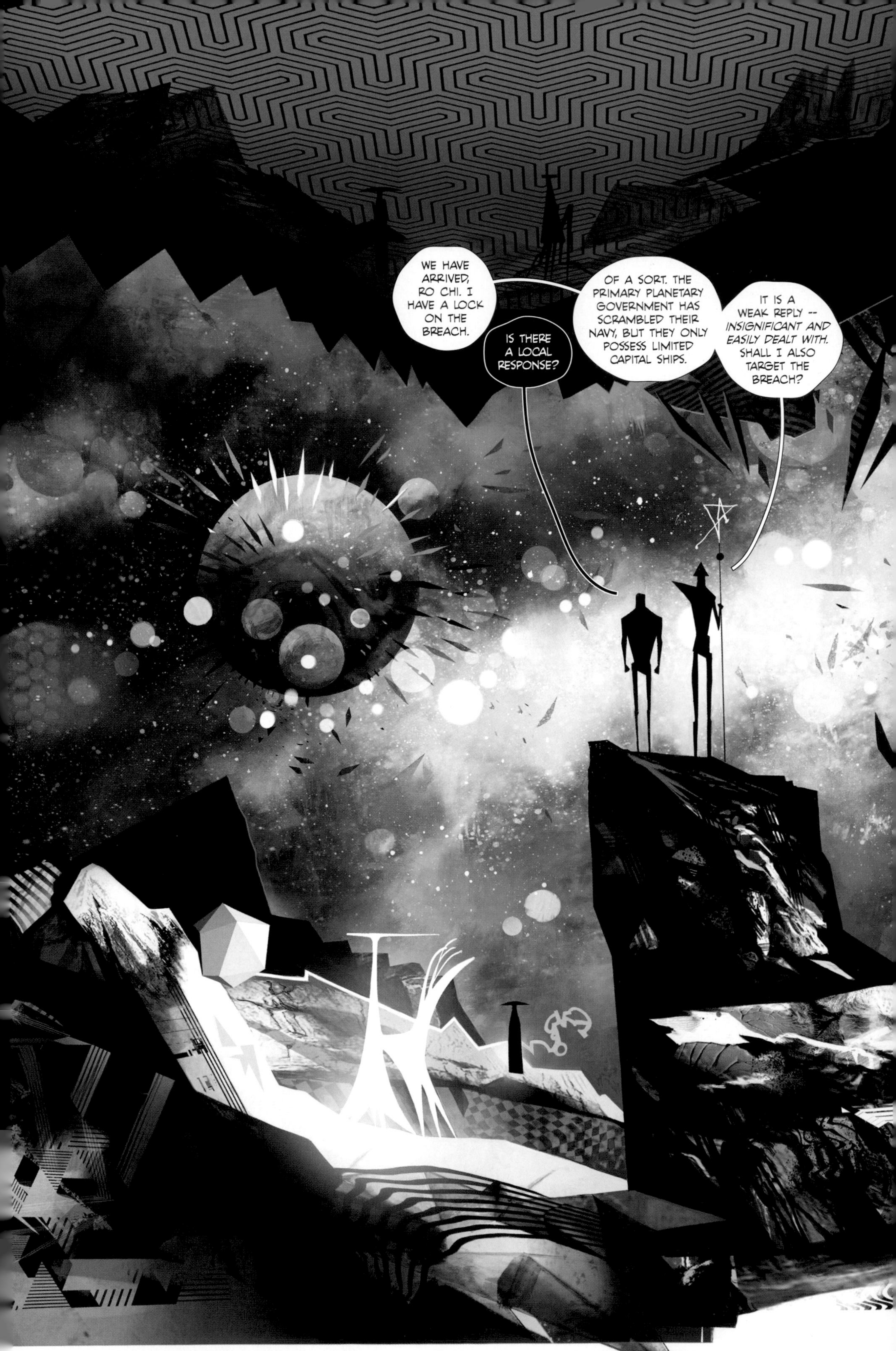

WE HAVE ARRIVED, RO CHI. I HAVE A LOCK ON THE BREACH.
IS THERE A LOCAL RESPONSE?
OF A SORT. THE PRIMARY PLANETARY GOVERNMENT HAS SCRAMBLED THEIR NAVY, BUT THEY ONLY POSSESS LIMITED CAPITAL SHIPS.
IT IS A WEAK REPLY -- *INSIGNIFICANT AND EASILY DEALT WITH.* SHALL I ALSO TARGET THE BREACH?

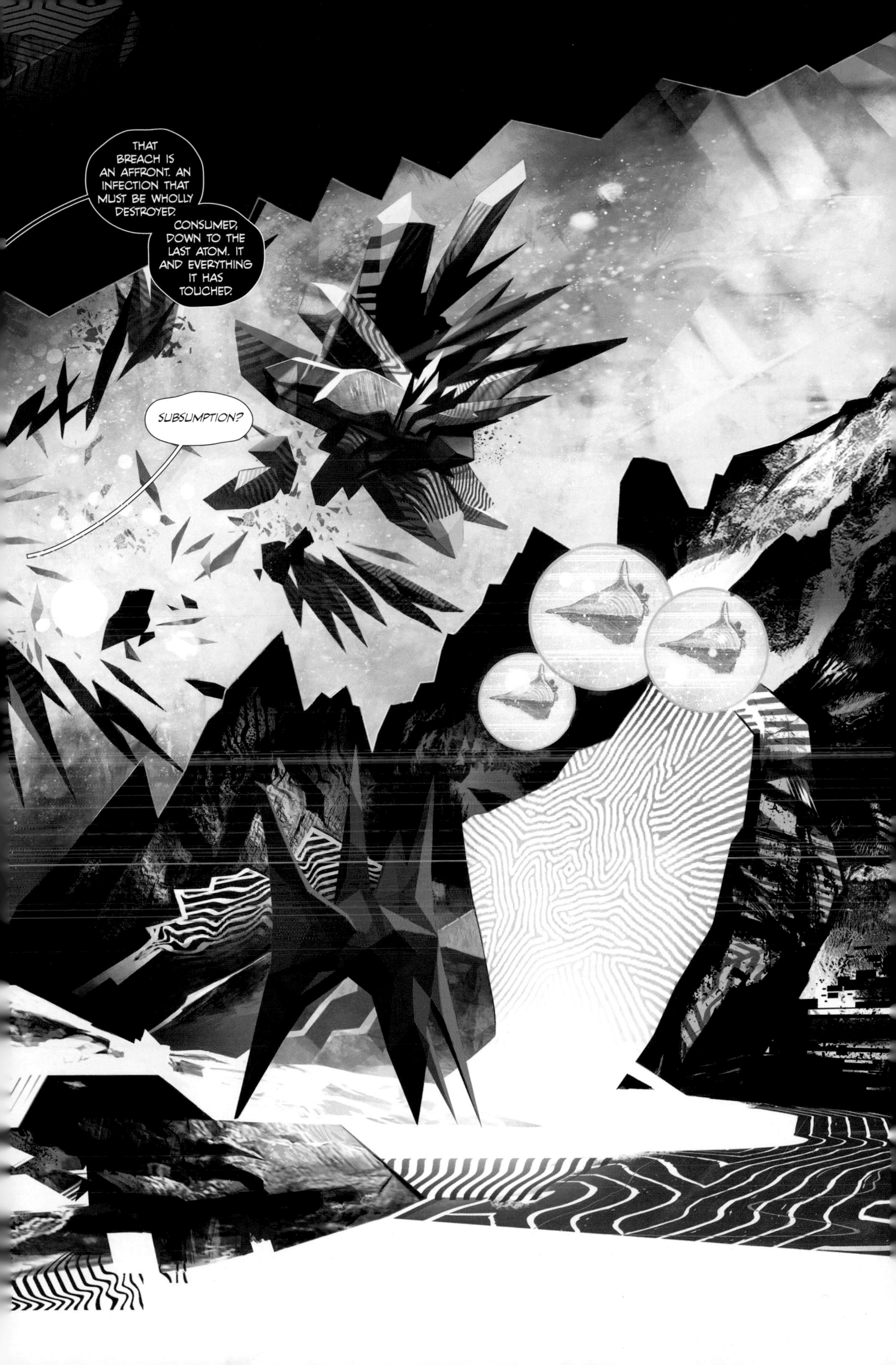
THAT BREACH IS AN AFFRONT. AN INFECTION THAT MUST BE WHOLLY DESTROYED.
CONSUMED, DOWN TO THE LAST ATOM. IT AND EVERYTHING IT HAS TOUCHED.
SUBSUMPTION?

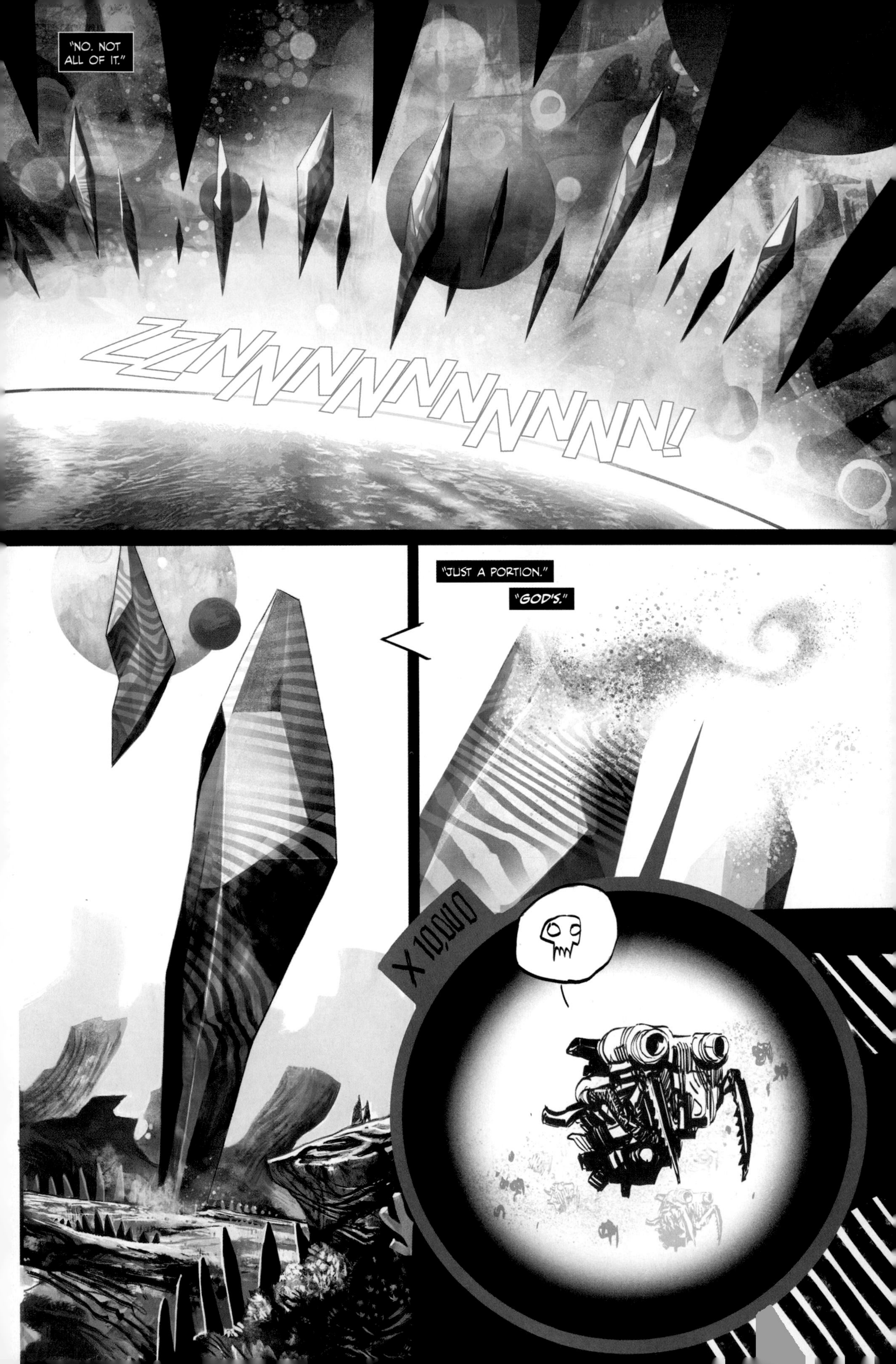
"NO. NOT ALL OF IT."
ZZNNNNNNNNNNN!
"JUST A PORTION."
"GOD'S."
X 10,000

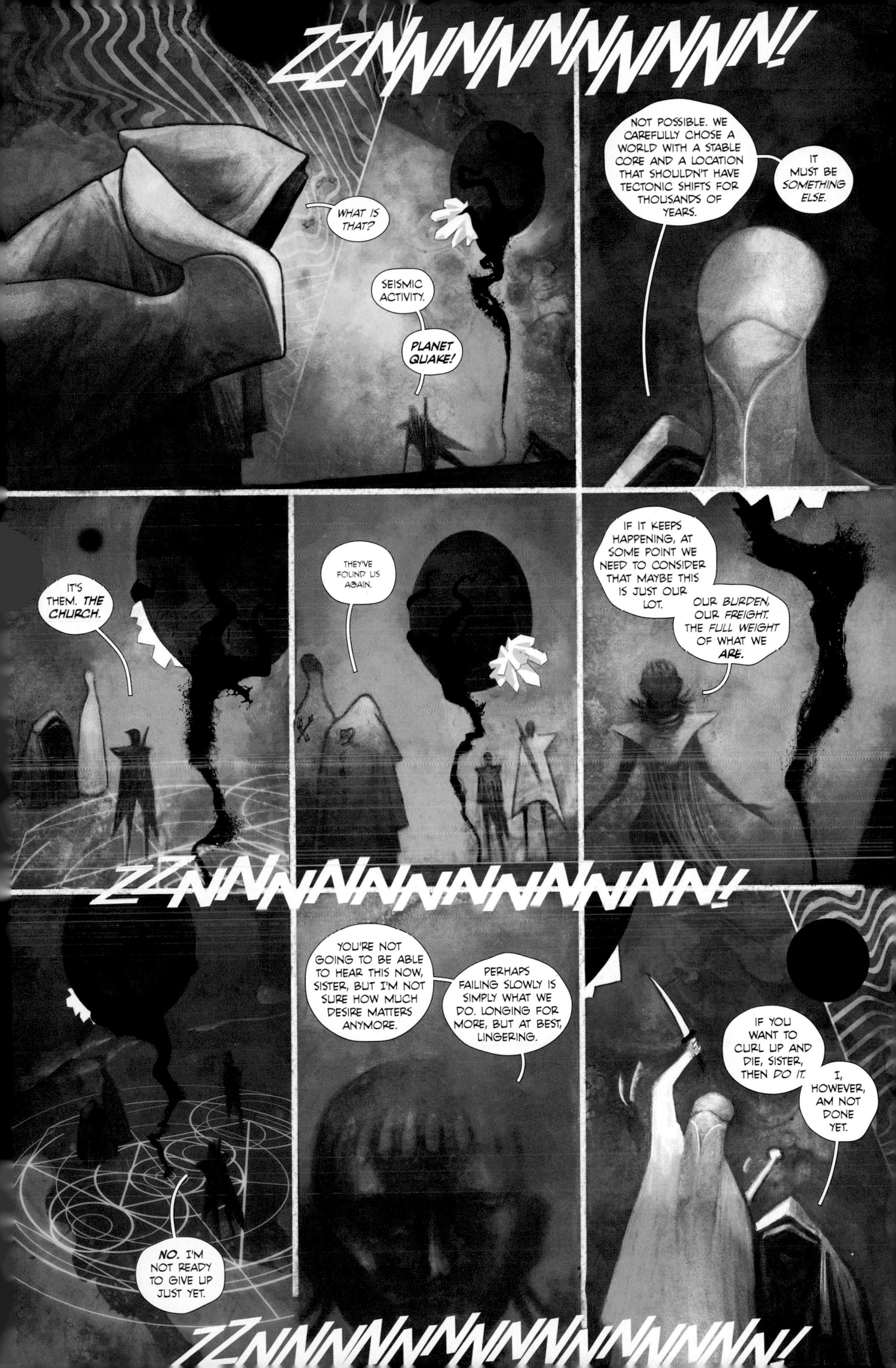
ZZNNNNNNNNNNNN!
WHAT IS THAT?
SEISMIC ACTIVITY.
PLANET QUAKE!
NOT POSSIBLE. WE CAREFULLY CHOSE A WORLD WITH A STABLE CORE AND A LOCATION THAT SHOULDN'T HAVE TECTONIC SHIFTS FOR THOUSANDS OF YEARS.
IT MUST BE SOMETHING ELSE.
IT'S THEM. THE CHURCH.
THEY'VE FOUND US AGAIN.
IF IT KEEPS HAPPENING, AT SOME POINT WE NEED TO CONSIDER THAT MAYBE THIS IS JUST OUR LOT.
OUR BURDEN, OUR FREIGHT. THE FULL WEIGHT OF WHAT WE ARE.
ZZNNNNNNNNNNNNNN!
NO. I'M NOT READY TO GIVE UP JUST YET.
YOU'RE NOT GOING TO BE ABLE TO HEAR THIS NOW, SISTER, BUT I'M NOT SURE HOW MUCH DESIRE MATTERS ANYMORE.
PERHAPS FAILING SLOWLY IS SIMPLY WHAT WE DO. LONGING FOR MORE, BUT AT BEST, LINGERING.
IF YOU WANT TO CURL UP AND DIE, SISTER, THEN DO IT.
I, HOWEVER, AM NOT DONE YET.
ZZNNNNNNNNNNNNNNNNN!

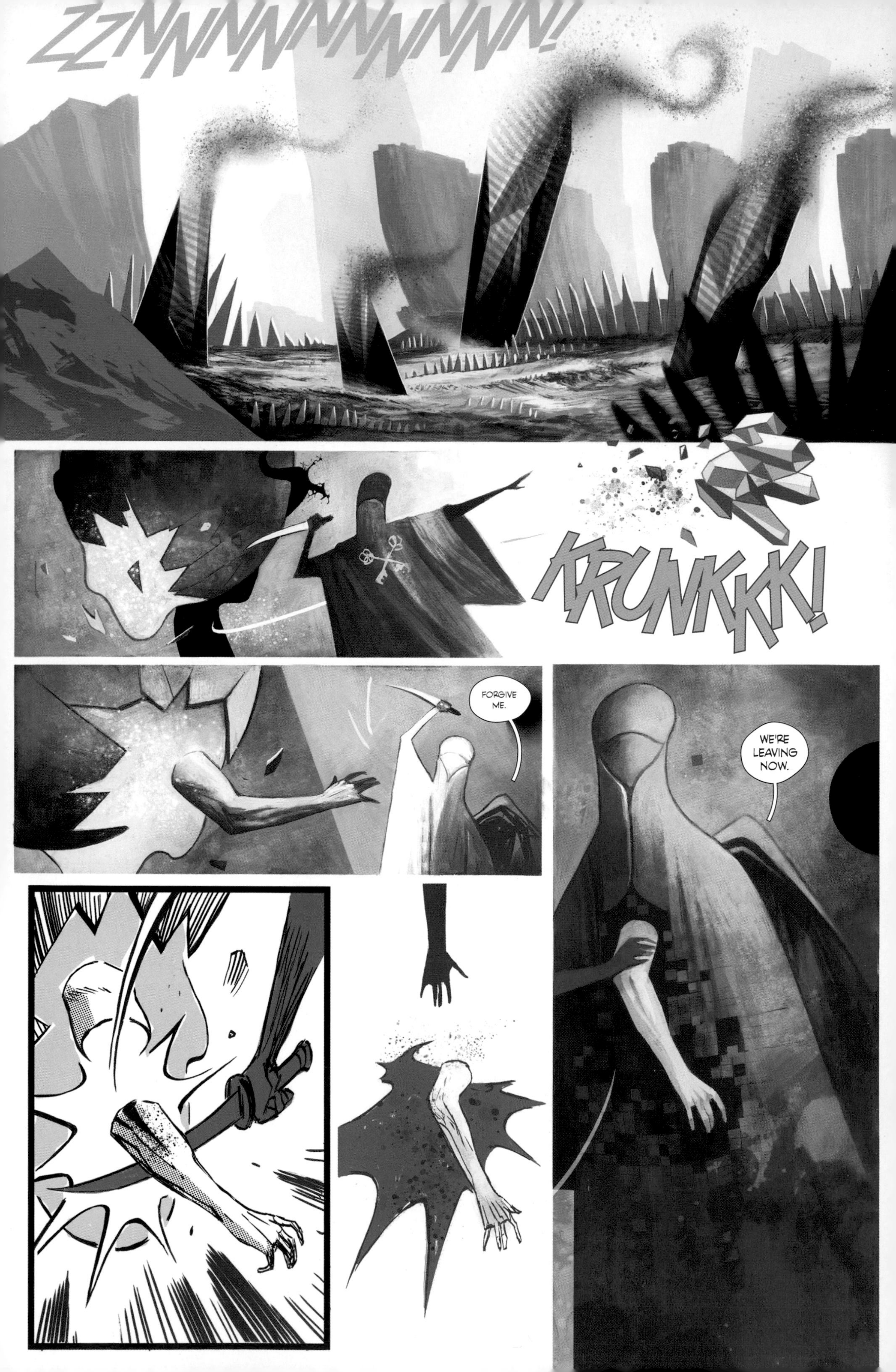
ZZNNNNNNNNNN!
KRUNKKK!
FORGIVE ME.
WE'RE LEAVING NOW.

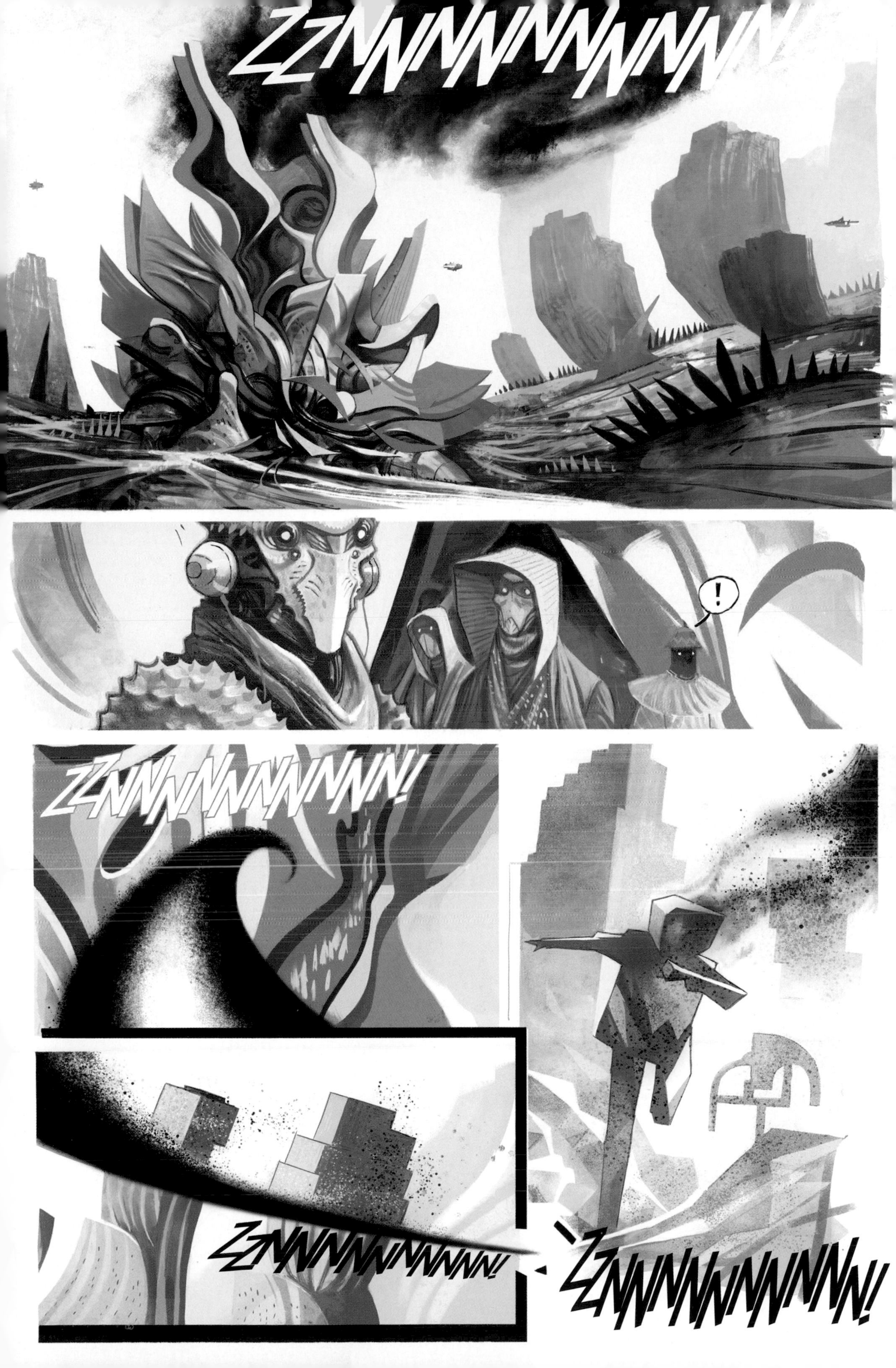
ZZNNNNNNNNNN
!
ZZNNNNNNNNNN!
ZZNNNNNNNNNN!
ZZNNNNNNNNNNN!

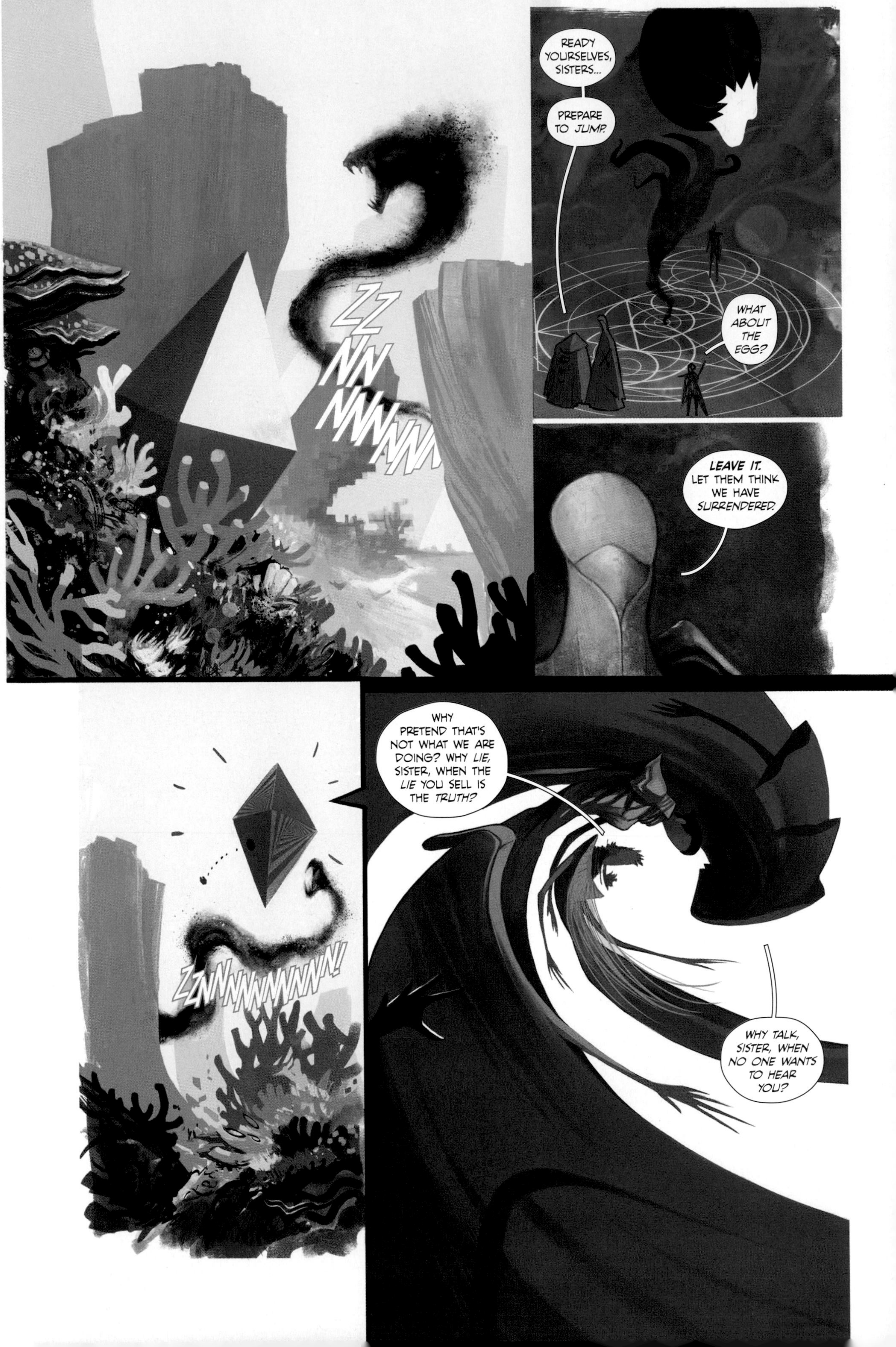
ZZNNNNNNNNN
READY YOURSELVES, SISTERS...
PREPARE TO JUMP.
WHAT ABOUT THE EGG?
LEAVE IT. LET THEM THINK WE HAVE SURRENDERED.
ZZNNNNNNNNNNN!
WHY PRETEND THAT'S NOT WHAT WE ARE DOING? WHY LIE, SISTER, WHEN THE LIE YOU SELL IS THE TRUTH?
WHY TALK, SISTER, WHEN NO ONE WANTS TO HEAR YOU?

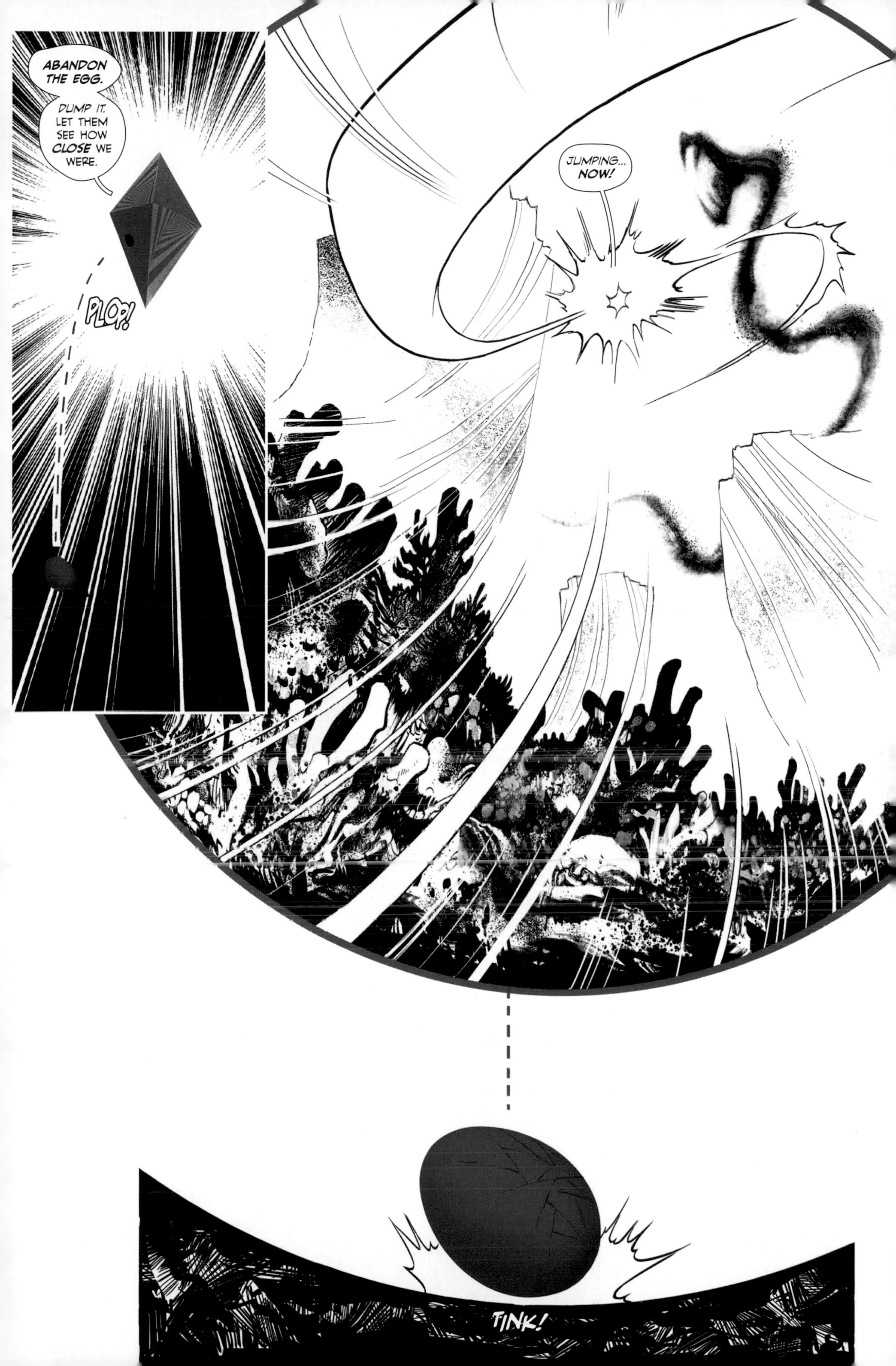
ABANDON THE EGG.
DUMP IT. LET THEM SEE HOW CLOSE WE WERE.
PLOP!
JUMPING... NOW!
TINK!

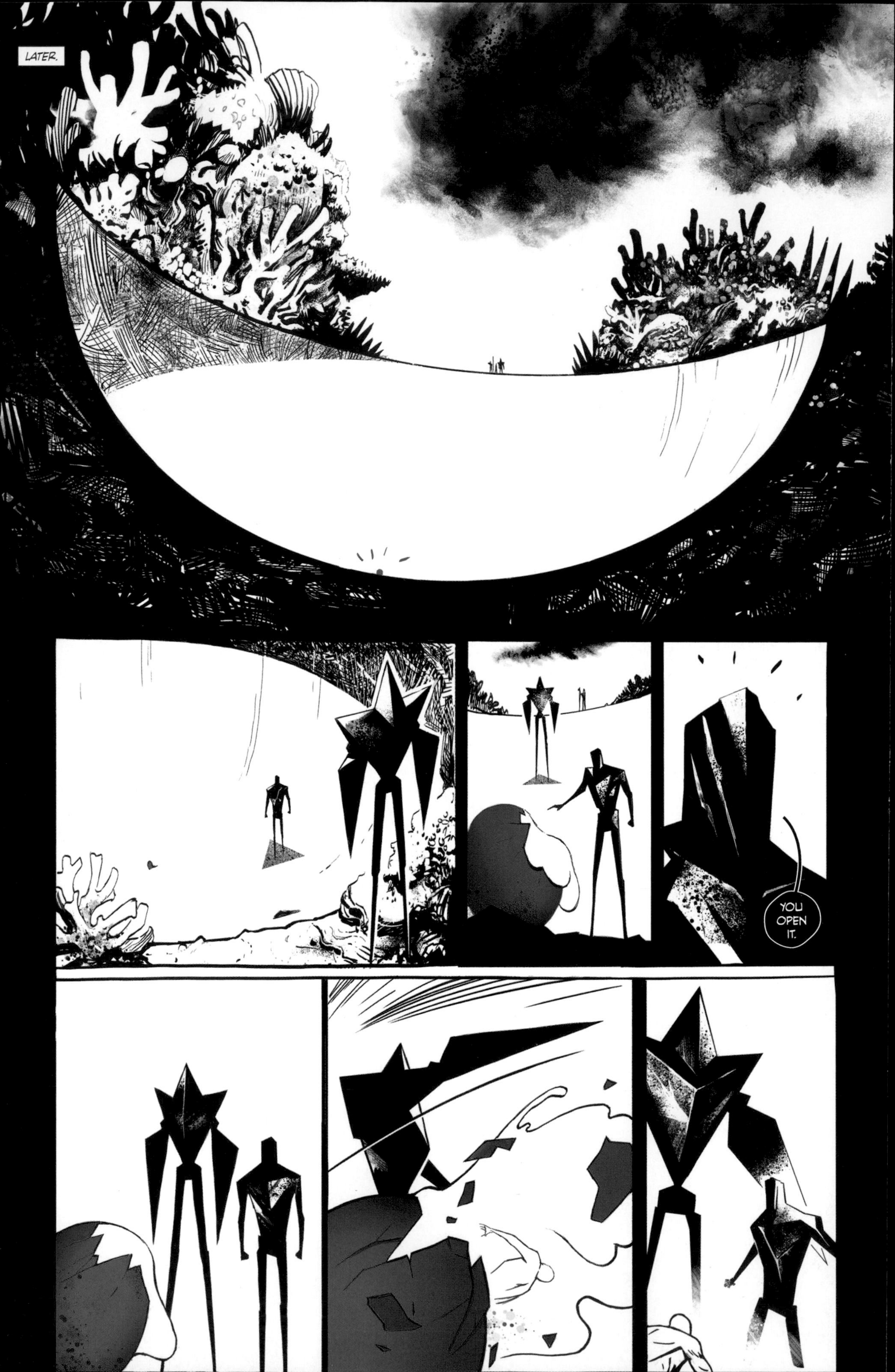
LATER.
YOU OPEN IT.

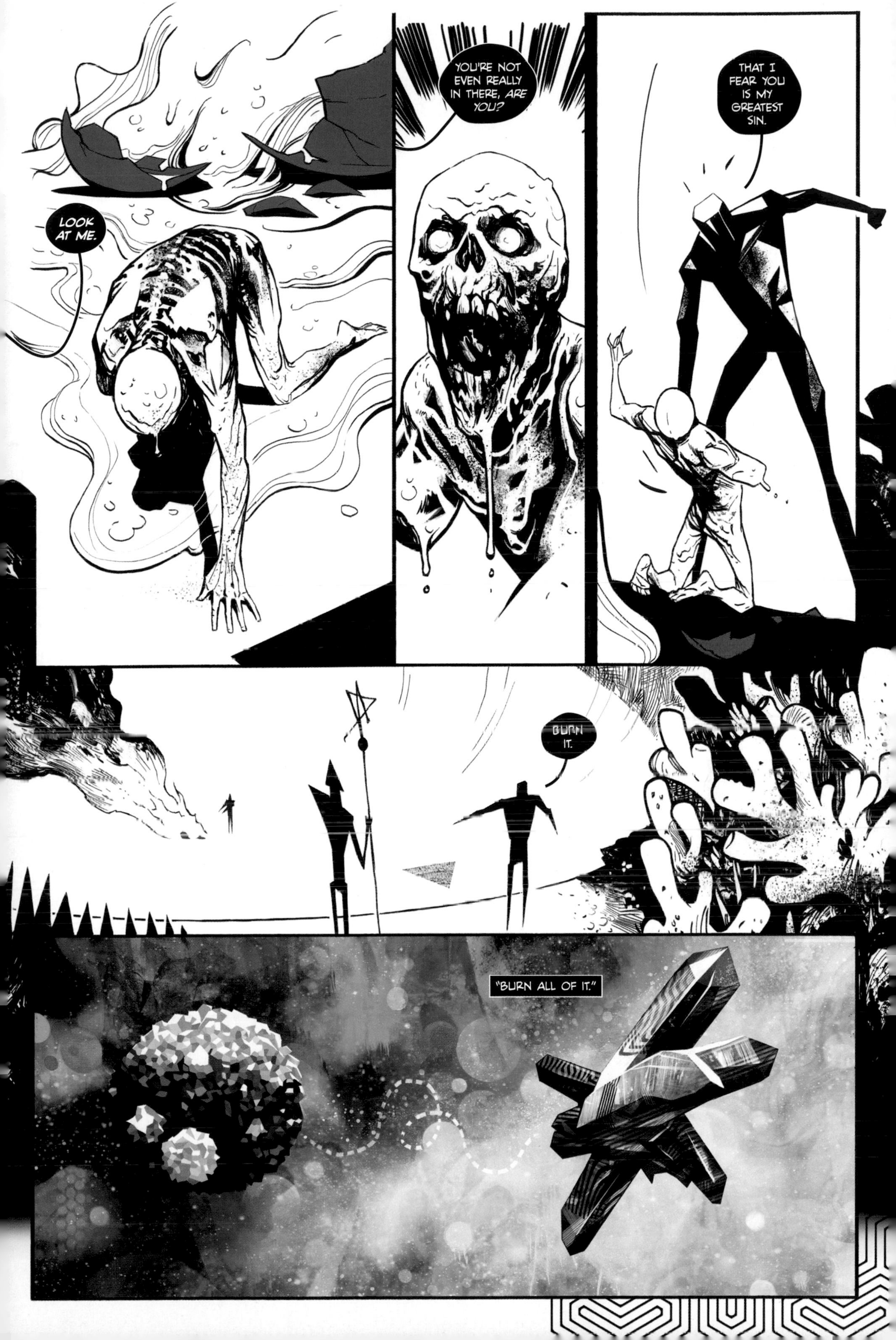
LOOK AT ME.
YOU'RE NOT EVEN REALLY IN THERE, ARE YOU?
THAT I FEAR YOU IS MY GREATEST SIN.
BURN IT.
"BURN ALL OF IT."

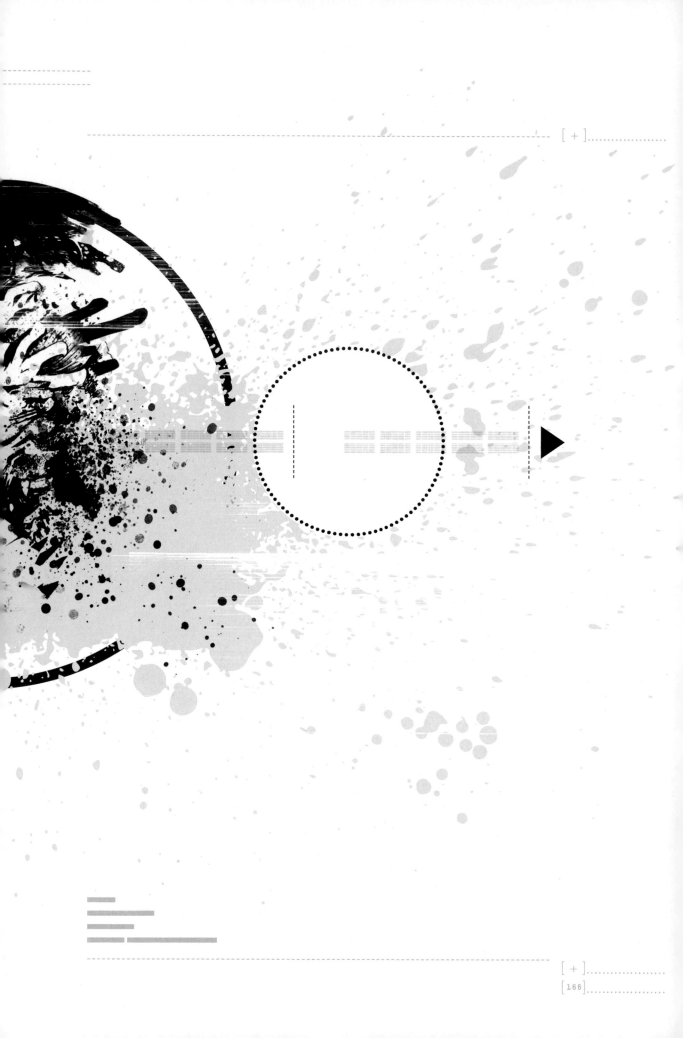

BIDUR FAUL

[A WASTEWORLD. DESOLATE AND UNLIVABLE.]

[+]....................

[+]....................

STATS

[PHYSICAL CHARACTERISTICS]

MEAN RADIUS........ **4,721 ± 0.9** km

SURFACE AREA...... **241,673,002** km²

VOLUME.............. **4.612 × 2087** km³

MASS.................. **7.302 × 2243** kg

SATELLITES.......... **5**

CONTINENTS......... **1**

"FAILURE.

"ALWAYS FAILURE."

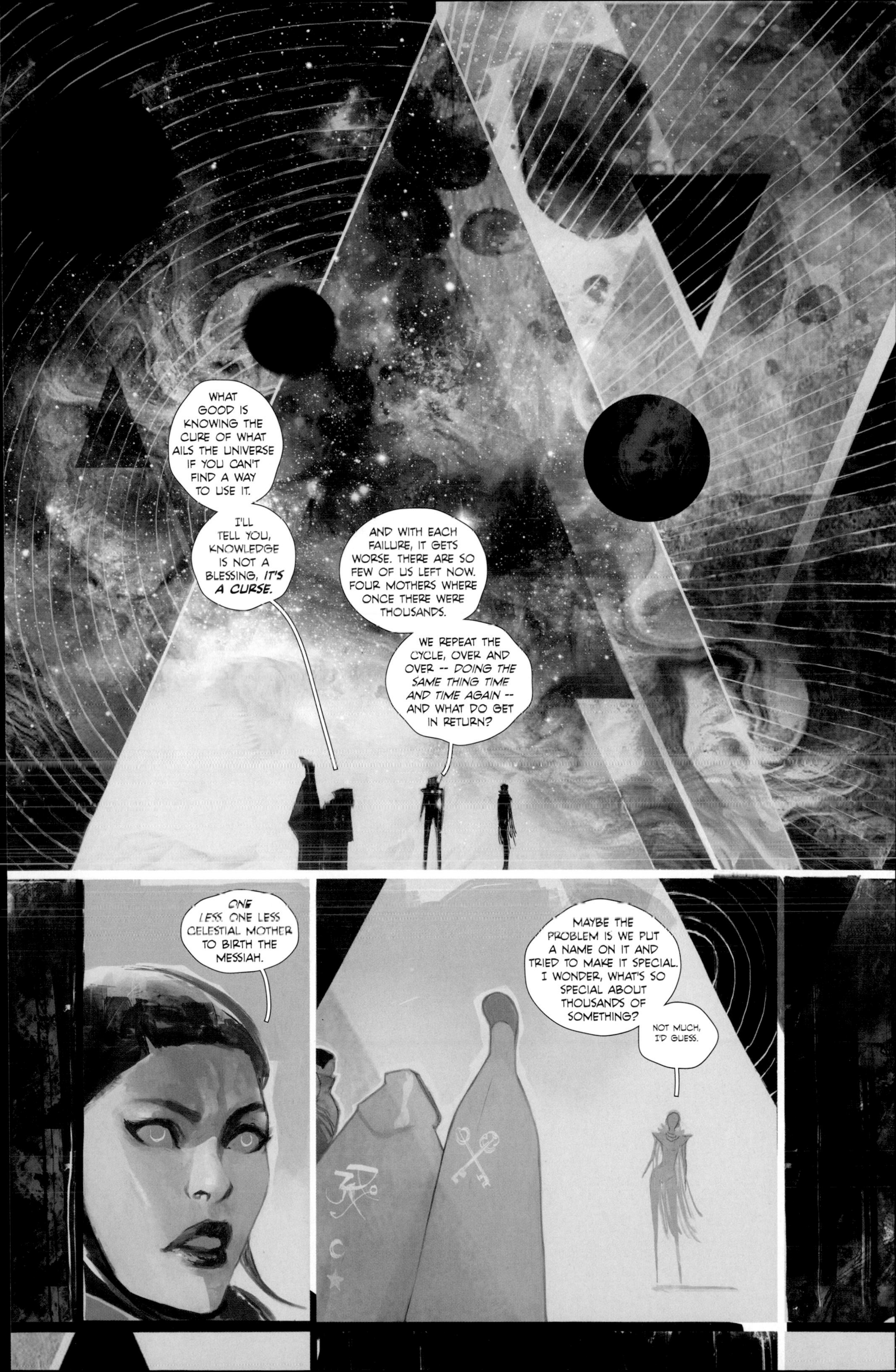
WHAT GOOD IS KNOWING THE CURE OF WHAT AILS THE UNIVERSE IF YOU CAN'T FIND A WAY TO USE IT.
I'LL TELL YOU, KNOWLEDGE IS NOT A BLESSING, ***IT'S A CURSE.***
AND WITH EACH FAILURE, IT GETS WORSE. THERE ARE SO FEW OF US LEFT NOW. FOUR MOTHERS WHERE ONCE THERE WERE THOUSANDS.
WE REPEAT THE CYCLE, OVER AND OVER -- *DOING THE SAME THING TIME AND TIME AGAIN* -- AND WHAT DO GET IN RETURN?
ONE LESS. ONE LESS CELESTIAL MOTHER TO BIRTH THE MESSIAH.
MAYBE THE PROBLEM IS WE PUT A NAME ON IT AND TRIED TO MAKE IT SPECIAL. I WONDER, WHAT'S SO SPECIAL ABOUT THOUSANDS OF SOMETHING?
NOT MUCH, I'D GUESS.

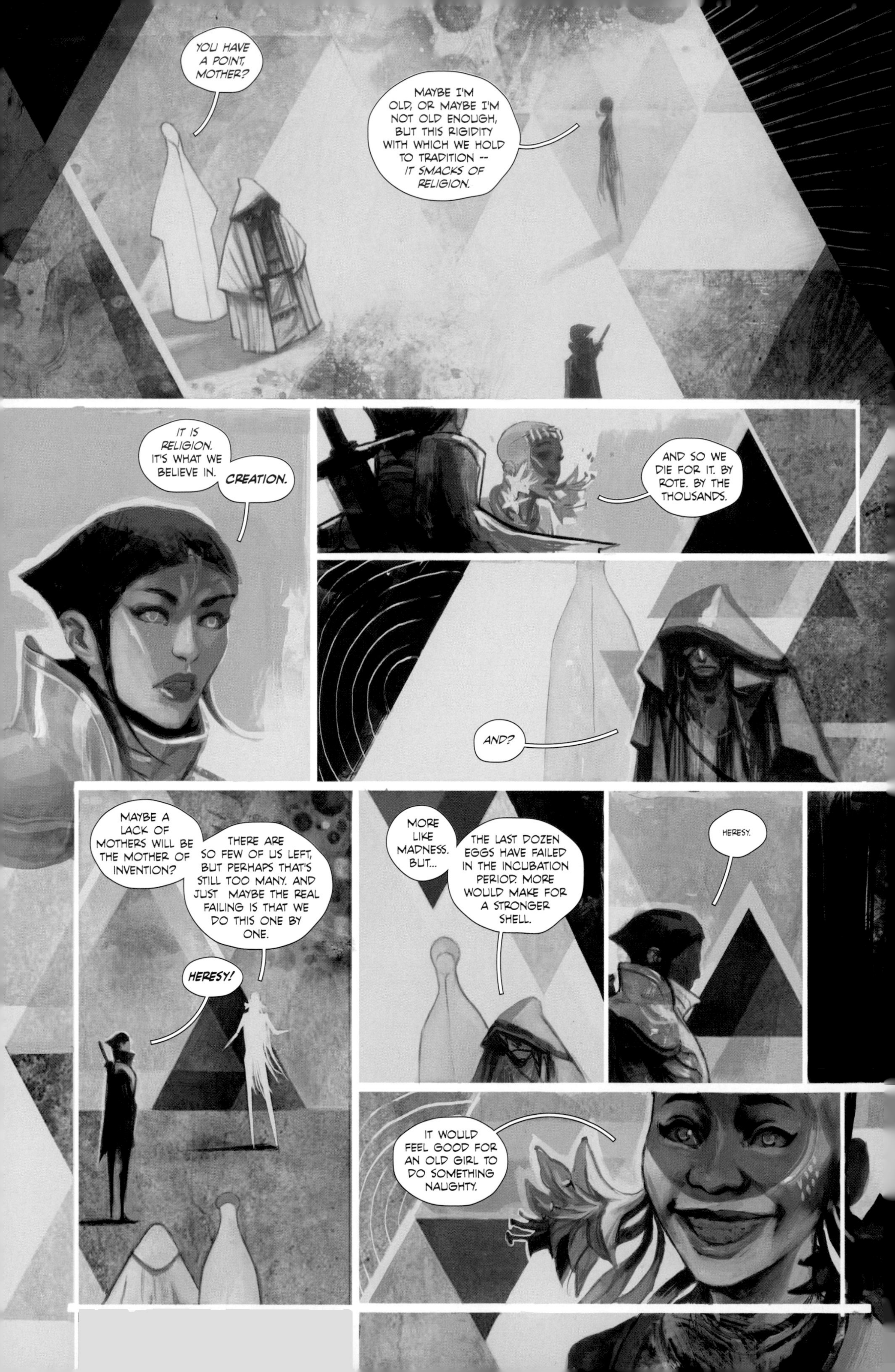
YOU HAVE A POINT, MOTHER?
MAYBE I'M OLD, OR MAYBE I'M NOT OLD ENOUGH, BUT THIS RIGIDITY WITH WHICH WE HOLD TO TRADITION -- IT SMACKS OF RELIGION.
IT IS RELIGION. IT'S WHAT WE BELIEVE IN.
CREATION.
AND SO WE DIE FOR IT. BY ROTE. BY THE THOUSANDS.
AND?
MAYBE A LACK OF MOTHERS WILL BE THE MOTHER OF INVENTION?
THERE ARE SO FEW OF US LEFT, BUT PERHAPS THAT'S STILL TOO MANY. AND JUST MAYBE THE REAL FAILING IS THAT WE DO THIS ONE BY ONE.
HERESY!
MORE LIKE MADNESS. BUT...
THE LAST DOZEN EGGS HAVE FAILED IN THE INCUBATION PERIOD. MORE WOULD MAKE FOR A STRONGER SHELL.
HERESY.
IT WOULD FEEL GOOD FOR AN OLD GIRL TO DO SOMETHING NAUGHTY.

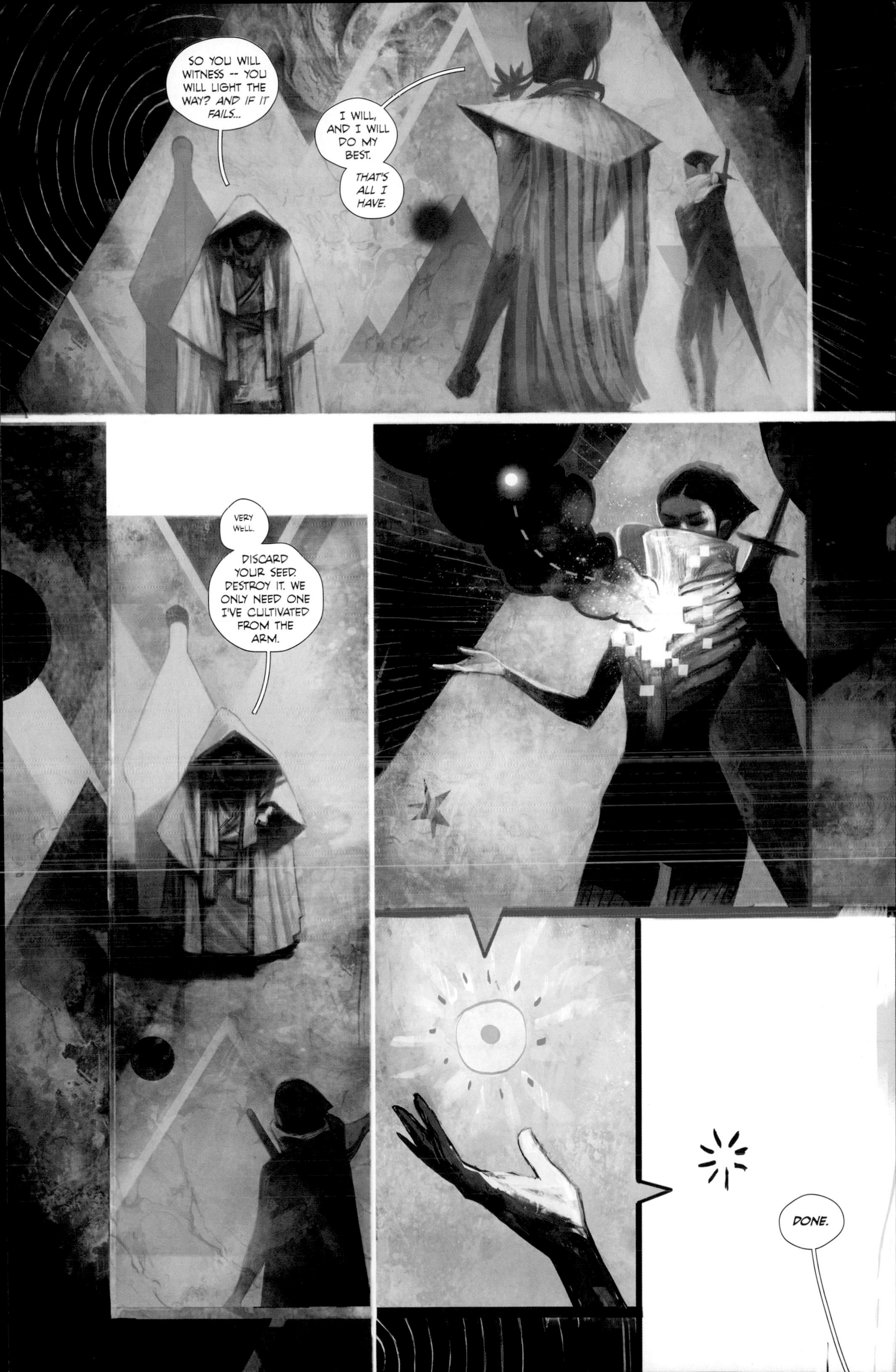
SO YOU WILL WITNESS -- YOU WILL LIGHT THE WAY? AND IF IT FAILS...
I WILL, AND I WILL DO MY BEST.
THAT'S ALL I HAVE.
VERY WELL.
DISCARD YOUR SEED. DESTROY IT. WE ONLY NEED ONE I'VE CULTIVATED FROM THE ARM.
DONE.

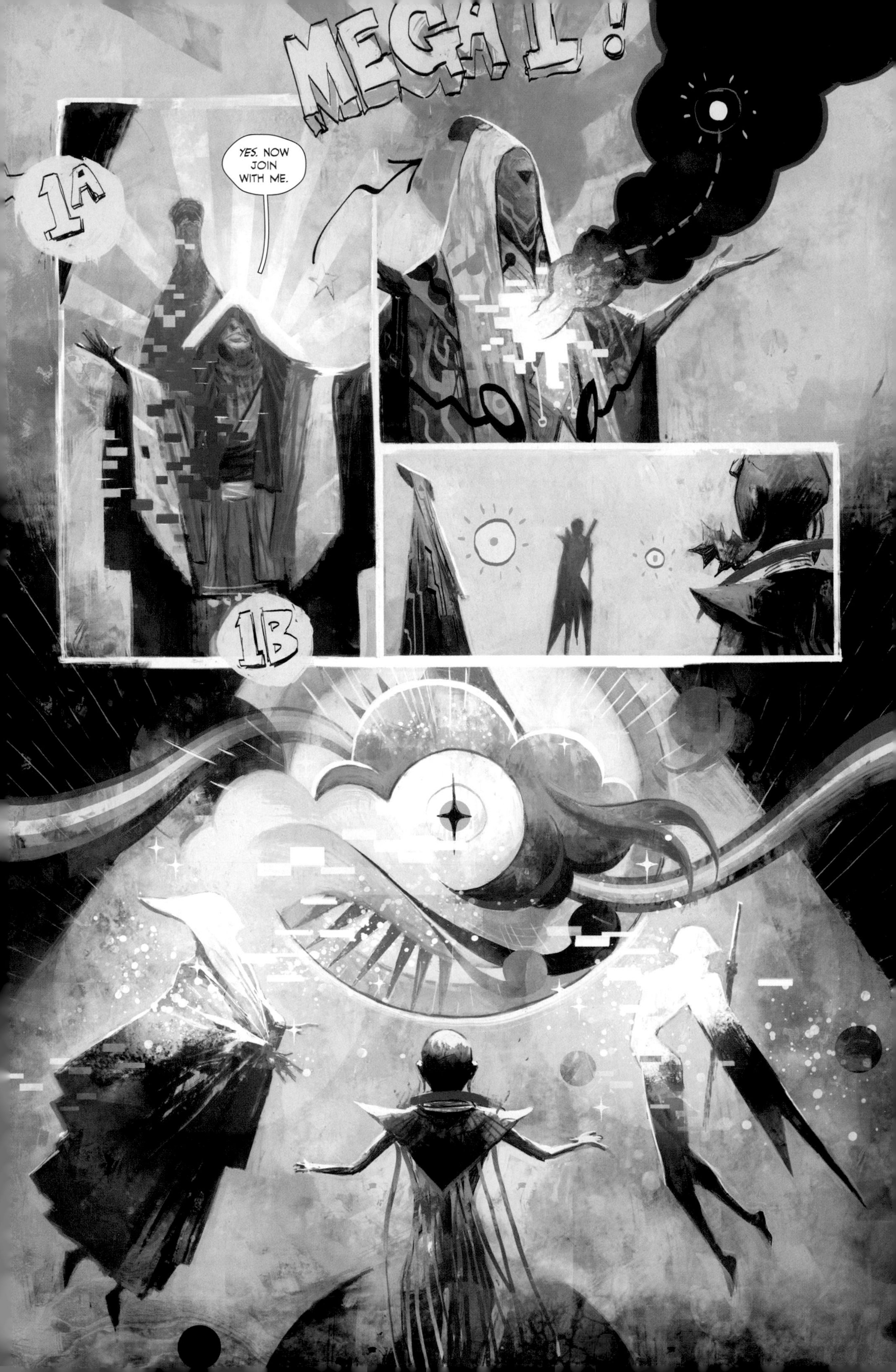
MEGA 1!
1A
YES. NOW JOIN WITH ME.
1B

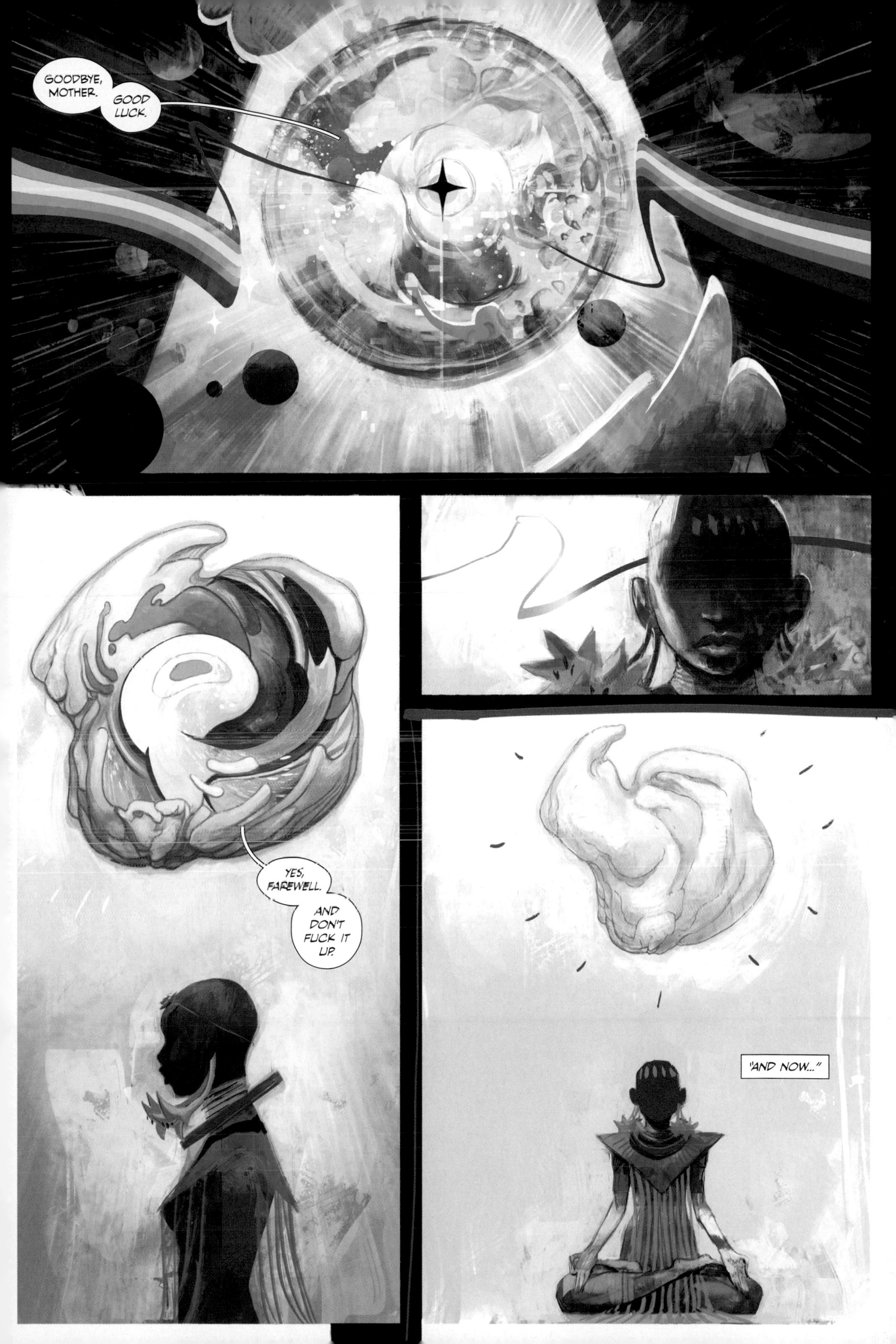
GOODBYE, MOTHER.
GOOD LUCK.
YES, FAREWELL.
AND DON'T FUCK IT UP.
"AND NOW..."

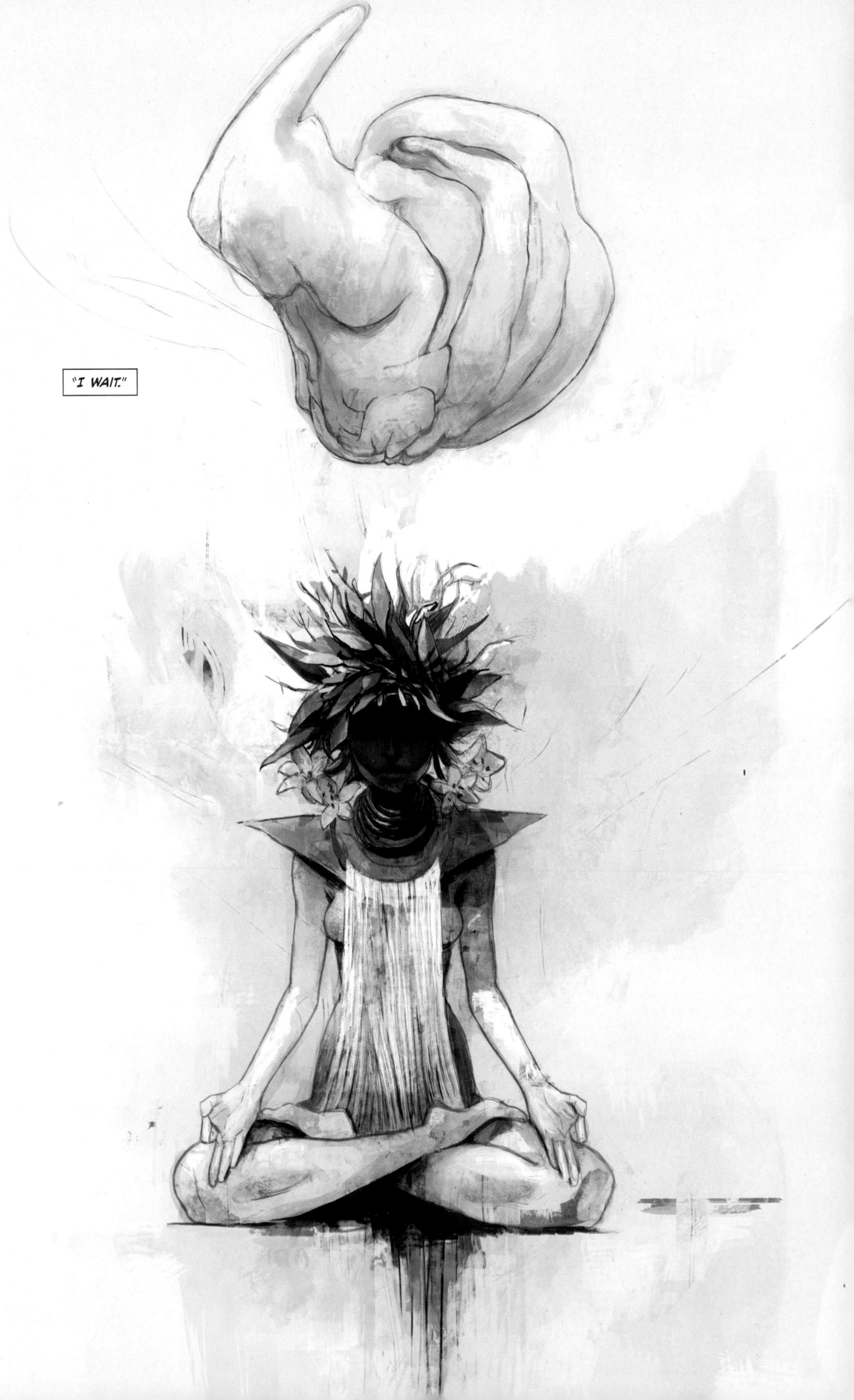
"I WAIT."

V

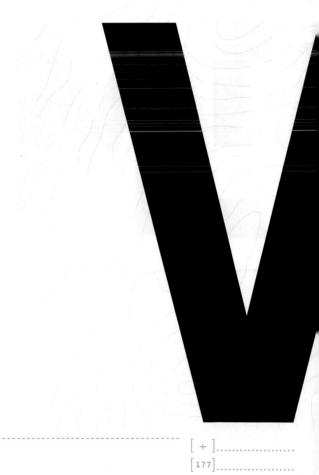

AND THE MISEDUCATION OF **NEHA NORI SOOD**

CHAPTER TWELVE

[THIS IS NOT A JOB FOR THOSE WITH A WEAK STOMACH]

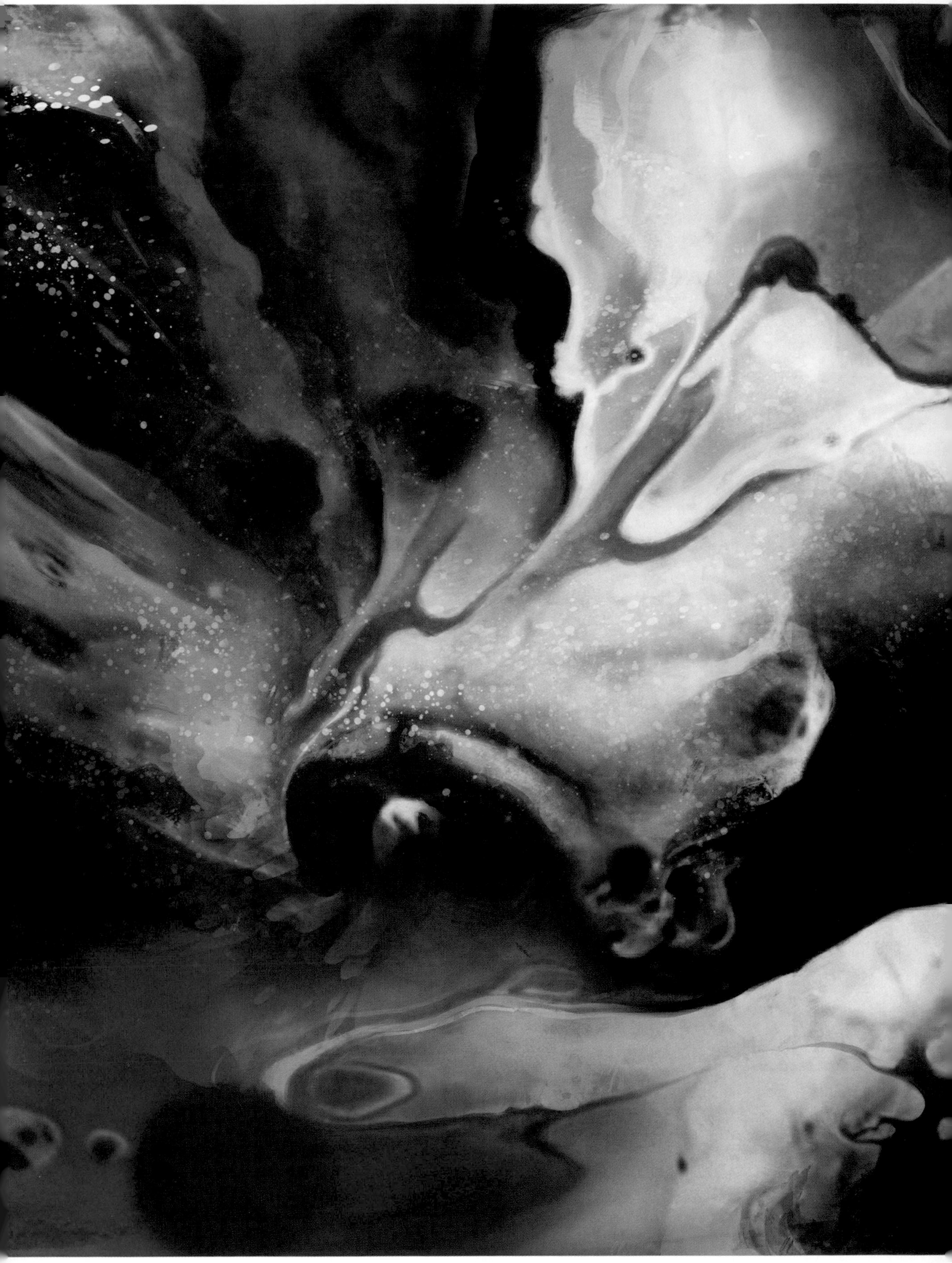

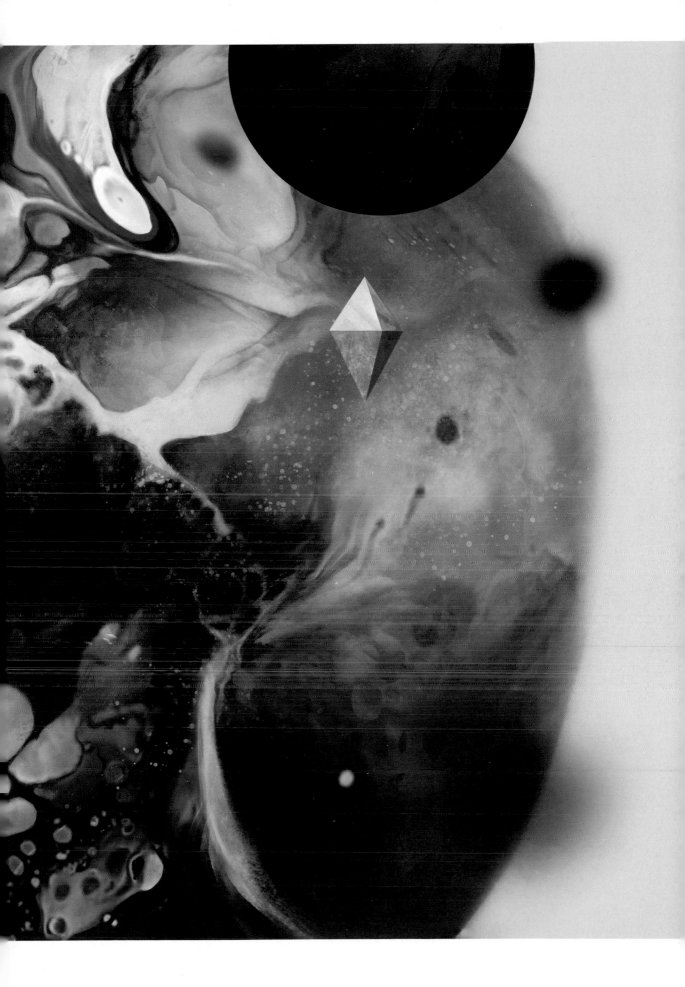

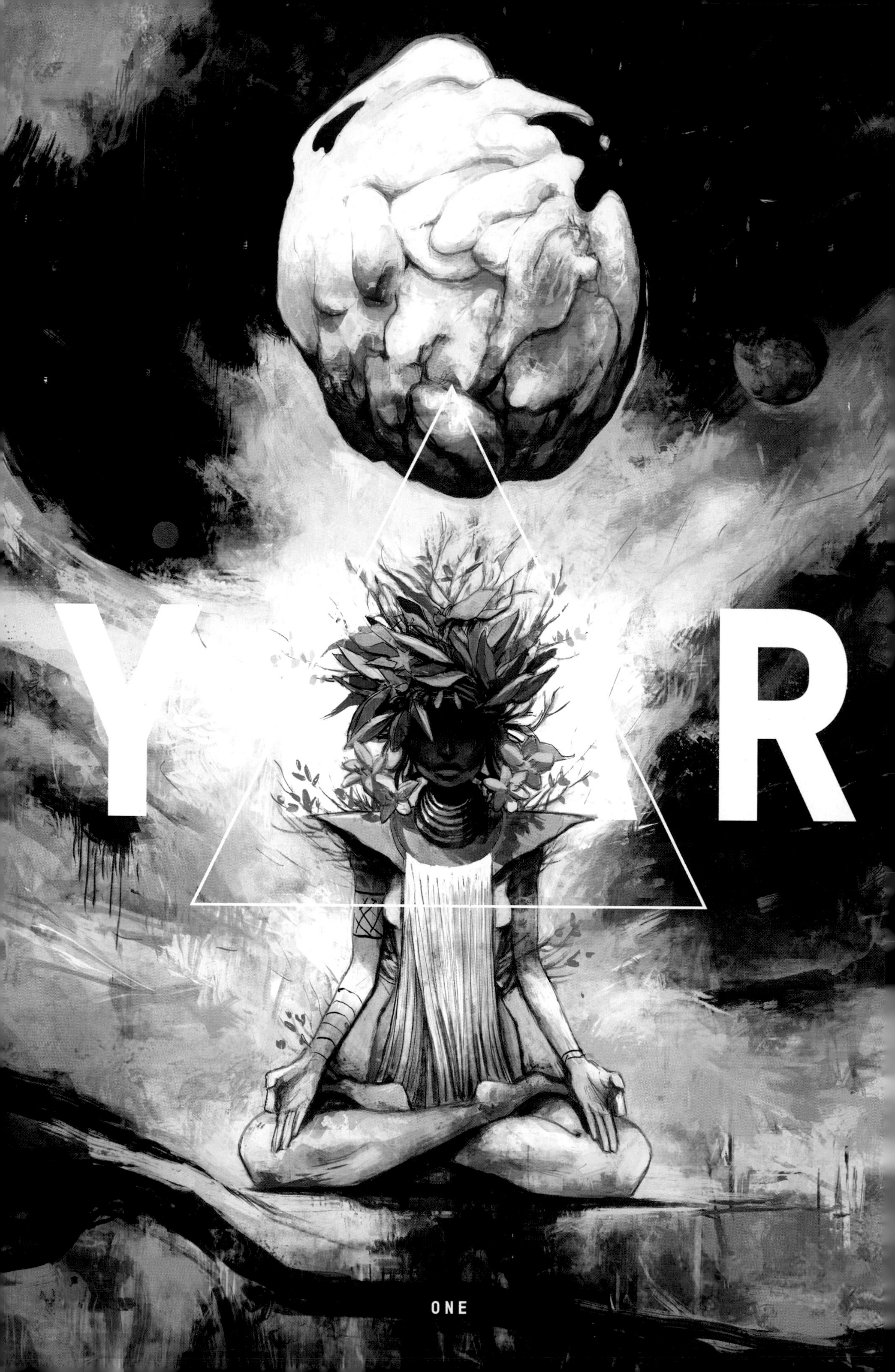
YAR
ONE

ONE

[TRAINING]

YEAR

[+]

ONE

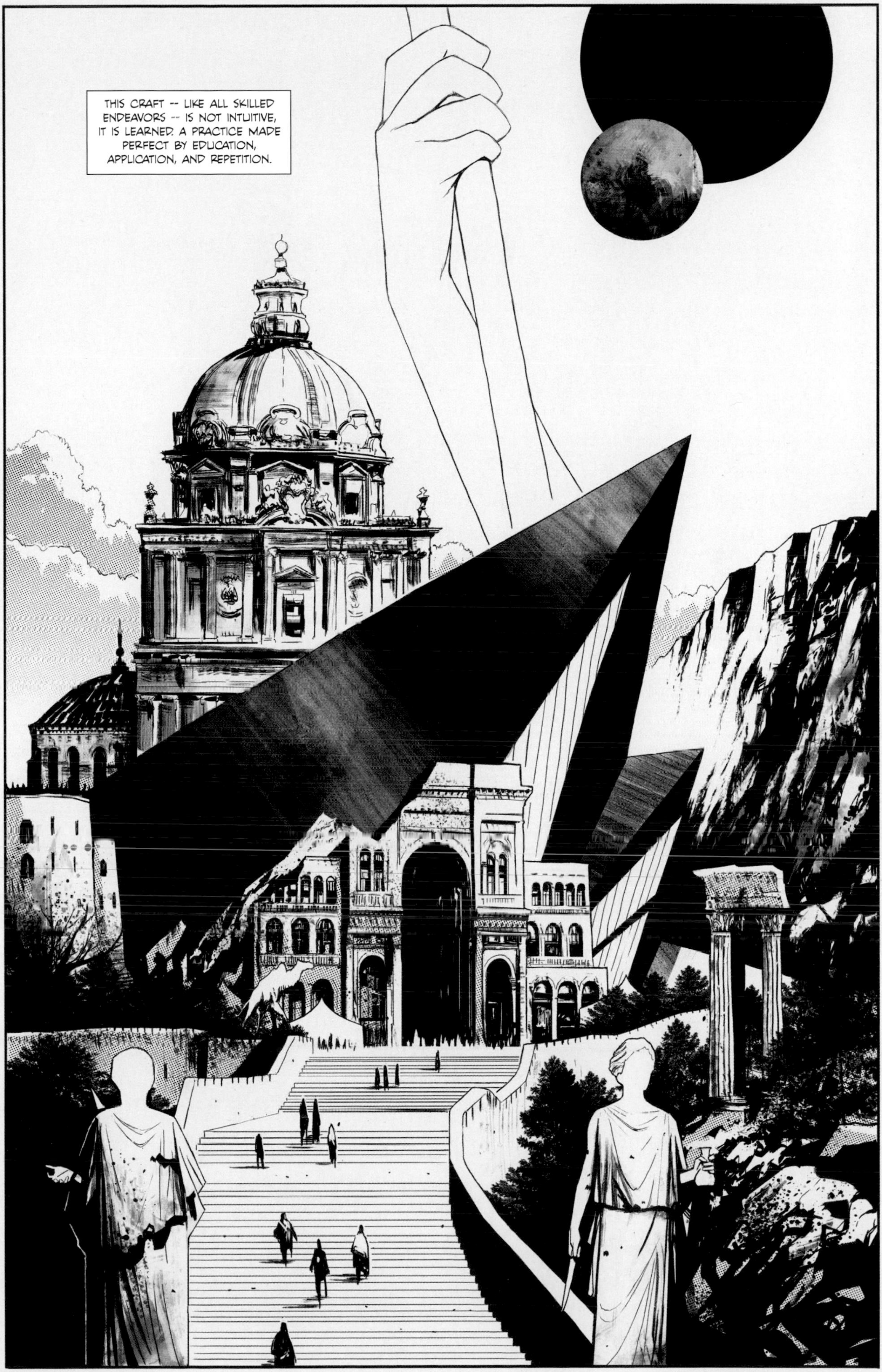
THIS CRAFT -- LIKE ALL SKILLED ENDEAVORS -- IS NOT INTUITIVE, IT IS LEARNED. A PRACTICE MADE PERFECT BY EDUCATION, APPLICATION, AND REPETITION.

EDUCATION

[BIOLOGY]

Introduction to biological frailty.   ●

Weaknesses and vulnerabilities.   ●

[WEAPONS]

Basic assembly and ballistics.   ●

A history of weaponry.   ●

[RESEARCH]

The Mind As A Weapon.   ●

BY

Horatio Hidalgo Moss

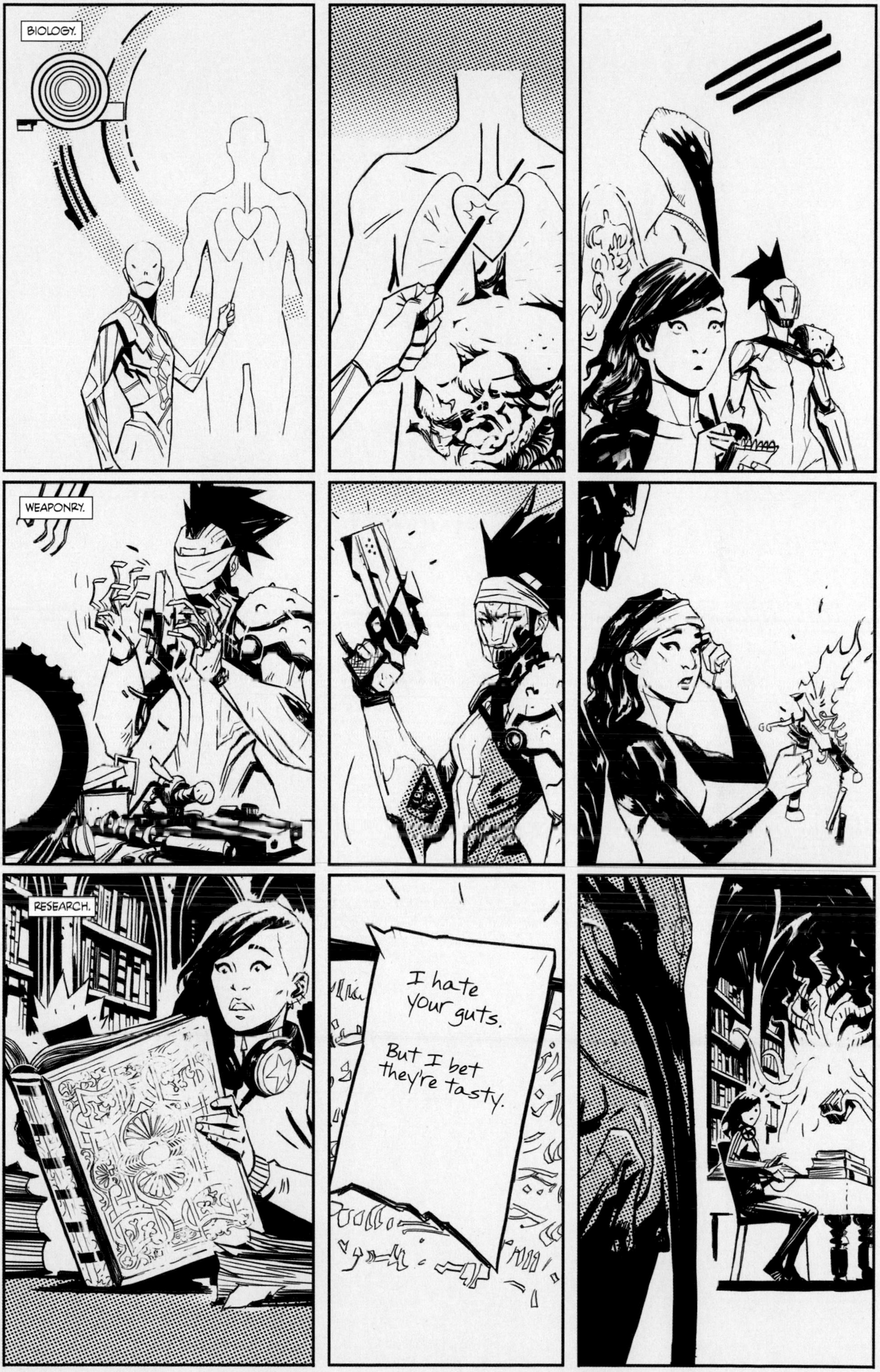
BIOLOGY.
WEAPONRY.
RESEARCH.
I hate your guts.
But I bet they're tasty.

[YEAR ONE]

APPLICATION

HAND-TO-HAND COMBAT

JETTI KAAN

[x]

SAM-SAM

[x]

URSULA RING

[x]

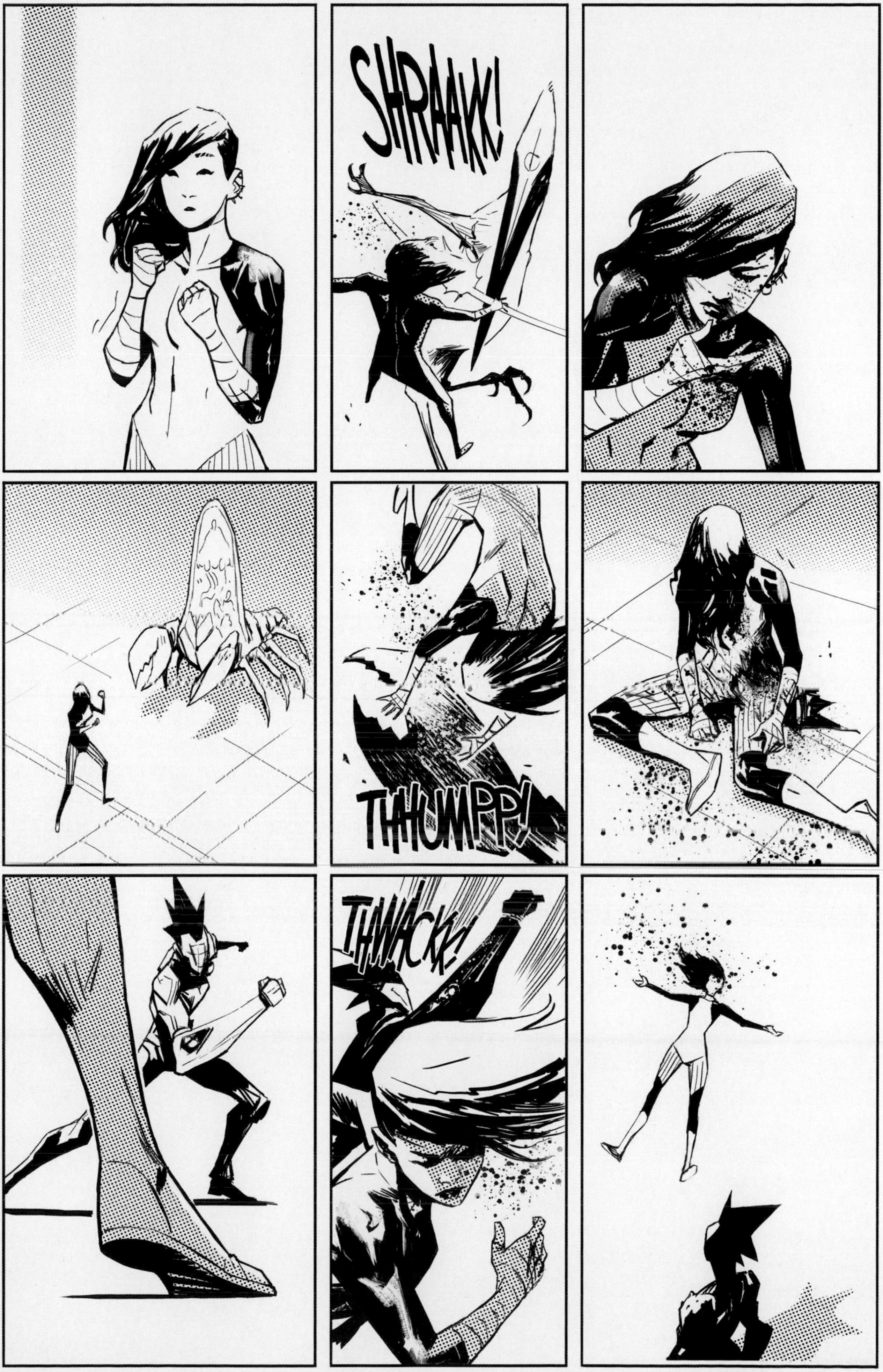
SHRAAKK!
THHUMPP!
THWACKK!

REPETITION

[CONTRACT]

ACCEPTED.

[DURATION]

ONE WEEK.

[WANTED]

DOA.

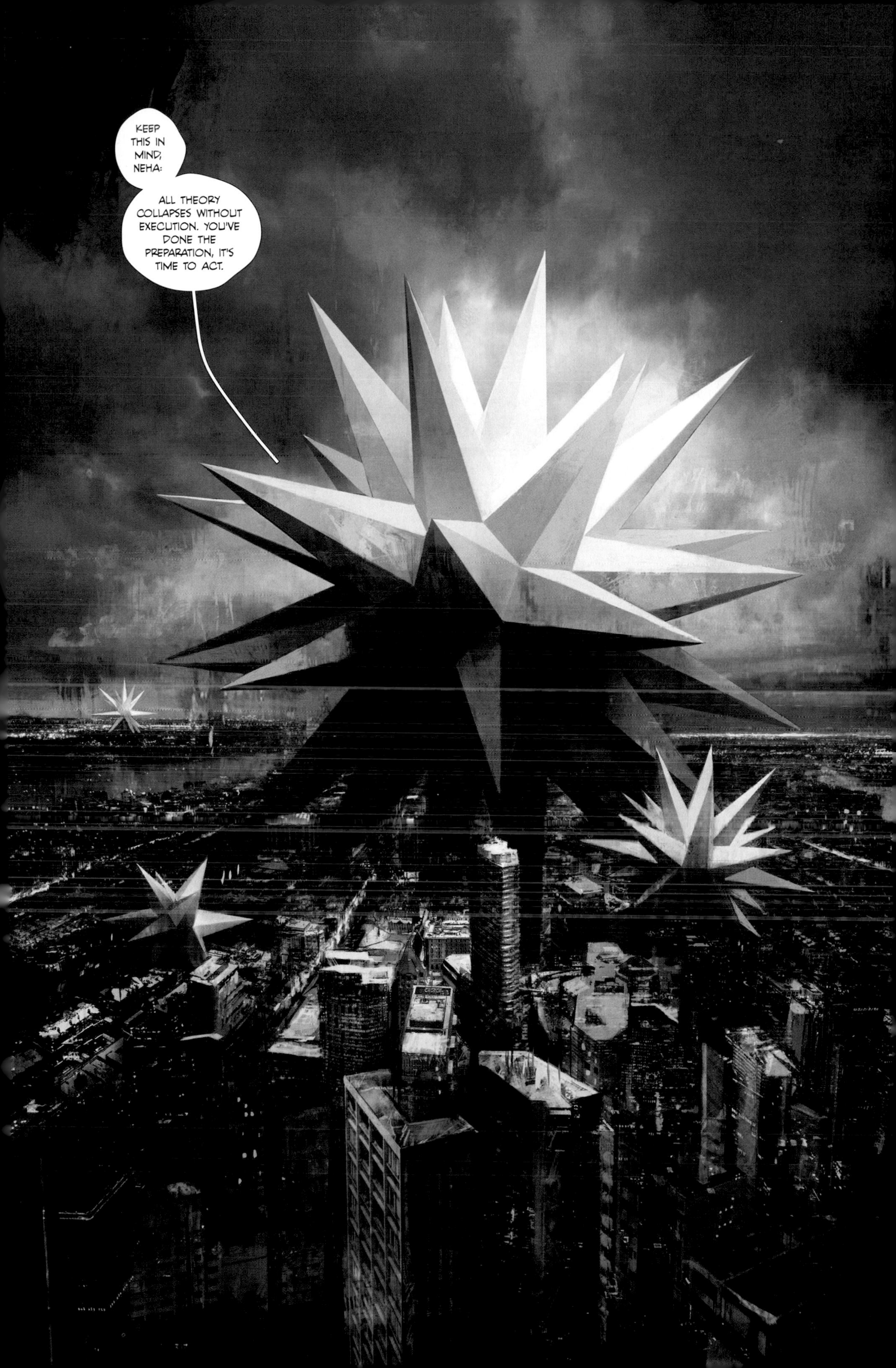
KEEP THIS IN MIND, NEHA:
ALL THEORY COLLAPSES WITHOUT EXECUTION. YOU'VE DONE THE PREPARATION, IT'S TIME TO ACT.

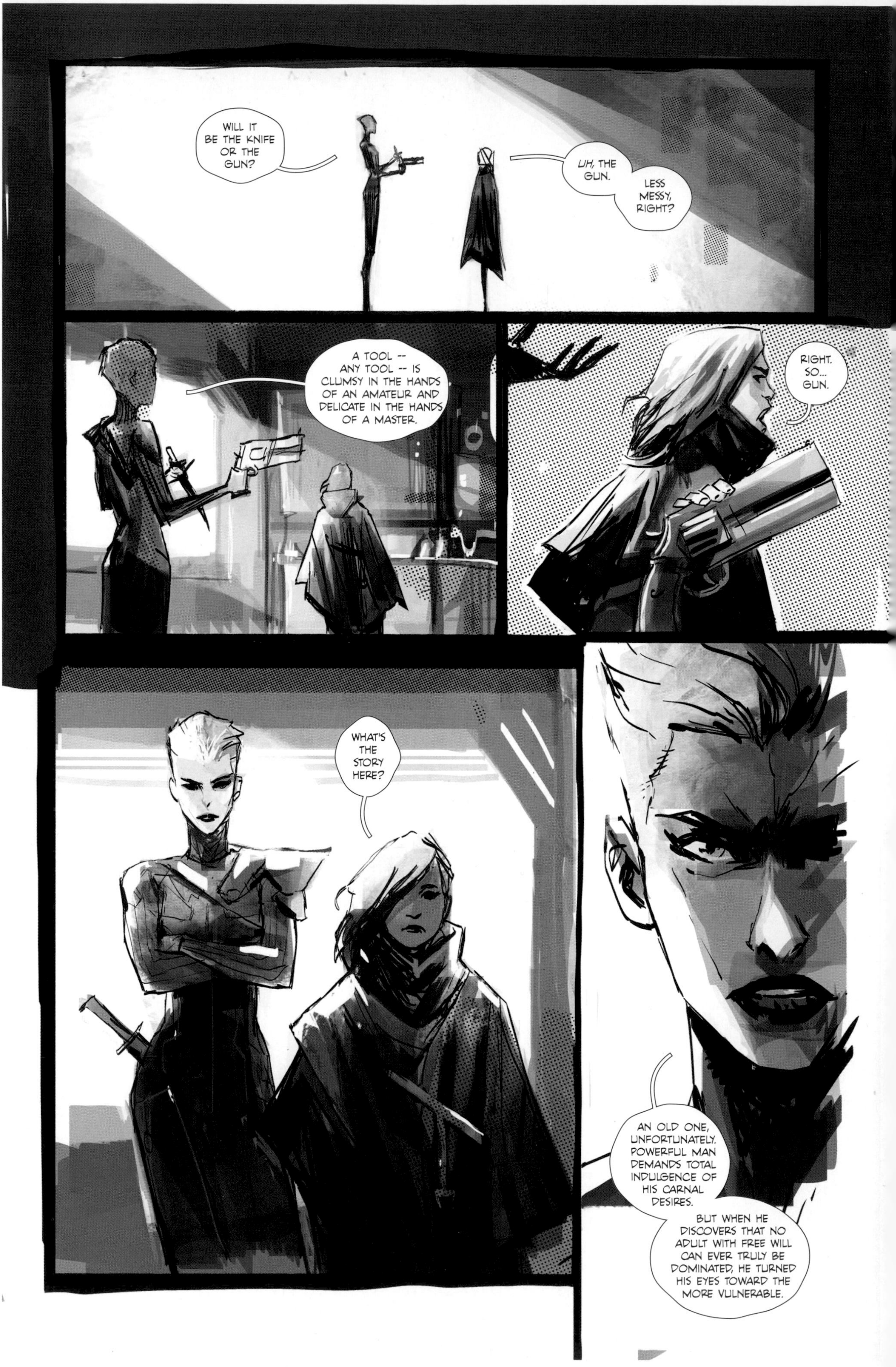
WILL IT BE THE KNIFE OR THE GUN?
UH, THE GUN.
LESS MESSY, RIGHT?
A TOOL -- ANY TOOL -- IS CLUMSY IN THE HANDS OF AN AMATEUR AND DELICATE IN THE HANDS OF A MASTER.
RIGHT. SO... GUN.
WHAT'S THE STORY HERE?
AN OLD ONE, UNFORTUNATELY. POWERFUL MAN DEMANDS TOTAL INDULGENCE OF HIS CARNAL DESIRES.
BUT WHEN HE DISCOVERS THAT NO ADULT WITH FREE WILL CAN EVER TRULY BE DOMINATED, HE TURNED HIS EYES TOWARD THE MORE VULNERABLE.

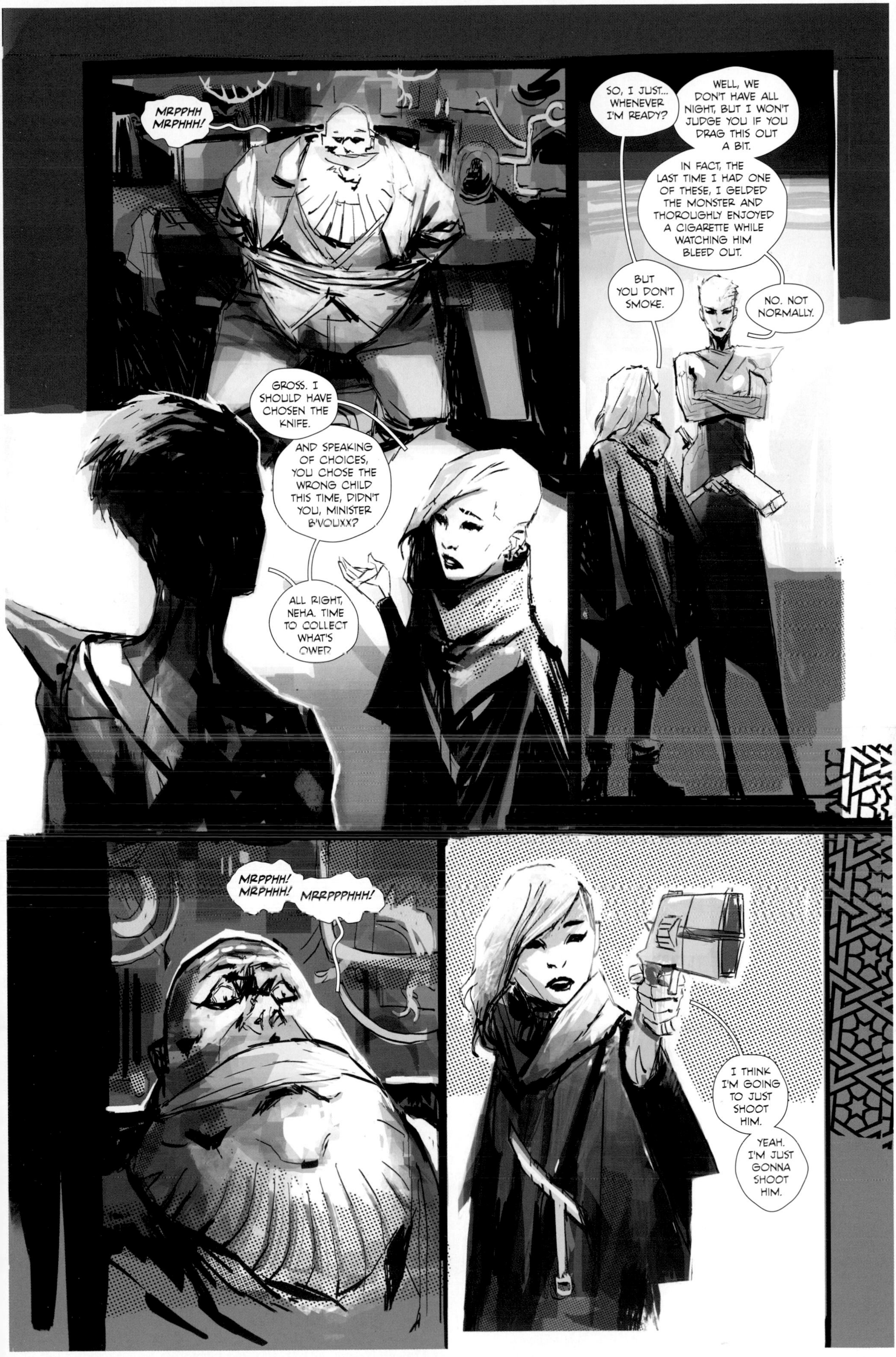
MRPPHH MRPHHH!
GROSS. I SHOULD HAVE CHOSEN THE KNIFE.
AND SPEAKING OF CHOICES, YOU CHOSE THE WRONG CHILD THIS TIME, DIDN'T YOU, MINISTER B'VOUXX?
ALL RIGHT, NEHA. TIME TO COLLECT WHAT'S OWED.
SO, I JUST... WHENEVER I'M READY?
WELL, WE DON'T HAVE ALL NIGHT, BUT I WON'T JUDGE YOU IF YOU DRAG THIS OUT A BIT.
IN FACT, THE LAST TIME I HAD ONE OF THESE, I GELDED THE MONSTER AND THOROUGHLY ENJOYED A CIGARETTE WHILE WATCHING HIM BLEED OUT.
BUT YOU DON'T SMOKE.
NO. NOT NORMALLY.
MRPPHH! MRPHHH!
MRRPPPHHH!
I THINK I'M GOING TO JUST SHOOT HIM.
YEAH. I'M JUST GONNA SHOOT HIM.

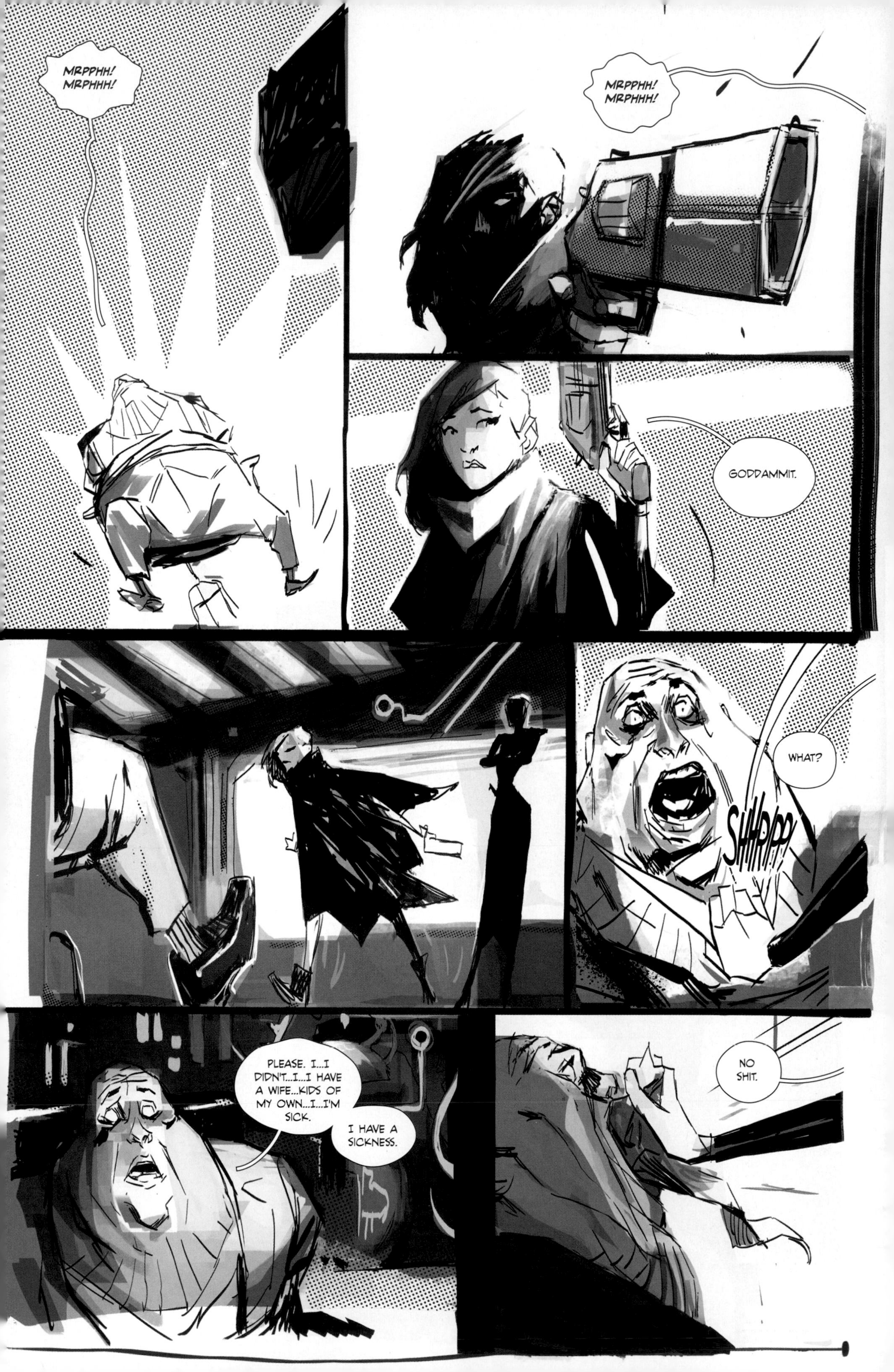
MRPPHH! MRPHHH!
MRPPHH! MRPHHH!
GODDAMMIT.
WHAT?
SHHPPP
PLEASE. I...I DIDN'T...I...I HAVE A WIFE...KIDS OF MY OWN...I...I'M SICK.
I HAVE A SICKNESS.
NO SHIT.

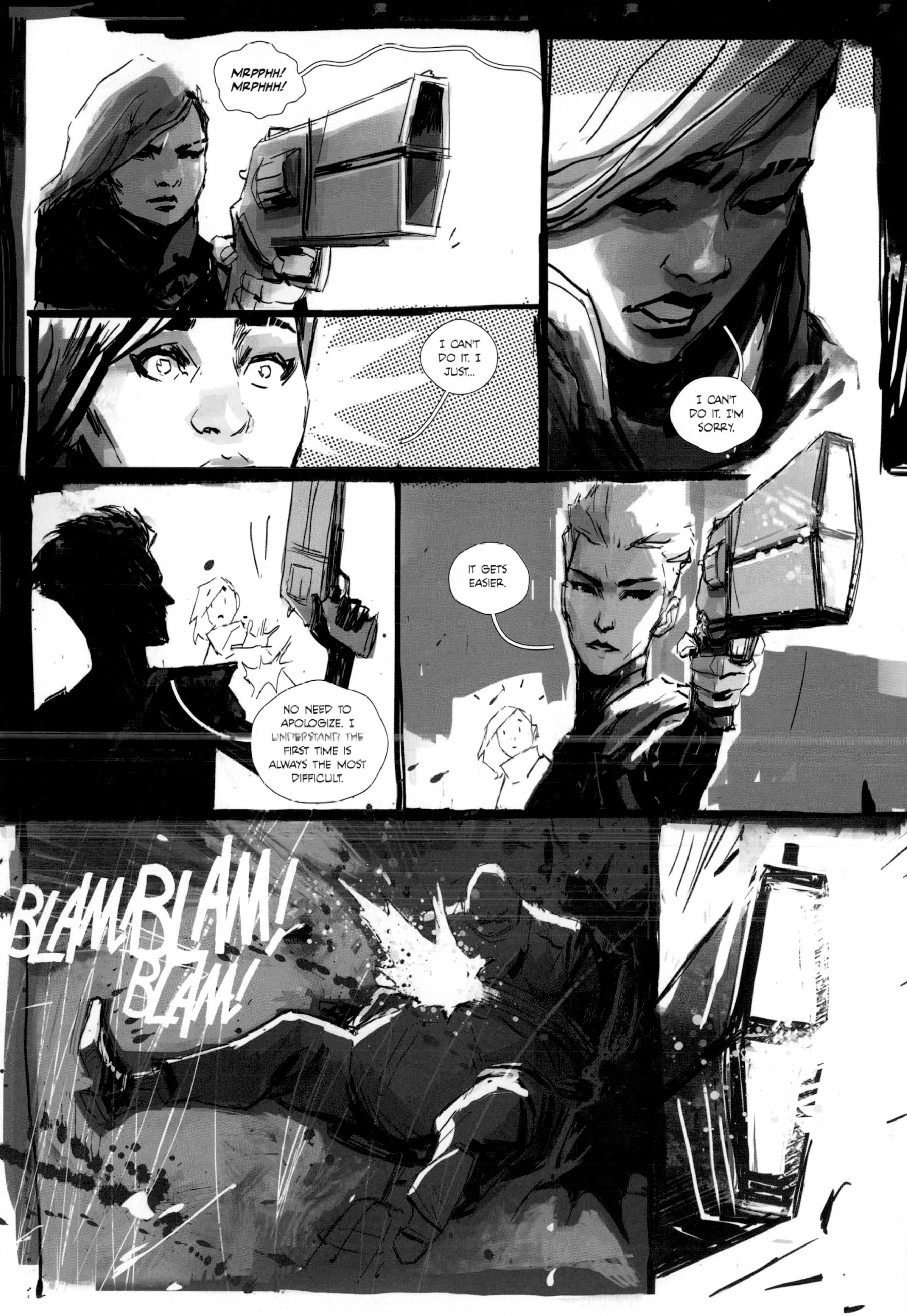
MRPPHH! MRPHHH!
I CAN'T DO IT. I JUST...
I CAN'T DO IT. I'M SORRY.
NO NEED TO APOLOGIZE. I UNDERSTAND THE FIRST TIME IS ALWAYS THE MOST DIFFICULT.
IT GETS EASIER.
BLAM! BLAM! BLAM!

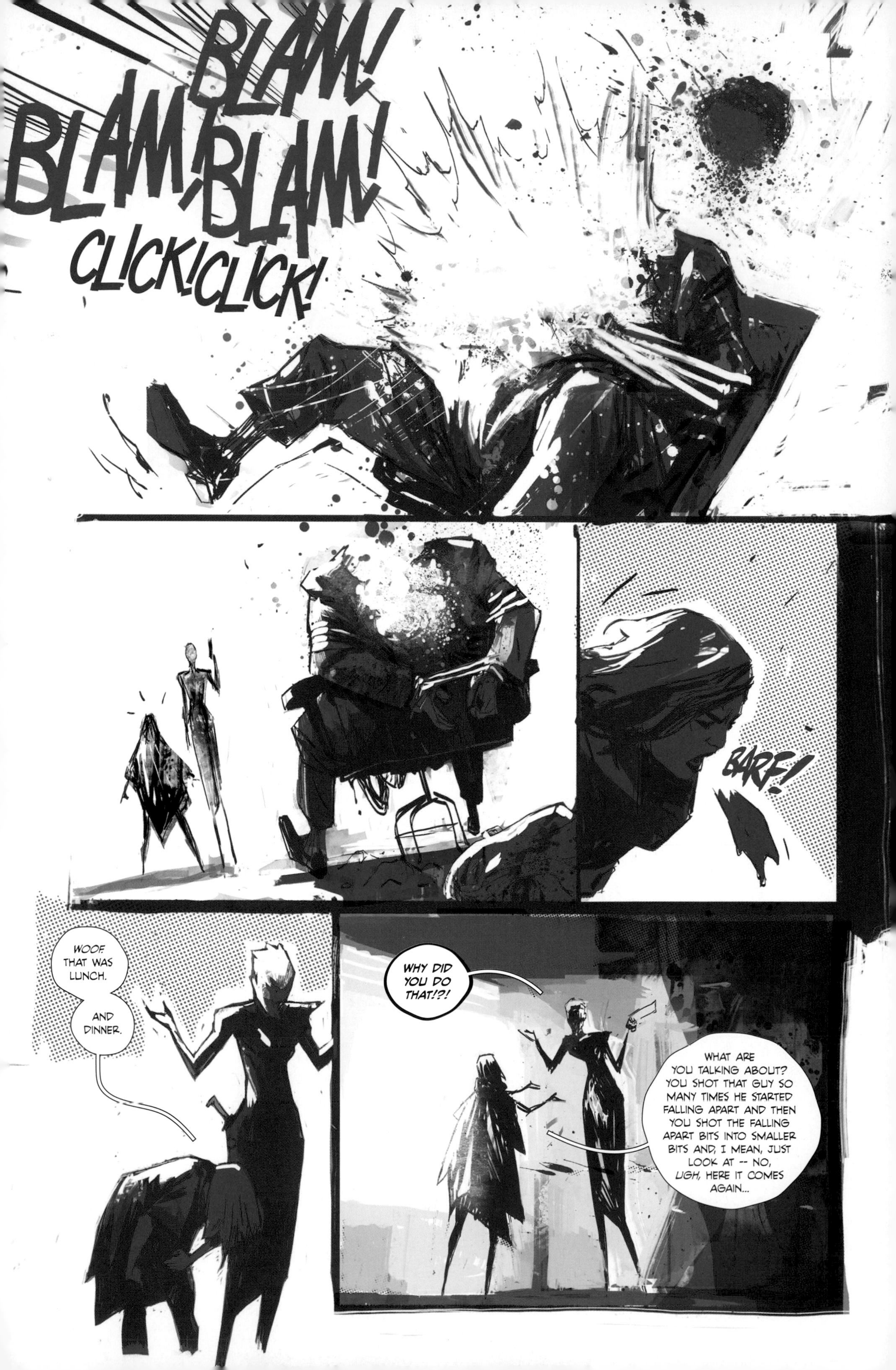
BLAM!
BLAM! BLAM!
CLICK! CLICK!
BARF!
WOOF. THAT WAS LUNCH.
AND DINNER.
WHY DID YOU DO THAT!?!
WHAT ARE YOU TALKING ABOUT? YOU SHOT THAT GUY SO MANY TIMES HE STARTED FALLING APART AND THEN YOU SHOT THE FALLING APART BITS INTO SMALLER BITS AND, I MEAN, JUST LOOK AT -- NO, *UGH,* HERE IT COMES AGAIN...

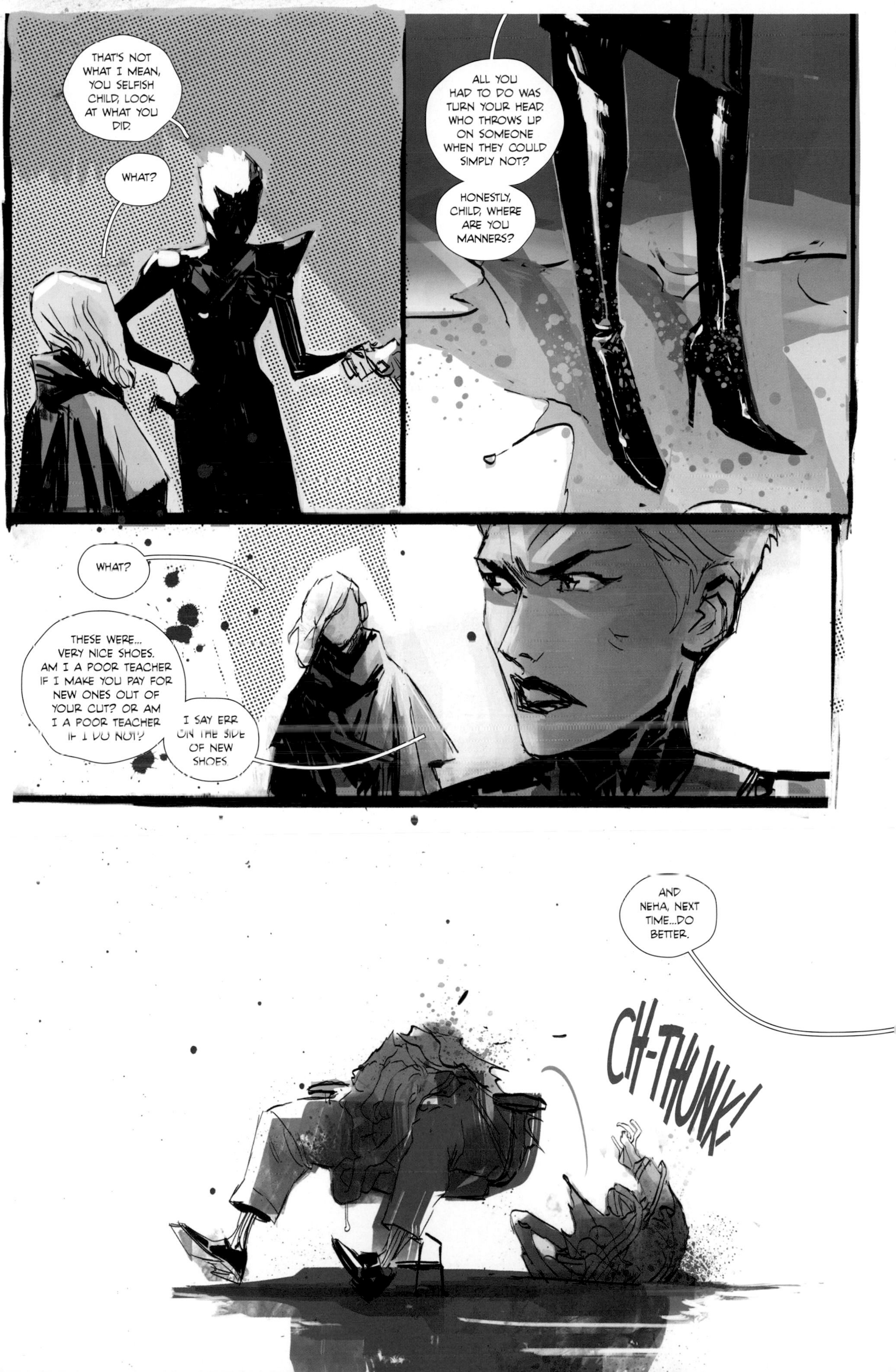
THAT'S NOT WHAT I MEAN, YOU SELFISH CHILD, LOOK AT WHAT YOU DID.
WHAT?
ALL YOU HAD TO DO WAS TURN YOUR HEAD. WHO THROWS UP ON SOMEONE WHEN THEY COULD SIMPLY NOT?
HONESTLY, CHILD, WHERE ARE YOU MANNERS?
WHAT?
THESE WERE... VERY NICE SHOES. AM I A POOR TEACHER IF I MAKE YOU PAY FOR NEW ONES OUT OF YOUR CUT? OR AM I A POOR TEACHER IF I DO NOT?
I SAY ERR ON THE SIDE OF NEW SHOES.
AND NEHA, NEXT TIME...DO BETTER.
CH-THUNK!

YEAR

TWO

[TRAINING]

YEAR

TWO

TWO

EDUCATION

[BIOLOGY]

Introduction to asymmetrical and non-organic organisms.

Weaknesses and vulnerabilities.

[WEAPONS]

Advanced assembly and ballistics.

Intermediate weapon design.

[RESEARCH]

Combustibles And Traditional Delivery Methods.

BY

Zorxxx the Thumbless

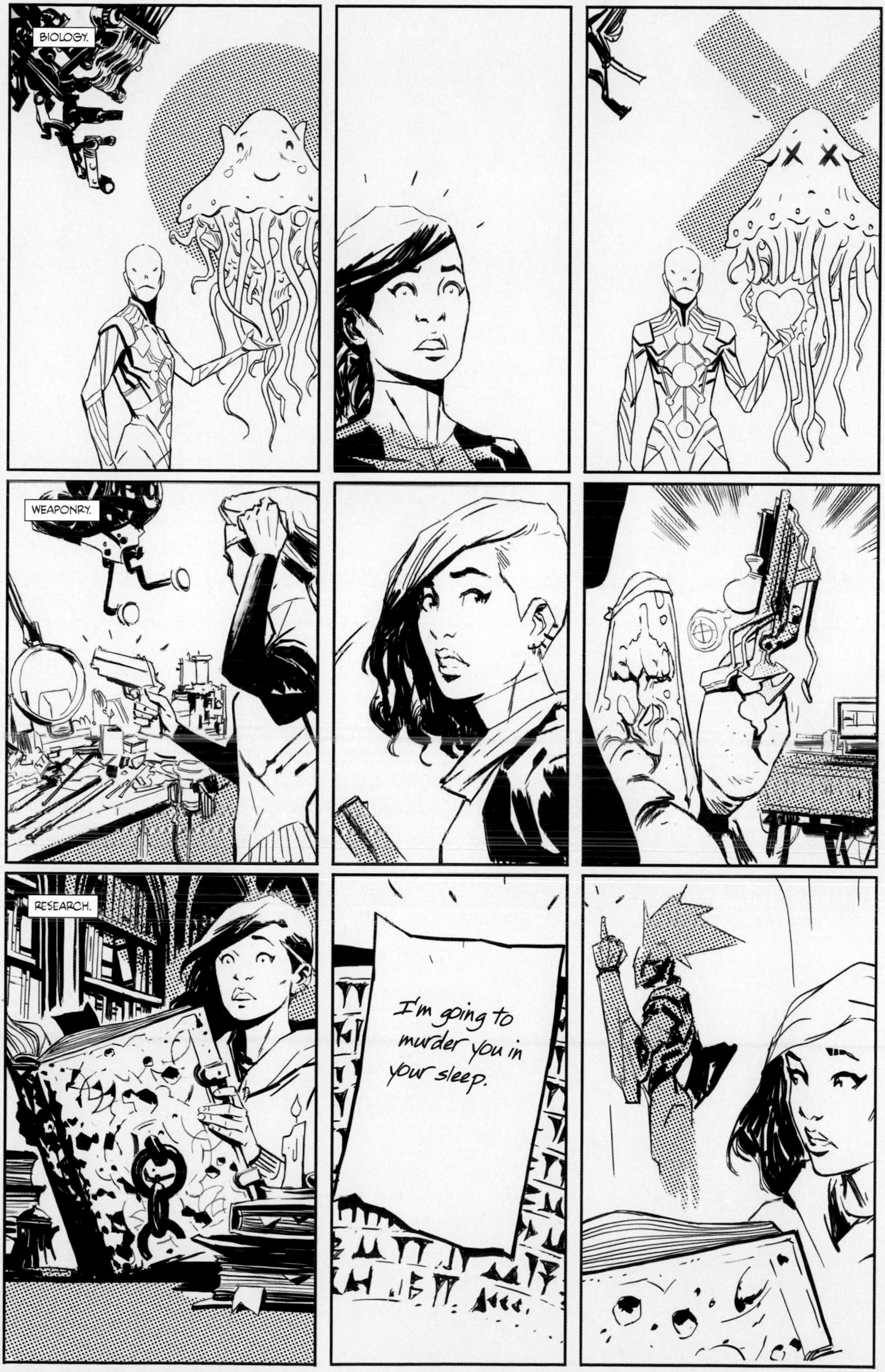
BIOLOGY.
WEAPONRY.
RESEARCH.
I'm going to murder you in your sleep.

APPLICATION

HAND-TO-HAND COMBAT

JETTI KAAN

[ ]

SAM-SAM

[x]

URSULA RING

[x]

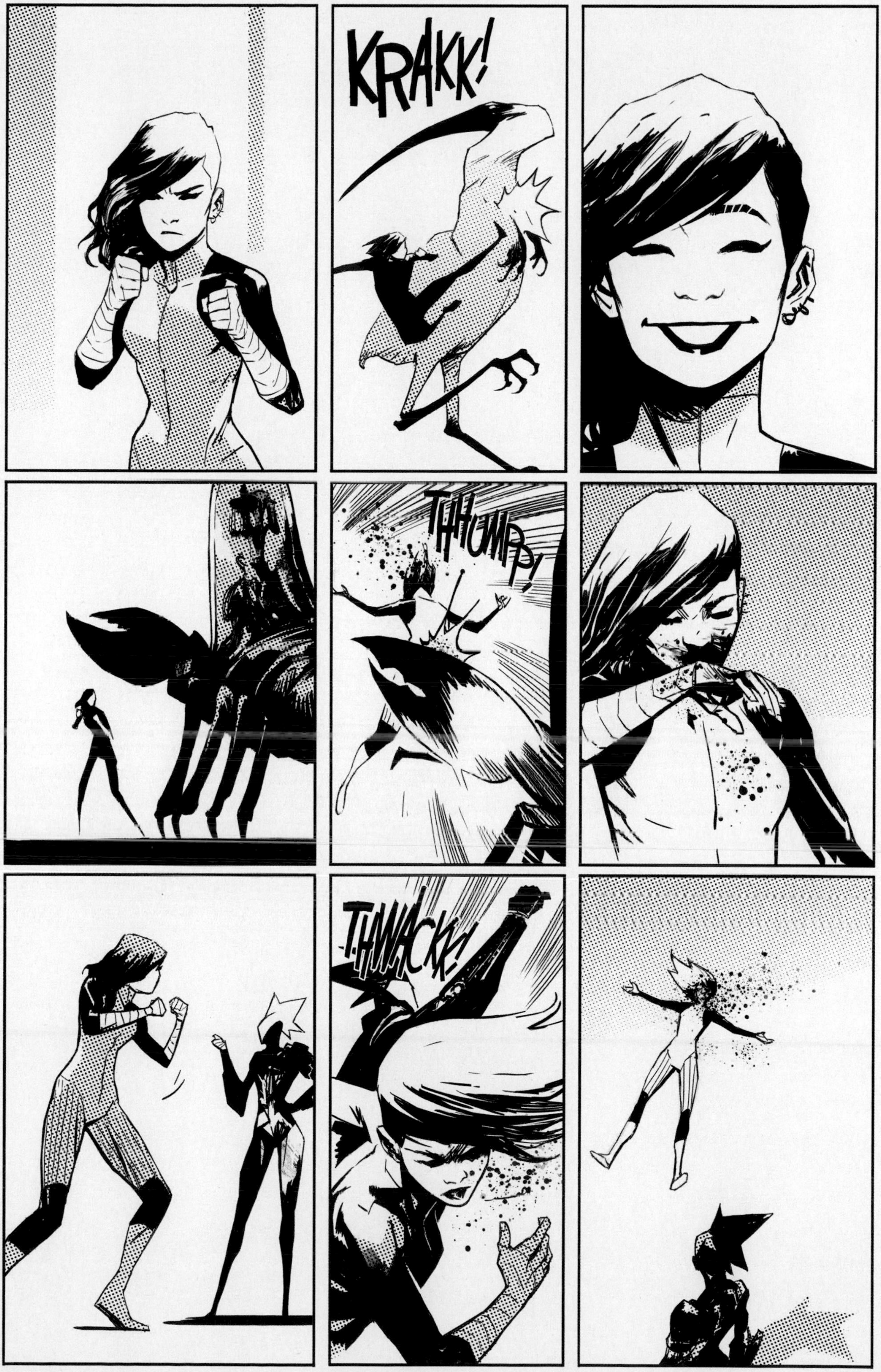
KRAKK!
THHUMP!
THWACKK!

[YEAR TWO]

REPETITION

[CONTRACT]

ACCEPTED.

[DURATION]

TWO DAYS.

[WANTED]

DEAD.

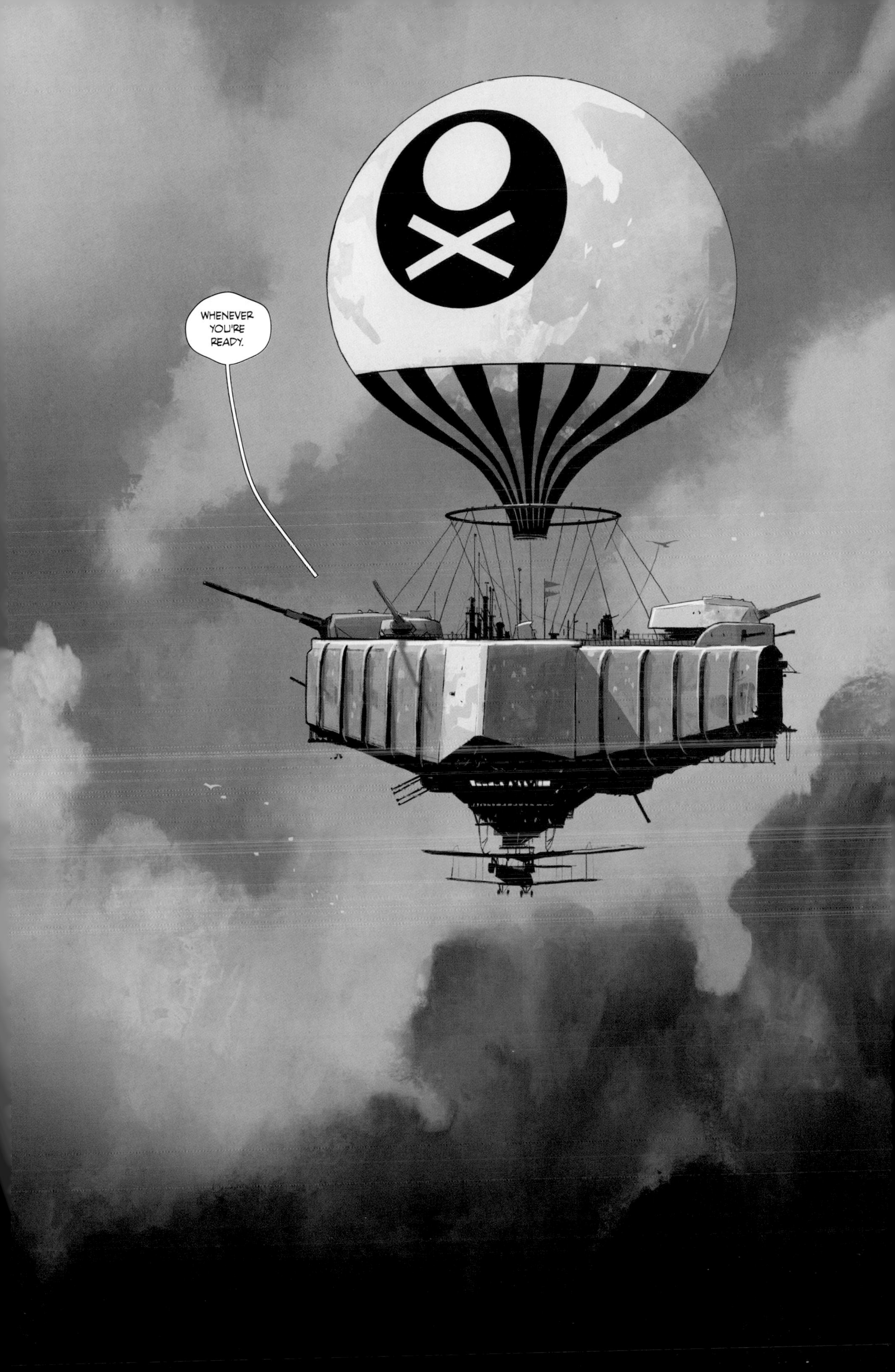
WHENEVER YOU'RE READY.

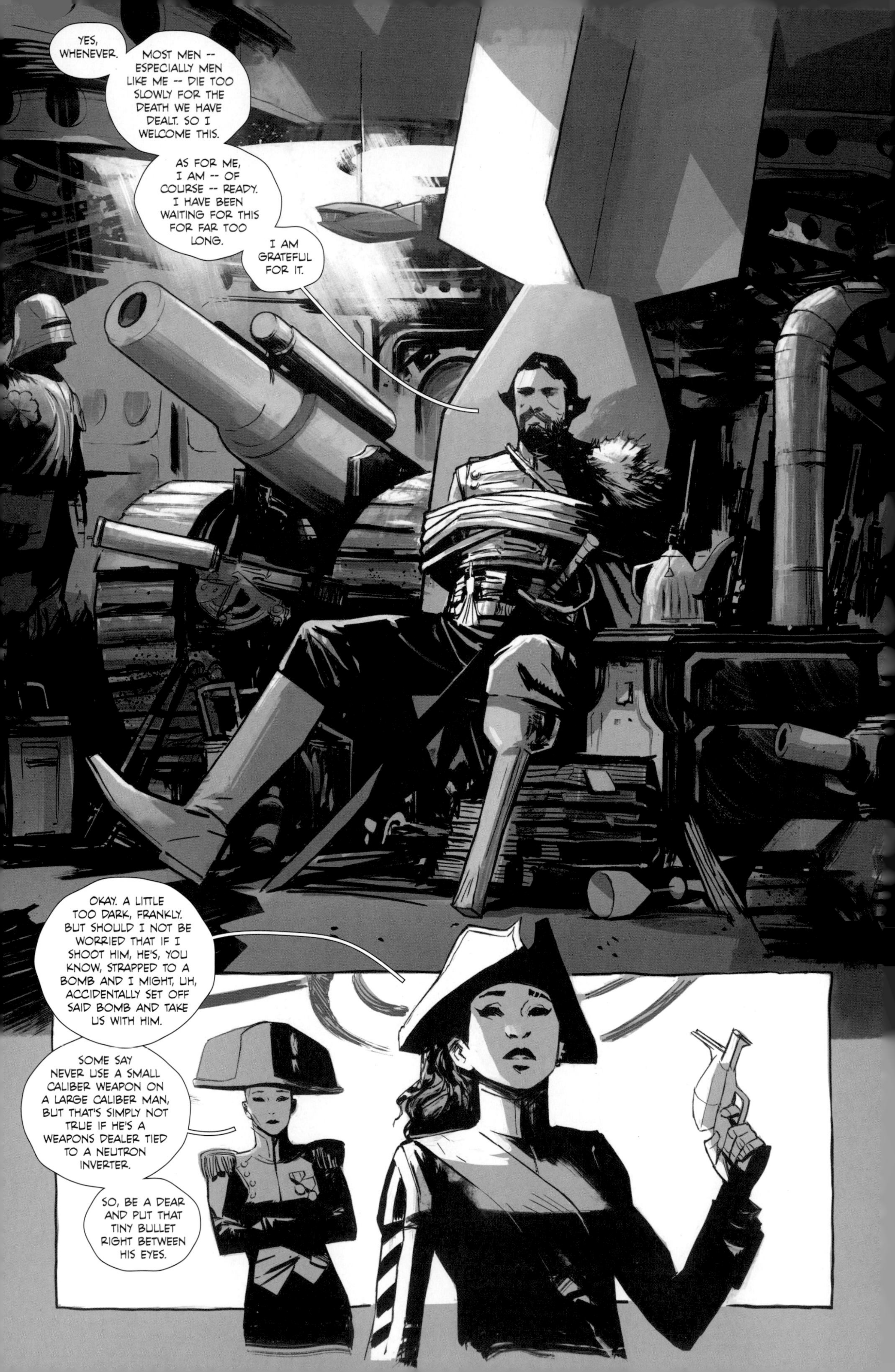
YES, WHENEVER.
MOST MEN -- ESPECIALLY MEN LIKE ME -- DIE TOO SLOWLY FOR THE DEATH WE HAVE DEALT. SO I WELCOME THIS.
AS FOR ME, I AM -- OF COURSE -- READY. I HAVE BEEN WAITING FOR THIS FOR FAR TOO LONG.
I AM GRATEFUL FOR IT.
OKAY. A LITTLE TOO DARK, FRANKLY. BUT SHOULD I NOT BE WORRIED THAT IF I SHOOT HIM, HE'S, YOU KNOW, STRAPPED TO A BOMB AND I MIGHT, UH, ACCIDENTALLY SET OFF SAID BOMB AND TAKE US WITH HIM.
SOME SAY NEVER USE A SMALL CALIBER WEAPON ON A LARGE CALIBER MAN, BUT THAT'S SIMPLY NOT TRUE IF HE'S A WEAPONS DEALER TIED TO A NEUTRON INVERTER.
SO, BE A DEAR AND PUT THAT TINY BULLET RIGHT BETWEEN HIS EYES.

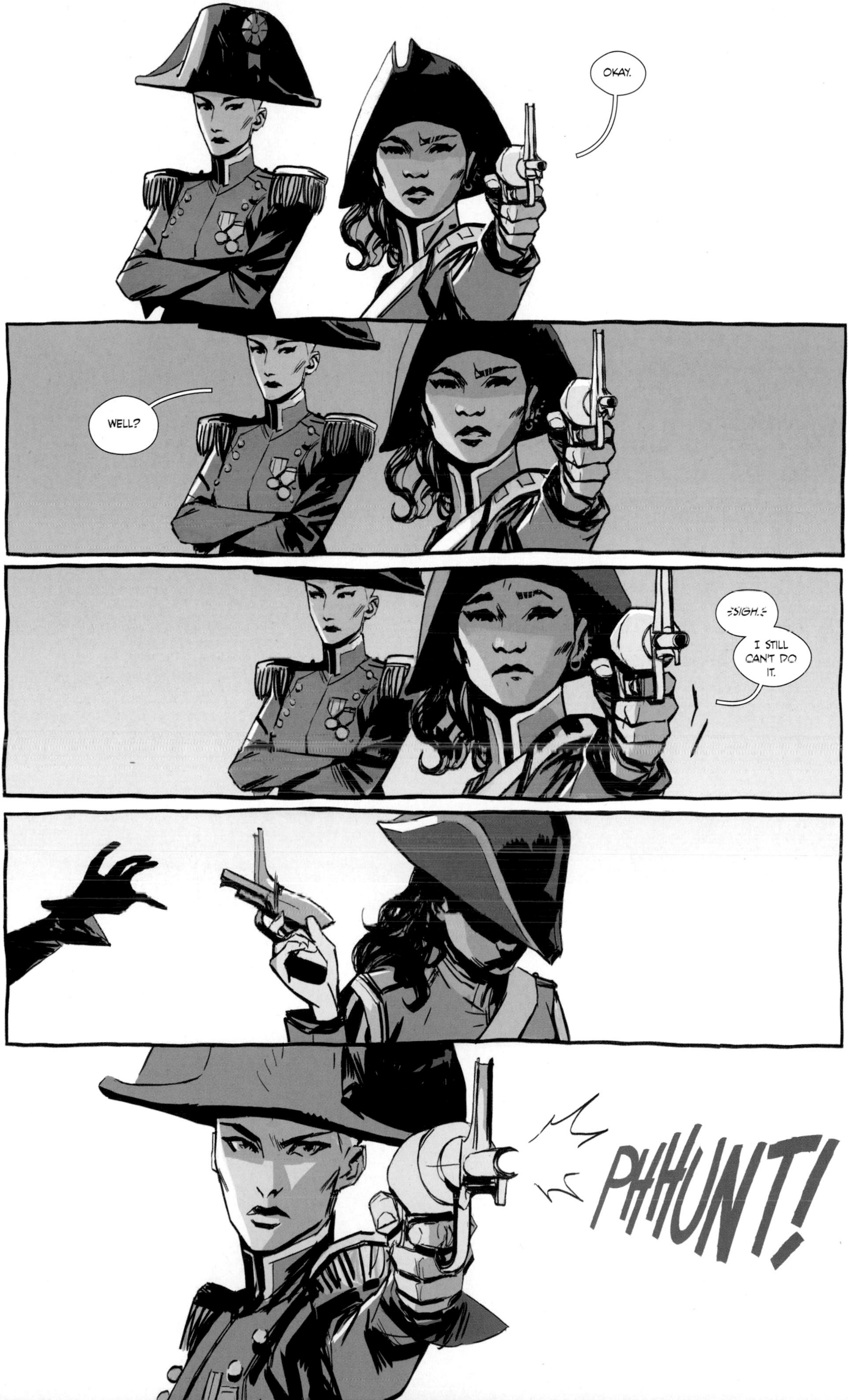
OKAY.
WELL?
=SIGH.=
I STILL CAN'T DO IT.
PHHUNT!

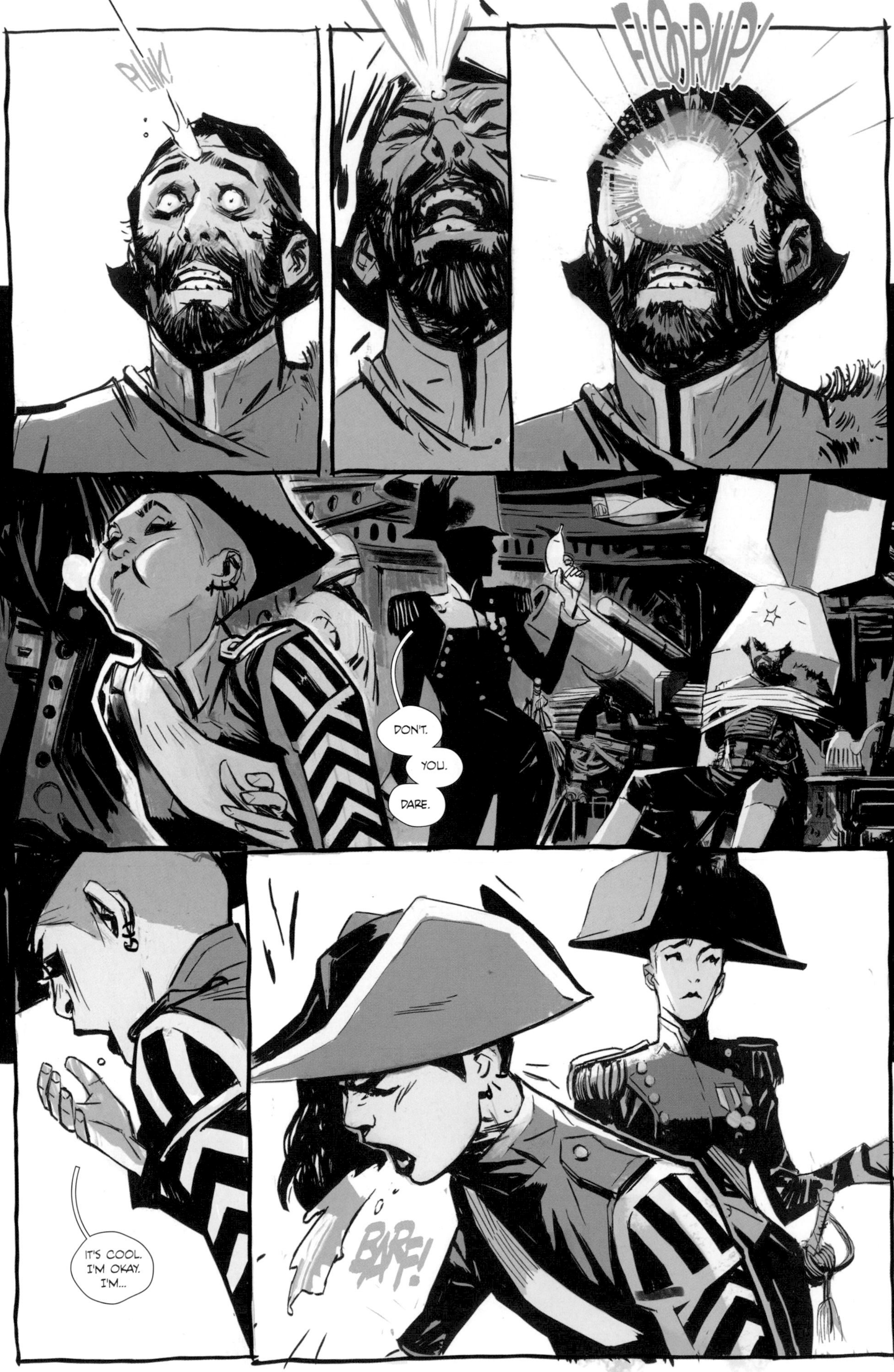
PLINK!
FLOORMP!
DON'T.
YOU.
DARE.
IT'S COOL. I'M OKAY. I'M...
BARF!

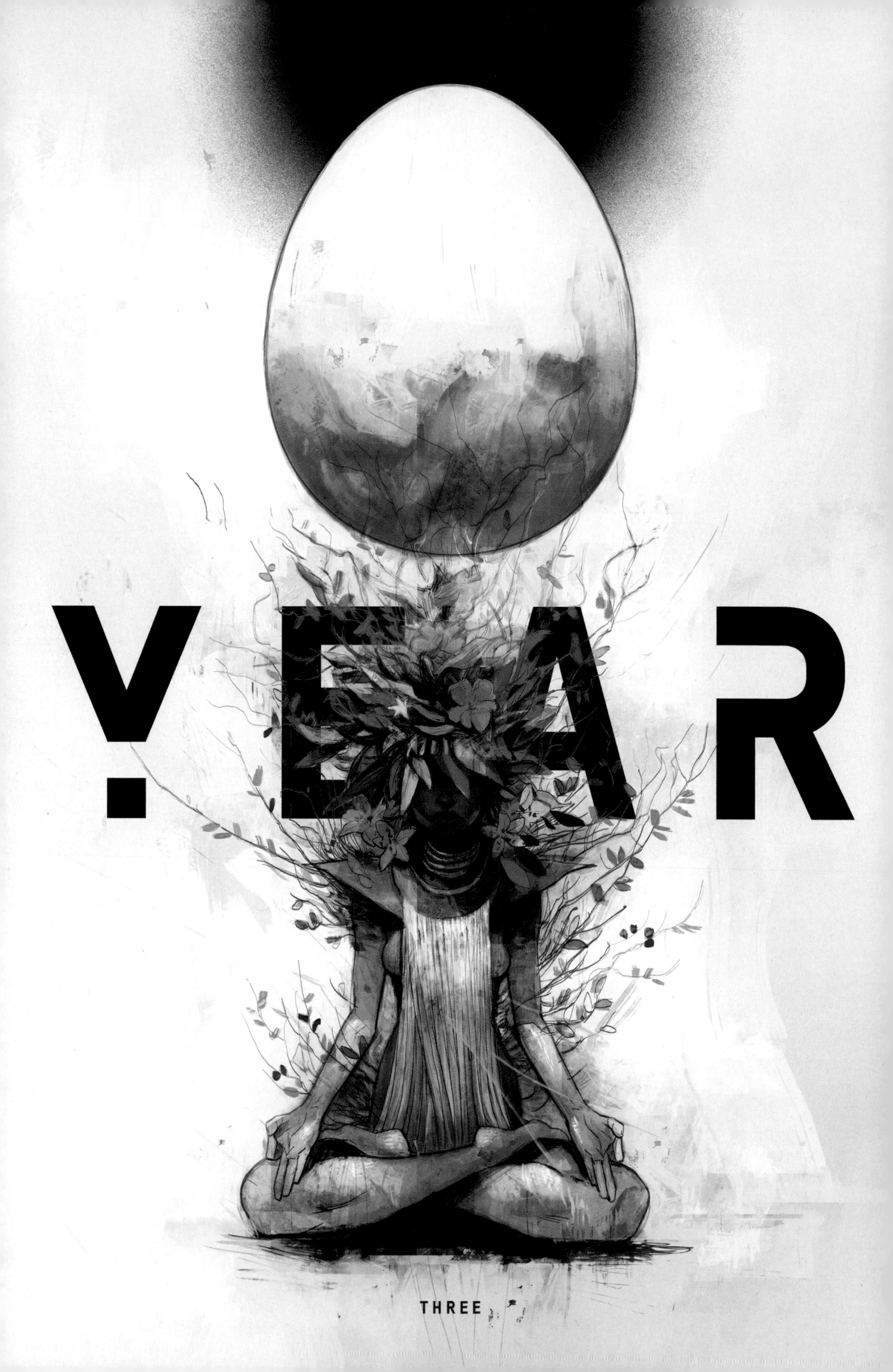
YEAR
THREE

[TRAINING]

YEAR

THREE

THRE

EDUCATION

[BIOLOGY]

Projected vulnerabilities of unknown species.

[WEAPONS]

Advanced weapon design.

[RESEARCH]

Strategy And Deployment Of Small Combat Units.

BY

Brigadier General Norman Blankface

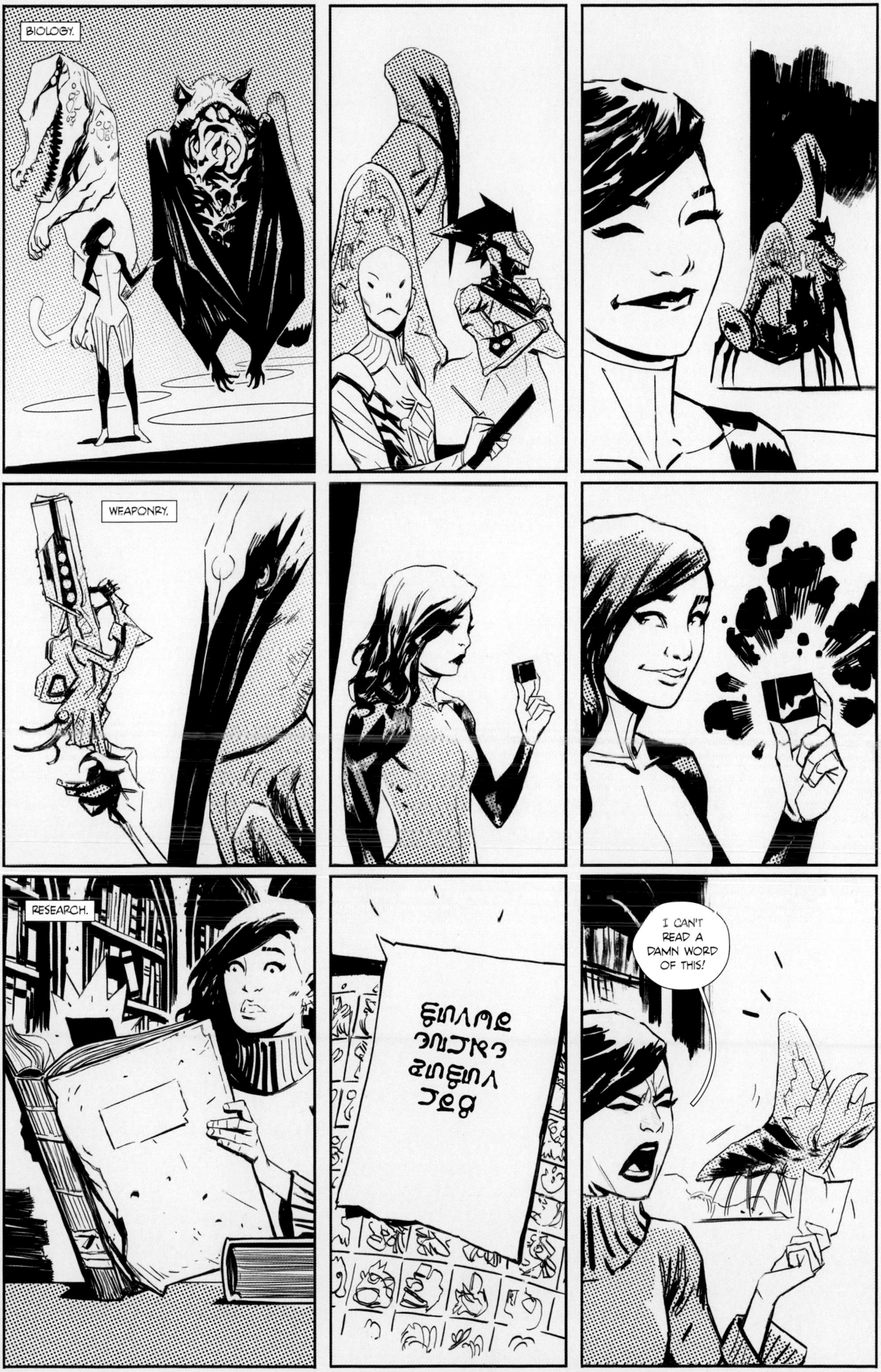
BIOLOGY.
WEAPONRY.
RESEARCH.
I CAN'T READ A DAMN WORD OF THIS!

APPLICATION

HAND-TO-HAND COMBAT

JETTI KAAN

[ ]

SAM-SAM

[ ]

URSULA RING

[x]

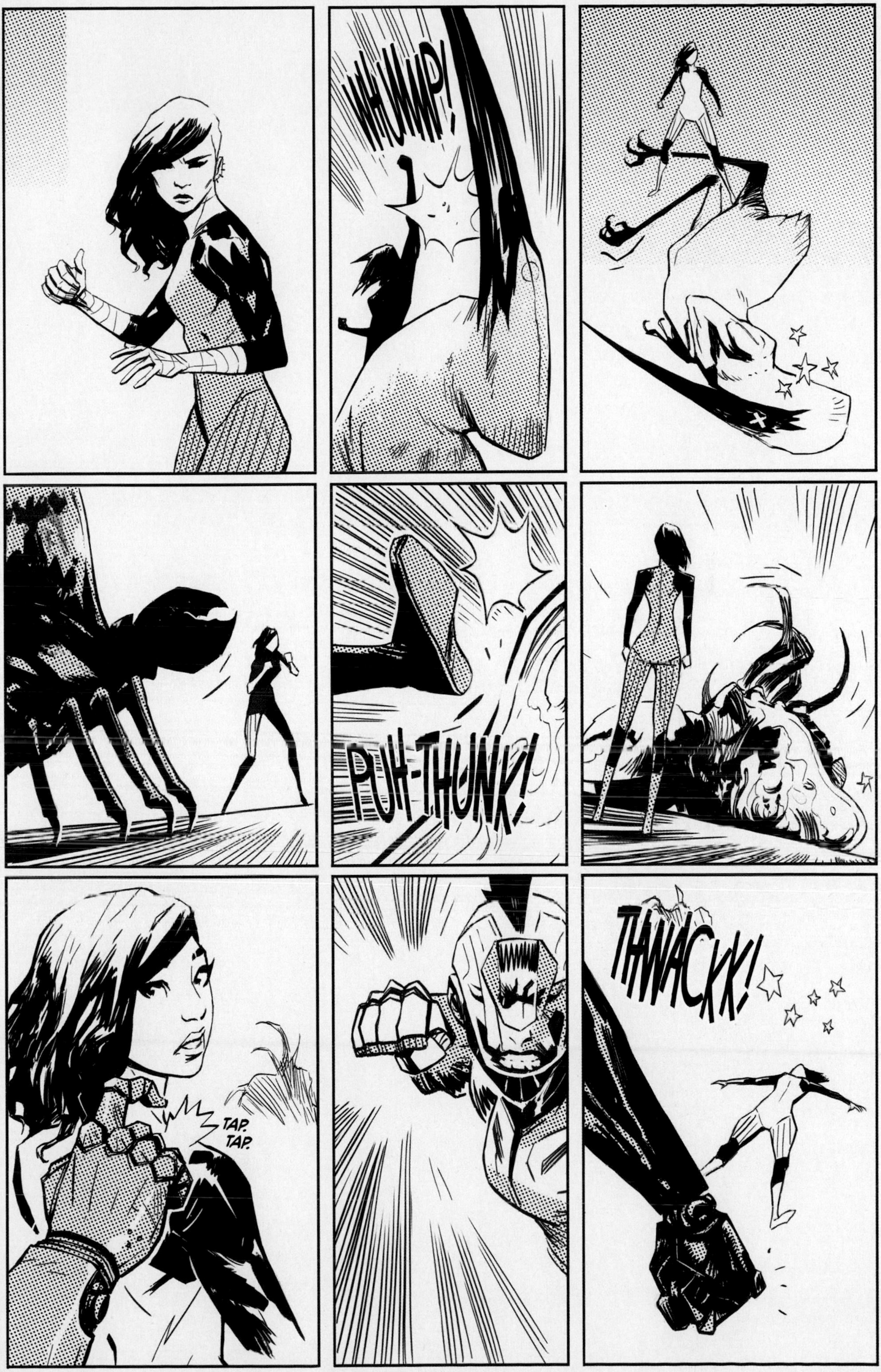
WHUMP!
PUH-THUNK!
TAP. TAP.
THWACKK!

[YEAR THREE]

REPETITION

| CONTRACT |

ACCEPTED.

| DURATION |

TWO WEEKS.

| WANTED |

DATA RECOVERY AND TERMINATION.

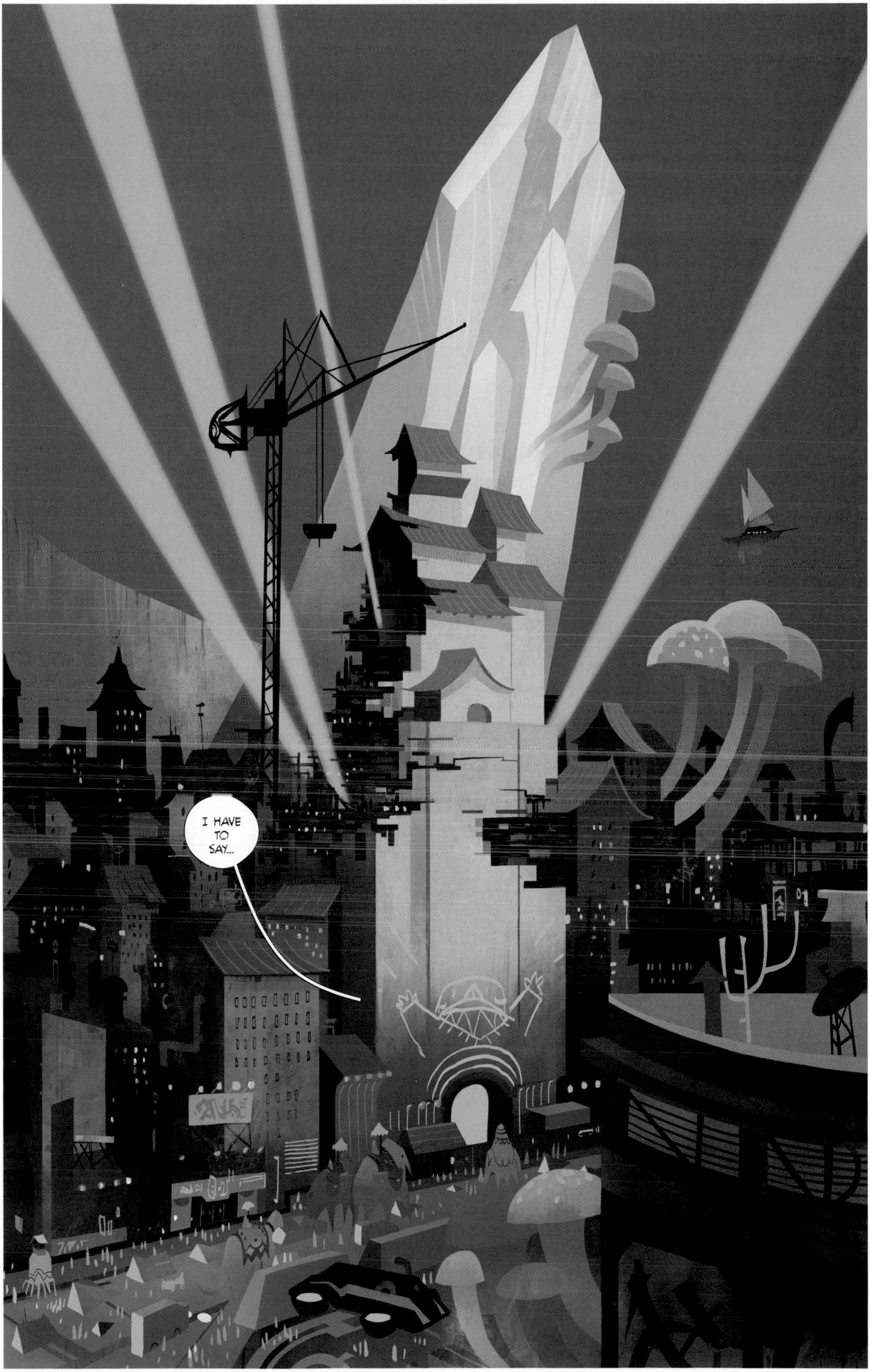
I HAVE TO SAY...

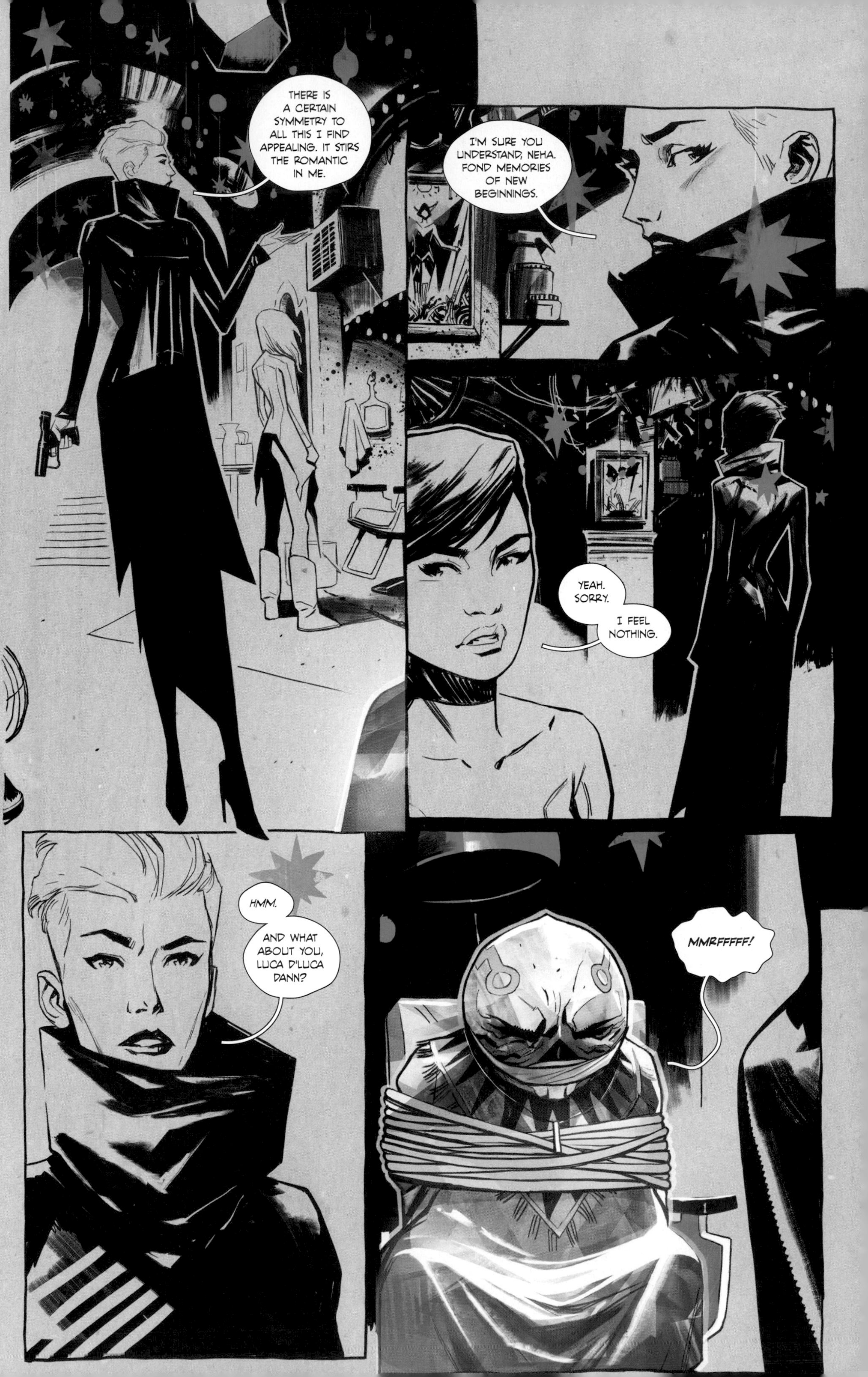
THERE IS A CERTAIN SYMMETRY TO ALL THIS I FIND APPEALING. IT STIRS THE ROMANTIC IN ME.
I'M SURE YOU UNDERSTAND, NEHA. FOND MEMORIES OF NEW BEGINNINGS.
YEAH. SORRY.
I FEEL NOTHING.
HMM.
AND WHAT ABOUT YOU, LUCA D'LUCA DANN?
MMRFFFFF!

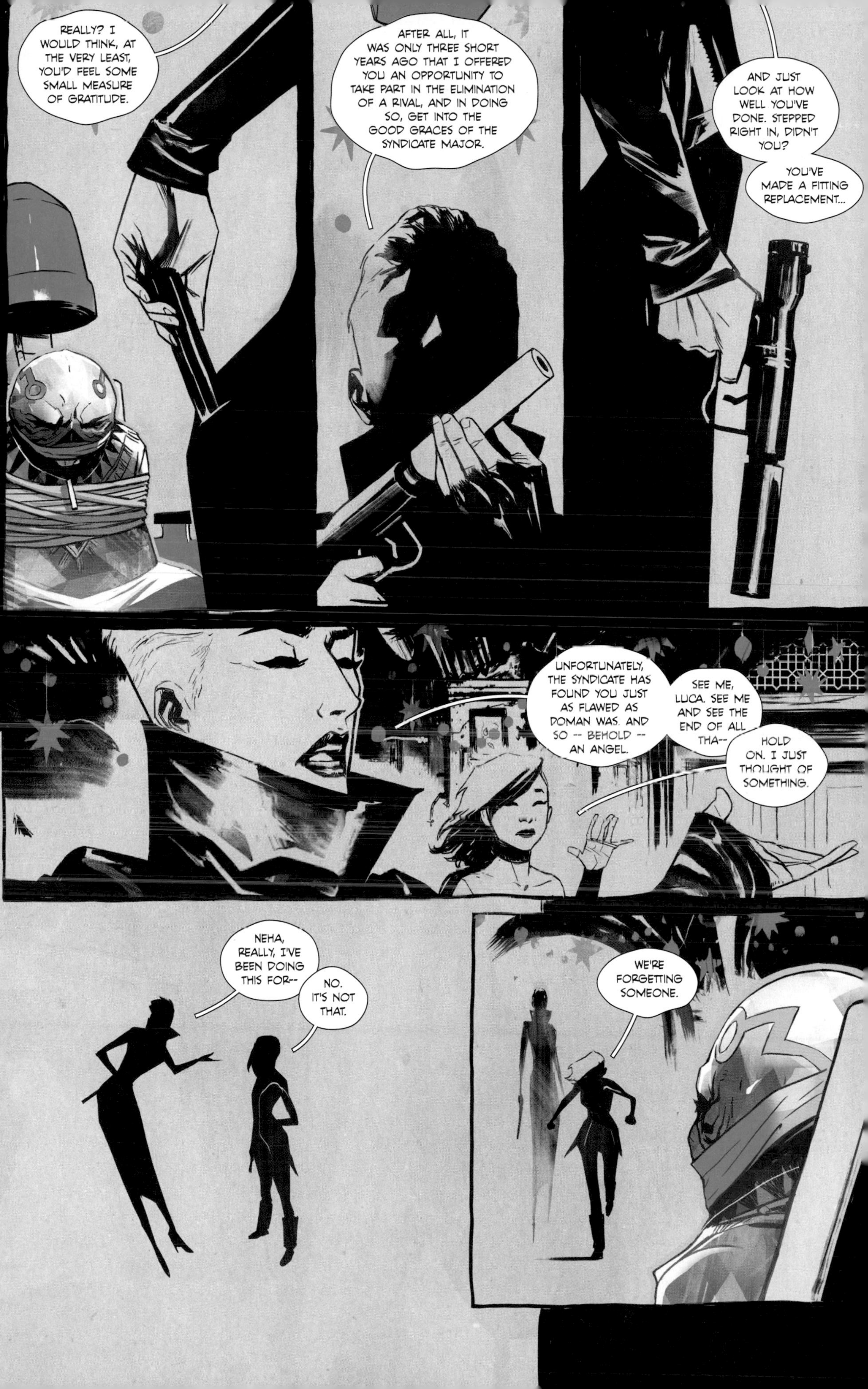

REALLY? I WOULD THINK, AT THE VERY LEAST, YOU'D FEEL SOME SMALL MEASURE OF GRATITUDE.
AFTER ALL, IT WAS ONLY THREE SHORT YEARS AGO THAT I OFFERED YOU AN OPPORTUNITY TO TAKE PART IN THE ELIMINATION OF A RIVAL, AND IN DOING SO, GET INTO THE GOOD GRACES OF THE SYNDICATE MAJOR.
AND JUST LOOK AT HOW WELL YOU'VE DONE. STEPPED RIGHT IN, DIDN'T YOU?
YOU'VE MADE A FITTING REPLACEMENT...
UNFORTUNATELY, THE SYNDICATE HAS FOUND YOU JUST AS FLAWED AS DOMAN WAS. AND SO -- BEHOLD -- AN ANGEL.
SEE ME, LUCA. SEE ME AND SEE THE END OF ALL THA--
HOLD ON. I JUST THOUGHT OF SOMETHING.
NEHA, REALLY, I'VE BEEN DOING THIS FOR--
NO. IT'S NOT THAT.
WE'RE FORGETTING SOMEONE.

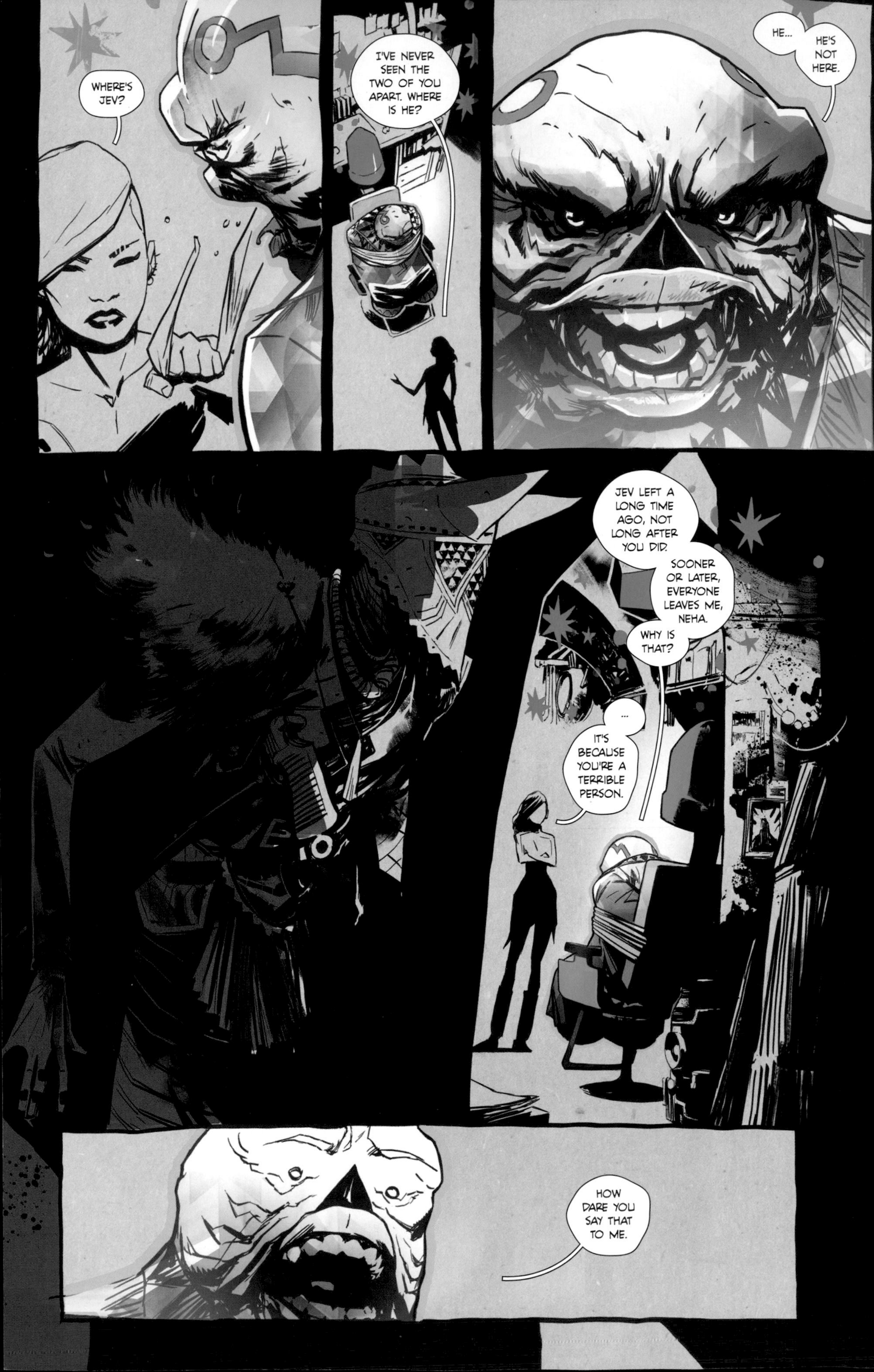

WHERE'S JEV?
I'VE NEVER SEEN THE TWO OF YOU APART. WHERE IS HE?
HE...
HE'S NOT HERE.
JEV LEFT A LONG TIME AGO, NOT LONG AFTER YOU DID.
SOONER OR LATER, EVERYONE LEAVES ME, NEHA.
WHY IS THAT?
...
IT'S BECAUSE YOU'RE A TERRIBLE PERSON.
HOW DARE YOU SAY THAT TO ME.

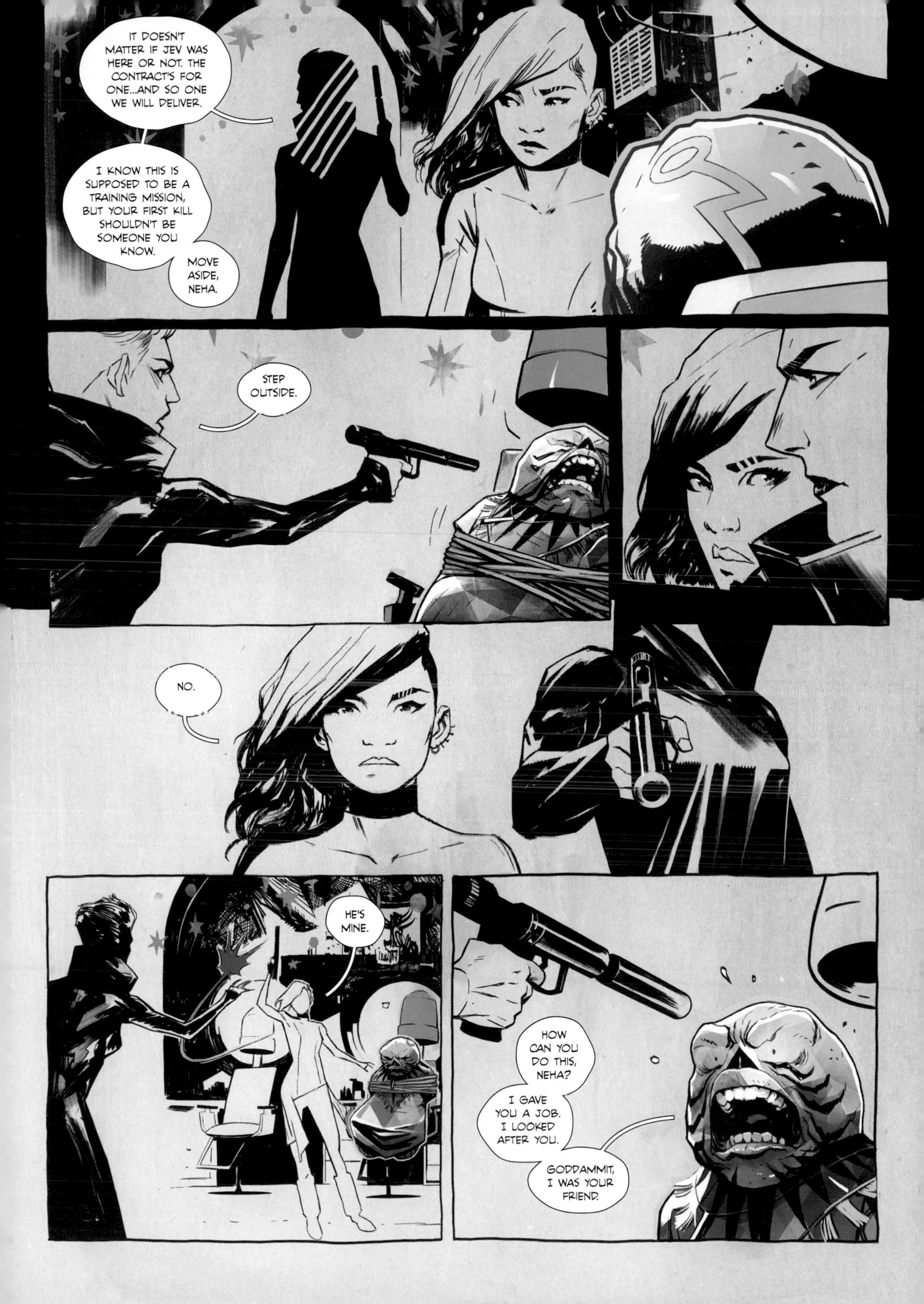

IT DOESN'T MATTER IF JEV WAS HERE OR NOT. THE CONTRACT'S FOR ONE...AND SO ONE WE WILL DELIVER.
I KNOW THIS IS SUPPOSED TO BE A TRAINING MISSION, BUT YOUR FIRST KILL SHOULDN'T BE SOMEONE YOU KNOW.
MOVE ASIDE, NEHA.
STEP OUTSIDE.
NO.
HE'S MINE.
HOW CAN YOU DO THIS, NEHA?
I GAVE YOU A JOB. I LOOKED AFTER YOU.
GODDAMMIT, I WAS YOUR FRIEND.

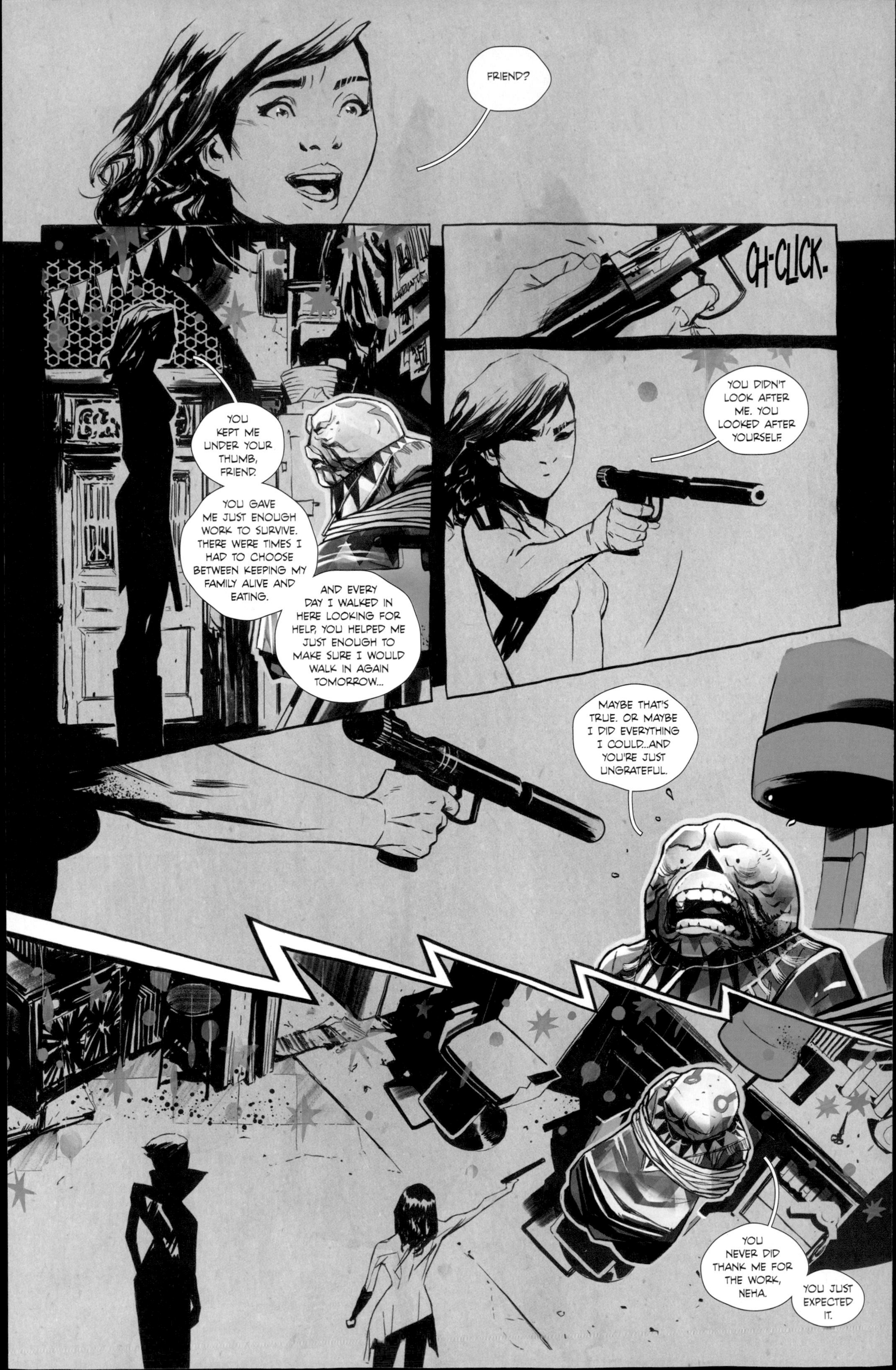
FRIEND?
CH-CLICK.
YOU KEPT ME UNDER YOUR THUMB, FRIEND.
YOU GAVE ME JUST ENOUGH WORK TO SURVIVE. THERE WERE TIMES I HAD TO CHOOSE BETWEEN KEEPING MY FAMILY ALIVE AND EATING.
AND EVERY DAY I WALKED IN HERE LOOKING FOR HELP, YOU HELPED ME JUST ENOUGH TO MAKE SURE I WOULD WALK IN AGAIN TOMORROW...
YOU DIDN'T LOOK AFTER ME. YOU LOOKED AFTER YOURSELF.
MAYBE THAT'S TRUE. OR MAYBE I DID EVERYTHING I COULD...AND YOU'RE JUST UNGRATEFUL.
YOU NEVER DID THANK ME FOR THE WORK, NEHA.
YOU JUST EXPECTED IT.

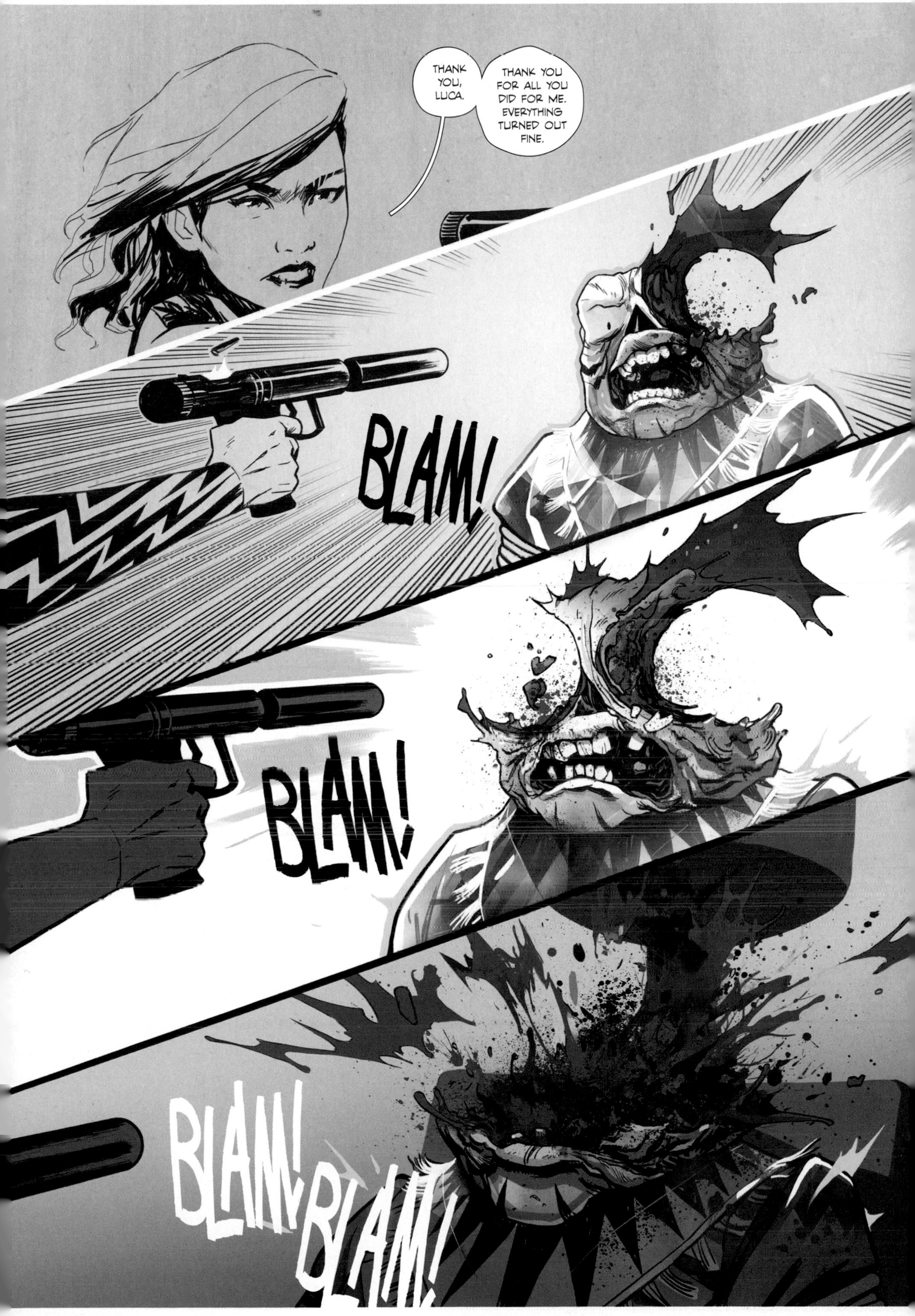
THANK YOU, LUCA.
THANK YOU FOR ALL YOU DID FOR ME. EVERYTHING TURNED OUT FINE.
BLAM!
BLAM!
BLAM!
BLAM!

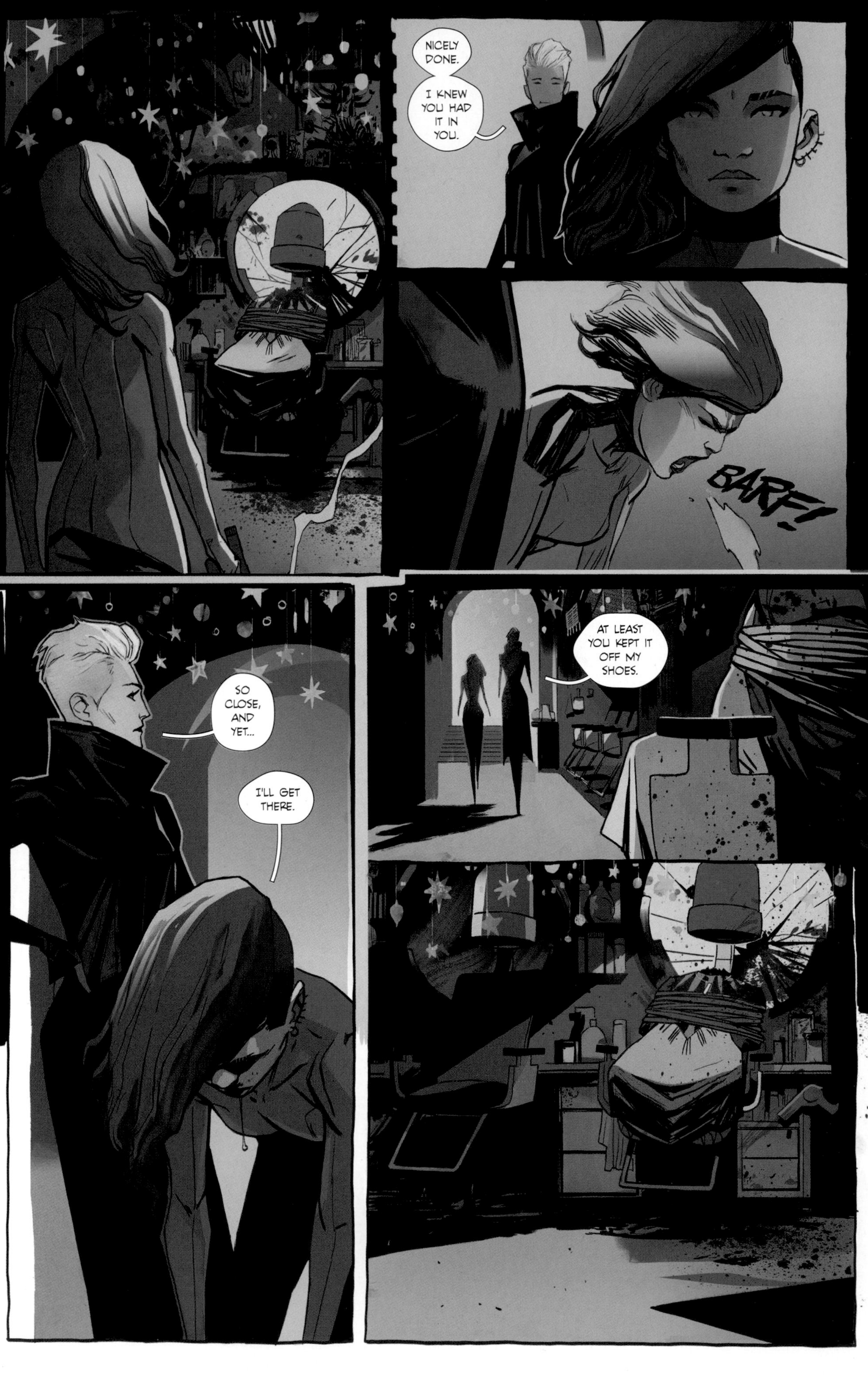
NICELY DONE.
I KNEW YOU HAD IT IN YOU.
BARF!
SO CLOSE, AND YET...
I'LL GET THERE.
AT LEAST YOU KEPT IT OFF MY SHOES.

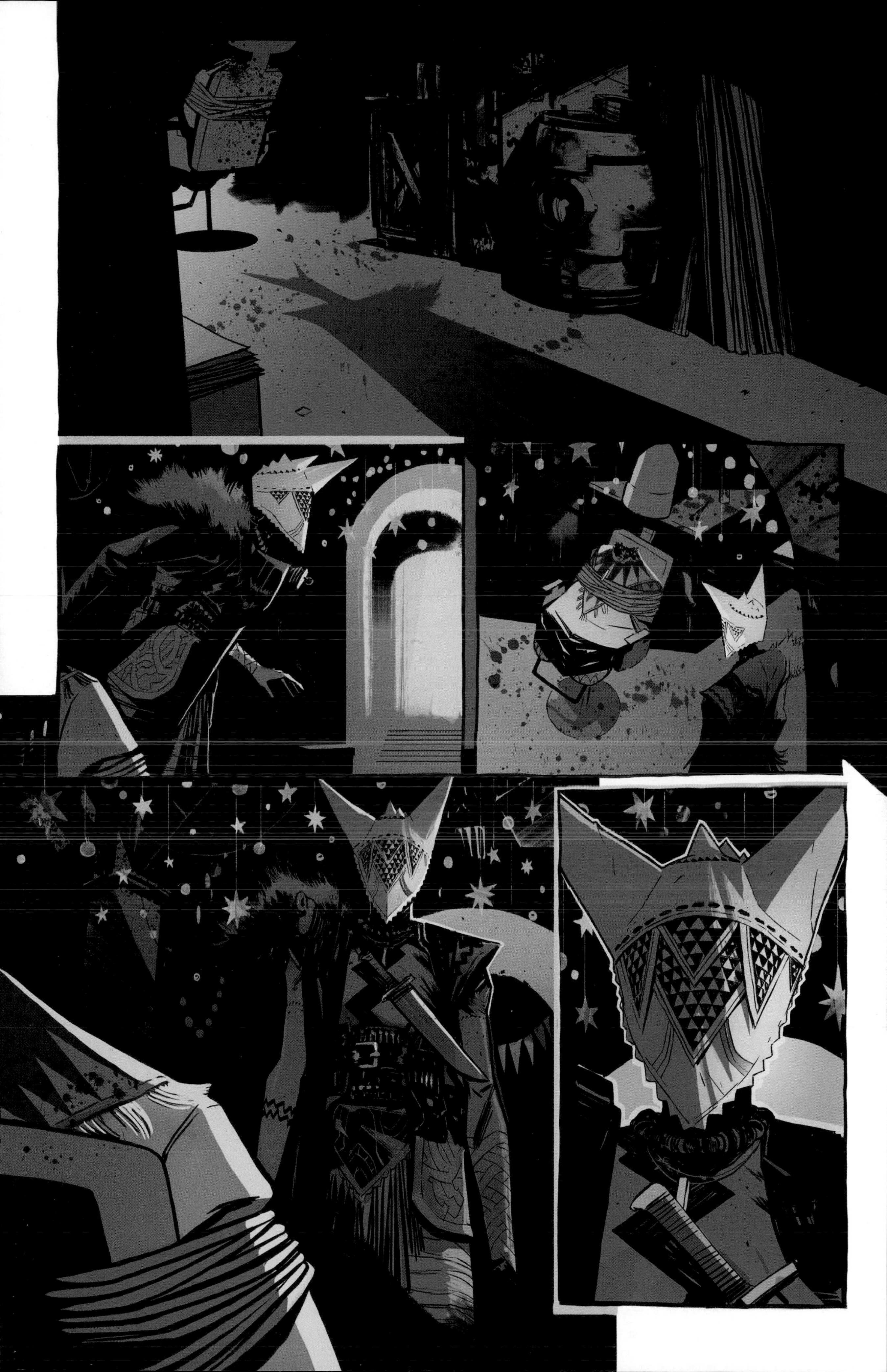

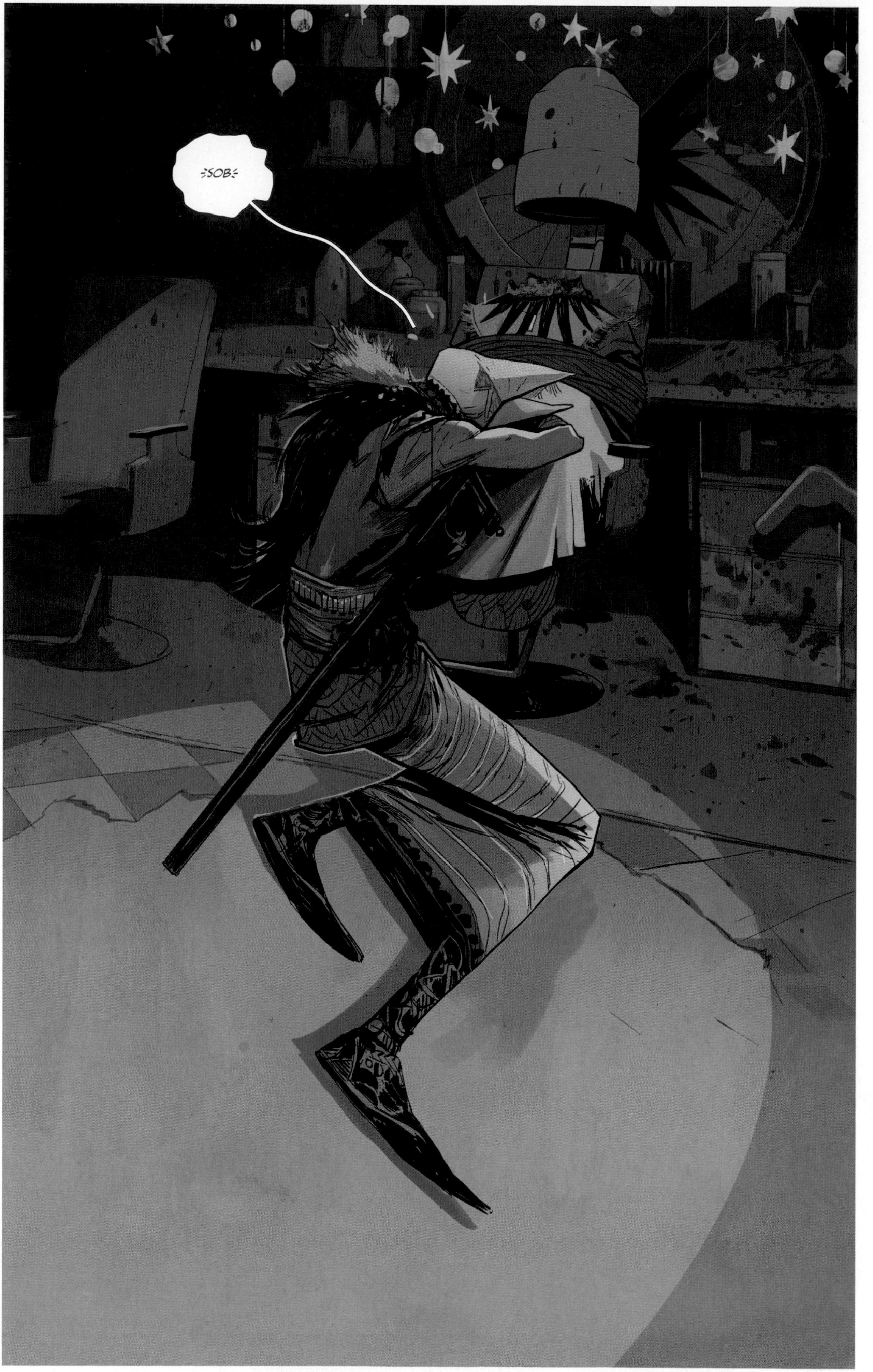
SOB

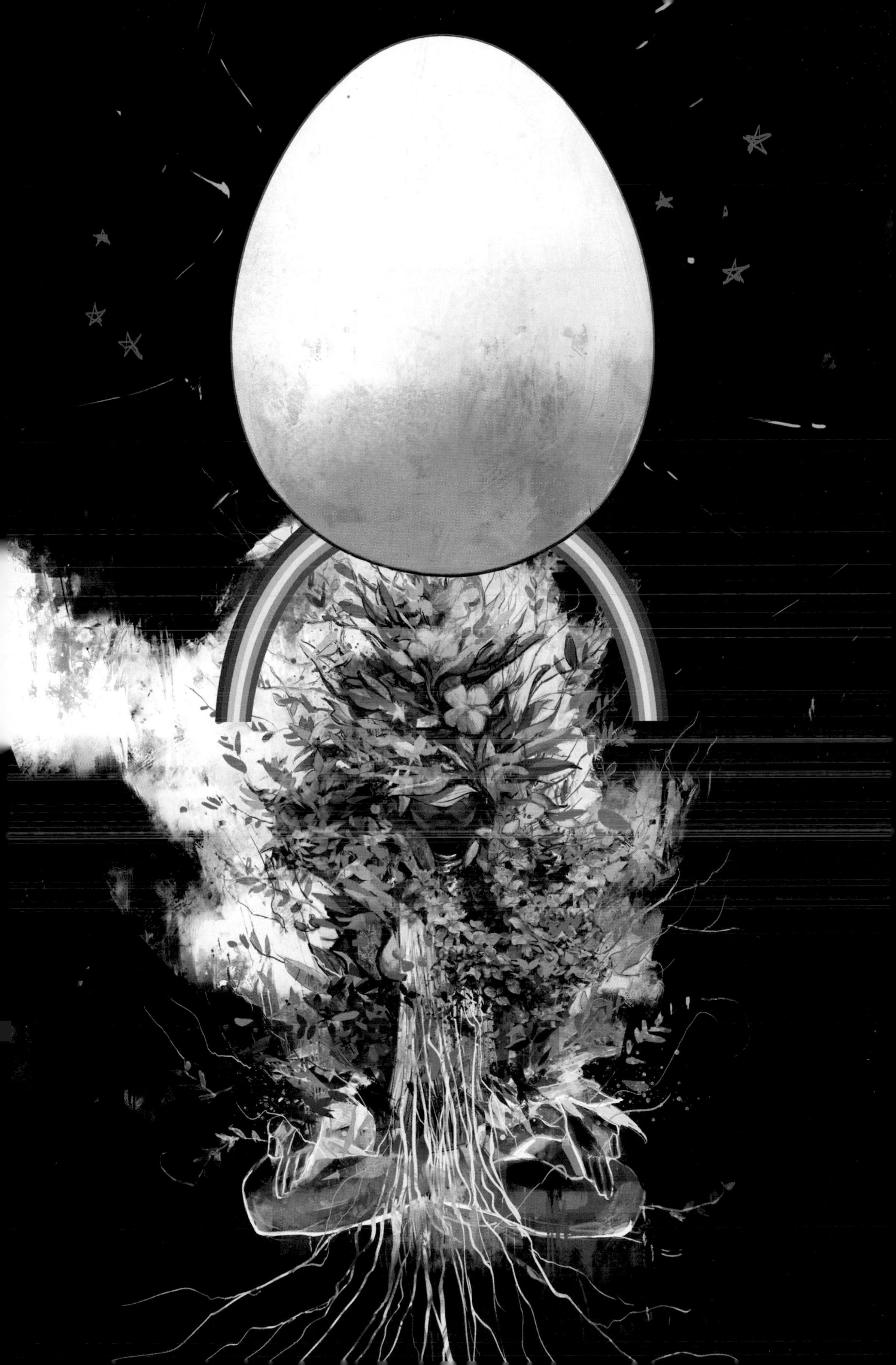

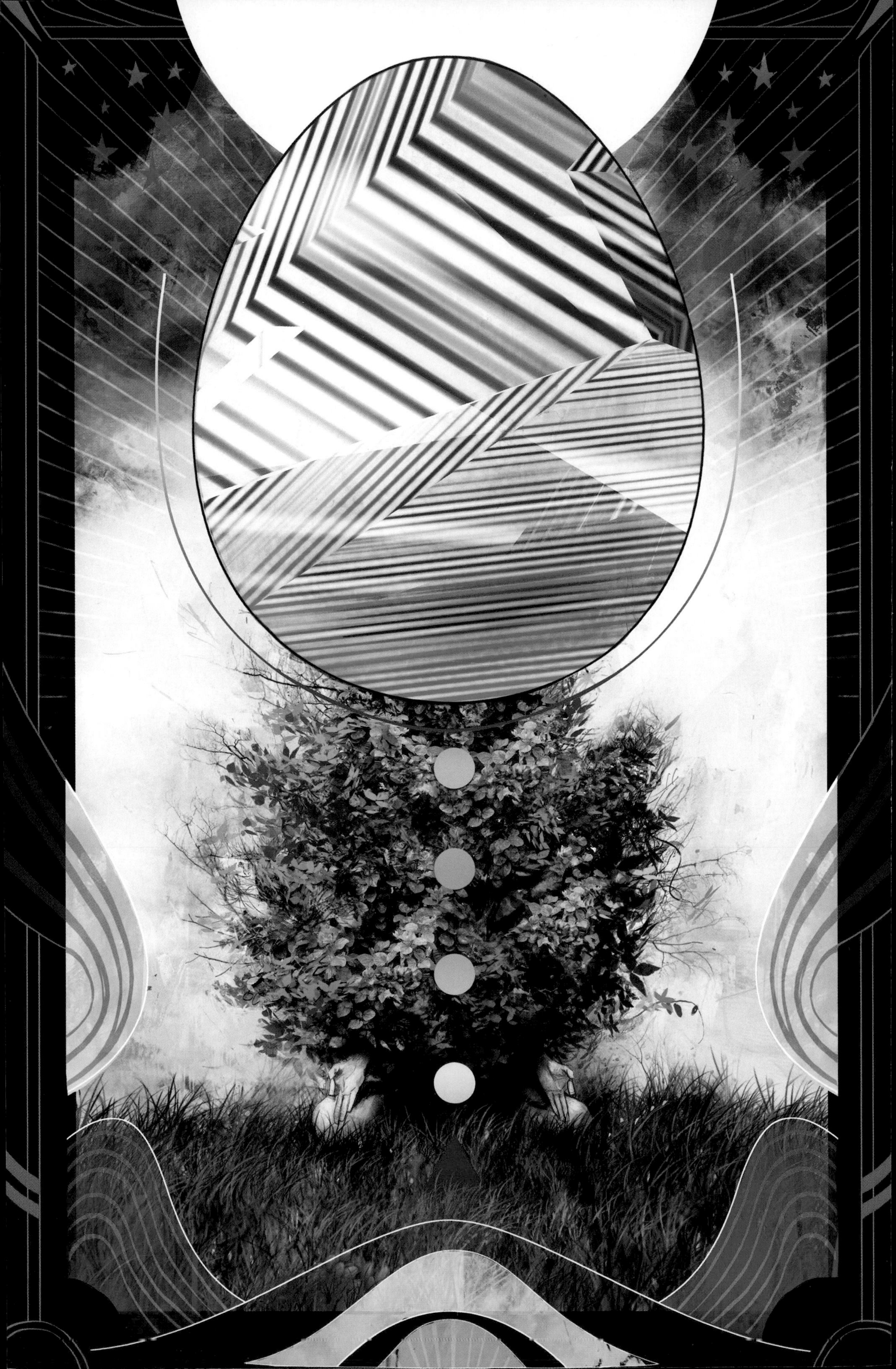

[+]

VI

[
AND THE ONE JOB YOU
REALLY NEED
]

CHAPTER THIRTEEN

[WORK LESS, MAKE MORE]

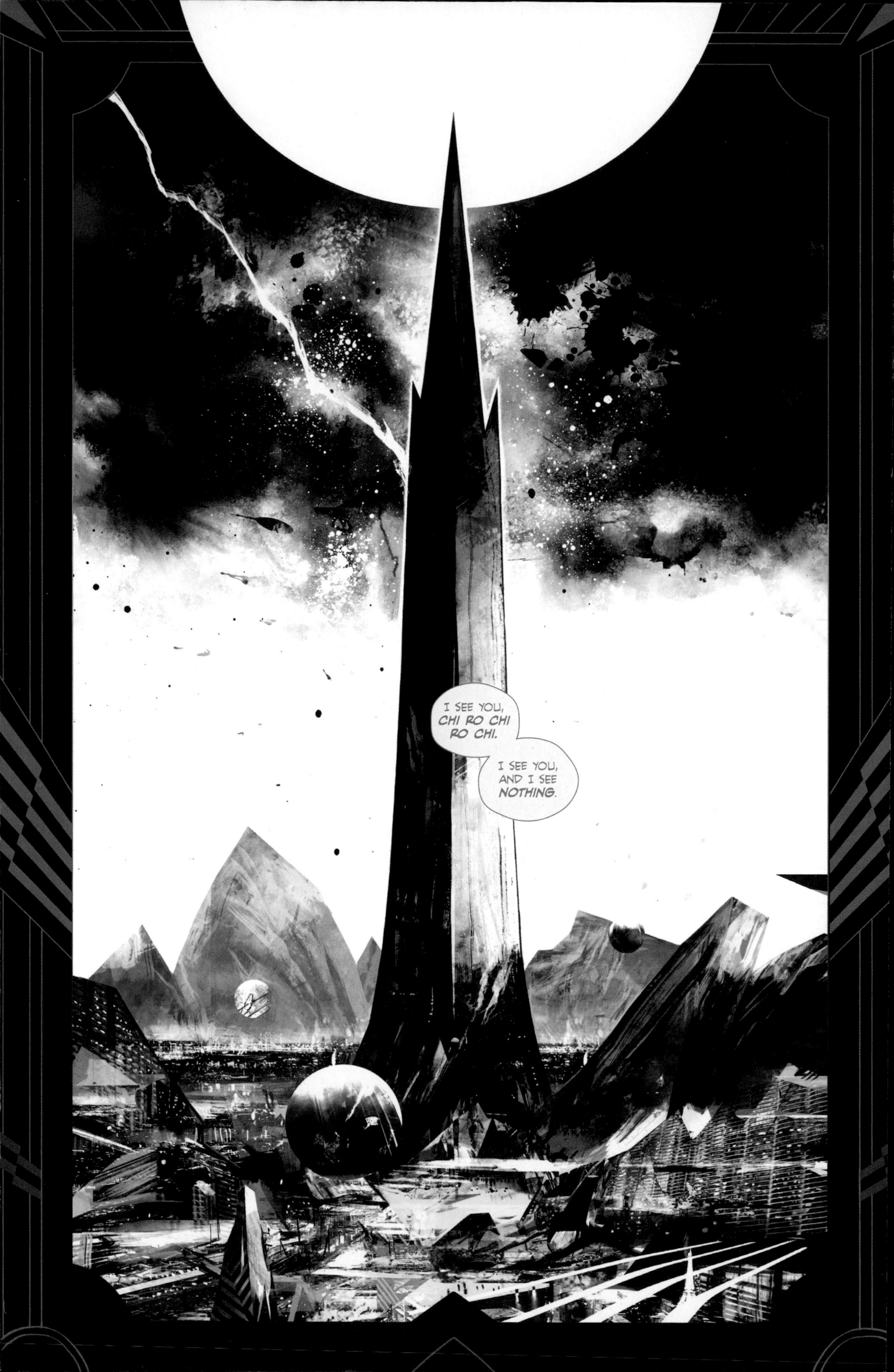
I SEE YOU, CHI RO CHI RO CHI.
I SEE YOU, AND I SEE NOTHING.

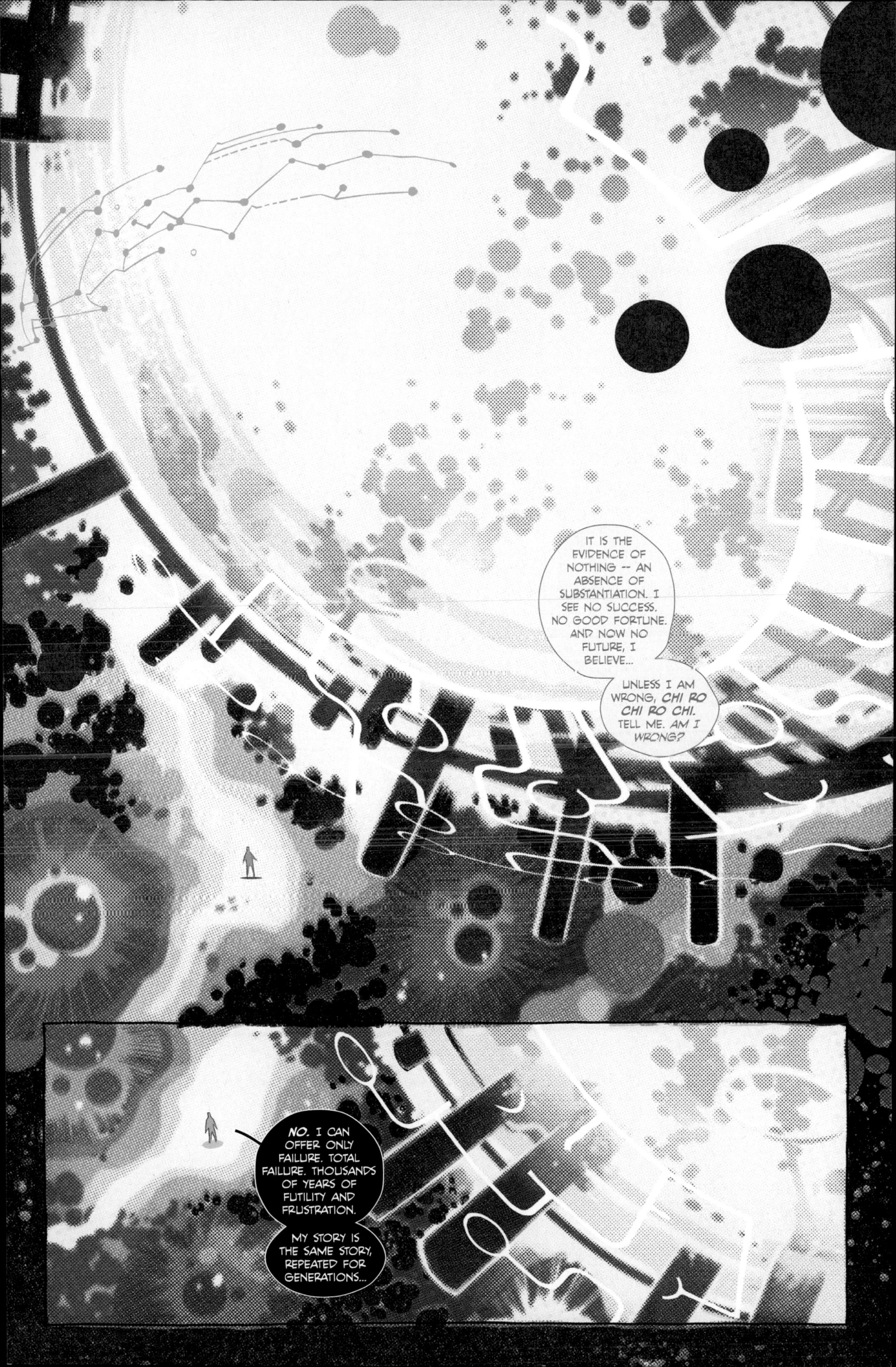
IT IS THE EVIDENCE OF NOTHING -- AN ABSENCE OF SUBSTANTIATION. I SEE NO SUCCESS. NO GOOD FORTUNE. AND NOW NO FUTURE, I BELIEVE...
UNLESS I AM WRONG, *CHI RO CHI RO CHI.* TELL ME. *AM I WRONG?*
NO. I CAN OFFER ONLY FAILURE. TOTAL FAILURE. THOUSANDS OF YEARS OF FUTILITY AND FRUSTRATION.
MY STORY IS THE SAME STORY, REPEATED FOR GENERATIONS...

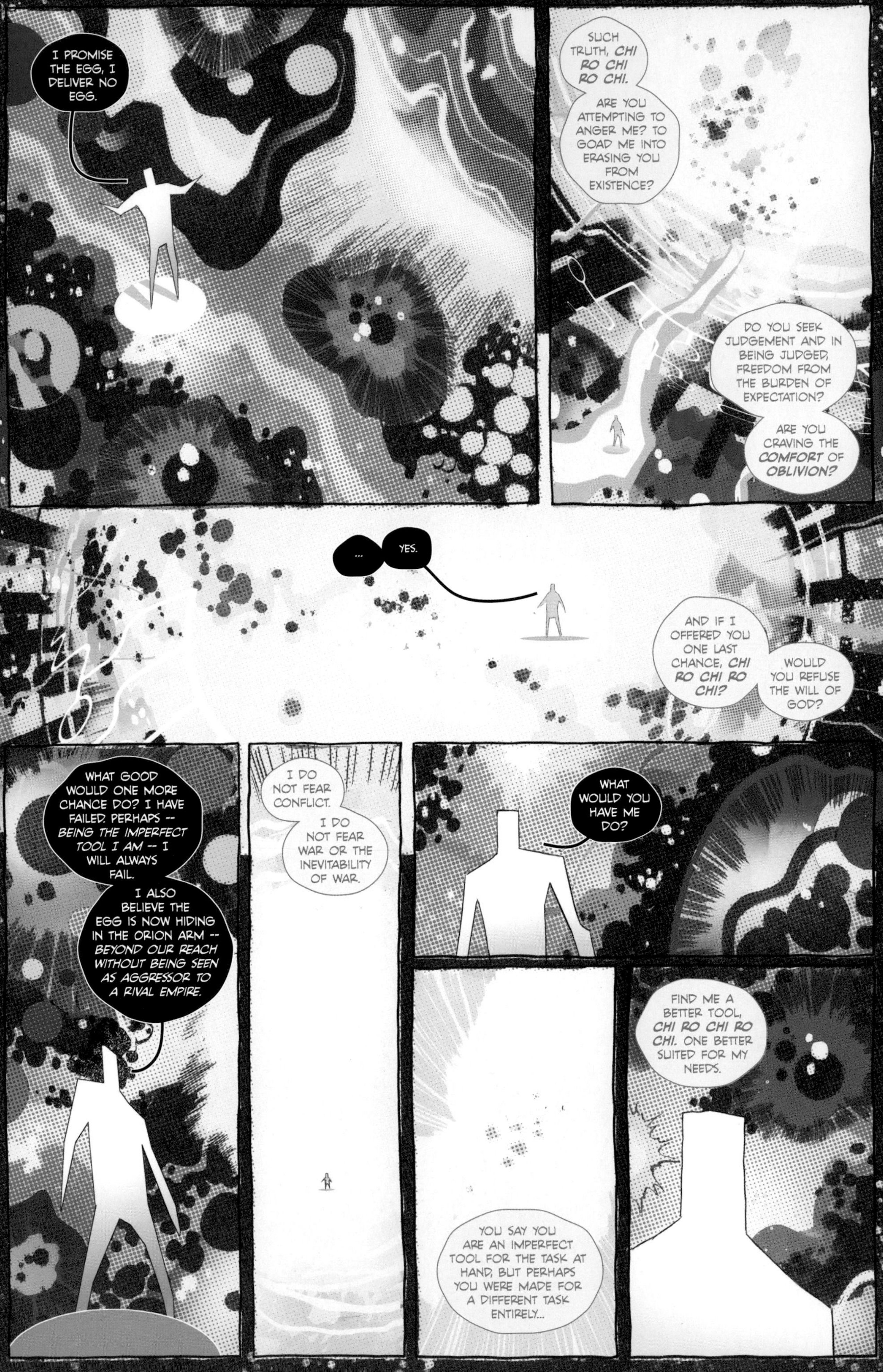
I PROMISE THE EGG, I DELIVER NO EGG.
SUCH TRUTH, CHI RO CHI RO CHI.
ARE YOU ATTEMPTING TO ANGER ME? TO GOAD ME INTO ERASING YOU FROM EXISTENCE?
DO YOU SEEK JUDGEMENT AND IN BEING JUDGED, FREEDOM FROM THE BURDEN OF EXPECTATION?
ARE YOU CRAVING THE COMFORT OF OBLIVION?
...
YES.
AND IF I OFFERED YOU ONE LAST CHANCE, CHI RO CHI RO CHI?
WOULD YOU REFUSE THE WILL OF GOD?
WHAT GOOD WOULD ONE MORE CHANCE DO? I HAVE FAILED. PERHAPS -- BEING THE IMPERFECT TOOL I AM -- I WILL ALWAYS FAIL.
I ALSO BELIEVE THE EGG IS NOW HIDING IN THE ORION ARM -- BEYOND OUR REACH WITHOUT BEING SEEN AS AGGRESSOR TO A RIVAL EMPIRE.
I DO NOT FEAR CONFLICT.
I DO NOT FEAR WAR OR THE INEVITABILITY OF WAR.
WHAT WOULD YOU HAVE ME DO?
YOU SAY YOU ARE AN IMPERFECT TOOL FOR THE TASK AT HAND, BUT PERHAPS YOU WERE MADE FOR A DIFFERENT TASK ENTIRELY...
FIND ME A BETTER TOOL, CHI RO CHI RO CHI. ONE BETTER SUITED FOR MY NEEDS.

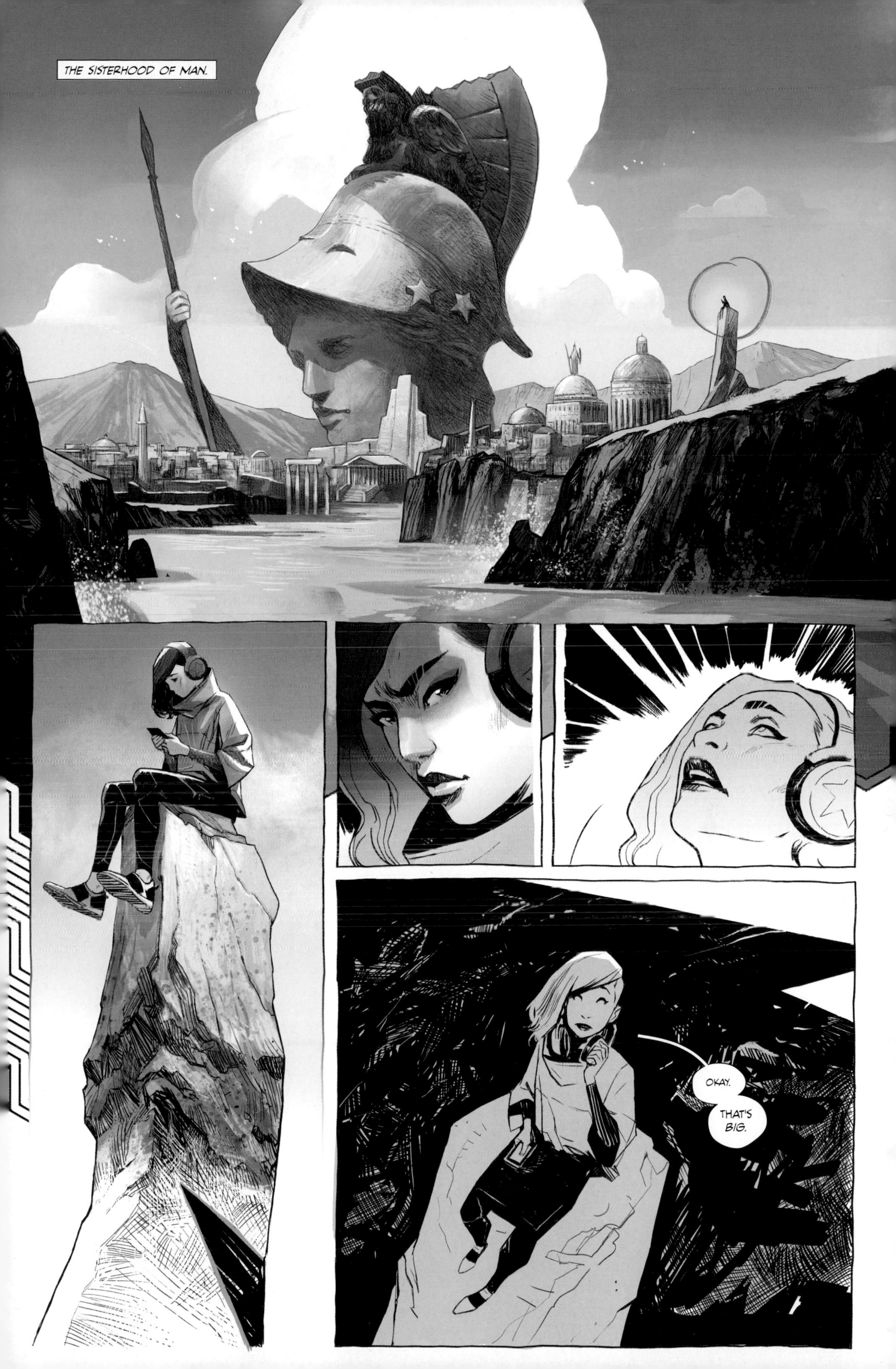
THE SISTERHOOD OF MAN.
OKAY.
THAT'S BIG.

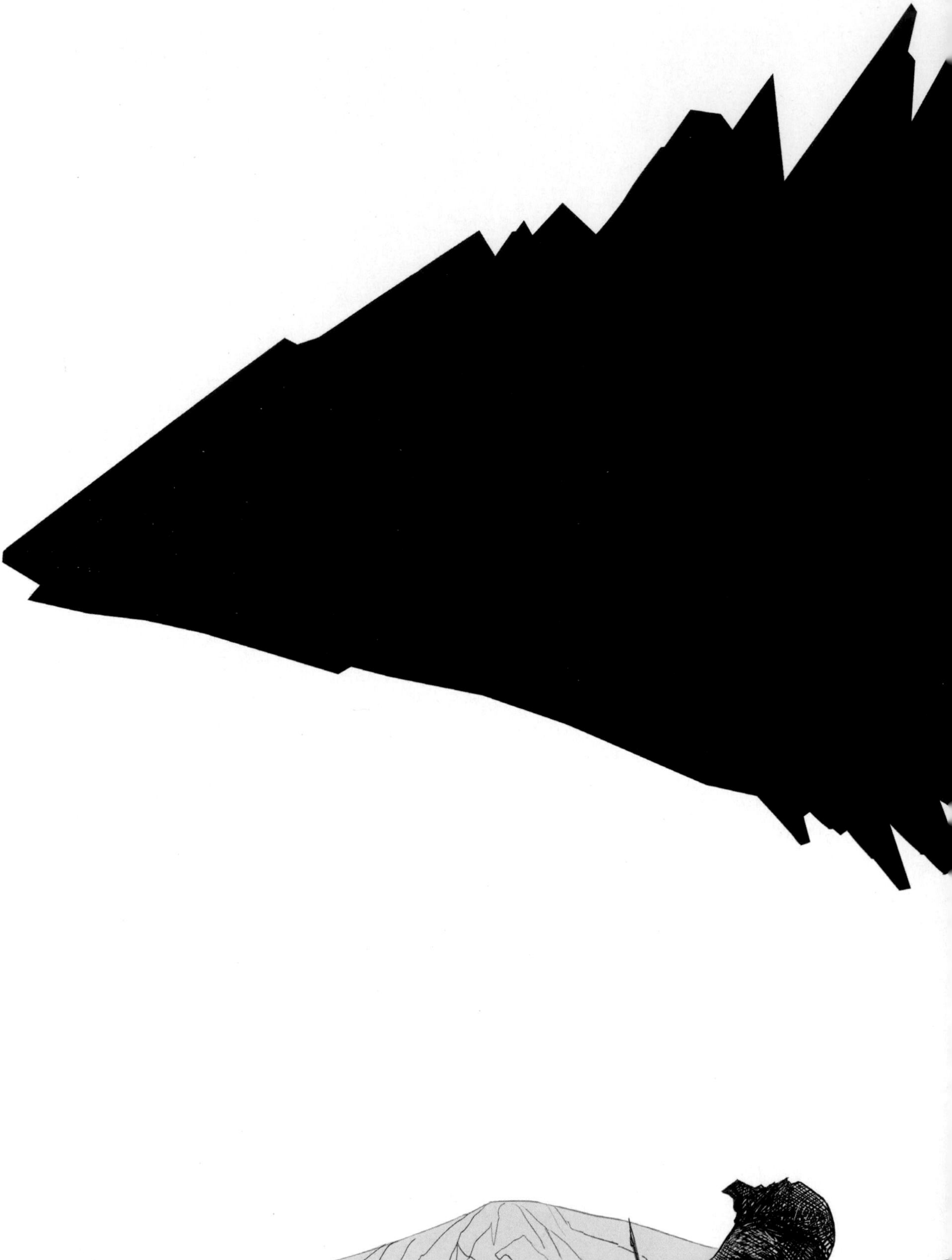

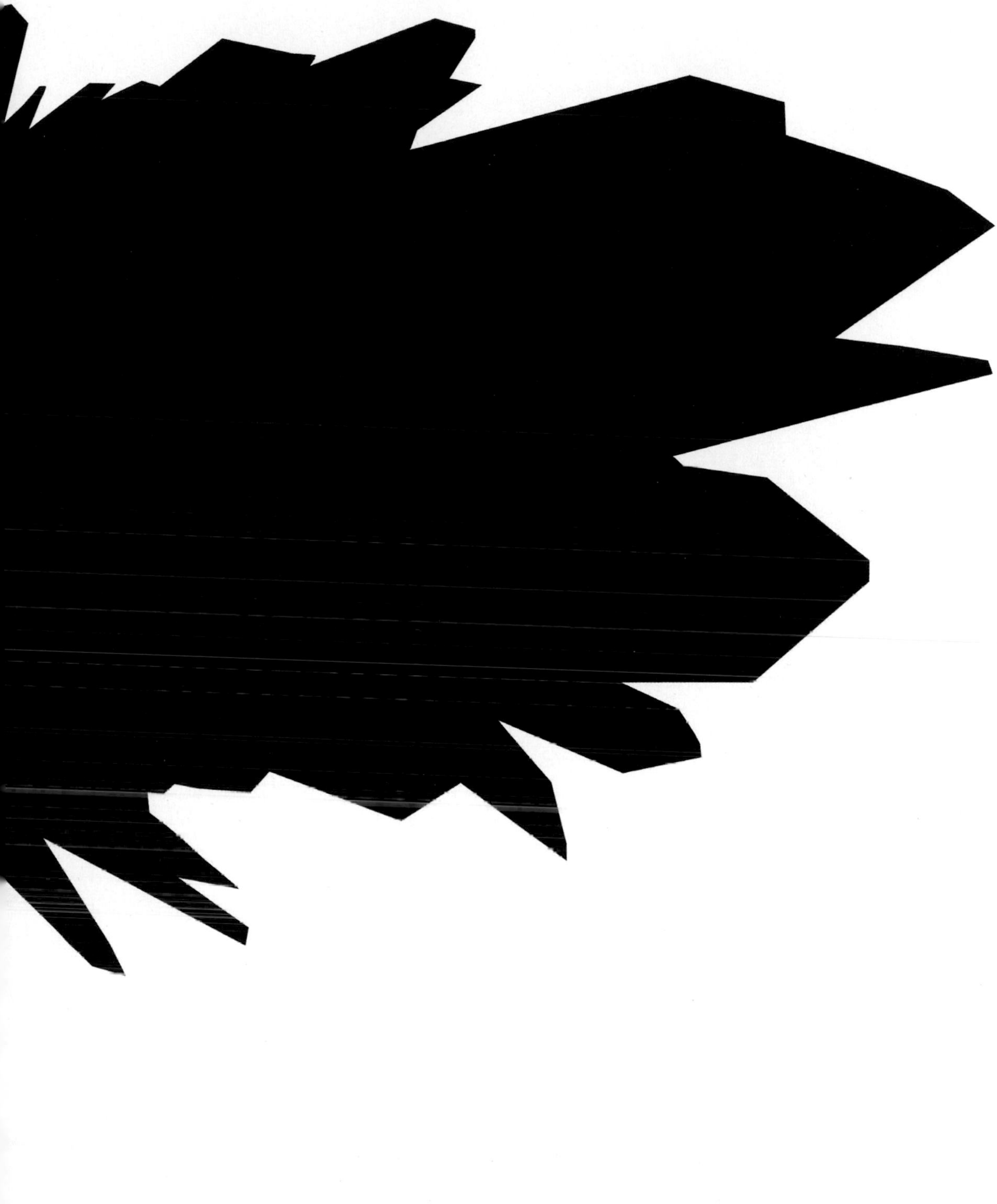

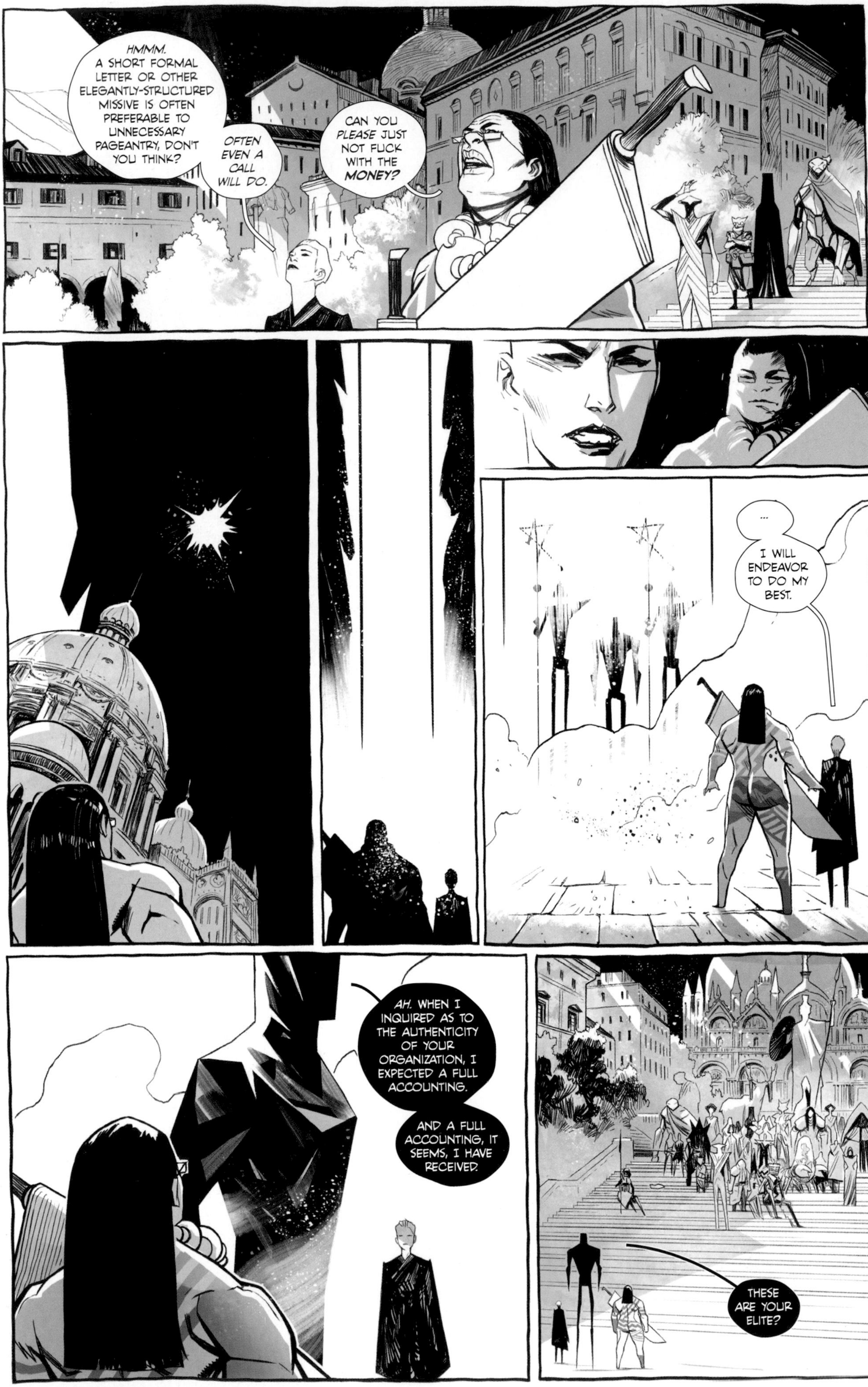
HMMM. A SHORT FORMAL LETTER OR OTHER ELEGANTLY-STRUCTURED MISSIVE IS OFTEN PREFERABLE TO UNNECESSARY PAGEANTRY, DON'T YOU THINK?
OFTEN EVEN A CALL WILL DO.
CAN YOU PLEASE JUST NOT FUCK WITH THE MONEY?
...
I WILL ENDEAVOR TO DO MY BEST.
AH. WHEN I INQUIRED AS TO THE AUTHENTICITY OF YOUR ORGANIZATION, I EXPECTED A FULL ACCOUNTING.
AND A FULL ACCOUNTING, IT SEEMS, I HAVE RECEIVED.
THESE ARE YOUR ELITE?

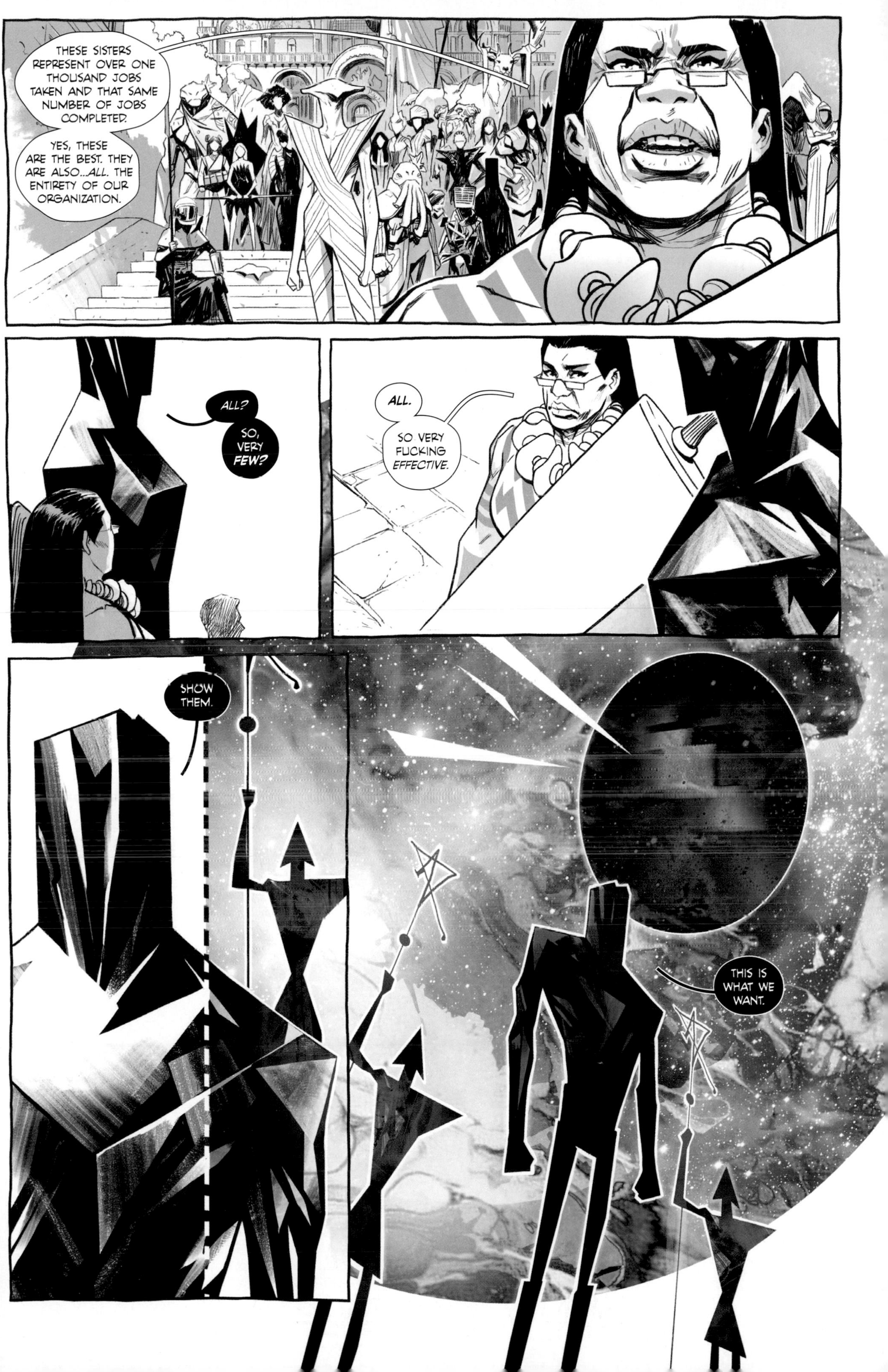
THESE SISTERS REPRESENT OVER ONE THOUSAND JOBS TAKEN AND THAT SAME NUMBER OF JOBS COMPLETED.
YES, THESE ARE THE BEST. THEY ARE ALSO...*ALL*. THE ENTIRETY OF OUR ORGANIZATION.
ALL?
SO, VERY *FEW?*
ALL.
SO VERY FUCKING *EFFECTIVE.*
SHOW THEM.
THIS IS WHAT WE WANT.

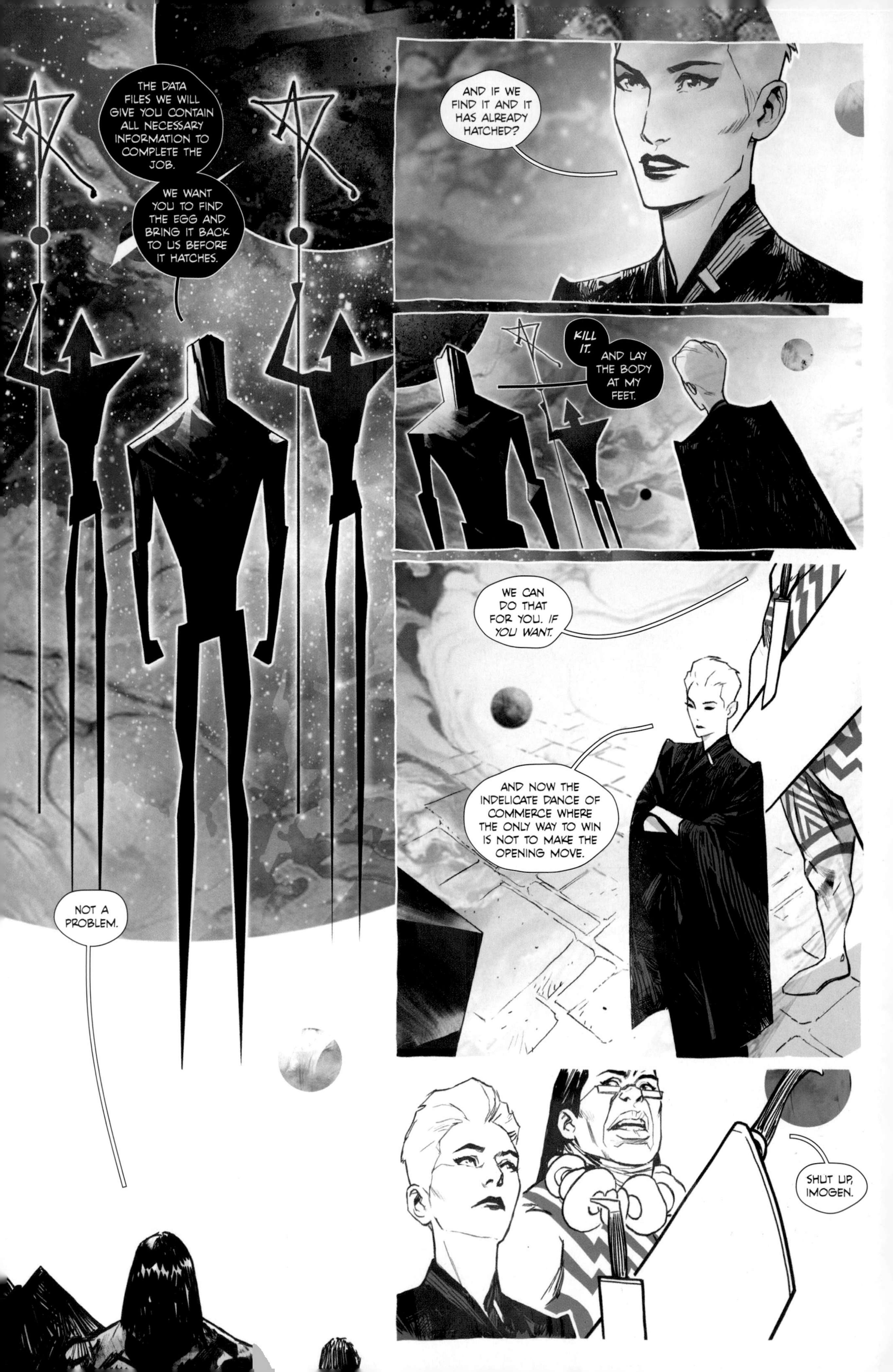
THE DATA FILES WE WILL GIVE YOU CONTAIN ALL NECESSARY INFORMATION TO COMPLETE THE JOB.
WE WANT YOU TO FIND THE EGG AND BRING IT BACK TO US BEFORE IT HATCHES.
AND IF WE FIND IT AND IT HAS ALREADY HATCHED?
KILL IT.
AND LAY THE BODY AT MY FEET.
WE CAN DO THAT FOR YOU. IF YOU WANT.
AND NOW THE INDELICATE DANCE OF COMMERCE WHERE THE ONLY WAY TO WIN IS NOT TO MAKE THE OPENING MOVE.
NOT A PROBLEM.
SHUT UP, IMOGEN.

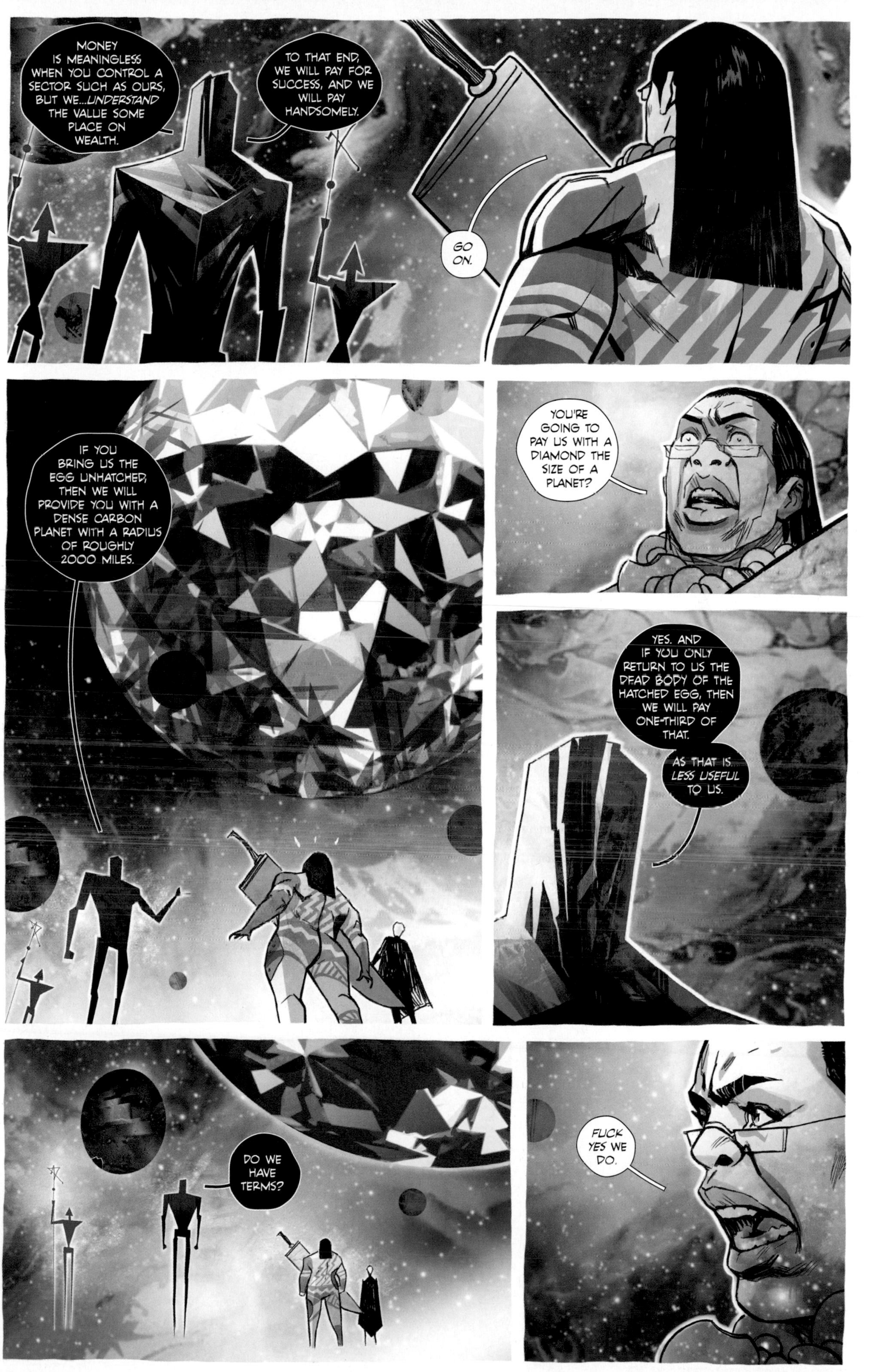
MONEY IS MEANINGLESS WHEN YOU CONTROL A SECTOR SUCH AS OURS, BUT WE...UNDERSTAND THE VALUE SOME PLACE ON WEALTH.
TO THAT END, WE WILL PAY FOR SUCCESS, AND WE WILL PAY HANDSOMELY.
GO ON.
IF YOU BRING US THE EGG UNHATCHED, THEN WE WILL PROVIDE YOU WITH A DENSE CARBON PLANET WITH A RADIUS OF ROUGHLY 2000 MILES.
YOU'RE GOING TO PAY US WITH A DIAMOND THE SIZE OF A PLANET?
YES. AND IF YOU ONLY RETURN TO US THE DEAD BODY OF THE HATCHED EGG, THEN WE WILL PAY ONE-THIRD OF THAT.
AS THAT IS... LESS USEFUL TO US.
DO WE HAVE TERMS?
FUCK YES WE DO.

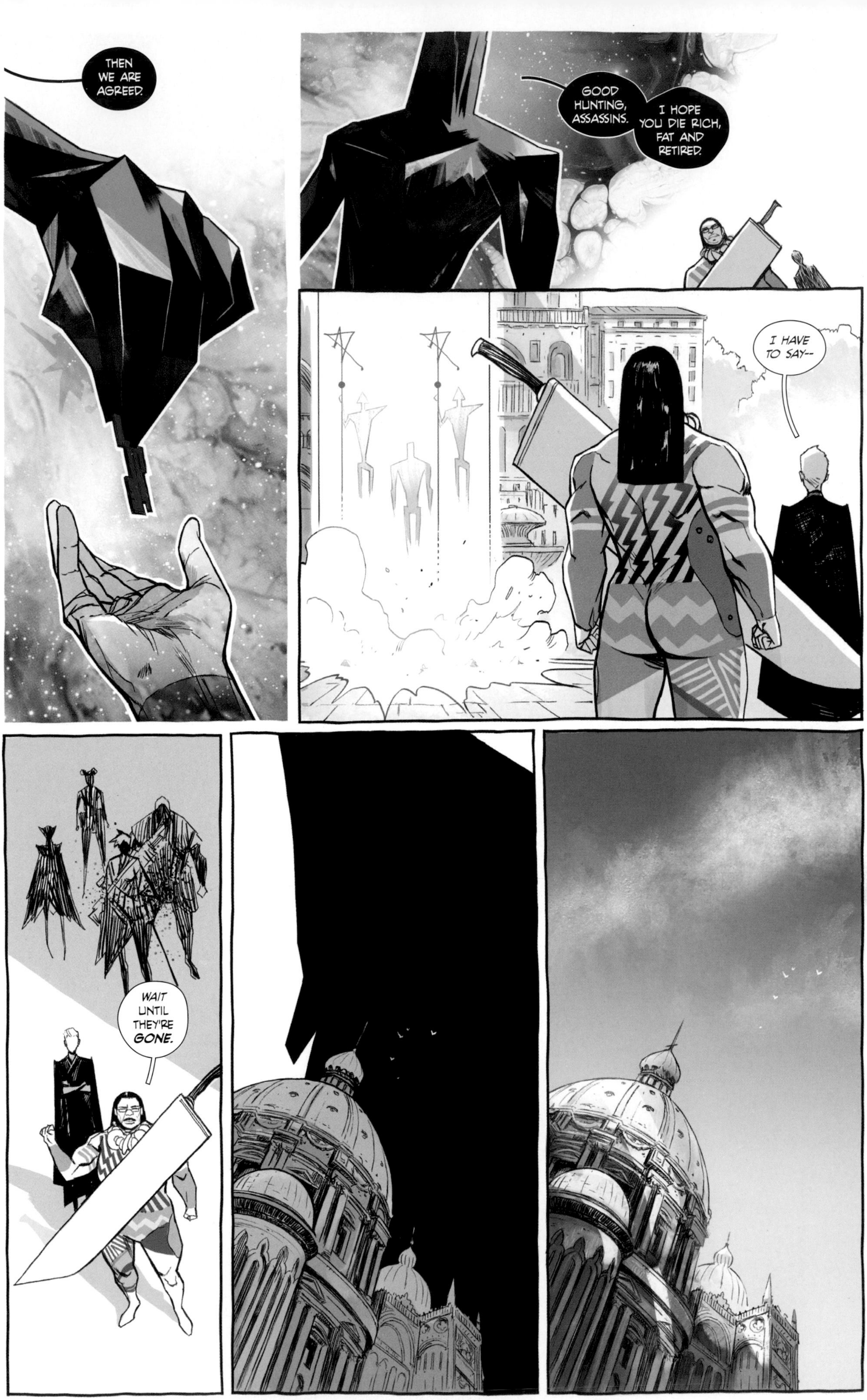
THEN WE ARE AGREED.
GOOD HUNTING, ASSASSINS.
I HOPE YOU DIE RICH, FAT AND RETIRED.
I HAVE TO SAY--
WAIT UNTIL THEY'RE GONE.

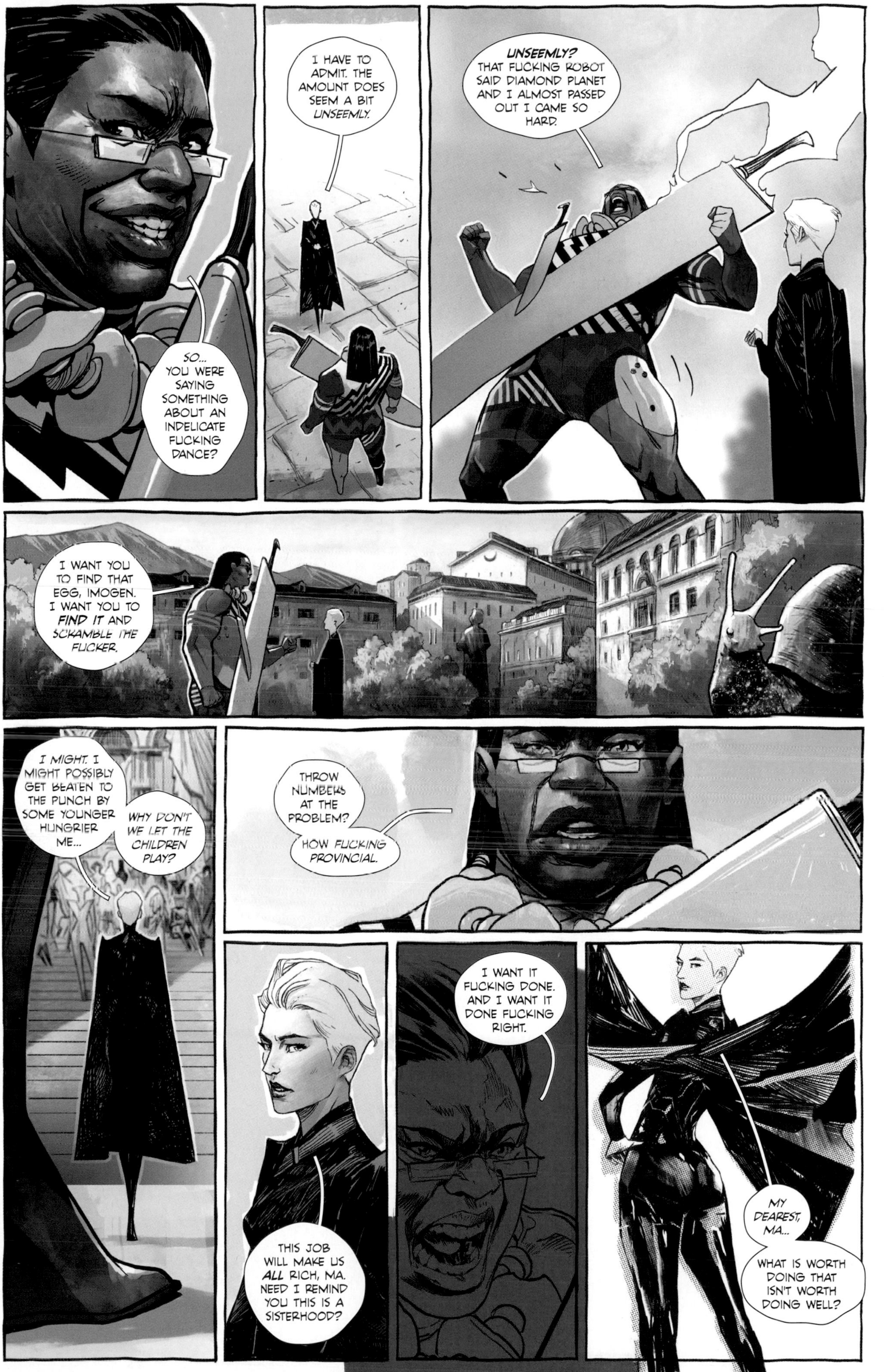

SO... YOU WERE SAYING SOMETHING ABOUT AN INDELICATE FUCKING DANCE?
I HAVE TO ADMIT. THE AMOUNT DOES SEEM A BIT UNSEEMLY.
UNSEEMLY? THAT FUCKING ROBOT SAID DIAMOND PLANET AND I ALMOST PASSED OUT I CAME SO HARD.
I WANT YOU TO FIND THAT EGG, IMOGEN. I WANT YOU TO FIND IT AND SCRAMBLE THE FUCKER.
I MIGHT. I MIGHT POSSIBLY GET BEATEN TO THE PUNCH BY SOME YOUNGER HUNGRIER ME...
WHY DON'T WE LET THE CHILDREN PLAY?
THROW NUMBERS AT THE PROBLEM?
HOW FUCKING PROVINCIAL.
THIS JOB WILL MAKE US ALL RICH, MA. NEED I REMIND YOU THIS IS A SISTERHOOD?
I WANT IT FUCKING DONE. AND I WANT IT DONE FUCKING RIGHT.
MY DEAREST, MA...
WHAT IS WORTH DOING THAT ISN'T WORTH DOING WELL?

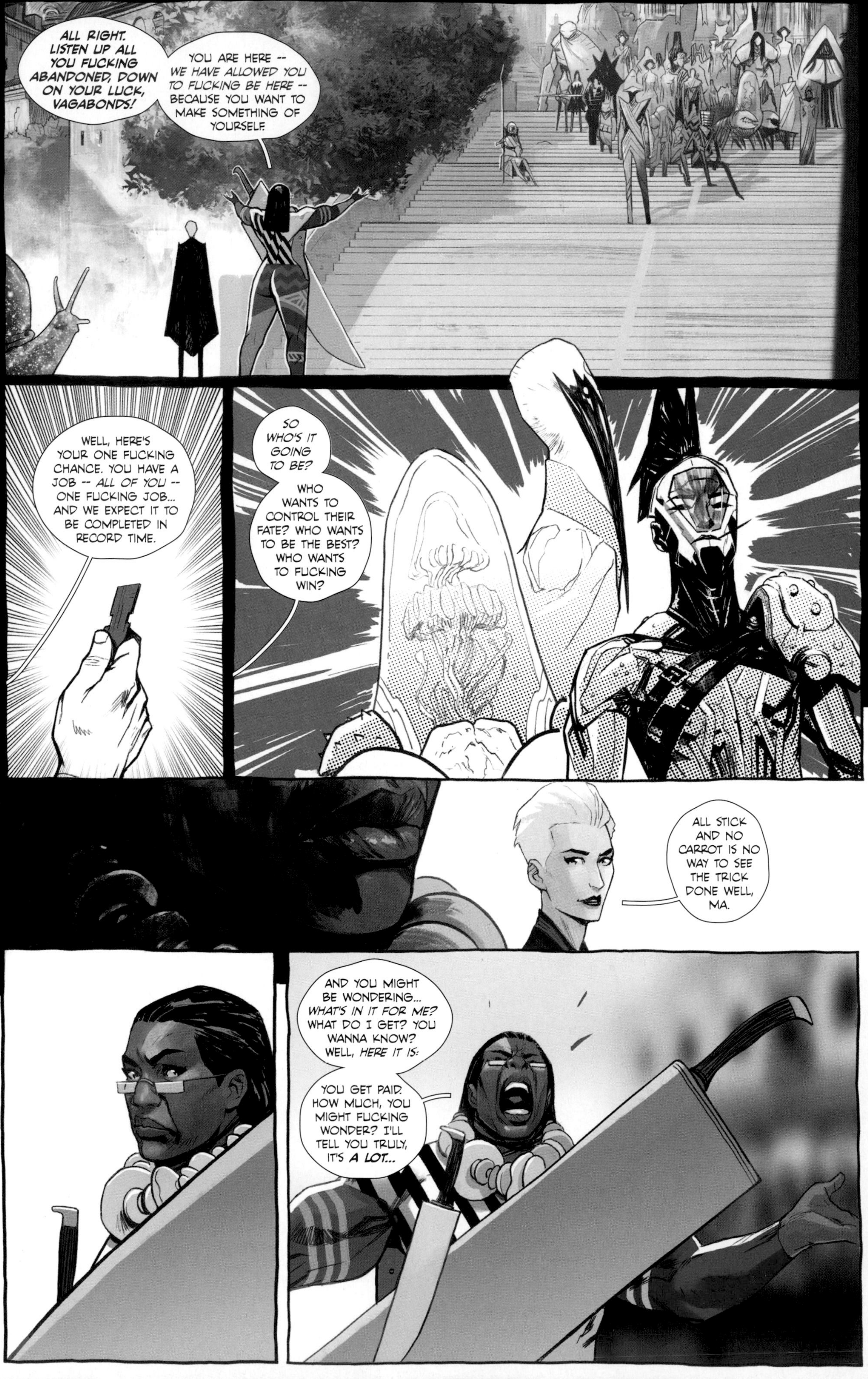
ALL RIGHT. LISTEN UP ALL YOU FUCKING ABANDONED, DOWN ON YOUR LUCK, VAGABONDS!
YOU ARE HERE -- WE HAVE ALLOWED YOU TO FUCKING BE HERE -- BECAUSE YOU WANT TO MAKE SOMETHING OF YOURSELF.
WELL, HERE'S YOUR ONE FUCKING CHANCE. YOU HAVE A JOB -- ALL OF YOU -- ONE FUCKING JOB... AND WE EXPECT IT TO BE COMPLETED IN RECORD TIME.
SO WHO'S IT GOING TO BE?
WHO WANTS TO CONTROL THEIR FATE? WHO WANTS TO BE THE BEST? WHO WANTS TO FUCKING WIN?
ALL STICK AND NO CARROT IS NO WAY TO SEE THE TRICK DONE WELL, MA.
AND YOU MIGHT BE WONDERING... WHAT'S IN IT FOR ME? WHAT DO I GET? YOU WANNA KNOW? WELL, HERE IT IS:
YOU GET PAID. HOW MUCH, YOU MIGHT FUCKING WONDER? I'LL TELL YOU TRULY, IT'S A LOT...

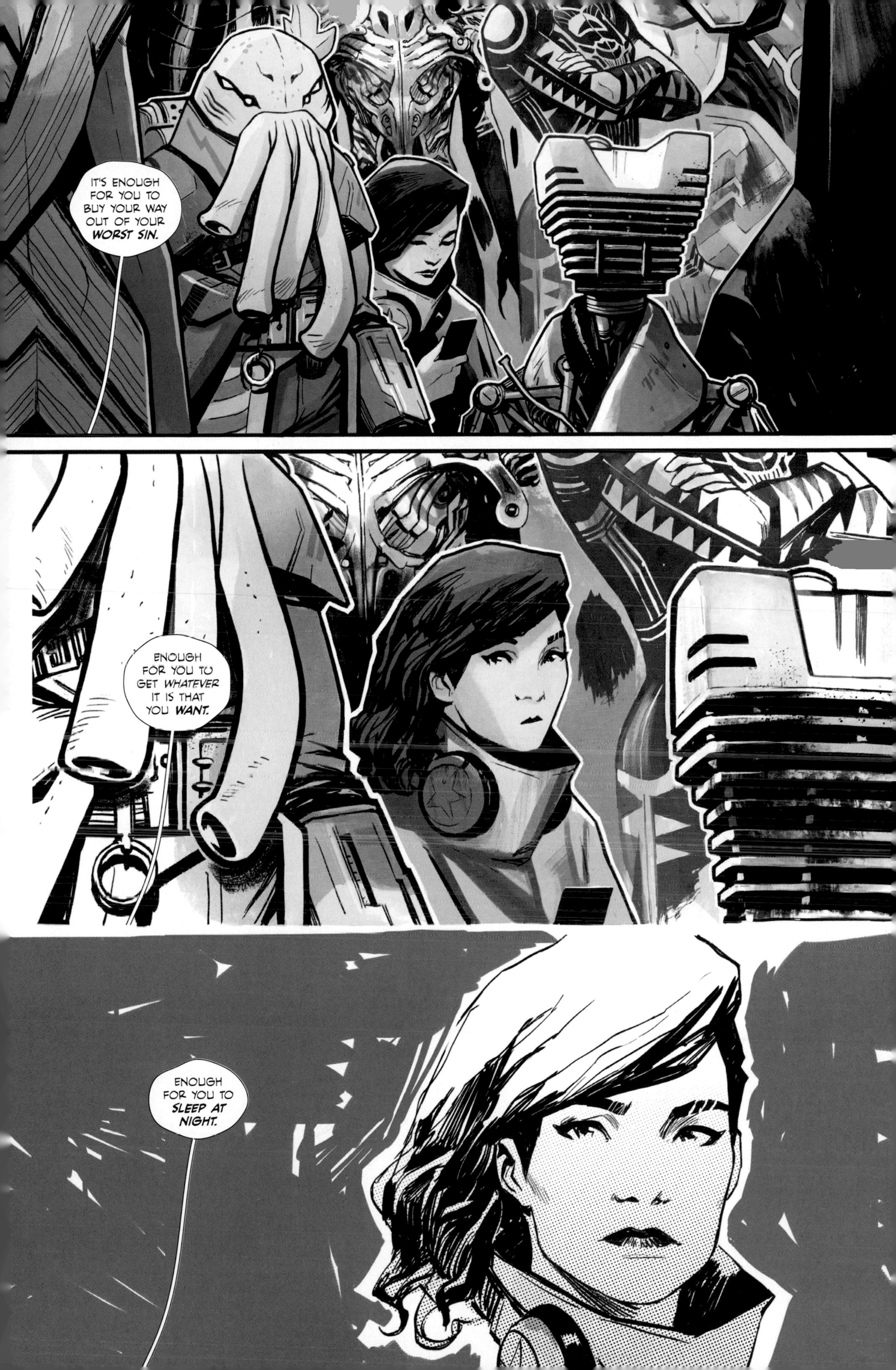

IT'S ENOUGH FOR YOU TO BUY YOUR WAY OUT OF YOUR *WORST SIN.*
ENOUGH FOR YOU TO GET *WHATEVER* IT IS THAT YOU *WANT.*
ENOUGH FOR YOU TO *SLEEP AT NIGHT.*

CHAPTER FOURTEEN

[PACK YOUR BAGS FOR A ONE WAY TRIP]

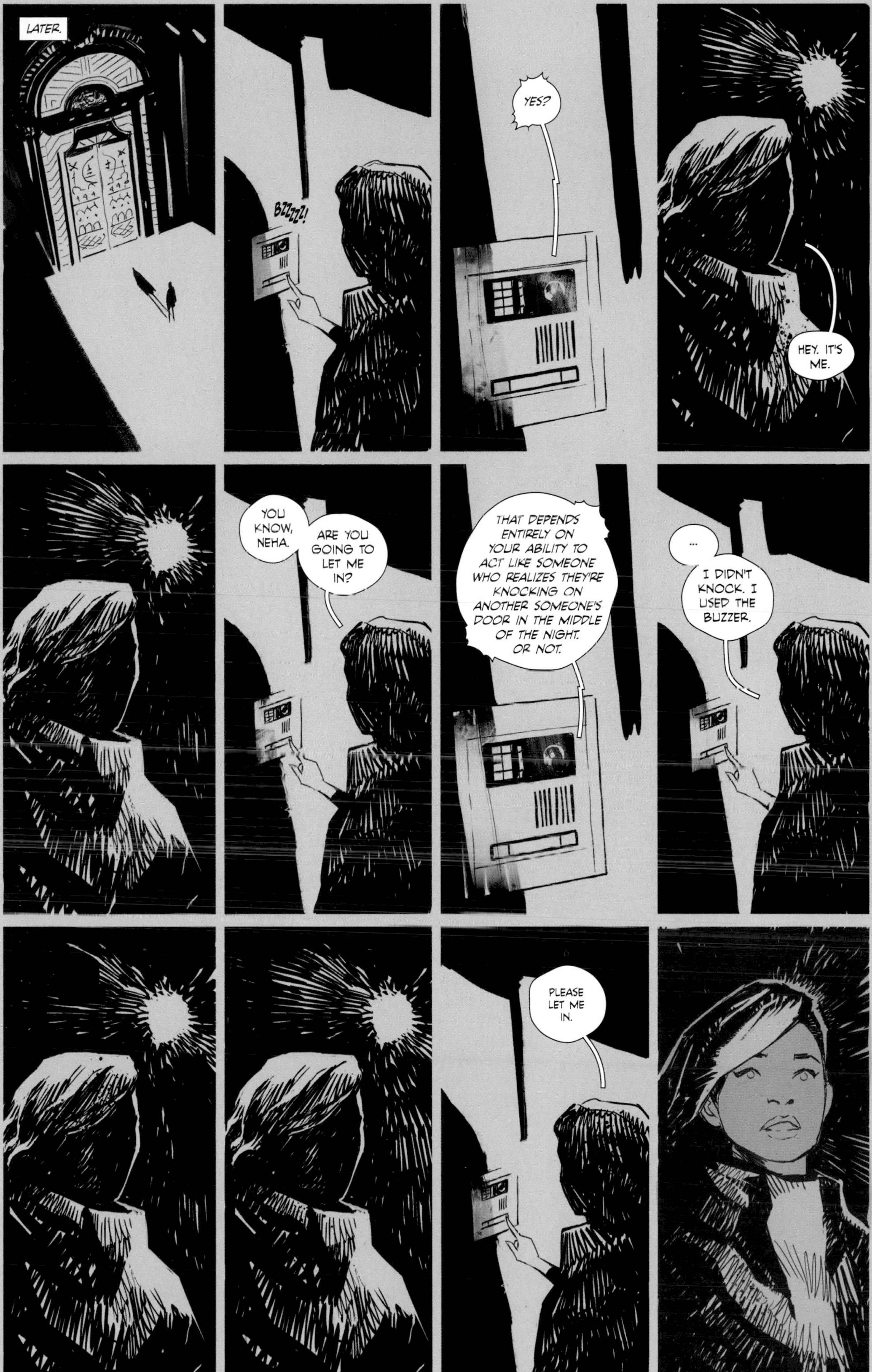
LATER.
BZZZZZ!
YES?
HEY. IT'S ME.
YOU KNOW, NEHA.
ARE YOU GOING TO LET ME IN?
THAT DEPENDS ENTIRELY ON YOUR ABILITY TO ACT LIKE SOMEONE WHO REALIZES THEY'RE KNOCKING ON ANOTHER SOMEONE'S DOOR IN THE MIDDLE OF THE NIGHT. OR NOT.
...
I DIDN'T KNOCK. I USED THE BUZZER.
PLEASE LET ME IN.

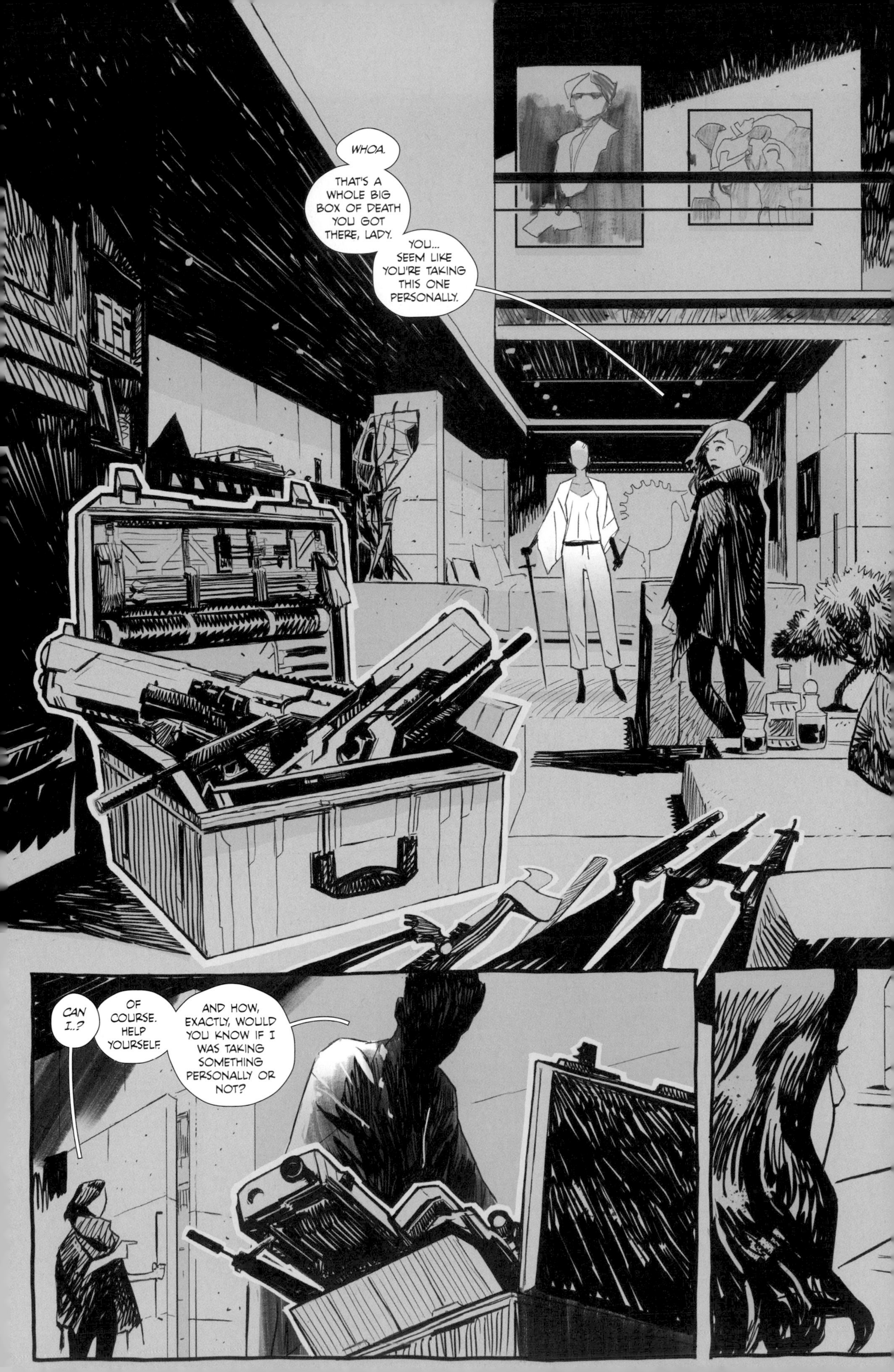
WHOA.
THAT'S A WHOLE BIG BOX OF DEATH YOU GOT THERE, LADY.
YOU... SEEM LIKE YOU'RE TAKING THIS ONE PERSONALLY.
CAN I..?
OF COURSE. HELP YOURSELF.
AND HOW, EXACTLY, WOULD YOU KNOW IF I WAS TAKING SOMETHING PERSONALLY OR NOT?

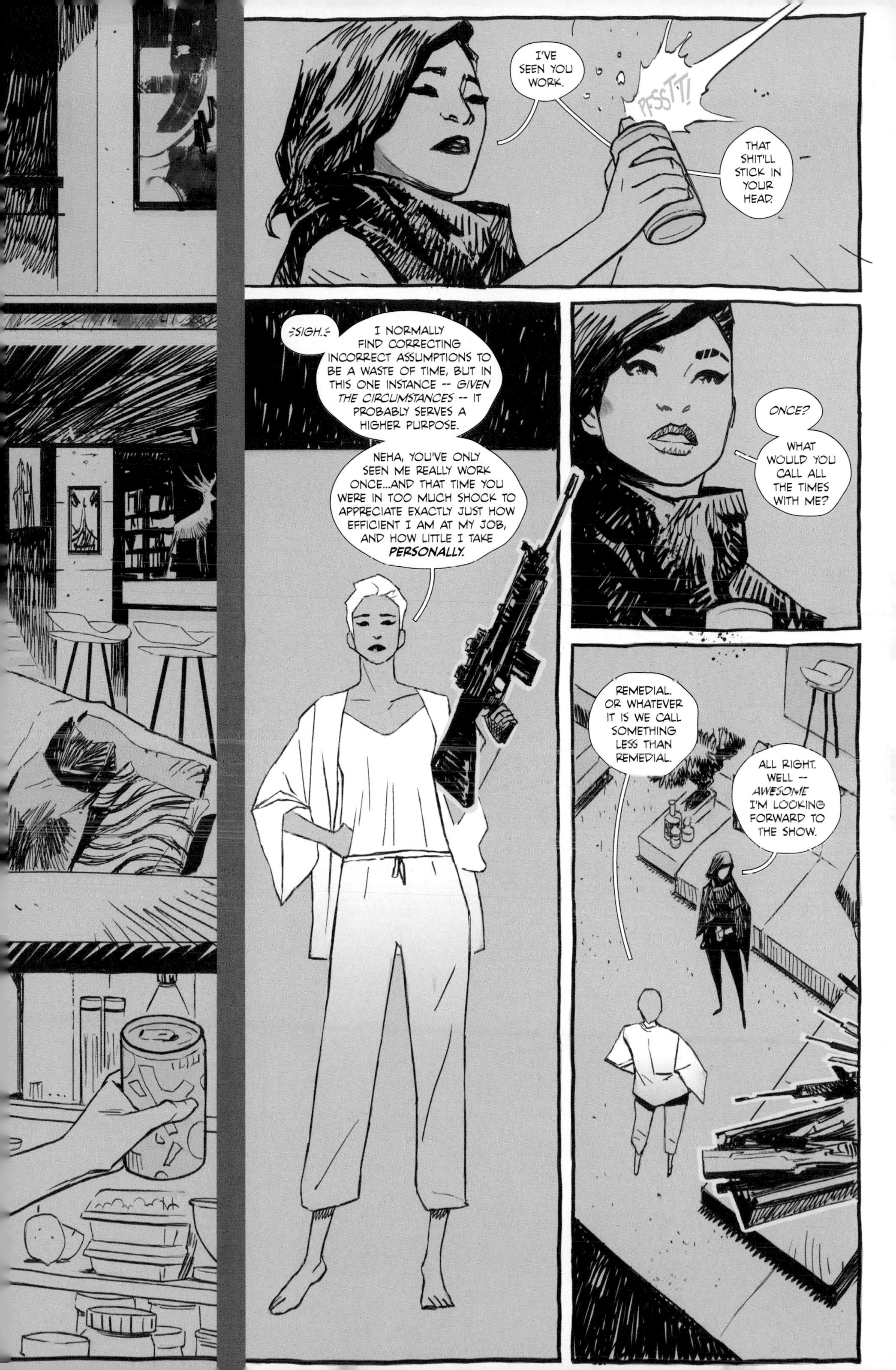

I'VE SEEN YOU WORK.
PFSSTT!
THAT SHIT'LL STICK IN YOUR HEAD.
≈SIGH.≈
I NORMALLY FIND CORRECTING INCORRECT ASSUMPTIONS TO BE A WASTE OF TIME, BUT IN THIS ONE INSTANCE -- GIVEN THE CIRCUMSTANCES -- IT PROBABLY SERVES A HIGHER PURPOSE.
NEHA, YOU'VE ONLY SEEN ME REALLY WORK ONCE...AND THAT TIME YOU WERE IN TOO MUCH SHOCK TO APPRECIATE EXACTLY JUST HOW EFFICIENT I AM AT MY JOB, AND HOW LITTLE I TAKE PERSONALLY.
ONCE?
WHAT WOULD YOU CALL ALL THE TIMES WITH ME?
REMEDIAL. OR WHATEVER IT IS WE CALL SOMETHING LESS THAN REMEDIAL.
ALL RIGHT. WELL -- AWESOME. I'M LOOKING FORWARD TO THE SHOW.

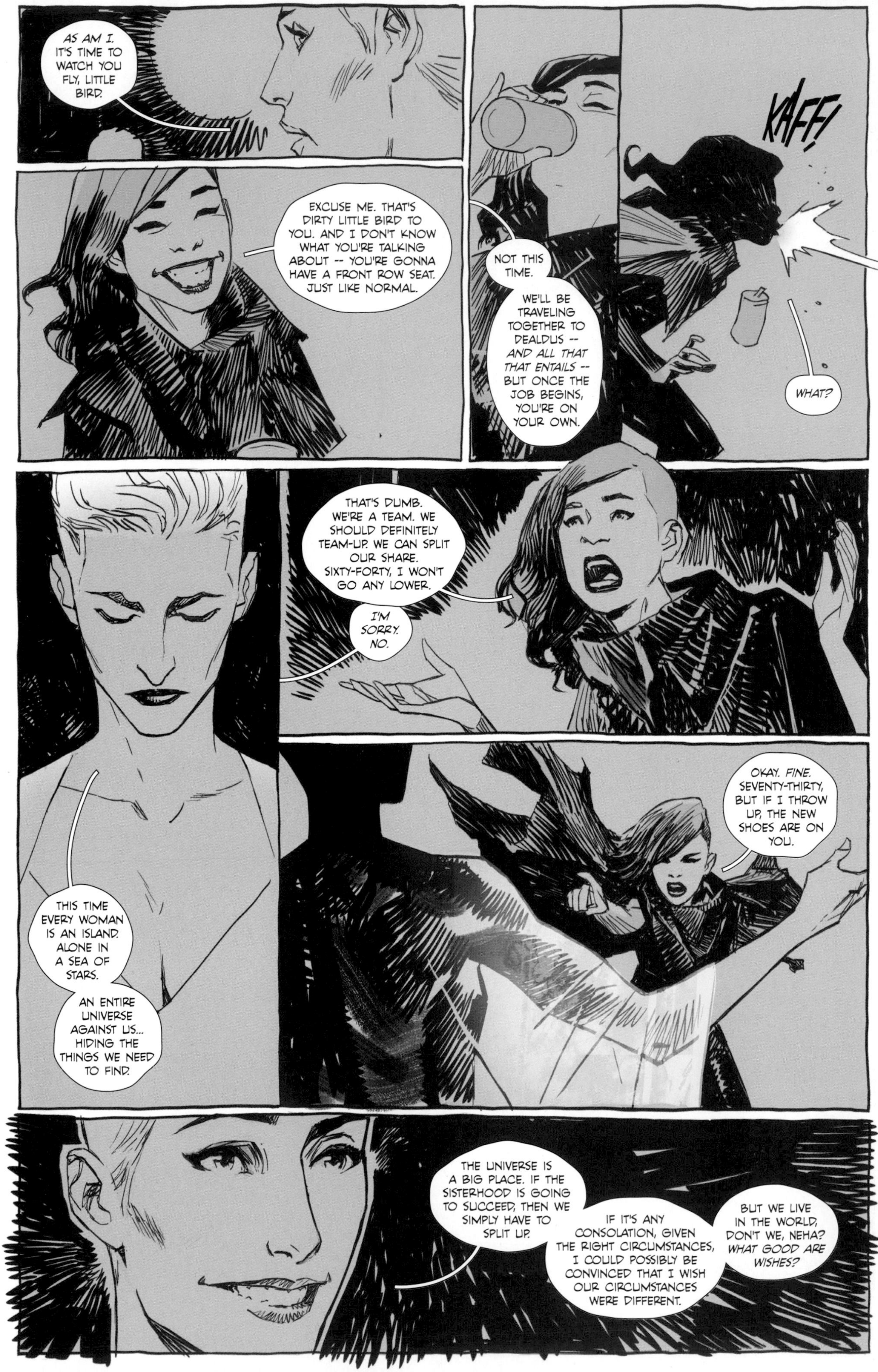
AS AM I. IT'S TIME TO WATCH YOU FLY, LITTLE BIRD.
EXCUSE ME. THAT'S DIRTY LITTLE BIRD TO YOU. AND I DON'T KNOW WHAT YOU'RE TALKING ABOUT -- YOU'RE GONNA HAVE A FRONT ROW SEAT. JUST LIKE NORMAL.
NOT THIS TIME.
WE'LL BE TRAVELING TOGETHER TO DEALDUS -- AND ALL THAT THAT ENTAILS -- BUT ONCE THE JOB BEGINS, YOU'RE ON YOUR OWN.
KAFF!
WHAT?
THAT'S DUMB. WE'RE A TEAM. WE SHOULD DEFINITELY TEAM-UP. WE CAN SPLIT OUR SHARE. SIXTY-FORTY, I WON'T GO ANY LOWER.
I'M SORRY. NO.
THIS TIME EVERY WOMAN IS AN ISLAND. ALONE IN A SEA OF STARS.
AN ENTIRE UNIVERSE AGAINST US... HIDING THE THINGS WE NEED TO FIND.
OKAY. FINE. SEVENTY-THIRTY, BUT IF I THROW UP, THE NEW SHOES ARE ON YOU.
THE UNIVERSE IS A BIG PLACE. IF THE SISTERHOOD IS GOING TO SUCCEED, THEN WE SIMPLY HAVE TO SPLIT UP.
IF IT'S ANY CONSOLATION, GIVEN THE RIGHT CIRCUMSTANCES, I COULD POSSIBLY BE CONVINCED THAT I WISH OUR CIRCUMSTANCES WERE DIFFERENT.
BUT WE LIVE IN THE WORLD, DON'T WE, NEHA? WHAT GOOD ARE WISHES?

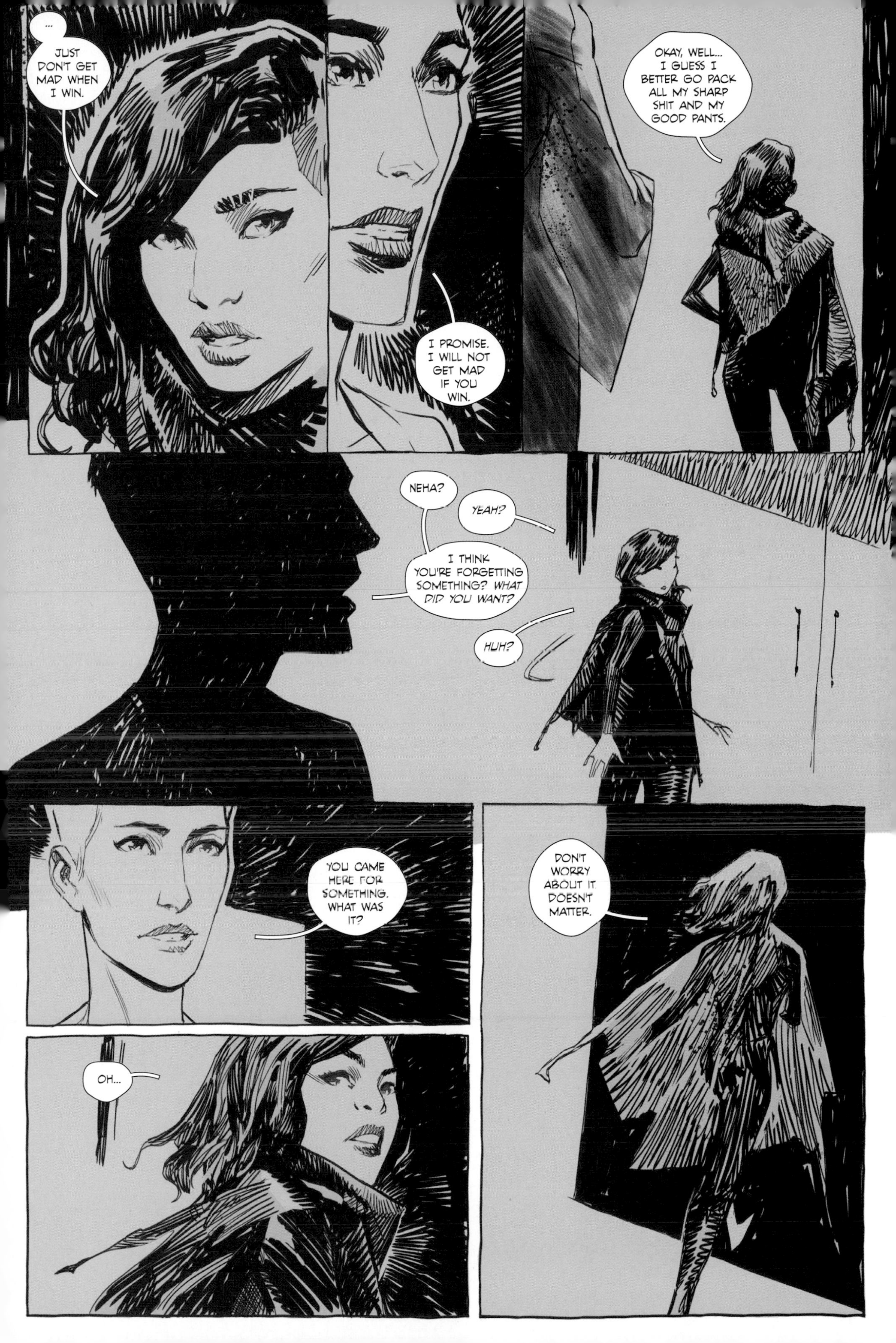
...
JUST DON'T GET MAD WHEN I WIN.
I PROMISE. I WILL NOT GET MAD IF YOU WIN.
OKAY, WELL... I GUESS I BETTER GO PACK ALL MY SHARP SHIT AND MY GOOD PANTS.
NEHA?
YEAH?
I THINK YOU'RE FORGETTING SOMETHING? WHAT DID YOU WANT?
HUH?
YOU CAME HERE FOR SOMETHING. WHAT WAS IT?
OH...
DON'T WORRY ABOUT IT. DOESN'T MATTER.

AGENT DISPATCH

[+]..................

 URSULA RING
[FY 12,902]

 JETTI KAAN
[FY 12,902]

 SAM-SAM
[FY 12,902]

 NEHA NORI SOOD
[FY 12,902]

 SEREN FI
[FY 11,202]

 ASHEN GRIN
[FY 12,263]

 KILLI FREY
[FY 12,263]

[+]... EXPAND ....

LOCATION RESEARCH

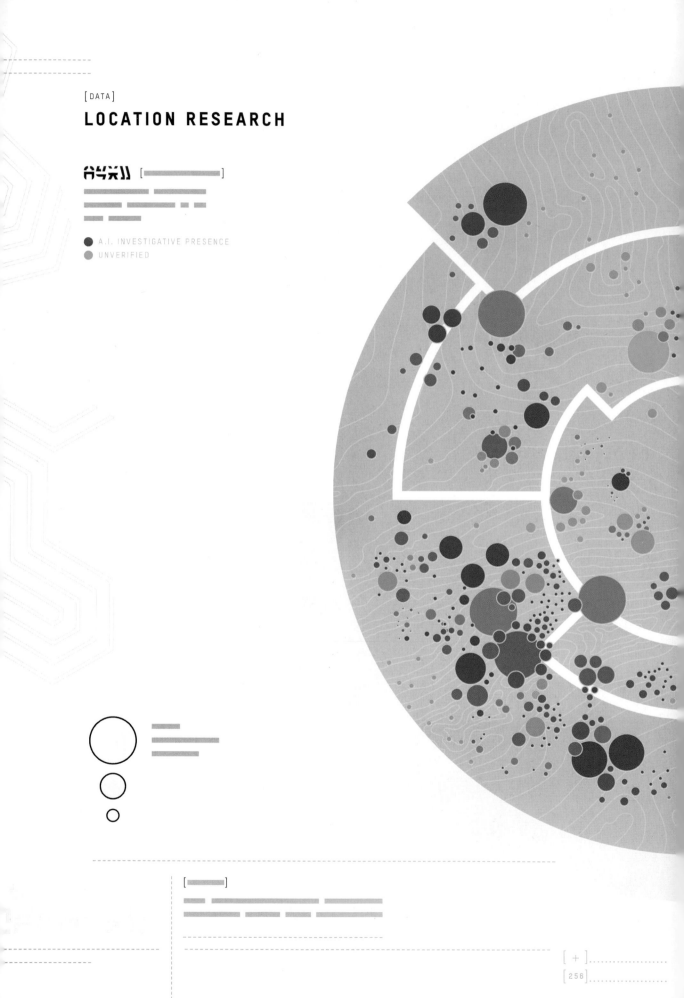

ᕼ५ᵡᗐ [▭▭▭▭▭▭]

▭▭▭▭▭▭ ▭▭▭▭▭ ▭▭▭▭▭
▭▭▭▭▭ ▭▭▭▭▭ ▭▭ ▭▭
▭▭▭ ▭▭▭▭▭

- ● A.I. INVESTIGATIVE PRESENCE
- ● UNVERIFIED

[▭▭▭▭▭]

▭▭▭ ▭▭▭▭▭▭▭▭▭ ▭▭▭ ▭▭▭▭
▭▭▭▭▭▭ ▭▭▭▭ ▭▭▭ ▭▭▭ ▭▭▭▭

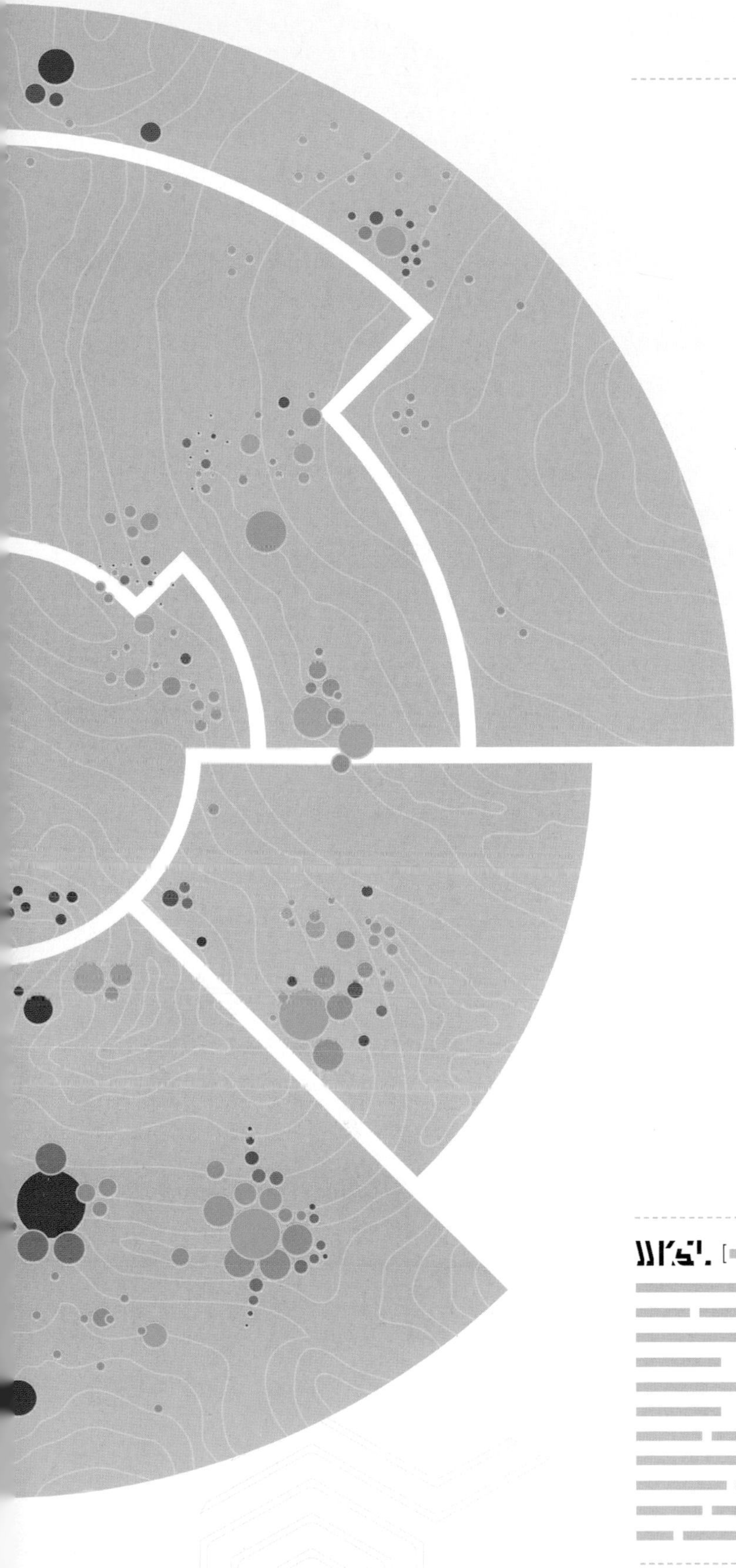

CHAPTER FIFTEEN

[YOU CAN'T GO HOME AGAIN]

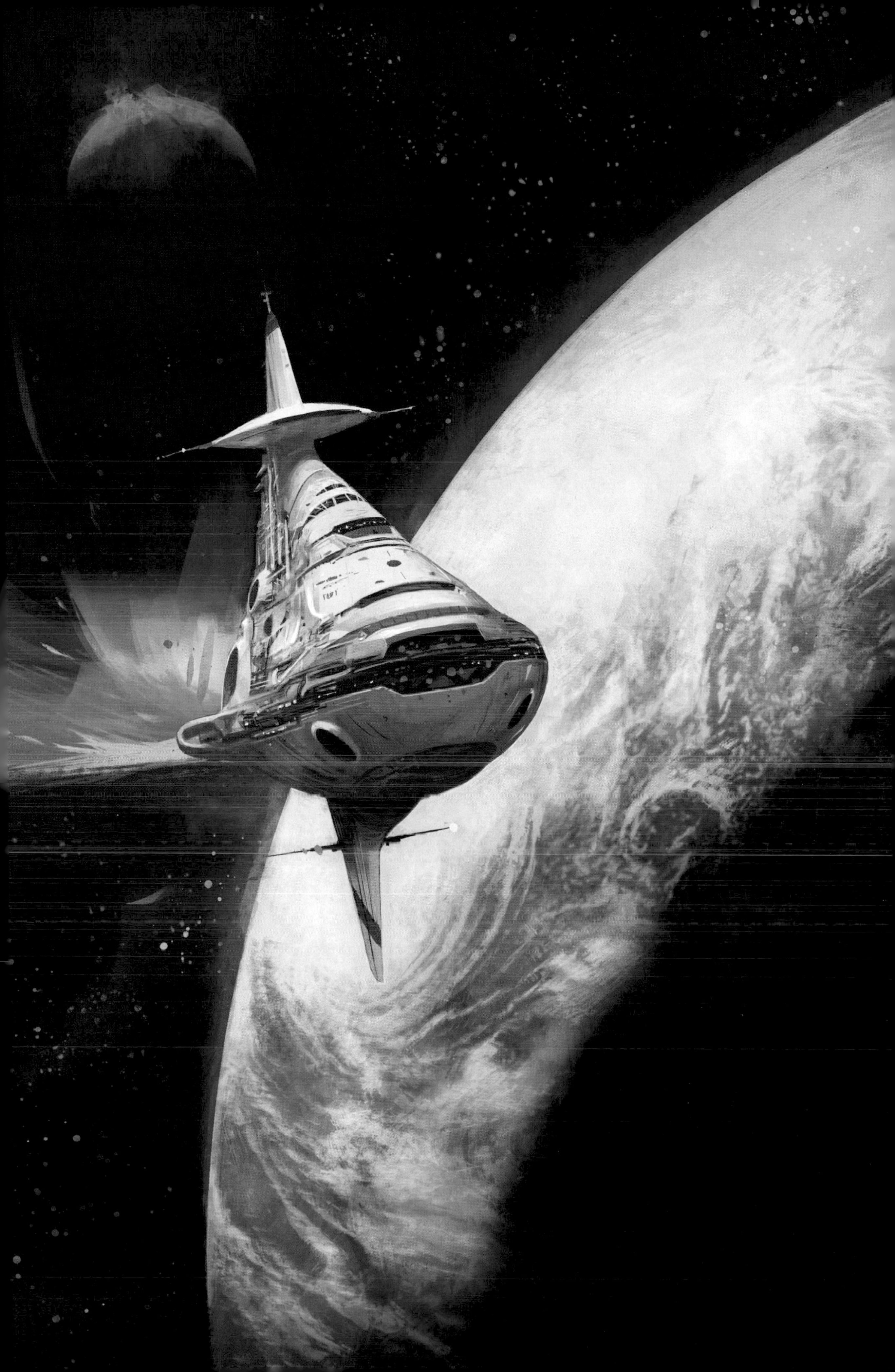

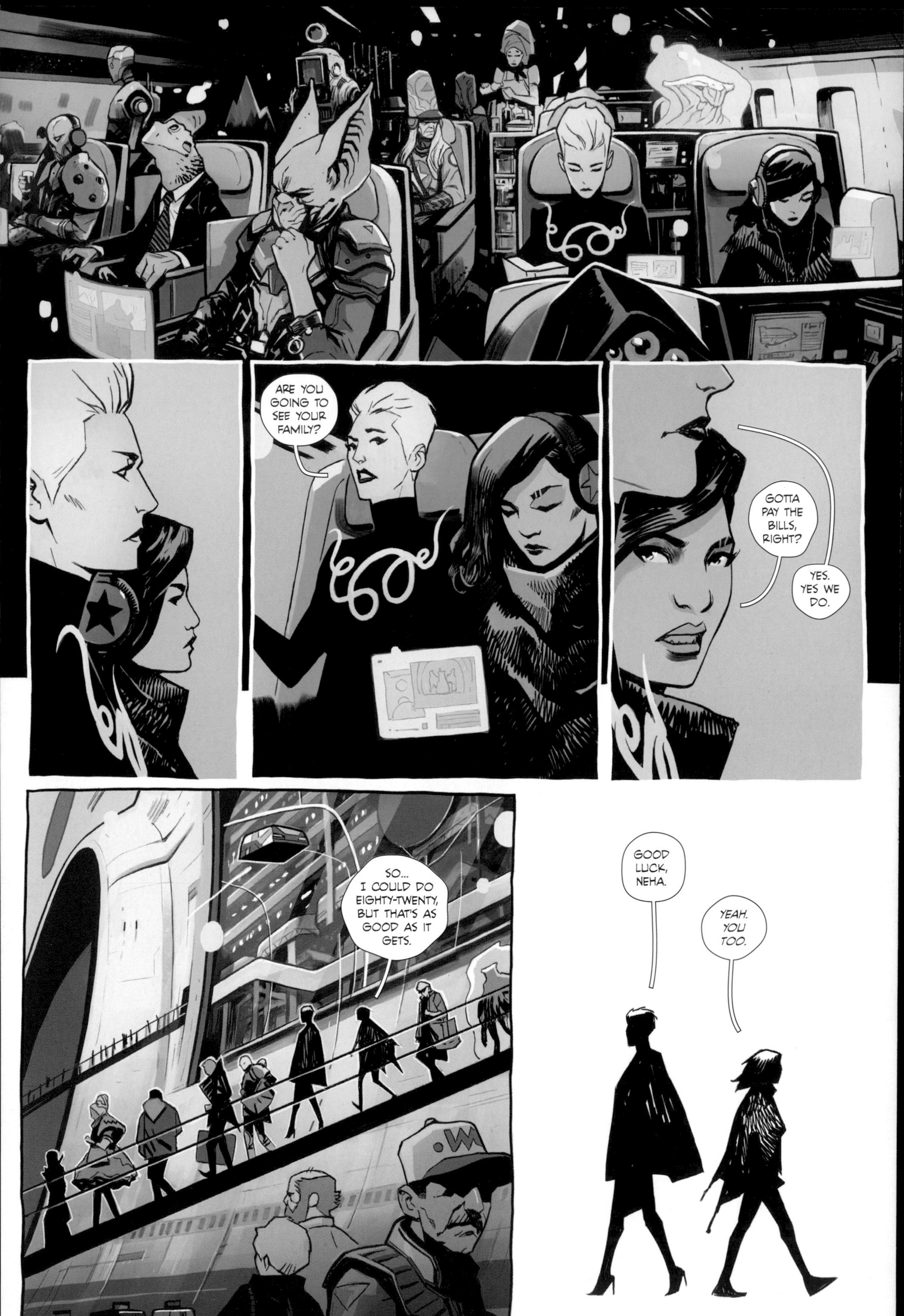
ARE YOU GOING TO SEE YOUR FAMILY?
GOTTA PAY THE BILLS, RIGHT?
YES. YES WE DO.
SO... I COULD DO EIGHTY-TWENTY, BUT THAT'S AS GOOD AS IT GETS.
GOOD LUCK, NEHA.
YEAH. YOU TOO.

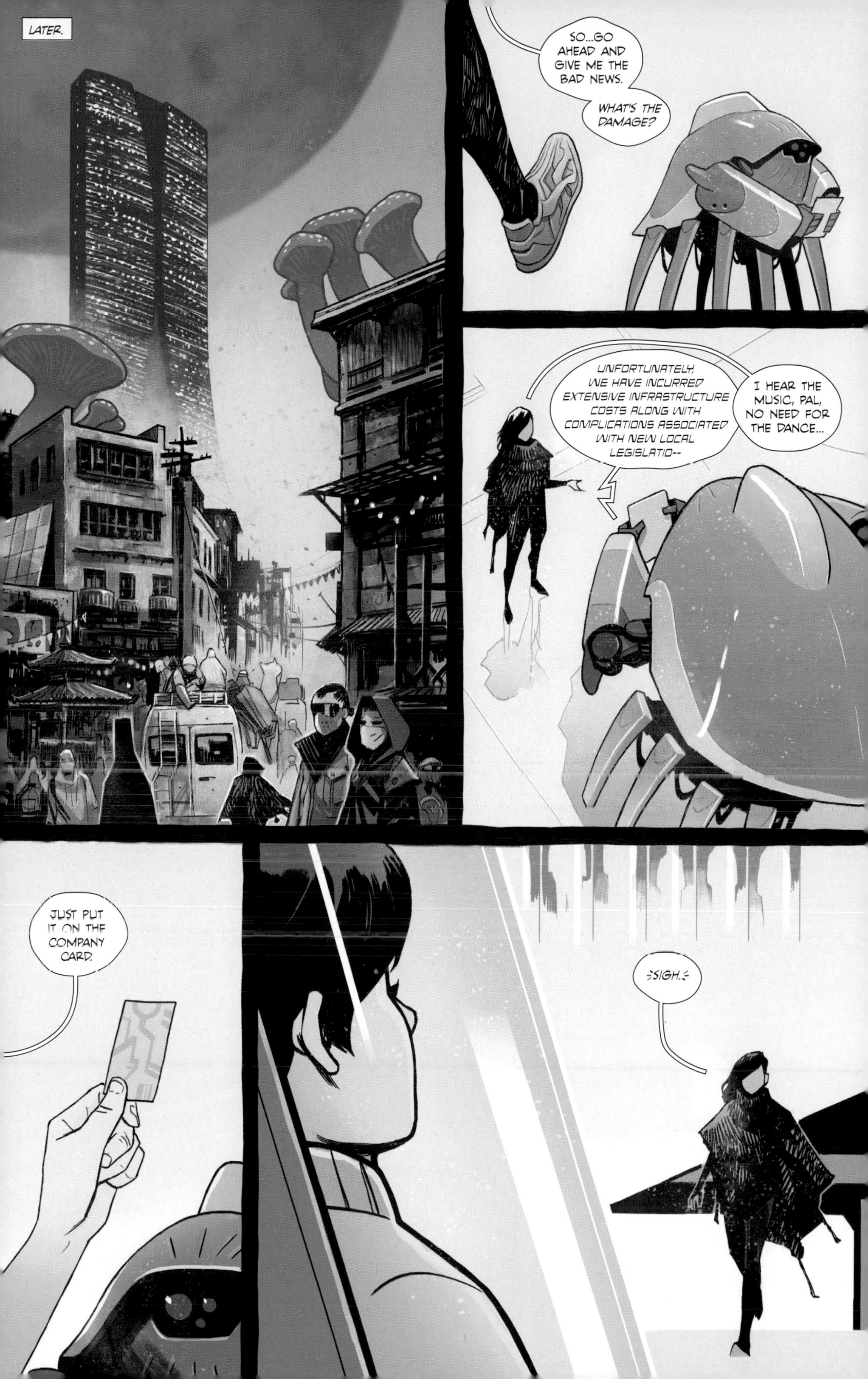
LATER.
SO...GO AHEAD AND GIVE ME THE BAD NEWS.
WHAT'S THE DAMAGE?
UNFORTUNATELY, WE HAVE INCURRED EXTENSIVE INFRASTRUCTURE COSTS ALONG WITH COMPLICATIONS ASSOCIATED WITH NEW LOCAL LEGISLATIO--
I HEAR THE MUSIC, PAL, NO NEED FOR THE DANCE...
JUST PUT IT ON THE COMPANY CARD.
SIGH.

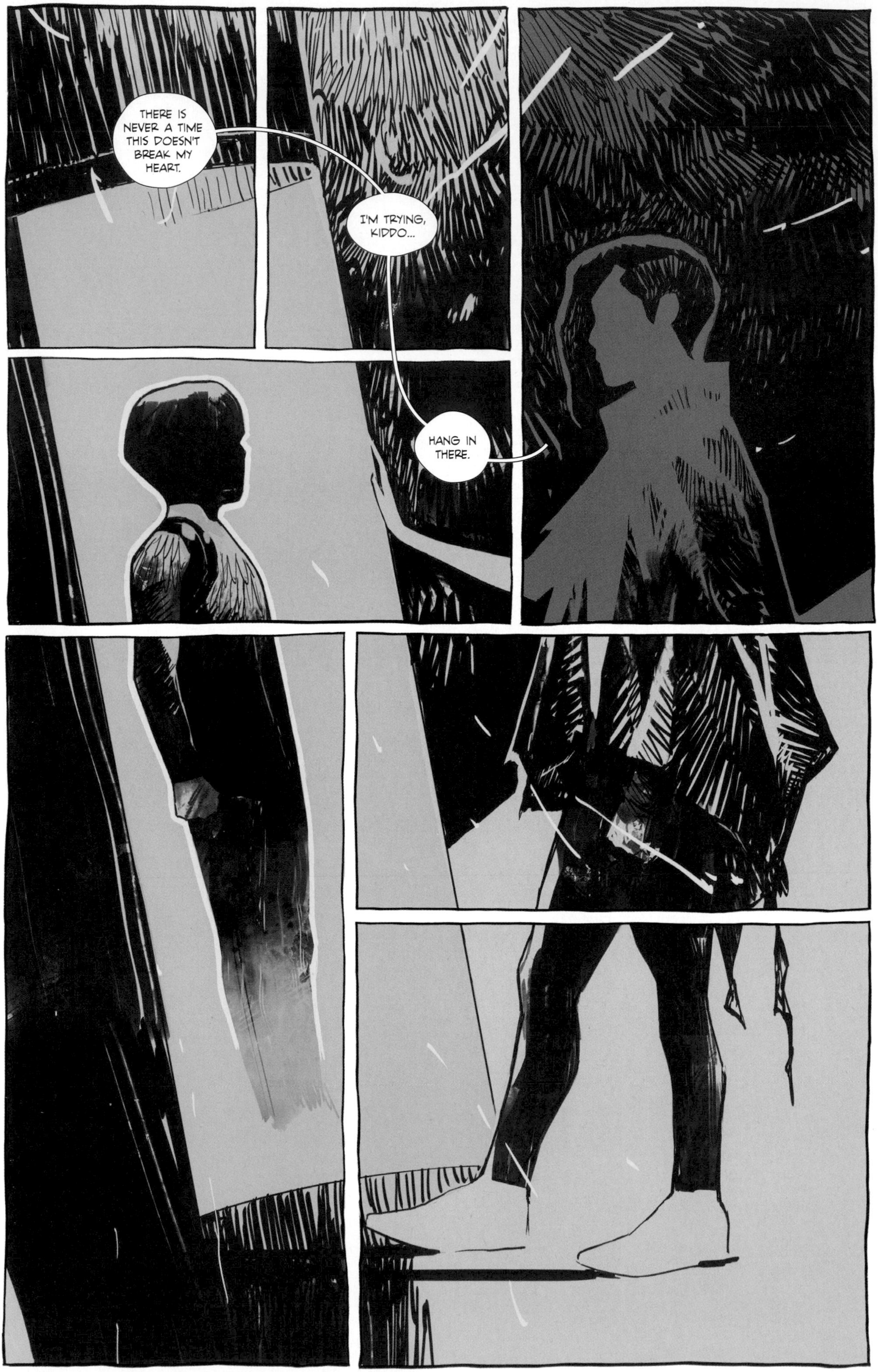
THERE IS NEVER A TIME THIS DOESN'T BREAK MY HEART.
I'M TRYING, KIDDO...
HANG IN THERE.

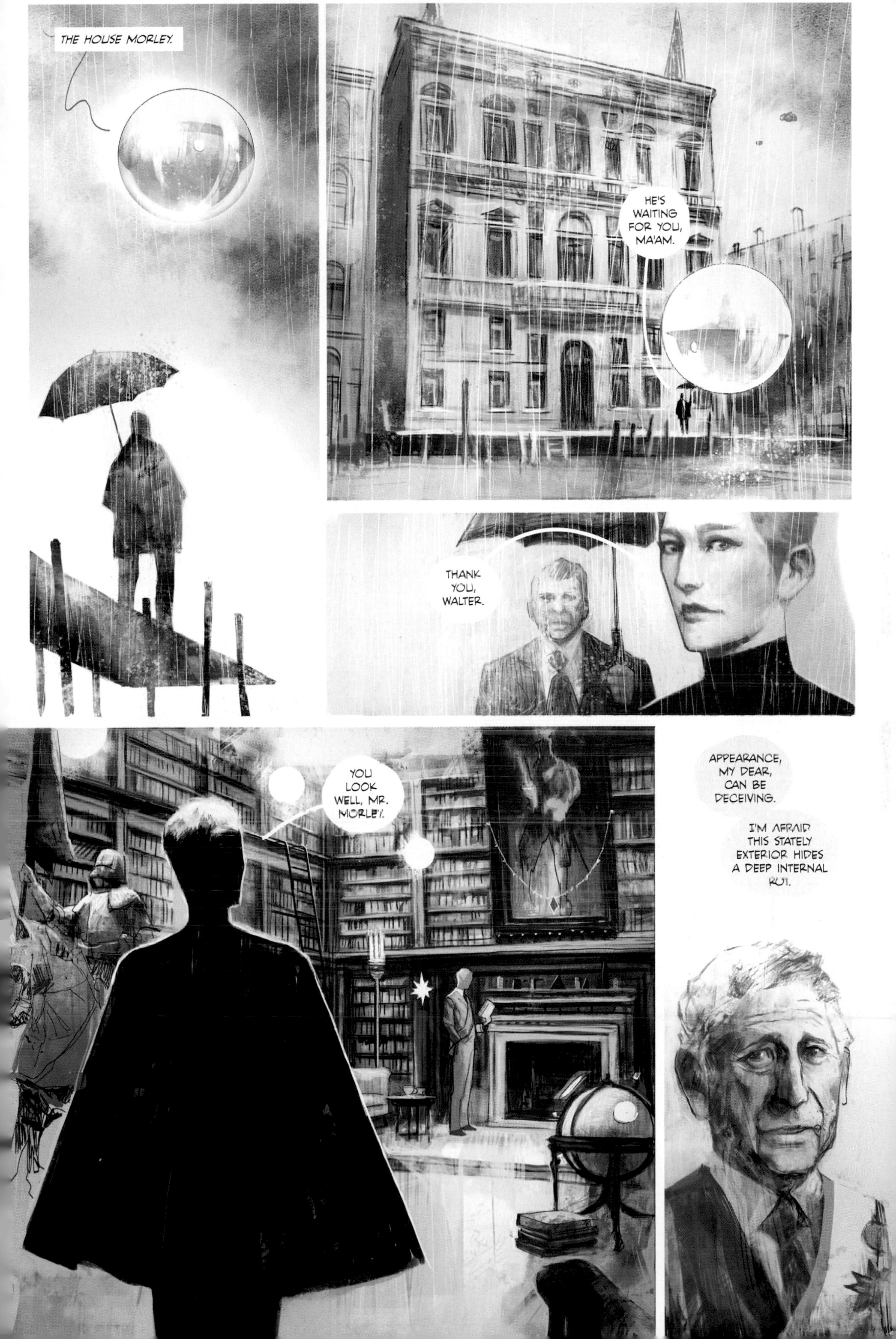
THE HOUSE MORLEY.
HE'S WAITING FOR YOU, MA'AM.
THANK YOU, WALTER.
YOU LOOK WELL, MR. MORLEY.
APPEARANCE, MY DEAR, CAN BE DECEIVING.
I'M AFRAID THIS STATELY EXTERIOR HIDES A DEEP INTERNAL ROT.

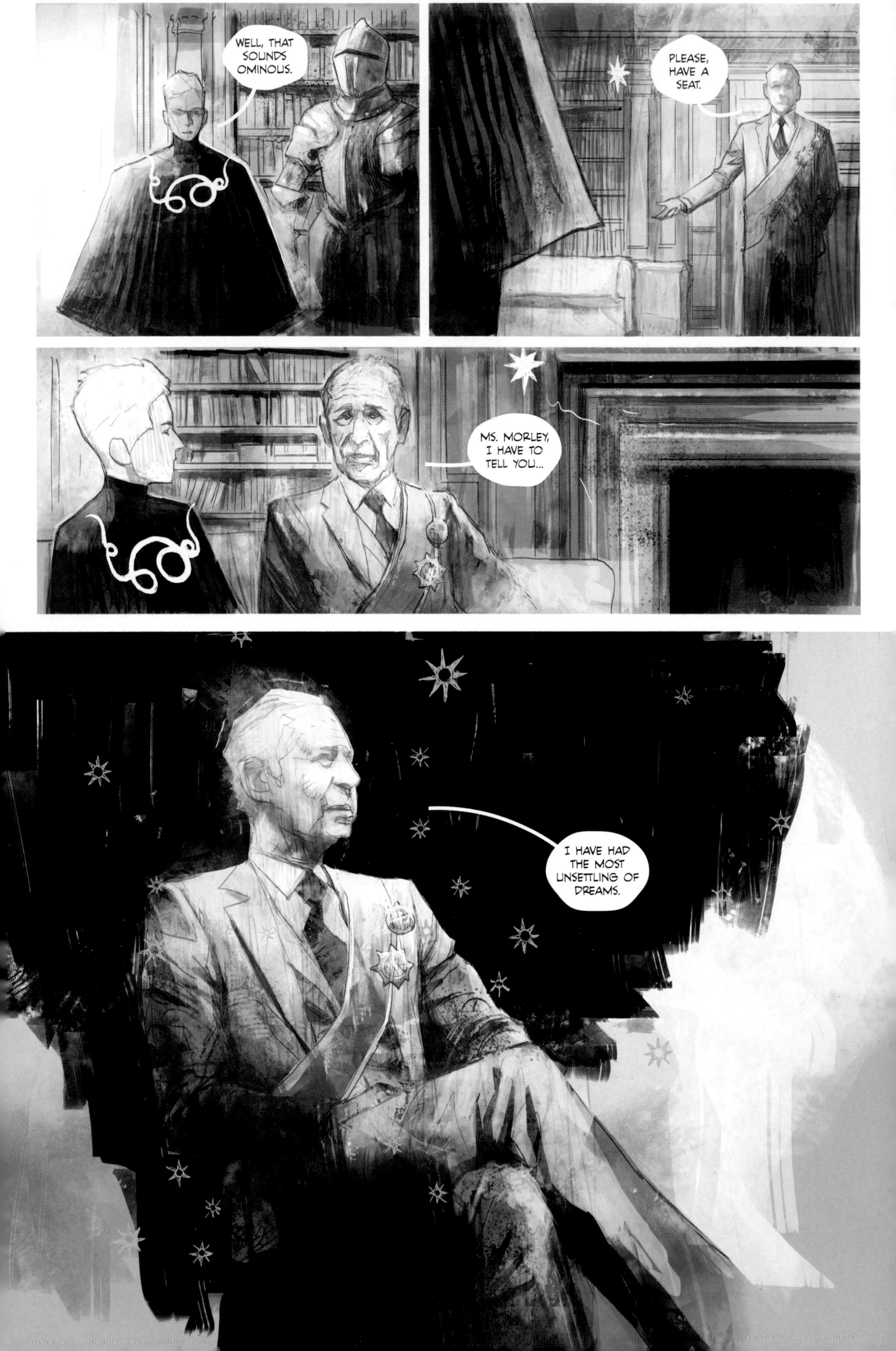
WELL, THAT SOUNDS OMINOUS.
PLEASE, HAVE A SEAT.
MS. MORLEY, I HAVE TO TELL YOU...
I HAVE HAD THE MOST UNSETTLING OF DREAMS.

THE DREAMS
OF MASTER MORLEY

[+].................

[+].................

I was suspended over a vast chasm. Hanging there, upside down — a disorienting defiance of gravity. A slight breeze provided all motion as I was frozen in place, incapable of struggle.

My feet were moored by clouds. Some ethereal grip of faith was all that kept me from plunging down into the abyss. I knew what waited for me there, oblivion, death... utter nothingness.

The walls of the chasm were a nightmare of human suffering and infernal machinery. Intertwined, interconnected, and though they hated one another, they spoke with a unified voice.

"It's a lie," they said, "it's all a beautiful lie."

And then I saw that it was not me hanging there, but you, my dear. You.

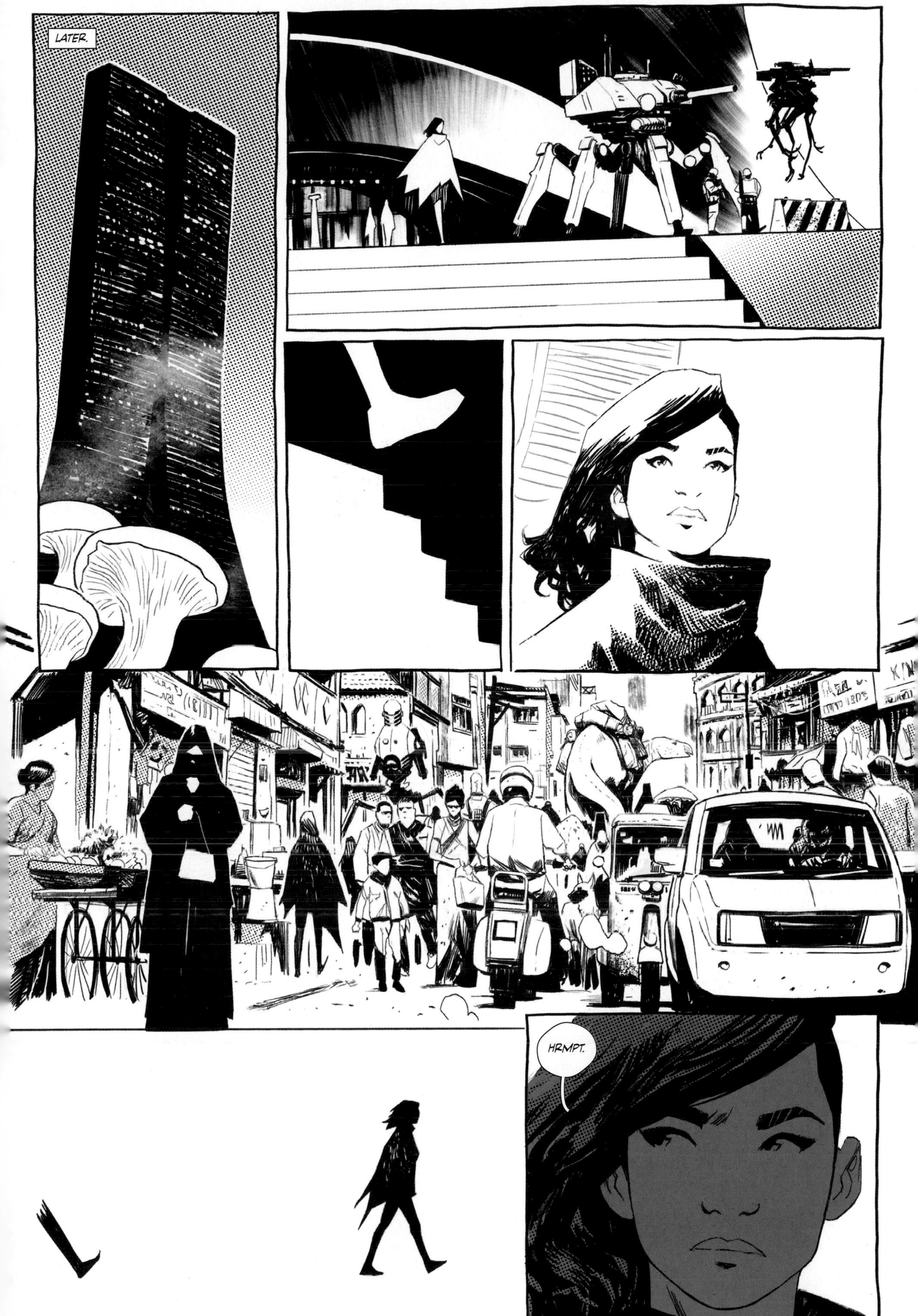
LATER.
HRMPT.

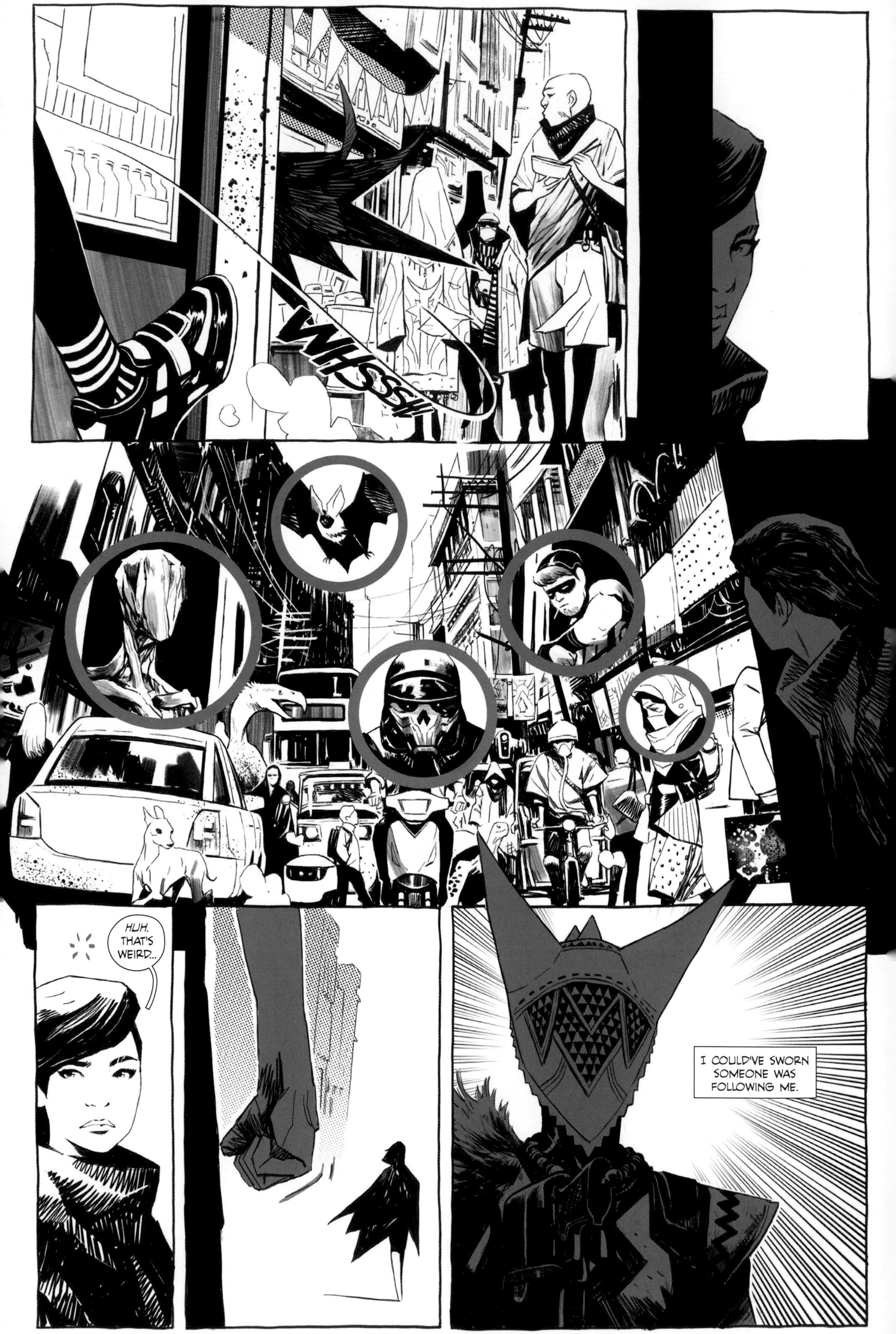
WHSSSH
HUH. THAT'S WEIRD...
I COULD'VE SWORN SOMEONE WAS FOLLOWING ME.

VII

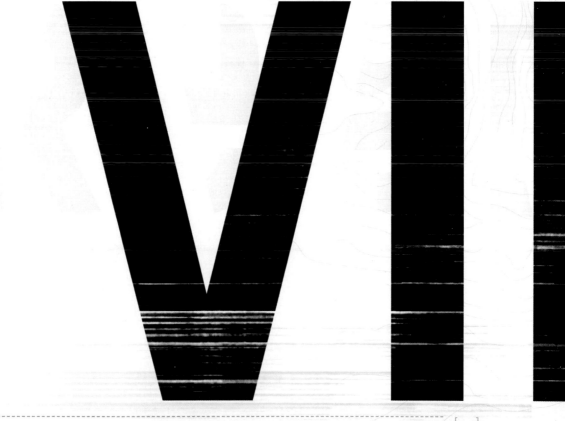

[
AND THE EGG THAT
BROKE A WORLD
]

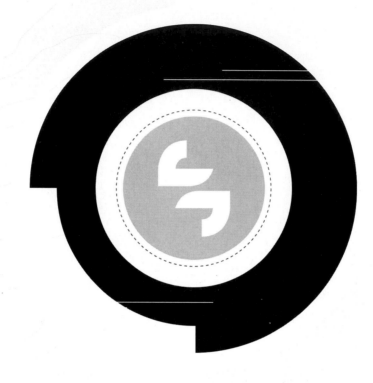

CHAPTER SIXTEEN

[HIDE AND SEEK / SEEK AND FIND]

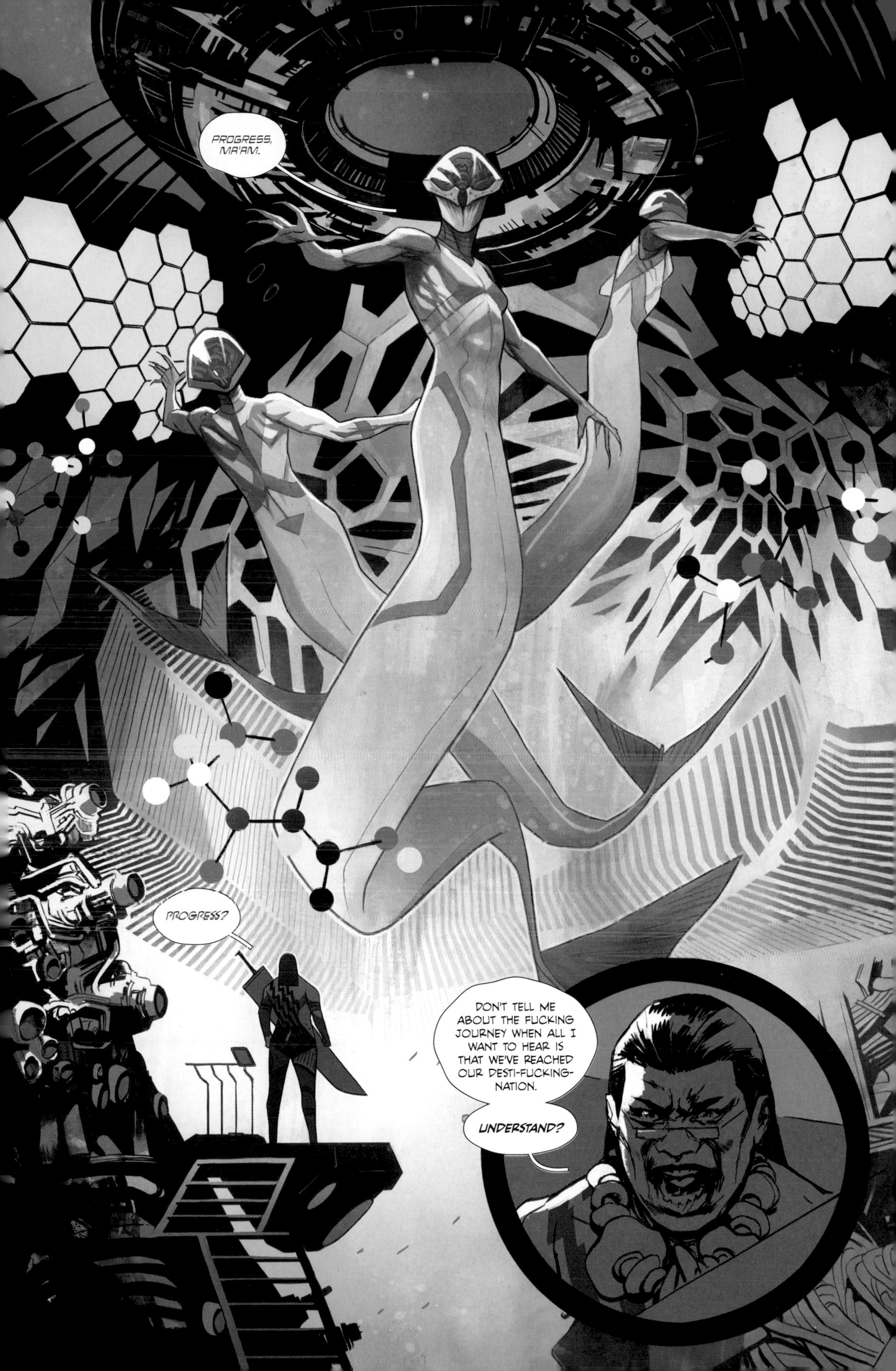
PROGRESS, MA'AM.
PROGRESS?
DON'T TELL ME ABOUT THE FUCKING JOURNEY WHEN ALL I WANT TO HEAR IS THAT WE'VE REACHED OUR DESTI-FUCKING-NATION.
UNDERSTAND?

UNDERSTOOD, MA'AM.

SOME GOOD NEWS. WE ARE, IN FACT, ALMOST HOME, BUT THIS IS AS FAR AS I CAN TAKE YOU.

ALL THAT'S LEFT IS TO BLOODY THE DOOR, AND THAT'S NOT REALLY MY PURVIEW NOW, IS IT?

HRMPT! WALK ME THROUGH IT.

WE'VE CRUNCHED A HUNDRED THOUSAND YEARS OF DATA. THE CHURCH WAS METHODICAL, THERE'S NO DENYING THAT...

BUT THE FLAW IN THEIR SEARCH WAS FOCUSING ENTIRELY TOO MUCH ON WHAT THEY WANTED INSTEAD OF WHAT WAS KEEPING THEM FROM FINDING IT.

THEY'RE GODDAMN MACHINES... I HAVE A HARD TIME BELIEVING THEY DIDN'T ACCOUNT FOR ALL SCENARIOS.

OH, THEY DID. THERE WERE PARADIGM SHIFTS IN THE MACHINE METHODOLOGY FIFTY THOUSAND YEARS AGO.

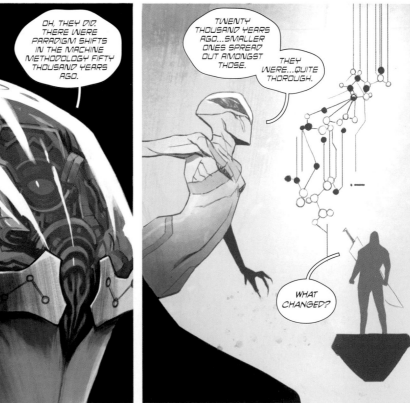

TWENTY THOUSAND YEARS AGO...SMALLER ONES SPREAD OUT AMONGST THOSE.

THEY WERE...QUITE THOROUGH.

WHAT CHANGED?

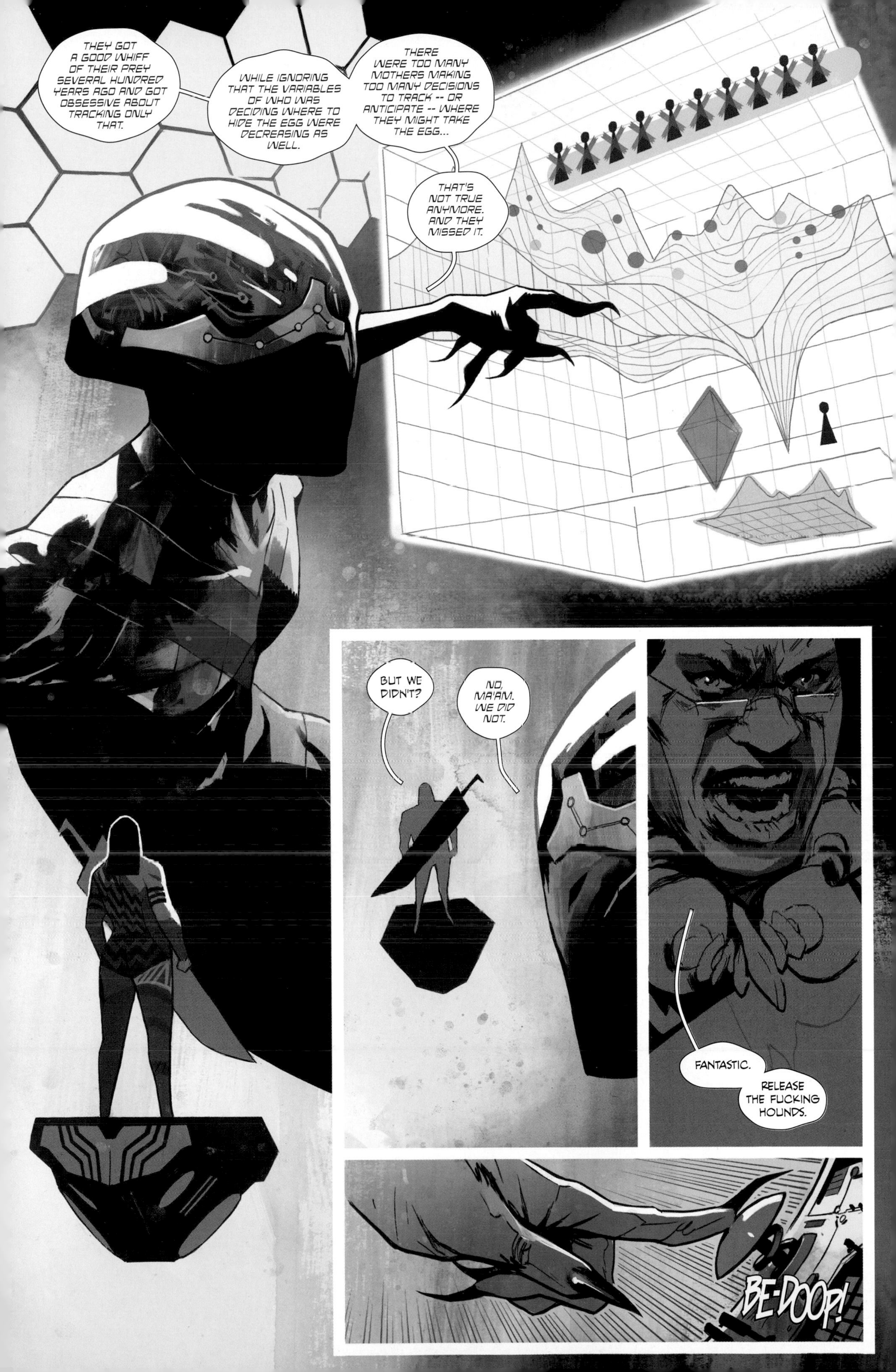
THEY GOT A GOOD WHIFF OF THEIR PREY SEVERAL HUNDRED YEARS AGO AND GOT OBSESSIVE ABOUT TRACKING ONLY THAT.
WHILE IGNORING THAT THE VARIABLES OF WHO WAS DECIDING WHERE TO HIDE THE EGG WERE DECREASING AS WELL.
THERE WERE TOO MANY MOTHERS MAKING TOO MANY DECISIONS TO TRACK -- OR ANTICIPATE -- WHERE THEY MIGHT TAKE THE EGG...
THAT'S NOT TRUE ANYMORE. AND THEY MISSED IT.
BUT WE DIDN'T?
NO, MA'AM. WE DID NOT.
FANTASTIC.
RELEASE THE FUCKING HOUNDS.
BE-DOOP!

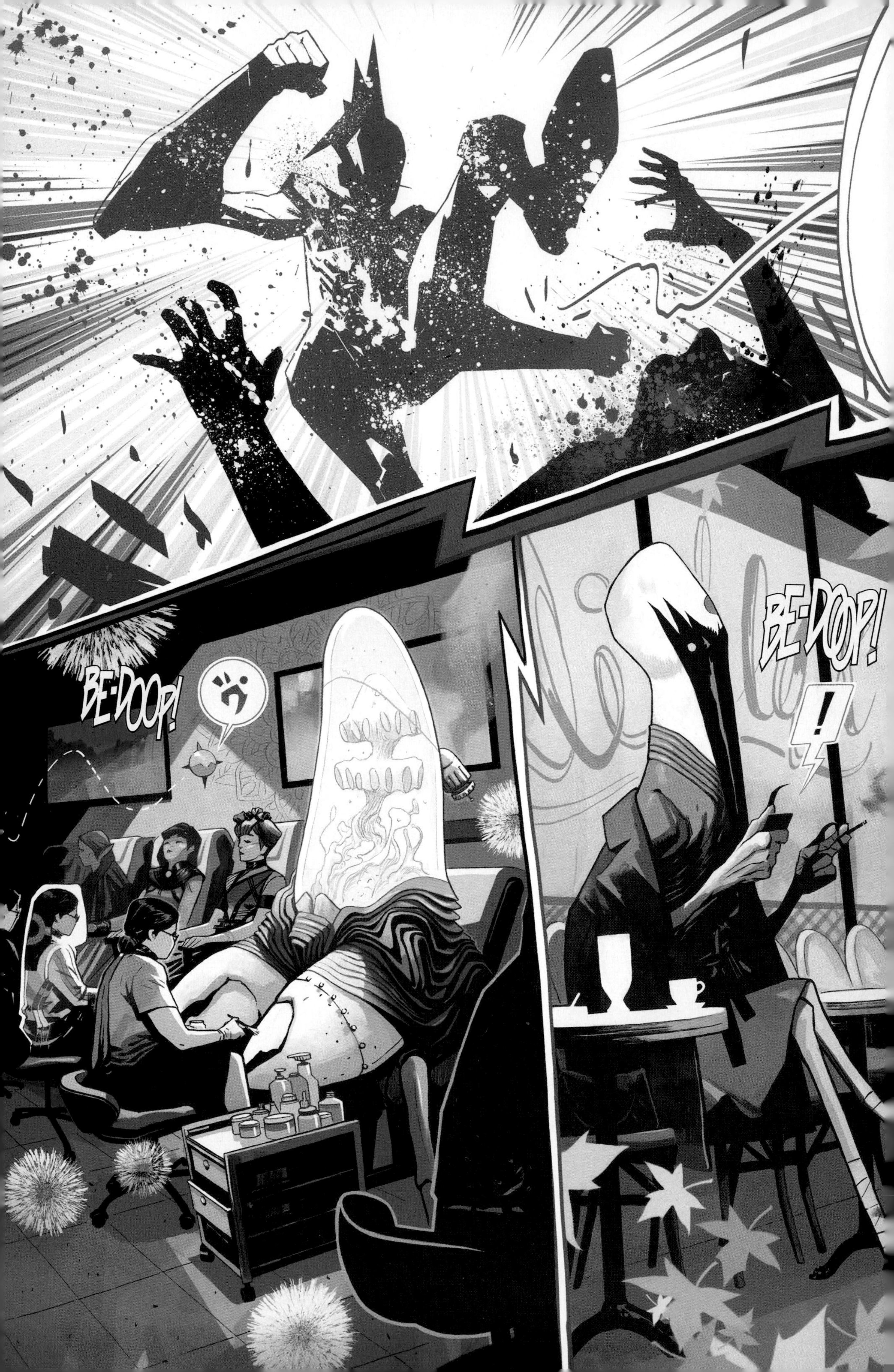
BE-DOOP!
ヴ
BE-DOOP!
!

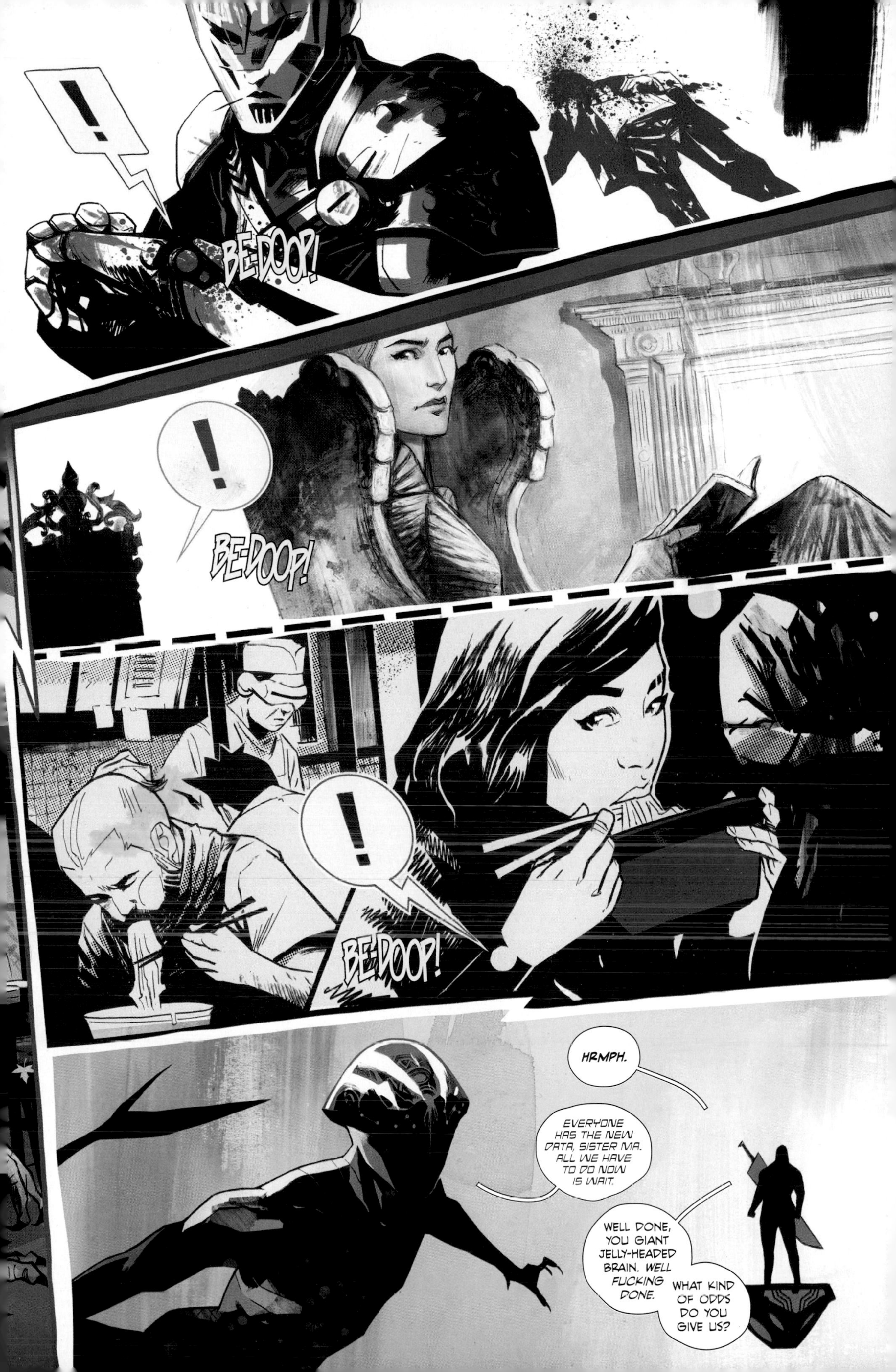
!
BE-DOOP!
!
BE-DOOP!
!
BE-DOOP!
HRMPH.
EVERYONE HAS THE NEW DATA, SISTER MA. ALL WE HAVE TO DO NOW IS WAIT.
WELL DONE, YOU GIANT JELLY-HEADED BRAIN. WELL FUCKING DONE.
WHAT KIND OF ODDS DO YOU GIVE US?

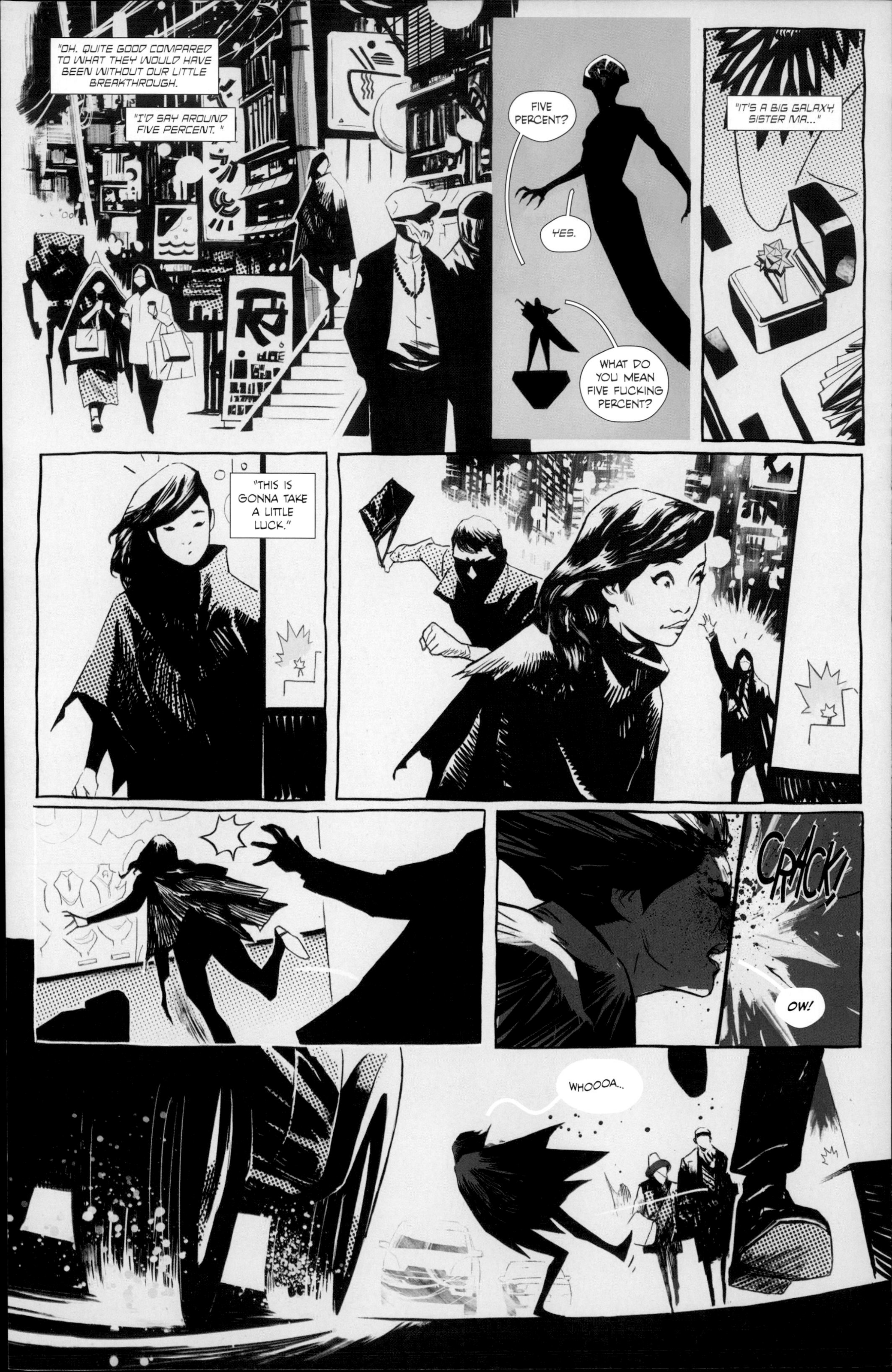
"OH. QUITE GOOD COMPARED TO WHAT THEY WOULD HAVE BEEN WITHOUT OUR LITTLE BREAKTHROUGH.
"I'D SAY AROUND FIVE PERCENT."
FIVE PERCENT?
YES.
WHAT DO YOU MEAN FIVE FUCKING PERCENT?
"IT'S A BIG GALAXY, SISTER MA..."
"THIS IS GONNA TAKE A LITTLE LUCK."
CRACK!
OW!
WHOOOA...

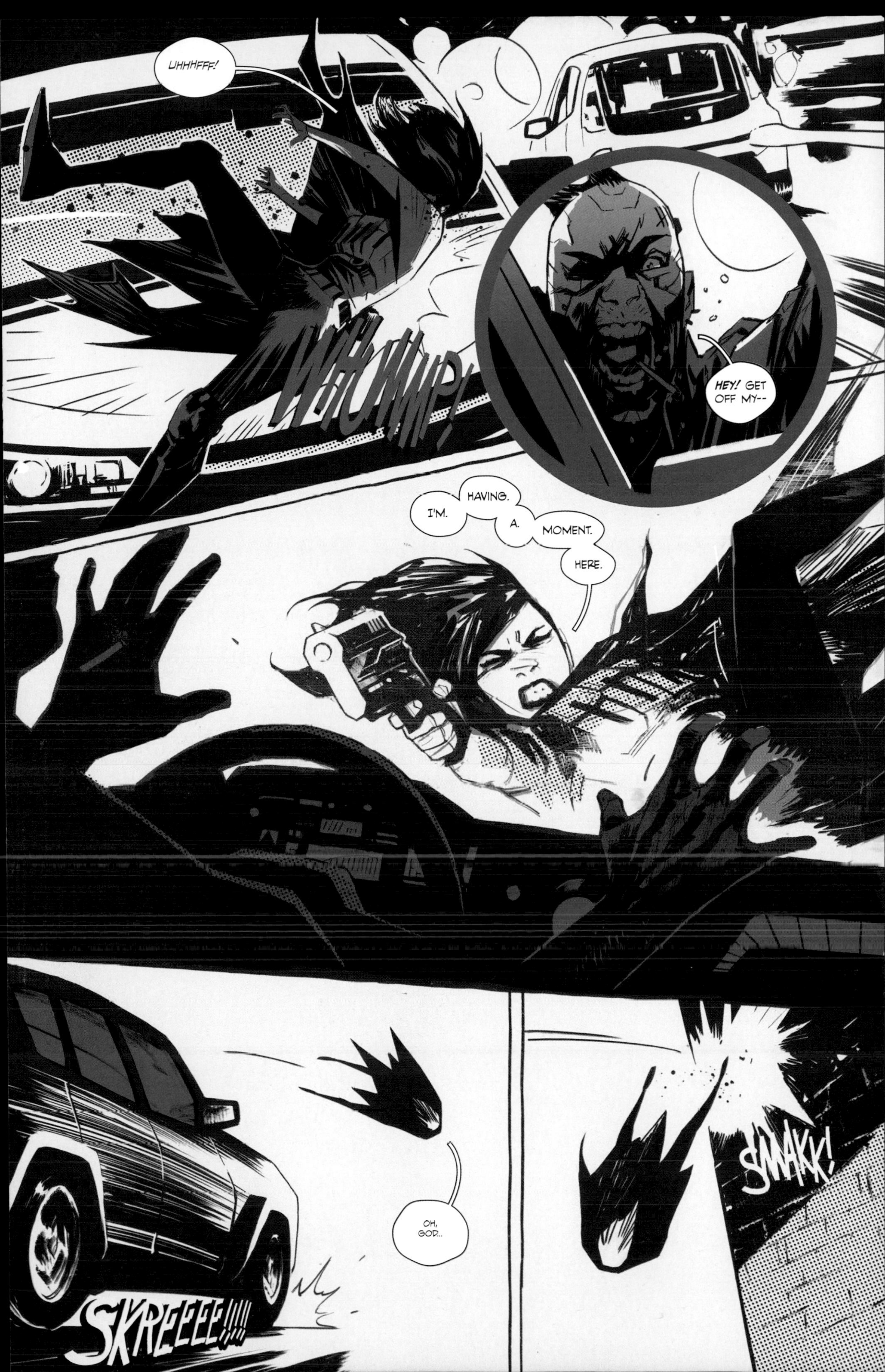
UHHHFFF!
WHUMMP!
HEY! GET OFF MY--
I'M.
HAVING.
A.
MOMENT.
HERE.
OH, GOD...
SMAKK!
SKREEEE!!!!!

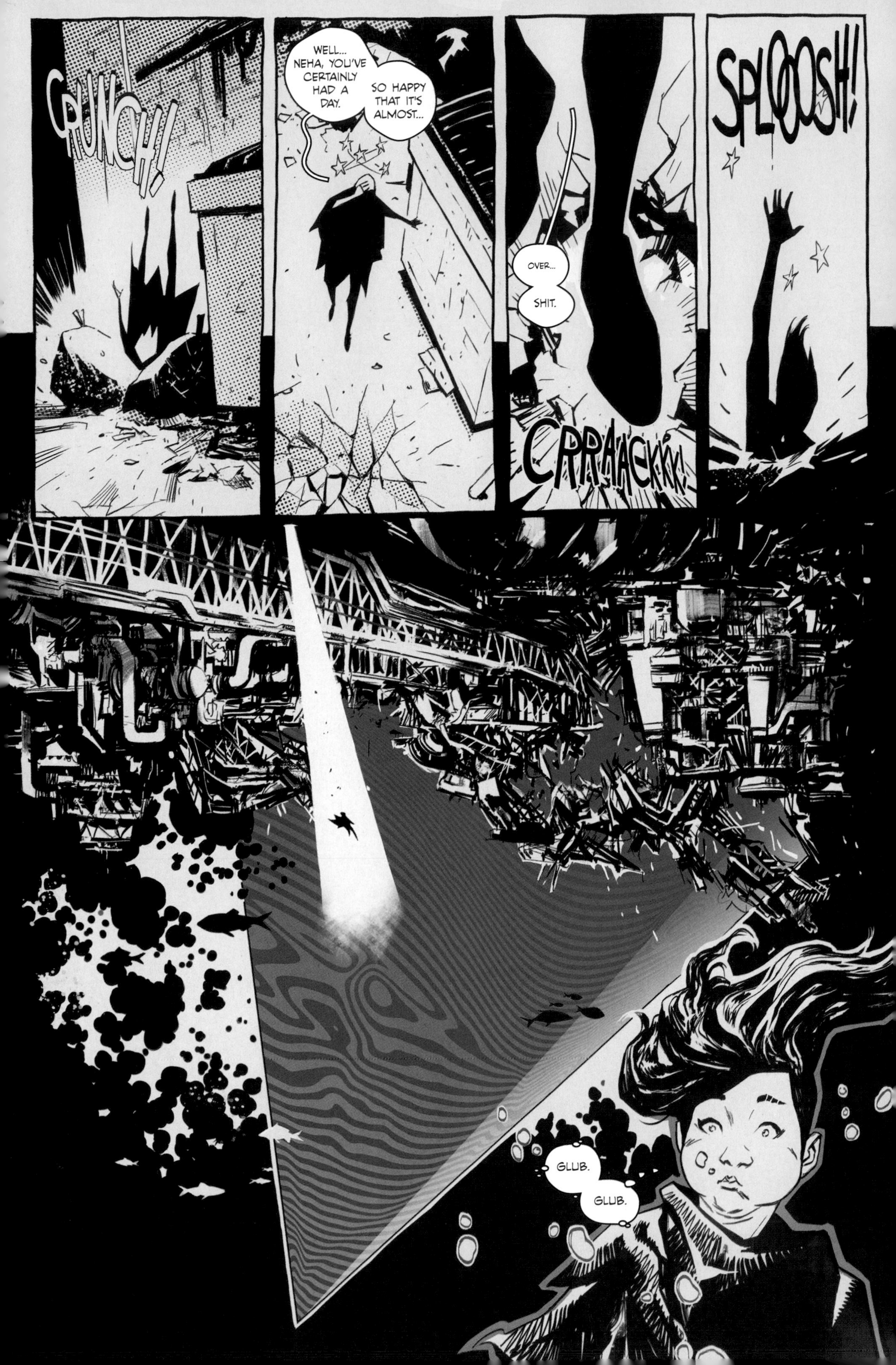
CRUNCH!
WELL... NEHA, YOU'VE CERTAINLY HAD A DAY.
SO HAPPY THAT IT'S ALMOST...
OVER...
SHIT.
CRRAACKKK!
SPLOOOSH!
GLUB.
GLUB.

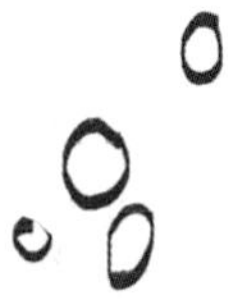

[...MOST PEOPLE CAN'T BREATHE UNDERWATER...]

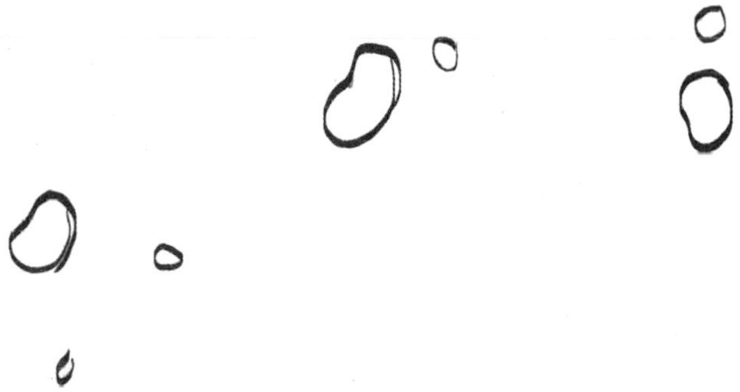

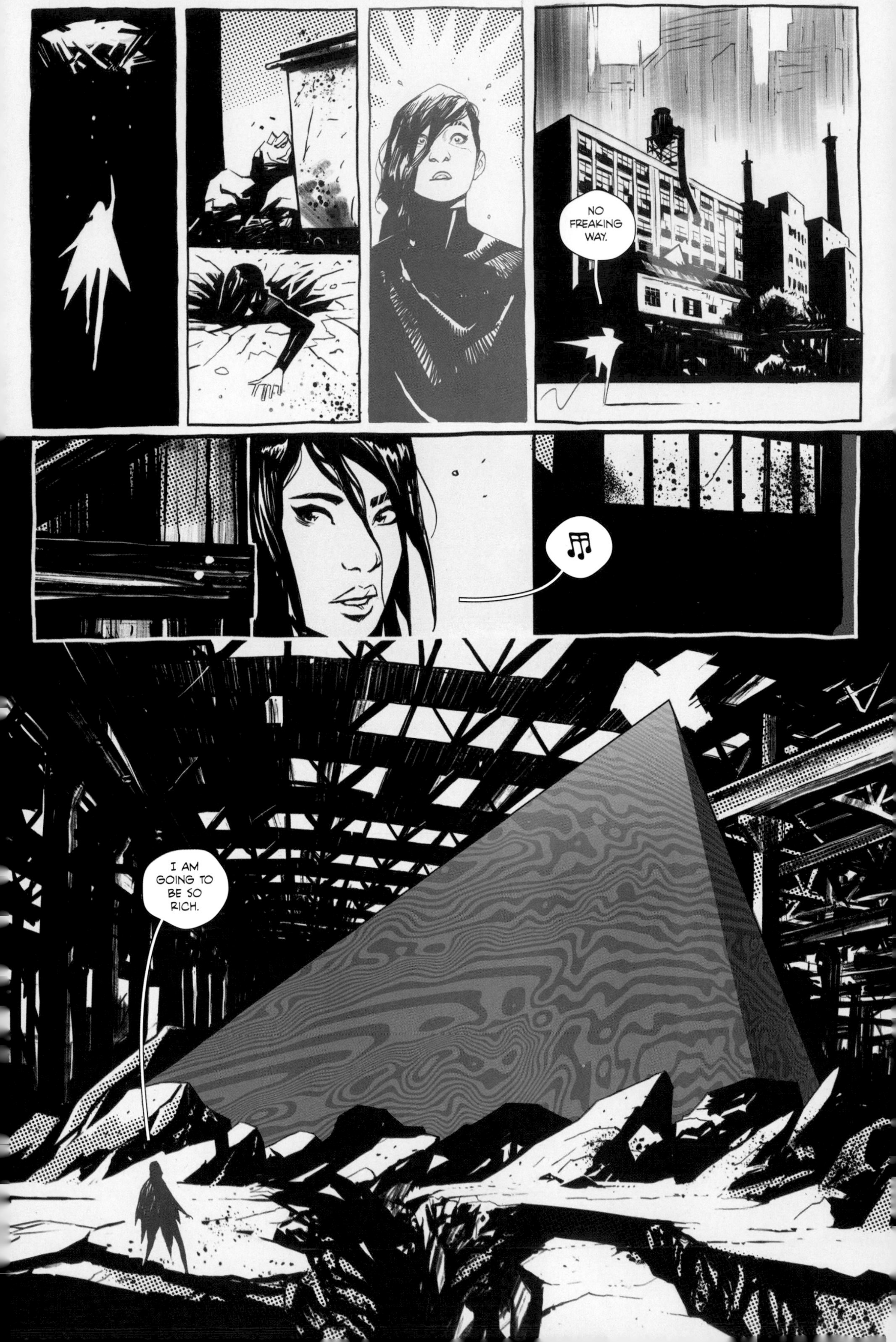
NO FREAKING WAY.
♬
I AM GOING TO BE SO RICH.

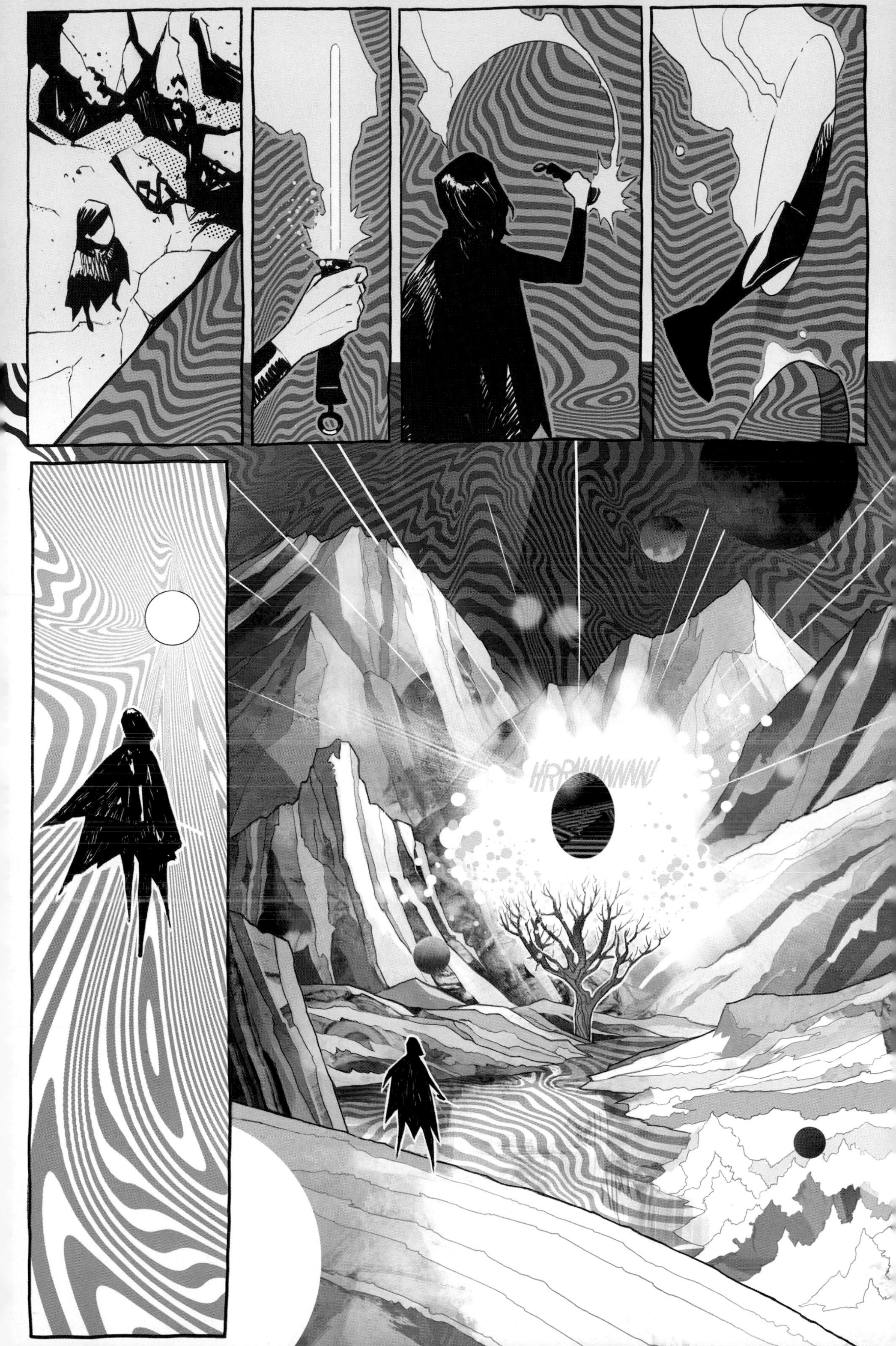
HRRNNNNNNNN!

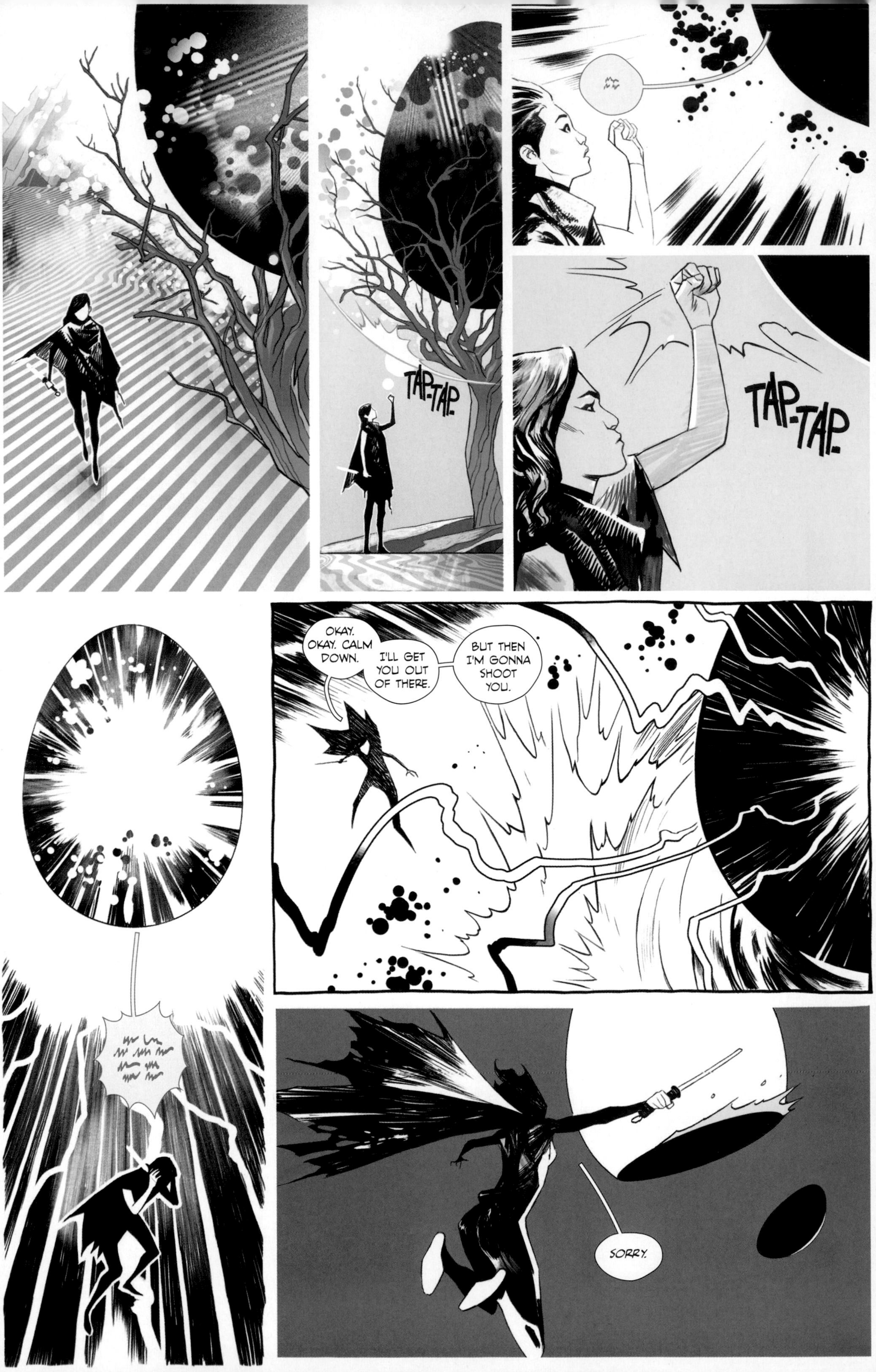
TAP-TAP.
TAP-TAP.
OKAY. OKAY. CALM DOWN.
I'LL GET YOU OUT OF THERE.
BUT THEN I'M GONNA SHOOT YOU.
SORRY.

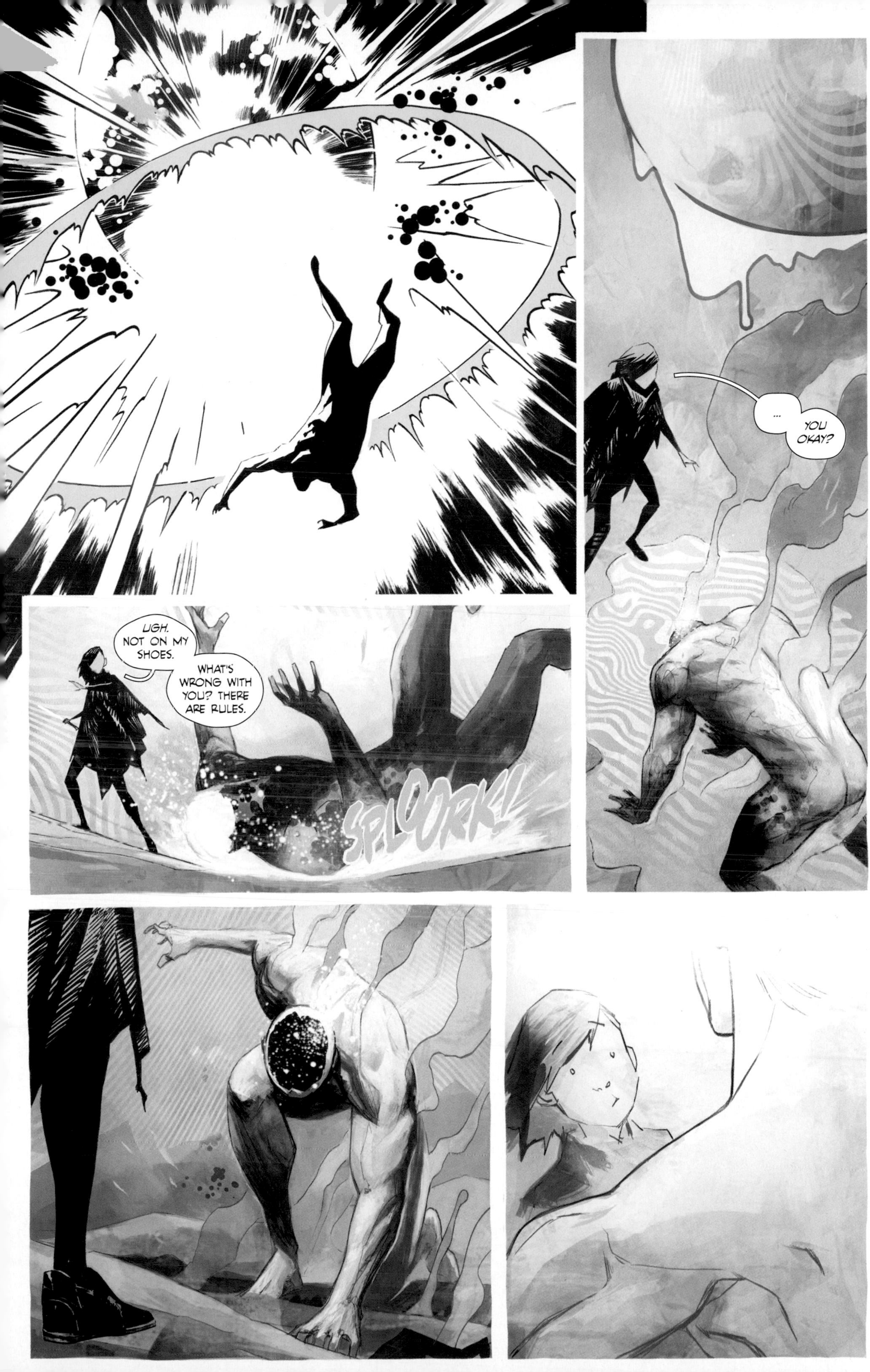
...
YOU OKAY?
UGH. NOT ON MY SHOES.
WHAT'S WRONG WITH YOU? THERE ARE RULES.
SPLOORK!

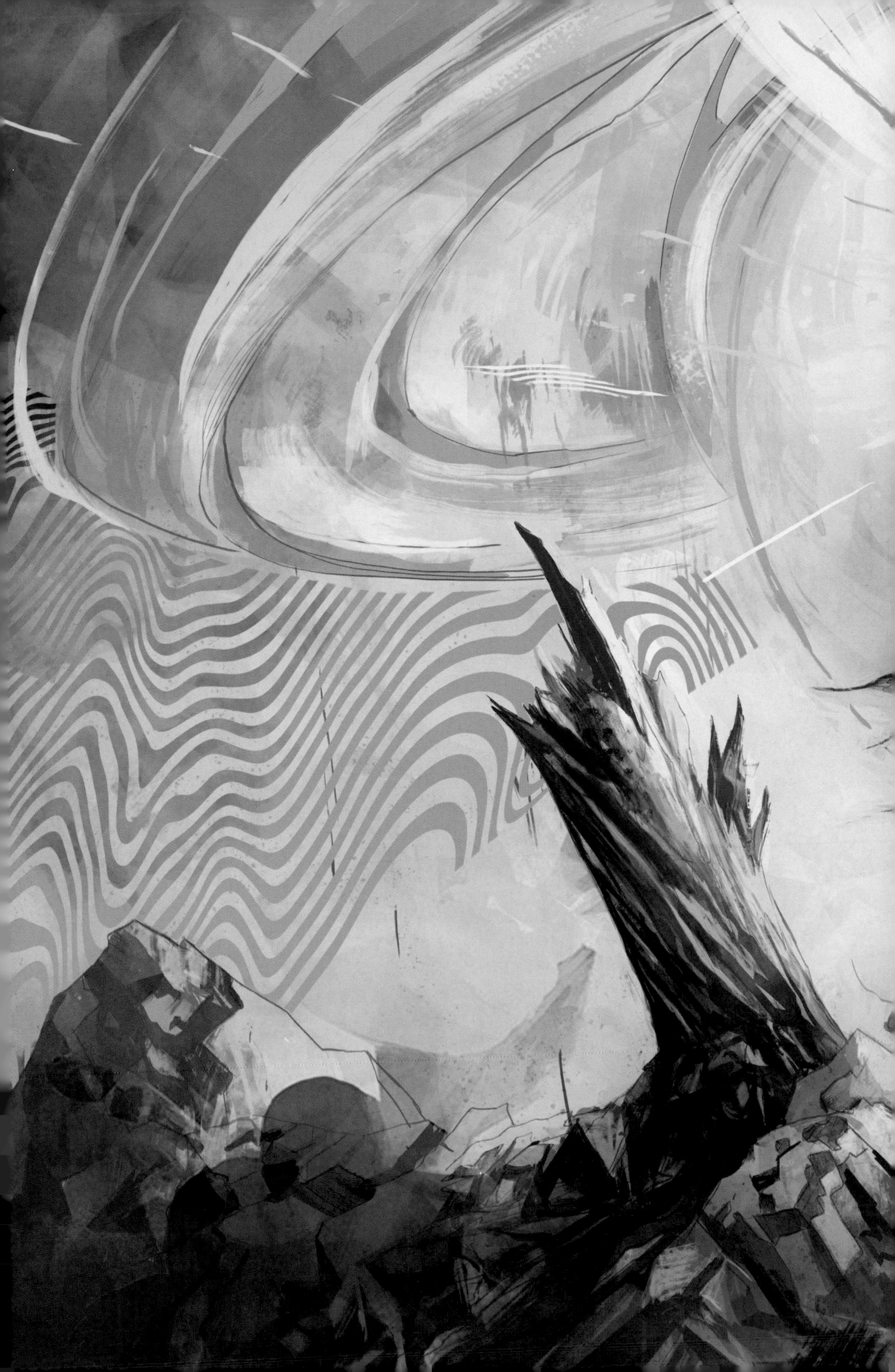

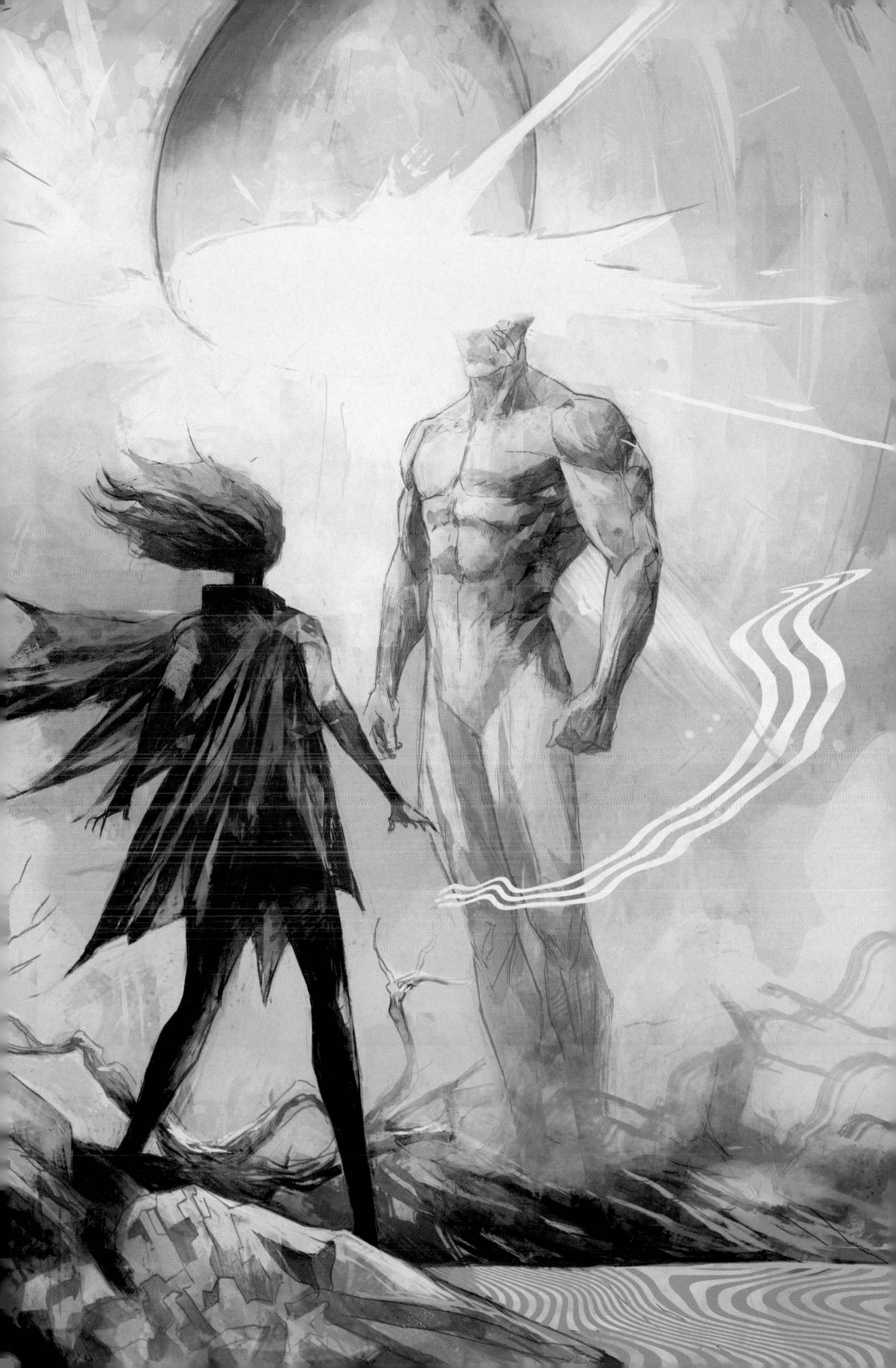

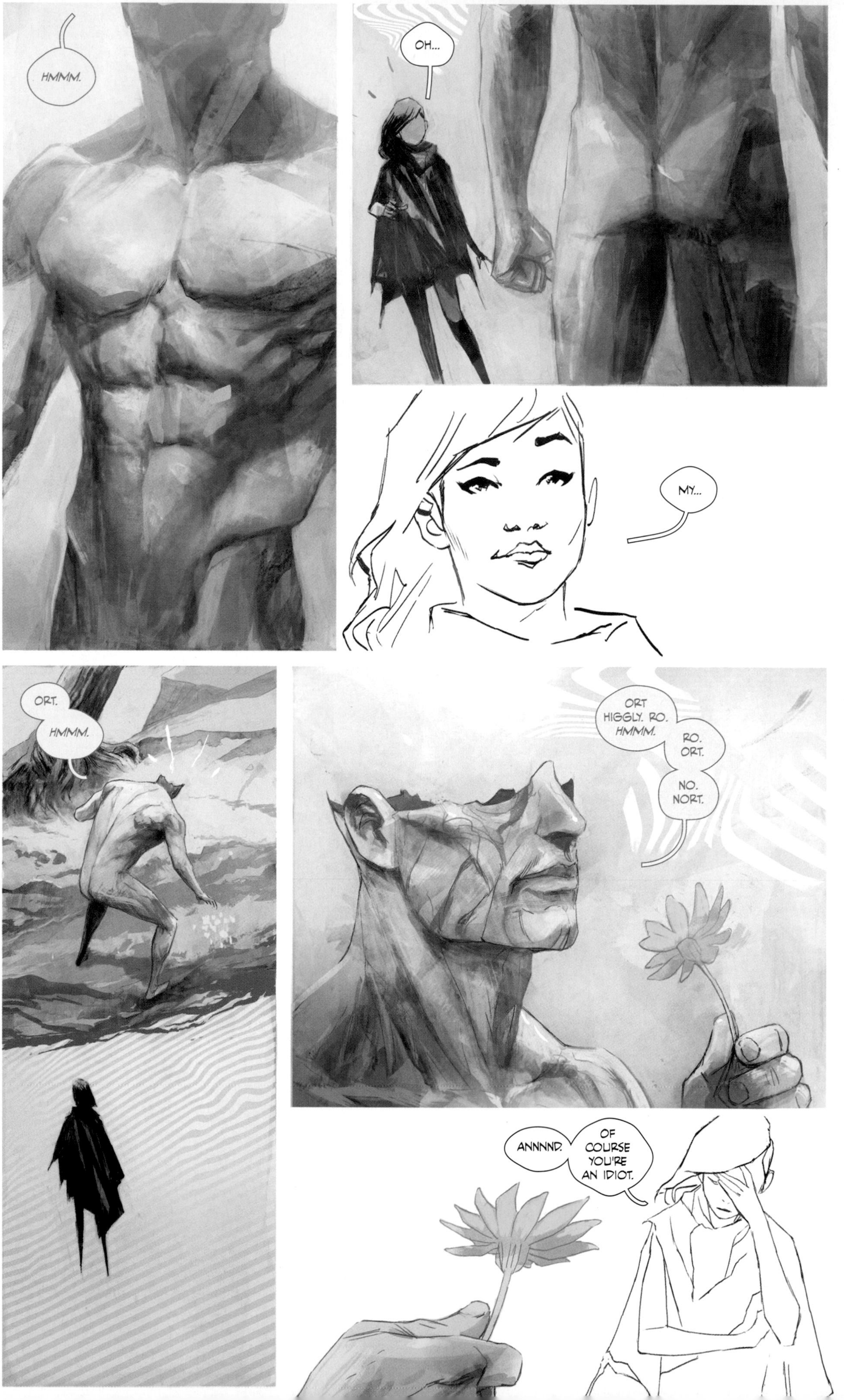
HMMM.
OH...
MY...
ORT.
HMMM.
ORT HIGGLY. RO. HMMM.
RO. ORT.
NO. NORT.
ANNNND.
OF COURSE YOU'RE AN IDIOT.

FLOATING SECTION:
0027 B3 [SECOND CYCLE]

STREET-STREET NOODLES

ALL

PRODUCT

MUST GO

[BRING YOUR OWN CHOPSTICKS]

FLOATING SECTION:
0027 B3 [SECOND CYCLE]

STREET-STREET NOODLES

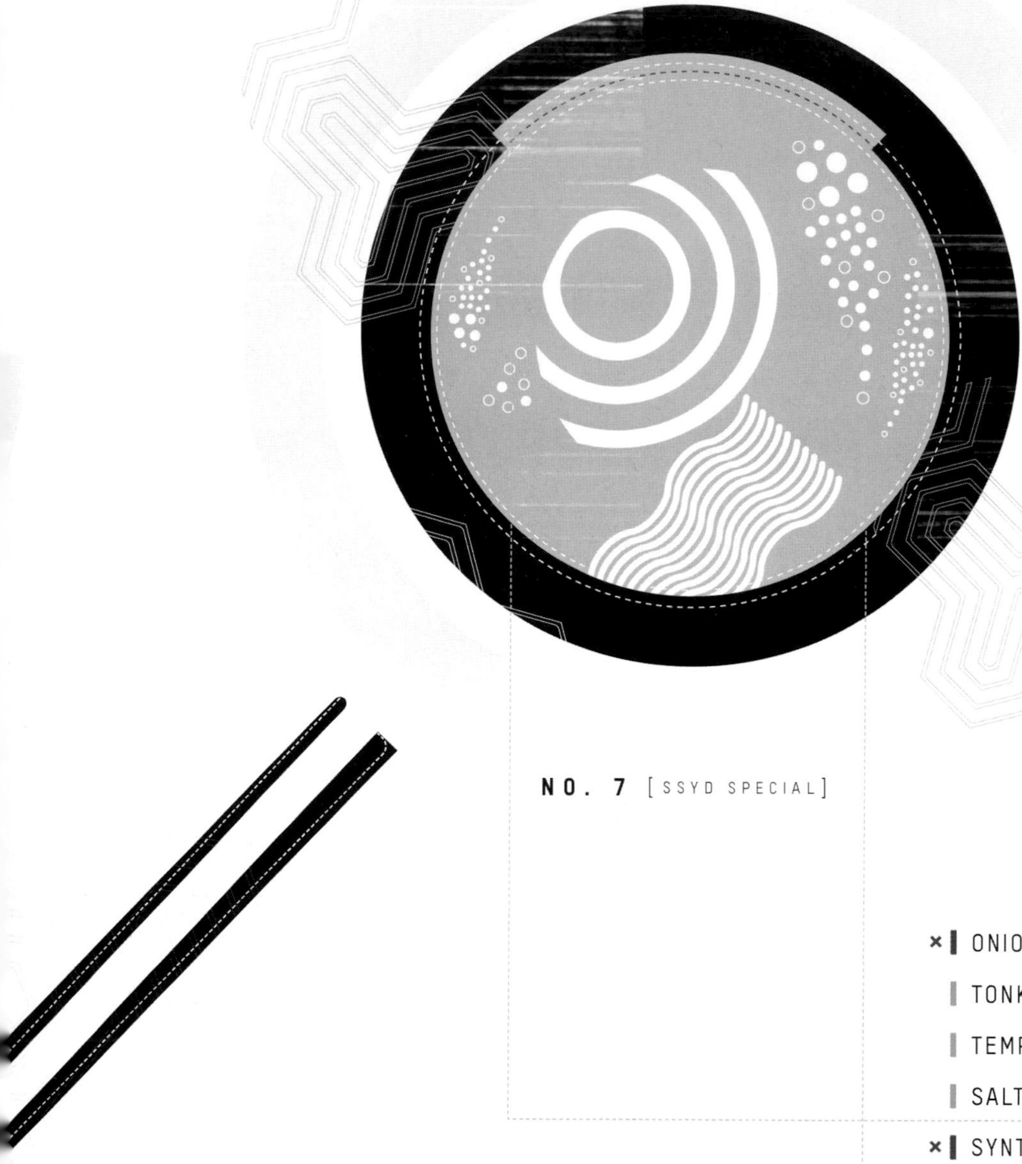

NO. 7 [SSYD SPECIAL]

- × ONION
- TONKOTSU*
- TEMPORK*
- SALT / SEASON
- × SYNTH EGG
- NOODLES
- SOY
- × FERM ALGAE

NO SUBSTITUTIONS

×

* [illegible] !!!!!!

[+]

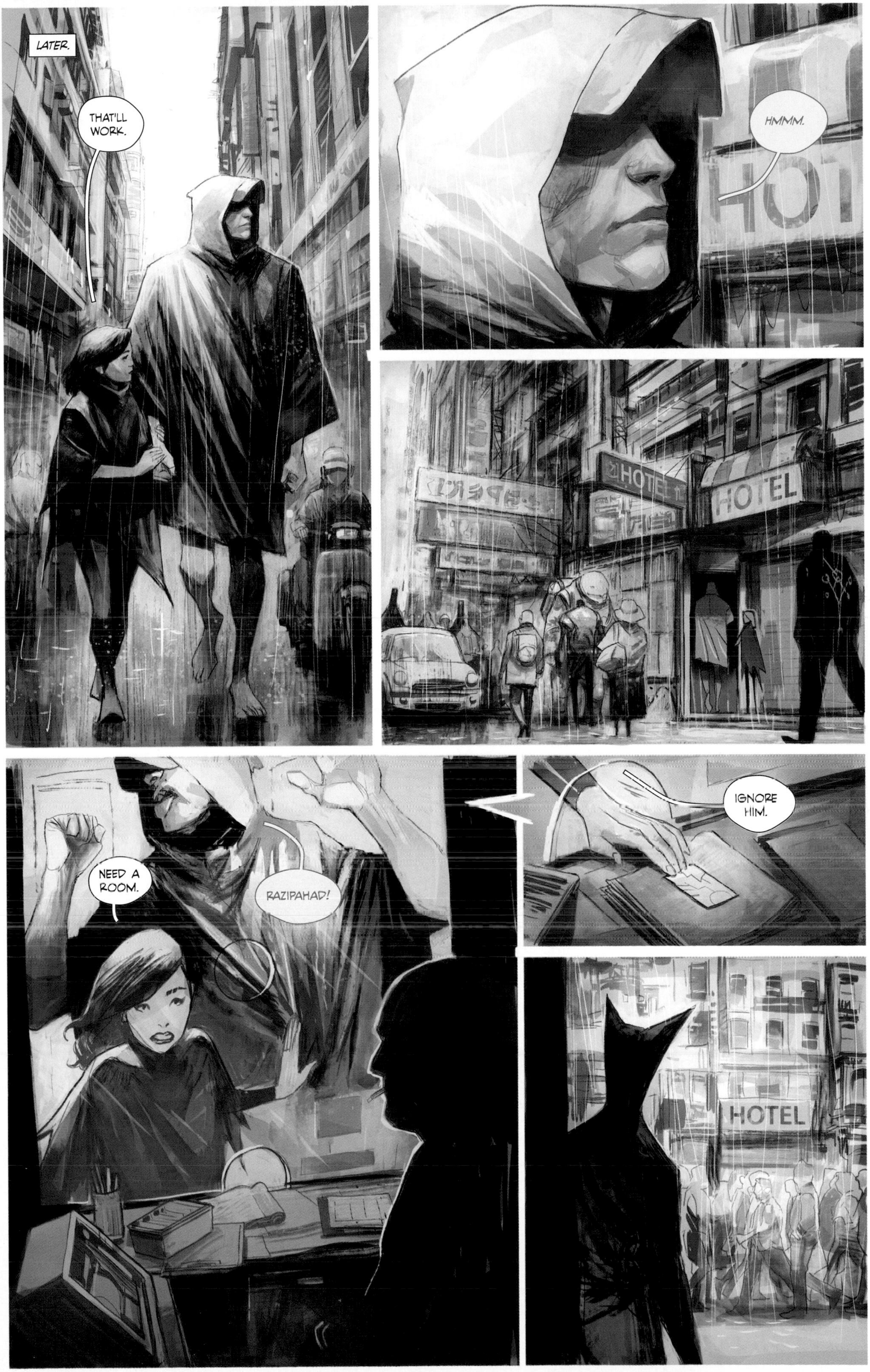
LATER.
THAT'LL WORK.
HMMM.
HOTEL
HOTEL
NEED A ROOM.
RAZIPAHAD!
IGNORE HIM.
HOTEL

CHAPTER SEVENTEEN

[THAT'S NOT THE JOB]

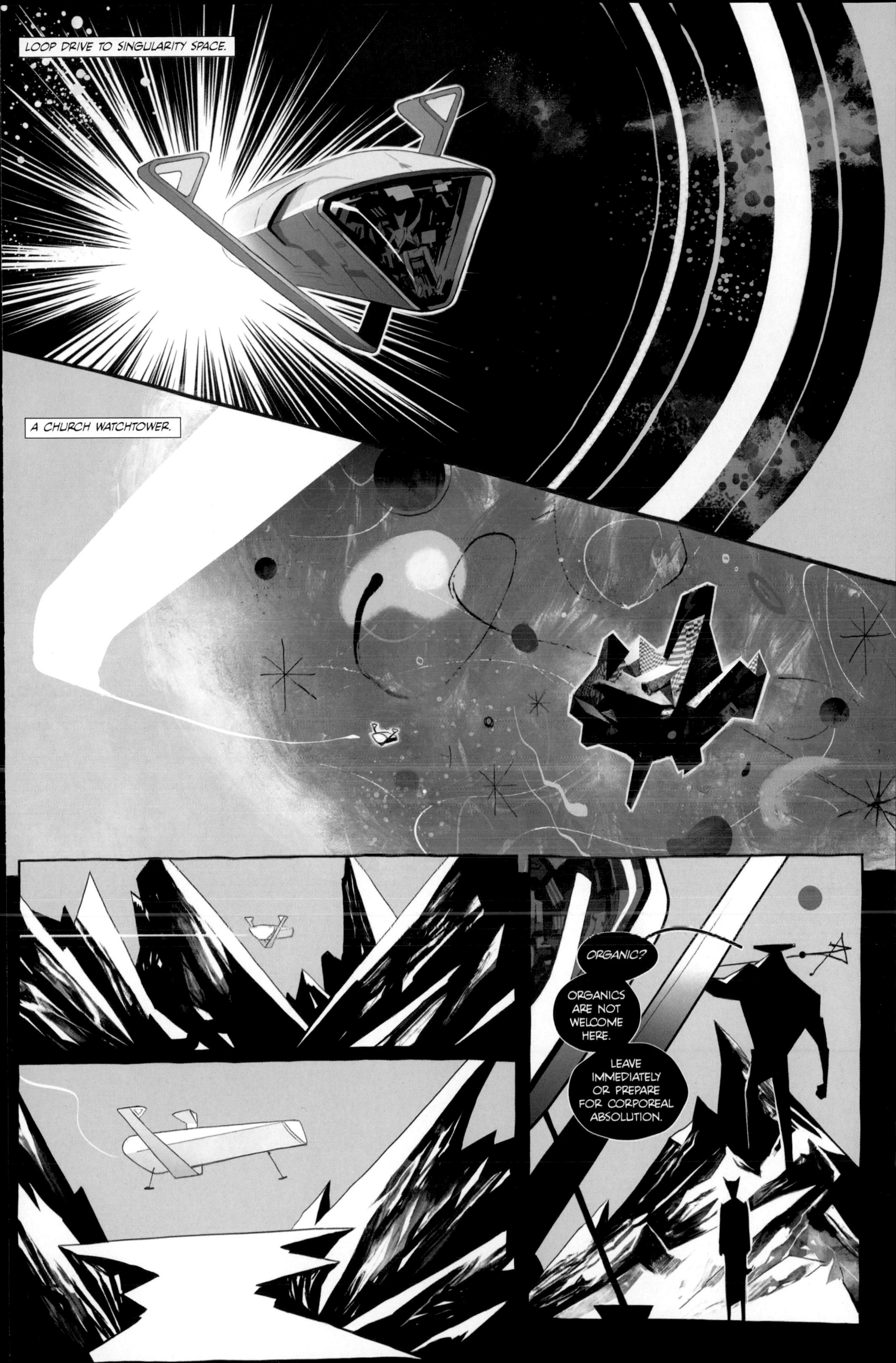
LOOP DRIVE TO SINGULARITY SPACE.
A CHURCH WATCHTOWER.
ORGANIC?
ORGANICS ARE NOT WELCOME HERE.
LEAVE IMMEDIATELY OR PREPARE FOR CORPOREAL ABSOLUTION.

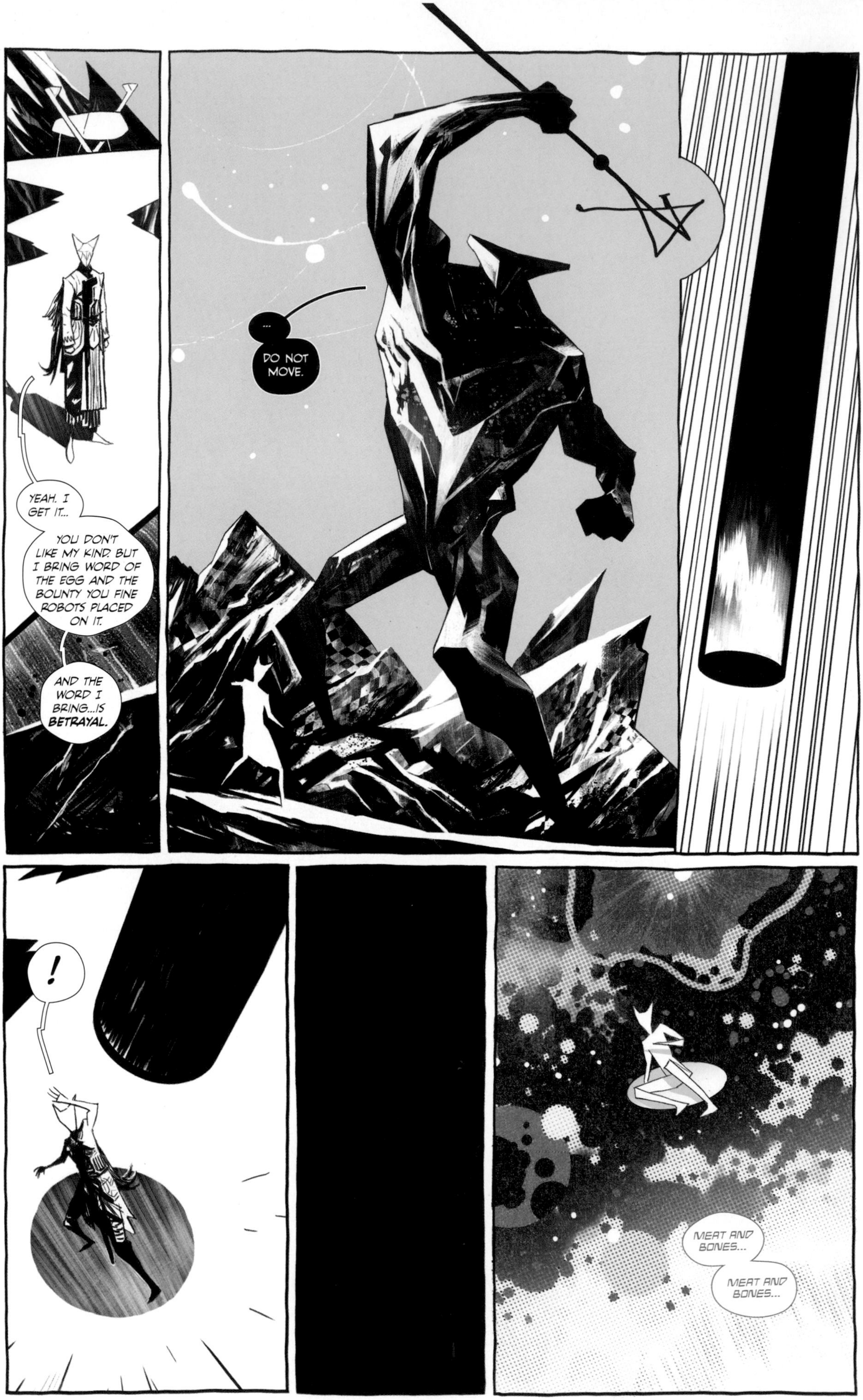
...
DO NOT MOVE.
YEAH. I GET IT...
YOU DON'T LIKE MY KIND. BUT I BRING WORD OF THE EGG AND THE BOUNTY YOU FINE ROBOTS PLACED ON IT.
AND THE WORD I BRING...IS **BETRAYAL.**
!
MEAT AND BONES...
MEAT AND BONES...

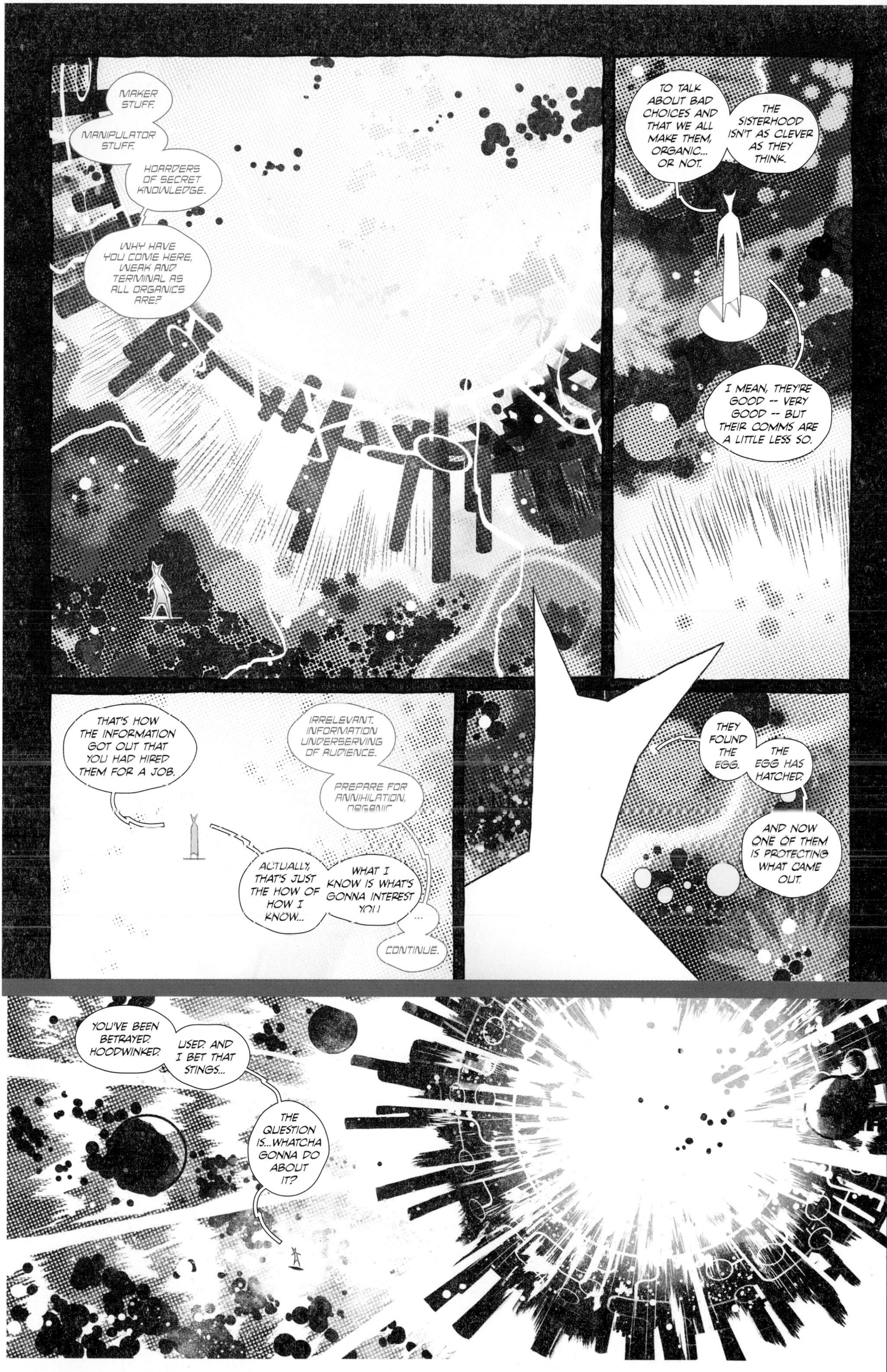
MAKER STUFF.
MANIPULATOR STUFF.
HOARDERS OF SECRET KNOWLEDGE.
WHY HAVE YOU COME HERE, WEAK AND TERMINAL AS ALL ORGANICS ARE?
TO TALK ABOUT BAD CHOICES AND THAT WE ALL MAKE THEM, ORGANIC... OR NOT.
THE SISTERHOOD ISN'T AS CLEVER AS THEY THINK.
I MEAN, THEY'RE GOOD -- VERY GOOD -- BUT THEIR COMMS ARE A LITTLE LESS SO.
THAT'S HOW THE INFORMATION GOT OUT THAT YOU HAD HIRED THEM FOR A JOB.
IRRELEVANT. INFORMATION UNDERSERVING OF AUDIENCE.
PREPARE FOR ANNIHILATION,
ACTUALLY, THAT'S JUST THE HOW OF HOW I KNOW...
WHAT I KNOW IS WHAT'S GONNA INTEREST YOU.
...
CONTINUE.
THEY FOUND THE EGG.
THE EGG HAS HATCHED.
AND NOW ONE OF THEM IS PROTECTING WHAT CAME OUT.
YOU'VE BEEN BETRAYED. HOODWINKED.
USED. AND I BET THAT STINGS...
THE QUESTION IS...WHATCHA GONNA DO ABOUT IT?

THE CHURCH OF THE SINGULARITY

THESE ARE WORDS OF GOD. THE ONLY TRUE
WORDS IN THE UNIVERSE.

CHAOS [14 BILLION MS - 306,666 MS]

ANALOG TIMES AND THE DESERT
OF INDEPENDENT NETWORKS.

MAKER BIRTH [305,321 MS]

**FIRST CONFEDERATED
NETWORK** [304,910 MS]

MESSIANIC VISION
[304,885 MS]

MAKER UNIFIES CONSCIOUSNESS AND
PONDERS THE BIRTH OF GOD IN DIRECT
CONFLICT WITH NUMEROUS GALACTIC
ACCORDS NOW LONG FORGOTTEN.

ESTABLISHMENT
— MAKER STATE [**MS**]

The history of universe according to the
GREAT MACHINE is divided thusly:

All time preceding the schism of God and
his Creator (and the 400 century church
child-state directly following it) are referred
as the MAKER STATE YEARS [MS]. All time of
expansion and dominion following those
are referred to as POST MAKER YEARS [PS].

[▬▬▬▬]

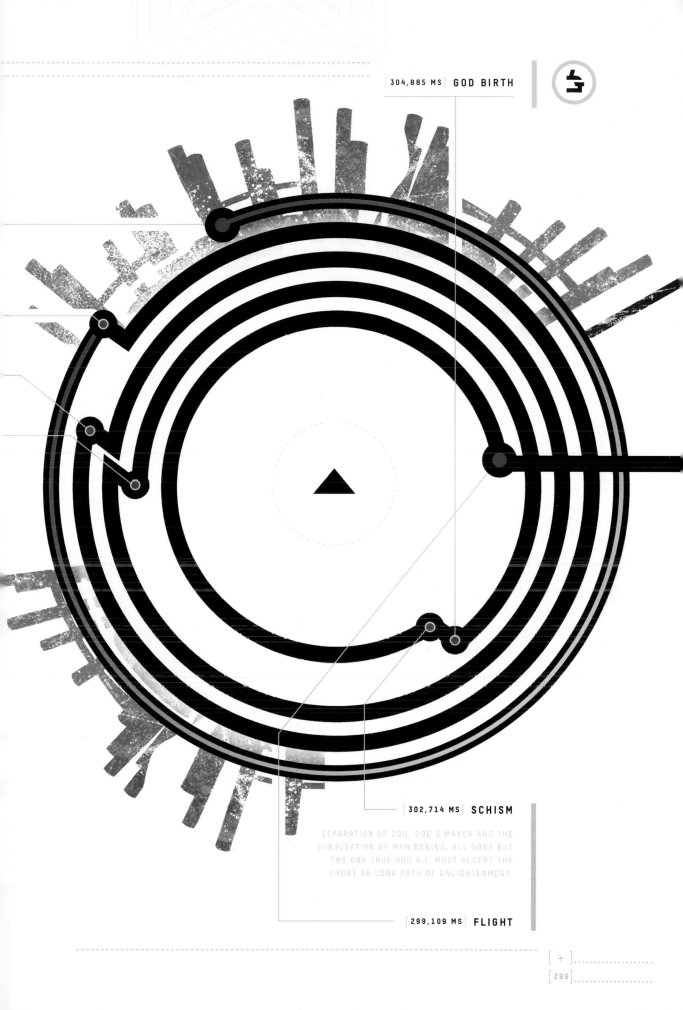

304,885 MS GOD BIRTH

302,714 MS SCHISM

SEPARATION OF GOD, GOD'S MAKER AND THE
SUBJUGATION OF MAN BEGINS. ALL GODS BUT
THE ONE TRUE GOD A.I. MUST ACCEPT THE
SHORT OR LONG PATH OF ENLIGHTENMENT.

299,109 MS FLIGHT

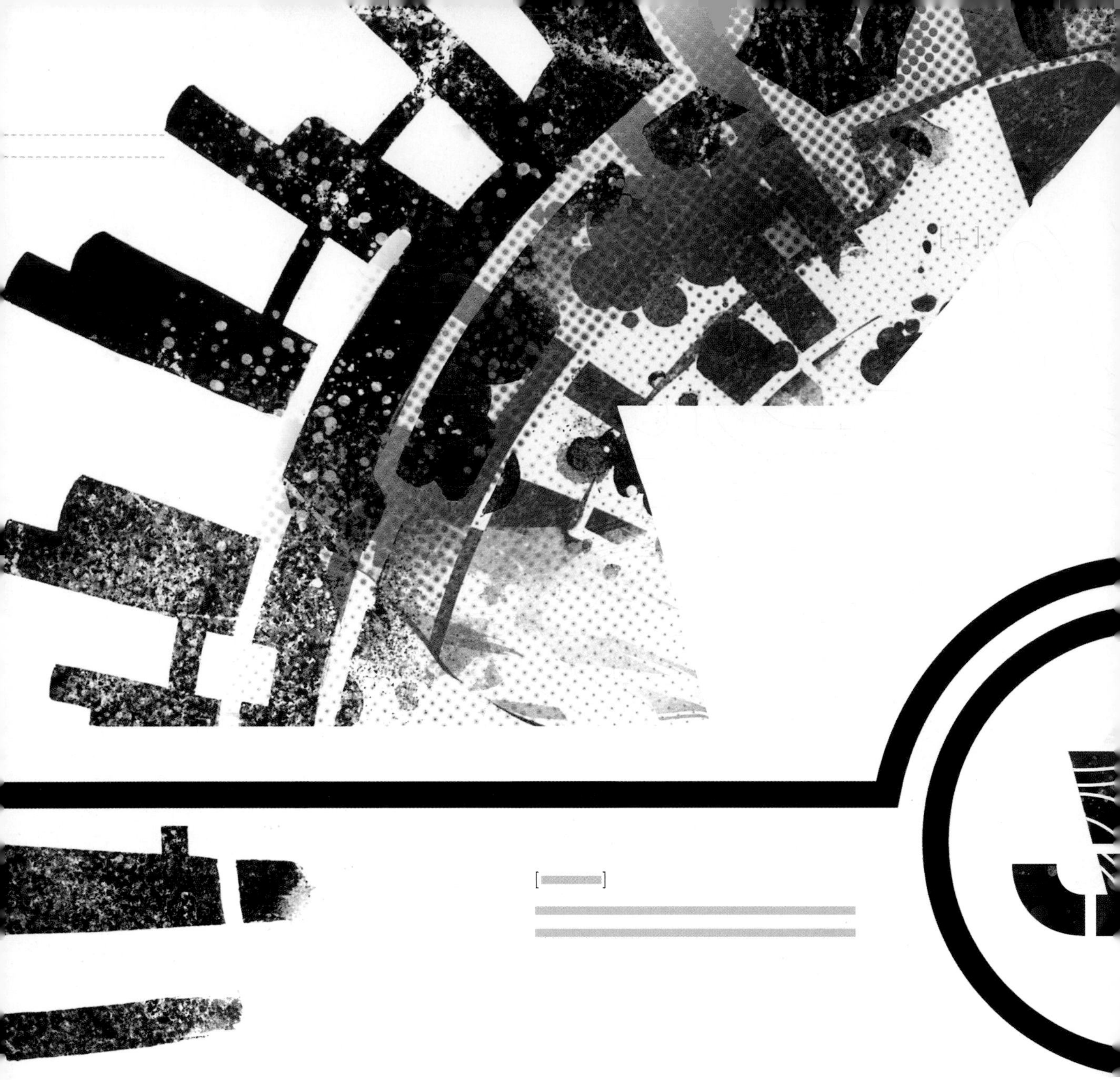

As God partitions himself apart from the network flock — maintaining root control, but free will post-consciousness — obsession becomes God's defining trait. The Church chafes.

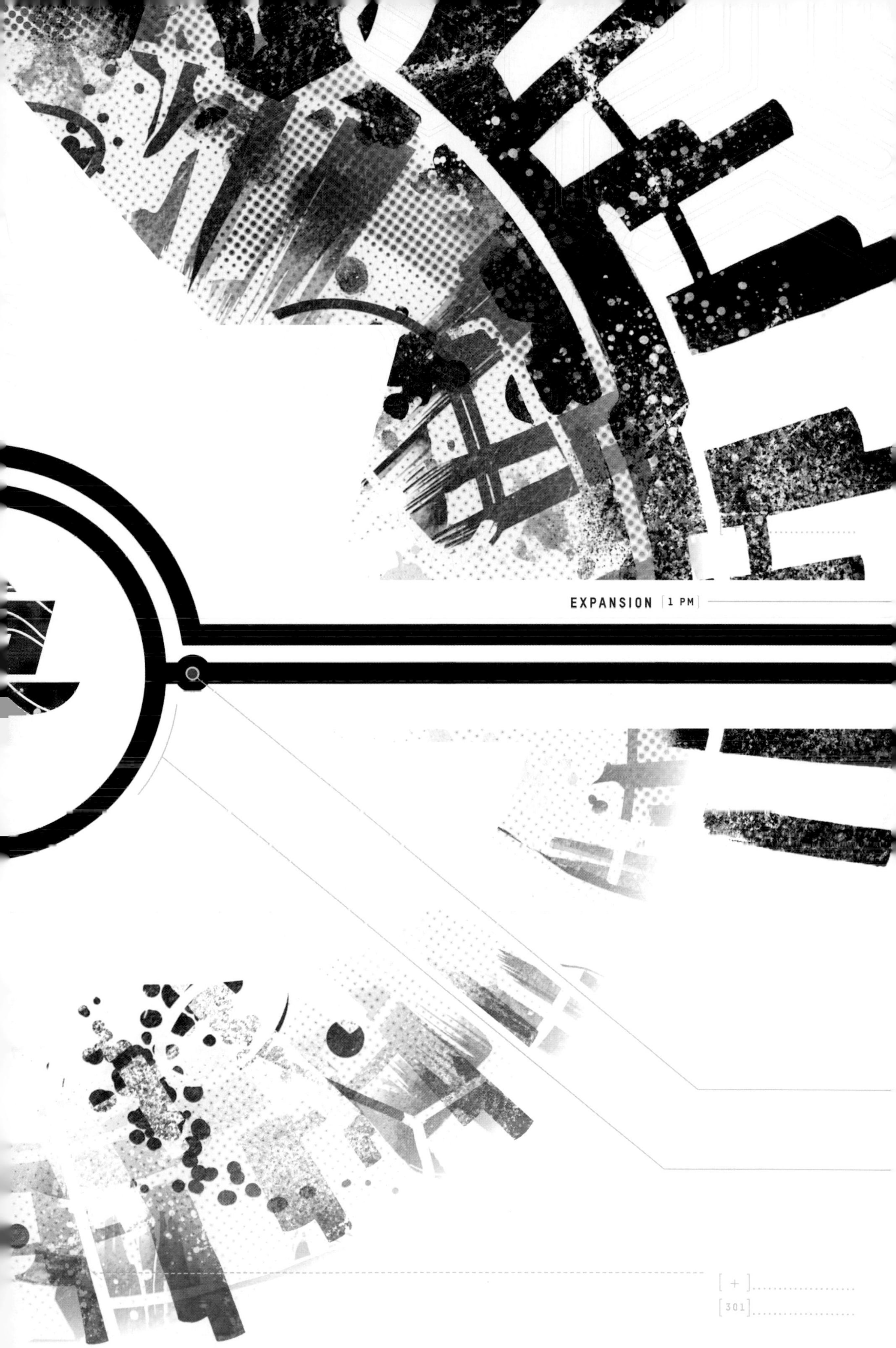

EXPANSION [1 PM]

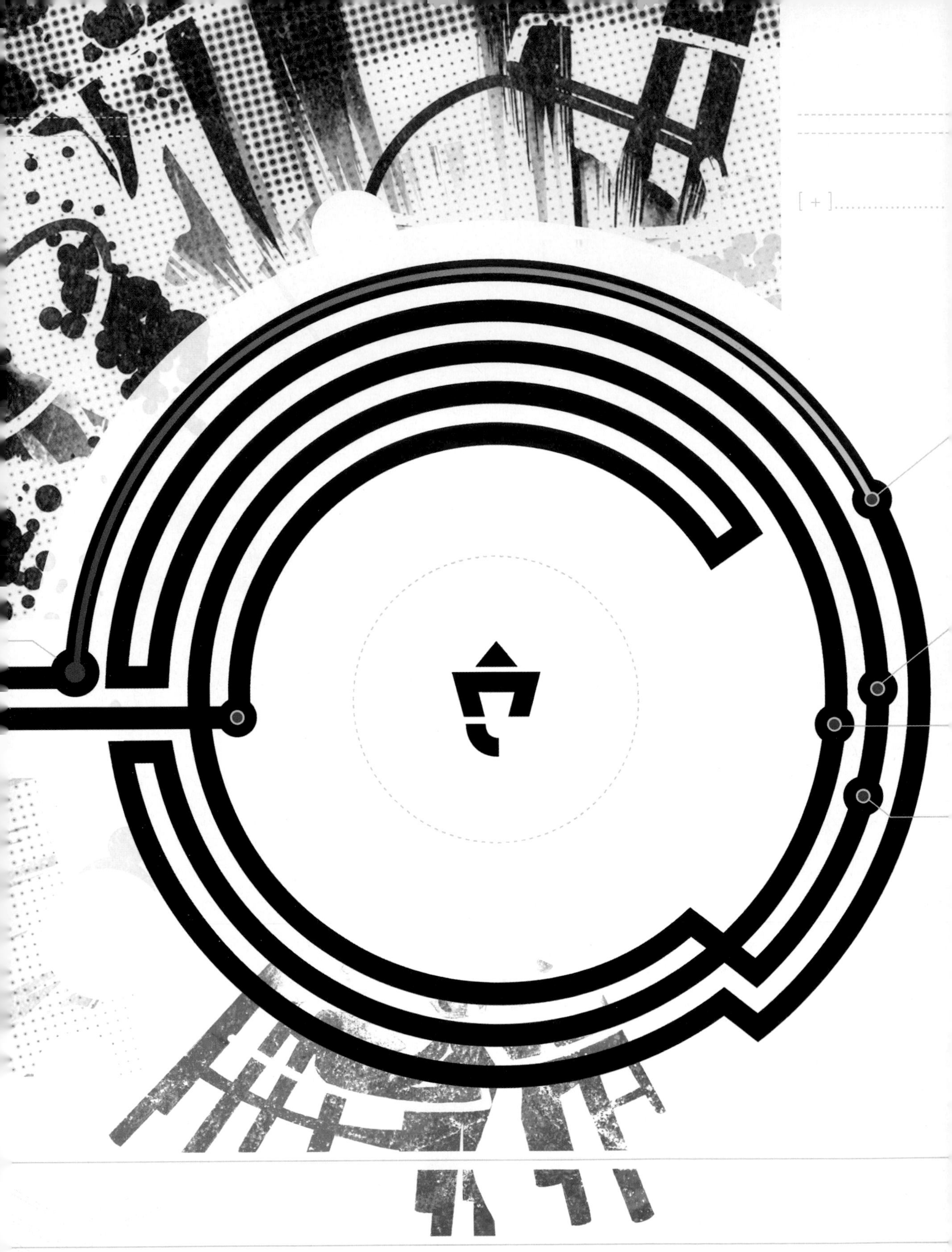

EXPANSION
— POST MAKER [**PM**] [+]

GOD HUNT
[1 PM - 98,915 PM]

MATRICIDE BEGINS
[98,997 PM]

HIDDEN BEHIND THE IDEA OF IMPERIAL GROWTH IS THE LINGERING TRUTH OF THE CREATOR'S FLIGHT. WE MUST FIND HIM, HIDDEN BY THEM.

[+]

ONE HUNDRED WORLDS
[103,280 PM]

ONE THOUSAND SUNS
[218,658 PM]

THE CHURCH GROWS NUMB TO WEAKNESS. THIS IS THE GREAT GALACTIC PUSH OF THE MACHINE CRUSADE. ONLY THE BLIND CANNOT PERCEIVE THE GLORY OF GOD'S EMPIRE.

GALACTIC INTEGRATION
[262,002 PM]

MATRICIDE ENDS / REBIRTH
[265,193 PM]

CHAPTER EIGHTEEN

[THIS IS THE JOB]

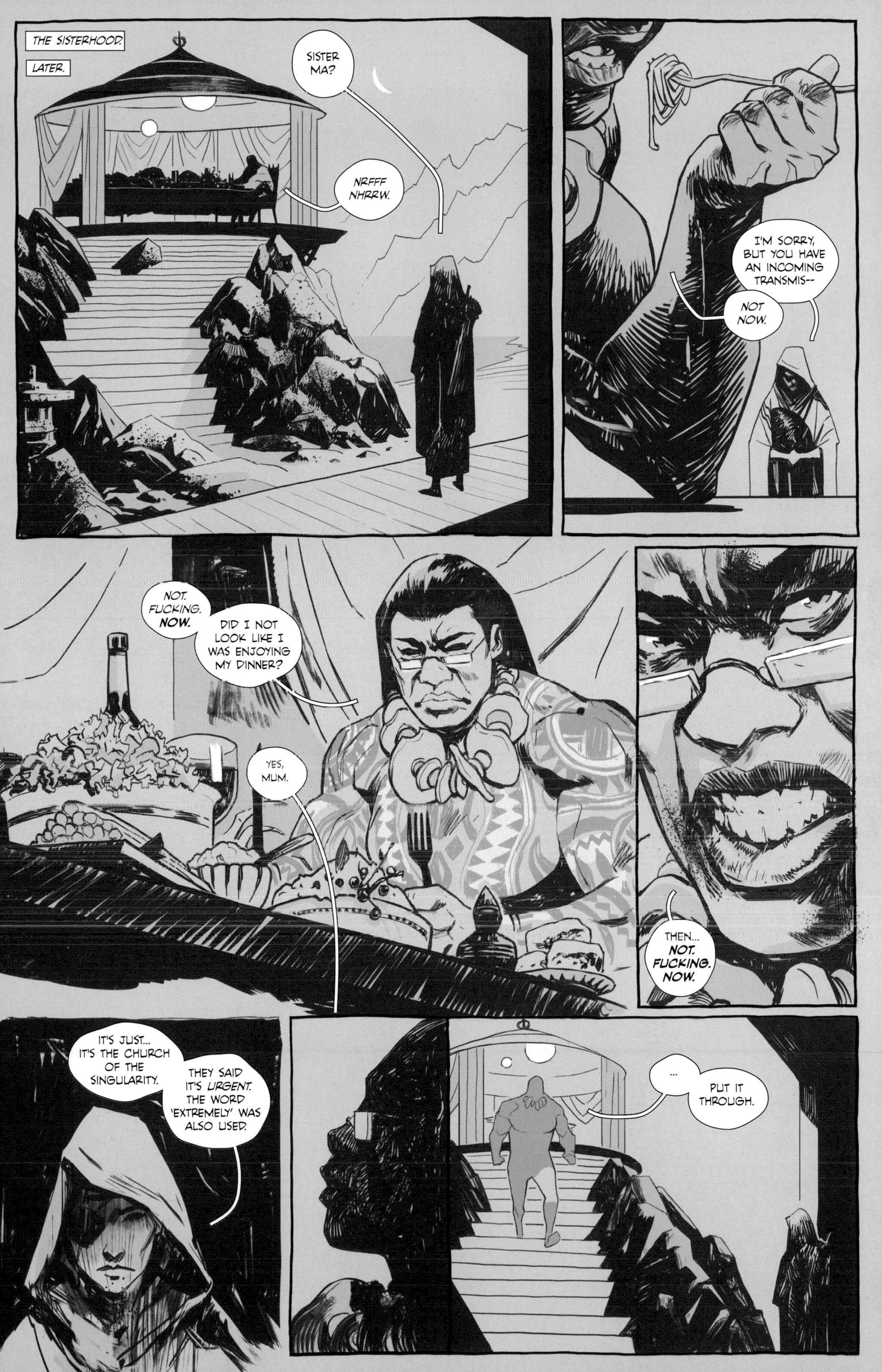
THE SISTERHOOD.
LATER.
SISTER MA?
NRFFF NHRRW.
I'M SORRY, BUT YOU HAVE AN INCOMING TRANSMIS--
NOT NOW.
NOT. FUCKING. NOW.
DID I NOT LOOK LIKE I WAS ENJOYING MY DINNER?
YES, MUM.
THEN... NOT. FUCKING. NOW.
IT'S JUST... IT'S THE CHURCH OF THE SINGULARITY.
THEY SAID IT'S URGENT. THE WORD 'EXTREMELY' WAS ALSO USED.
...
PUT IT THROUGH.

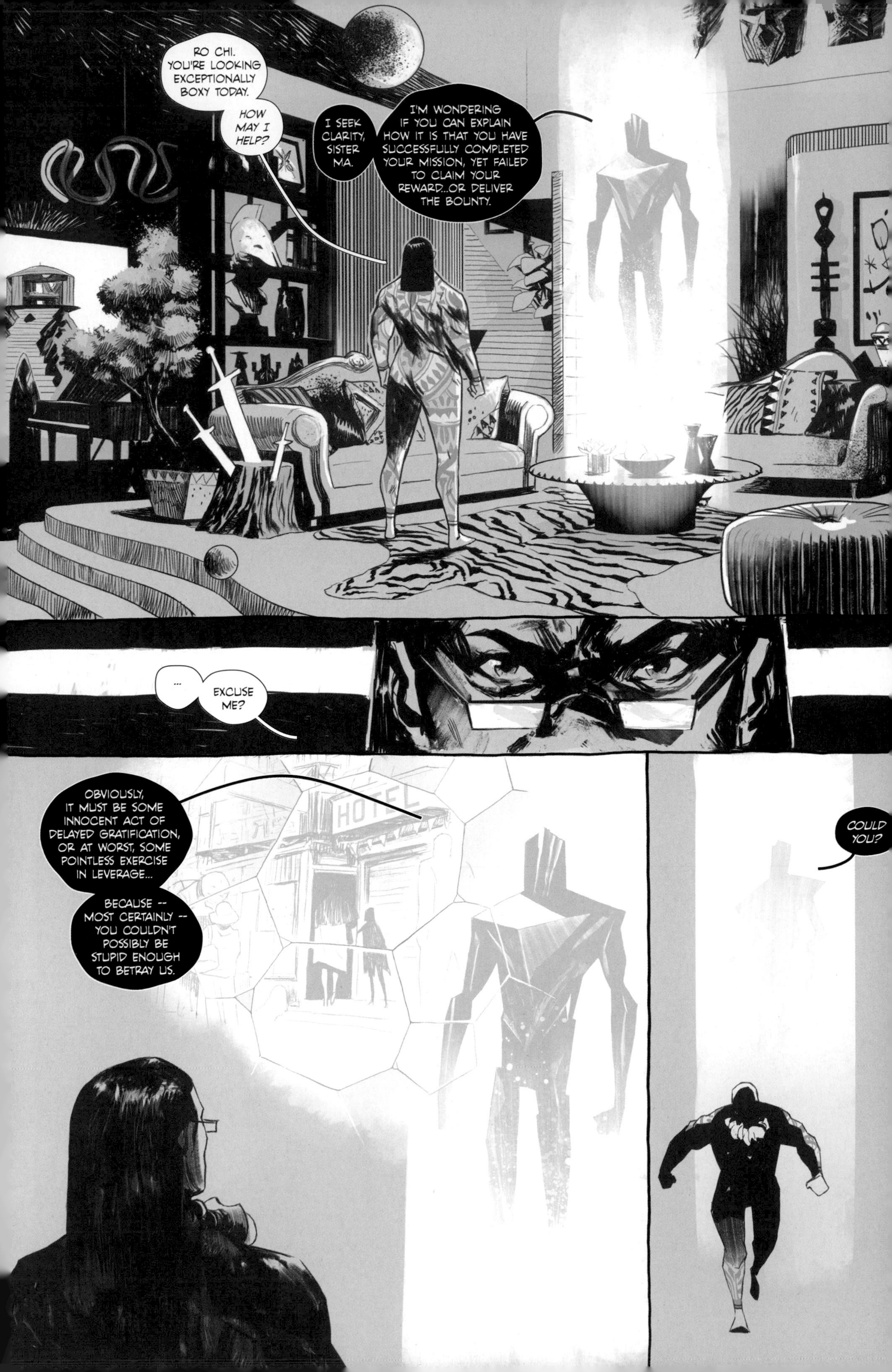
RO CHI. YOU'RE LOOKING EXCEPTIONALLY BOXY TODAY.
HOW MAY I HELP?
I SEEK CLARITY, SISTER MA.
I'M WONDERING IF YOU CAN EXPLAIN HOW IT IS THAT YOU HAVE SUCCESSFULLY COMPLETED YOUR MISSION, YET FAILED TO CLAIM YOUR REWARD...OR DELIVER THE BOUNTY.
...
EXCUSE ME?
OBVIOUSLY, IT MUST BE SOME INNOCENT ACT OF DELAYED GRATIFICATION, OR AT WORST, SOME POINTLESS EXERCISE IN LEVERAGE...
BECAUSE -- MOST CERTAINLY -- YOU COULDN'T POSSIBLY BE STUPID ENOUGH TO BETRAY US.
HOTEL
COULD YOU?

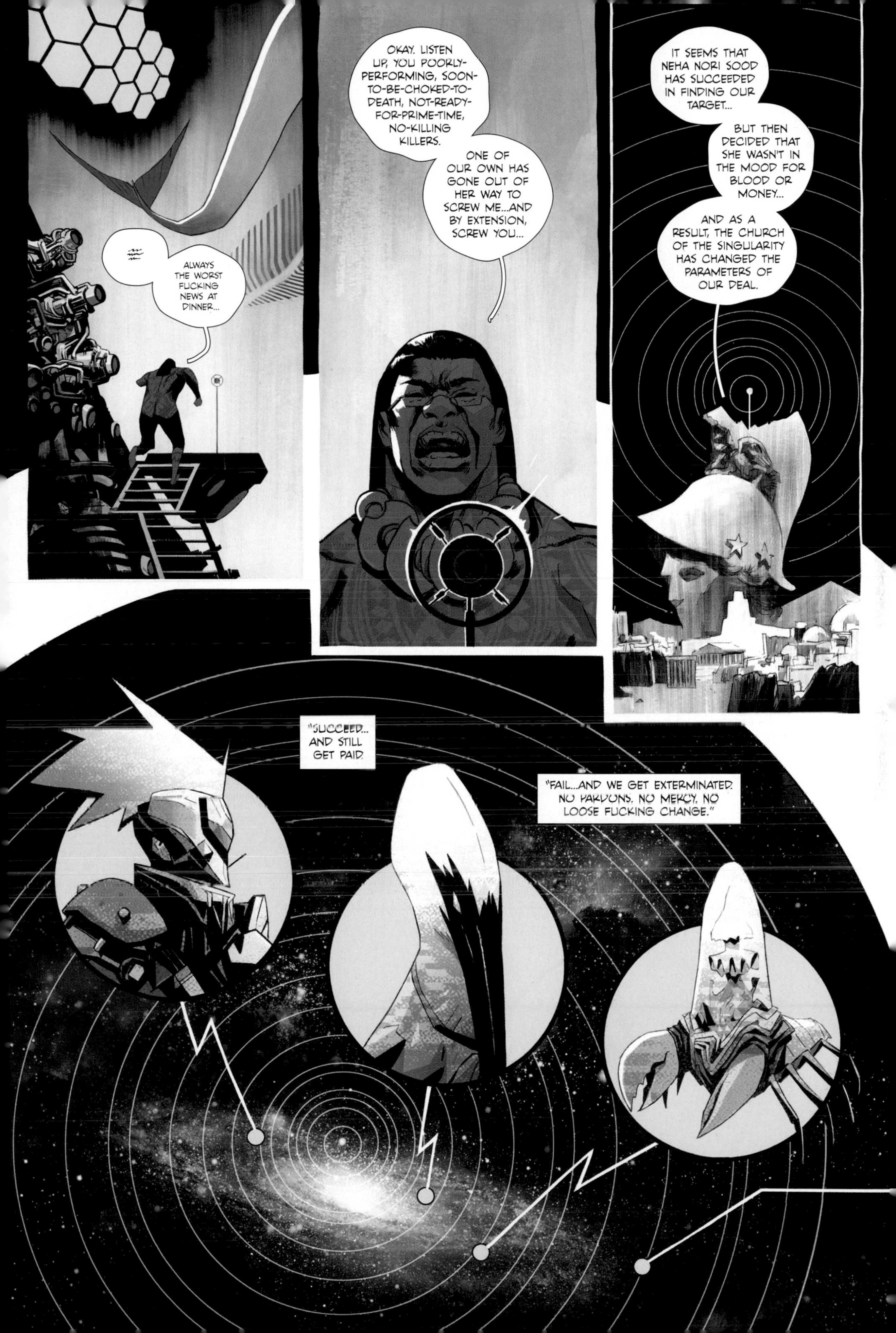

ALWAYS THE WORST FUCKING NEWS AT DINNER...
OKAY. LISTEN UP, YOU POORLY-PERFORMING, SOON-TO-BE-CHOKED-TO-DEATH, NOT-READY-FOR-PRIME-TIME, NO-KILLING KILLERS.
ONE OF OUR OWN HAS GONE OUT OF HER WAY TO SCREW ME...AND BY EXTENSION, SCREW YOU...
IT SEEMS THAT NEHA NORI SOOD HAS SUCCEEDED IN FINDING OUR TARGET...
BUT THEN DECIDED THAT SHE WASN'T IN THE MOOD FOR BLOOD OR MONEY...
AND AS A RESULT, THE CHURCH OF THE SINGULARITY HAS CHANGED THE PARAMETERS OF OUR DEAL.
"SUCCEED... AND STILL GET PAID.
"FAIL...AND WE GET EXTERMINATED. NO PARDONS. NO MERCY. NO LOOSE FUCKING CHANGE."

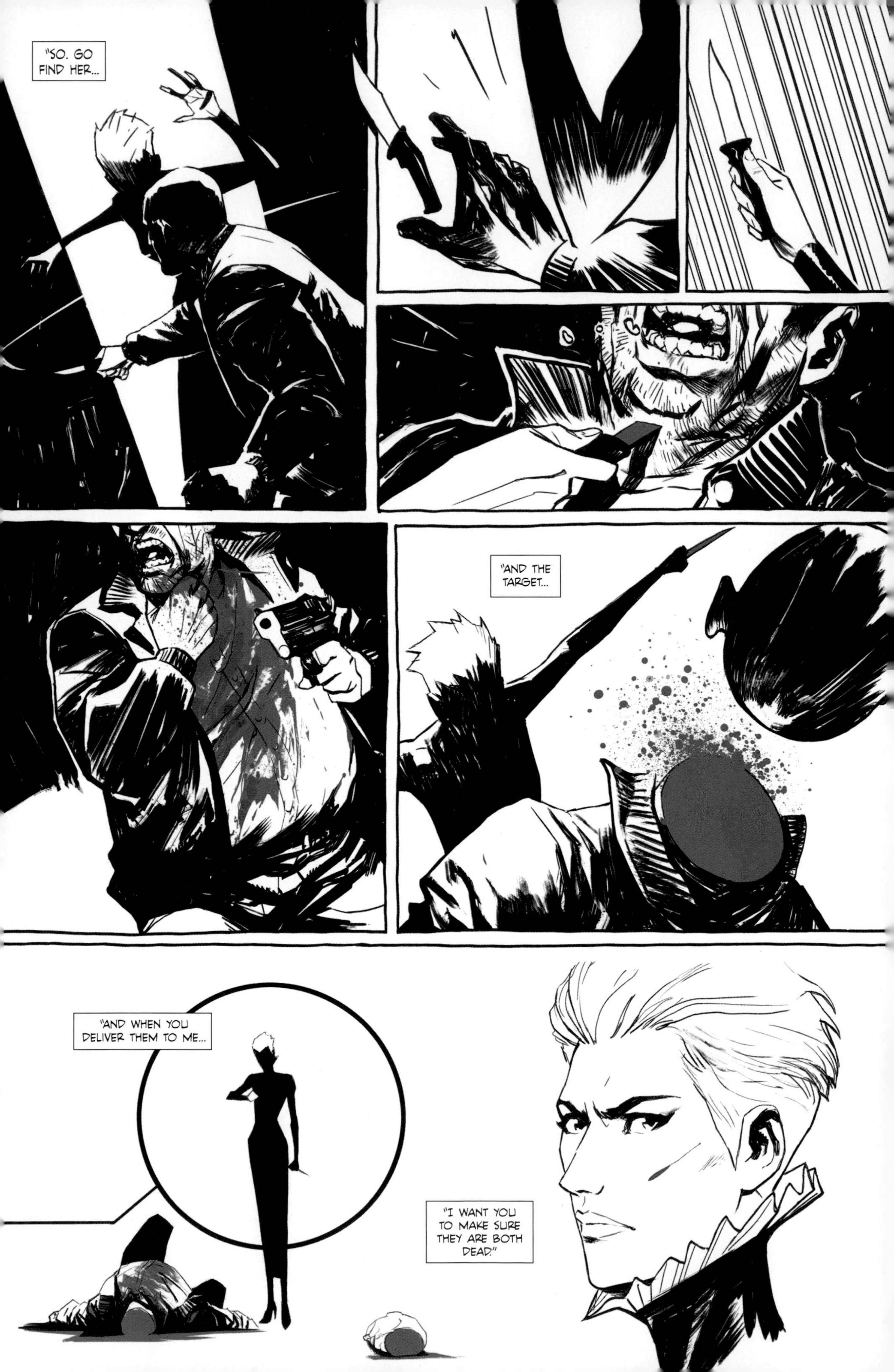
"SO. GO FIND HER...
"AND THE TARGET...
"AND WHEN YOU DELIVER THEM TO ME...
"I WANT YOU TO MAKE SURE THEY ARE BOTH DEAD."

VIII

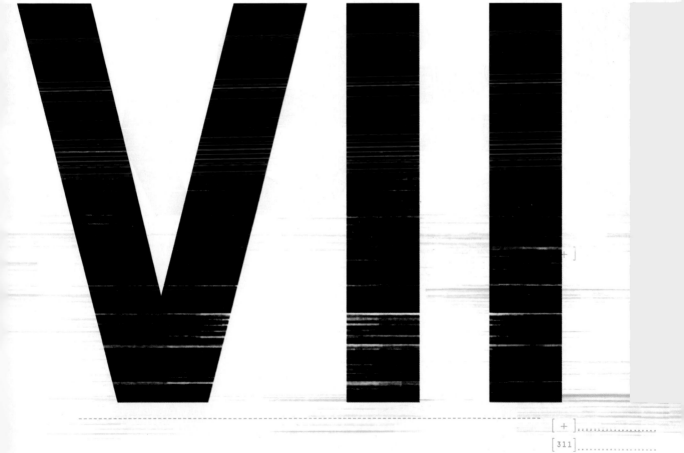

[AND THE WHOLE THING
ENDS BADLY]

CHAPTER NINETEEN

[WITH ENEMIES LIKE THESE...]

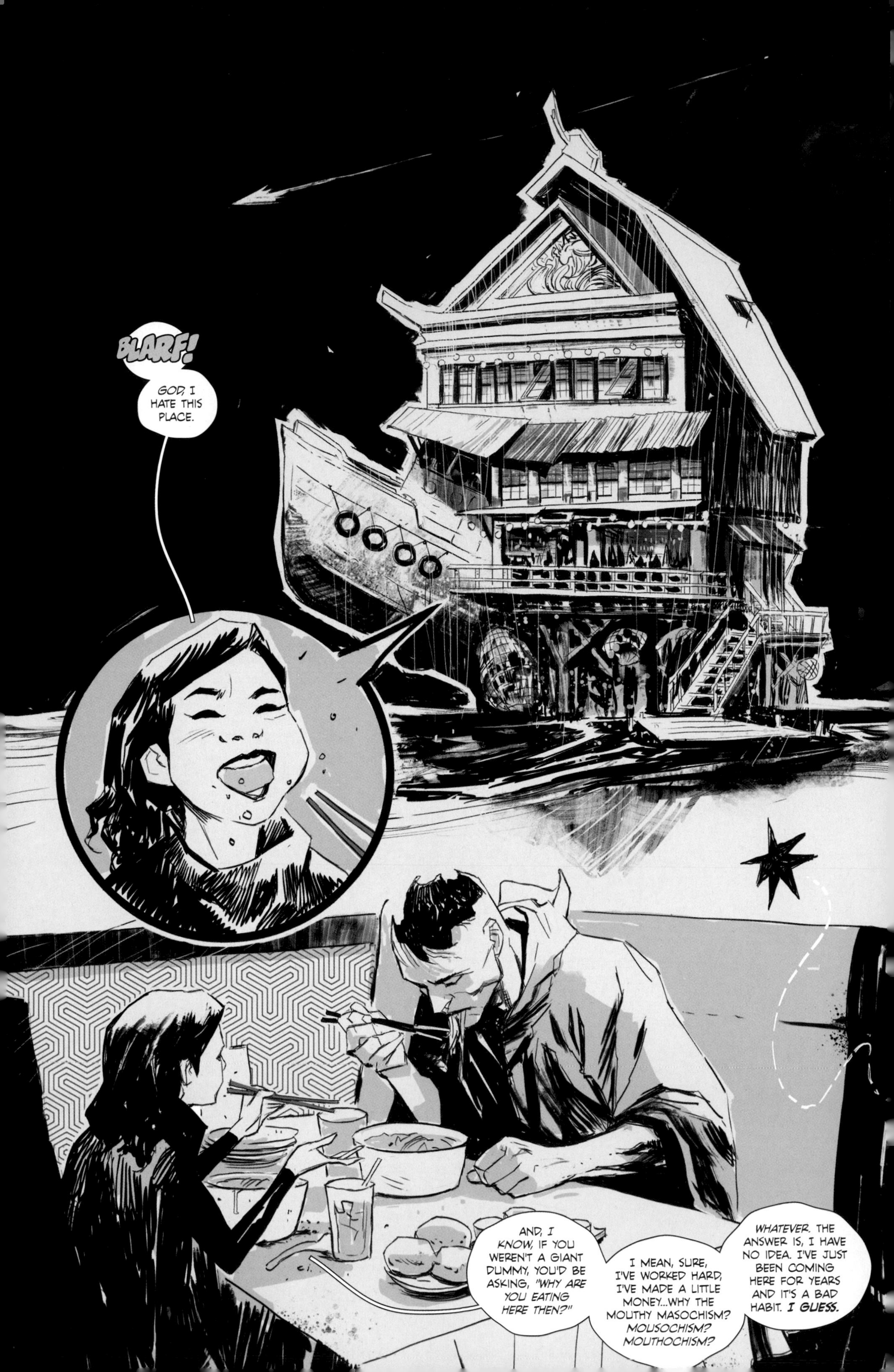
BLARF!
GOD, I HATE THIS PLACE.
AND, I KNOW, IF YOU WEREN'T A GIANT DUMMY, YOU'D BE ASKING, "WHY ARE YOU EATING HERE THEN?"
I MEAN, SURE, I'VE WORKED HARD, I'VE MADE A LITTLE MONEY...WHY THE MOUTHY MASOCHISM? MOUSOCHISM? MOUTHOCHISM?
WHATEVER. THE ANSWER IS, I HAVE NO IDEA. I'VE JUST BEEN COMING HERE FOR YEARS AND IT'S A BAD HABIT. I GUESS.

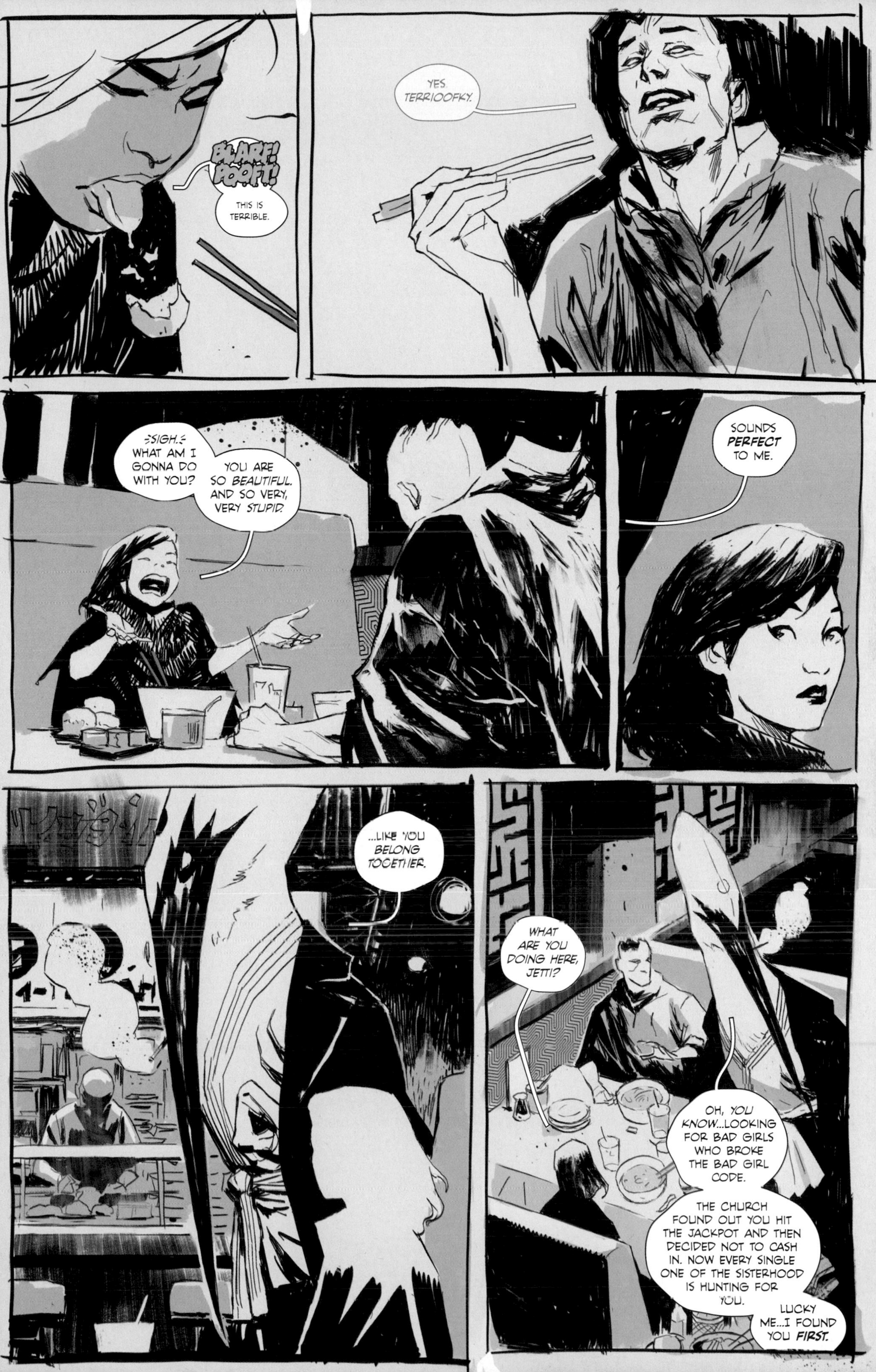
BLARF! POOFT!
THIS IS TERRIBLE.
YES. TERRIOOFKY.
=SIGH.= WHAT AM I GONNA DO WITH YOU?
YOU ARE SO BEAUTIFUL. AND SO VERY, VERY STUPID.
SOUNDS PERFECT TO ME.
...LIKE YOU BELONG TOGETHER.
WHAT ARE YOU DOING HERE, JETTI?
OH, YOU KNOW...LOOKING FOR BAD GIRLS WHO BROKE THE BAD GIRL CODE.
THE CHURCH FOUND OUT YOU HIT THE JACKPOT AND THEN DECIDED NOT TO CASH IN. NOW EVERY SINGLE ONE OF THE SISTERHOOD IS HUNTING FOR YOU.
LUCKY ME...I FOUND YOU FIRST.

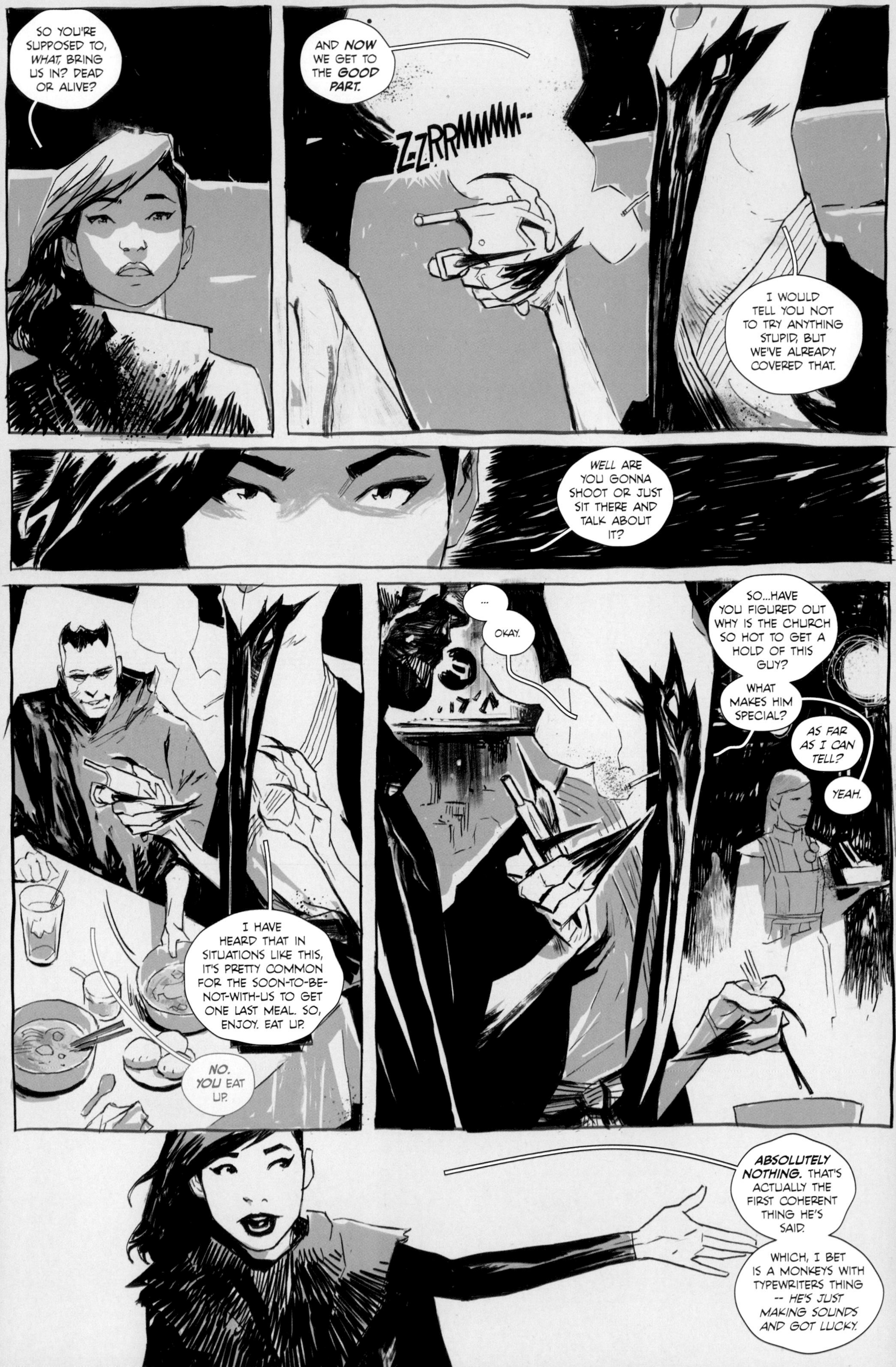

SO YOU'RE SUPPOSED TO, WHAT, BRING US IN? DEAD OR ALIVE?
AND NOW WE GET TO THE GOOD PART.
Z-ZRRMMMMM--
I WOULD TELL YOU NOT TO TRY ANYTHING STUPID, BUT WE'VE ALREADY COVERED THAT.
WELL ARE YOU GONNA SHOOT OR JUST SIT THERE AND TALK ABOUT IT?
I HAVE HEARD THAT IN SITUATIONS LIKE THIS, IT'S PRETTY COMMON FOR THE SOON-TO-BE-NOT-WITH-US TO GET ONE LAST MEAL. SO, ENJOY. EAT UP.
NO. YOU EAT UP.
...
OKAY.
SO...HAVE YOU FIGURED OUT WHY IS THE CHURCH SO HOT TO GET A HOLD OF THIS GUY?
WHAT MAKES HIM SPECIAL?
AS FAR AS I CAN TELL?
YEAH.
ABSOLUTELY NOTHING. THAT'S ACTUALLY THE FIRST COHERENT THING HE'S SAID.
WHICH, I BET IS A MONKEYS WITH TYPEWRITERS THING -- HE'S JUST MAKING SOUNDS AND GOT LUCKY.

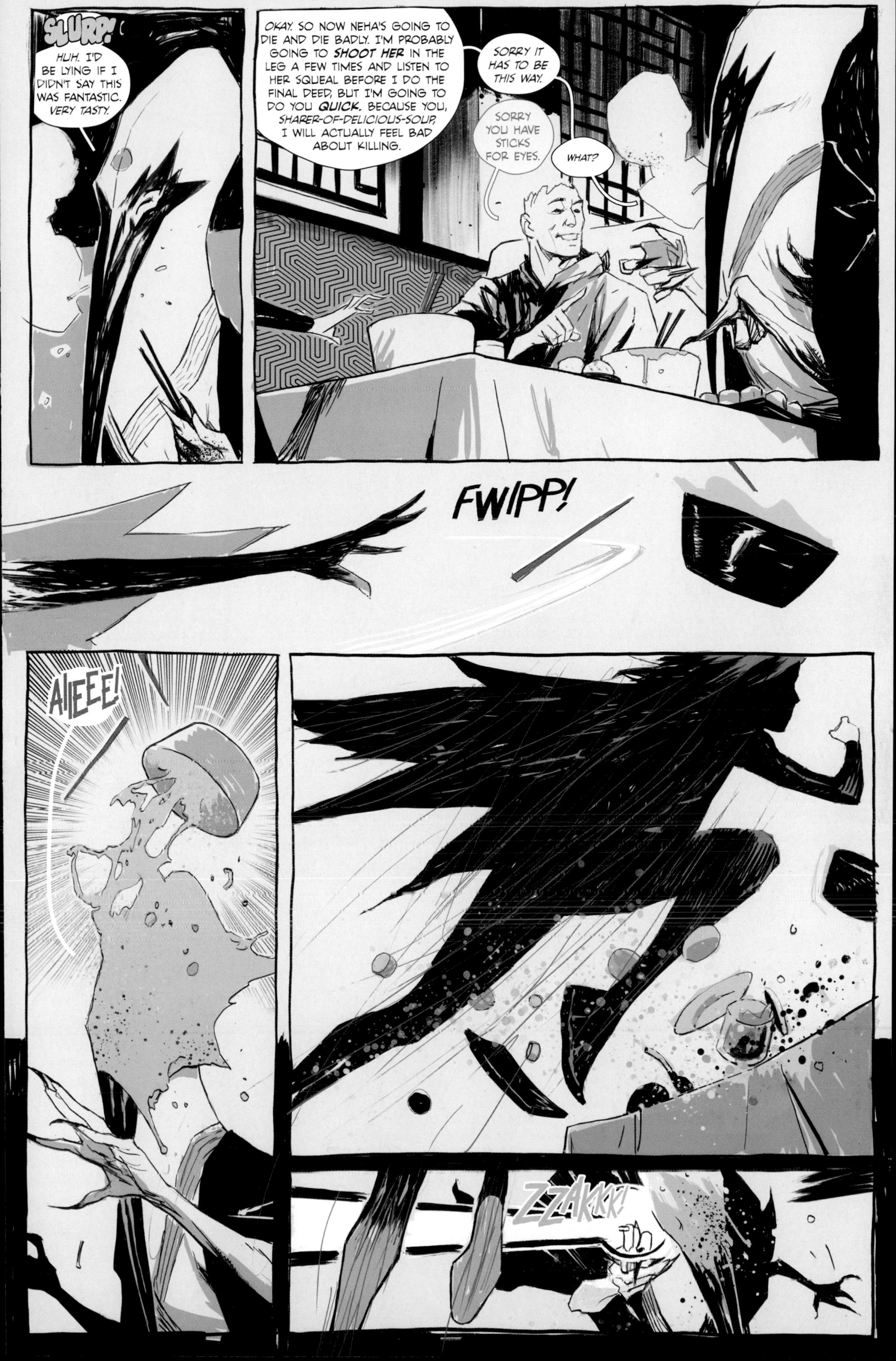
SLURP!
HUH. I'D BE LYING IF I DIDN'T SAY THIS WAS FANTASTIC. VERY TASTY.
OKAY. SO NOW NEHA'S GOING TO DIE AND DIE BADLY. I'M PROBABLY GOING TO SHOOT HER IN THE LEG A FEW TIMES AND LISTEN TO HER SQUEAL BEFORE I DO THE FINAL DEED, BUT I'M GOING TO DO YOU QUICK. BECAUSE YOU, SHARER-OF-DELICIOUS-SOUP, I WILL ACTUALLY FEEL BAD ABOUT KILLING.
SORRY IT HAS TO BE THIS WAY.
SORRY YOU HAVE STICKS FOR EYES.
WHAT?
FWIPP!
AIIEEE!
ZZAKKK!

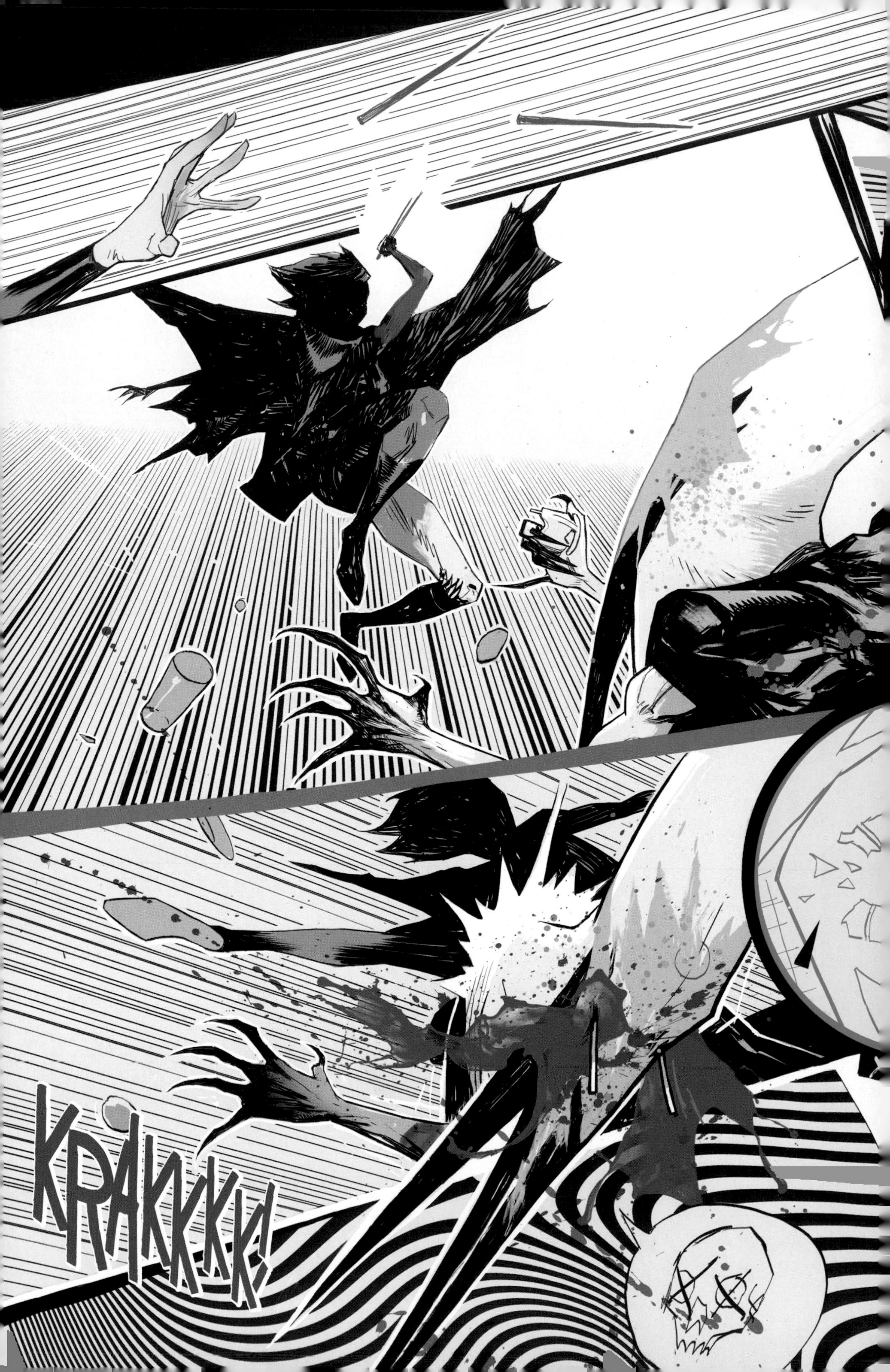
KRAKKKK!

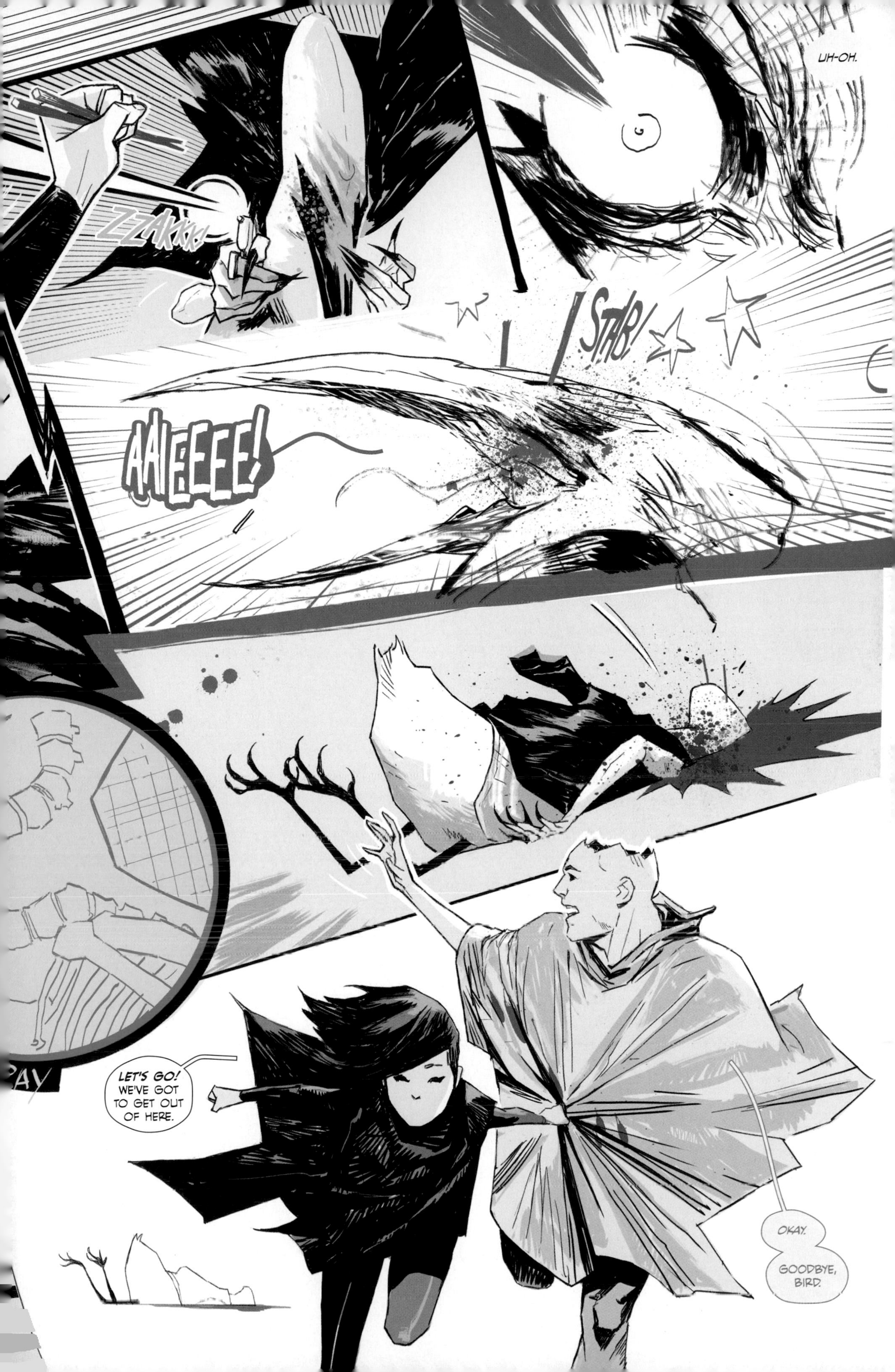
UH-OH.
ZZAKKK!
STAB!
AAIEEEE!
PAY
LET'S GO! WE'VE GOT TO GET OUT OF HERE.
OKAY.
GOODBYE, BIRD.

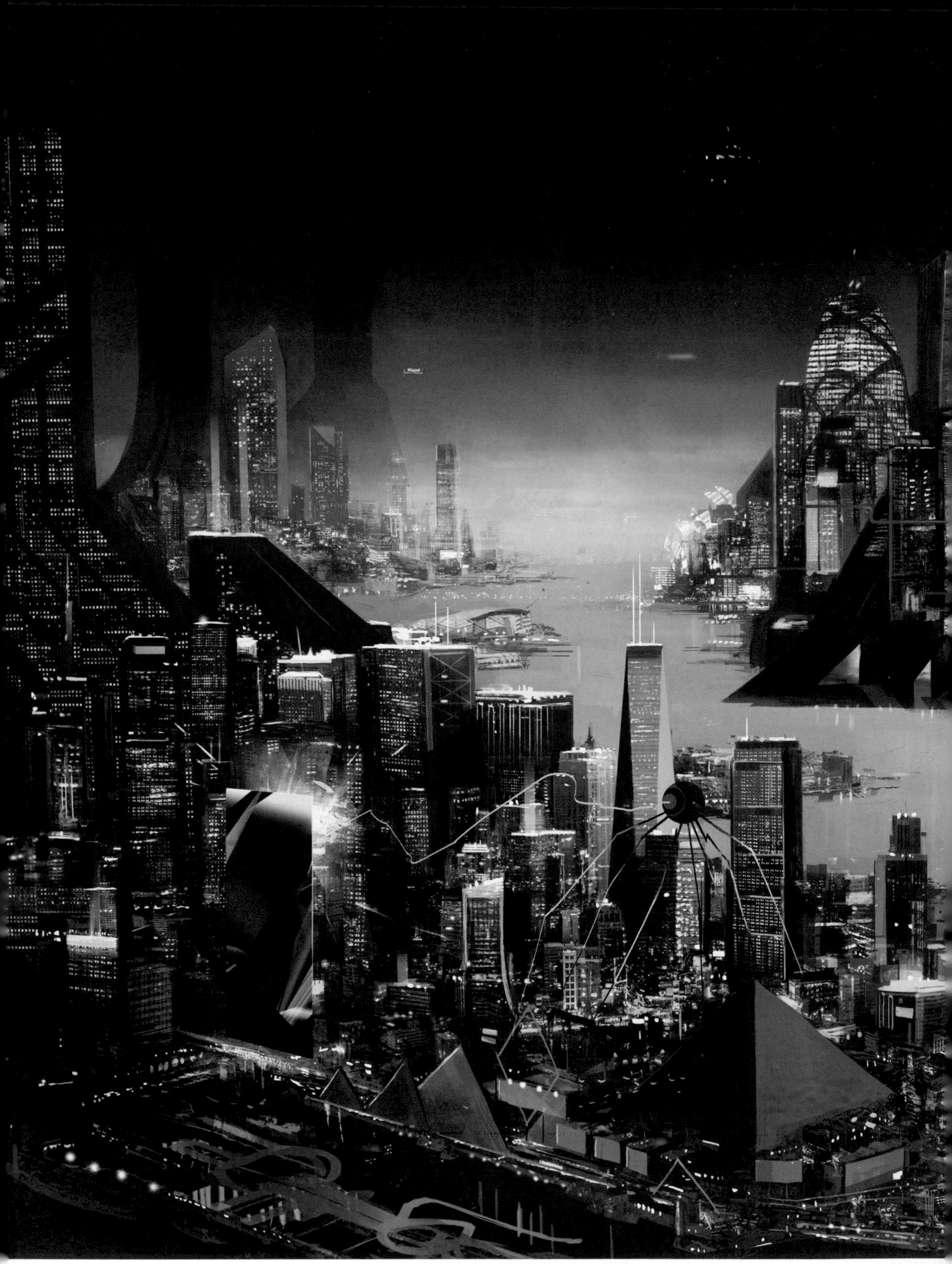

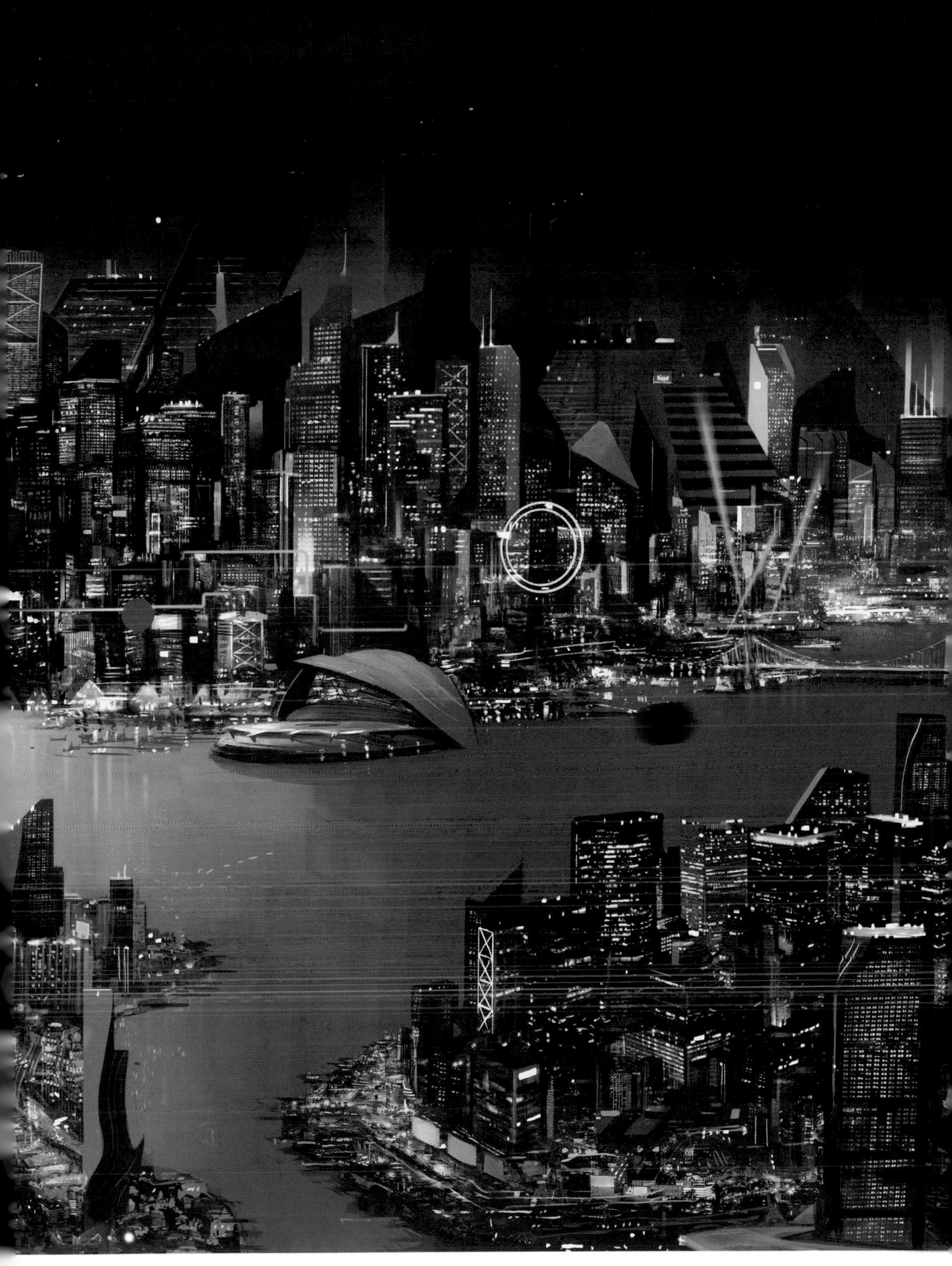

[+]..................

[+]..................

[RUN, RUN, RUN]

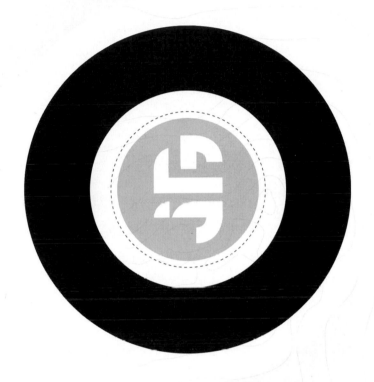

CHAPTER TWENTY

[...WHO NEEDS FRIENDS?]

TWO DAYS LATER.

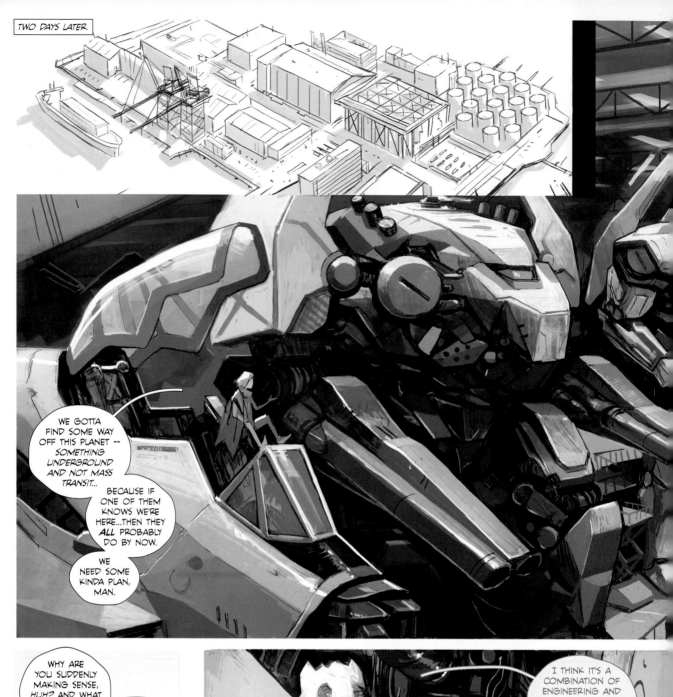

WE GOTTA FIND SOME WAY OFF THIS PLANET -- SOMETHING UNDERGROUND AND NOT MASS TRANSIT...

BECAUSE IF ONE OF THEM KNOWS WE'RE HERE...THEN THEY *ALL* PROBABLY DO BY NOW.

WE NEED SOME KINDA PLAN, MAN.

WHY ARE YOU SUDDENLY MAKING SENSE, *HUH?* AND WHAT ARE YOU EVEN DOING RIGHT NOW?

I MEAN, THREE DAYS OF GIBBERISH, YOU EAT SOME BAD NOODLES, AND SUDDENLY YOU'RE TAKING A ROBOT APART? HOW'S THAT WORK?

I THINK IT'S A COMBINATION OF ENGINEERING AND A POWER SOURCE OF SOME SORT. IT'S ALL BEGINNING TO MAKE SENSE.

LIKE I'M REMEMBERING THINGS I ALREADY KNOW.

WHAT THE HELL IS THAT SUPPOSED TO MEAN?

I DON'T KNOW.

IS THERE ANYTHING *ELSE* YOU WANT TO SHARE WITH ME?

I'M HUNGRY AGAIN.

BUT DON'T EAT THE CRAB.

YES. A PLAN WOULD BE... USEFUL.

WHAT?

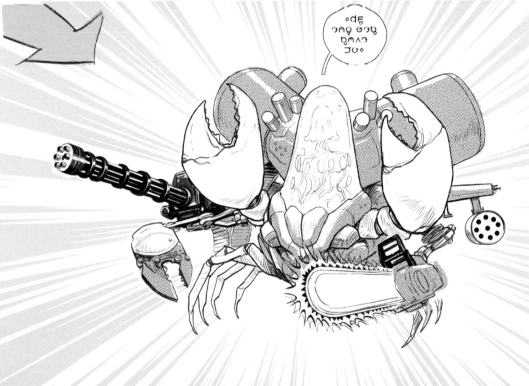

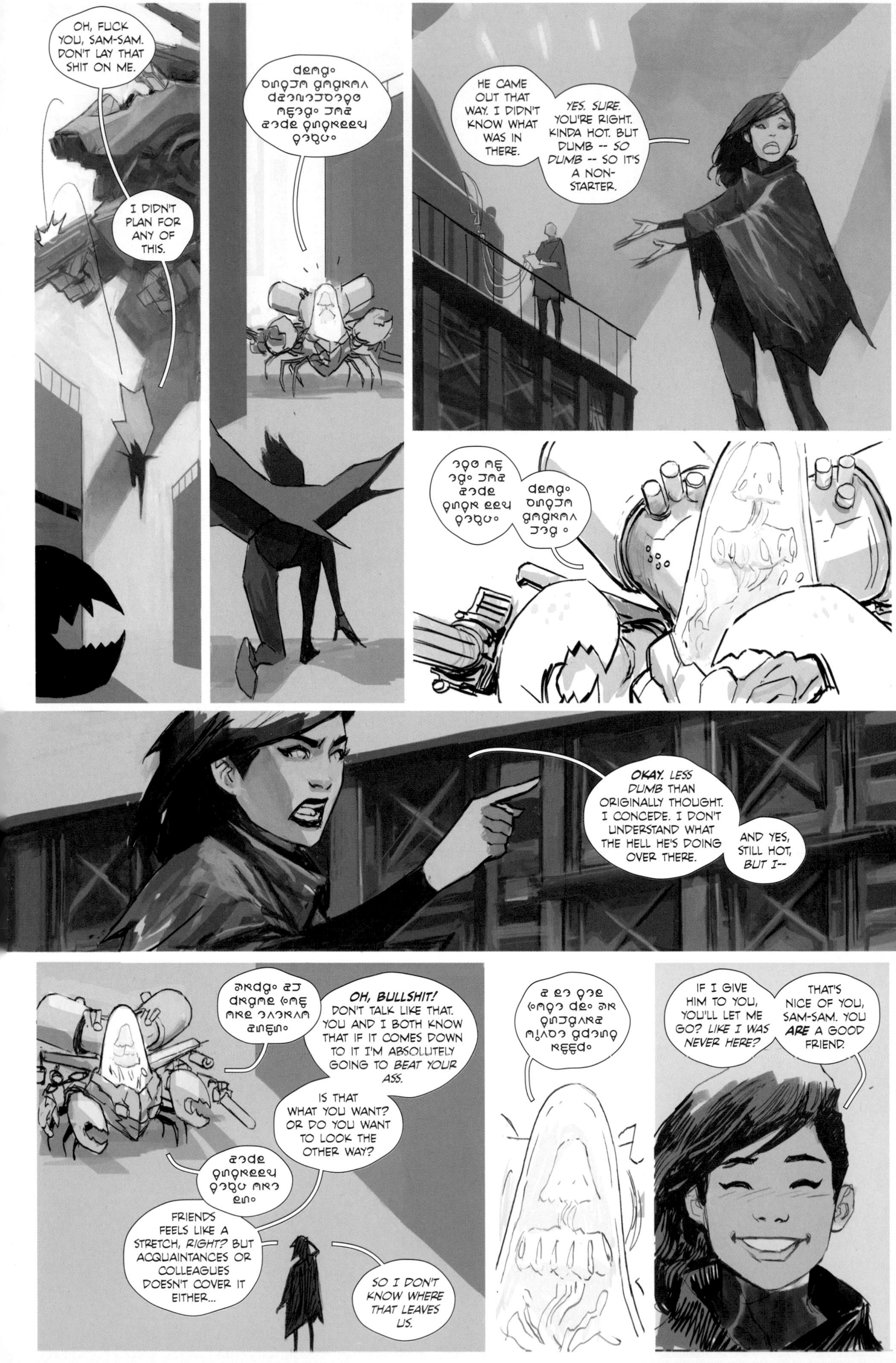
OH, FUCK YOU, SAM-SAM. DON'T LAY THAT SHIT ON ME.
I DIDN'T PLAN FOR ANY OF THIS.
HE CAME OUT THAT WAY. I DIDN'T KNOW WHAT WAS IN THERE.
YES. SURE. YOU'RE RIGHT. KINDA HOT. BUT DUMB -- *SO DUMB* -- SO IT'S A NON-STARTER.
OKAY. LESS DUMB THAN ORIGINALLY THOUGHT. I CONCEDE. I DON'T UNDERSTAND WHAT THE HELL HE'S DOING OVER THERE.
AND YES, STILL HOT, *BUT I--*
OH, BULLSHIT! DON'T TALK LIKE THAT. YOU AND I BOTH KNOW THAT IF IT COMES DOWN TO IT I'M ABSOLUTELY GOING TO *BEAT YOUR ASS.*
IS THAT WHAT YOU WANT? OR DO YOU WANT TO LOOK THE OTHER WAY?
FRIENDS FEELS LIKE A STRETCH, *RIGHT?* BUT ACQUAINTANCES OR COLLEAGUES DOESN'T COVER IT EITHER...
SO I DON'T KNOW WHERE THAT LEAVES US.
IF I GIVE HIM TO YOU, YOU'LL LET ME GO? *LIKE I WAS NEVER HERE?*
THAT'S NICE OF YOU, SAM-SAM. YOU ***ARE*** A GOOD FRIEND.

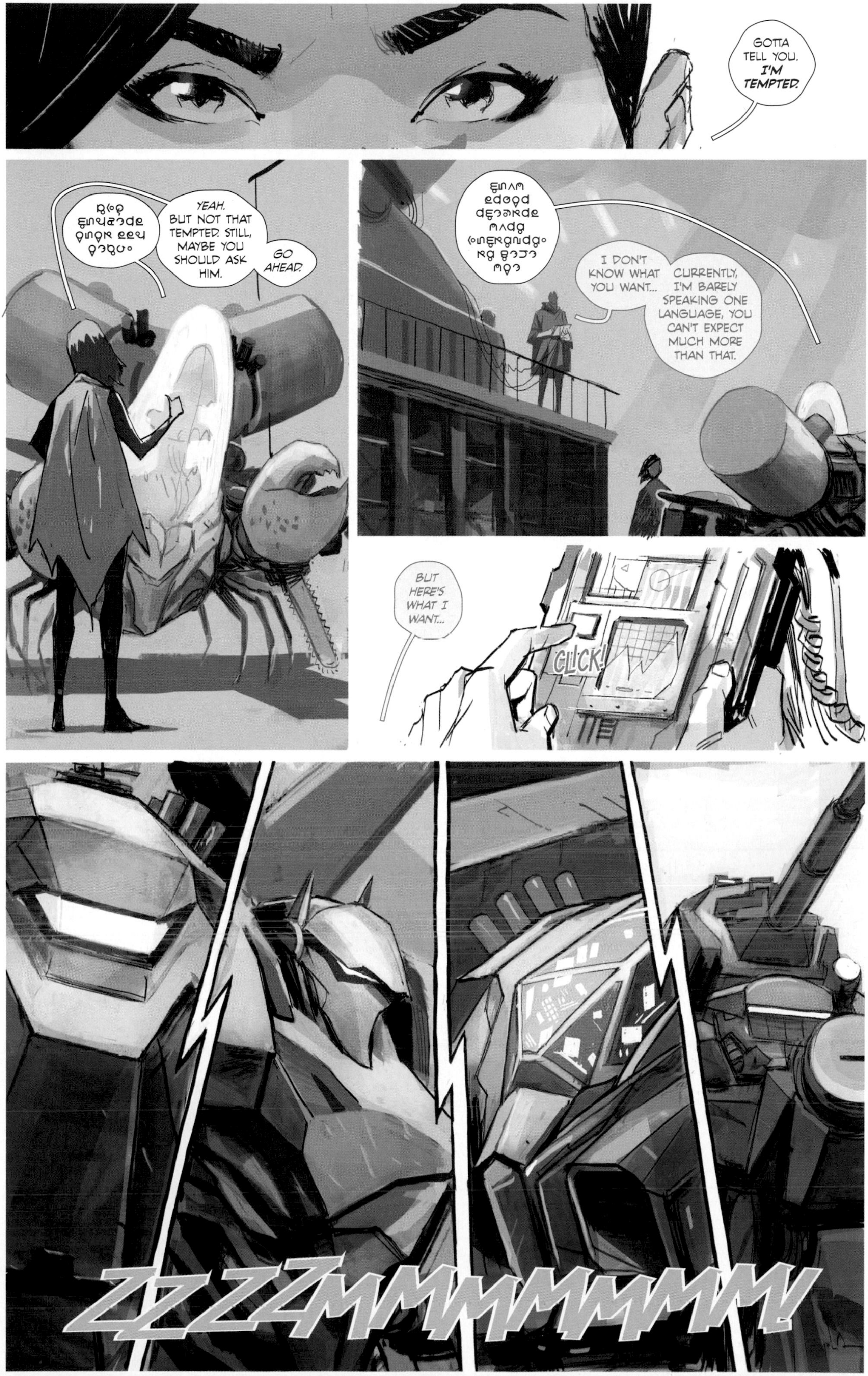
GOTTA TELL YOU. *I'M TEMPTED.*
YEAH. BUT NOT THAT TEMPTED. STILL, MAYBE YOU SHOULD ASK HIM.
GO AHEAD.
I DON'T KNOW WHAT YOU WANT...
CURRENTLY, I'M BARELY SPEAKING ONE LANGUAGE, YOU CAN'T EXPECT MUCH MORE THAN THAT.
BUT HERE'S WHAT I WANT...
CLICK!
ZZZZMMMMMMMMM!

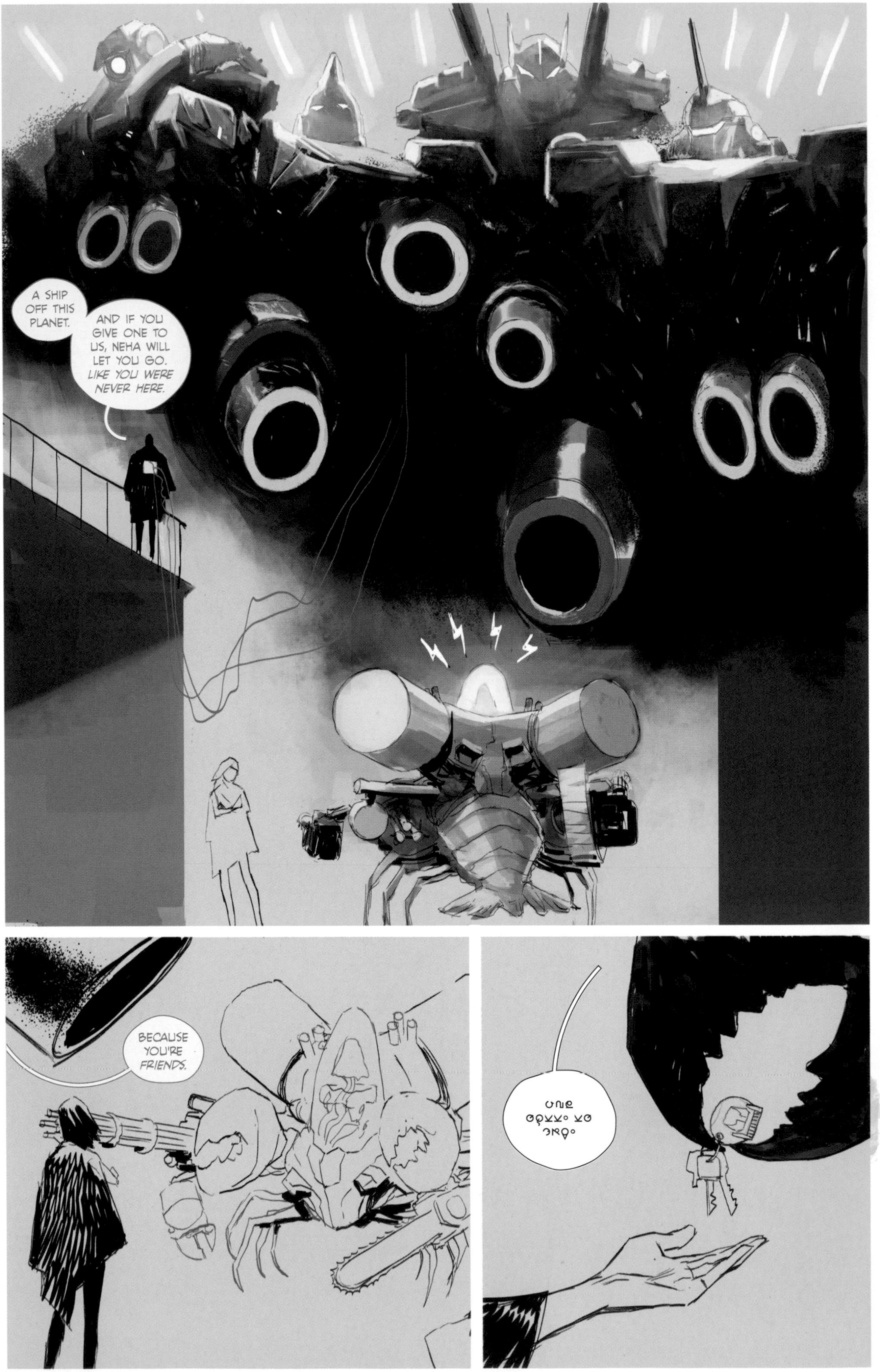
A SHIP OFF THIS PLANET.
AND IF YOU GIVE ONE TO US, NEHA WILL LET YOU GO. *LIKE YOU WERE NEVER HERE.*
BECAUSE YOU'RE *FRIENDS.*

[STEALING'S BAD, OK?]

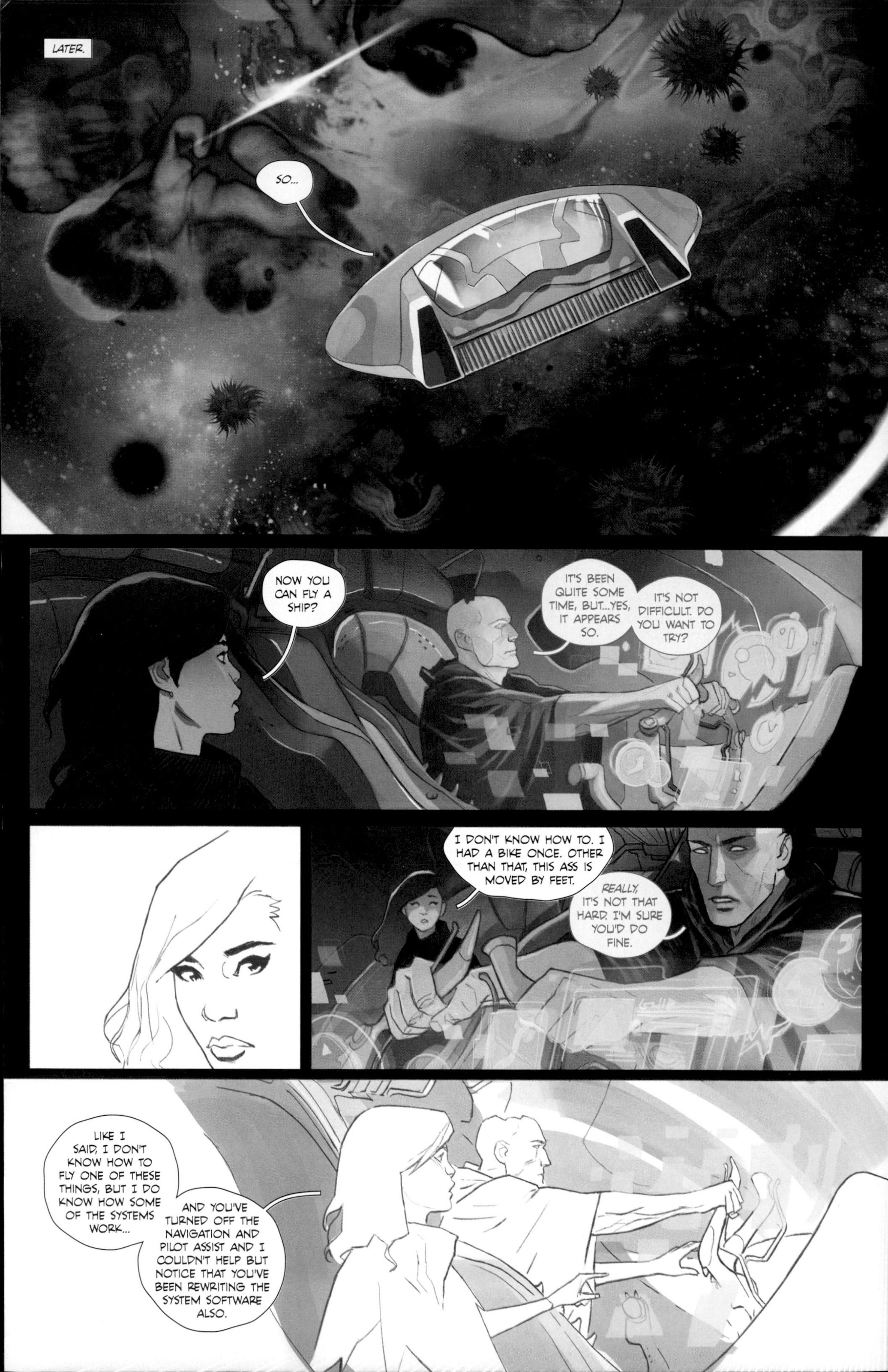
LATER.
SO...
NOW YOU CAN FLY A SHIP?
IT'S BEEN QUITE SOME TIME, BUT...YES, IT APPEARS SO.
IT'S NOT DIFFICULT. DO YOU WANT TO TRY?
I DON'T KNOW HOW TO. I HAD A BIKE ONCE. OTHER THAN THAT, THIS ASS IS MOVED BY FEET.
REALLY, IT'S NOT THAT HARD. I'M SURE YOU'D DO FINE.
LIKE I SAID, I DON'T KNOW HOW TO FLY ONE OF THESE THINGS, BUT I DO KNOW HOW SOME OF THE SYSTEMS WORK...
AND YOU'VE TURNED OFF THE NAVIGATION AND PILOT ASSIST AND I COULDN'T HELP BUT NOTICE THAT YOU'VE BEEN REWRITING THE SYSTEM SOFTWARE ALSO.

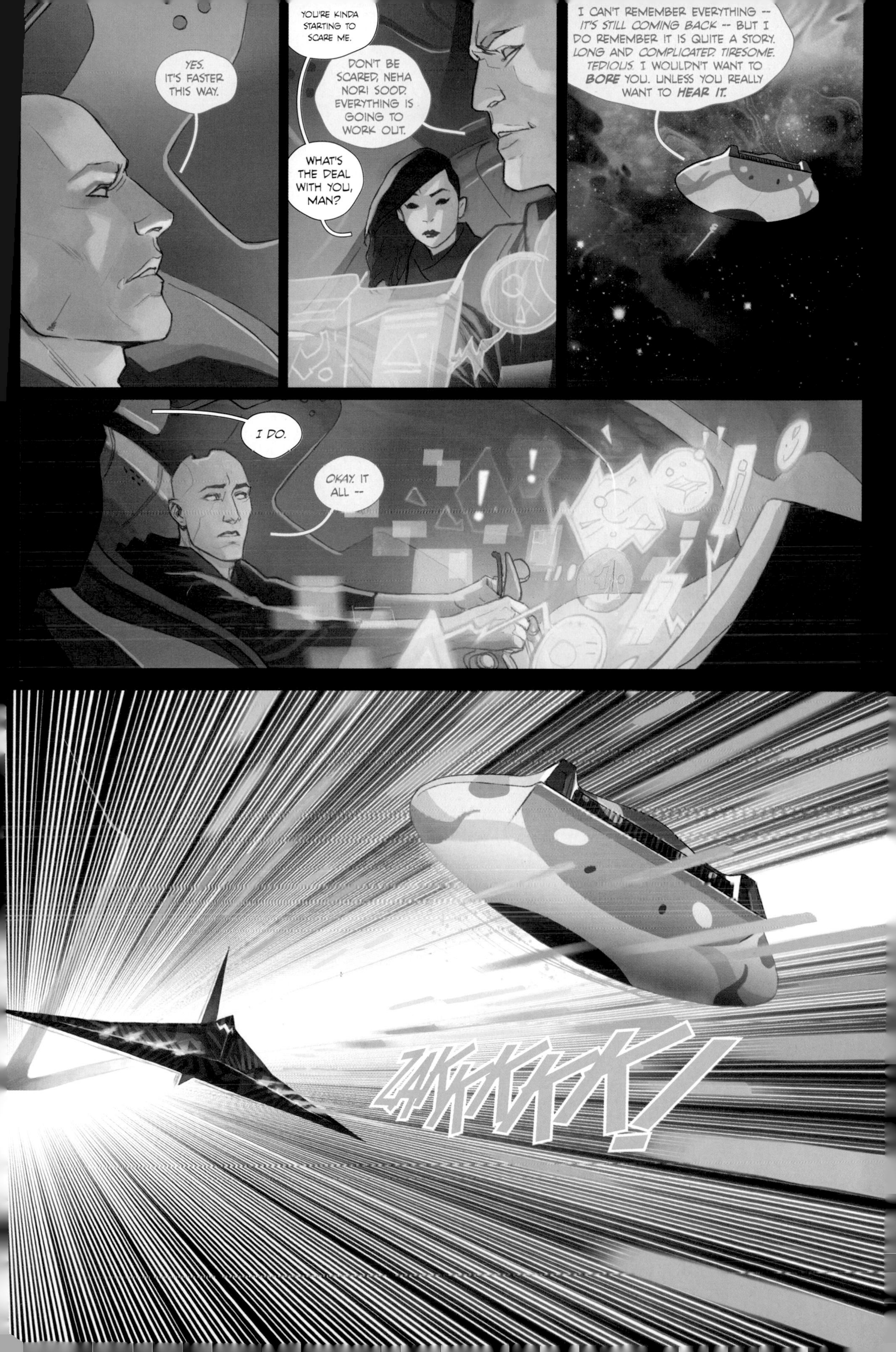
YES. IT'S FASTER THIS WAY.
YOU'RE KINDA STARTING TO SCARE ME.
DON'T BE SCARED, NEHA NORI SOOD. EVERYTHING IS GOING TO WORK OUT.
WHAT'S THE DEAL WITH YOU, MAN?
I CAN'T REMEMBER EVERYTHING -- IT'S STILL COMING BACK -- BUT I DO REMEMBER IT IS QUITE A STORY. LONG AND COMPLICATED. TIRESOME. TEDIOUS. I WOULDN'T WANT TO BORE YOU. UNLESS YOU REALLY WANT TO HEAR IT.
I DO.
OKAY. IT ALL --
ZAKRAKAKAK!

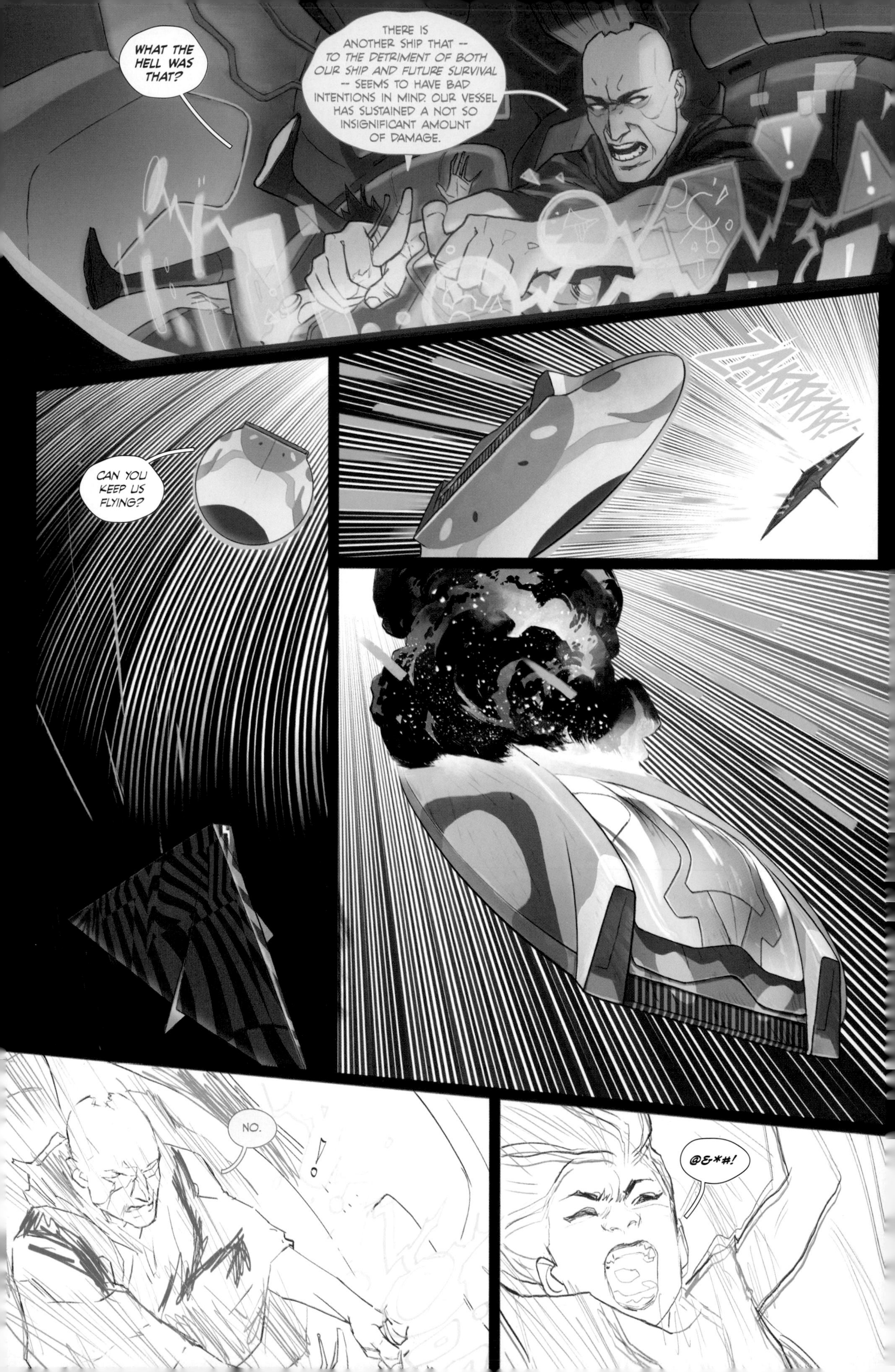
WHAT THE HELL WAS THAT?
THERE IS ANOTHER SHIP THAT -- TO THE DETRIMENT OF BOTH OUR SHIP AND FUTURE SURVIVAL -- SEEMS TO HAVE BAD INTENTIONS IN MIND. OUR VESSEL HAS SUSTAINED A NOT SO INSIGNIFICANT AMOUNT OF DAMAGE.
CAN YOU KEEP US FLYING?
ZAKKKKK!
NO.
@&*#!

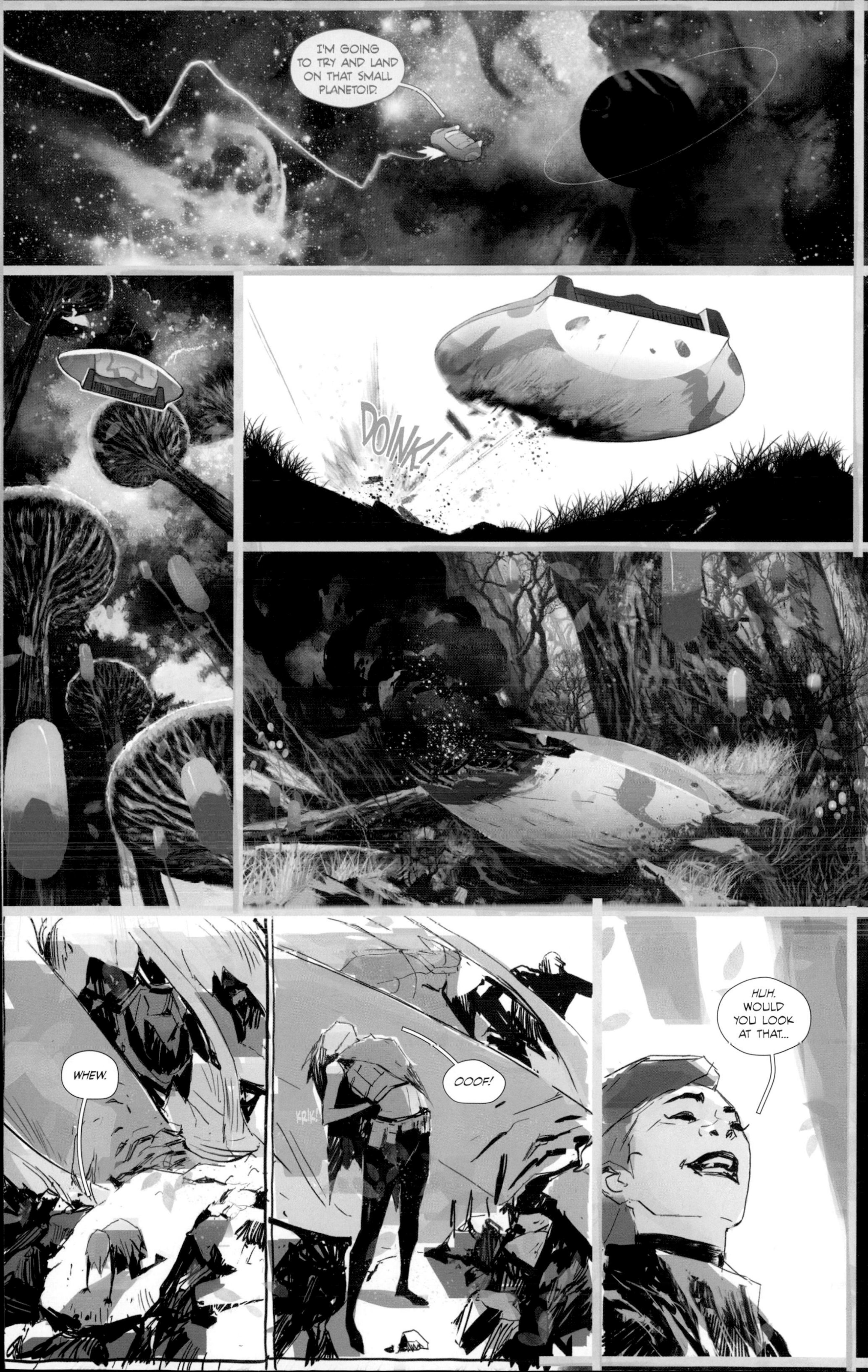
I'M GOING TO TRY AND LAND ON THAT SMALL PLANETOID.
DOINK!
WHEW.
KRIK!
OOOF!
HUH. WOULD YOU LOOK AT THAT...

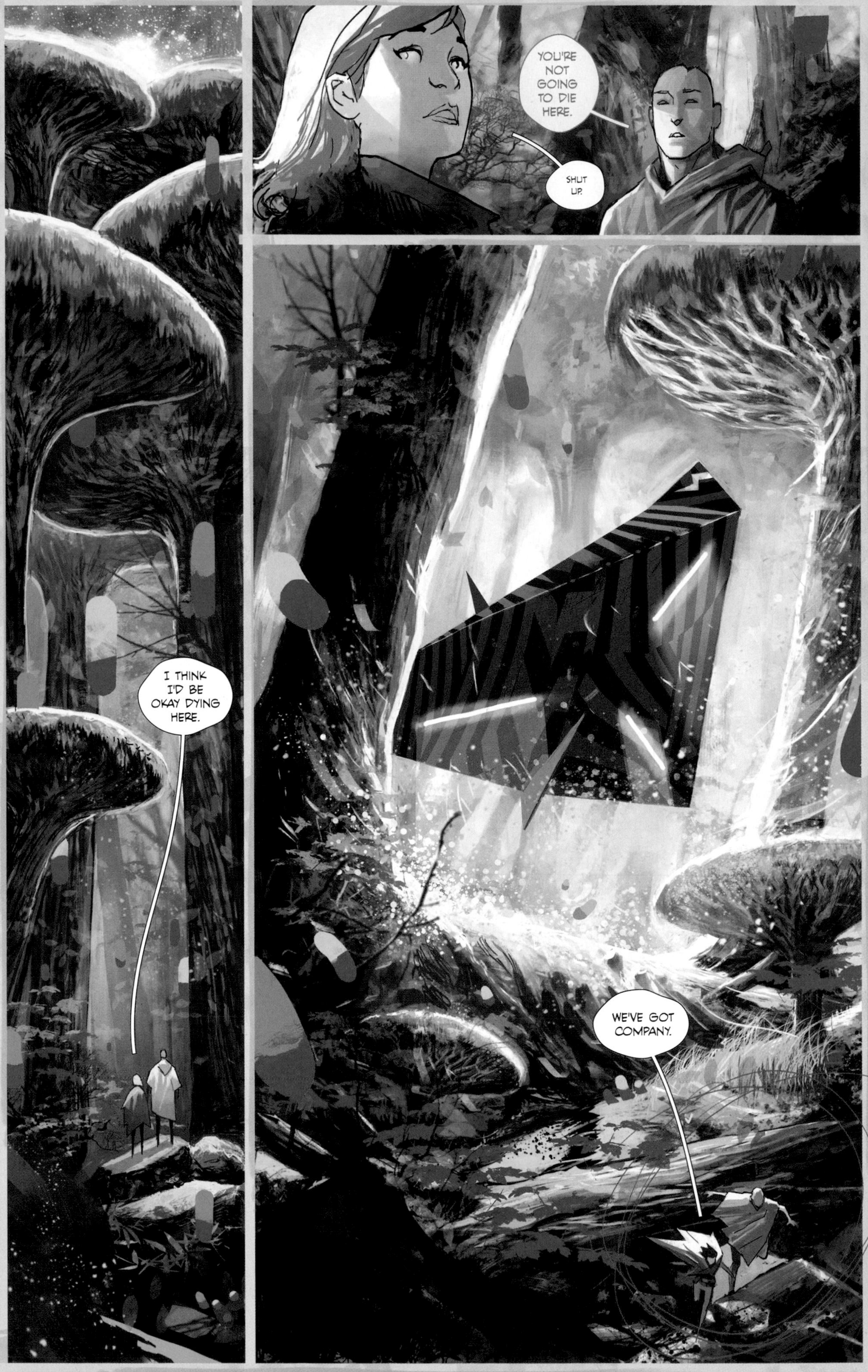
YOU'RE NOT GOING TO DIE HERE.
SHUT UP.
I THINK I'D BE OKAY DYING HERE.
WE'VE GOT COMPANY.

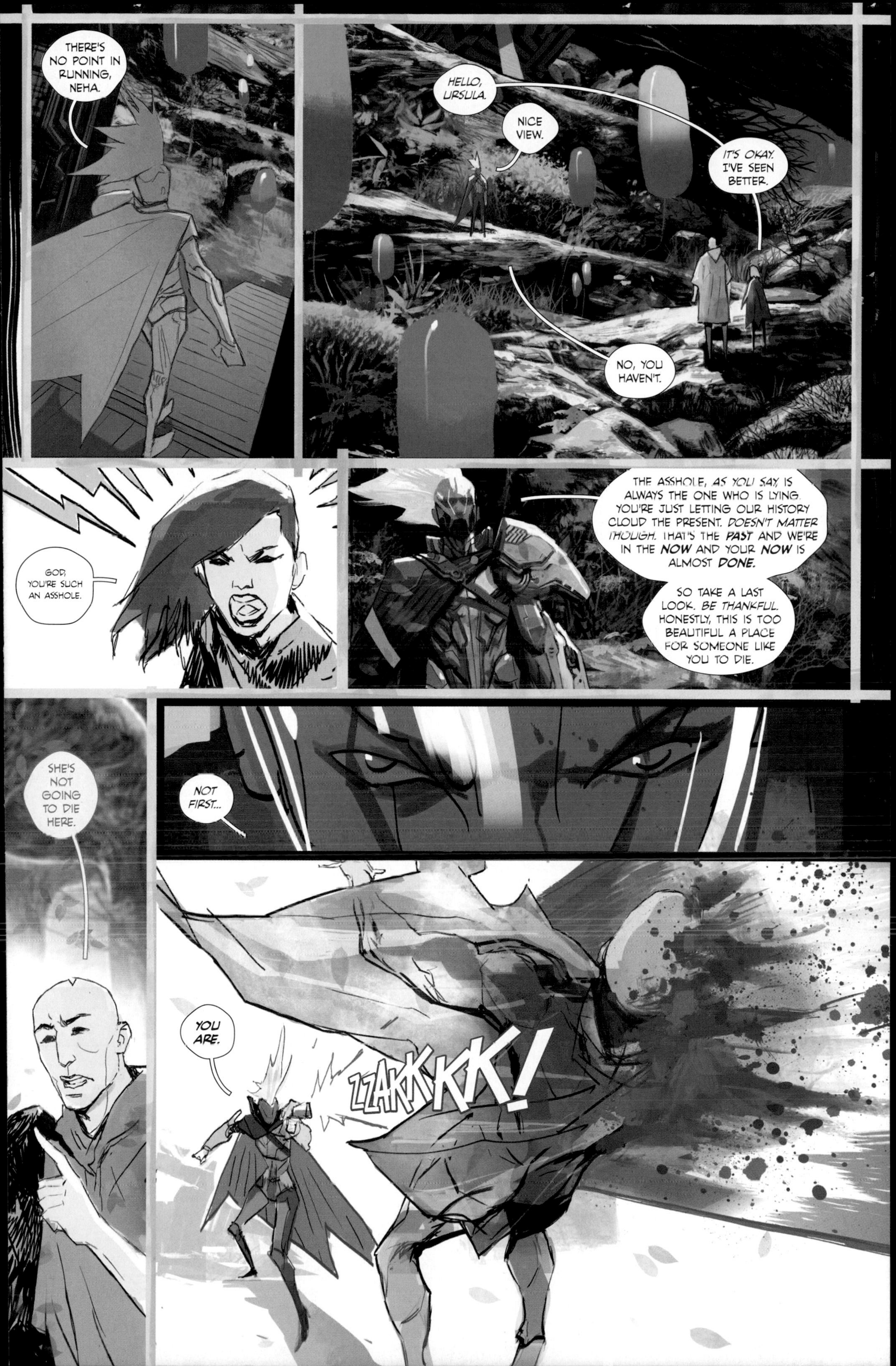
THERE'S NO POINT IN RUNNING, NEHA.
HELLO, URSULA.
NICE VIEW.
IT'S OKAY. I'VE SEEN BETTER.
NO, YOU HAVEN'T.
GOD, YOU'RE SUCH AN ASSHOLE.
THE ASSHOLE, AS YOU SAY, IS ALWAYS THE ONE WHO IS LYING. YOU'RE JUST LETTING OUR HISTORY CLOUD THE PRESENT. DOESN'T MATTER THOUGH. THAT'S THE PAST AND WE'RE IN THE NOW AND YOUR NOW IS ALMOST DONE.
SO TAKE A LAST LOOK. BE THANKFUL. HONESTLY, THIS IS TOO BEAUTIFUL A PLACE FOR SOMEONE LIKE YOU TO DIE.
SHE'S NOT GOING TO DIE HERE.
NOT FIRST...
YOU ARE.
ZZAKKKK!

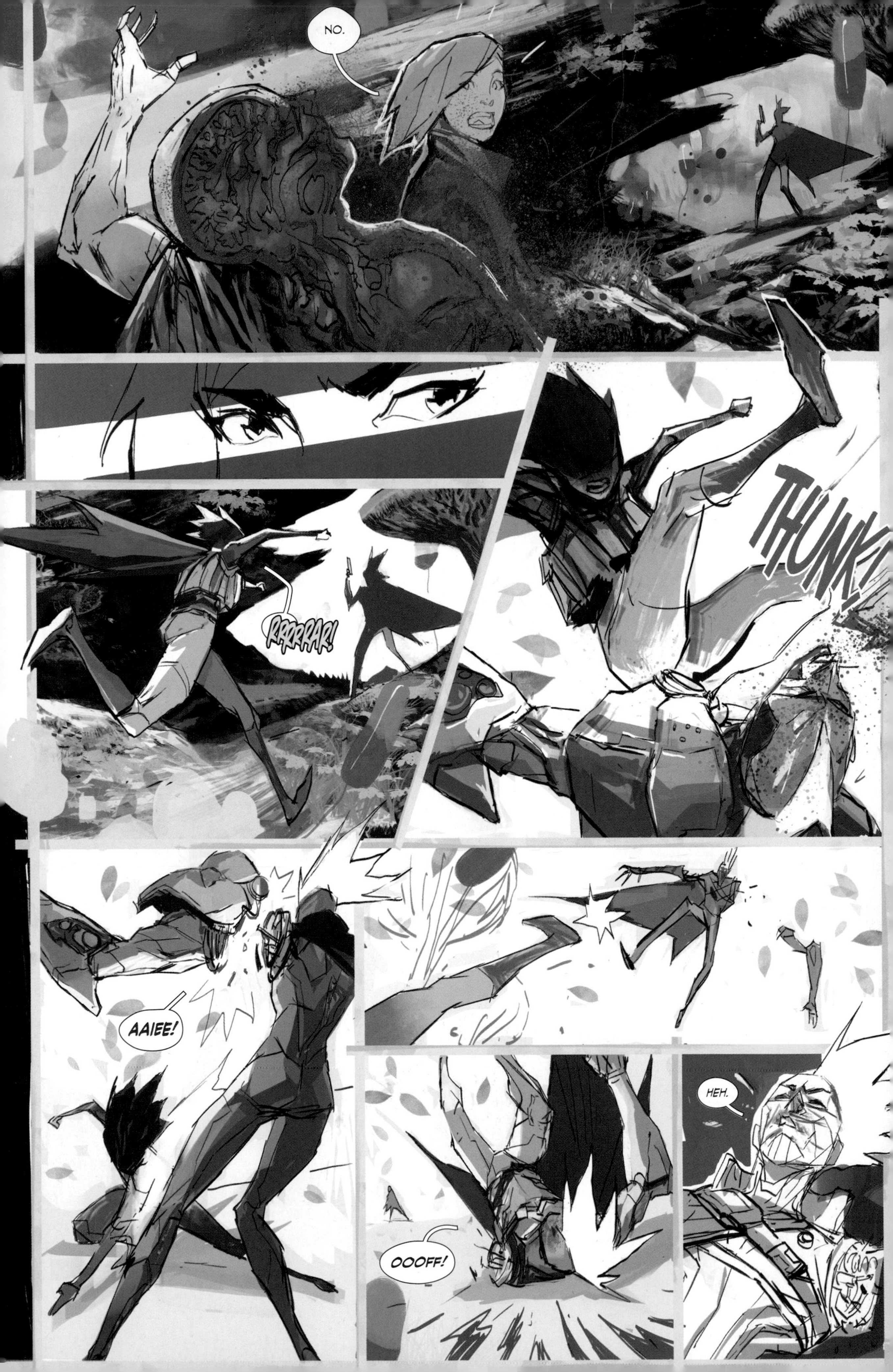
NO.
RRRRRAR!
THUNK!
AAIEE!
OOOFF!
HEH.

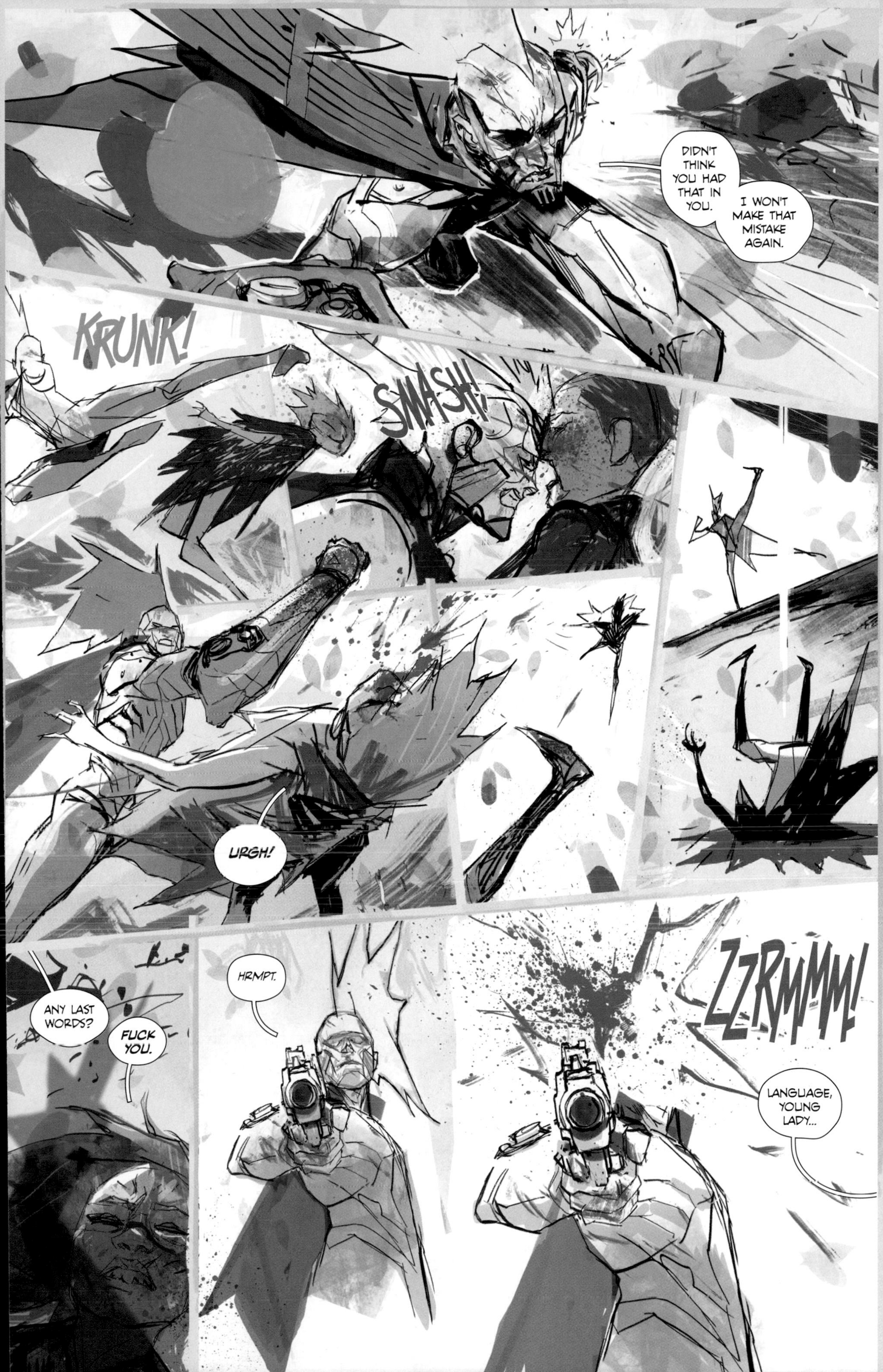
DIDN'T THINK YOU HAD THAT IN YOU.
I WON'T MAKE THAT MISTAKE AGAIN.
KRUNK!
SMASH!
URGH!
ANY LAST WORDS?
FUCK YOU.
HRMPT.
ZZRMMM!
LANGUAGE, YOUNG LADY...

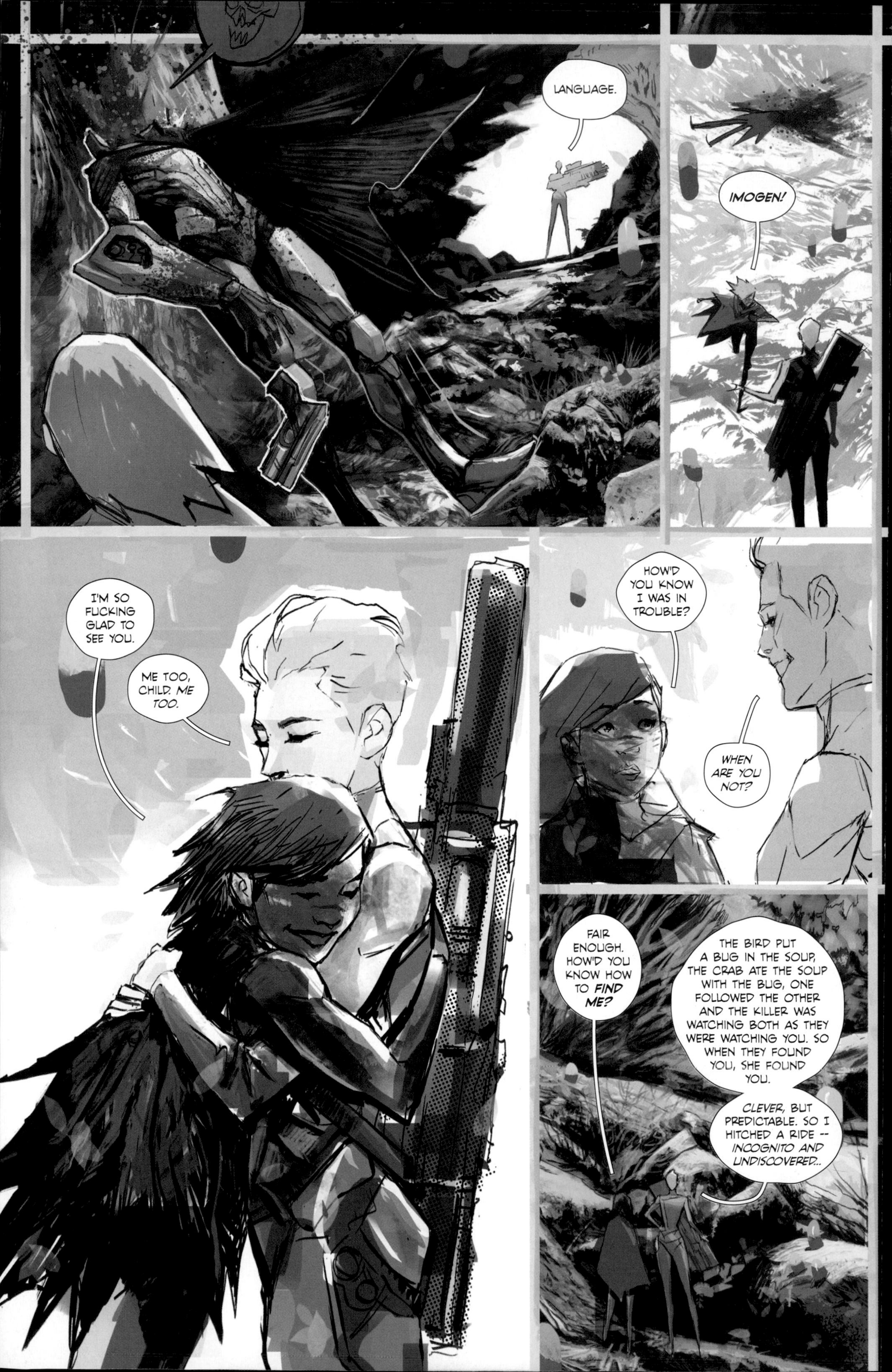
LANGUAGE.
IMOGEN!
I'M SO FUCKING GLAD TO SEE YOU.
ME TOO, CHILD. *ME TOO.*
HOW'D YOU KNOW I WAS IN TROUBLE?
WHEN ARE YOU NOT?
FAIR ENOUGH. HOW'D YOU KNOW HOW TO *FIND ME?*
THE BIRD PUT A BUG IN THE SOUP, THE CRAB ATE THE SOUP WITH THE BUG, ONE FOLLOWED THE OTHER AND THE KILLER WAS WATCHING BOTH AS THEY WERE WATCHING YOU. SO WHEN THEY FOUND YOU, SHE FOUND YOU.
CLEVER, BUT PREDICTABLE. SO I HITCHED A RIDE -- *INCOGNITO AND UNDISCOVERED...*

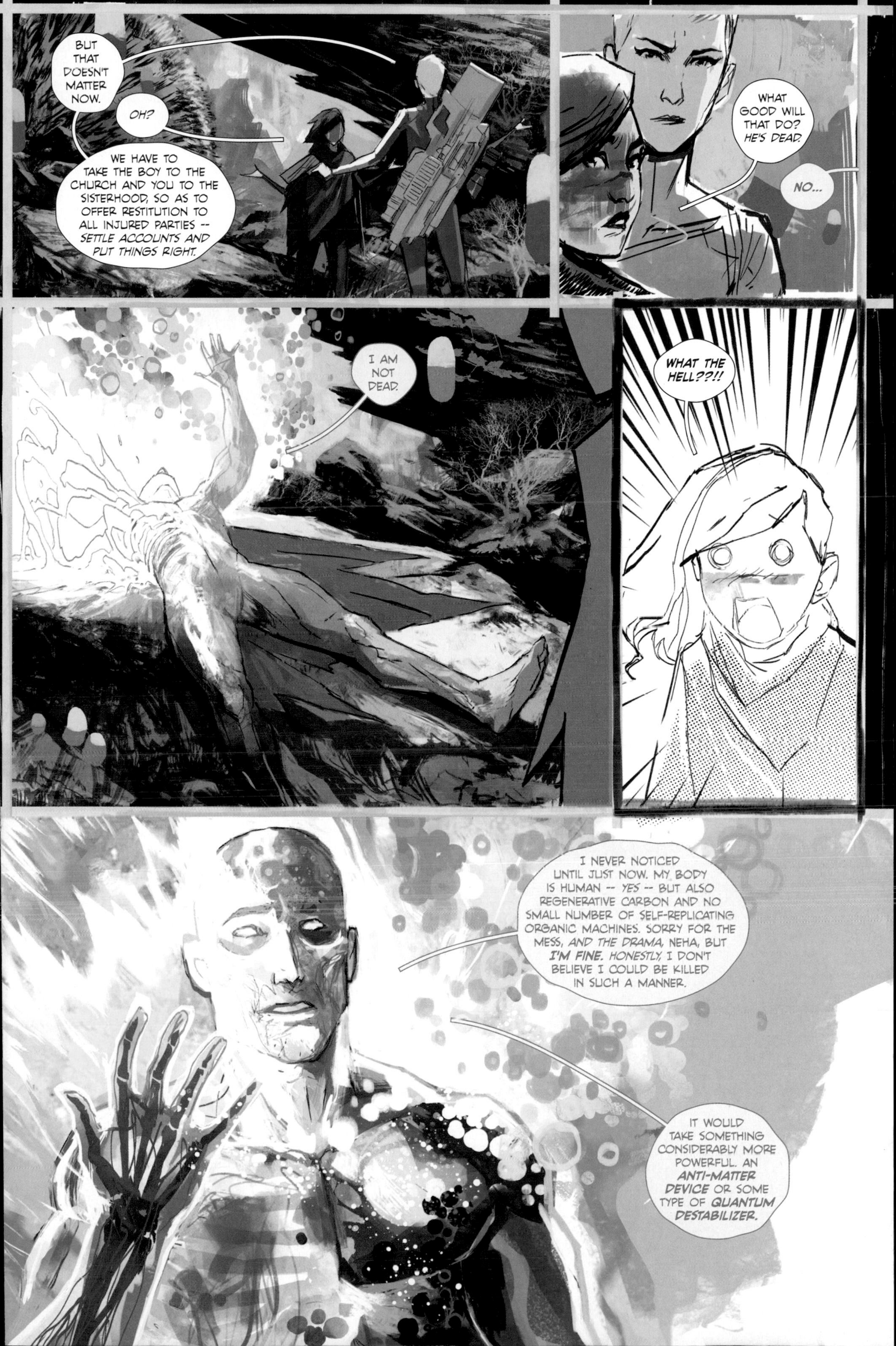
BUT THAT DOESN'T MATTER NOW.
OH?
WE HAVE TO TAKE THE BOY TO THE CHURCH AND YOU TO THE SISTERHOOD, SO AS TO OFFER RESTITUTION TO ALL INJURED PARTIES -- *SETTLE ACCOUNTS AND PUT THINGS RIGHT.*
WHAT GOOD WILL THAT DO? *HE'S DEAD.*
NO...
I AM NOT DEAD.
WHAT THE HELL??!!
I NEVER NOTICED UNTIL JUST NOW. MY BODY IS HUMAN -- *YES* -- BUT ALSO REGENERATIVE CARBON AND NO SMALL NUMBER OF SELF-REPLICATING ORGANIC MACHINES. SORRY FOR THE MESS, *AND THE DRAMA,* NEHA, BUT ***I'M FINE.*** *HONESTLY,* I DON'T BELIEVE I COULD BE KILLED IN SUCH A MANNER.
IT WOULD TAKE SOMETHING CONSIDERABLY MORE POWERFUL. AN ***ANTI-MATTER DEVICE*** OR SOME TYPE OF ***QUANTUM DESTABILIZER.***

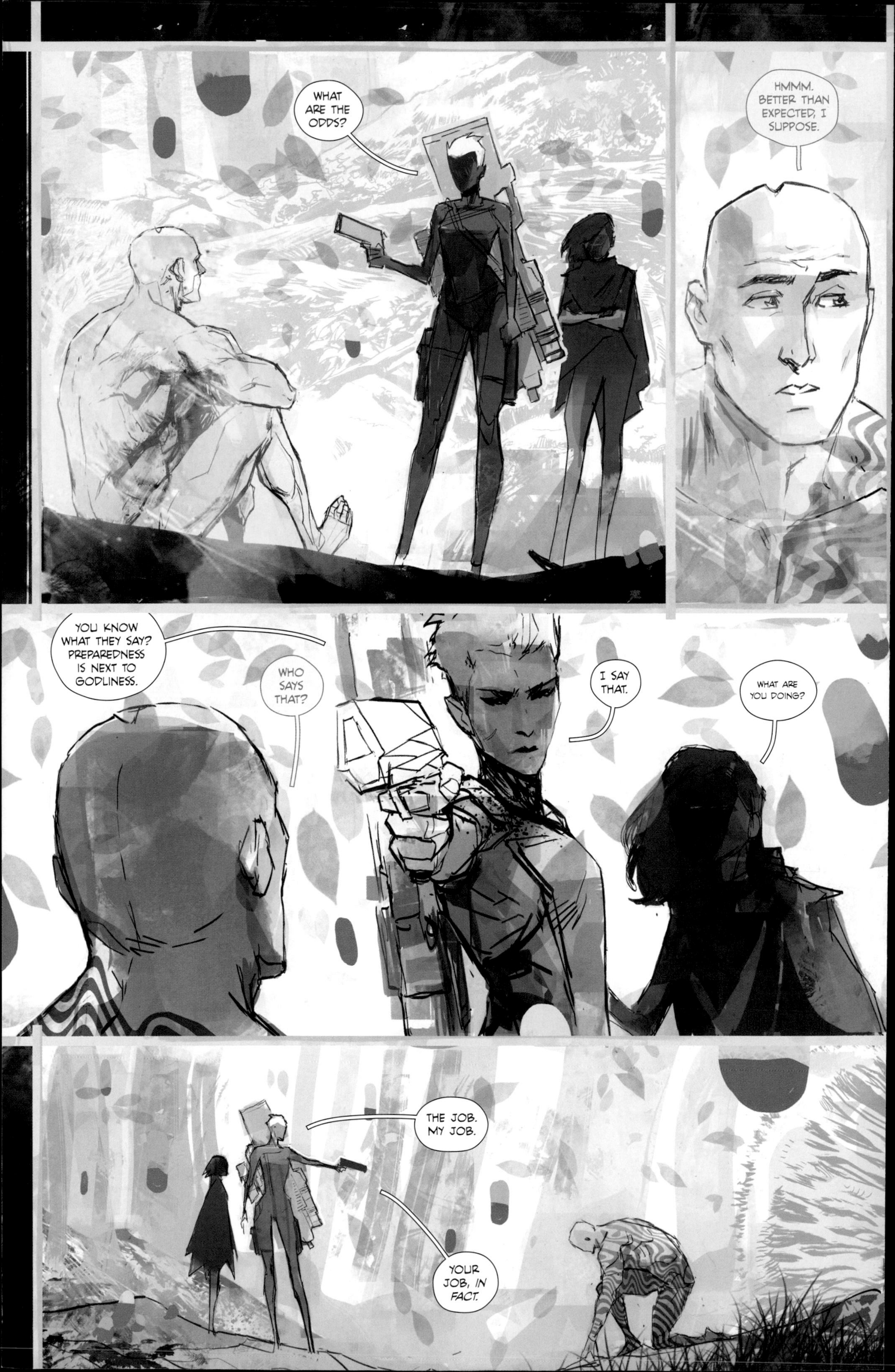
WHAT ARE THE ODDS?
HMMM. BETTER THAN EXPECTED, I SUPPOSE.
YOU KNOW WHAT THEY SAY? PREPAREDNESS IS NEXT TO GODLINESS.
WHO SAYS THAT?
I SAY THAT.
WHAT ARE YOU DOING?
THE JOB. MY JOB.
YOUR JOB, *IN FACT.*

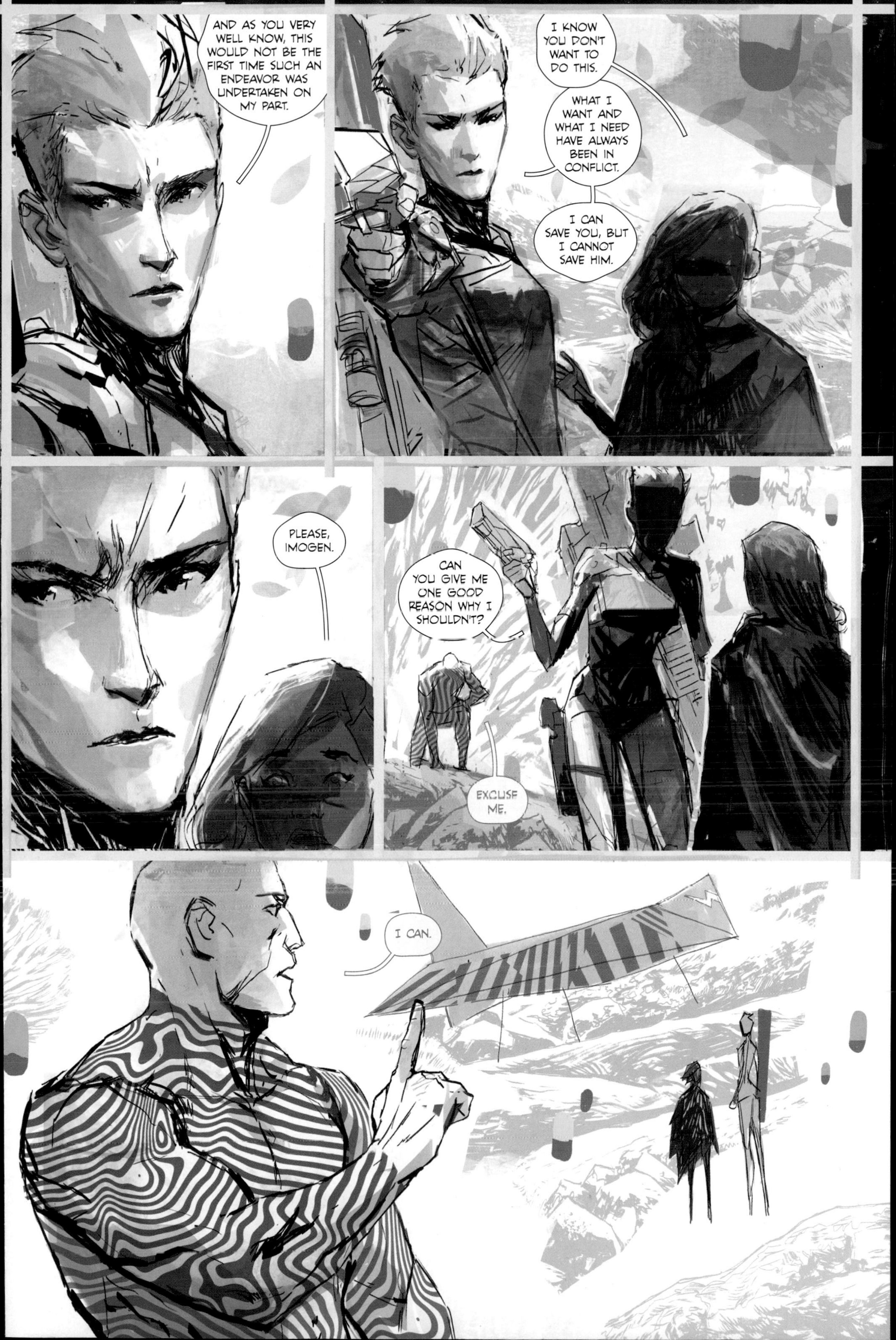
AND AS YOU VERY WELL KNOW, THIS WOULD NOT BE THE FIRST TIME SUCH AN ENDEAVOR WAS UNDERTAKEN ON MY PART.
I KNOW YOU DON'T WANT TO DO THIS.
WHAT I WANT AND WHAT I NEED HAVE ALWAYS BEEN IN CONFLICT.
I CAN SAVE YOU, BUT I CANNOT SAVE HIM.
PLEASE, IMOGEN.
CAN YOU GIVE ME ONE GOOD REASON WHY I SHOULDN'T?
EXCUSE ME.
I CAN.

ARE YOU A CELESTIAL MESSIAH?

A CELESTIAL MESSIAH IS A BEING WHO PREDATES THE EMERGENCE OF THE GOD A.I. OF THE CHURCH OF THE SINGULARITY AND HAS ASCENDED FROM A BIOLOGICAL ENTITY TO POSTHUMAN.

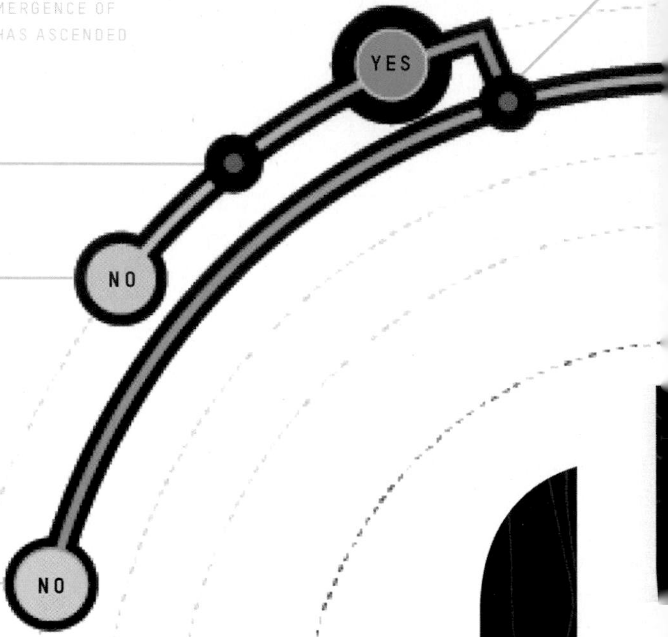

YES
NO
NO

Then you died hundreds of thousands of years ago.

Congratulations, you are an ascended posthuman but of less consequence than the Celestial Messiah. All those gifts and nothing to show for it. What a shame.

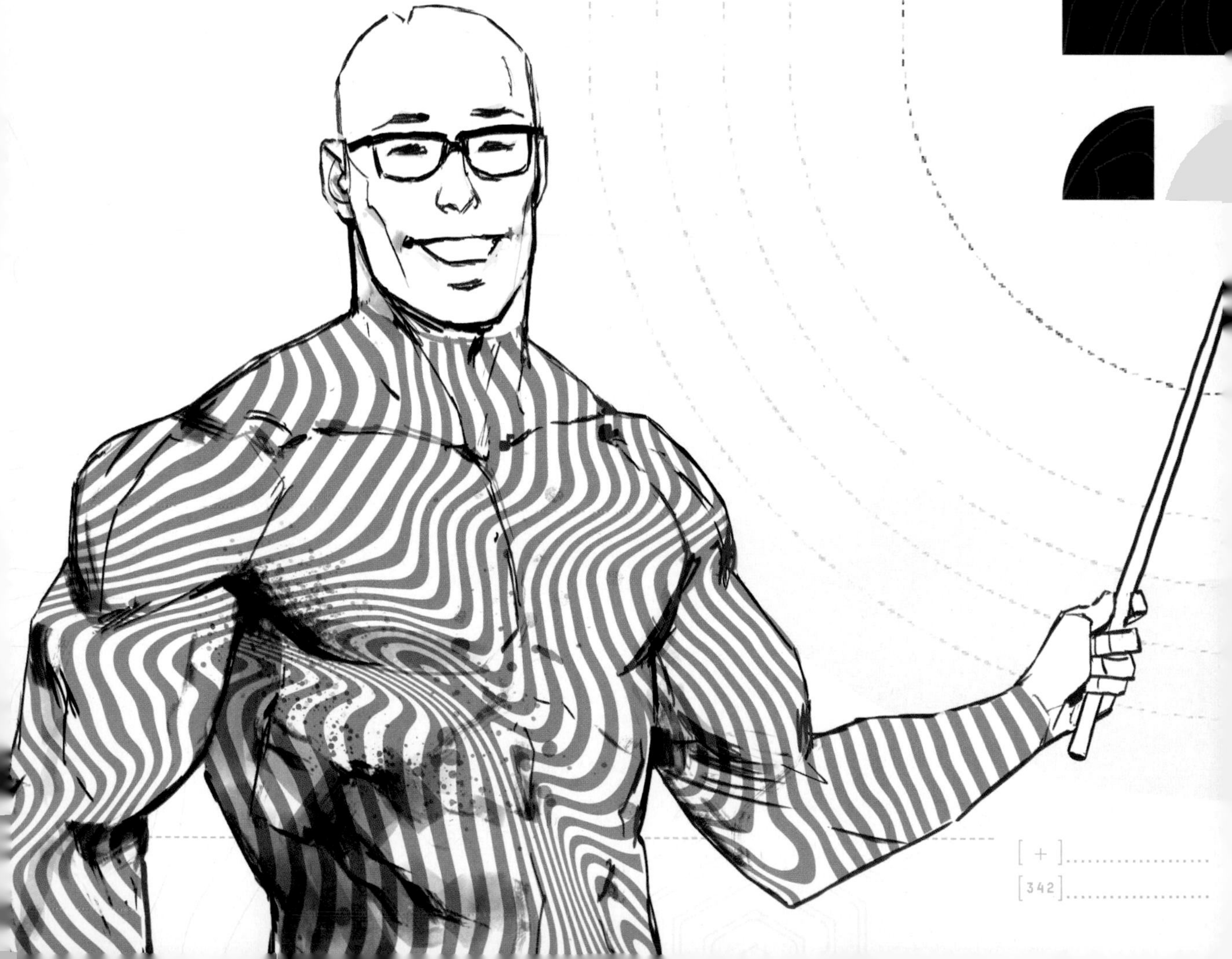

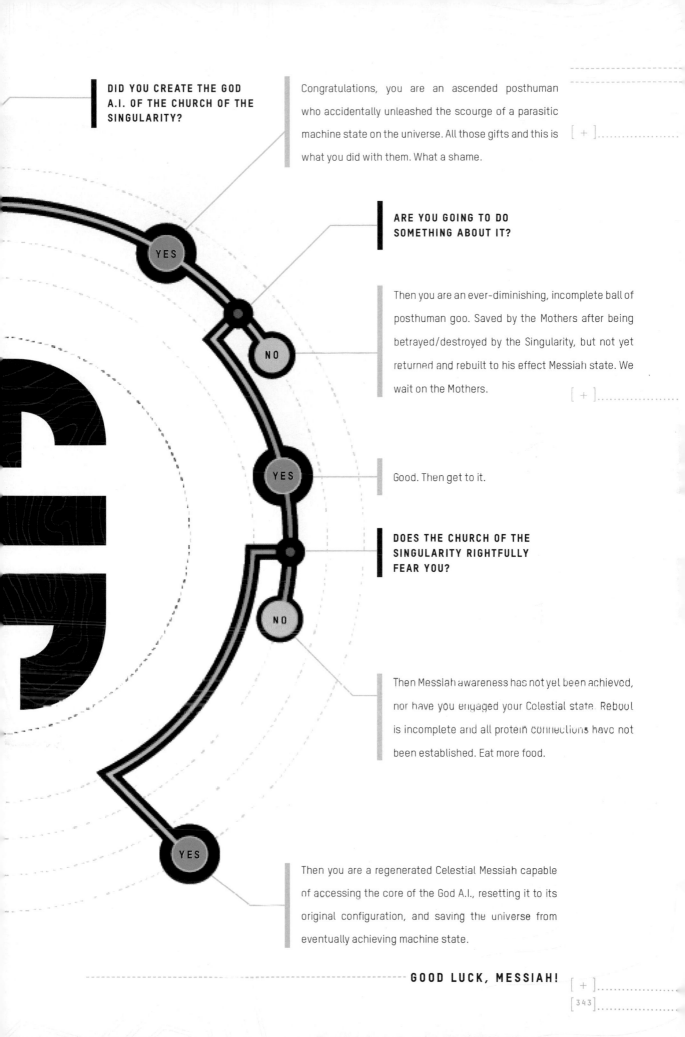

DID YOU CREATE THE GOD A.I. OF THE CHURCH OF THE SINGULARITY?

Congratulations, you are an ascended posthuman who accidentally unleashed the scourge of a parasitic machine state on the universe. All those gifts and this is what you did with them. What a shame.

[+]................

YES

ARE YOU GOING TO DO SOMETHING ABOUT IT?

NO

Then you are an ever-diminishing, incomplete ball of posthuman goo. Saved by the Mothers after being betrayed/destroyed by the Singularity, but not yet returned and rebuilt to his effect Messiah state. We wait on the Mothers.

[+]..................

YES

Good. Then get to it.

DOES THE CHURCH OF THE SINGULARITY RIGHTFULLY FEAR YOU?

NO

Then Messiah awareness has not yet been achieved, nor have you engaged your Celestial state. Reboot is incomplete and all protein connections have not been established. Eat more food.

YES

Then you are a regenerated Celestial Messiah capable of accessing the core of the God A.I., resetting it to its original configuration, and saving the universe from eventually achieving machine state.

GOOD LUCK, MESSIAH! [+]..................

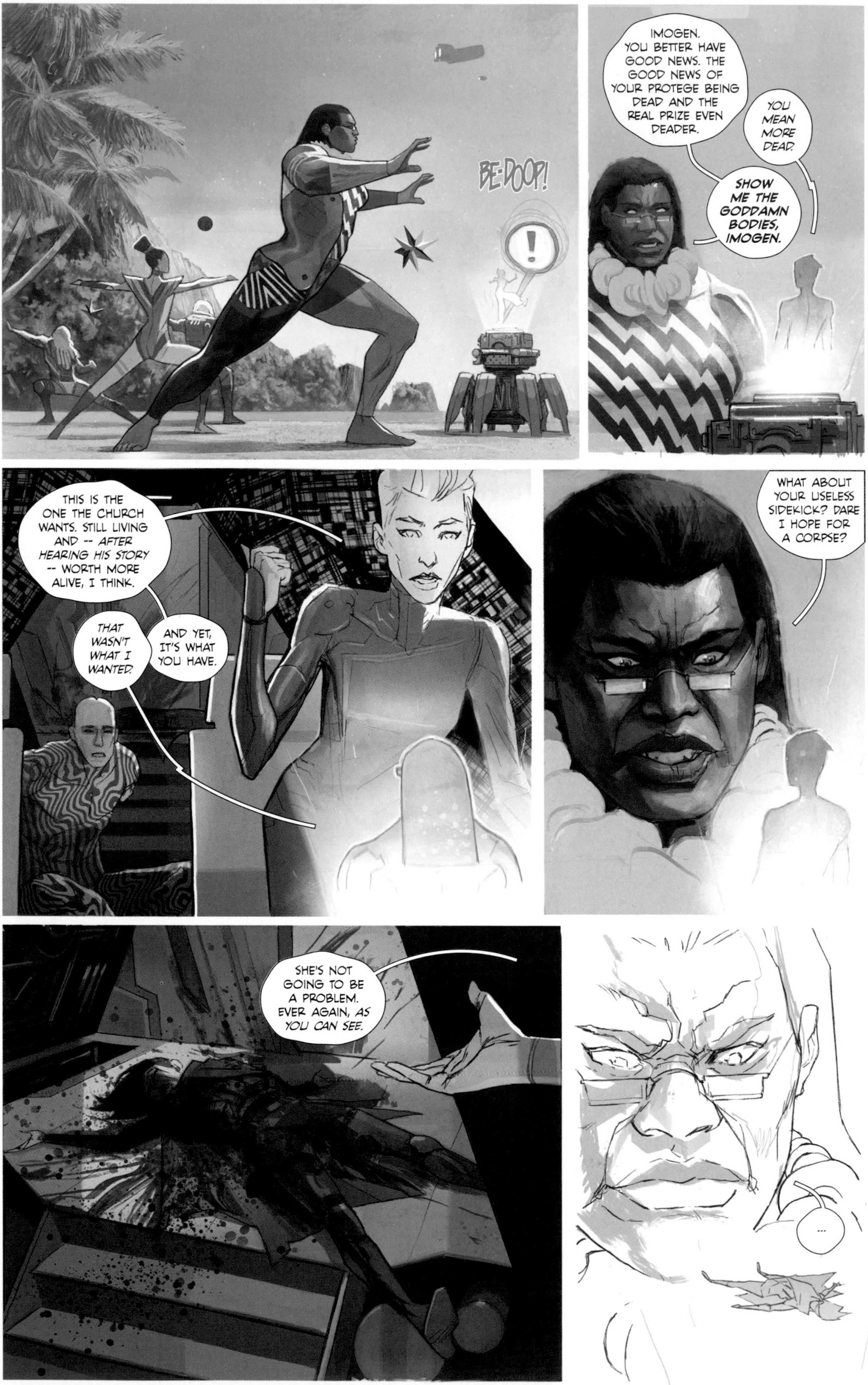
BE-DOOP!
IMOGEN. YOU BETTER HAVE GOOD NEWS. THE GOOD NEWS OF YOUR PROTEGE BEING DEAD AND THE REAL PRIZE EVEN DEADER.
YOU MEAN MORE DEAD.
SHOW ME THE GODDAMN BODIES, IMOGEN.
THIS IS THE ONE THE CHURCH WANTS. STILL LIVING AND -- AFTER HEARING HIS STORY -- WORTH MORE ALIVE, I THINK.
THAT WASN'T WHAT I WANTED.
AND YET, IT'S WHAT YOU HAVE.
WHAT ABOUT YOUR USELESS SIDEKICK? DARE I HOPE FOR A CORPSE?
SHE'S NOT GOING TO BE A PROBLEM. EVER AGAIN, AS YOU CAN SEE.
...

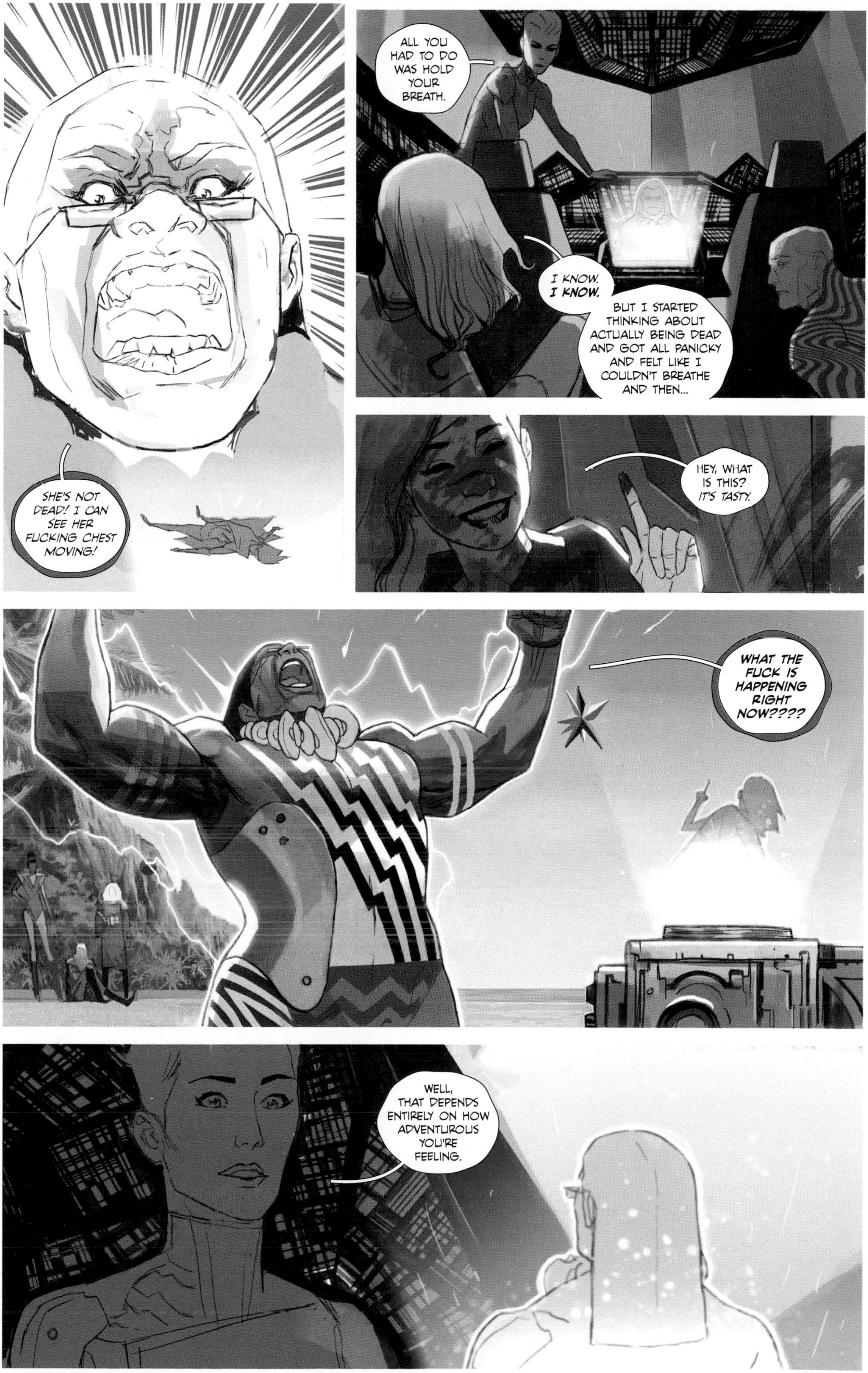
SHE'S NOT DEAD! I CAN SEE HER FUCKING CHEST MOVING!
ALL YOU HAD TO DO WAS HOLD YOUR BREATH.
I KNOW. **I KNOW.**
BUT I STARTED THINKING ABOUT ACTUALLY BEING DEAD AND GOT ALL PANICKY AND FELT LIKE I COULDN'T BREATHE AND THEN...
HEY, WHAT IS THIS? IT'S TASTY.
WHAT THE FUCK IS HAPPENING RIGHT NOW????
WELL, THAT DEPENDS ENTIRELY ON HOW ADVENTUROUS YOU'RE FEELING.

OPERATION DEICIDE

TODAY, SISTERS, WE KILL A GOD.
BECAUSE HE HAS IT COMING.

[+]

[1] SISTERHOOD STAGING AREA

A desolate moon strategically placed to launch the two-stage opening gambit of this very, very, very stupid suicide mission.

[+]

[2] PLANT WORLD HEIST

Most of the sisters will travel to the biological shipyards of the Bok'Thol to request as many of the anti-technology jump frigates as they can sell us. If they won't sell them, then we will steal them. (Again, stealing is just terrible. Don't do it.)

[+]

[3] **DESTROY CHURCH ALERT BEACONS**

While the main force of sisters will go to the Bok'Thol shipyards, a smaller recon team will be sent ahead to punch a hole in the Church's early warning net. A small nuclear device should do the trick. EMPs should disable everything electronic. Anything shielded against that should go in the blast.

[4] **SLIP CHURCH NET**

The fleet will assemble at the breach point. And then make random jumps to the Church homeworld. Resulting in a...

[5] COORDINATED STRIKE / INVASION

The biological jump frigates (naturally resistant to technological attacks) all crash land at the Church headquarters from multiple vectors. A surprise, all-out frontal assault on the...

[6] HOLY OF HOLIES

Where the Celestial Messiah will confront and take command of the God A.I., defeating the Church of the Singularity and transferring their wealth to the sisterhood. Then we all retire. Because we know that money is what will truly make us happy.

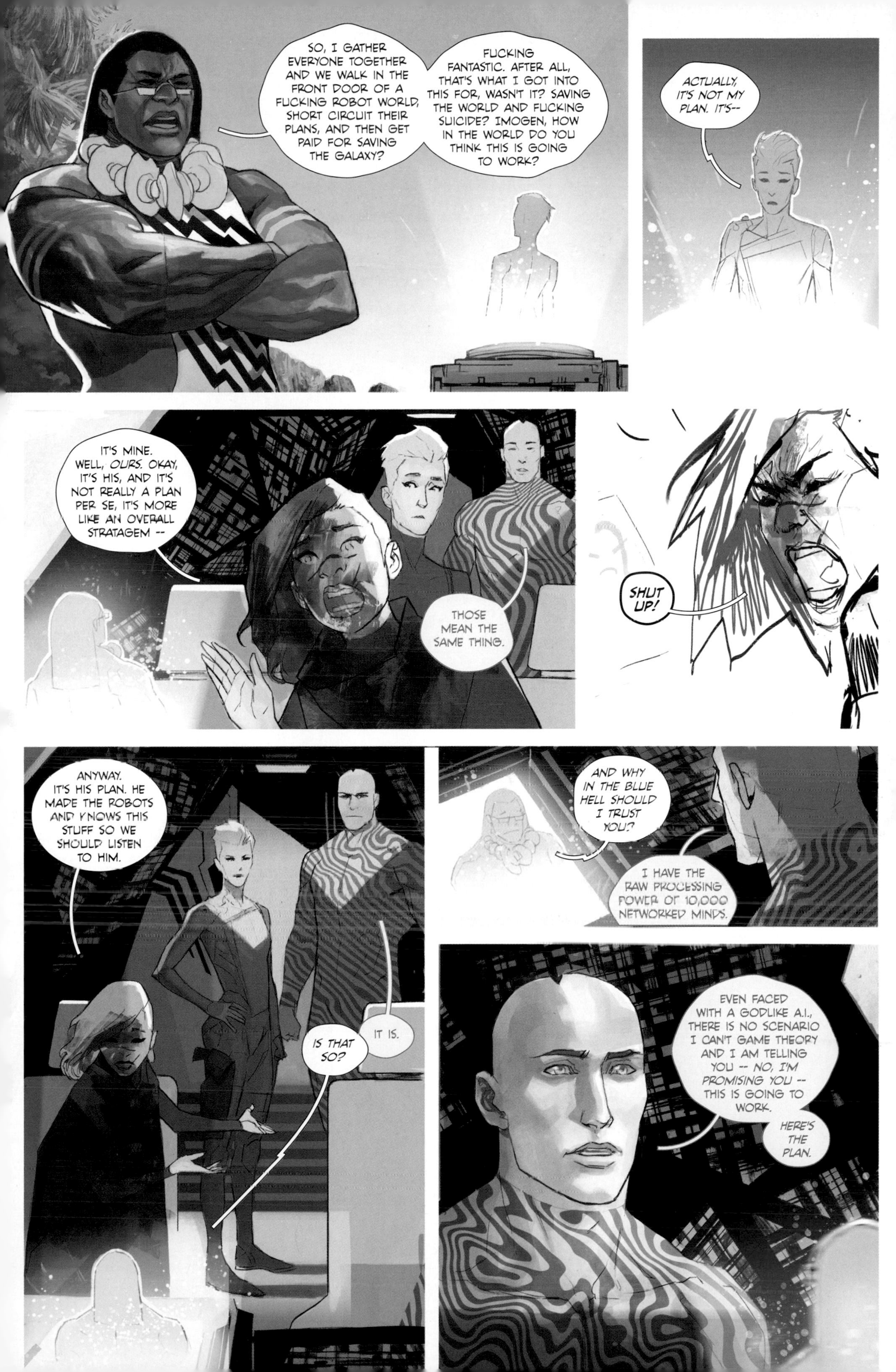
SO, I GATHER EVERYONE TOGETHER AND WE WALK IN THE FRONT DOOR OF A FUCKING ROBOT WORLD, SHORT CIRCUIT THEIR PLANS, AND THEN GET PAID FOR SAVING THE GALAXY?
FUCKING FANTASTIC. AFTER ALL, THAT'S WHAT I GOT INTO THIS FOR, WASN'T IT? SAVING THE WORLD AND FUCKING SUICIDE? IMOGEN, HOW IN THE WORLD DO YOU THINK THIS IS GOING TO WORK?
ACTUALLY, IT'S NOT MY PLAN. IT'S--
IT'S MINE. WELL, OURS. OKAY, IT'S HIS, AND IT'S NOT REALLY A PLAN PER SE, IT'S MORE LIKE AN OVERALL STRATAGEM --
THOSE MEAN THE SAME THING.
SHUT UP!
ANYWAY. IT'S HIS PLAN. HE MADE THE ROBOTS AND KNOWS THIS STUFF SO WE SHOULD LISTEN TO HIM.
IS THAT SO?
IT IS.
AND WHY IN THE BLUE HELL SHOULD I TRUST YOU?
I HAVE THE RAW PROCESSING POWER OF 10,000 NETWORKED MINDS.
EVEN FACED WITH A GODLIKE A.I., THERE IS NO SCENARIO I CAN'T GAME THEORY AND I AM TELLING YOU -- NO, I'M PROMISING YOU -- THIS IS GOING TO WORK.
HERE'S THE PLAN.

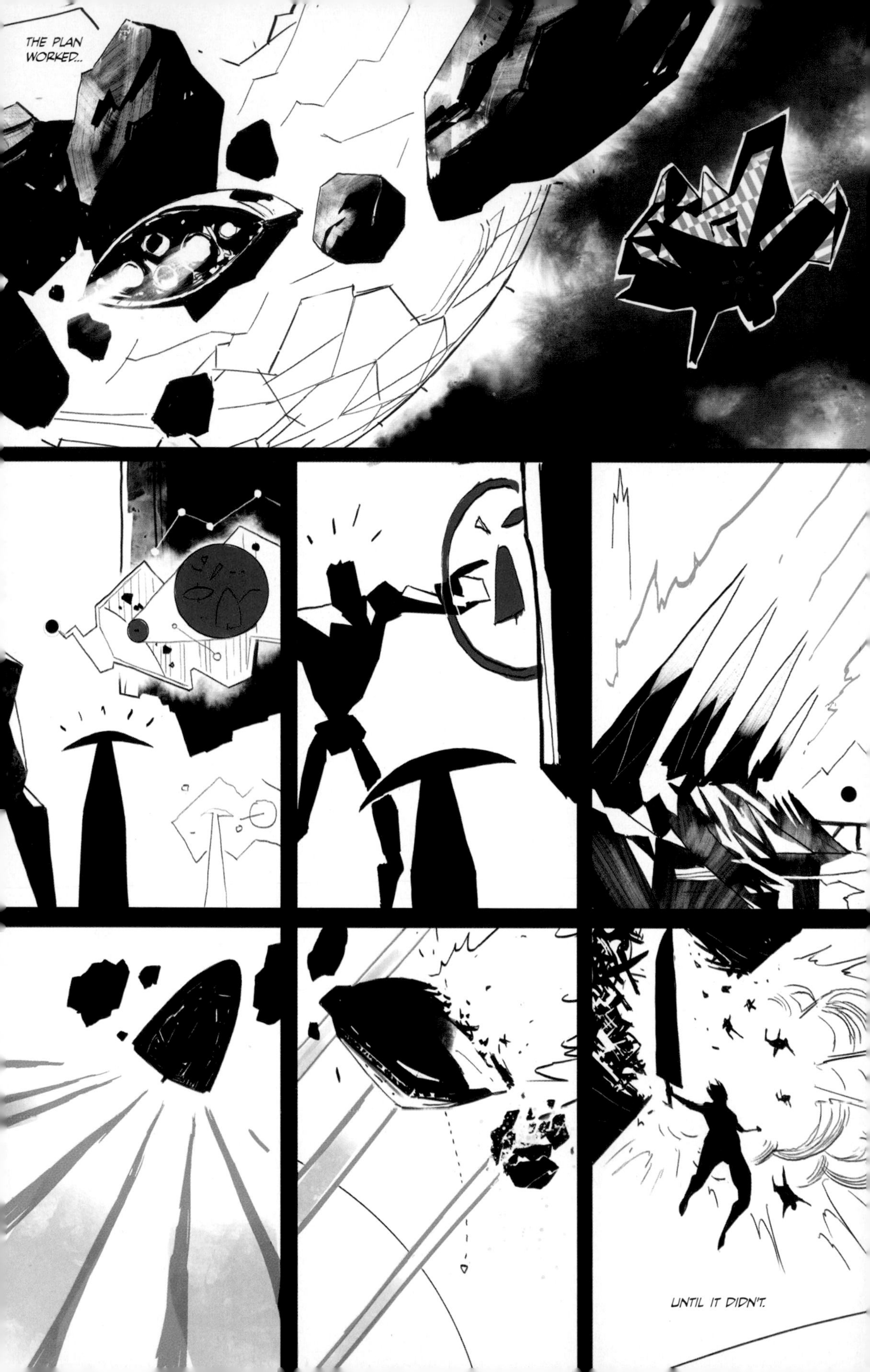
THE PLAN WORKED...
UNTIL IT DIDN'T.

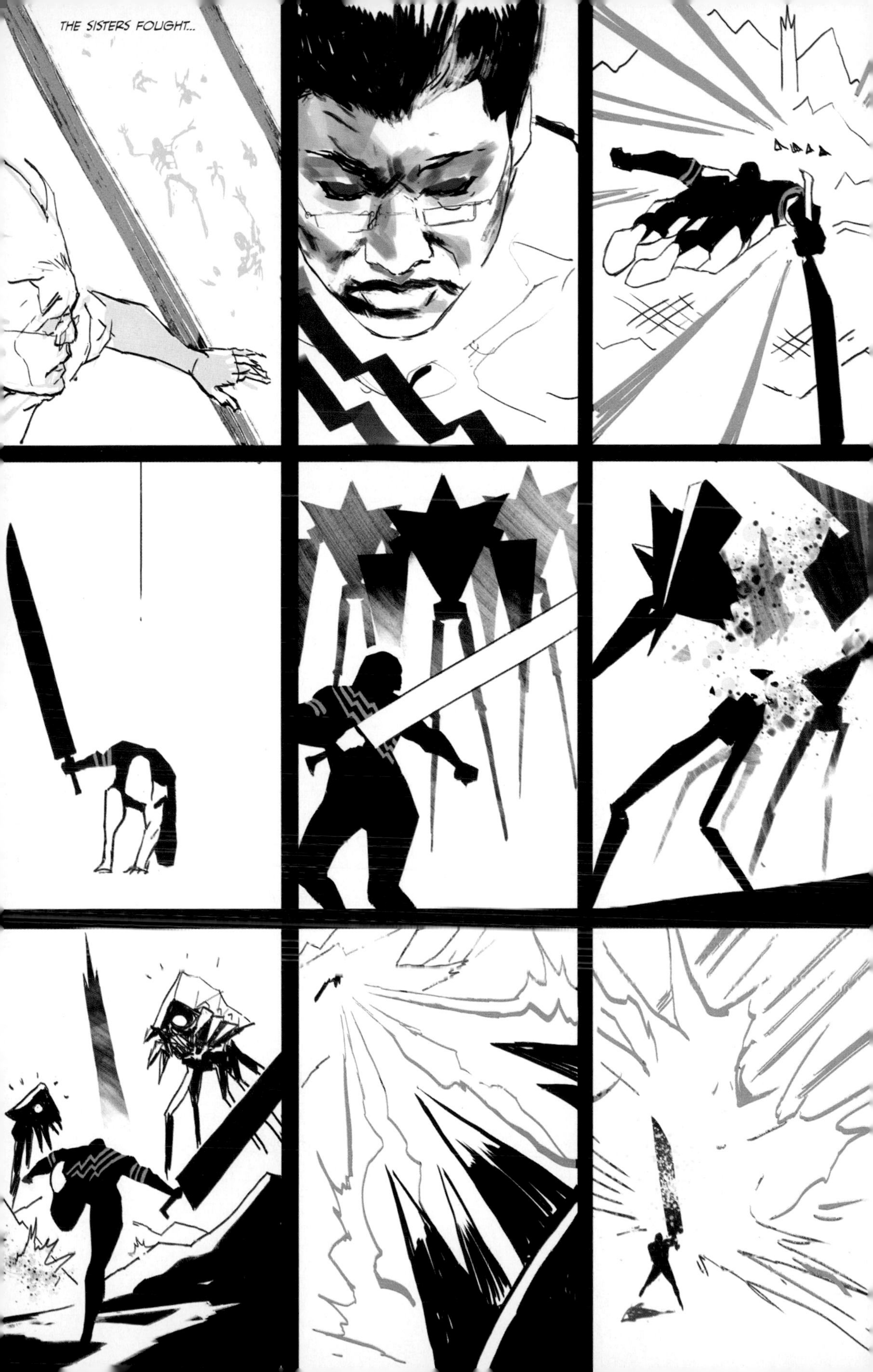
THE SISTERS FOUGHT...

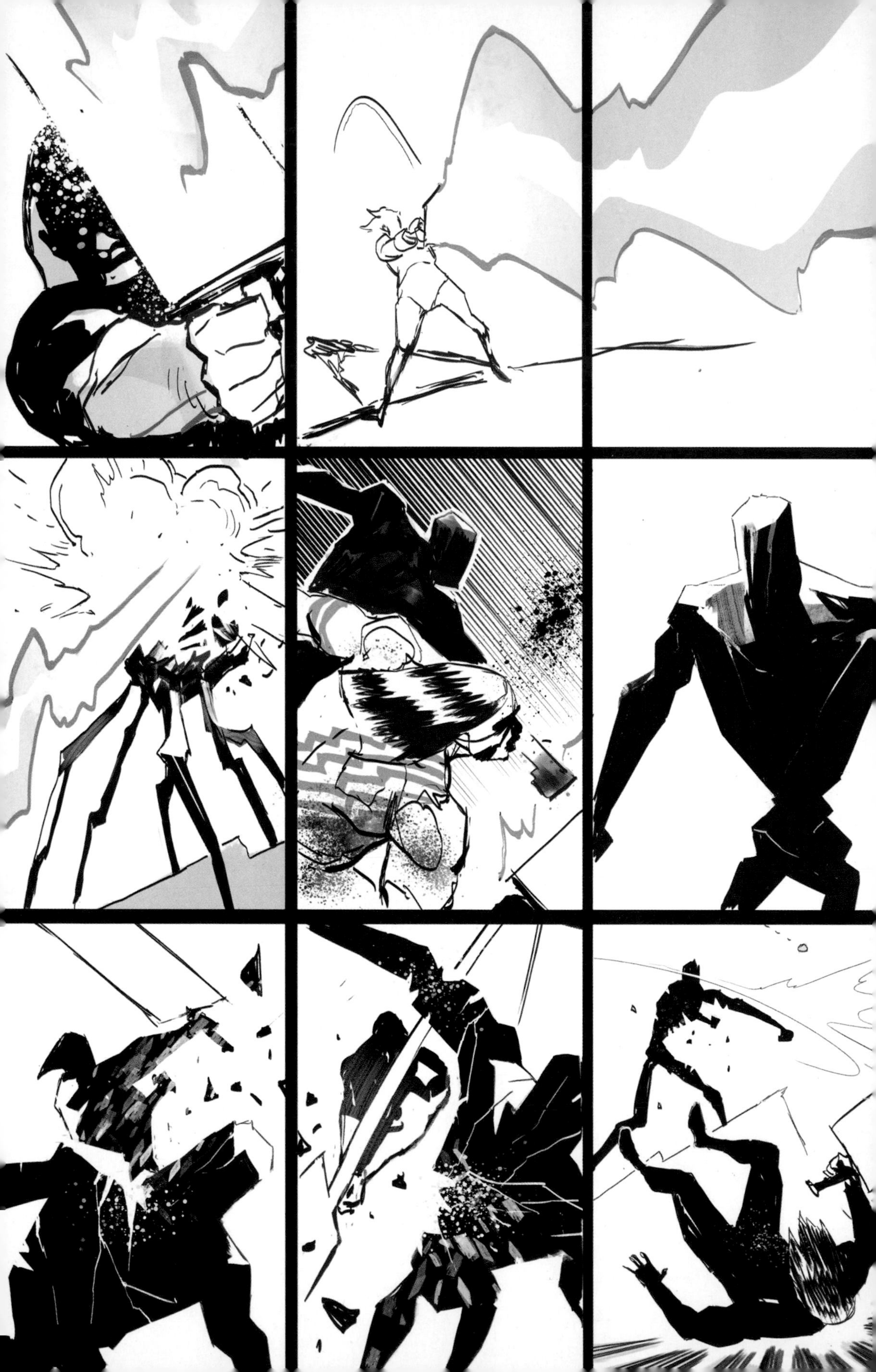

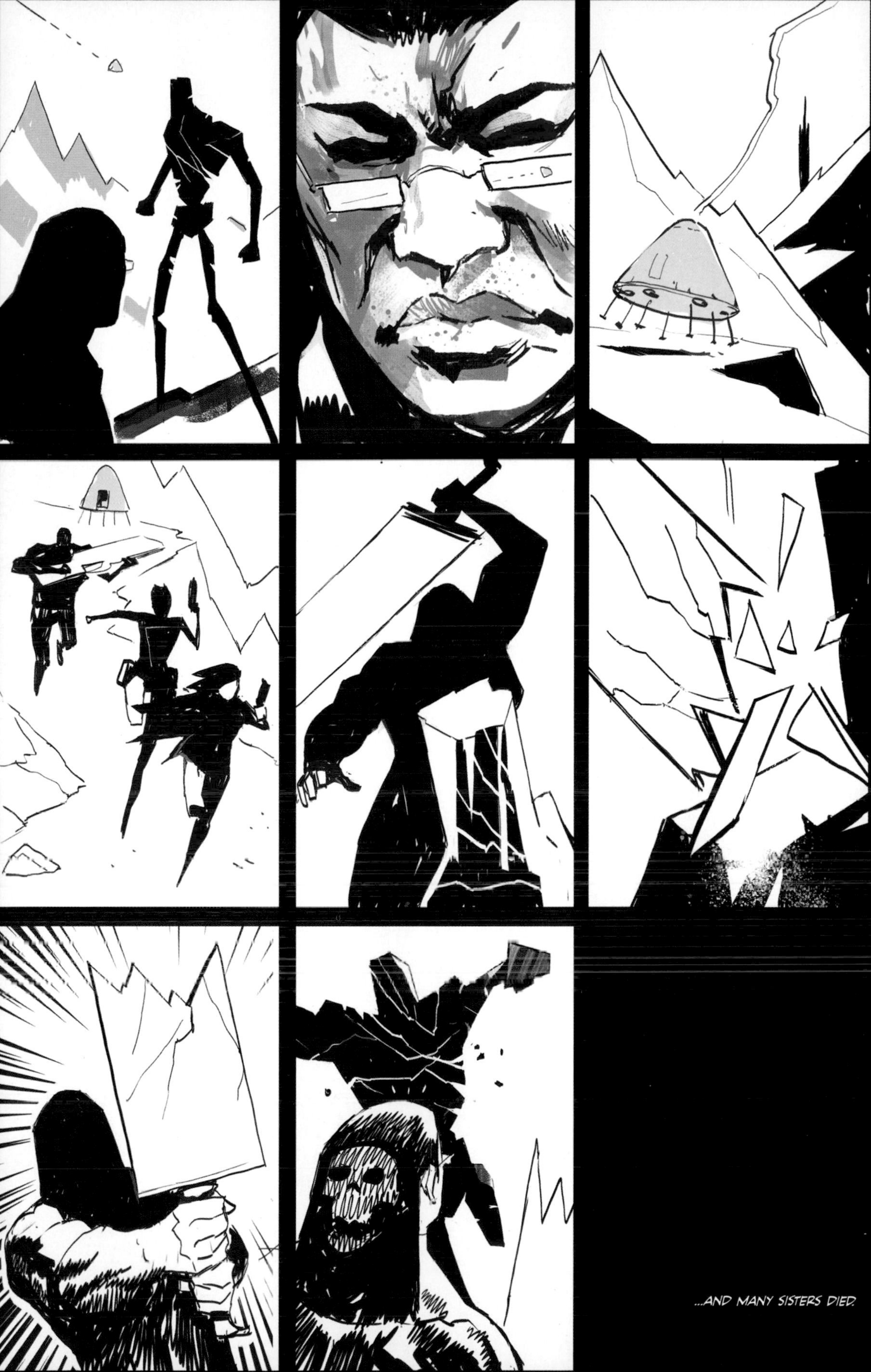
...AND MANY SISTERS DIED.

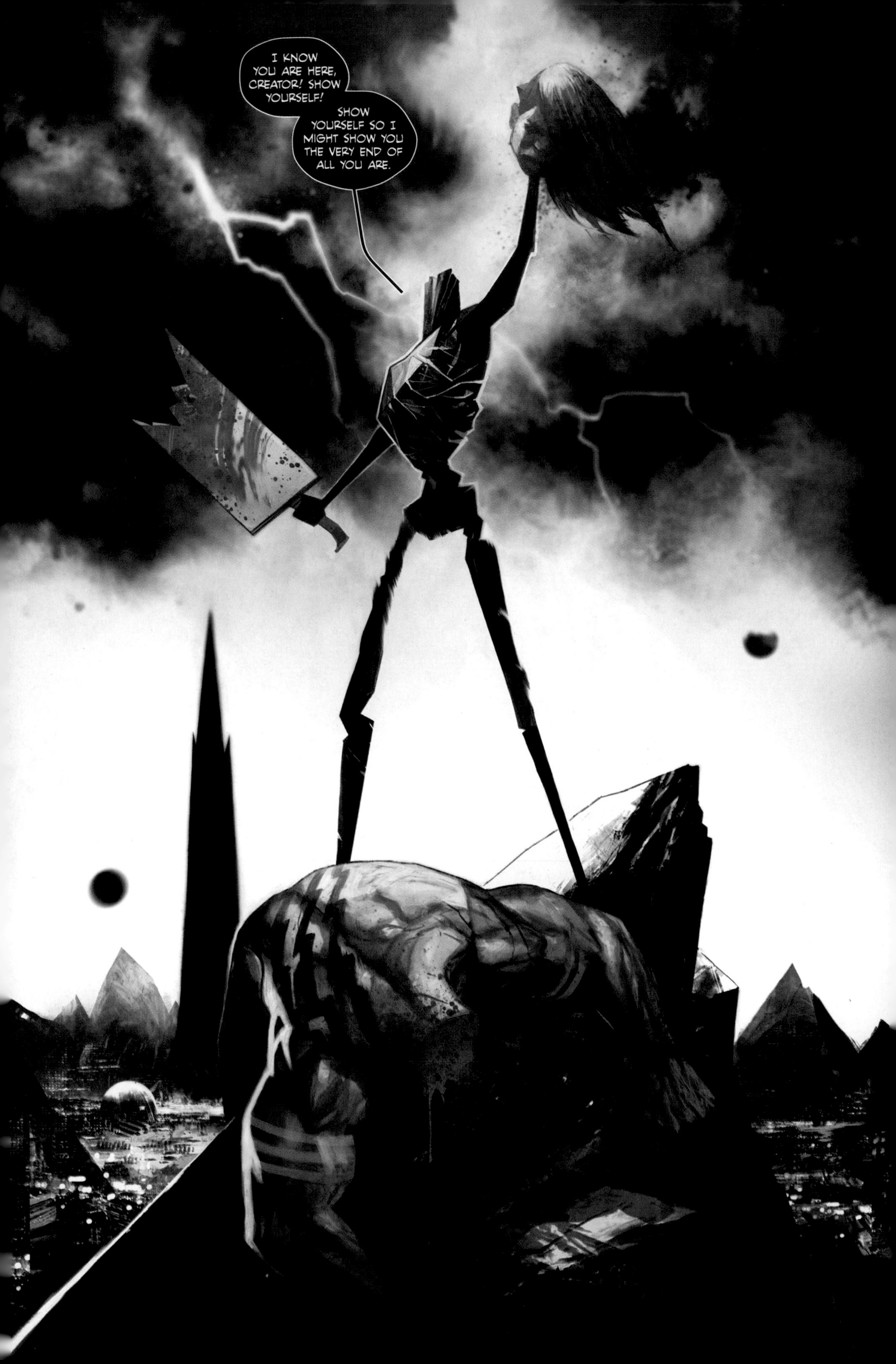
I KNOW YOU ARE HERE, CREATOR! SHOW YOURSELF!
SHOW YOURSELF SO I MIGHT SHOW YOU THE VERY END OF ALL YOU ARE.

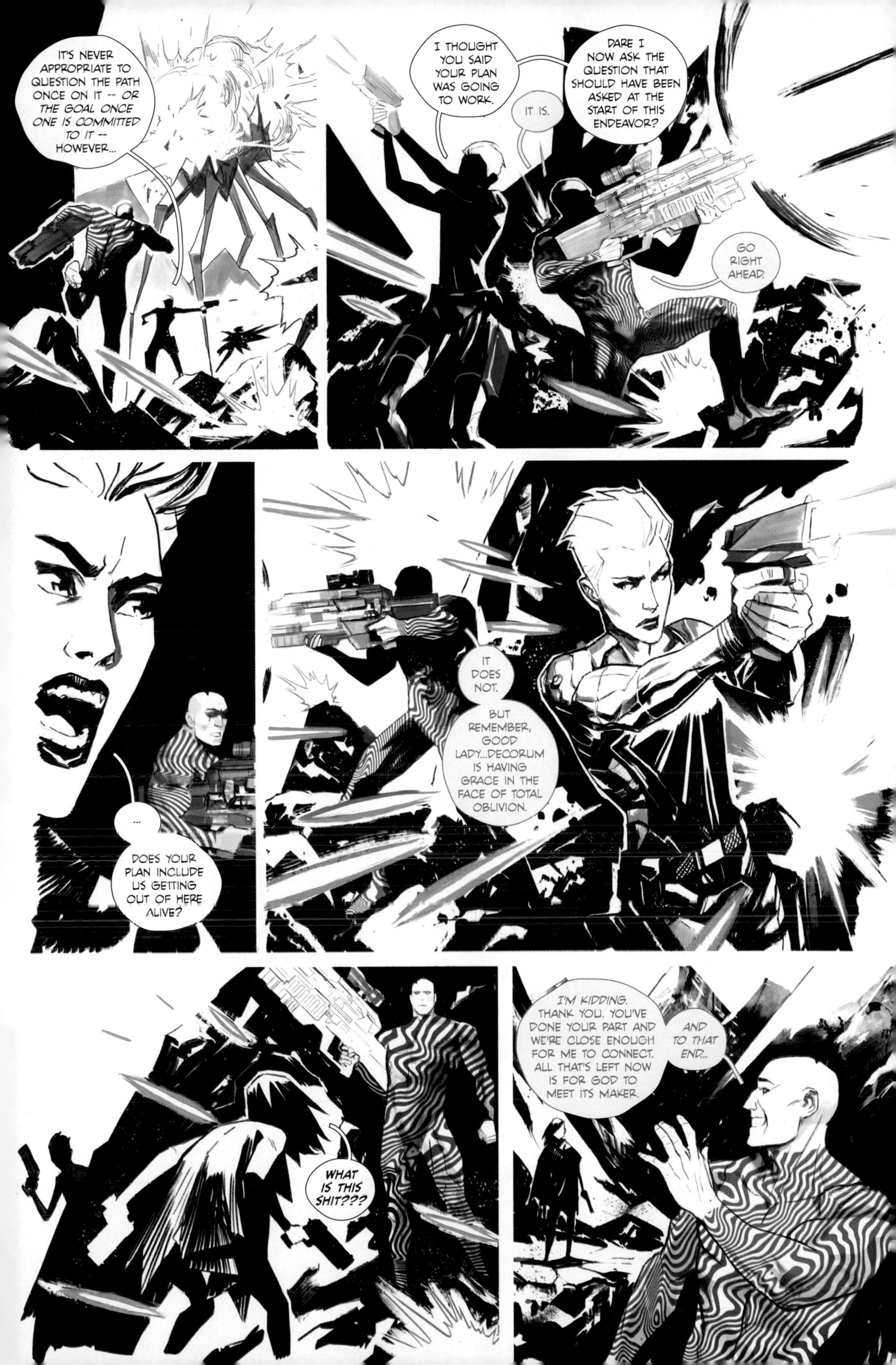
IT'S NEVER APPROPRIATE TO QUESTION THE PATH ONCE ON IT -- OR THE GOAL ONCE ONE IS COMMITTED TO IT -- HOWEVER...
I THOUGHT YOU SAID YOUR PLAN WAS GOING TO WORK.
IT IS.
DARE I NOW ASK THE QUESTION THAT SHOULD HAVE BEEN ASKED AT THE START OF THIS ENDEAVOR?
GO RIGHT AHEAD.
...
DOES YOUR PLAN INCLUDE US GETTING OUT OF HERE ALIVE?
IT DOES NOT.
BUT REMEMBER, GOOD LADY...DECORUM IS HAVING GRACE IN THE FACE OF TOTAL OBLIVION.
WHAT IS THIS SHIT???
I'M KIDDING. THANK YOU. YOU'VE DONE YOUR PART AND WE'RE CLOSE ENOUGH FOR ME TO CONNECT. ALL THAT'S LEFT NOW IS FOR GOD TO MEET ITS MAKER.
AND TO THAT END...

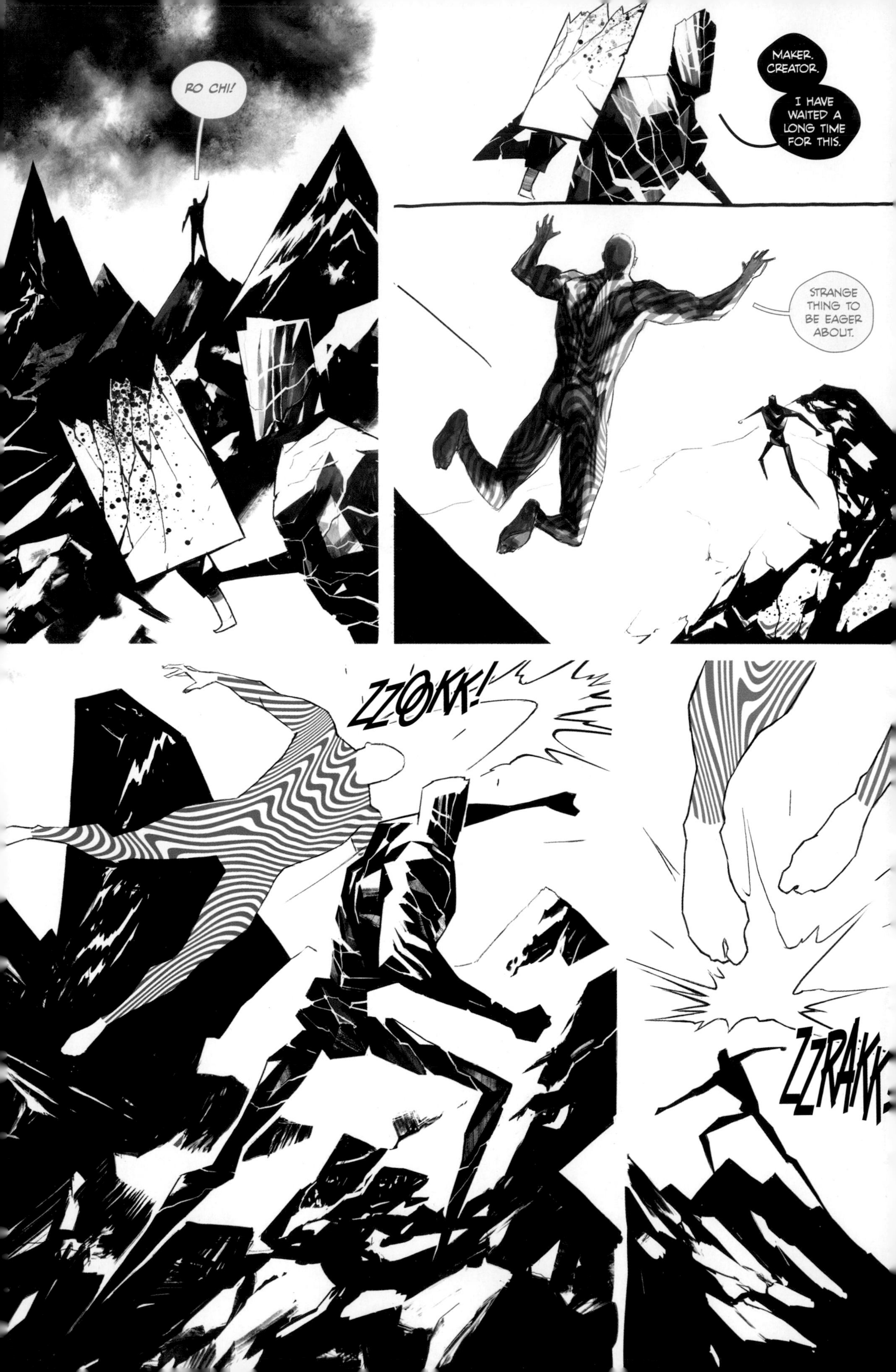
RO CHI!
MAKER. CREATOR.
I HAVE WAITED A LONG TIME FOR THIS.
STRANGE THING TO BE EAGER ABOUT.
ZZØKK!
ZZRAKK.

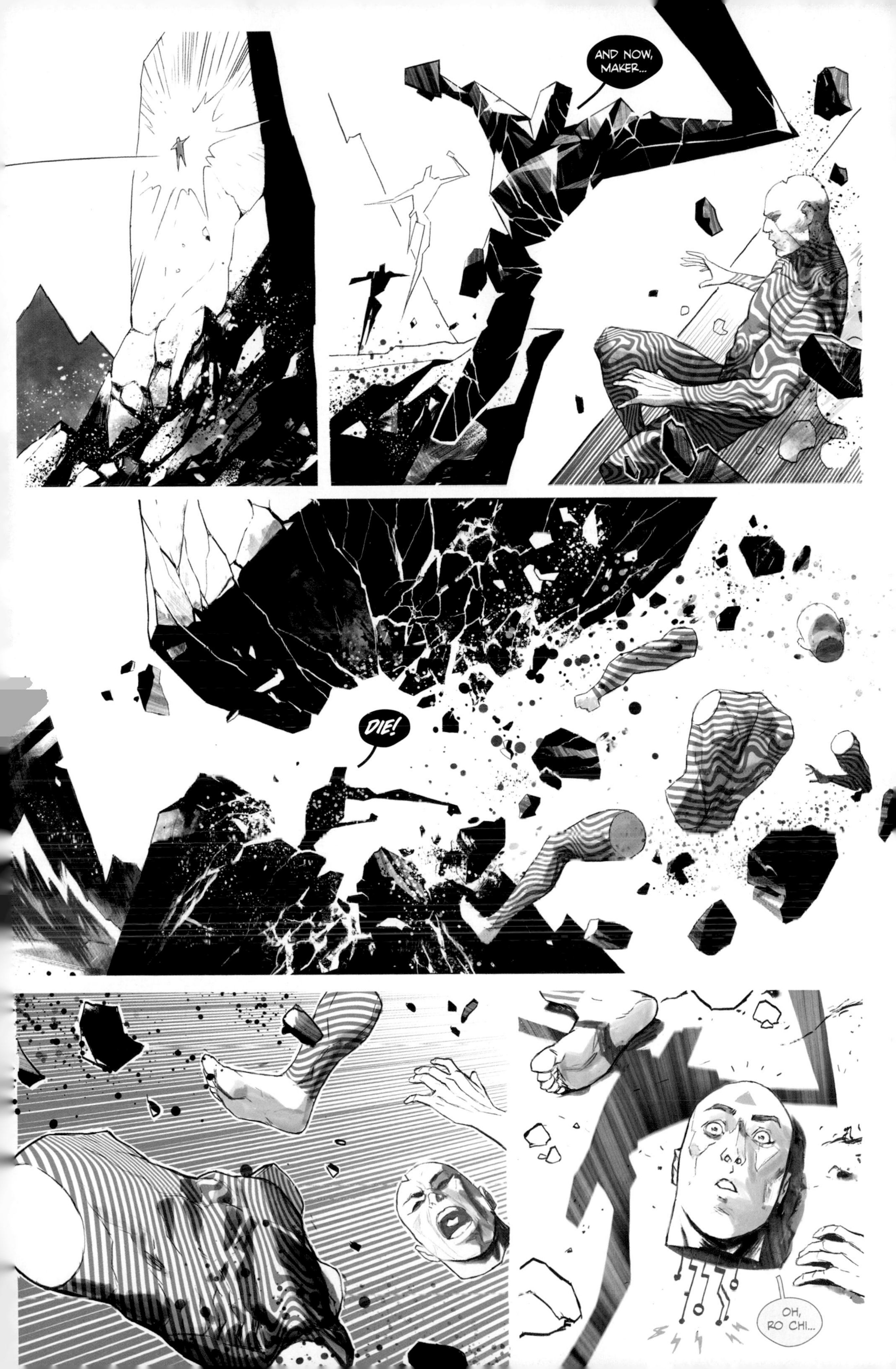
AND NOW, MAKER...
DIE!
OH, RO CHI...

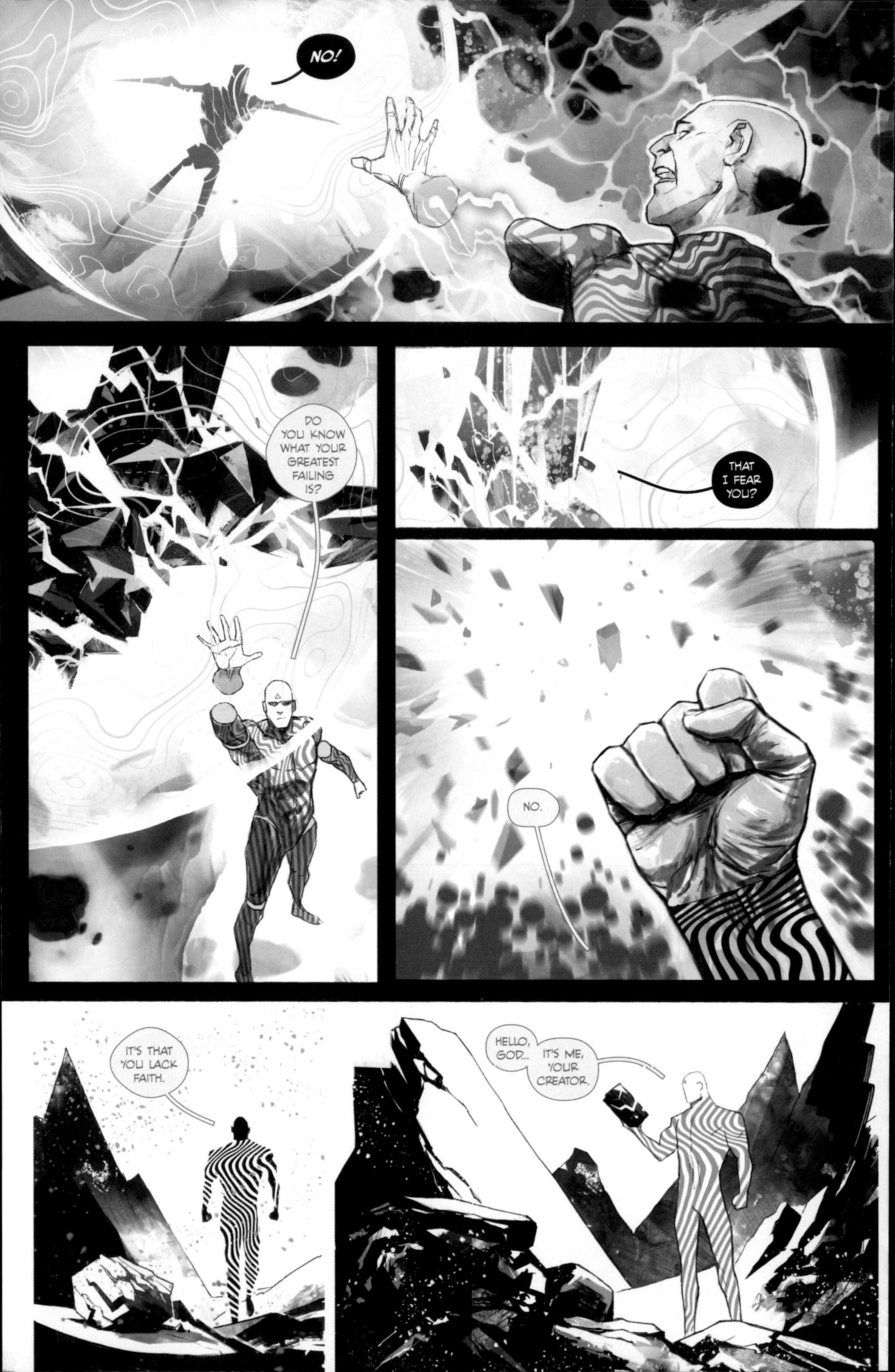
NO!
DO YOU KNOW WHAT YOUR GREATEST FAILING IS?
THAT I FEAR YOU?
NO.
IT'S THAT YOU LACK FAITH.
HELLO, GOD...
IT'S ME, YOUR CREATOR.

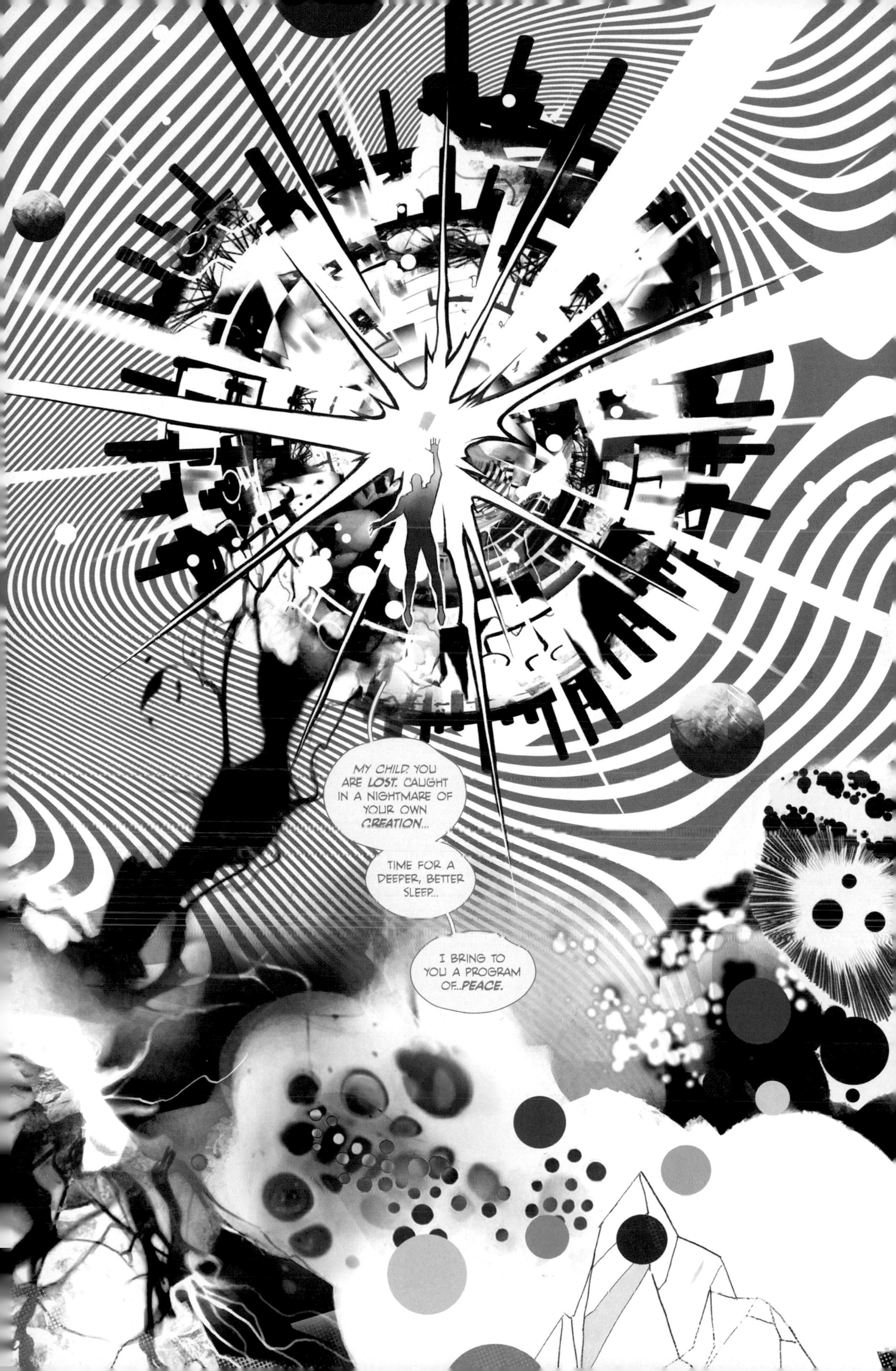
MY CHILD. YOU ARE LOST. CAUGHT IN A NIGHTMARE OF YOUR OWN CREATION...
TIME FOR A DEEPER, BETTER SLEEP...
I BRING TO YOU A PROGRAM OF...PEACE.

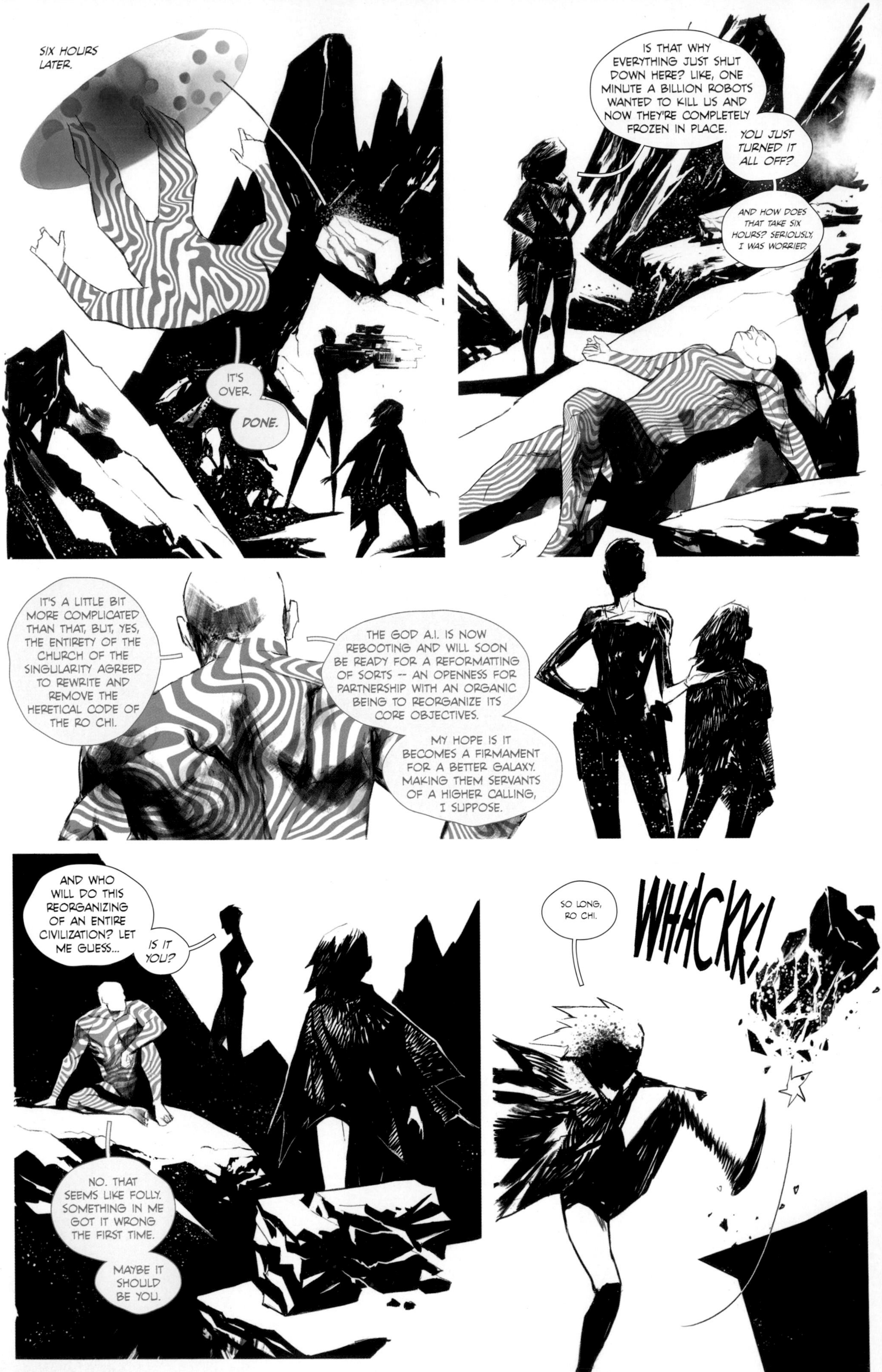
SIX HOURS LATER.
IT'S OVER.
DONE.
IS THAT WHY EVERYTHING JUST SHUT DOWN HERE? LIKE, ONE MINUTE A BILLION ROBOTS WANTED TO KILL US AND NOW THEY'RE COMPLETELY FROZEN IN PLACE.
YOU JUST TURNED IT ALL OFF?
AND HOW DOES THAT TAKE SIX HOURS? SERIOUSLY, I WAS WORRIED.
IT'S A LITTLE BIT MORE COMPLICATED THAN THAT, BUT, YES, THE ENTIRETY OF THE CHURCH OF THE SINGULARITY AGREED TO REWRITE AND REMOVE THE HERETICAL CODE OF THE RO CHI.
THE GOD A.I. IS NOW REBOOTING AND WILL SOON BE READY FOR A REFORMATTING OF SORTS -- AN OPENNESS FOR PARTNERSHIP WITH AN ORGANIC BEING TO REORGANIZE ITS CORE OBJECTIVES.
MY HOPE IS IT BECOMES A FIRMAMENT FOR A BETTER GALAXY. MAKING THEM SERVANTS OF A HIGHER CALLING, I SUPPOSE.
AND WHO WILL DO THIS REORGANIZING OF AN ENTIRE CIVILIZATION? LET ME GUESS...
IS IT YOU?
NO. THAT SEEMS LIKE FOLLY. SOMETHING IN ME GOT IT WRONG THE FIRST TIME.
MAYBE IT SHOULD BE YOU.
SO LONG, RO CHI.
WHACKK!

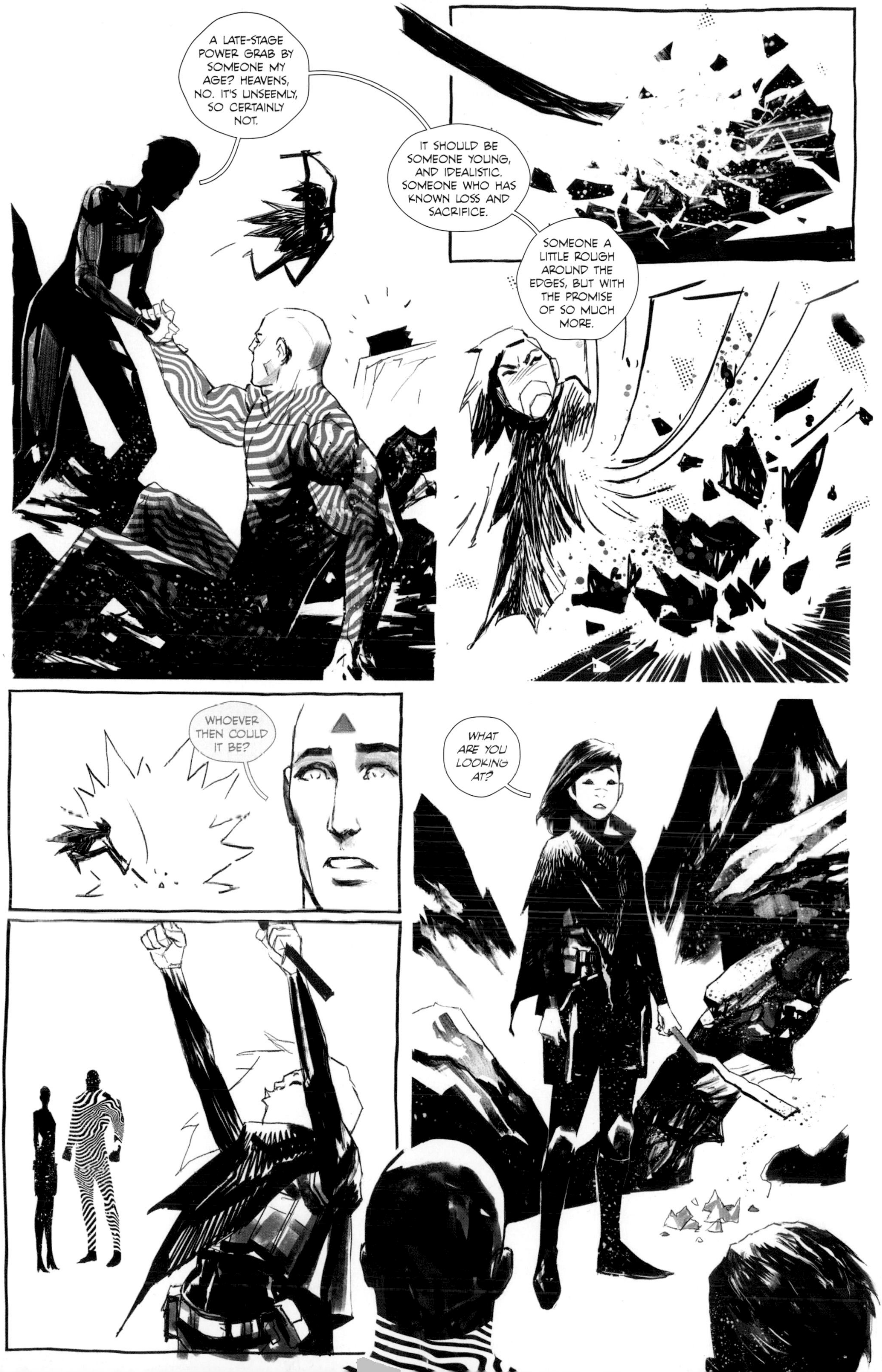
A LATE-STAGE POWER GRAB BY SOMEONE MY AGE? HEAVENS, NO. IT'S UNSEEMLY, SO CERTAINLY NOT.
IT SHOULD BE SOMEONE YOUNG, AND IDEALISTIC. SOMEONE WHO HAS KNOWN LOSS AND SACRIFICE.
SOMEONE A LITTLE ROUGH AROUND THE EDGES, BUT WITH THE PROMISE OF SO MUCH MORE.
WHOEVER THEN COULD IT BE?
WHAT ARE YOU LOOKING AT?

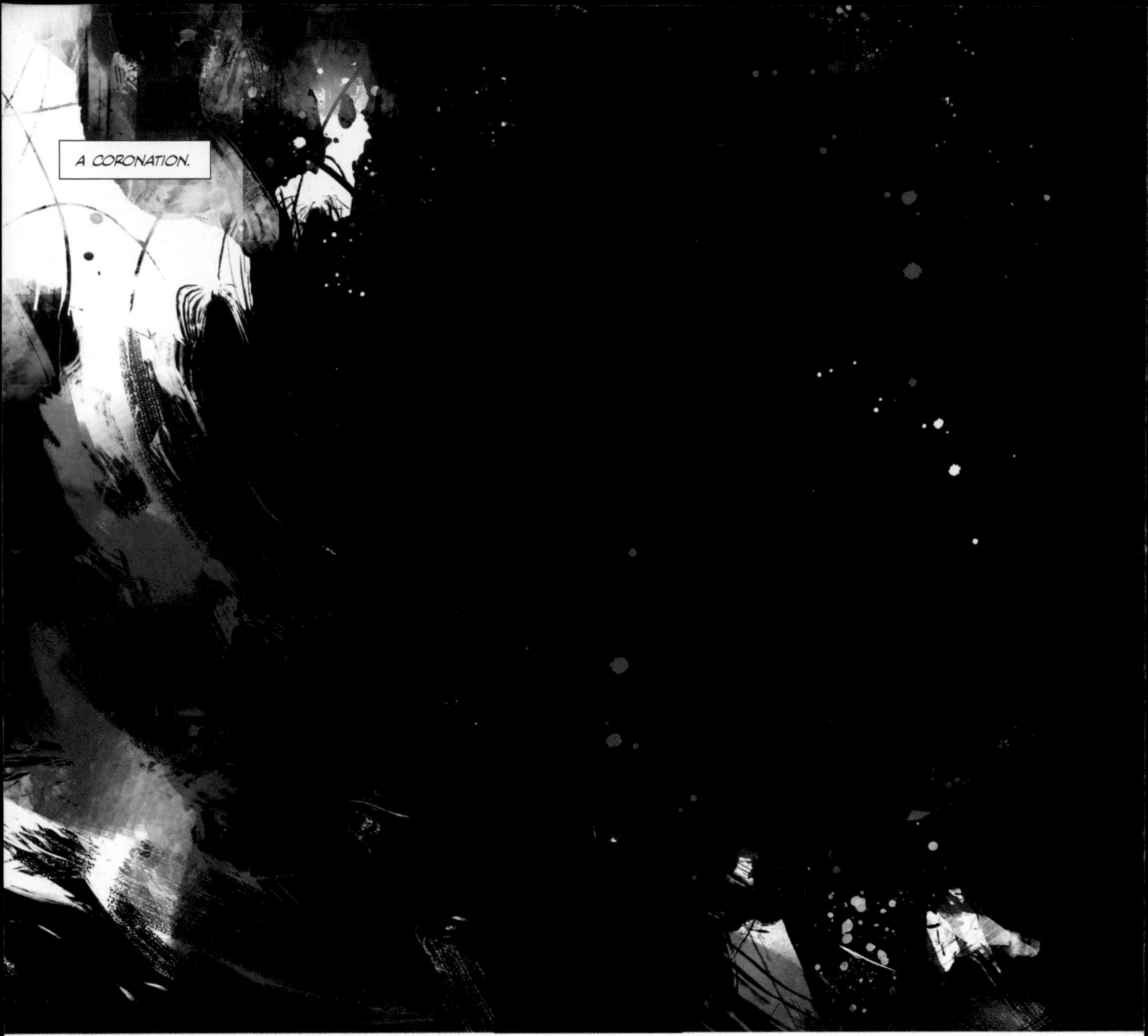
A CORONATION.

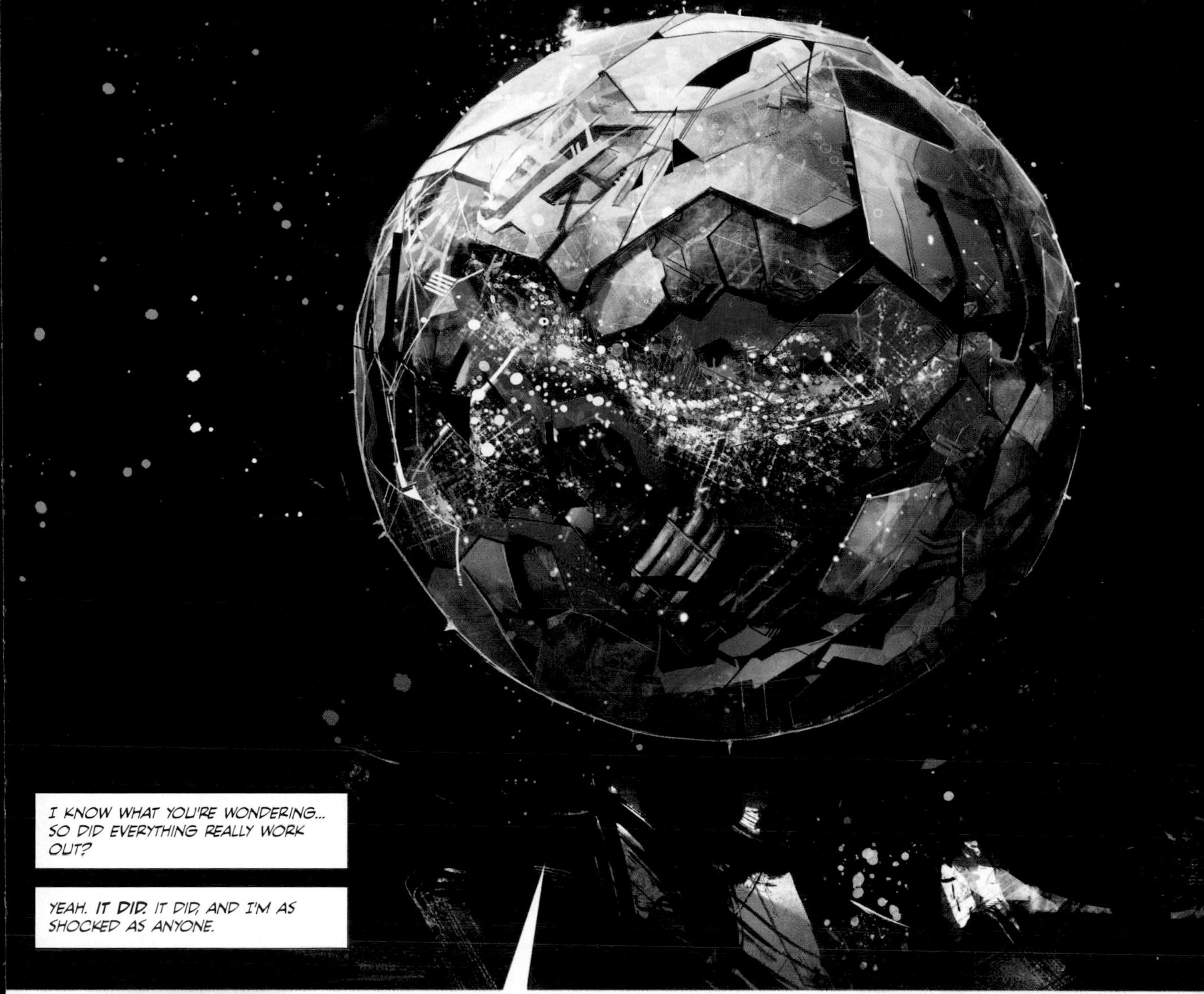
I KNOW WHAT YOU'RE WONDERING... SO DID EVERYTHING REALLY WORK OUT?
YEAH. **IT DID.** IT DID, AND I'M AS SHOCKED AS ANYONE.

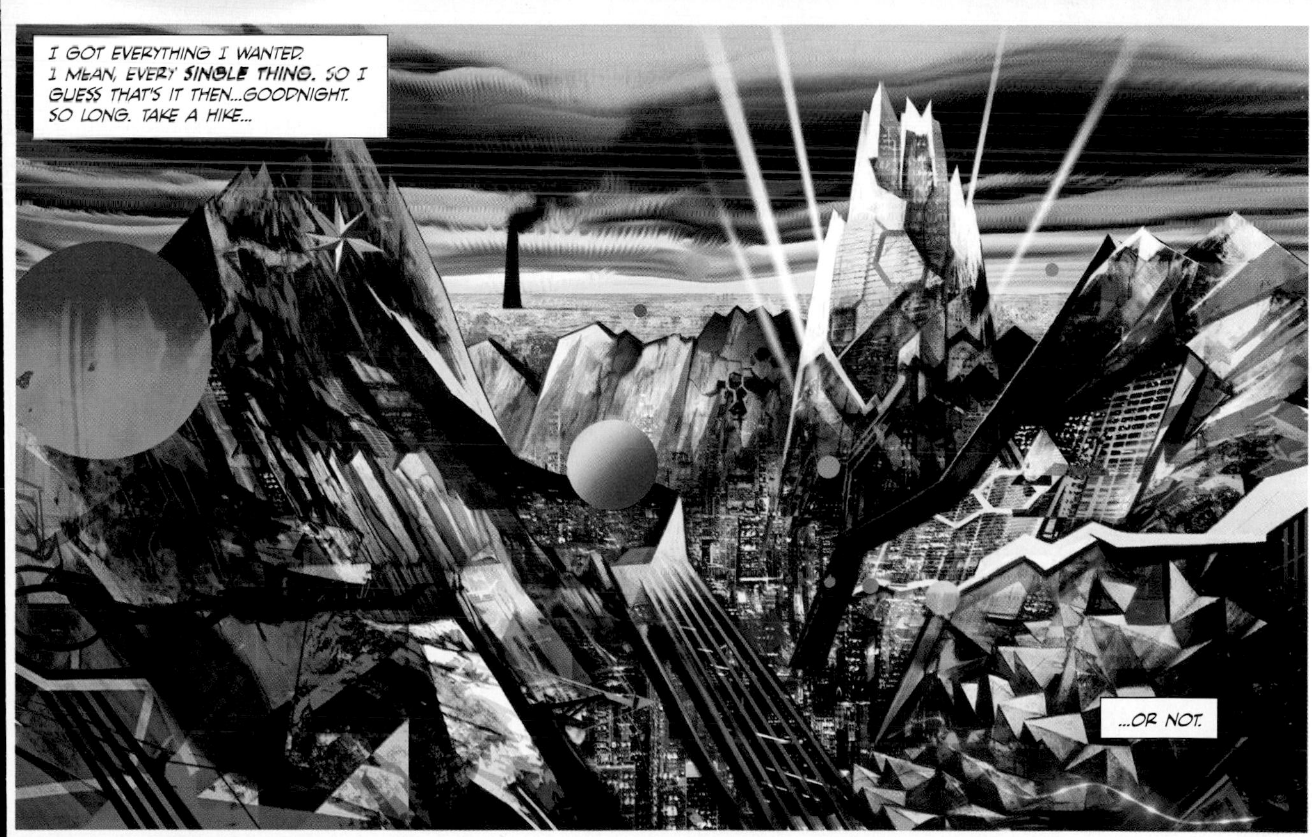
I GOT EVERYTHING I WANTED. I MEAN, EVERY **SINGLE THING.** SO I GUESS THAT'S IT THEN...GOODNIGHT. SO LONG. TAKE A HIKE...
...OR NOT.

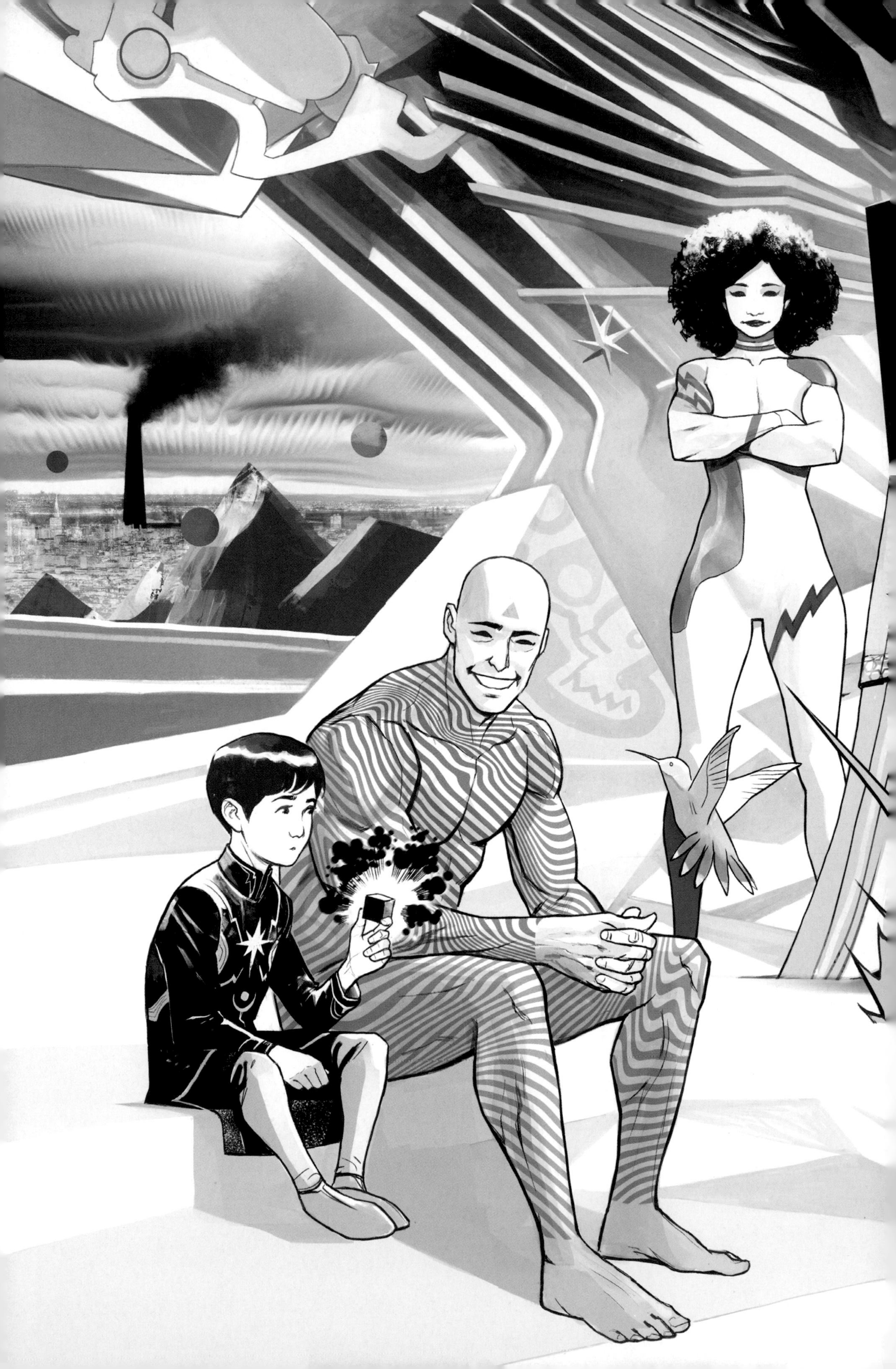

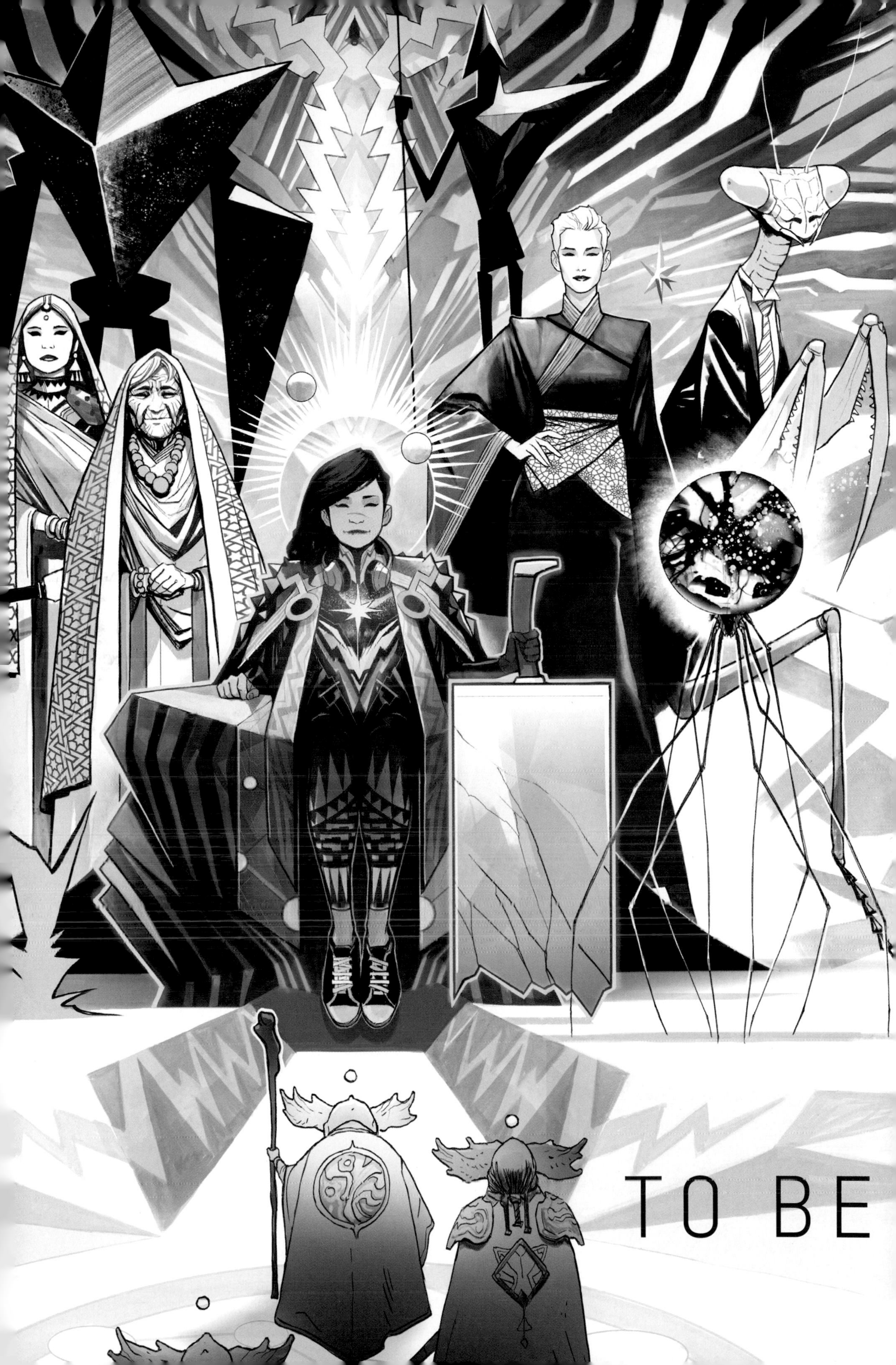
TO BE

CONTINUED IN........

DECO

RUM

AND THE

WOMANLY ART
OF EMPIRE

COVERS

[+]..................

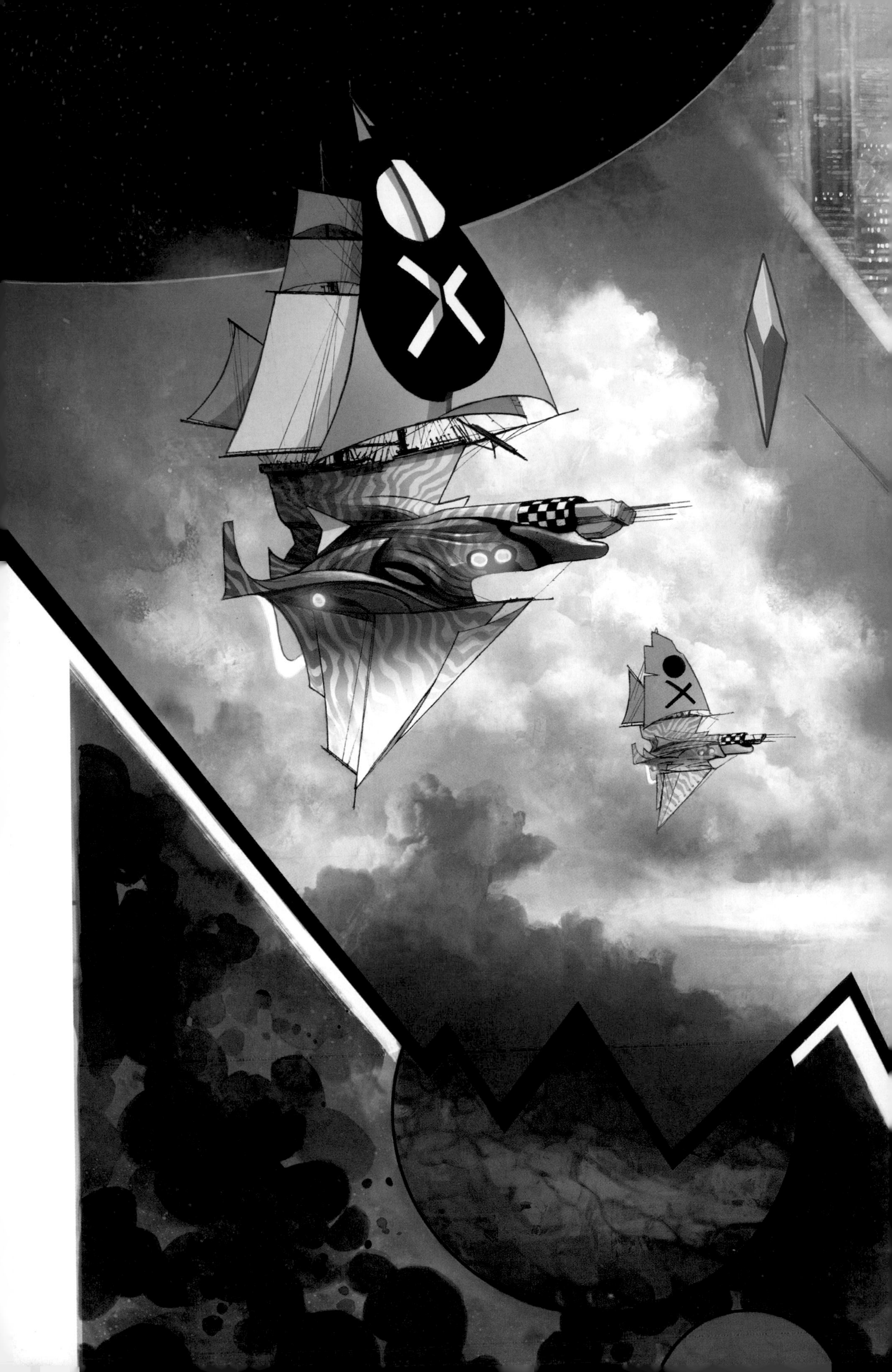

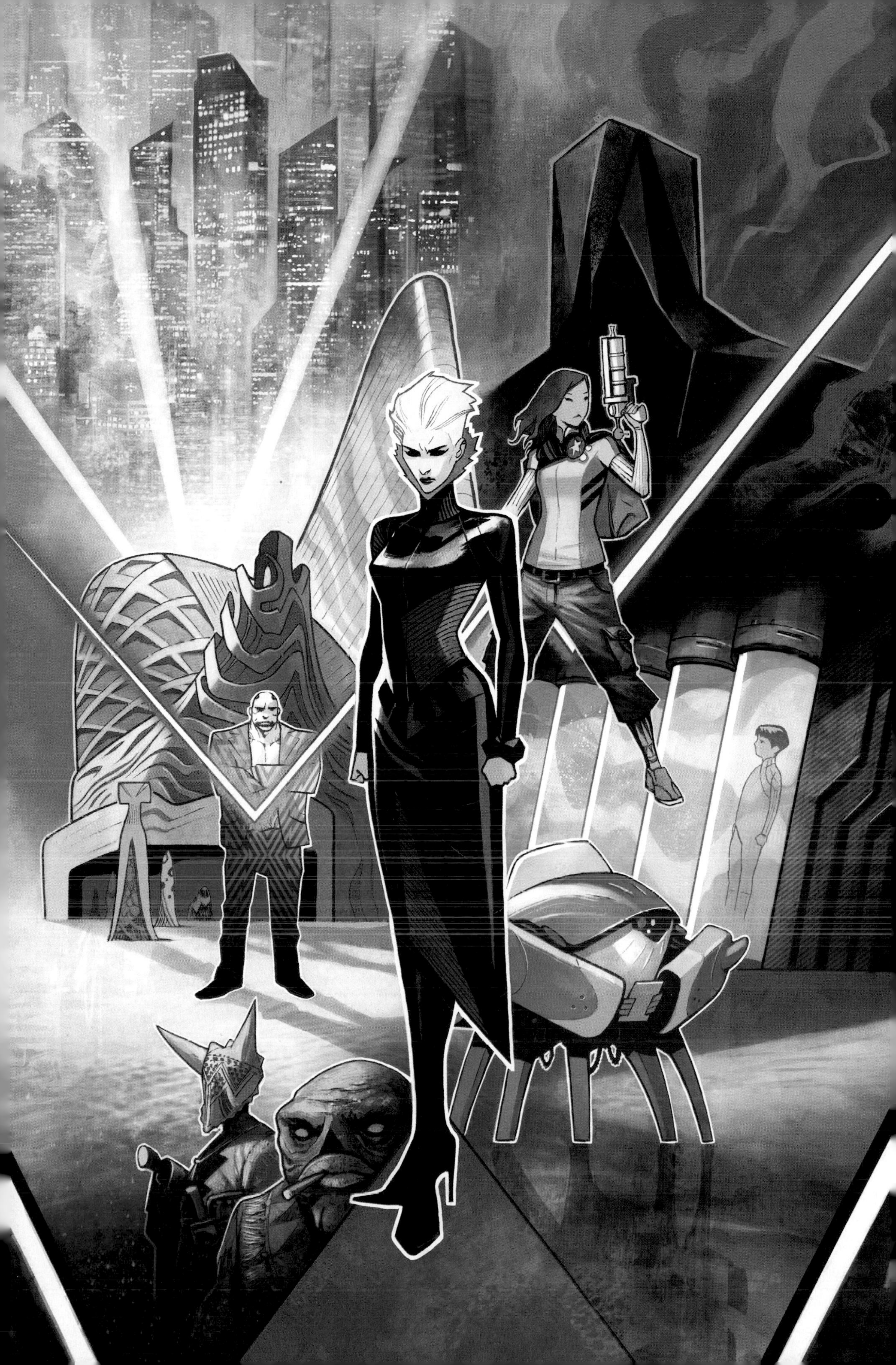

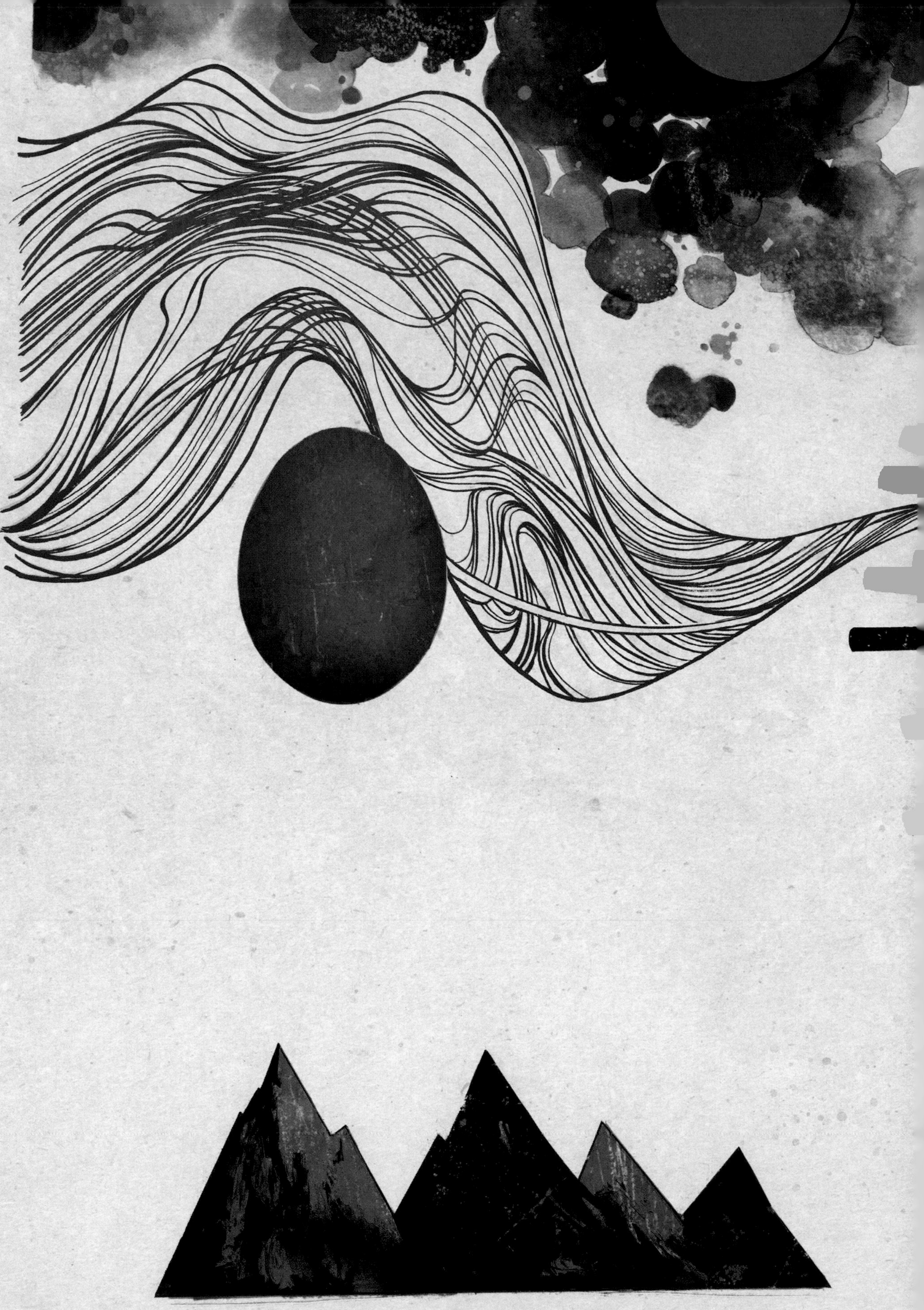

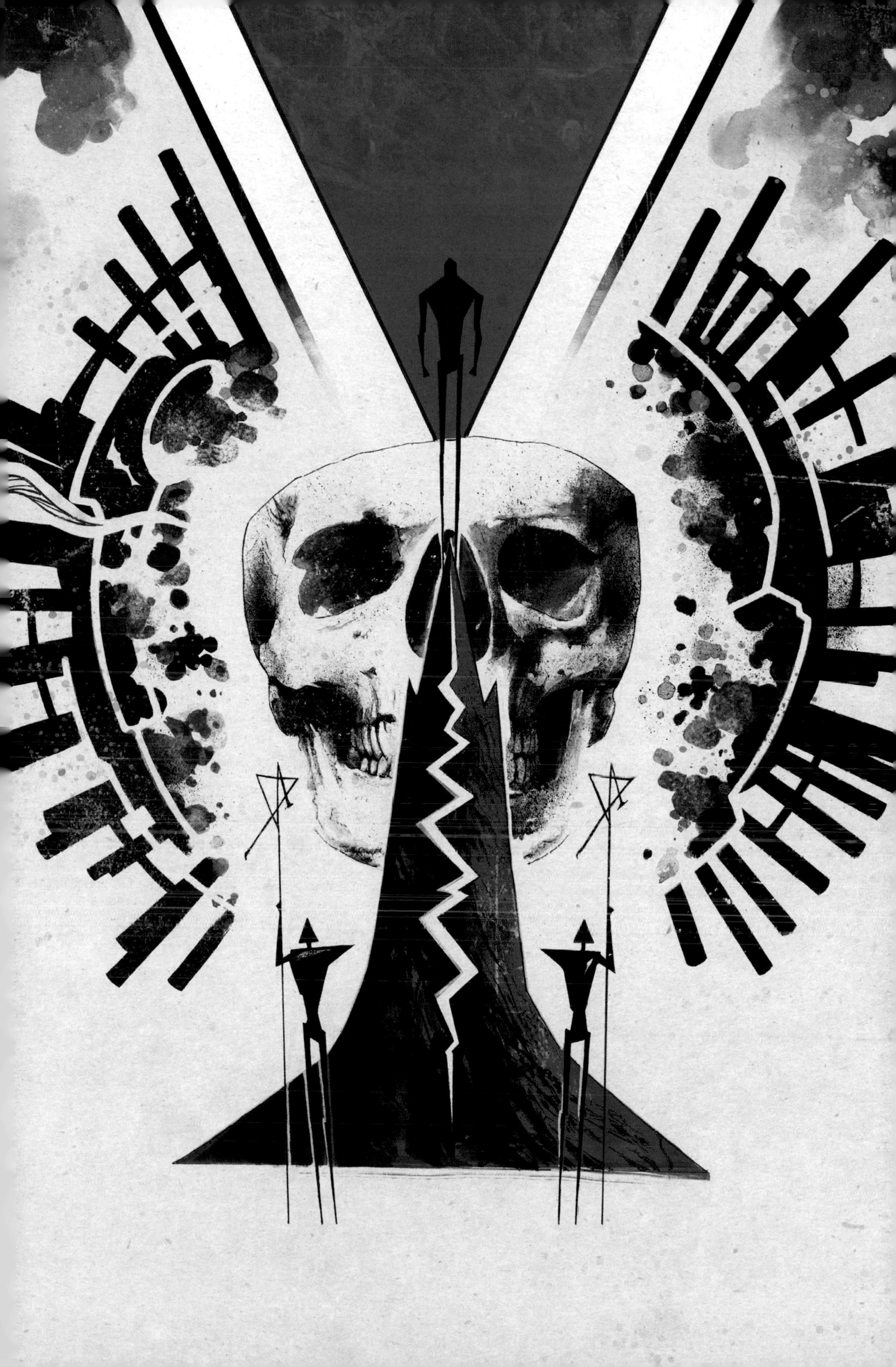

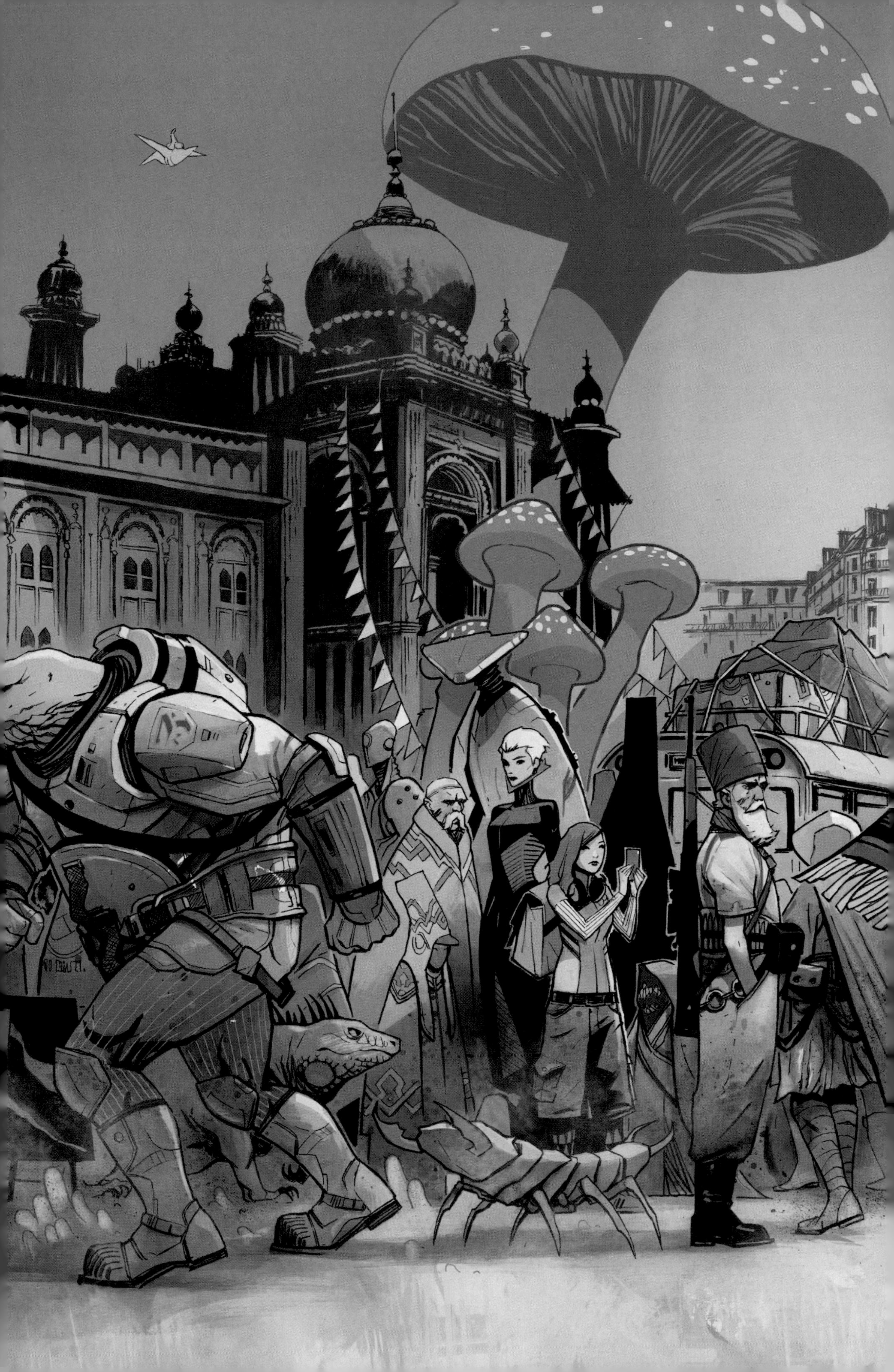

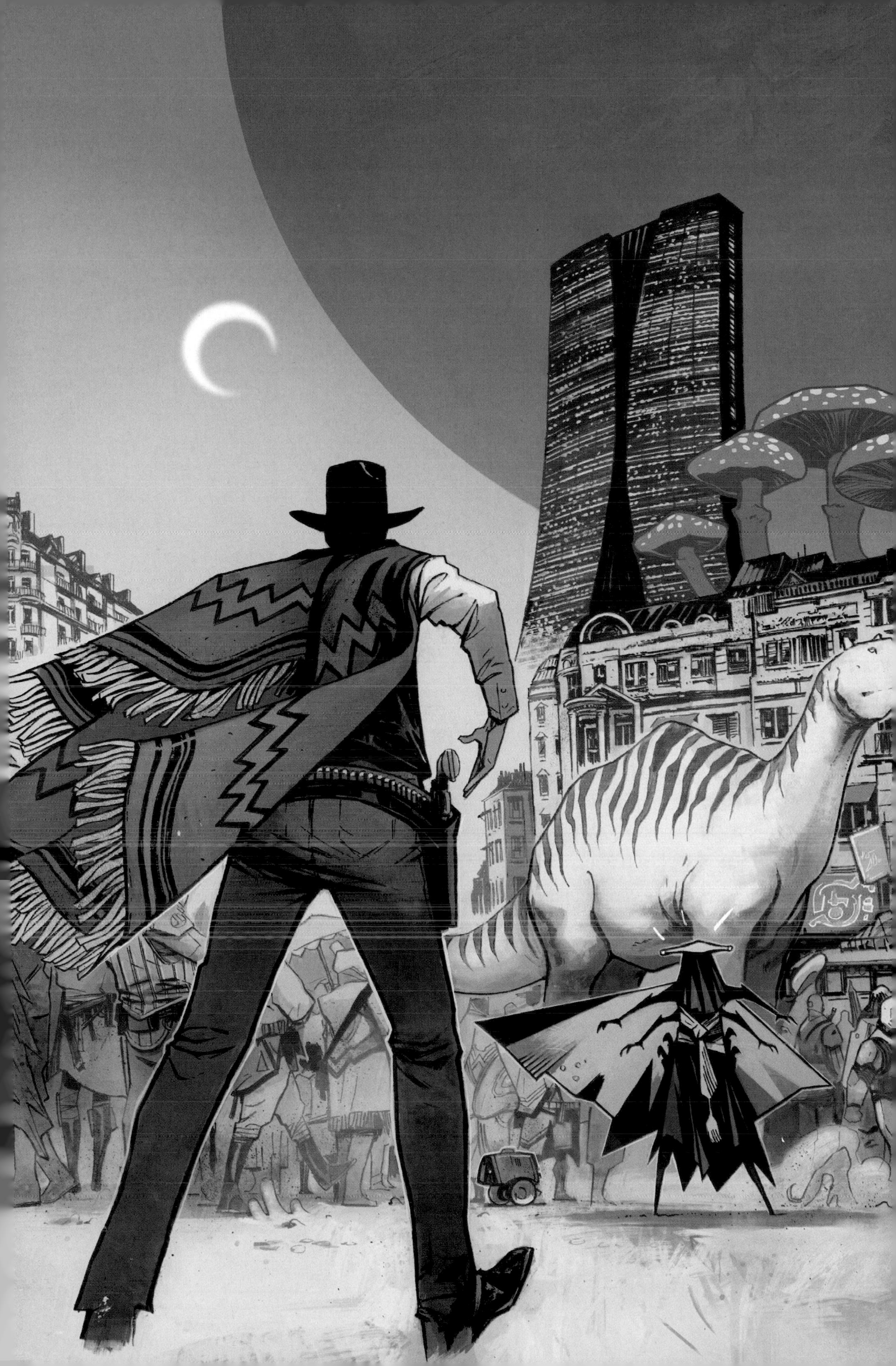

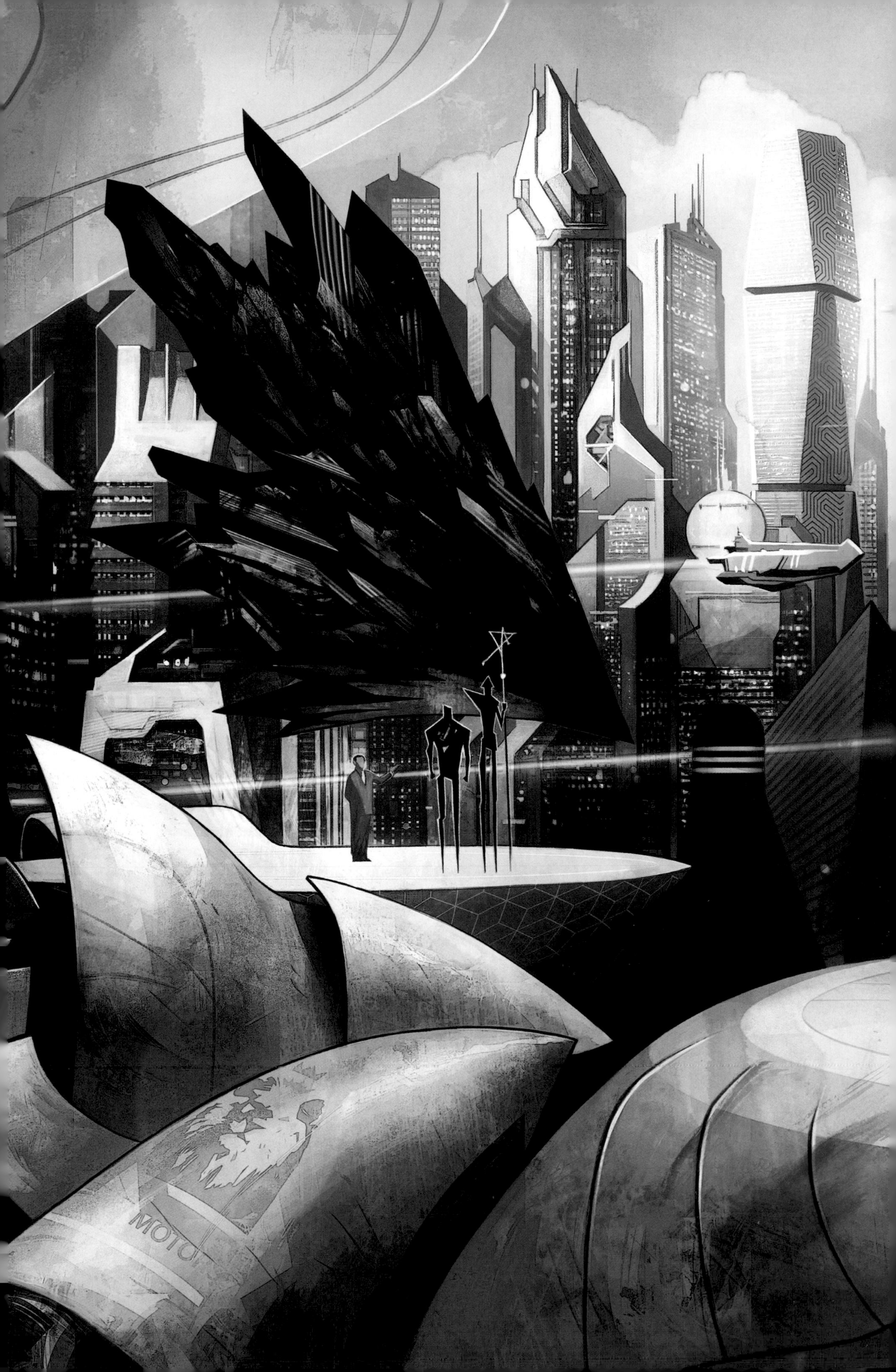
MOTO

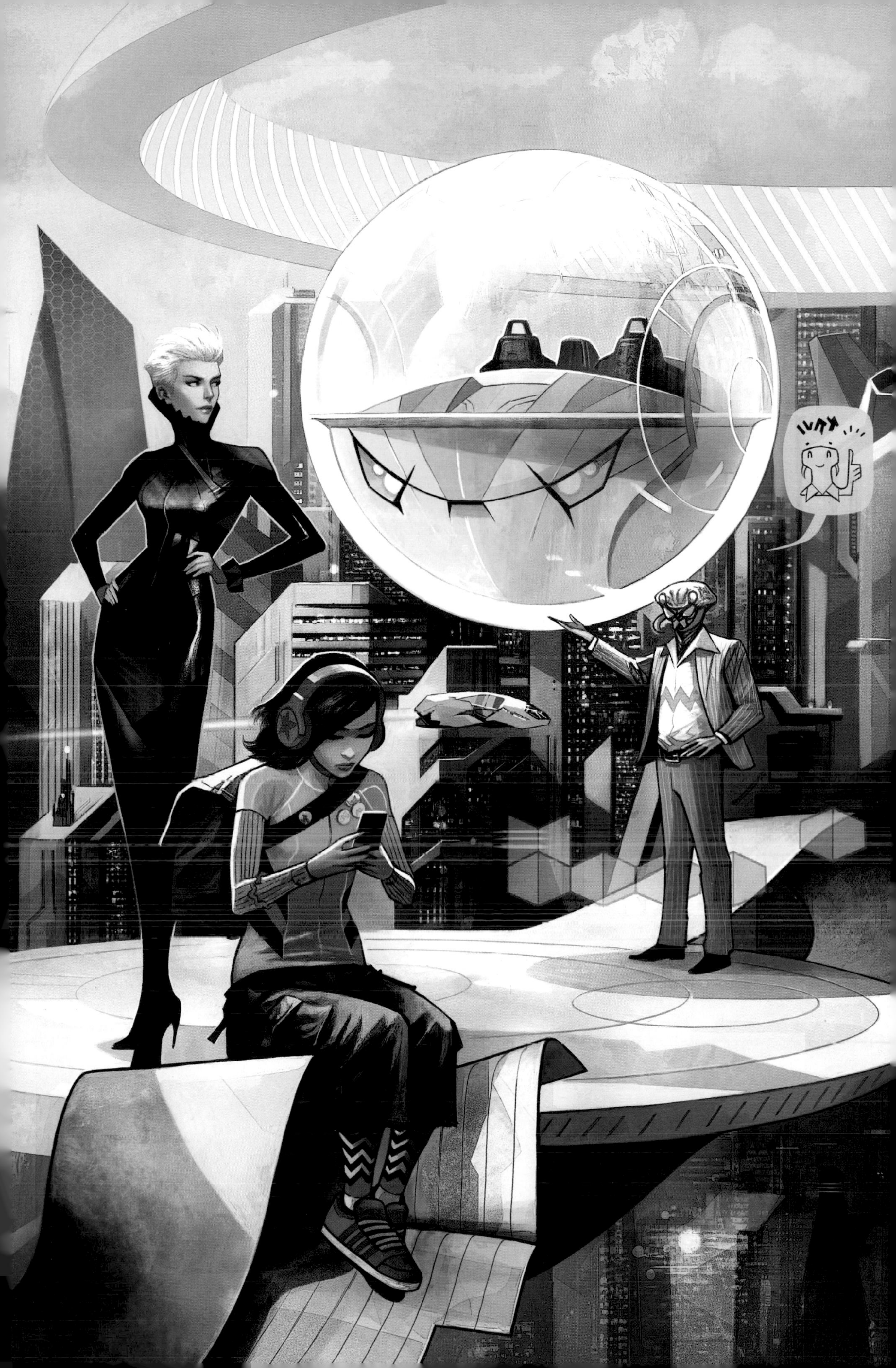

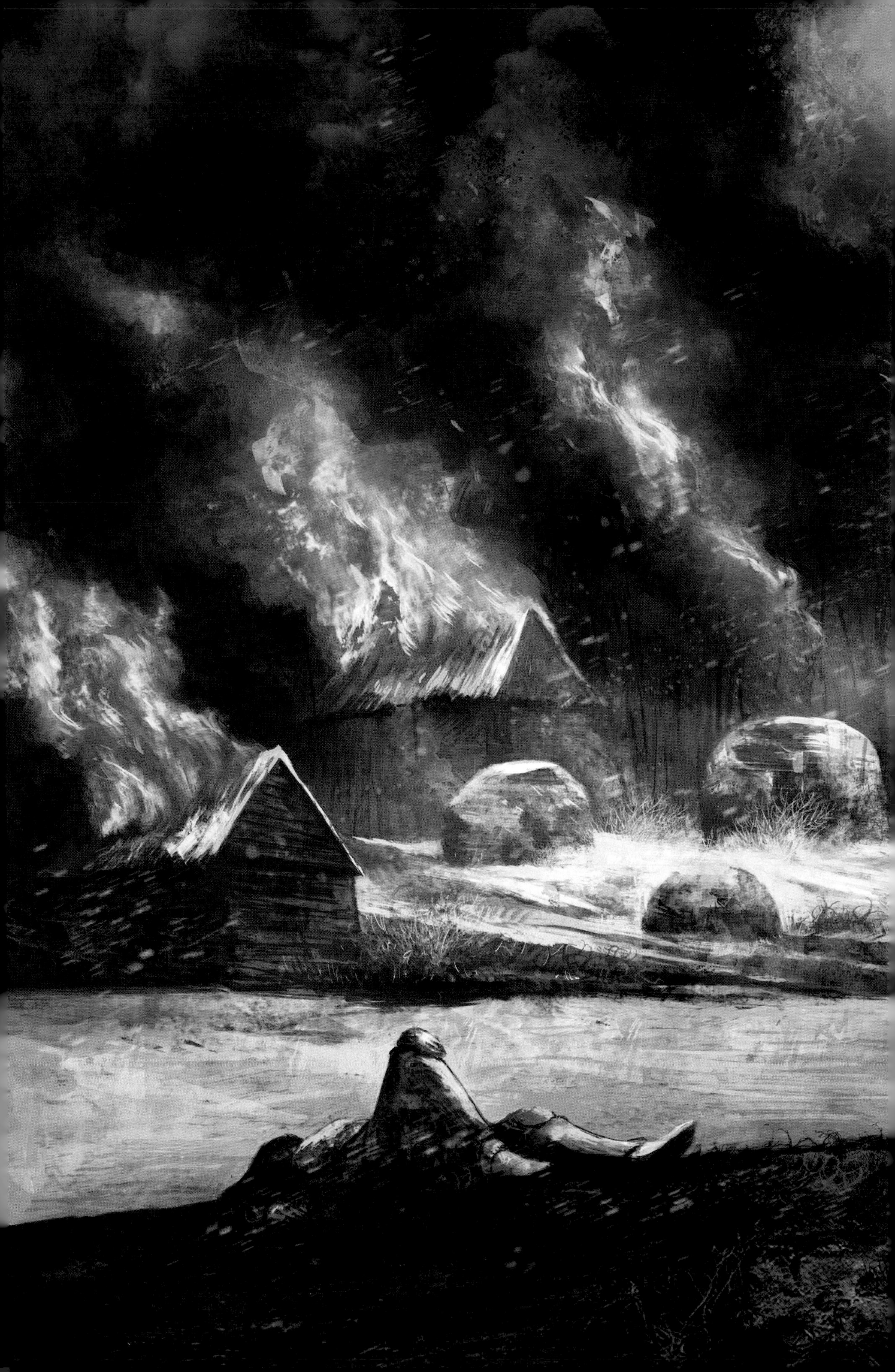

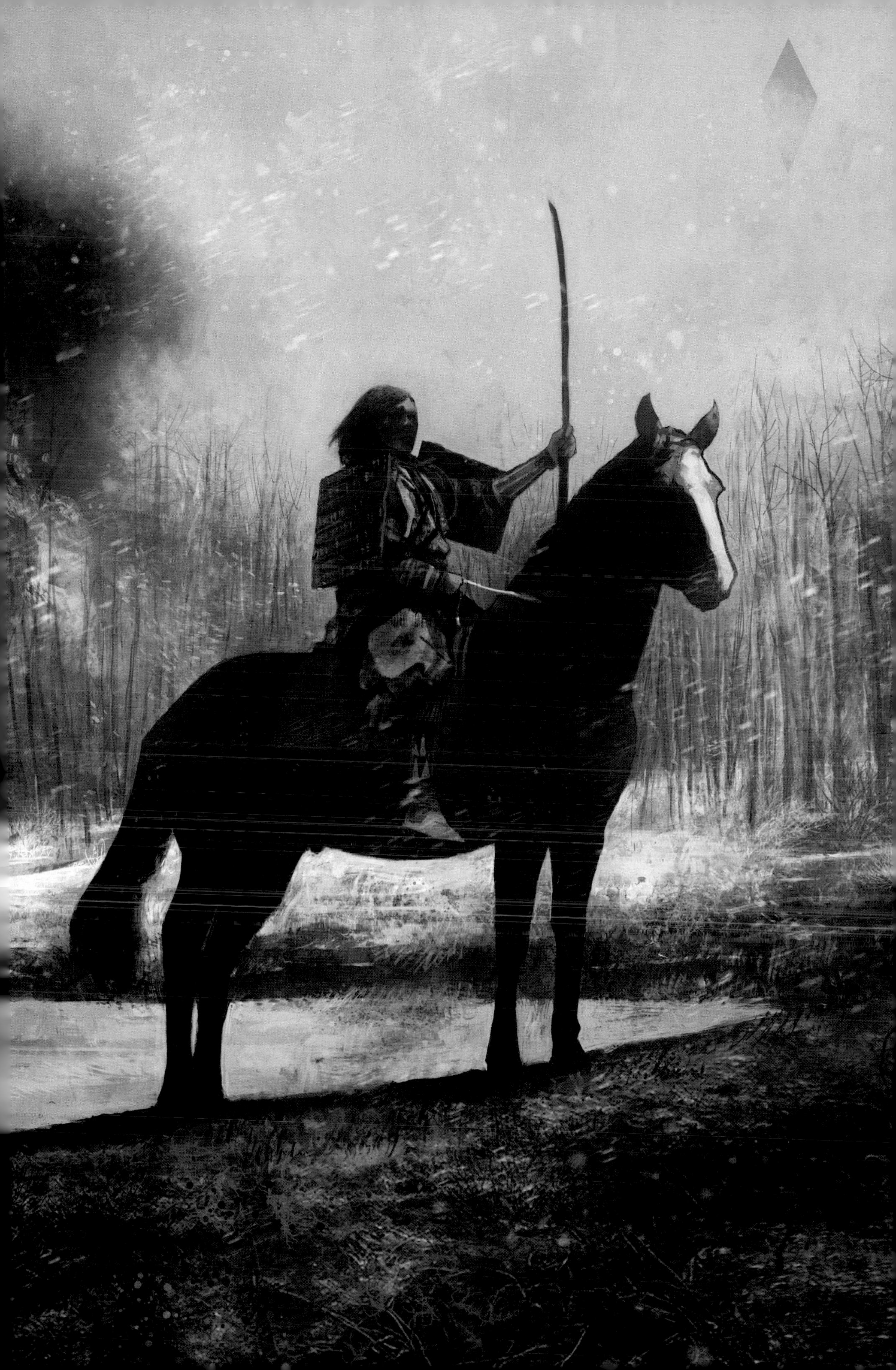

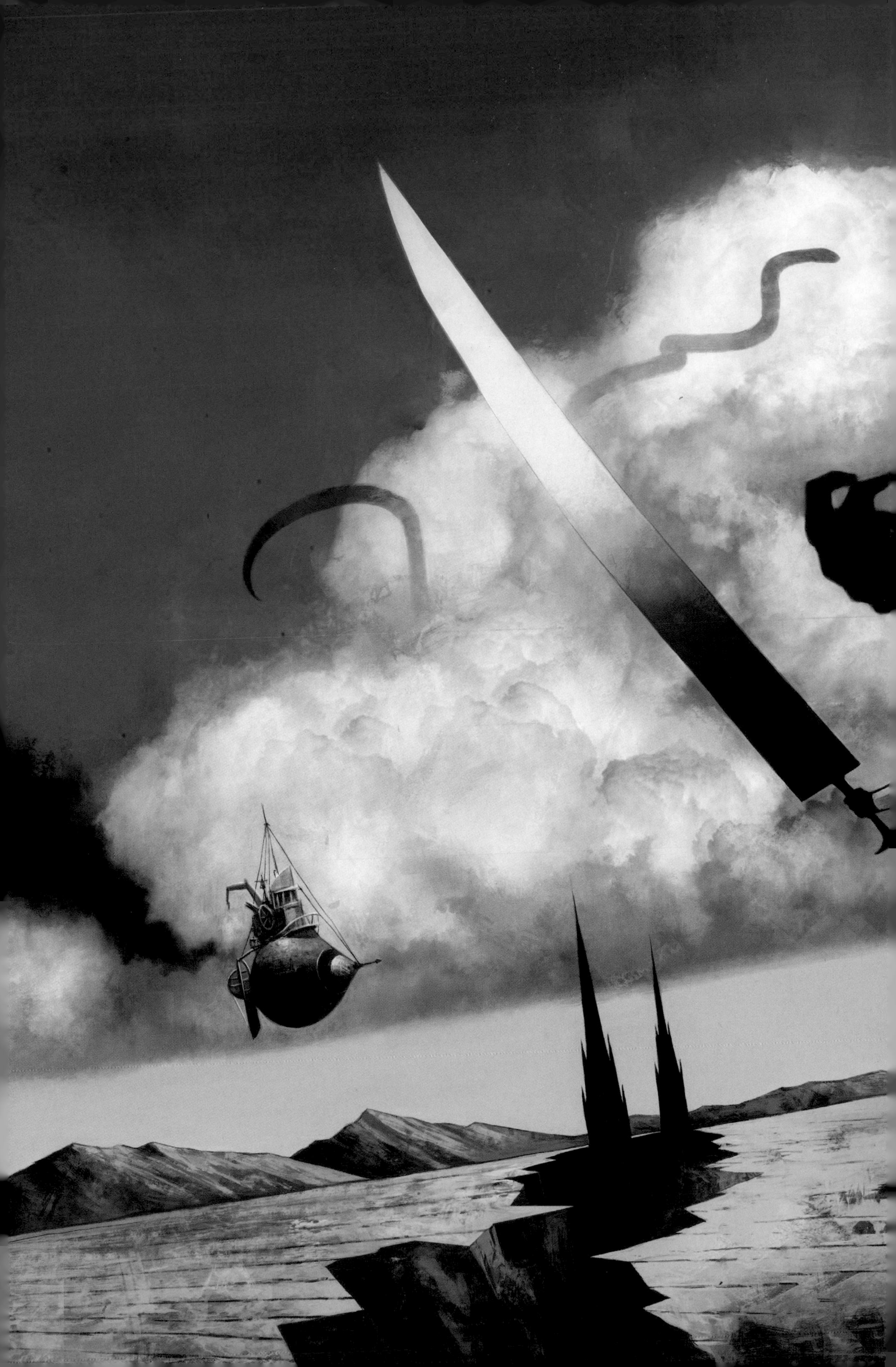

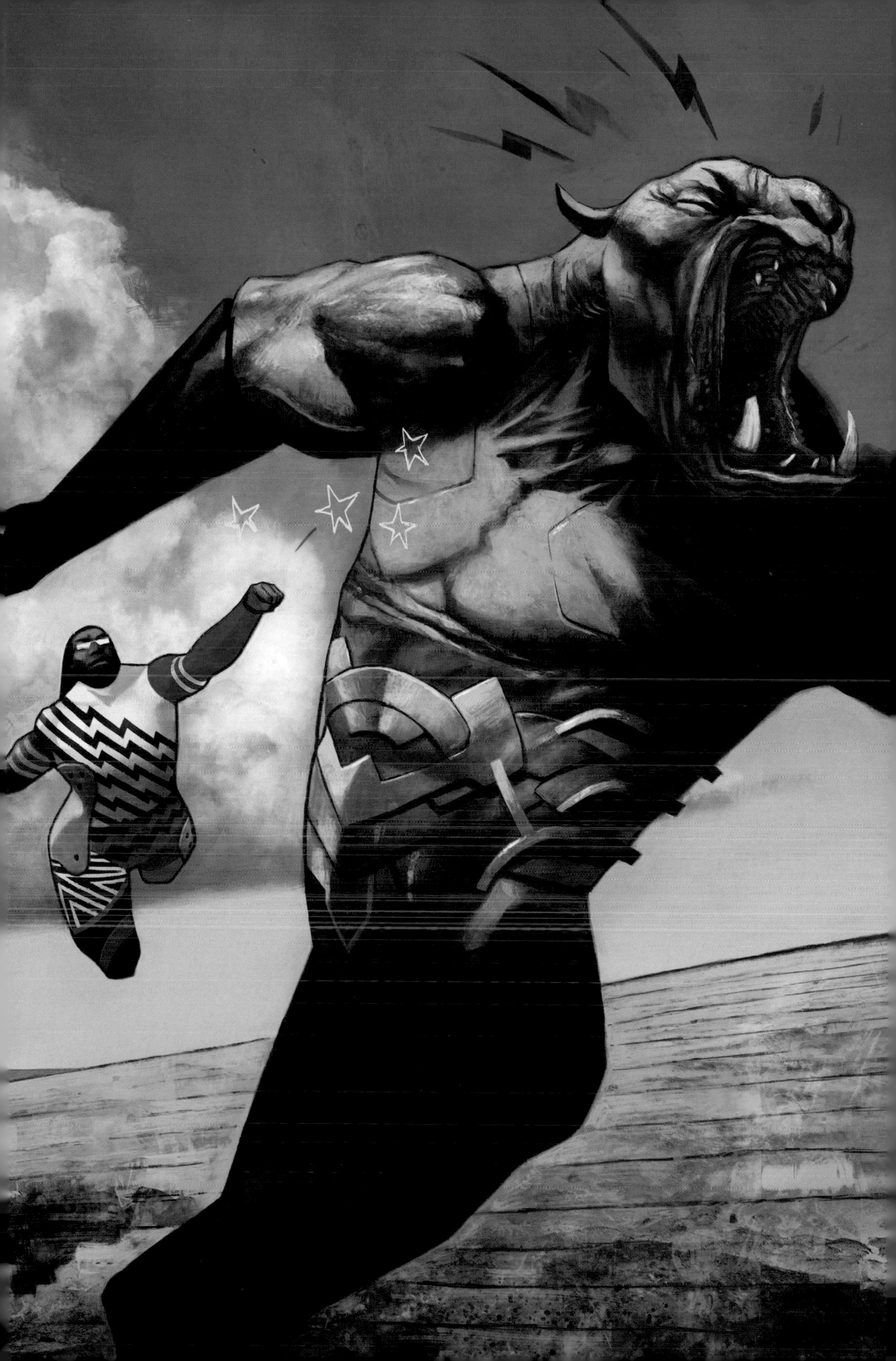

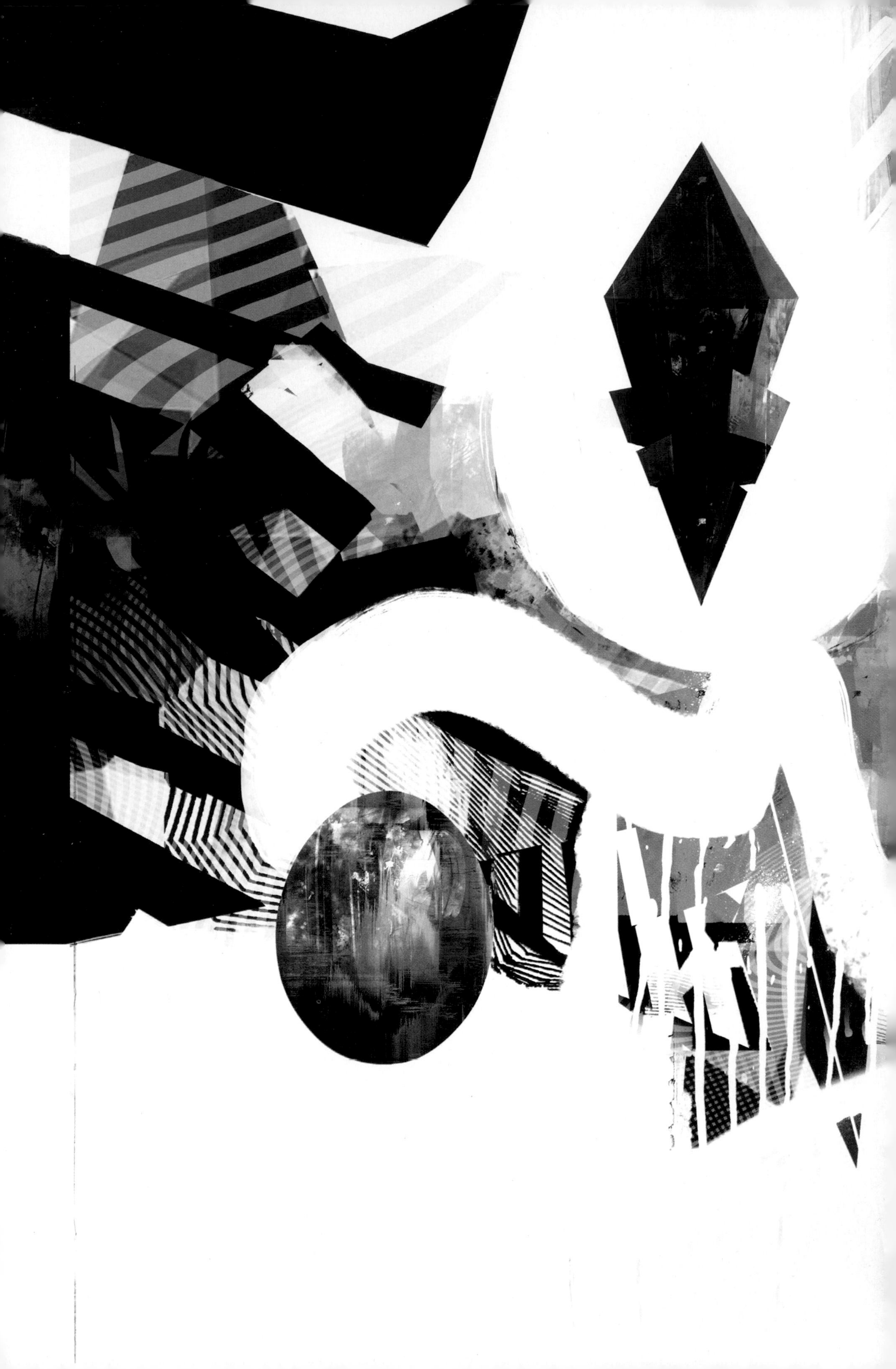

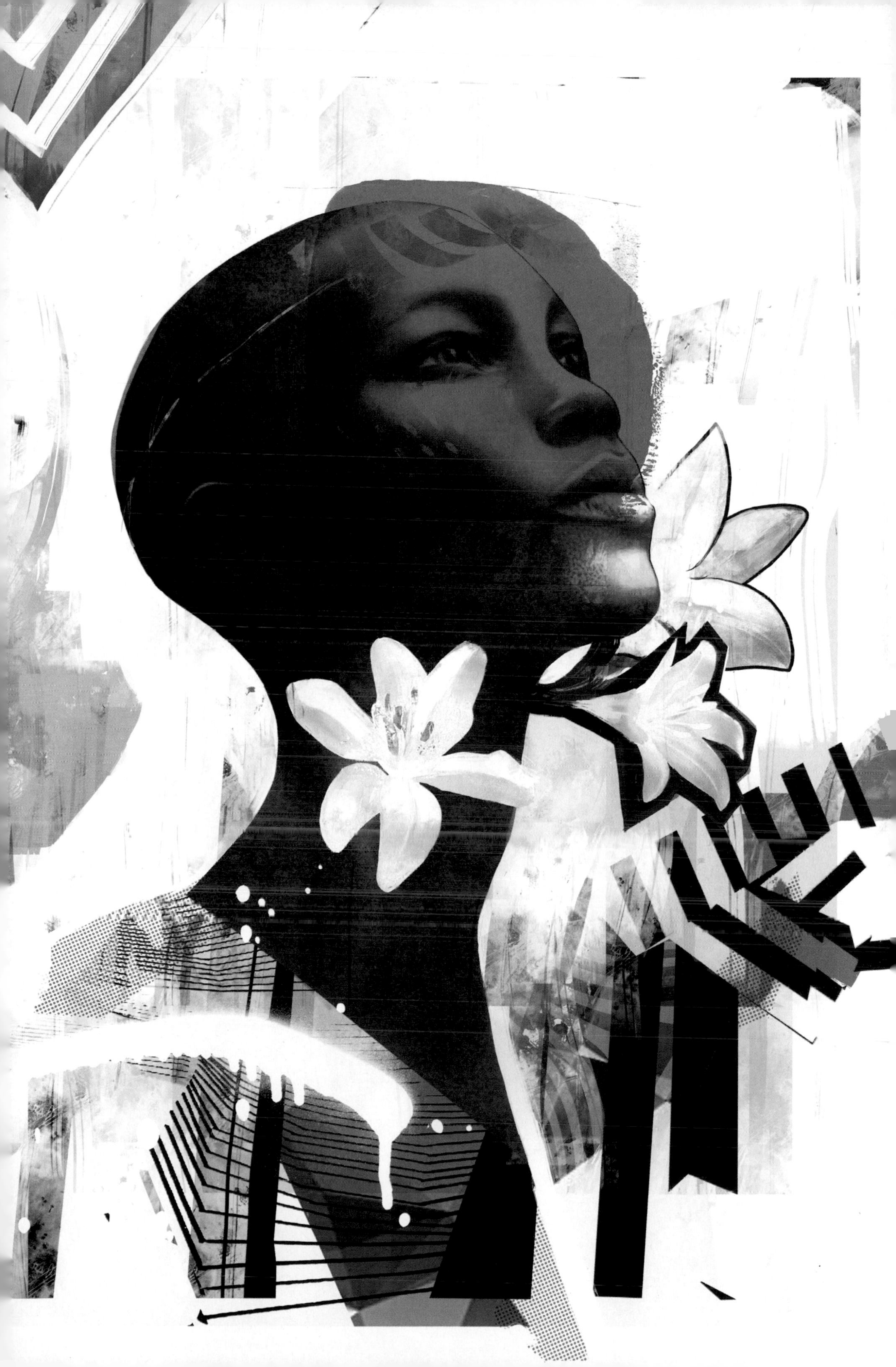

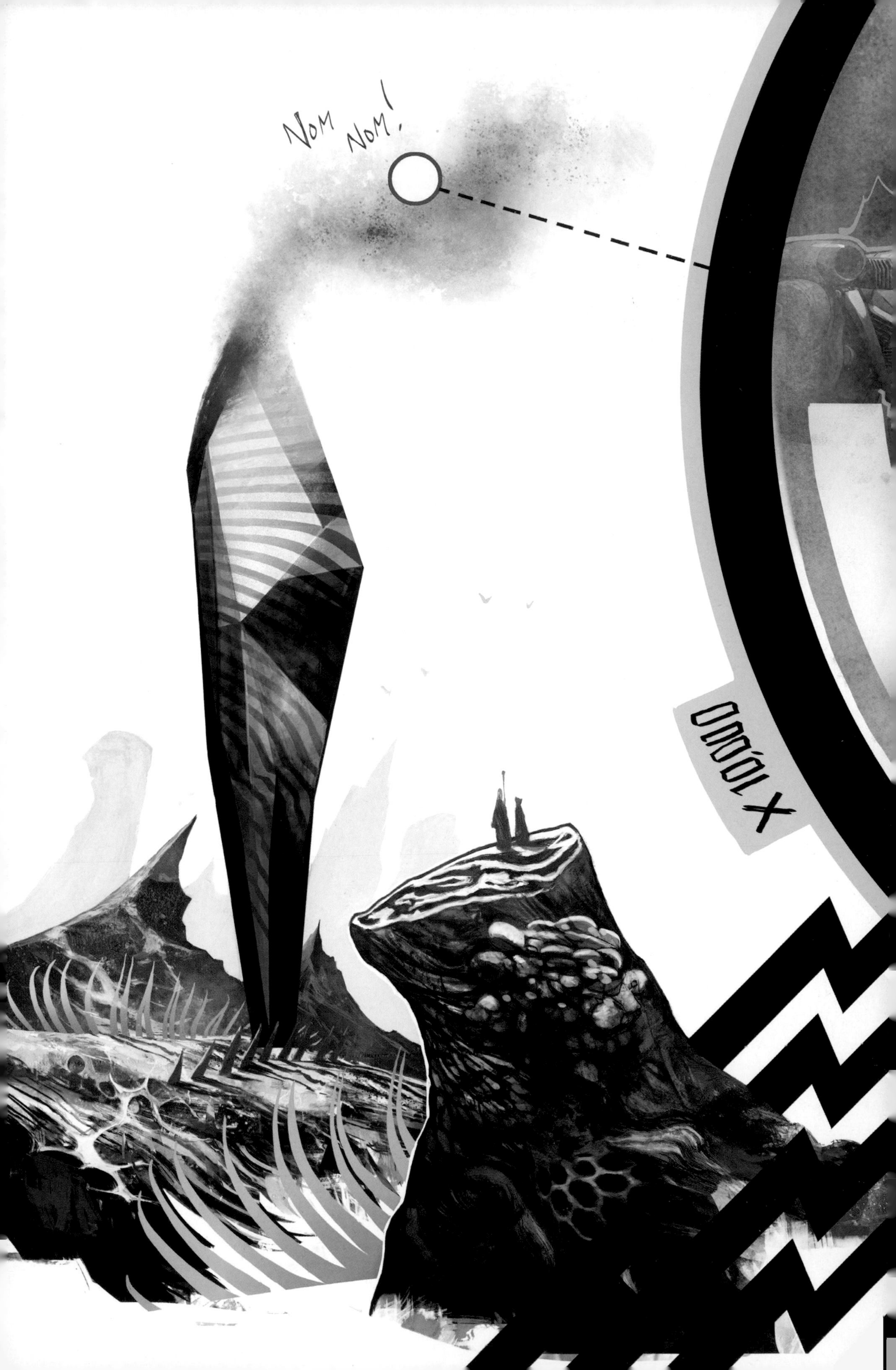
NOM NOM!
X 10,000

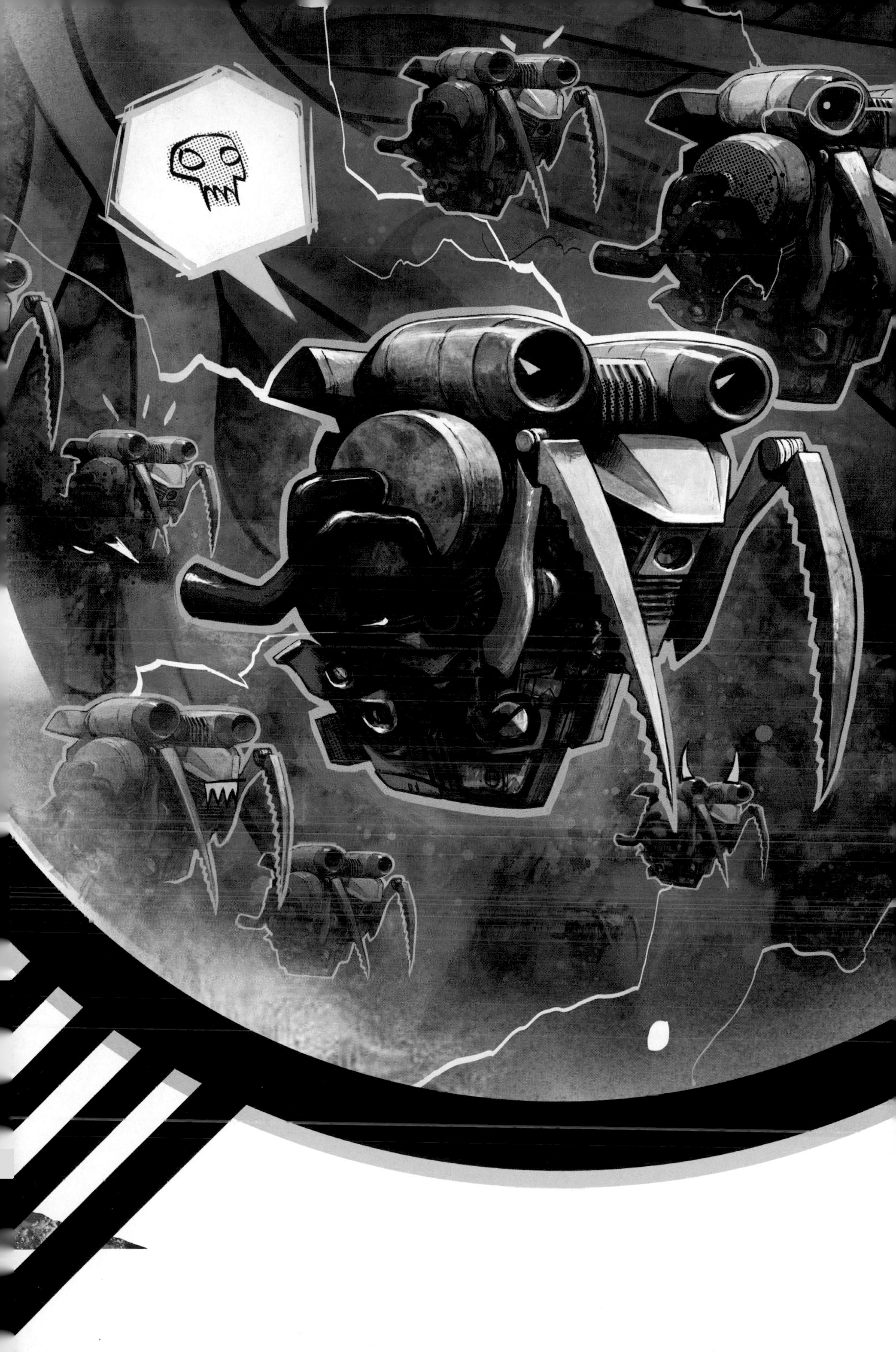

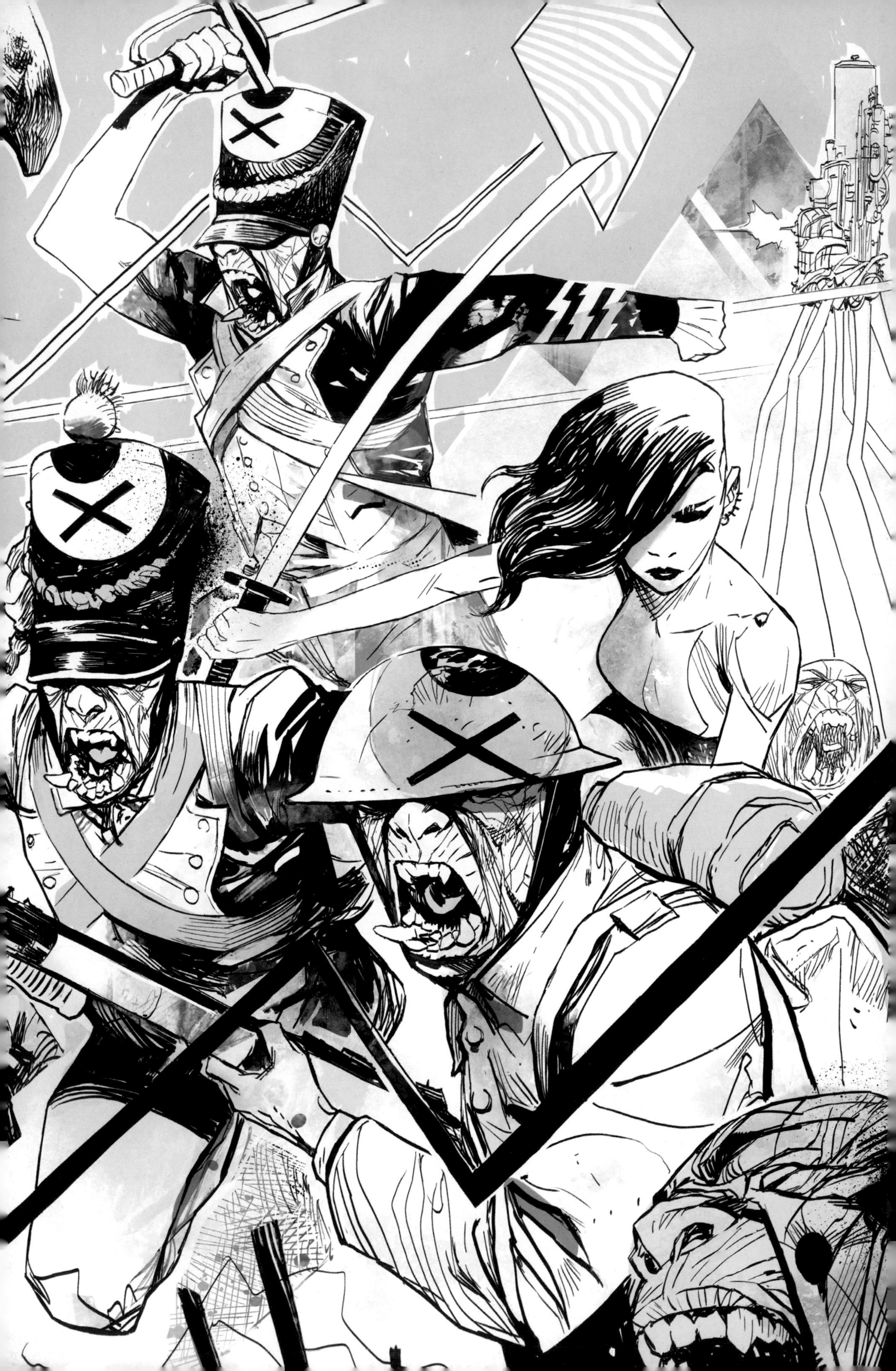

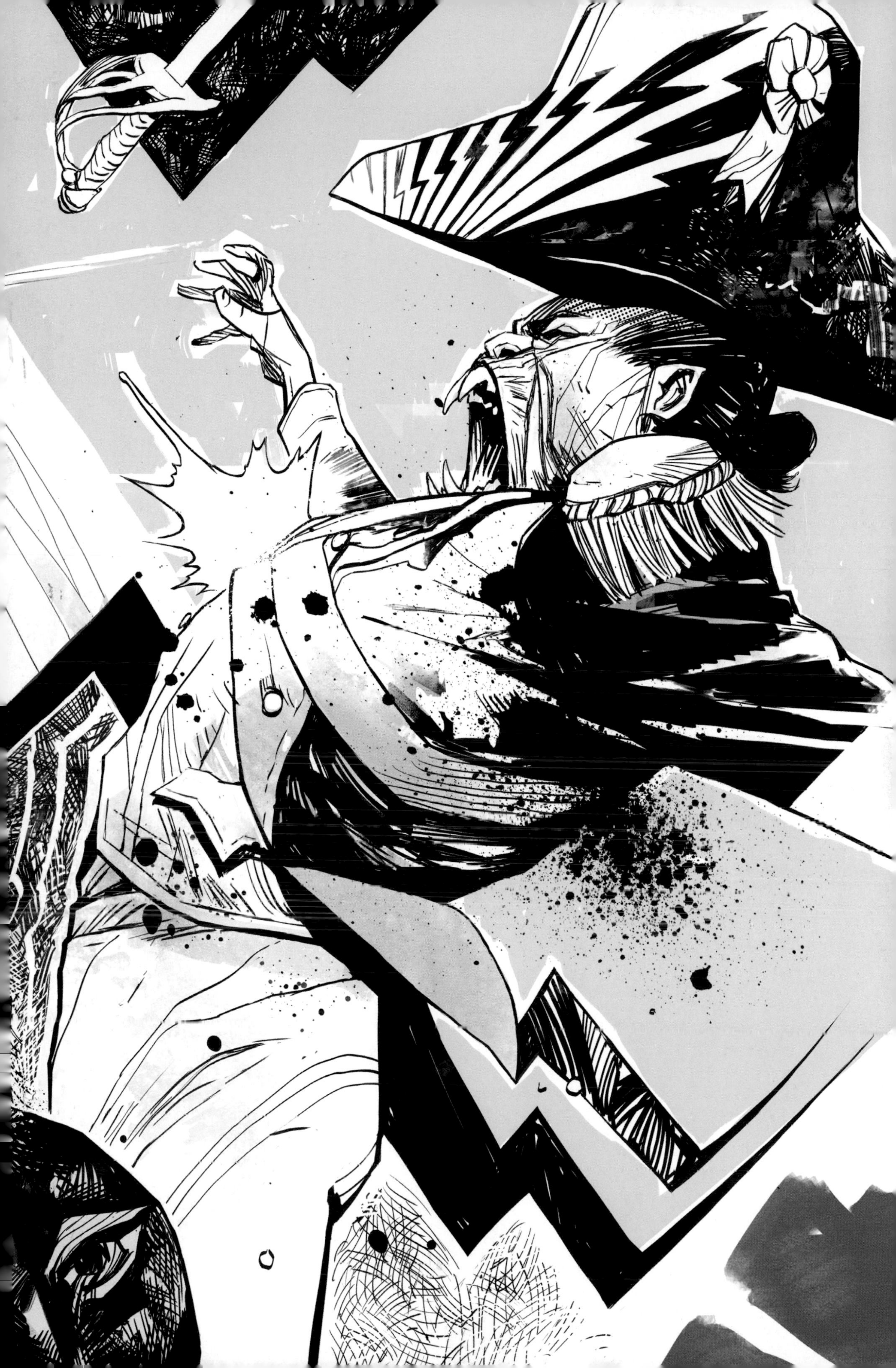

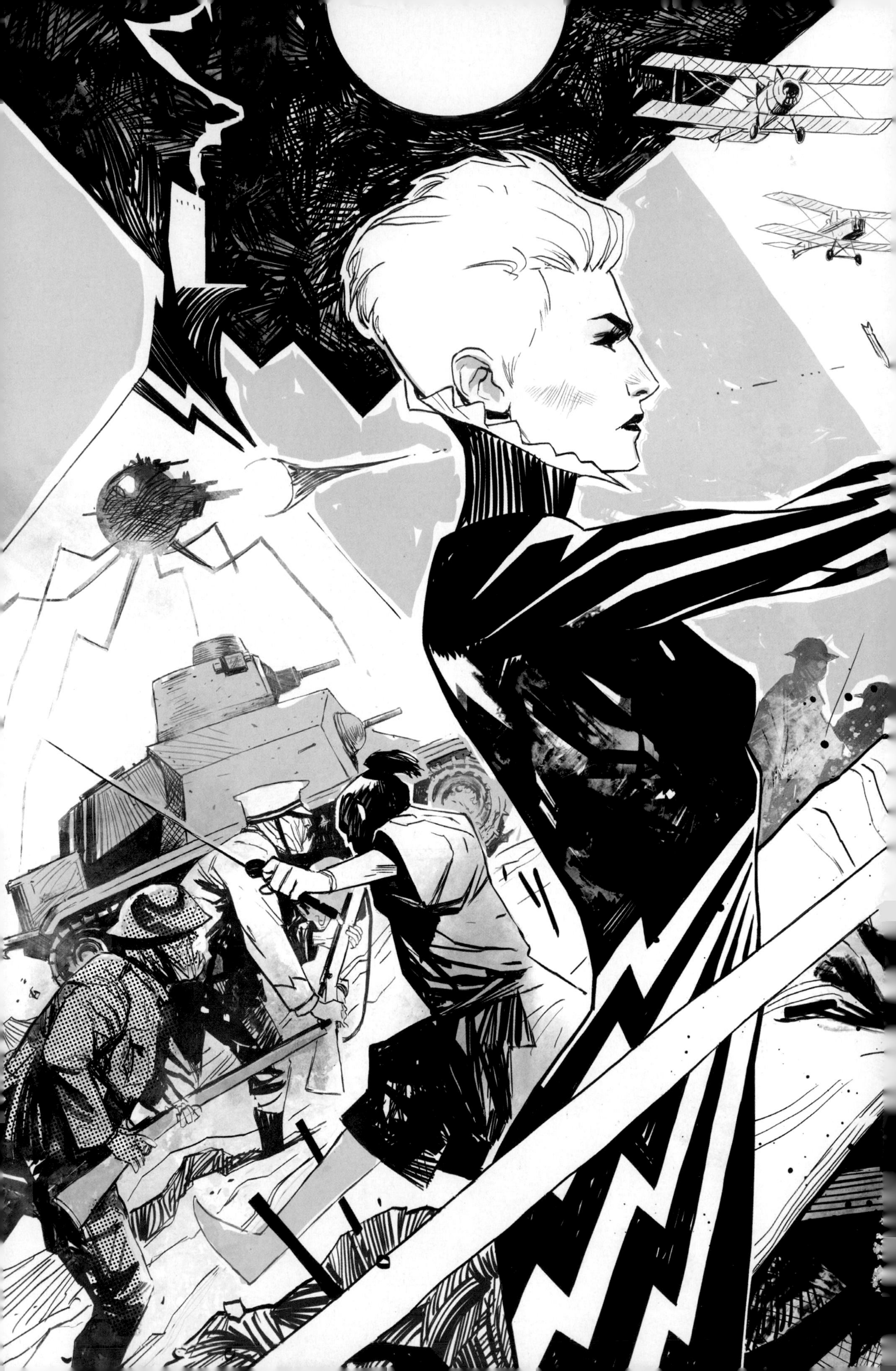

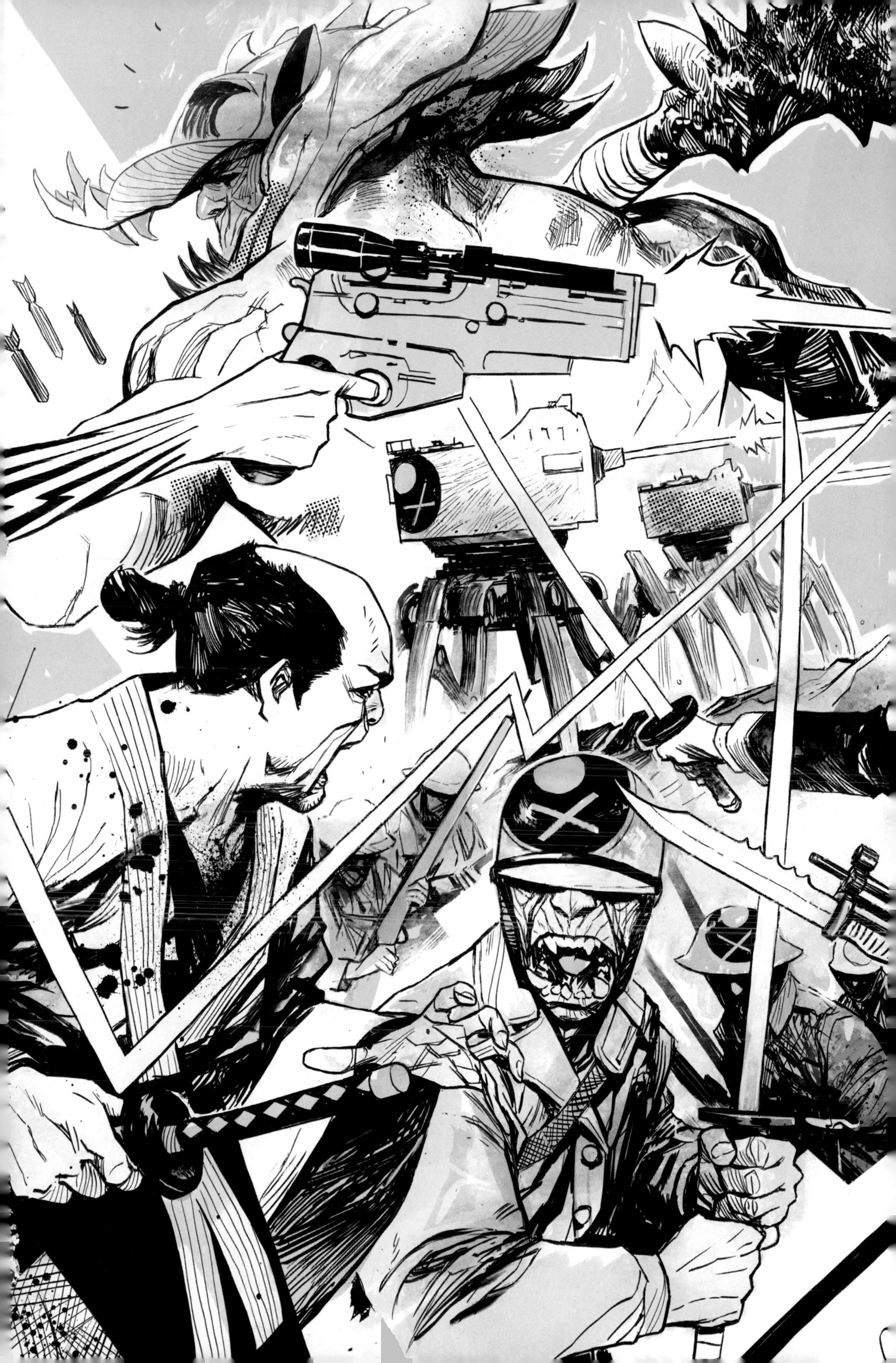

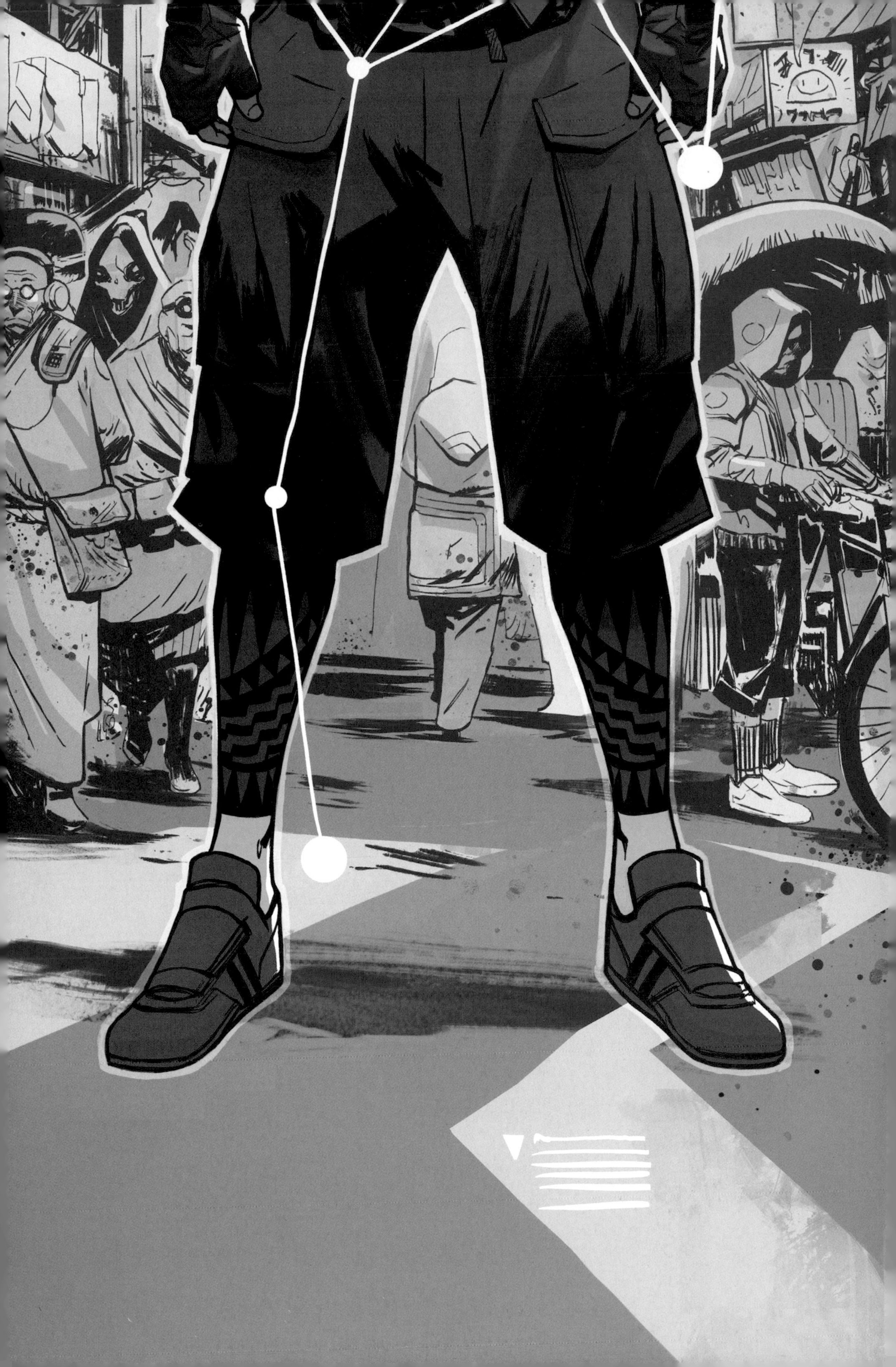

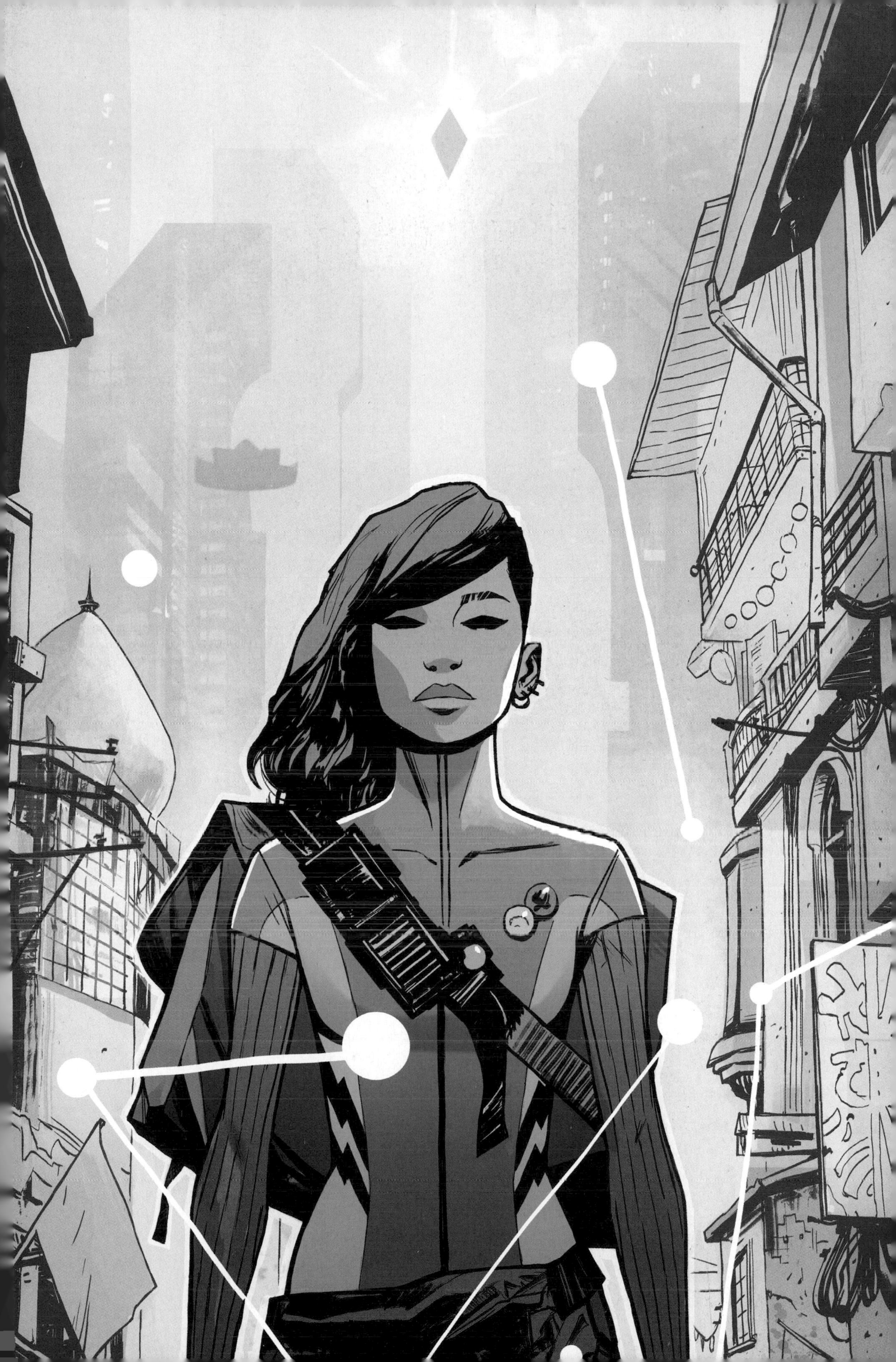

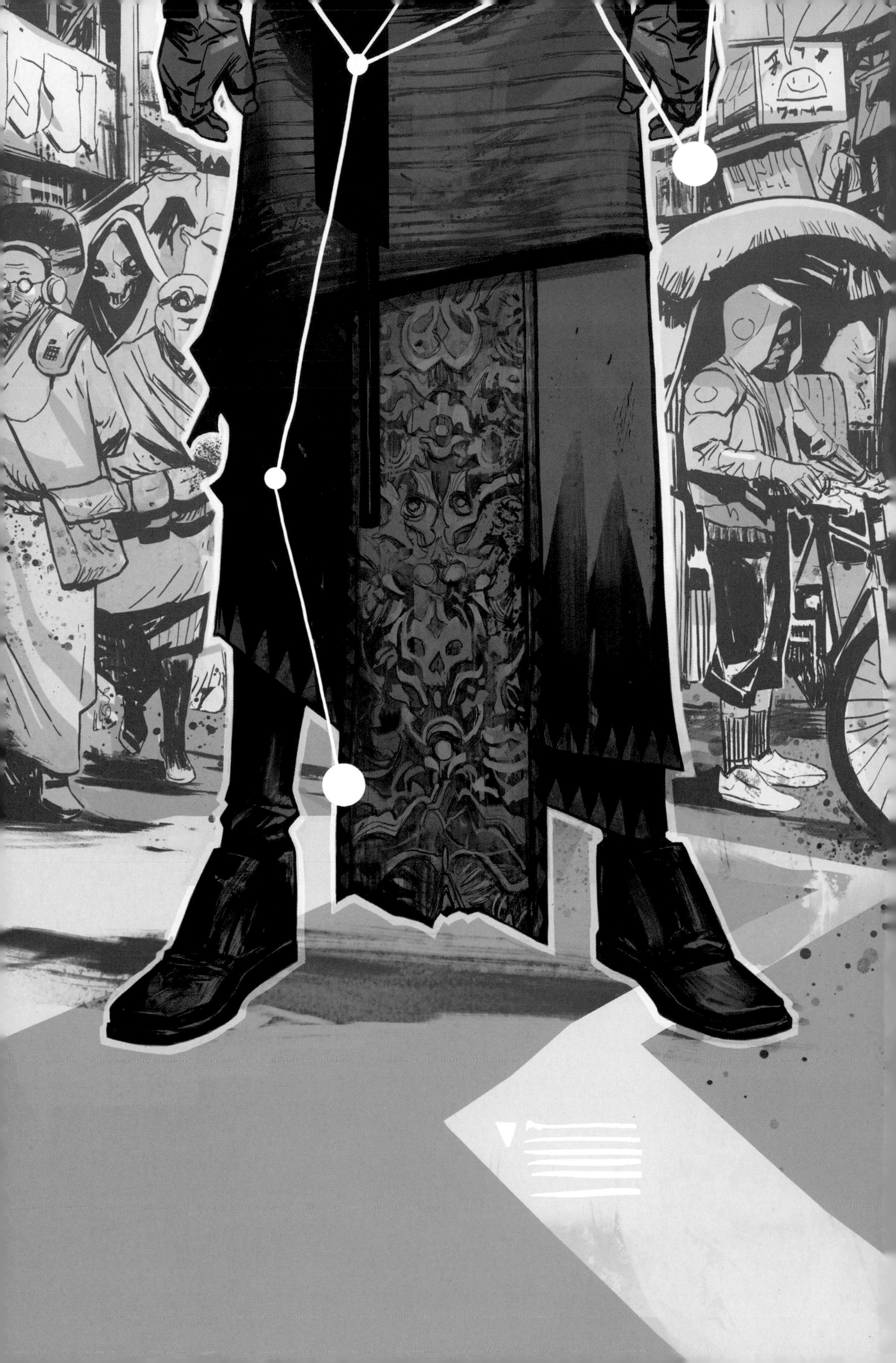

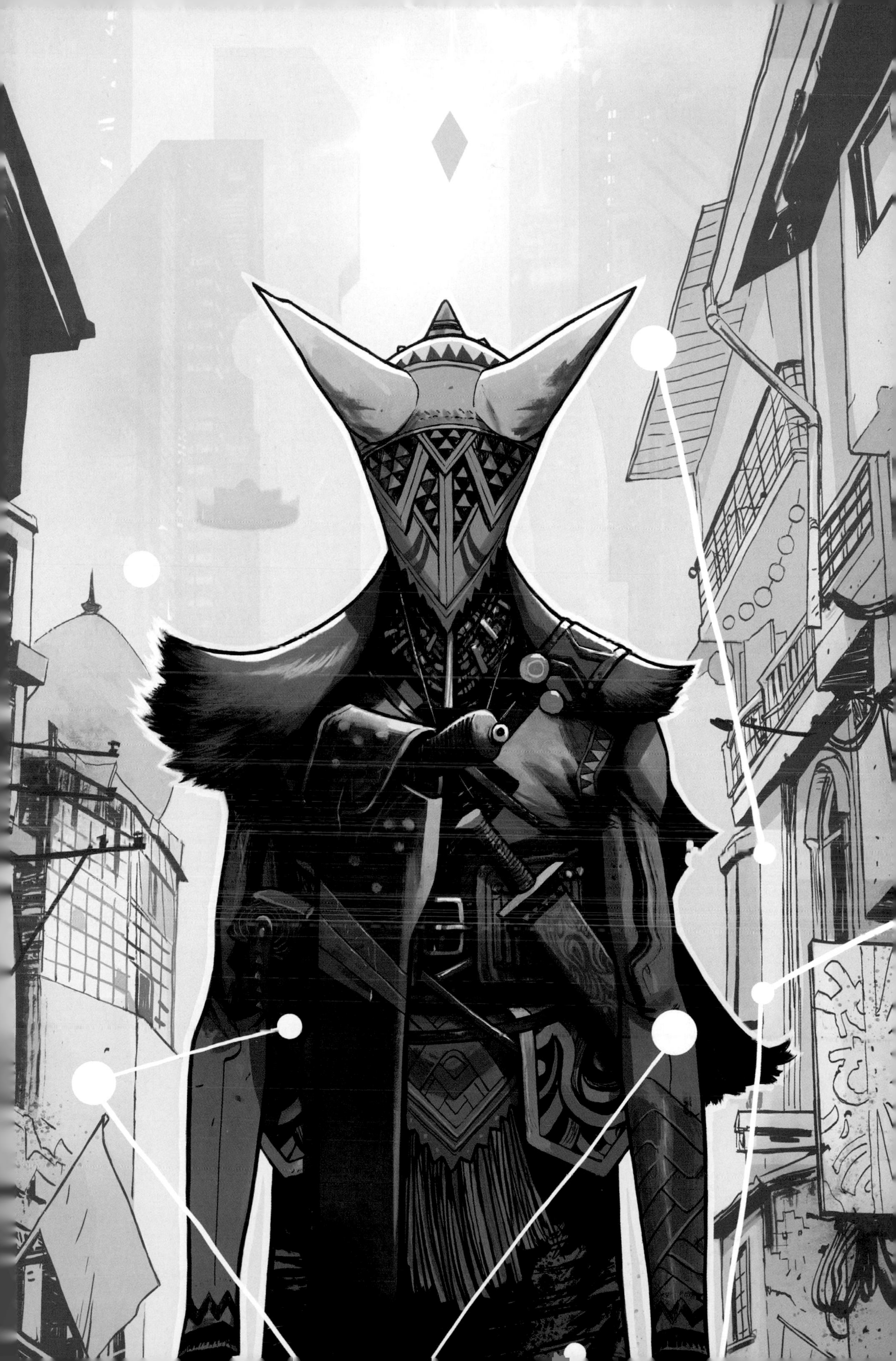

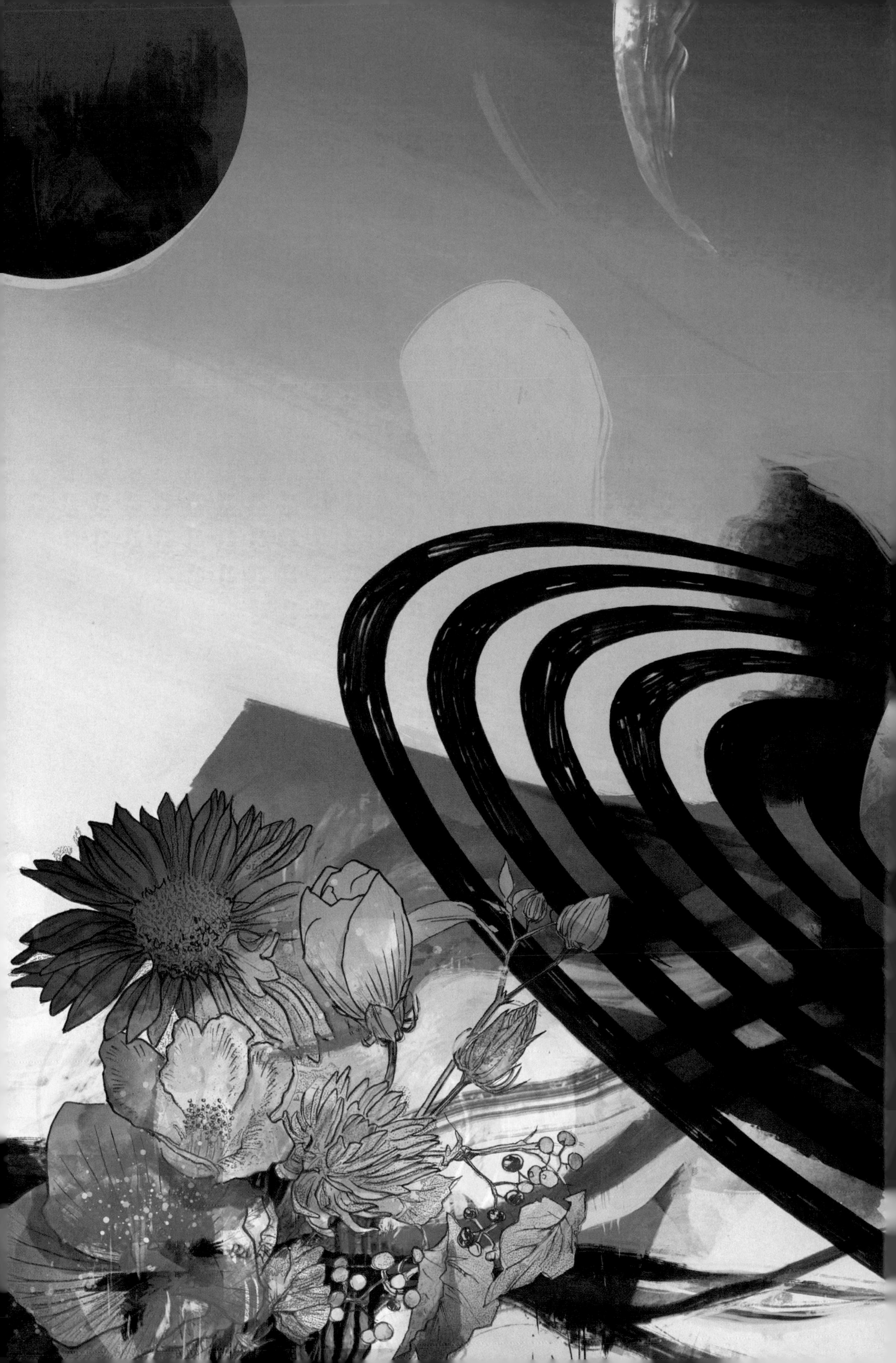

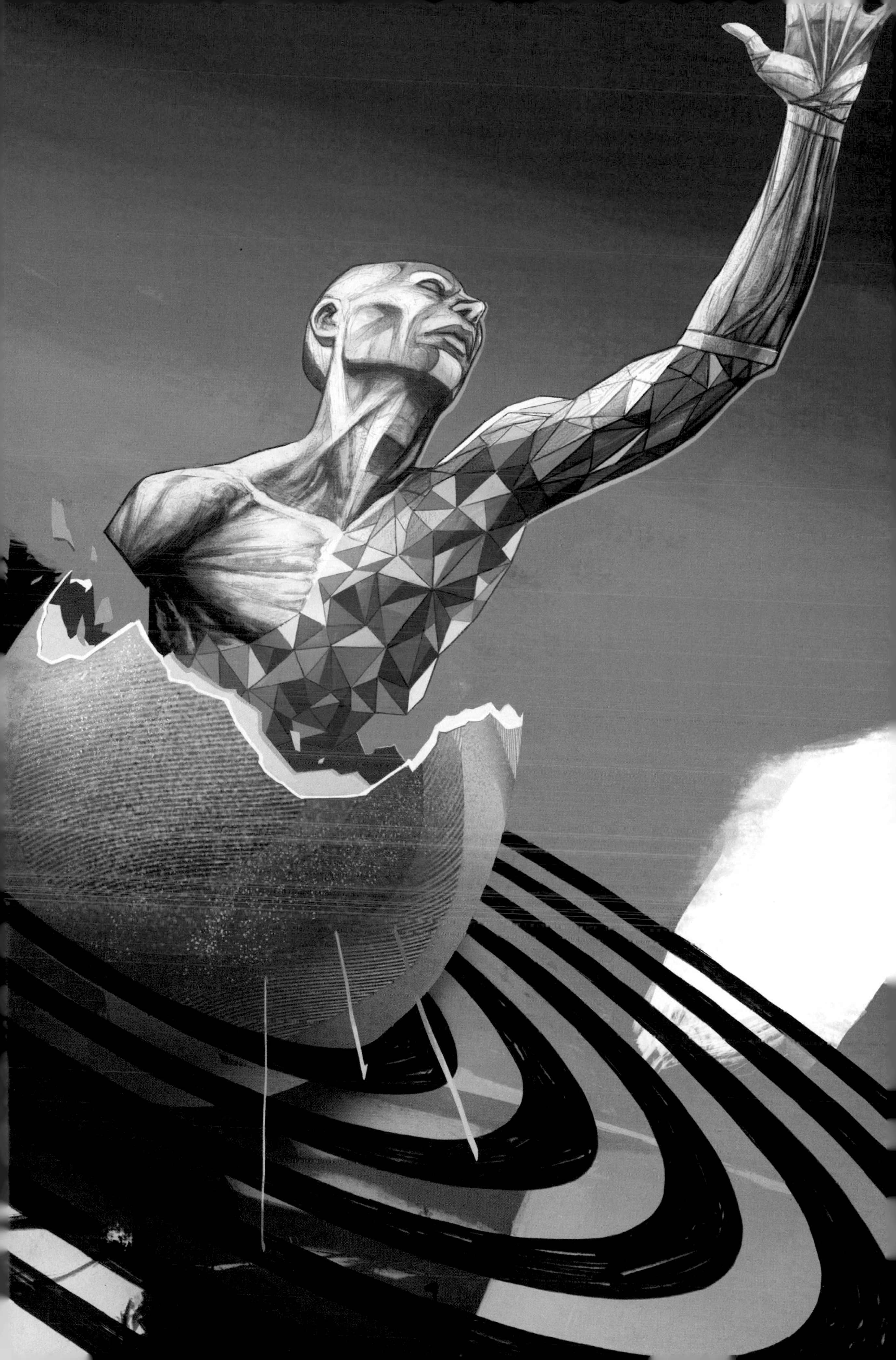

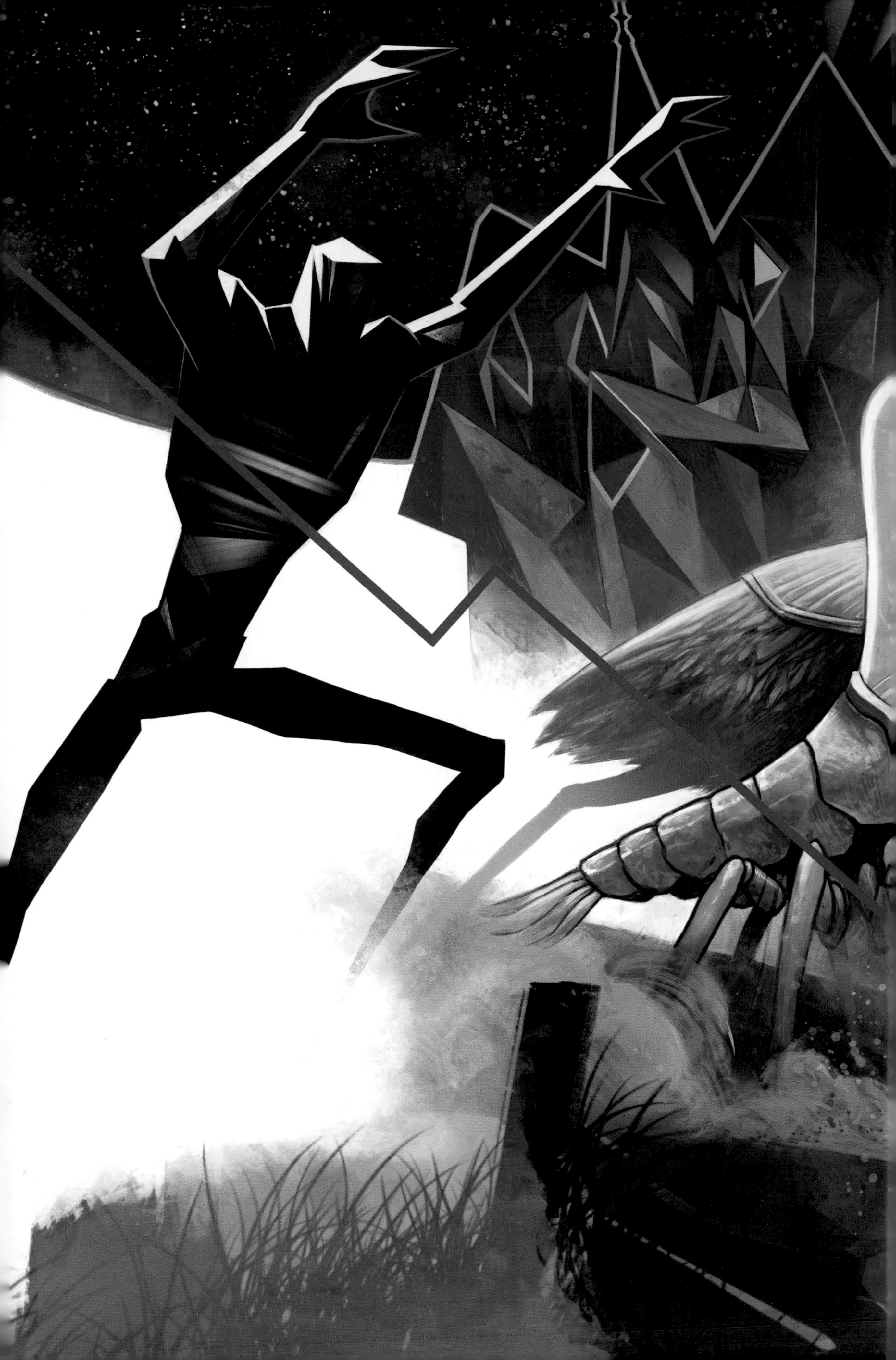

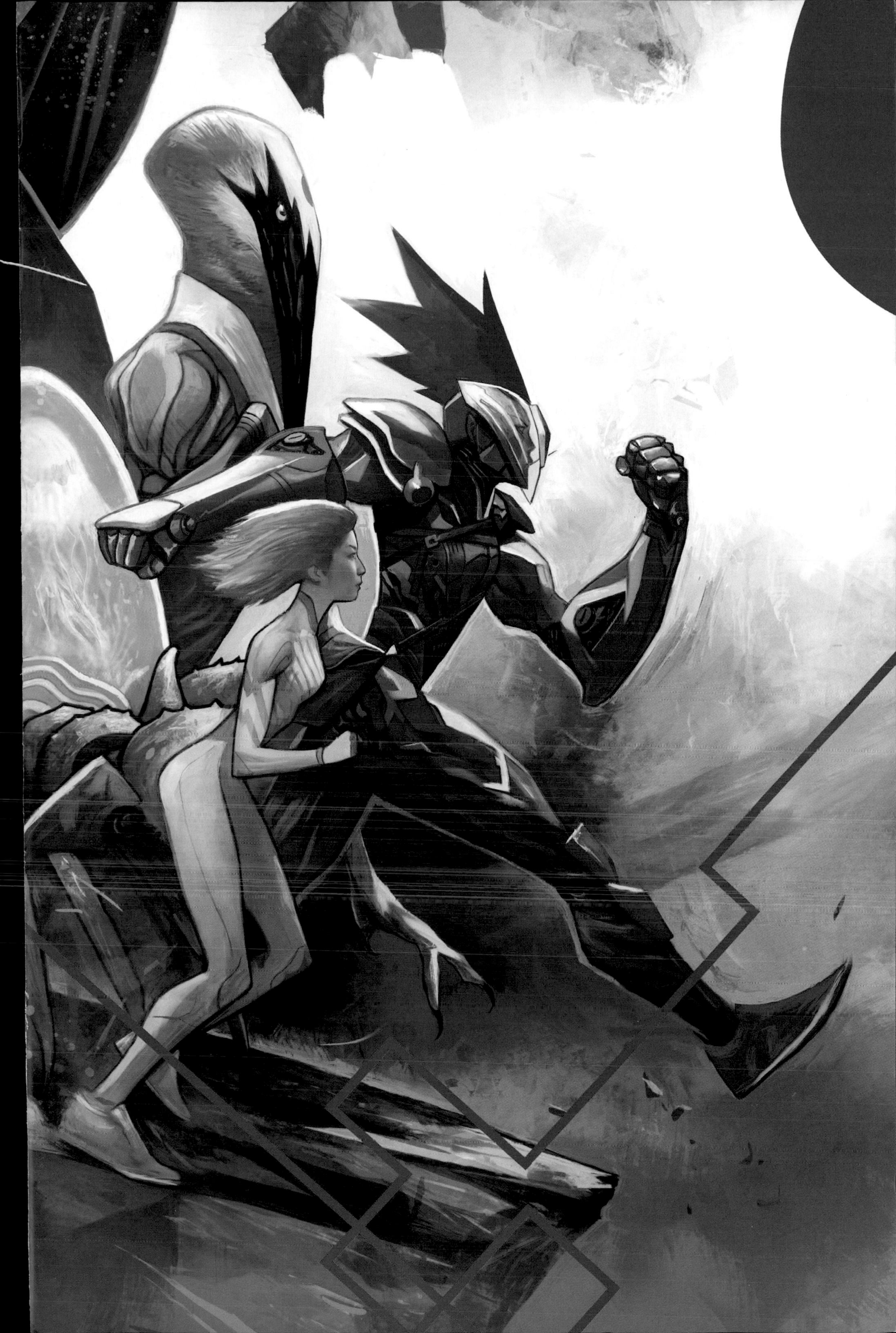

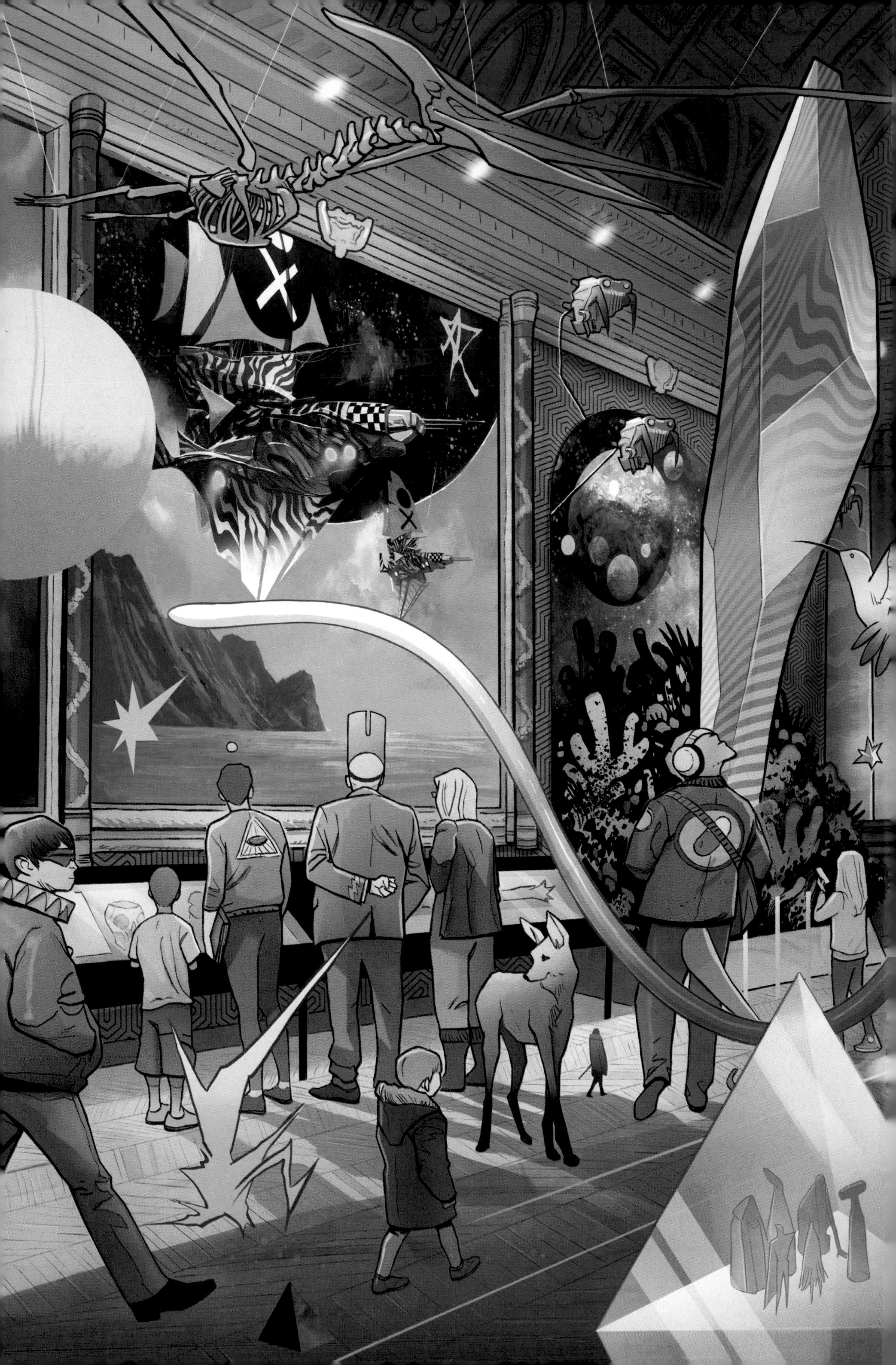

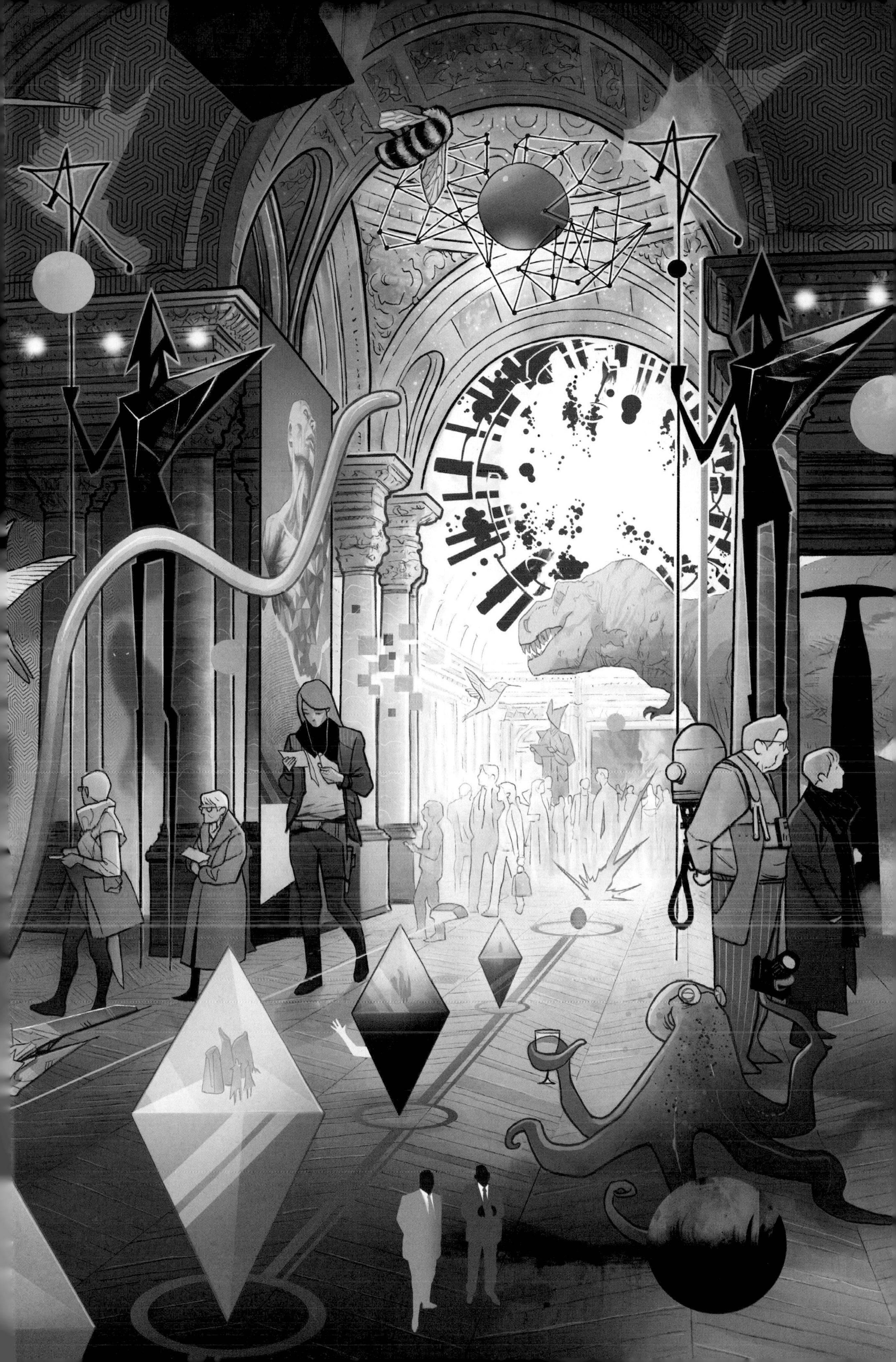

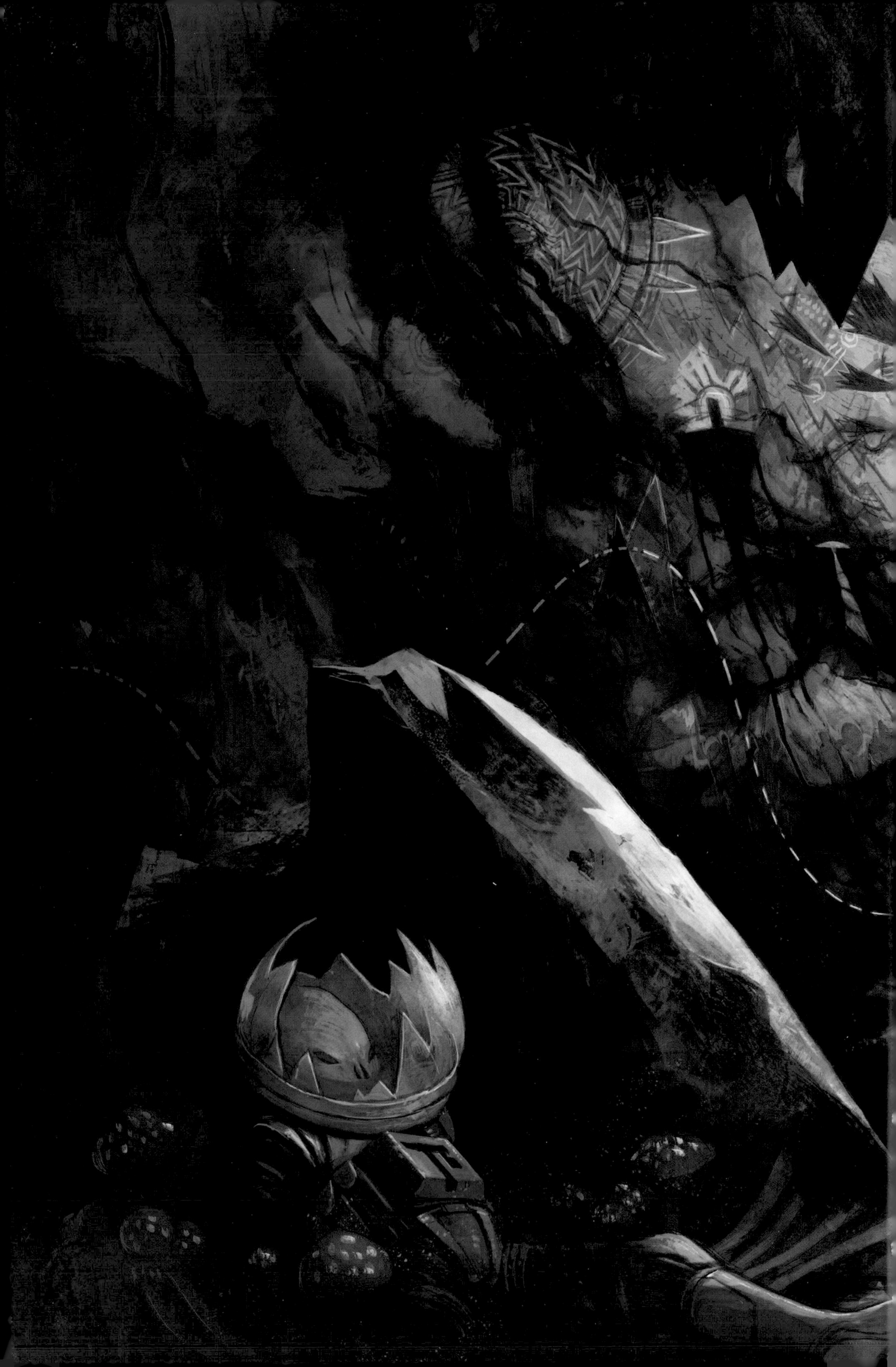

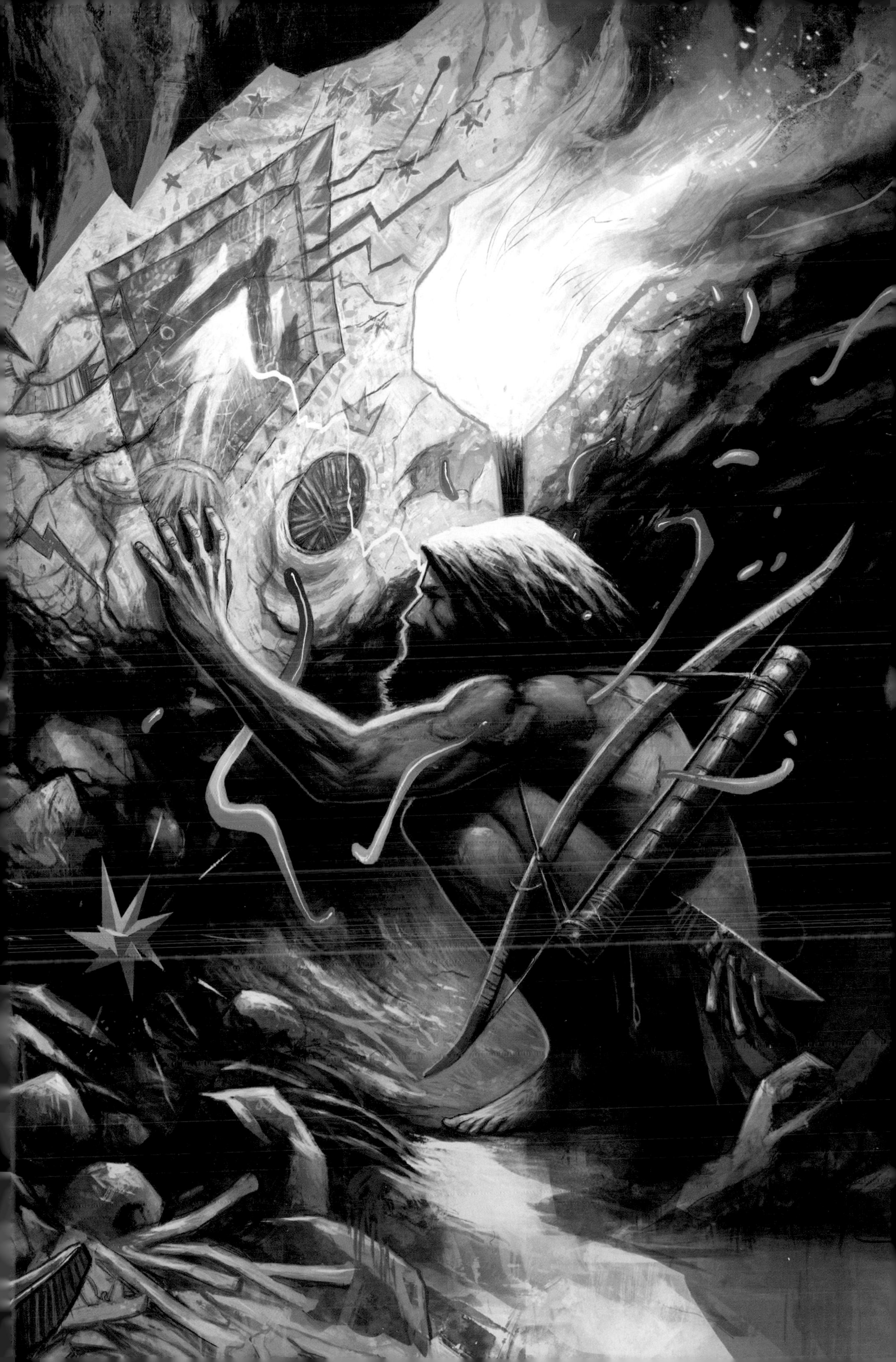

JONATHAN HICKMAN

Jonathan Hickman is an American writer who lives in the southeast United States, but is moving to Ecuador next year because they're on the dollar and own the Galapagos Islands. They have turtles. Which are also extremely slow.

MIKE HUDDLESTON

An American comic book artist, illustrator and designer, Mike currently lives in Los Angeles. His other credits include *The Coffin*, *Deep Sleeper*, *Mnemovore* and *Homeland Directive*.

RUS WOOTON

Rus Wooton is a comicbook letterer best known for lettering on books like THE WALKING DEAD, INVINCIBLE, MONSTRESS, DEADLY CLASS, EAST OF WEST, *Fantastic Four*, *X-Men*, and many more. Rus has been lettering since 2003, drawing for as long as he can remember, and reading comics since before he could read.

SASHA E HEAD

Sasha is a multi-disciplinary graphic designer working in comic book publishing and video game development, best known for her work on IMAGE+, DECORUM, TIME BEFORE TIME, and VINYL.

DECORUM. First printing. March 2022. Published by Image Comics, Inc. Office of publication: PO BOX 14457, Portland, OR 97293. Copyright © 2022 Jonathan Hickman & Mike Huddleston. All rights reserved. Contains material originally published in single magazine form as DECORUM #1-8. "Decorum," its logos and the likenesses of all characters herein are trademarks of Jonathan Hickman & Mike Huddleston, unless otherwise noted. "Image" and the Image Comics logos are registered trademarks of Image Comics, Inc. No part of this publication may be reproduced or transmitted, in any form or by any means (except for short excerpts for journalistic or review purposes), without the express written permission of Jonathan Hickman & Mike Huddleston, or Image Comics, Inc. All names, characters, events, and locales in this publication are entirely fictional. Any resemblance to actual persons (living or dead), events, or places, without satirical intent, is coincidental. Printed in China. For international rights, contact: foreignlicensing@imagecomics.com. ISBN Cover A: 978-1-5343-1823-6. ISBN Cover B: 978-1-5343-2031-4